SPIRIT OF LOVE

Snow Blossom smiled up at Cade. "If you want me as your wife, know this, warrior of my heart. I would follow you to all the ends of the earth. I would stay by your side with you as we walked the path to the Great Spirit together."

Cade felt the agony of pure joy. He could not speak any words to tell her how he felt. He drew her into his arms and held her, then gently, like the whisper of the water, he took her mouth with his. Her mouth was soft and pliant and her arms circled his neck holding him more and more closely. Snow Blossom was not afraid of the passion she could feel in his hard lean body. She had waited too long, dreamed too often, to be afraid now. Her lips opened to his in joyous giving and she heard his soft murmured groan as he bound her against him with arms that felt like iron.

When he released her, they stood looking at each other, more aware of each other than they had ever been before. It seemed to Cade as if every sense he owned touched her. In his mind, he could feel the smooth texture of her skin, smell the sweet scent of her, and taste her soft honeyed mouth. . . .

THE BEST IN HISTORICAL ROMANCE
by Sylvie F. Sommerfield

SAVAGE RAPTURE (1085, $3.50)
Beautiful Snow Blossom waited years for the return of Cade, the handsome halfbreed who had made her a prisoner of his passion. And when Cade finally rides back into the Cheyenne camp, she vows to make him a captive of her heart!

REBEL PRIDE (1084, $3.25)
The Jemmisons and the Forresters were happy to wed their children—and by doing so, unite their plantations. But Holly Jemmison's heart cries out for the roguish Adam Gilcrest. She dare not defy her family; does she dare defy her heart?

TAMARA'S ECSTASY (998, $3.50)
Tamara knew it was foolish to give her heart to a sailor. But she was a victim of her own desire. Lost in a sea of passion, she ached for his magic touch—and would do anything for it!

DEANNA'S DESIRE (906, $3.50)
Amidst the storm of the American Revolution, Matt and Deanna meet—and fall in love. And bound by passion, they risk everything to keep that love alive!

ERIN'S ECSTASY (861, $2.50)
Englishman Gregg Cannon rescues Erin from lecherous Charles Duggan—and at once realizes he must wed and protect this beautiful child-woman. But when a dangerous voyage calls Gregg away, their love must be put to the test . . .

TAZIA'S TORMENT (882, $2.95)
When tempestuous Fantasia de Montega danced, men were hypnotized. And this was part of her secret revenge—until cruel fate tricked her into loving the man she'd vowed to kill!

RAPTURE'S ANGEL (750, $2.75)
When Angelique boarded the *Wayfarer*, she felt like a frightened child. Then Devon—with his captivating touch— reminded her that she was a woman, with a heart that longed to be won!

Available wherever paperbacks are sold, or order direct from the Publisher. Send cover price plus 50¢ per copy for mailing and handling to Zebra Books, 475 Park Avenue South, New York, N.Y. 10016. DO NOT SEND CASH.

BY SYLVIE F.
SOMMERFIELD

ZEBRA BOOKS
KENSINGTON PUBLISHING CORP.

To Frenchie Suber, a very special friend.

ZEBRA BOOKS

are published by

KENSINGTON PUBLISHING CORP.
475 Park Avenue South
New York, N.Y. 10016

Printed in the United States of America

Prologue

The wind-swept hill was bare of anything but the tall grass that waved like a luxurious green blanket and the two figures that stood together. He was tall, broad of shoulder and narrow-hipped. The immaculate blue military uniform he wore made him look even larger. She was small and very slender. Her dress was of soft brown fringed buckskin, and her long black hair hung in two thick braids that fell to her hips.

His strong arms held her close, crushed her to him as if he would never let her go. She clung to him, her arms about his waist and her head pressed against his broad chest. He could feel her body tremble and without seeing her face, he knew she was crying.

He cupped one hand under her chin and lifted her face so that he could see her eyes. They were large brown eyes swimming in tears she was trying unsuccessfully to contain.

"I will return, Waterflower; no matter what, I will return. One day when I have fulfilled the mission upon which I go, I will come back. My heart will always be here with you and with our son. Do you know how it breaks my heart to leave you? You and my son are the center of my heart. Don't . . . don't let him forget me."

"No, my heart," she whispered. "The son should know of the father who is willing to sacrifice himself for others. I will sing him songs of his father's courage and tell him the stories of his bravery. Never will I let him forget he is the son of Michael Holliday."

"I will send messages to learn of his progress and your well-being. When he is old enough, you must inform me and we will begin his education. I want him to learn both worlds. I want him to someday be a link between my world and yours. Maybe we can find a way to live together in peace."

"Oh, Michael," she said softly.

"I know." His arms tightened about her again and his lips sought hers in a long and hungry kiss. They clung to each other in desperate longing for they knew it was the last time for a very long time. There were no words left to be said between them for they had all been said; there was only the burning need now to cling to each other this one last time. He held her, pressing his cheek against her hair and feeling her draw the strength from him that she would need to face the days to come.

She lifted her head and looked up at him. The tears were there, but so was determination and pride.

"I love you, Waterflower—you and Cade. More than my life. We will do what we have to do for our people, but one day we will be together again. I love you, I love you."

His words died to a whisper as he again pressed her warm giving lips with his and rocked her against him.

They were standing so, locked in their own quiet pain-filled world, when they heard someone approach. Michael turned, his arm still about Waterflower's waist, and he looked at the man who stood a few feet from them. Michael smiled, his crystal-blue eyes bright with friendship for the man who approached them.

Long Arrow was about the same age as Michael, both being in their late twenties. He was lean and tall, his face handsome and bright with intelligence.

"It is time, my brother." He said the words softly to Michael, but his black eyes were warm with sympathy as he gazed at Waterflower.

"Long Arrow, my brother, my friend. I leave my wife and my son in your care. I will not leave with such a heavy heart when I know they will be under your guard."

He placed his hand on Long Arrow's shoulder. Long Arrow's eyes brightened with pride and the deep love and respect he felt for this tall handsome man who had lived among them for such a short time. He placed his hand on Michael's shoulder.

"I will guard them with my life, brother, until you return. Let your heart rest easy; they will be protected from harm as long as the Great Spirit gives me the strength."

Michael chuckled. "I know of the strength of Long Arrow's

arm, just as I know of the honor in his heart. It is the reason I would not leave them with any other."

"I have put your baggage on the horses. We will ride with you to the river."

"Good, I shall be with you soon."

Long Arrow nodded and turned away from them. Michael watched him walk away; then he turned to Waterflower. Without a word, he reached for her. She came to his arms and he kissed her. For a long moment their eyes held, then he turned and walked away.

She remained on the hill, eyes blurred with tears as she saw him mount, and in the company of three other braves, he rode away—rode away to a place far away and for a long long time.

Fifteen Years Later . . .

Chapter One

The two young Indian boys squatted on their haunches at the top of the hill. They watched with keen eyes the five tepees that nestled in the small valley. Although they both belonged to the same tribe, there was a subtle difference in their appearance. Both were about seventeen, but this and their clothes were the only things that were the same. Their bronzed bodies, naked except for breechcloths, were lean and muscled and there was a shade or two of difference in the color of their skin.

The larger of the two chewed his lip thoughtfully then turned his deep black eyes toward the other. "They have more horses than I thought; can we handle them if we succeed?"

The question was spoken in a whisper. There was a soft, light chuckle from the second boy.

"We will simply head them toward home and follow. It is not important if we lose a few along the way, they will find their way home."

The first one nodded as bright humorous laughter filled his eyes. They rose and went silently back to the horses they had kept out of sight. They mounted, and kicking their horses into motion, they crested the hill at breakneck speed; loud shrill shouts from their lips sent the small encampment into momentary confusion.

They rode saddleless ponies and the only control was a rope bridle tied to the lower jaw, yet they rode as if they were part of the animals under them.

Their shrill yipps startled the small herd of horses as they rode around them and sent them stampeding away.

The few men in the encampment, taken by surprise, could

do little but watch as their horses ran, with the two attackers yelling wildly behind them.

Later that afternoon, the thundering herd stormed through the village to which the two boys belonged. They were exhausted enough now to be herded into a circle and calmed until they stood placidly munching the green grass around them.

The two young, would-be warriors dismounted and unbridled their ponies and let them graze among the others. They stood together looking at the group of horses, their eyes lit with pride.

"Ayee, Brother," the large one said, "we have done well this day. Surely we will be allowed to take part in the sun dance the next time."

The second boy made an irritated sound. "At least you have had your vision, you know how you will paint your shield. How can I be a warrior if the Great Spirit will not give me a sign?"

"You have no patience, my Brother, the Great Spirit will give you your vision in his own good time; besides"—he grinned—"you need not have a sign to draw the looks of the women; you need only gaze in their direction."

The second boy chuckled, his humor renewed. "Are you again insulting my white blood, Brother, or do you envy me my good looks and courage?"

The larger one laughed outright, sharing a long-lasting comradeship with the other. He took and gave no offense by his words for the two were the closest of friends. The larger one pointed toward the village.

"My sister comes, to see another of her brothers' accomplishments, and," he said slyly glancing at the other boy, "to look again into the light eyes of her warrior."

The girl who ran across the open ground was about twelve. She was slim and extremely fine-boned and beautiful. But to the tall young warriors, she was a child. She came panting to their side; her words were for her natural brother, the larger of the two, but her eyes were for his silent companion.

"You have captured many horses this time, Brother. Father has spoken and you will join the ceremonies at harvest."

Excitement filled both pairs of eyes as they looked at her.

She was aware, as she always had been since she could remember, of the intent blue gaze that held hers.

"Did he speak of me, Snow Blossom?"

She would gladly sacrifice her life to spare him any hurt, so she searched all the words she had heard to find the most acceptable to tell him. Her eyes brightened as she smiled at him and said, "My father says that one day the son of Michael Holliday will bring great honor to his people."

Cade could barely hide the swift look of disappointment and her smile died when she saw it. Without a word, he turned to walk away. With a soft sound, Snow Blossom started after him, but her brother's strong arm held her.

"No, Snow Blossom, leave him be. He would not like you to see him so."

Deep pride was a thing Snow Blossom understood so she remained, but her eyes followed Cade until he disappeared into his tepee.

Slowly, brother and sister walked together toward the tepee of the chief, for they were the son and daughter of Chief Tekata.

"You have painted my shield?" he asked.

"Yes, Brother, and I have decorated it with white eagle feathers as you asked. It is a beautiful thing and I'm sure you will be proud to carry it into battle when you have received permission to be called White Eagle."

The young brave was proud; yet his heart went out to his blood brother. At the age of fifteen each of them had gone from the village in separate directions. For three days, they had communed with nature and the Great Spirit in search of the sign that would guide their lives.

Without food or water, they had prayed and waited for the Great Spirit to reach out to them. For the one, it was successful for he could remember vividly the great White Eagle who in his dreams had lifted him from the earth and soared above his people's lands. Having returned he told his dream to the medicine man who instructed him that this was the sign for which he searched. He would take it as his name and his own personal emblem. It would be painted on his tepee and his shield. It would also be the guide for his future because the medicine man had told him of the great courage and eternal freedom of the eagle, and the same qualities would be expected from him for the balance of his life.

It was not the same for Cade who returned in an exhausted state and with confused dreams that the medicine man was still trying to unravel for the right sign.

If it did not happen soon, harvest time would come and Cade would have to wait until the following summer to repeat his quest for his future. It confused him, Cade's dream, but he did not linger on it for it was the province of his father, Chief Tekata, and the medicine man.

Cade went inside the tepee he shared with his mother, Waterflower. Next to their tepee sat the tepee of Long Arrow. To Cade, Long Arrow was the closest thing to a father he had known. He had been taught by Long Arrow from the first steps he took the traits of character he would carry with him through a long eventful life.

Carefully, he hung his equipment, consisting of a bow, quiver of arrows, and a coil of rope. The tepee was empty at the moment and he walked to the center where the fire burned. He knelt to examine what his mother was cooking, for like all boys his age, he seemed to be in a state of perpetual hunger. He was about to taste what bubbled in the pot and smelled so enticing when his mother entered the tepee. She smiled at Cade as he turned his startling blue eyes toward her. He smiled, his teeth white and even and his features softened by affection. As he looked at her, he rose and went to her.

"Our raid was successful, my Mother; we have taken many horses. If we divide them, I shall have at least fifteen. I am almost wealthy."

She laughed. "And have you finished the lessons you were given by your teacher?"

"No . . . Mother . . . the lessons . . . are they really necessary? I can do much for my people by staying here. I am a warrior, my arm is strong, I can fight, hunt, do whatever is necessary."

"Cade . . ." her dark eyes smiled sympathetically into his, "what disturbs you so? You have not questioned my decisions before."

He turned from her, uncertainty in his eyes. "I . . . I don't feel the lessons are necessary any longer. I don't want to leave my people and the life I know."

"Cade, you must think with your mind, not your heart. You must remember that you have obligations you must fulfill. You are chosen by the circumstances of your birth to carry on work that is needed by your people."

"Chosen," he said softly, "when the Great Spirit will not even look upon my face and give me a sign, when he gives me dreams and visions in a form not even our chief can understand."

She was silent again for a few minutes. Then she said quietly, "I have received a message this day from your father. He wants to know if your teacher has been successful, if you have learned all he has requested, and . . . when you will be coming to join him."

She saw the quiver of his muscles and the tightening of his jaw.

"My father . . ." he whispered, "a man I do not know . . . a world I do not know. Why must I go, can I not learn medicine from our medicine man?"

It took her only a moment to understand what he was feeling. Fear. He was afraid to be transplanted into a world where he could not function as well as he did here. She remained silent for a moment watching him. "How handsome he is," she thought, "and how much he is like his father." He was tall, towering over her even at his young age. His shoulders were broad and his lithe, well-controlled muscles rippled under the smooth deep-bronze skin. He was slim-hipped and his legs were long and firm. His mane of thick black hair hung just below his shoulders and was tied back with a strip of rawhide while a white- and red-beaded band of leather circled his head. From this, two white-and-black feathers hung downward over his left ear. His face was smooth and clear with a wide easily smiling mouth in a square firm jaw. His black, winged brows arched over a pair of clear blue intelligent eyes—eyes, at his youthful age, that were a mirror to the mind of the boy behind them. She read them clearly and easily as she always could, as she could read his father's before him.

"Cade, I have told you over and over; you understand. I realize it is difficult for you to accept, this changing in your world; your father has sacrificed much. He deserves now to have you with him, to teach you what he wants you to know."

Disobedience never even occurred to him. His training at the hand of Long Arrow was complete. "How . . . how soon did you tell him I would come?"

"I have left that decision to you."

"Can . . . can I wait until I have received my vision sign, until I have taken my name? I hate to leave my life here unfinished."

"It will never be finished, my son. Your life among us is just beginning. Your father only wants to train you so that when you return you can bring with you his gift for healing."

Cade didn't want to tell her that his interest in his father's medicine was less than his interest in his place among his people.

"As you wish, my mother. I shall go when it pleases you."

He turned to leave the tepee.

"Will you not eat now?"

"No, I will go to the river and wash first." He left, but she was sure of what he would do. His mind troubled, he would turn to the closest thing to a father he had, Long Arrow.

Cade did exactly what she had thought. He went to the river and washed; then gathering his clothes and re-dressing, he made his way to Long Arrow's tepee where he requested permission to enter.

Long Arrow sat beside his fire working on the creation of new weapons. All warriors of the tribe made everything they used. He handled his weapons with great care and an eye toward perfection, a perfection necessary if he were going to be successful as a hunter.

Without words, Cade sat down opposite him and waited to be spoken to first. Long Arrow watched him surreptitiously for several minutes before he spoke.

"Your heart is heavy, Cade." It was a statement, not a question. "Is it because of the message your mother received today?"

Cade looked at Long Arrow. This man had cared for him as a

son all his life. From Cade, he had all the respect and admiration the boy's heart could give. Besides the fact that he was a courageous and strong man whose prowess as a hunter and warrior were unsurpassed in the entire tribe, was the fact that he had given up everything, out of friendship to Cade's father, for the sole purpose of caring for Waterflower and himself.

He was less than forty years old, but looked much younger. His face was firm and chiseled, giving him a stern look that belied the humor that always lingered below the surface. It was his fine sense of mental balance, his way of facing any problem with a firm and quiet determination that always had given Cade the feeling that Long Arrow knew what to do about any problem.

"I don't want to leave my people. I can do more here than I can by traveling to a far place where I will be useless."

Long Arrow smiled gently, his face filled with compassion.

"Is it that, my son?" he questioned. "Or are you afraid?"

Cade's ever-present pride was stung, mostly because Long Arrow was right and had come directly to the point.

"Long Arrow has never taught me to be afraid of anything," he said stiffly.

"You are right, but Long Arrow has never taught you to lie to yourself either. Look inside your heart, Cade; you will find your way clearly marked. I have told you all about your father and why it is necessary for you to do this. No one here could or would want to force you to do anything. The choice now and always must be yours."

Cade sat in deep thought and Long Arrow watched, reading the boy easily; he smiled again.

"You are right." Cade smiled. "You are always right."

"There is no right or wrong here, only the choice of duty."

"I feel . . . incomplete," Cade said thoughtfully, "as if I were being separated. I want to become a warrior with my own vision before I go. It is the only way I will feel that I still belong here."

"Yes, but maybe that will happen soon. I have come recently from the tepee of Chief Tekata. He has talked of you with the medicine man and I feel they will send for you soon."

"Long Arrow," he said hopefully.

"It is all I know, my Son." Long Arrow grinned. "They are speaking. But I think you should be ready to be sent for."

A tingle of expectancy combined with a little fear again nudged Cade's consciousness. The hope to stand beside his brother White Eagle as a warrior, to have his own vision to follow, his own sign to guide his life was, at this point in his life, his greatest desire.

"I will return to my tepee," he said quietly. "I will stay there and prepare myself. Maybe they will still speak with me this night."

He rose and left Long Arrow's tepee. He walked slowly through the dusky evening light. The activities about him went unheard and unseen as his mind drifted to the jumbled dreams he had had, to the confused vision he had presented to the medicine man.

He remembered so vividly the clouded visions. He was walking through a large group of his people. He sensed they were his people yet the faces were vague. They seemed to be reaching for him as if in supplication. Why then did he walk with a bloodied knife in his hand and feel the terrible choking pain? Then he sensed that someone was walking beside him. He turned his head. On either side of him walked a man. One was dark and the other light. As they walked, he realized their arms crossed in front of him and they were bound to each other. In a swift movement, he reached out with the bloodied knife and severed the bonds that held them together. The dark one staggered and fell, but the light one seemed to stand straighter and taller and walk with a more purposeful stride. Then, the vagueness disappeared and he was looking into the eyes of his brother, White Eagle.

He could not understand it; he only knew it had caused some consternation to the medicine man and his chief when he had told them. Now, as he had for the past few weeks, he waited.

Inside his own tepee, he sat while his mother prepared his meal. She knew he was considering the words Long Arrow had spoken to him, so she left him to his thoughts and remained silent.

The meal was barely over when they heard a voice from just

outside the tepee. It was Snow Blossom, and she quietly requested permission to enter. Waterflower called to her and she came in. Her eyes were wide and bright as they searched for Cade. He rose and stood looking at her for he knew it had to be an extremely important thing for the daughter of the chief to be sent.

"Snow Blossom?"

"My father wishes you to come to him," she said and her voice was filled with a mystifying awe as she gazed at him with a look closely akin to worship.

Cade gulped and steadied himself as a sudden trembling excitement almost overcame him. He looked at his mother who was smiling. Without a word, he left with Snow Blossom behind him.

At the entrance to Chief Tekata's tepee, he requested permission to enter. When it was granted, he stepped inside and waited by the entranceway for the great chief, who was seated on the fur-covered bench by his fire, to motion for him to come forward. He was not surprised to see the medicine man was also present. In their tribe, the medicine man was second to no one but the chief.

Cade stepped forward and waited, holding his breath in an agony of suspense. Chief Tekata was a large bronze man. His face was the granite face of a leader who was sure both of his power and his strength to handle it. He looked at Cade with agate, unreadable eyes. He motioned Cade to sit before him, and Cade obediently dropped down cross-legged on the ground in front of the chief.

"It has taken us long to consider your vision. We have had to give it much thought for the signs were confusing. Now, they are understood clearly and we are ready to give you your vision sign."

Cade could feel the excitement boil within him, but he waited in stoic silence until the chief continued. Tekata held out a piece of soft buckskin to Cade who took it, unfolded it, and blinked in surprise at what he saw. In red, there was an elongated diamond, inside this was another, and within this the picture of the rising sun with its rays. Underneath the large diamond was a long-bladed knife.

The red diamonds were the coveted signs of the medicine man. The sun within was the sign for constancy and loyalty. The knife was to be Cade's own sign.

"You are to be Sun Knife, blood brother to White Eagle, chosen to be medicine man not only among your people but to others. Word has come to us that your father now sends for his son so that he can give to him the medicine we need. It is our wish that you go after the first harvest moon. You will take word to your father that he is missed by his friends. Know this, Sun Knife; you carry within you the blood of a great man. Go in peace, my Son, and one day, return to us and bring with you your father's medicine."

There was absolutely no thought of disobedience in Cade's mind. No matter how he felt, he would do as Tekata commanded. He rose and left the tepee. Outside, the joy overwhelmed him; he raised his fist to the sky and shouted his wild cry at the top of his voice.

Inside her tepee, Waterflower heard and smiled. Snow Blossom also heard and her young heart leaped with the pleasure of sharing Cade's happiness. No matter if he thought of her as a child, he was the warrior of her dreams and he walked in a special place in her heart no other could reach.

The next day, with infinite care, Cade took his shield from the wall of his tepee. The shield was several layers of buckskin over a frame made of buffalo bones. It could withstand an arrow or the blow from a war club. Anything painted on its surface was considered a sacred sign that would in some supernatural way, protect the bearer from harm.

Laboriously, he painted on it the sign given him. He did it with the greatest patience and care. When he was finished, he attached feathers from the hawk around the edges. Each feather had a special meaning, denoted by the color it was dyed and how it was notched.

His heart sang and he was sure he had never felt happier in his life.

As the days went on, he walked among his people with a pride that bordered closely on strutting. He knew he would stand beside his blood brother White Eagle at the ceremony of okipa. The rite was both a vision quest and a celebration of their creation. To stand beside the chief's son, to suffer through the ceremony together would make them more than blood brothers.

Then the day finally came. Okipa began with the arrival of a lone man who recited tribal myths while Hoita presided over the ceremonies within the okipa lodge.

Sun Knife and White Eagle presented themselves proudly. For several days, they had fasted and prepared for the torturous ceremony.

Two sharp knives were used to slash their chests. Neither spoke a word or made a sound. Then, they were skewered through the loosened skin and raised toward the roof of the lodge on thongs attached to lengths of rawhide. There they hung, lifting their eyes toward the sun until they fainted.

Lowered to the ground in an unconscious state, they were now receptive to vision.

Sun Knife was to remember his for the rest of his life. Through the waves of excruciating pain, walked two figures. Both were women. When they neared him, Sun Knife could see that one was white and the other Indian. They spoke, but he could not hear the words. Then he could hear weeping and he could see the Indian girl's tears. She reached for him, her dark hair blowing about her. The white girl laughed scornfully. She held out her hand to him and glittery gold coins fell from them.

Before blackness enclosed him, he felt his hands touched, but he did not know which one had done so. They faded into the mists of his mind, but not before he felt the sense of being, of belonging as he had never felt before and he heard her soft whisper. "You are home, Cade . . . you are home." Then darkness enfolded him and he released his touch on his vision and the searing tearing pain he had endured.

When White Eagle and Sun Knife had recuperated from their ordeal, they spent many days together. Days Cade wanted to cling to, for the day he had to face leaving the security of his home was rapidly approaching. Before it came, Cade was to stumble into a situation that was as pleasing as the okipa was painful.

Among his tribe, as among all others, there was a fine degree of morality. He would never have considered approaching a maiden in sexual desire for fear of shaming both his name and hers. But, as always, there was the other woman. The one who, as they put it, "straddled the road." He had heard of them, and imagined them as coarse ugly women who could not get a man otherwise. Maybe that is why he was in a state of suspended shock when he met her.

He had been hunting, alone this time only because White Eagle had other duties to which he had to attend, and was on his way home, letting his pony pick his way delicately down a shallow stream when he rounded a curve in the stream and froze in his tracks.

The stream widened a little, and standing in a waist-deep pool, bathing, was a girl. Her naked body caught his stunned attention, both what he could see above the water and what he could imagine below. He was even more surprised when she saw him and instead of fleeing, she smiled.

Her body glistened in the late-afternoon sun; her long wet hair clung to her wet skin in thick tendrils. She was a little older than he and her smile was wide and knowing. She walked slowly from the water, knowing his eyes were upon her, and leisurely reached for the buckskin dress she had left on the bank. Raising her arms, she let it drop about her. It was only when her slender figure was covered that he realized he had been sitting still staring at her. He could hear the soft murmur of her laughter and it stung his youthful pride. He kicked his pony into motion and rode to her side. She smiled up at him and his scrambled thoughts searched words to make him sound more like a warrior and less like a trembling boy.

"You are alone here, without protection?"

"Why do I need protection, warrior, do you intend to harm me?"

"I am Sun Knife. Our tribe lives near here. Where are you from?"

Her eyes became shadowed. "My tribe lives many miles from here. I am alone."

Her words told him exactly why she was where she was. She had been excluded from her village as was always done with a woman whose morals were loose. He knew what she was; he just didn't know how to handle it. She saw this, too, and smiled again.

"My tepee is near and I have food; are you hungry?"

He was, but it was not for food. His body was busy remembering her lovely golden body in the light of the dying sun.

"Yes."

"Come and eat," she said softly, her words meaning more than they said.

He slid down from his horse and led it as he walked beside her into the shade of the woods that bordered the stream. He tied his horse outside and went into the tepee with her. She prepared him a dish of food and he ate. It would have been impossible an hour later for him to say what he ate.

She laughed and talked with him, questioning him about himself. Soon, he was talking freely, telling her all about himself and relaxing with her. The tepee had darkened with the setting sun and the glow of the fire was the only light. He knew he should go, but no power on earth could pull his eyes away from her pretty face or the memory of what was beneath the dress.

She rose and walked to the mat covered with thick furs. She smiled at him again and reaching down, she took the hem of her dress and pulled it over her head, casting it aside. If she had been lovely in the sunlight, to him, she was a goddess in the golden glow of the fire.

Drawn by her beauty, he rose and went to her side. He reached for her and she laughed pressing her small warm hands against his broad chest.

"You must learn, Sun Knife," she whispered, "and Tzia will teach you. Patience, warrior, it is a thing of joy if you learn patience."

Slowly, she began to undress him, her warm gentle fingers causing sensations that drew from him a murmured sound of pleasure. Naked, he stood as she came into his arms, her cool rounded body pressing against his heated one.

His hungry mouth caught hers in a kiss so furiously demanding that she was surprised. His arms held her so tightly against him, she could hardly breathe. Tzia had taken many men, but she realized Sun Knife's uniqueness immediately. She had looked at his bronze muscular body with the eye of an expert and found nothing wanting. Obviously, he was a brave warrior for she could see from the only scars on his body that he had taken part in the okipa. She felt the strength in the arms that held her and the pressure of his swollen manhood as it pressed urgently against her belly.

His hands were beginning to wander, searching as hers were, for the pleasure he was feeling. They dropped to the furs together and he began an exploration that set her gasping and began to build a heat in her she had not found before.

Gently, she led him, feeling the need for her build in him until he gripped her with hands of iron and drew her body against his. Giving in to the searching pleasure, she felt his lips brush her face, touch her lips, then begin a heated path to more sensitive areas. The more he sensed her enjoyment, the more it heightened his. He wanted to prolong this magically awakening journey as long as possible. The fire within him was beyond control as he felt her hands caressing his back and shoulders and drawing him tighter to her.

The need was greater than anything he had ever felt before and it drew a groan of ecstasy from him when he felt his body join with hers. Sheathed within her, he moved with a force that shook her. She clung to him and met his thrusts halfway with a passion that matched his. The fire engulfed them both and they journeyed to the edge of the volcano and tumbled into its molten depths together. In that one brilliant moment, Cade felt as if he were going to die. The pleasure was so great that he crushed her to him and held her trembling body in an embrace that blended them together like one.

In a state of near exhaustion, he rolled from her and lay beside her, both of them silent—he in amazed wonder at what had just happened, and she contemplating many nights in the future when her brave new warrior had learned all the secrets she possessed.

And so, Sun Knife began to learn another secret of living; he was an apt and very willing pupil.

During the last of the summer days, he kept her supplied with meat and other things she needed to live, and she supplied him with the most unforgettable summer of his life. She taught him the patience of an expert lover and the ways to give the most pleasure. It was not many weeks until he was leading and she, to her surprise, was following.

Sun Knife took much in the way of jesting by White Eagle and some of his other friends who surmised what was happening, but kept a respectful distance out of care for him.

He had a life in which he was completely happy; yet hovering on the outer sphere of his consciousness was the knowledge that soon, he would be forced to separate himself from all he knew and loved and to exist in a strange new world with people he did not know or understand.

Tzia knew and understood the separate ways of their lives even if he did not. At this stage, he deluded himself with the idea that he was in love with Tzia. When he spoke of it, he paid no attention to the strange quiet look in her eyes. Now, she knew all there was to know about Sun Knife, and she realized what his future would be. She also realized it would soon be the end of the only relationship she had ever truly enjoyed. They lay together one night, after a beautiful and breathtaking hour of love-making. She lay quietly and let him talk of plans for a future she would never share.

"Soon, the harvest moon will be full, Tzia, and I will go to join my father. I will return as soon as I can. You will wait for me here and when I come back, we will go to my village. There we will join and live together."

"Already you talk like a warrior. You give commands and expect them to be obeyed." She laughed, but it was a soft broken laugh. "You have a great and exciting future ahead of you, Sun Knife. I am pleased and very proud of you. It has been good for me to have shared these weeks with you."

He turned on his side and braced his elbow against the mat on which they lay, and looked down into her eyes.

"I would share it with you, Tzia. You will wait for me. I will have someone come and care for you while I am gone."

She reached up and caressed the side of his face, her eyes touched with tears. He was surprised and brushed them away with the tips of his fingers.

"Why do you weep, Tzia? Is it that you don't love me

enough to wait for me? Is there someone else?"

"I love you, Sun Knife," she whispered. "I love you enough that I will do for you whatever I have to do to make you happy."

He accepted this in the way he wanted and not in the way she meant. With a triumphant laugh, he pulled her into his embrace, covering her face with kisses and clasping her to him. She clung to him, knowing it was for the last time, knowing the hurt he would feel when he returned and found her gone. She would hurt him now to save him the pain and shame a man of his strong pride would feel when he found that neither of them would be accepted by the tribe if she returned with him.

She surrendered to his heated passion in a way she had never done before. She had always restrained herself, keeping herself strong enough for the day she must go. It had come, and she wanted now to hold it away for just a little longer. This time, she gave him Tzia, her heart and her body.

Sun Knife realized something was different, but he was so caught in the magic of their passion, so engulfed in the flame of her body that he let everything else escape his mind but the possession of the soft loveliness he held.

For her, the night ended too soon. With the morning light, she must face the fact of Sun Knife's loss. They rose early and ate the breakfast she prepared.

"I shall go back to the village and make my plans to go. Tonight, I will come and we will be together until I leave. Then you will be under the protection of my blood brother, White Eagle."

Her eyes watched him. She wanted to memorize every line of his sleek muscular body, the quick smile and light laughing eyes. He had such an aura of overpowering strength and confidence that she was tempted for a moment to go with him, but she loved him too much to do so. She was wise enough to know that what he thought was love, was his first brush with passion and she envied the woman who would share the balance of his life.

She held him for a long moment before he left. He laughed at her, chiding her on her feelings for him.

"I shall be back soon."

"Good-by, Sun Knife," she whispered as she pressed her mouth to his.

She watched him walk to his horse. With one lithe move, he was up on its back. She held the picture of him in her mind. His white smile, the beauty of his bronzed symmetry and his proud arrogance that gave him such an air of masculine confidence. He waved, and she returned the wave. She stood silently watching him until he was out of sight. Then she turned away, hot tears blending her eyes. She gathered her things together. Within two hours after Sun Knife had left, the area in which he had found such warm passion was as devoid of life as the heart of Tzia.

Sun Knife rode back to his village with a light heart and a broad smile. When he arrived, he sought out White Eagle. When he told him all that he had planned, White Eagle wanted to tell him of the impossibilities of such a situation. That Sun Knife would have an unwinnable battle on his hands he knew, but he did not have the heart to destroy his pleasure. He wanted to look into Tzia's eyes and see if she was a woman who could give his friend what he needed to fill his life.

They rode together to the small stream and White Eagle watched the smile fade from Sun Knife's face when he found her gone. They tried to trace her trail, but she was as expert as they and no trace of her could be found.

White Eagle's estimation of her jumped a few notches and even though Sun Knife was first angry then desperate, White Eagle knew it was for the best. He swore to himself that should he ever cross the path of a woman named Tzia, he would somehow reward her for the sacrifice she had made.

After a fruitless three-day search, Sun Knife and White Eagle returned to the camp. There, at his mother's tepee, Sun Knife found a stranger in a blue uniform who rose to his feet to welcome him.

"I am Lt. Grant Jameson. I've been sent by your father to help you over any . . . ah . . . difficulties."

Sun Knife smiled. "Did he expect the transition to be hard for an ignorant savage?"

Grant's smile remained. "Your father is the man who lived here for years, he's the man who sent the teacher to educate you. By no means does he think of you as an ignorant savage. He thought, since you have never been east before, I might be able to help you over the rough spots."

Sun Knife chuckled and extended his hand in grudging friendship to the first white friend he would have. The firm handshake increased his curiosity about the white man in general. A new experience was about to open before him, to lead him down a path filled with excitement, joy . . . and pain.

Chapter Two

Grant spent three days in the village while Cade made preparations for travel. The morning they were to leave, Grant sat in wide-eyed wonder at the elaborate preparations Cade was making. The clothes that he donned were of white buckskin, heavily fringed, and about the neck and wrists were elaborate bands of beadwork. His hair was braided on each side of his face allowing the back to hang to his shoulders. A beaded band encircled his head and from it three feathers hung downward.

"Well," Grant chuckled. "I must say you do look beautiful, but are you going to travel all the way east in that outfit?"

Cade laughed. "No, this is only for leaving. I will leave my village like a proud warrior. It will make my mother proud and give my people something to talk about. The brave they are sending to the white man's world to get his medicine. They will expect me to come back the way I leave."

Grant watched the emotions flicker across what was usually an unreadable face. For the first time, it registered with him what a step Cade was taking and he wondered how he would feel if he were suddenly to be transplanted into a new world filled with people he did not know or understand.

"Cade, I will be living close to your father's home. If you ever feel you need a friend to talk to, you know where I am."

Cade looked at him, his eyes unreadable now in self-protection. He would admit to no man that he was afraid. His young pride was touched, and for a moment he stiffened. But the past few years with the teacher his father had sent had opened Cade's eyes to the white man's ways. He smiled. "Thanks, Grant. I'll be all right. Shall we go?"

Their horses were tied outside and they left the tepee. All family good-bys had been said. His mother stood by his horse; next to her was Long Arrow and White Eagle. He barely noticed Snow Blossom who stood just behind her brother, her large dark eyes filled with tears.

Tekata stood at his son's side. "Go in peace, my son, and bring our good wishes to your father. Tell him we wish he would return to us soon."

"I will speak your words to him, my Chief. I am sure they will lighten his heart."

Tekata nodded. He clapped his heavy hand on Cade's shoulder for a moment, then he turned away. Cade watched him walk back toward his tepee and realized how much he was going to miss the older man's guidance.

"Return soon, Sun Knife," White Eagle said. "My brother will be missed."

Cade nodded as his and White Eagle's eyes held for a moment of understanding. The sorrowful good-bys spoken to all others, he turned to his mother. Without a word, he held her to him, his strong arms about her; then he silently mounted and rode from the village. They did not stop and Cade did not speak until the sun was high overhead. Grant left him alone with his thoughts allowing him to adjust his mind to the future.

They stopped by a river for the noontime meal. Cade removed his clothes and folded them carefully, packing them away. They would not be worn again for a long time.

It would be many days of travel before they sighted the first fort. For these days, Cade wore only his breechcloth. It was more comfortable and Grant found himself envying the freedom he must have felt for he could feel the sweat trickle down his body under the confining clothes. Cade smiled, and the twinkle of laughter in his eyes told that he knew exactly how Grant felt.

Fort Stanton was the last outpost of the white man's world. It sat, insecure and bolted against the fear of the "savages" that existed between them and the sea. Peace between the white and the Indian was a precarious thing, and everyone at the fort lived in expectation of the unknown. Past stories of the bloodthirsty savages were always spread about and an unconscious fear of them was overly enlarged in every mind. That, and the natural prejudice of the "superior" white over all others was the reason there was a deadened silence as Grant and Cade rode through the doors of the fort.

From the fort, they would take a stagecoach to Bridger City, the first touch of "civilization."

Cade had dressed in buckskin pants and a fringed buckskin shirt. The boots were of leather and each piece of clothing fit his tall muscular frame. He conceded to their civilization only on this point, for he retained the headband and the feathers that spoke of his tribe and his pride.

Cade sensed the emotions through every pore in his body, but no one would have known it as he slid from his horse in one lithe movement, tied it, and followed Grant into the commanding officer's office.

Inside, the corporal rose to his feet and saluted Grant.

"Tell Major Riles we're here, Corporal Dawson."

"Yes, sir."

The man rose from his desk and with his eyes still on Cade's form, he went inside and closed the door. Cade chuckled.

"I had the urge to scream a war cry and jump at him. What do you think would have happened?"

Grant could hardly control his smile. "He would have lost control of his body functions and embarrassed the U.S. Cavalry."

Cade threw back his head and laughed. It eased a lot of the tension he had carried within him for the past few days.

The door opened and the corporal returned. "Major Riles wants you to come in, sir."

Grant saw the wicked gleam in Cade's eye. He took him by the arm and urged him toward the door.

Inside, Major Riles rose to his feet and extended his hand first to Grant, and then, to Cade's surprise, to him. The surprised look did not go unnoticed by Maj. George Riles. He was a man of about fifty. It was easy to see that he had led a very physical life for his body was trim and straight. He had clear dark brown eyes that were assessing Cade as closely as he was being assessed.

"So," he said softly, "you are Michael's son."

"You know my father?"

"Yes, I'm proud to say I do. I would not be on the last spot of the civilized world if I did not know and admire the man. He is doing more to keep peace here than any other I know. I'm here because he trusts me and wants a man here who will not let a situation happen. I would not have come to this godforsaken place for any other man."

"It is not a godforsaken place," Cade said gently. "Here the gods have been good to us. We live in peace. It is the white man's greedy reaching that only brings the trouble. Why can they not be satisfied with what they have? Why must they always be reaching to take what belongs to another?"

Major Riles sighed and sat back down in his chair. "If I had the answer to that, boy, I would put an end to the reaching. You are quite good with our language."

"My father sent a teacher when I was a boy. I have learned much of your ways."

Major Riles smiled, the word "boy" amused him for Cade was, at eighteen, not much beyond a boy. "You are going to finish your education; then what?"

"I will, if the Great Spirit wishes, follow my father's footsteps. I will be a medicine man."

"A doctor?"

"No," Cade said softly, "a medicine man."

Major Riles's eyes met Grant's and he saw the amusement there. Cade may have been afraid of the transition, but he was prepared to stand for what he loved and believed in.

"A medicine man," the major repeated, then he rose again, the smile reappearing in his eyes. "The stage will arrive tomorrow morning and leave tomorrow afternoon. I wish you well, son, and when you have decided to return home, will you stop here? I should like to meet a . . . medicine man."

"Yes, sir, I will."

The major chuckled. "Good luck, boy, but I fear you are going to be more of a challenge than you think you are."

"A challenge, sir? I don't understand. I don't want to challenge anyone. I only want to know my father and do as he wishes. Why is that a challenge to the whites?"

"I wish to explain to you," Riles said almost angrily, "but I'm sure you will find the answer to that question soon enough." He looked at Grant. "You have quarters arranged across the compound. Will you two share a room or should I arrange separate quarters?"

"One room is enough," Grant said. "Cade and I have a lot of talking to do. It's time I made myself useful. Are the things I sent for here?"

"Yes, they came a week or so ago."

"What talking, what did you send for?" Cade asked.

"We're going to talk about what you have to do, and I sent for some clothes. It's time you took the step. Tomorrow, you take off freedom and put on civilization."

Three hours later, after they had eaten and returned to their room, Grant sat on the edge of the bed and watched Cade, shaking his head in disbelief of what he was trying to do. Cade stood before him. He had changed into the clothes Grant had gotten for him, but adamantly refused to cut his hair or remove the signs of his tribe.

"Damn it, you can't walk around back east in braids with feathers in your hair."

"Why?"

"Because . . . because you just can't."

"I have put on all of the white man I intend to. I will keep also the part of me that is Indian," Cade said firmly.

Grant could see he was getting nowhere, so for the time being, he gave up. He looked at Cade critically. Despite the fact that the clothes fit him well, there was no way to hide the wild, free look of the boy. He looked like a young eagle held in a cage and continually watching for a way to fly away. It was a look, though he would learn to control it, that would never leave him. He exuded an aura of controlled violence that would in time draw the ire of many men, and the hungry gazes of numbers of women who seemed to sense the savage man behind the exterior. They talked long into the night, yet Cade was up with the dawn. It was nearing noon when the coach arrived and it was two hours later when they boarded and began the long journey home.

Cade, who had never seen a city before, watched in fascination as they went from one to the other, each becoming larger than the one before. It was a fair exchange of fascination, for they were as interested in him as he was in them. He was quick to learn and by the time they reached Washington, Grant felt he could have left Cade to himself and he would have been fine. Again, he wondered if he could have absorbed the Indian culture as fast as Cade was absorbing the whites'.

As they neared Washington, Grant sensed a tension in Cade that he was trying to keep under control. He couldn't understand what was wrong; then suddenly it dawned on him. In a few days, he would meet his father for the first time and the meeting, for some reason, was worrying him. Again, it took a few minutes for it to dawn on him that to Cade, Michael was very nearly a legend. They arrived in Washington, a city of more hustle and bustle than Cade had ever seen before. No one would have suspected he was spellbound except Grant, who could see the way he was trying to control his vibrant enthusiasm and not gape in open-mouthed wonder at the scenes unfolding about him.

Grant watched with amusement the tight control Cade was using. He felt Cade would be fine once the first meeting with his father was over.

The coach came to a rocking halt and Grant opened the door and stepped down. Michael Holliday stood watching the coach door as if his life depended upon it. Then Cade filled the doorway and father's and son's eyes met for the first time.

Cade was unsure whether to be Indian or white. He chose the safest course, just to be himself. He walked to his father and stood before him, his ingrained attitude of respect and honor obvious. He waited for Michael to acknowledge his presence. Michael's heart leaped with joy and he smiled and placed his hand on Cade's shoulder. He could feel the tremor in the boy's body, and saw the happiness dance in the mirror of his own blue eyes.

"Welcome to my home, my Son," Michael said. He tried to grasp and remember the gentle ways of the Indian. "You have made an old man very happy."

Cade smiled. "The age sets well with you, my Father. My heart is gladdened by the welcome you have given. It is good to see the man who gave me life. I hope I can bring joy and pride to your home."

"You have, Son," Michael said softly, unshedable tears in his eyes. "You have."

He could bear the strain of this overly polite greeting no longer. He grasped the boy in his arms and held him to him. For one small second he could feel the joyous clinging of the strong arms of his son as they held him to him fiercely as if he had found something valuable and was afraid he might lose it.

"Come," Michael said in a voice choked with emotion. "You must both be tired and hungry."

They went to Michael's carriage and started home. When Michael began to question Cade, he could not stop, question after question, most of them about his mother and the conditions at home. The realization came to Cade, maybe for the first time, how completely his father loved his mother and her people. The sacrifice he had made came through to Cade with its full force and his heart swelled with pride that this tall handsome man was his father. At that moment, the seed of intense love and respect began to blossom—a love that grew day by day in the years he would spend with his father.

They spent the first two weeks getting Cade accustomed to life in the city. He got along well, with the exception of the constraining clothes and the sense of the loss of freedom. He kept his windows open at night and refused to sleep clothed. He found that there was a park near his father's house and he could ride there; consequently, dawn found him there every morning. About three weeks later, Michael decided to join him. Cade had already gone so he arrived alone. When he got his horse he followed the bridle path. He was shaking with laughter when he finally came across Cade, who, when out of eyesight of the horse's owner, had calmly unsaddled the horse and was riding like the wind across meadows and fields that had no connection to the well-laid-out bridle paths. Michael never let him know he was there, but let him keep his one remembered joy of home.

When Michael felt sufficient time had passed to get Cade settled, he broached the subject of his continued education. This was met with a great deal of enthusiasm from Cade, so Michael began letting Cade observe as he cared for patients. This was done four days a week; for two others he hired a tutor to continue his scholastic development.

Within two months, they were on a relaxed schedule and Michael was amazed at the rapidity with which Cade absorbed everything he had to offer.

Grant returned to duty, but less than a year later, he was transferred and Cade was not to see him for a long time. They corresponded sporadically and after a year, Grant wrote that he was being sent to Fort Stanton for an unknown amount of time.

Cade left himself little time for social activities, and Michael was a firm believer that all work and no play was not good for any boy who was nearing twenty.

Michael was a welcome person in the homes of everyone of consequence in New York. He was respected and loved both as a doctor and a man. Few people knew anything about his past and he kept it that way, but it left him open to the predatory gazes of many women.

At forty-three, Michael was still very handsome, and he had kept his large muscular body in good condition.

When he began introducing his son to people, it first surprised them; then began to overwhelm them with curiosity. It was no surprise when he decided to have a party in celebration of Cade's twentieth birthday; no one even considered refusal.

It was Cade who was slightly rebellious at the idea of a huge crowd of people he did not know and with whom he felt no affinity.

He dressed for the party with elaborate care. Michael had finally convinced him to shorten his hair and remove, albeit temporarily, the feathers and the band of tribal heritage.

It was a night Cade would not only remember for a long time, but it was a night that was going to make many changes both in his attitude and his life.

He came down the stairs of his father's huge house when most of the guests had already arrived. He drifted about the room for a while, his alert eyes sensing everyone about him. He had his back to his father when he felt his hand on his shoulder. He turned with a smile. His father was accompanied by two people; one was a tall distinguished man, and the other was a beautiful auburn-haired vision he had never seen before.

"Cade, I want you to meet Alexander Brent and his daughter, Lauren."

Cade shook hands and spoke to Alexander Brent, but his eyes were on the slim girl that stood at his side and met the look in his eyes with the same depth of curiosity as his.

Lauren Brent smiled slightly, but her mind was busy contemplating Cade. "He is so ungodly handsome," she thought. There was something intrinsically different between him and any other man she had met.

As an extremely wealthy and very beautiful heiress, Lauren had met many men. She knew most of them for what they were, fortune hunters, who wanted the privilege of crawling into her bed and spending her money—and not necessarily in that order. Somehow, she felt this man was different. There was an air about him, as if he held in sharp control, deep and very violent passions that if left unchecked could consume those near him. "Savage" was the first word that popped into her mind.

He smiled, his bronze skin a perfect foil for his white square teeth. She found herself smiling in response and her hand held in a large strong hand that sent a lightning current through her. She also saw the startled look register in his amazingly blue eyes, and wondered if he, too, felt the strong magnetic attraction.

"Miss Brent," he said softly.

"How do you do, Mr. Holliday?"

"So, Michael, this is the son I have heard so much about. How do you like our city, Cade?" Alexander asked.

"Well . . . it's . . . large," he said with a quick laugh.

Alexander shrugged. "Yes, it's large and prosperous, and your father could have it at his feet if he were not so stubborn."

"Oh?" Cade questioned.

"I am on the board of directors at both of our hospitals. I've offered the position of head of surgery to your father several times."

"And he's refused?" Cade looked questioningly at his father and was surprised to see his usually smiling face was grim and his lips were pressed together as if he were restraining himself with a great deal of effort.

"Continually," Alexander said, "politely, and firmly and without any logical reasons."

Cade had a swift thought about what his father's reasons might have been, but he would say nothing until they were alone. Lauren smiled as she realized from Cade's look that he was loyal to his father.

"Father, you have promised to behave tonight," Lauren said with as sweet a smile as she could muster. "If you two are going to discuss business I shall just have to rescue Cade from your clutches." She turned her sunny smile on Cade and extended her hand, a gesture he could not refuse. He took it. "You will rescue me from all this boring talk and dance with me, won't you?"

It was the first time since his arrival that Cade was at a complete loss, for he had not even given a moment's thought to learning how to dance. Lauren slipped her hand through his arm and they excused themselves and walked toward the dance floor. After a few steps, Cade stopped and turned to her.

"Miss Brent?"

"Lauren," she said with a smile that made him respond.

"I'm . . . I'm afraid I don't know how to dance."

Her eyes sparkled with mischief and she pressed his arm against her. "Good, we can take a walk in the garden and you can satisfy all my very, very unladylike curiosity."

She laughed lightly. "Right now, I'm the envy of every pretty girl in this room. Let me turn them green by walking away with you. It will drive them insane."

Cade grinned. "I'm sure you're exaggerating, Lauren, but I would be very stupid not to take advantage of it."

They walked out through the large French doors, across the veranda and down the steps to a small but exquisite garden.

"Tell me about you, Cade Holliday."

"Me? There's nothing interesting about me. I'm an average person trying to get enough education to fill a dream . . . that's me."

"An average person," she said softly. She stopped walking and turned to him. "You are the farthest thing from an average man I've ever met. I know more about you than you think. Your mother was a very beautiful Indian girl and your father wanted to stay there more than he ever wanted anything he could have here. What I really would like to know is . . . what did he find there, what holds his heart there and . . . I suspect you would be the same."

"Yes, I guess you are right. My heart will always be there. I am only here to learn. When my father thinks I am ready, I will go home."

"You say home in that very special way. Tell me, I have been so many places, seen so many things and I can never have that very . . . special feeling about that mythical place called home. Tell me."

"I don't know if I can, Lauren. Yes, home to me is something very special. I'd never been more than twenty miles away from it at any time until I came here. I've never seen a white man outside of the teacher my father sent, until Grant came for me. Yet I've never felt lonely or unhappy; I've never felt restricted and smothered like I am here. There is a peace there. It's . . . I can't explain it."

"How very luck you are," she whispered.

"Yes, I guess I am. Someday, maybe you would like to come and see for yourself."

"That would be beautiful. Now, since you have made such a gallant offer to me, I am going to return to favor."

"Oh?" He laughed. "How?"

"I'm going to teach you to dance."

"I shall probably step on your feet." He chuckled.

"I'll take that chance."

The soft strains of the waltz drifted through the window. Lauren stepped close looking up into his eyes.

"Put your arm about me."

He did, slowly drawing her close. She put her other hand in his.

"It's easy," she said softly and began slowly to sway to the music. "One-two-three, one-two-three, one-two-three."

A natural grace and physical control was instinctive in Cade. It took him only a moment to catch the rhythm and begin to move with her. He could feel her supple body in the curve of his arm and slowly he drew her close enough for their bodies to touch. Without speaking, they moved to the music. Lauren could feel her pulse begin to race as she felt the latent strength of him and was held in the magnetic pull of his blue eyes. He was like no man whom she had ever known and she began to wonder if she could unleash that control for a moment and see the man she sensed was just below the civilized nerves.

The music stopped and they both stood still, yet he did not drop his arm from about her. His hand caressed her cheek in the gentlest of touches, then he slowly bent his head and brushed her lips lightly with his. The tingling shock of it held them both mesmerized for a moment, then his arms enclosed her in a grip of iron and his mouth came down on hers, a hard demanding mouth from which her senses seemed to have no protection. Her lips parted under his questioning ones and she could feel the length of his body pressed against hers.

Always, Lauren had been in command of all her faculties no matter what the situation, but now, she felt all sense of reason slip away. She closed her eyes and let the heat of his passion enfold her. She was only brought back to startling awareness when she realized that his hands were gently exploring. It was not that that startled her, but the fact that she was thoroughly enjoying it and wanted to feel him touch her. It alarmed her, for Lauren was never an easy conquest. Others had tried and failed . . . but others did not reach the sensuous and tempestuous center of Lauren Brent. She stepped back from him and for a moment, they stood, breathlessly caught in the stillness of time, and looked at each other. Each realized the passion in which they had nearly become enmeshed.

"I'm sorry," Cade said.

"No . . . no, don't be sorry, Cade. I'm not . . . it's just that it's . . ." She was aware of the inadequacy of words. What she wanted to say she couldn't, what she wanted to do, she couldn't.

"Shall we go back in?" he said in a voice filled with gentleness. "We could practice our dancing in a safer place."

"Yes."

They reentered the house. It was no less difficult on the dance floor than it had been in the garden. And Lauren was grateful when the party was over and her father escorted her to the carriage.

They were riding home, the carriage enclosed in darkness. She realized her father could not see her face so she tentatively began to question him.

"You've known Michael Holliday for a long time, Father?"

"Yes, over fifteen years, since he came back from the West."

"Did you mean it about the offers you've made?"

"I surely did. He is the best surgeon I've ever had the privilege of knowing and if he is training his son, I should not be surprised if when he puts a scalpel in that boy's hand, he isn't better than the father."

"Do you believe that?"

"I've heard talk; Michael has taken a lot of time and patience with the boy. Around the hospital, Cade is his father's shadow. He is bright and he learns quickly. They have been telling me he has all the potential to be as good as his father."

"If . . . if he were, would you offer him the same posts as you did his father?"

"If he turned out as good, I would do my very best to get him to continue his work here."

"Don't you think he would want to?"

"No. Lauren, the boy is like a caged animal. He is wild and no civilization is going to hold him. He is on some sort of quest. When he finds his Holy Grail, he will be gone, like the wind. There is nothing—and no one—who will stop him from doing what he starts out to do."

Lauren rested her head against the back of the seat and closed her eyes. She could still feel the strength of the arms that held her and the heat of his demanding lips that had searched hers so thoroughly.

"Wouldn't it be wonderful," she thought, "if Cade would become the doctor her father obviously thought he could be, and if she could convince him to stay here, stay here with her and make a life together. To be a famous surgeon's wife, to be Cade Holliday's wife, and to have everything she had ever wanted at her fingertips," filled her mind.

Lauren was reputed to be one of the most beautiful young

debutantes in Washington. Her eyes, wide and sea green sat in an oval face. Her thick auburn hair glowed with a muted flame. Her mouth, wide and sensuous gave her the classic appearance of an unapproachable goddess. She was slim, yet her body was softly curved and definitely sensual.

She had lived with wealth all her life. Her father had a financial interest in so many things that she could not even realize the extent of it. She was an only child and her mother had died at her birth. Alexander had loved his wife completely and when she had died, he had transferred all that love to his daughter. There was nothing she wanted that he would not supply. Although she developed into a very beautiful woman, she was spoiled atrociously. By sixteen, she had seen every part of the civilized world, and had experienced many attempts both at marriage and seduction. By the time she was nineteen, she had developed a hard inner core and an eye that could spot a man's intent across a crowded room, for most of their intentions had always been the same.

Maybe that was why Cade had taken her so completely by surprise, for he had given her the impression that if she wanted to come to him, he would gladly accept what she offered, but that he offered nothing in return.

It jolted her with the fact that here was a man she could not just reach out and take, for he would not be taken. Here was a man who would take only a woman of his choice and on his terms. Yet she could still sense the deep hungry passion within him and something within her stirred to life and taunted her to see if she could change him.

"Father?"

"Yes?"

"If . . . if Cade should decide to stay, and if he is a good doctor, would you promise me to offer him that position?"

"What are you planning, Lauren?"

"Nothing, Father," she said innocently. "It was just a question; would you?"

"If he is as good as the father, I would be a fool not to. Yes, I would make that promise. But I want to warn you, Lauren, I don't want to see you get hurt."

"Warn me about what?"

"He doesn't belong here. Can't you sense it? Can't you feel it when he's near you? He will take what his father wants him to have, but he will live only on his own terms, and those terms will never include this civilization."

"I would not count on that, Father. Any man can change his plans if he's offered the right incentive. He's no different from any other man. All men want to be rich or famous—or both. Make him that kind of an offer and I'll wager he will not refuse."

Her father remained quiet for some time and then he said quietly, "Do you honestly believe that, Lauren—that all men have their price?"

"Yes, don't you?"

"I used to, once."

"And then?"

"And then I met Michael Holliday."

"And how is he different from any other man?"

Alexander told her all of Michael's past before he came to New York. "He's become a very wealthy man. Most of his money has been spent buying legislators, senators, other businessmen, anyone who will help him keep the land of his wife's people from being opened to settlers. A lot of money has gone to purchase food supplies and things those people need. At this moment, and for the past several years, he has been the only protective shield they have. Now, he wants to train his son to be a doctor for them. I have offered him more in the past few years, and I might add, so have others, than I have ever offered anyone for anything and yet he refuses. He lives only to return someday. No, he has no price for his honor and his pride and I don't believe his son does either. I should hate to see you get hurt when you find that he would walk away from you and wealth for his people."

"I believe if I'm given enough time, I could convince him that it is best for him to stay here. He could have a world men would envy."

"I just don't believe he could be happy in that world."

"But why? It is impossible not to be."

"Oh, Lauren, don't you see? He's not like these other men. The civilization has taken something from him. He is a free spirit. He cannot be contained in our world. He would die here, like an eagle, fettered forever and unable to fly. Leave him to his own world for I know he will never change and I don't want you to have to cry over the disappointment when he has gotten what he came for and decides to return to the only home he will ever love. Leave him be, child."

She was silent. It was not that she accepted his words, but that she was searching for the way to begin her conquest of Cade Holliday. All her father had said had whetted both her desire for him and the challenge he presented. She would find a way to reach him, and in the process, she would prove that Cade's pride and hers were a perfect match and she could get anything she wanted. At that moment, she wanted him more than she had ever wanted anything in her life and she was grimly determined that one day he would come to her on her terms. He would cast aside his father's dreams and stay with her. They would marry and be rich and famous. She closed her eyes again, enjoying the pictures she was creating.

Cade and his father sat in the library over a last drink in silence. Cade was thinking of a beautiful green-eyed girl and why he had the strange feeling he had seen her somewhere before. He could still taste the sweetness of her mouth on his and feel the soft body he had held so close for a moment.

"A moment now," he thought, but he knew there would be a moment again and he would not let the sweetness of Lauren Brent go untasted.

Chapter Three

It was two weeks before Lauren saw Cade again and it was at a large lawn party thrown for the benefit of the addition of a wing to the hospital. She had only gone because she knew Cade would be there.

She had taken great care in dressing, wearing a deep-green dress that accentuated her wide green eyes and enhanced the deep-wine color of her hair. She and her father walked about the huge crowded lawn that extended from the back of the hospital. There was a very large crowd and she searched the sea of faces for one.

She saw him standing with his father and two other men about his age. Again she sensed the vibrant difference between him and any of the others as he threw back his head and laughed at something someone had said. His smile flashed in his bronzed face. He stood half a head taller than the others, with the exception of his father. He was wearing a white shirt with ruffles at the cuffs and throat and a deep-blue jacket that made everyone more startlingly aware of his magnetic blue eyes. The fawn-colored pants hugged his lean muscular frame like a second skin and his black boots shone with an immaculate shine. It was obvious that he took care of himself.

She knew all the people in the group so she smiled up at her father as if she had just accidentally seen someone she knew.

"Father, there is Martin Preston and Lawrence Greely. I haven't seen either of them for ages. Shall we go and talk with them?"

Her father chuckled. "And the fact that they both happen to be in the vicinity of the man to whom you really want to talk has gone completely unnoticed by you?"

"Cade Holliday?"

"Cade Holliday, and don't play that innocent game with me, my girl. You forget I've been the victim of it far too often not to recognize it."

She laughed lightly, her green eyes aglow with mischief. "Lauren, do you remember what I told you on the way home from the party?"

"Yes, I remember."

"I don't want to see you get hurt, but—"

"But what?"

"I don't want to see him get hurt either. He is a fine boy, and he is well on his way to becoming an excellent doctor. He's not a man to take things as a frivolous game."

"Why, Father?" She looked up at him, the laughter gone from her eyes. "Who ever said this was a game?"

Alexander looked down into the eyes of the person he loved most in the world, this time with a worried frown on his face. "Lauren—"

"Don't always protect me, Father. I've been a pretty little doll on a white pedestal long enough. If I make a mistake, let it be my mistake. If I have the chance to reach for something special, let me reach. If I fall, I promise you I will pick myself up. I'm not so easily broken as you think."

He sighed deeply and escorted her toward the group. Lawrence Greely saw them approaching first and his smile brightened. Lawrence had tried once for Lauren's attention, but soon realized he was far out of her league. He knew without a doubt that it would take a special breed of man to conquer the heart of Lauren Brent, just as he knew, deep within, it was not him. Larry was just a little over average height, with sandy brown hair and a wide humorous smile. A bridge of fine freckles marched across his nose and his brown eyes were alive and interested in everything about him.

He had come from a poor family, which was another reason he felt Lauren was beyond him, and he had worked diligently to earn enough money to pay for his medical education.

He and Cade worked together well at the hospital, Larry's bright humor balancing Cade's quiet determination. The two were well on the way to becoming good friends. In some mysterious way, two men, from completely different cultures had breeched the void between them and had nearly reached a point of complete understanding. Nearly . . . for the presence of Martin Preston usually unbalanced everything. He was a tall slender man with dark hair and even darker eyes. His face was long and rather thin and his features, mostly angular, gave him a somewhat predatory look. He was a year or so ahead of both Cade and Larry and he never missed an opportunity to slight either of them if it could be done in a way that would not rouse their anger.

It was a fact that both Martin and Larry were in love with Lauren. Larry knew her unattainability for him so he had long ago retreated to a safe distance to admire her. Martin knew no such word as defeat. He wanted Lauren and her wealth and he was not the kind of man either to step aside for another or to fight fair if someone got between him and something he wanted.

"Good afternoon, Mr. Brent," Larry called. "And Lauren, you're looking prettier than ever today."

"Thank you, Larry." Lauren smiled, then she turned to Cade's father. "Mr. Holliday, it is so nice to see you again. This time I promise you my father will not barrage you with offers."

"Thank you, Lauren." Michael smiled. "If I had known you would be so effective, I would have asked for your help a long time ago."

Lauren laughed and turned her eyes to Cade to find he was watching her intently, his eyes serious and completely unreadable.

"And how are you today, Cade?"

"I'm fine, Lauren, and I agree with Larry; you do look exceptionally beautiful today." The words were said softly and she felt a quickening within her as if he had somehow reached out and caressed her.

Many may have missed the swift hungry look in her eyes, but two did not. Martin sensed it . . . and so did Cade.

A summer with Tzia had given Cade an acute awareness of a woman's inner feelings. He could feel a stir within him as he remembered vividly the feel of her in his arms. He was about to speak to her again when Martin spoke first.

"Lauren, I've been meaning to call on you," he said arrogantly. "I wanted to say that if you were not otherwise engaged tomorrow, I would love to escort you to the races."

Lauren smiled her brightest, most charming smile, but she gently laid her hand on Cade's arm. "Oh, I'm so sorry, Martin, but I have already accepted Cade's invitation."

Martin stiffened slightly, but Cade's face was completely impassive.

"I see. It seems our future doctor has time on his hands. I should think you would have to use it to catch up with the rest of us . . . considering your . . . ah . . . obvious background."

The insult to his Indian blood registered as rage in Michael, but he quietly stood his ground and let Cade handle himself.

"Yes," Cade said gently, "I do have time on my hands, and it is more than a pleasure to spend it with Lauren. As for catching up"—he chuckled—"it seems most of the medicine our shaman taught me as a child has already put me in the position of being just a little ahead. But of course, since the Indian has been practicing good medicine since before the white man came down from the trees, it is no surprise to find us advanced. My father has given me access to what you will agree is an exceptional surgical mind. All in all," he said, his eyes becoming cold, "I'm very proud of my . . . ah . . . obvious background."

Michael smiled, and hid it behind the glass of wine he held. Larry and Alexander remained silent, but laughter was in their eyes. Martin's eyes were deadly as he turned and walked away.

Cade realized he had made his first real enemy among the whites, but he did not regret one word. Martin's arrogant prejudice had rubbed him the wrong way just once too often. He extended his arm to Lauren.

"Lauren, would you care for some refreshments?"

"Yes, thank you," she replied as she tucked her hand under his arm and they walked away together. After a few minutes, Cade chuckled and in a moment Lauren's soft laughter joined him.

"Why did you lie to him, Lauren?"

"Lie to him?"

"Yes, telling him I'd asked you to the races."

"Do you want to take me to the races?"

"Of course, I'd like nothing better."

"Then, are you asking me?"

"Yes," he laughed, "I am."

"Good, then I didn't lie. You did ask me."

Now he laughed aloud. "Do you always arrange for things to come out the way you want them?"

"Of course, if I can; what's wrong with that? If you truly want something in the world, you should be prepared to find a way to get it."

"It's not always that easy."

"Oh, but it is if you've the money to pay for it."

He looked at her with the same deep intent look she had caught in his eyes before. "Lauren, isn't there anything you don't think your money will buy?" he said softly.

"I . . . I didn't mean it to sound so cold, Cade," she said. "You will admit that your father's money has done a great deal, both for your people and for you."

"Yes, I guess it can open doors, but it's different with people. A person with integrity can't be bought."

Lauren didn't want to arouse anger in him, so she kept silent, but her thoughts were as far from his as was humanly possible.

They had walked away from most of the crowd and stood beneath the shade of a tree. She leaned against it and looked up at him.

"Do you really believe that, Cade?"

"That real integrity can't be bought? Yes, I do."

"But I've seen it, probably much more often than you. I know. You're a dreamer, Cade. Someday you will have to put away those dreams and realize that every man has his price."

"I'll never accept that."

She reached up and gently touched the side of his face.

"I had thought you mightn't," she said.

It had finally occurred to Cade that she was implying that every man, including him, had his price. First it angered him, then it turned to amusement as he began to wonder just what she thought his price might be.

She could not read his gaze, and was somewhat surprised when he placed a hand on each side of her against the tree and bent toward her. His lips gently brushed against hers and she again felt the surging flood of warmth that threatened to overpower her. Before she could speak, she was suddenly lifted against a hard chest and his seeking lips found hers in a kiss that rocked the foundations of her world. His arms held her bound to him and she could only cling as she felt her senses reel under the onslaught of his hungry, seeking mouth. Her lips softened and her body molded to his in urgent giving. As suddenly as he had taken her, he released her and she fell back against the tree. She was breathless and at that moment wanted nothing more than to return to the arms that had just held her. He came close enough that their bodies were almost touching. The look of the intense savagery he held in check had returned. He cupped her chin in one hand.

"Don't try to buy me, Lauren," he whispered, "unless you're willing to pay my price. Since you think I have one you might be surprised to find it's more than you care to pay."

Again, he bent forward and captured her soft pliant mouth with his, but this time, the kiss was gentle and seeking. He parted her lips and let his tongue explore. His hand slid down and caressed her breasts gently, then slid down to her belly and down until it pressed firmly against her. She felt weak and trembling and a soft murmur escaped her as she clung desperately. Then he released her and she stood tremblingly aware of him as she had never been aware of any other man in her life. For the first time, she faced a man who could storm her defenses, a man who would take things only on his terms; a man who challenged all her ideals and tore them apart. Yet, she was filled with a desire for him that threatened to consume her. If Cade had done nothing else, he had solidified the fact in her mind that she would fight this battle and she would have him . . . on her terms.

"Shall we go back before we're missed?" he said quietly.

Without a word, she walked beside him back to the crowd of merrymakers.

She was not the least surprised when he arrived the next day to take her to the races which they both thoroughly enjoyed.

It was the day following the races that he and Larry were working together at the hospital. Cade, as usual, was trying to accomplish three times more than what was expected of him.

"You know, Cade, you've made quite an enemy of old Martin?" Larry said.

"Yes, I know."

"Doesn't that bother you?"

"Not really. If a man can face his enemies, he has nothing to fear."

"Damn it, Cade, you're so damned honest and proud you think you can face any enemy. What about the enemy who strikes from behind?"

"Will he strike from behind?"

"You bet your life he will."

"Then"—Cade smiled—"I must trust a friend to keep his eye on my back."

Larry grinned. "Yes . . . you're cool as a cucumber aren't you? He wants Lauren Brent—and her money. But you know that."

"Of course, but don't you think the choice of the man she wants should be up to her?"

Larry sighed hopelessly, and shaking his head at Cade's laughter, he walked away.

Cade's duties kept him exceptionally busy for the next six weeks. He spent them in such exhaustive work that when he did go home at night he was too tired to do anything but fall into bed and sleep.

He came down to an early breakfast one morning to find his father waiting for him. He sat slowly down in his chair; despite his sleep, he still felt drained.

"Good morning, Cade, sleep well?"

"If you call four hours sleep well, yes, I guess I did."

Michael chuckled and Cade grinned wryly. A young maid came to stand beside him.

"Just bring me some coffee, Martha," he told her. Cade rested his elbows on the table and his chin in his hands and closed his eyes.

Michael watched him, the glint of some mysterious thing in his eyes. Cade opened one eye slightly.

"You," he said, "look like the proverbial cat that just ate the canary."

Michael laughed. "Drink some of your coffee and try to wake up. I have some news for you and I want you to be fully awake to appreciate it."

At this, Cade opened both eyes. He looked at his father for a minute, then picked up his cup and drank. When he set the cup down, he waited in expectant silence for what his father had to say.

"Cade, you've completed three years of study."

"Yes."

"You've done well; I've kept a close check on your record."

Cade waited.

"Starting today," his father said slowly and softly, "you will begin your surgical training next to me. For the next three years, we will be working together. You are ready, and it's time I began to give you what you came for."

Cade remained speechless, not sure that the words that were registering in his mind were not a dream he had conjured up in his tired mind.

"Cade?"

"You . . . you mean it? I'm to work with you?"

"Yes."

Cade leaped to his feet and raising both hands to the sky, he gave vent to a shrill victory cry that rattled the rafters in the house and frightened to death every servant within the walls. He came around the table as Michael laughingly rose from his seat and he threw himself into his father's arms hugging him with a bear hug that brought a groan from Michael.

"I take it, you're pleased?"

Cade laughed exuberantly. "I have never been so happy in my life."

"Good, then get yourself dressed and ready. I'm due at the hospital to operate by ten and I'd like you to be by my side."

Cade would swear he had never washed and dressed faster in his lifetime. They rode to the hospital and walked down the long halls toward the surgical area, their feet making a sharp clicking noise on the hardwood floor.

An hour later, Cade stood beside his father for the first time and listened to Michael talk as he explained what he was doing.

If Cade had thrown himself into learning before, he did more this time. He was literally his father's shadow in surgery, watching his every move and asking questions about anything he did not understand.

It went on like this for six months; then Michael insisted he take a break. Realizing he was nearing exhaustion, Cade agreed.

Later that week, he called on Lauren and asked her if she would share a picnic with him. Without a moment's hesitation, Lauren agreed.

It was a warm Sunday morning. Cade had their cook pack an excellent lunch and he took the buggy and rode to the Brent estate. Surprised, he found Lauren waiting for him.

They rode for a while chatting of unimportant things until Cade found a place to share their lunch. He pulled the buggy off the small dirt road and guided it down through a thick stand of trees to stop by a small gurgling stream.

Cade unharnessed the horse and hobbled it so it could graze. Taking a blanket and the lunch they went to a grassy spot, spread the blanket and set the basket upon it.

"Shall we take a walk before we eat?" he suggested.

She agreed and they began to walk down the pebbled edge of the stream. Lauren watched him from under her long lashes. She was not going to be foolish enough to make the same mistake with him again. Her claws were sheathed; she was a purring kitten, not a cat.

"Cade, it's been so long since I heard from you. I thought you might still be angry with me."

"I was never angry with you, Lauren. A man would be very foolish to waste anger on a girl as pretty as you. It's much nicer to walk with you here."

"Tell me what you've been doing. I should like to know what can draw all your undivided attention."

"No, no work today. I came here to relax and enjoy your beautiful company."

They stopped just to enjoy the surroundings. Against this backdrop, Cade seemed to Lauren to be more at home, more relaxed. He belonged to this kind of environment. His smile brightened and his bronzed skin glowed in the sunlight. He wore a white shirt, open at the throat, and a pair of dark pants that seemed to be tailored to his lean muscular frame.

She bent to pluck some flowers that grew near. He watched. There was no doubt in his mind that Lauren was the loveliest vision he had seen since he'd arrived in Washington. Again, she wore a pale-green dress and her auburn hair, brushed loose, hung below her waist, tied back with a green ribbon. They walked along in a comfortable silence enjoying the peace around them.

"Cade, what will you do when you've finished your surgical training with your father?"

"Take what I know home and make it all worth the effort."

"Don't you think you could help your people more by doing what your father is doing. You two together would be twice the protection for them."

He took her hand and they started to walk back. "I have never thought of it that way and I don't intend to. When my father thinks I'm ready, I will go home."

"I see," she said gently. "Tell me about home, Cade."

All the way back to their blanket, Cade talked. He talked and she watched his face, feeling his love for his home and his people flow from him. A sense of jealousy coursed through her; she wanted him to feel that way about her. She wanted to reach out and hold him somehow. And then the way slipped into her mind as easy as her next breath. Cade's sense of honor. Her path into Cade's heart, Cade's world, and Cade's future.

They sat on the blanket and ate the meal that had been provided. Lauren suggested he lie back on the blanket and rest while she put the balance of the food away. As tired as he was and as peaceful as it was there, it did not take long until he closed his eyes in restful sleep.

The first haze of dusk was in the air when he opened his eyes. He was disoriented for a moment; then he remembered where he was . . . and who he was with. Lauren!

He turned his head to find her sitting beside him. She smiled.

"I'm sorry; I didn't mean to do that. I guess I was more tired than I thought. Will you forgive me?"

"It's all right, Cade. You needed the rest, and it's given me time to think."

"Think about what?"

She turned to him and put her hand against his chest. She had loosened the ribbon from her hair and it fell about them as she lowered her head and touched her lips to his. She made a soft sound of pleasure as she felt him reach up and tangle his hands in her hair and draw her more firmly against him.

"Lauren," he whispered against her throat as his lips began to press kisses along her ivory skin. "God, you are so very beautiful."

He pulled her down beside him and rose on one elbow to gaze down into her eyes. Gently, he caressed her face and while their eyes held, his hand moved down to the buttons of her dress and slowly began to unbutton it. She did not move until she felt his hand slide within and gently cup her breast. His thumb pressed in a gentle circular motion against the nipple that hardened and rose in a surge of passion. Again he bent his head and took her lips with his. The kiss grew in intensity as her lips parted and she returned willingly the warmth he found.

His mouth strayed down her throat and pressed warm, seeking kisses on the soft curves of her breasts. He found one hardened nipple and captured it with his lips, drawing forth a gasping sigh from her as she pressed his head more firmly against her.

While she closed her eyes, allowing herself only to feel the growing need that flooded her, his hand moved to the hem of her dress and slid it up until he found one silken thigh. His hands caressed gently, not rushing, and creating a tingle that set her trembling and made her cling to him. That she desired him as much as he did her, he knew. His body cried out for the joining with hers, but he wanted this special moment to be good for her.

He sat up and looked down into her passion-heated eyes; then he took hold of her shoulders and drew her up beside him. He kissed her again slowly and gently, before, with expert hands, he began to remove the restricting clothes that stood between them. She made no move either to stop him or to help him; she seemed mesmerized by the sweet agony of wanting that consumed her.

He dropped the last piece of their clothing aside and drew her body into his arms. This time, the kiss was filled with a brilliant flame as he pressed her back against the blanket. Her arms encircled his neck and she closed her eyes, feeling her need for him grow to an overpowering emotion as his hands sought the sensitive spots that caused her to moan gently in response.

Seeking hands caressed, hungry lips possessed, and together they rose to a plane of ecstasy their minds could hardly contain. She felt the hard muscles of his back with gentle caressing fingers that turned into possessive demanding hands, drawing him closer to the white heat he was building in the center of her existence. Her words urged him to a deeper more fulfilling possession, words she was completely unconscious of.

Gently, he found the center of her need and touched her with flame-tipped fingers until she writhed in his arms, her body searching for the final and deeper possession.

He was close to the threshold of complete abandon, yet he held himself under an iron control so that he could carry her along. He was rewarded for his patience when she abandoned any threads of restraint and, gasping, begged him to love her.

"Cade . . . oh, Cade . . . love me."

His mouth caught hers in a fiery demanding kiss at the same moment he pressed himself within her. He felt more than heard her sobbing moan of both pain and pleasure as she twined herself about him. His hands slid to her hips holding her against him and they moved together in a white flame that sent them spiraling to a world where there were only two people in existence—Cade and Lauren . . . lovers.

They lay clinging to one another while their senses spiraled down to reality. Their sweat-slicked bodies entwined; they were engrossed in one another as sated lovers.

"Cade," she whispered softly as she caressed his cheek with her slender fingers. "I've never known . . . never felt so in my life."

Cade pulled her closer in his arms and touched his lips lightly to her cheek. He caressed her slender body with a gentle touch.

"You're so very sweet, Lauren," he said, and again she could not read the look in his eyes. "I'm so glad I never missed you in my life. You are a very special woman."

She smiled. "I'm glad you appreciate me. It took me long enough to get your attention."

"Lauren"—he laughed—"you've had my undivided attention since the very first day we met."

"Undivided?" she said with a mock doubtful look.

"Well . . . maybe not exactly undivided."

She slid her hands down from his shoulders where they had been resting, to his broad chest. It was then she saw the two ragged scars.

"Cade! Good heavens, what happened to you?" Her fingers traced the rigid scars gently, then her eyes rose to him.

"It's part of a tribal ceremony."

"A tribal ceremony! It must have been painful. Tell me about it."

He doubted if he could make her understand the value of the ceremony in his culture, but he tried. Her eyes widened in shock as he told her how the ceremony had proceeded. As he had expected, she was horrified by the brutal ceremony and missed completely the religious and personal value.

If she did not, Cade realized that it would be difficult, if not impossible for their two cultures to meet on common ground. One of them would have to surrender his or her way of life. He knew he could not, would not, desert his father and his people and their need for him. He made the mistake then of letting himself believe he could make her change. Maybe it was the warm gentle feel of her in his arms that blinded him to a fact he inwardly knew: Lauren had as strong a spirit as he; she had dreams of her own.

She herself was turning her mind away from the reality that one day Cade would turn his face toward home. She felt in time she could convince him that his life and the lives of his people would be better if he stayed in Washington—with her.

They circled the matter, each of them shying away from a subject too sensitive to discuss yet.

She laughed as he told her some of his escapades as a boy,

listened intently as he told her about his blood brother, White Eagle, his foster father, Long Arrow, and his mother whom he so obviously loved, Waterflower.

"You have had a happy childhood, Cade."

"I have. My memories draw me home more than anything else."

Treading on dangerous ground again, she put both hands on his face and drew his lips to hers. It was all the incentive Cade needed; it ignited his passion and his arms drew her tight against him as his hungry mouth possessed hers in a deep probing kiss.

It was past ten o'clock when they gathered their scattered clothing and rode slowly home.

Cade woke the next morning before dawn. He allowed himself the luxury of remaining in bed until the sun rimmed the horizon. When he rose, washed, and dressed, he went down to breakfast. His father waited for him.

"Morning, Cade."

"Morning."

"Feeling well?"

Cade grinned. "I feel fine."

"Feel like taking your first step in surgery?"

Their eyes met and Michael smiled at Cade's obvious efforts to contain his overpowering excitement.

"My, my"—Michael laughed—"I do believe my son is becoming civilized. No war cry, Sun Knife, no victory shout?"

"I'm too excited even for that. Do you think I'm ready?"

"I'll be at your shoulder, but I've every confidence you'll do well. If I did not you would not be there." Michael's voice was serious and Cade felt an even stronger sense of accomplishment for he knew what his father said was true, and to have Michael tell him that he was to be rewarded for all the hours of work filled his heart with joy.

They went to the hospital together and as the patient was prepared for surgery, Michael watched his son closely. Despite his inner feelings of tension and excitement, Cade's hands were steady and he seemed to have complete control over himself.

Soon they stood across the operating table from each other over a patient who had been put to sleep with a new discovery called ether. Until now, patients had been drugged with as much as could be given them and strapped to the table to go through the ordeal until they lost consciousness. Ether permitted them to be left unstrapped and made their bodies more relaxed so the surgeon's job was much easier.

Their eyes held for a moment and Cade saw his father smile with confidence in him. He took a deep breath and lifted the scalpel for the first time.

In deep concentration, time and place slipped away from him. Nothing else existed in his mind except the man who lay on the table and the job he had to perform. Nimble fingers worked almost as if they had a knowledge of their own. His mind sorted and held instructions his father had pounded into him.

He knew as soon as he started to work that what he was doing was not a matter of life and death for the patient, but a less serious case where his father could observe his work without endangering life. What mattered to him was not the seriousness of the operation, but the cool blue gaze that watched his every move.

When he had finished tying off the last stitch, he stepped back breathing a sigh of relief. He looked across at his father and realized his own body was wet with perspiration and that his shoulders ached with the tension he had been working under. His father took his pocket watch out and looked at it.

"Two and a half hours," he said softly, and his eyes smiled across the table. Cade could feel himself swell with pride at his father's look. "Quite good, boy, quite good."

Michael had more surgery to perform himself that day and Cade stayed on to observe. In fact, wild horses couldn't have dragged him away from his father's side the balance of the day.

That night, he took Lauren to dinner and then when he took her home they sat on a bench in the Brent garden while he enthusiastically tried to explain to her what he felt that day. She was overjoyed to see his enthusiasm for his work, for she hoped it would be her key to solve the problems they faced.

That day heralded progressive days of hard work. Lauren

controlled all her impatience with the tremendous number of hours he spent involved with it. It was a means to an end for her so she wisely kept her thoughts to herself, promising herself that when Cade opened his own practice in Washington, she would see to it they made up for all the lost time.

Working with a completely different set of ideas, Cade and Lauren spent what spare time they had together. The times were few and far between, but that only heightened the intensity of their enjoyment of each other when they were together.

Often they would sit in front of the fireplace in the Brent home and talk softly of immediate things. Lauren wisely kept away from the future. She knew Cade cared deeply for her and that he enjoyed the time they were together, but a sixth sense told her that he was still not completely hers.

The days drifted into weeks, then into months. Cade was surprised when he realized it had been almost five years since he had left home. It began to kindle the desire in him to see home again. He missed the freedom and the old way of life. Sometimes, it depressed him to think that he wanted two ways of life and didn't, in reality, have either. Slowly, Michael began to enlarge the work load of cases Cade handled. He watched each operation with a critical eye, trying to keep his pride from showing each time he realized that the young man, with the seemingly magic fingers, who stood across the table from him, was his son.

His pleasure grew when he found other doctors recommending as many patients to Cade as they did to him. It pleased him, yet it gave him sorrow, for he loved Cade and he knew as Cade's skill improved, the day was drawing nearer and nearer when he must release his son and let him return to his people.

He knew Cade was hearing that faraway call from home for he could sometimes sense that his mind was far away as if he were listening to some distant sound.

Cade's ability, pleasing Michael, caused the hatred for him in Martin's mind to grow completely out of proportion. Martin sensed one thing that Lauren did not. The fact that the ties that drew Cade were not going to be broken by anything or anyone here. He waited for the opportunity to make that clear to

Lauren. The day came when he found success, and started the only serious and final argument between Cade and Lauren—an argument that was going to begin Cade's renewal of his old life, and open a whole new and surprising future for Lauren Brent.

Cade and Michael stood in Michael's office, neither of them noticing the door was ajar, and neither of them knowing about the tall dark figure listening intently to the words exchanged.

"Cade, have you spoken to Alexander Brent lately?"

"No, why?"

"It seems he's checking about to see where and how he can find the best place for a new physician to open a practice. For a minute I thought he might be thinking of you. You haven't given him the idea that you might consider staying here permanently and opening a practice?"

"No, I've never even discussed the idea with him," Cade replied, but his thoughts immediately jumped to Lauren. A strange premonitional feeling twisted within him and he began to wonder if Lauren was making plans she was not telling him about.

"If I had any such idea, I would have come to you. You know we have always worked together toward one goal. Nothing can keep me from going back and fulfilling my obligations. My people—our people—need me. Nothing could change that, Father. You know I'm grateful for all you've given me just as you know I don't belong here."

"Yes, Cade, I know. I shall regret seeing you go. Maybe soon, I shall join you. I am tired of fighting the fight alone. I would rather spend my last days with you and your mother."

"How much longer do you expect me to stay?"

"You need more work on the perfection of some techniques, but that will not take long. Six to eight months is all that is likely."

"Six to eight months," Cade repeated. "After almost six years, it seems like nothing. I cannot believe the time has gone so quickly."

"Cade, can I ask you one more question?"

"Of course."

"What about you and Lauren Brent?"

"What about us?"

"What are your plans for the future?"

"I haven't asked Lauren to marry me, but when the time comes for me to go, I will. We can go home together."

"Cade"—his father hesitated. "Do you think it will work? Lauren has always been used to luxury. I don't believe she could be happy living in your world."

"Don't you think that if she loves me, luxury just won't matter? Lauren is strong, we could make a good life together."

"What if . . . if she refused to go with you? What if she stands her ground and insists that you stay here and continue your work here?"

Cade was silent for a long time and the figure outside the door bent forward slightly, impatient to hear the answer.

"If she doesn't come with me, then her love for me is not strong enough. If the good life means so much to her that she would expect me to sacrifice all our people for it, then it is not the kind of love we need to build on and in that case, even if it hurt, I would go alone. I have to do this and if Lauren loves me she will understand."

"I see," Michael said softly. "For your sake, Cade, I hope it works. I know you care deeply about her."

"Well," Cade replied, his voice low and cold, "in six or eight months, we'll all know what our futures will hold."

The figure outside the door smiled and walked silently away. "Yes," he thought maliciously and with pleasure, "you will know, Cade Holliday." He laughed softly with pleasure as he left the hospital and headed his buggy toward the home of Lauren Brent.

Chapter Four

Martin began a campaign that day. Knowing that the time Cade and Lauren could find to spend together was rare, he began calling on Lauren anytime he knew Cade was occupied. Subtly, he filled her mind with the idea that she deserved nothing but the best. He talked to her of the beauties their life had to offer. He spoke of parties, fine clothes, the arts, and the joyous friendships—never once implying that Cade had no intention of offering her any of these things.

He filled her head with these things, knowing she was associating it with Cade and their future. He knew with a malicious certainty that the disappointment would be bitter and impossible for her to accept.

As the weeks went by, Cade was unaware of the plans Lauren, with the aid of her father, was making. Alexander did not realize that Cade meant to leave as soon as his training was over. He thought Lauren and Cade had discussed it and he had decided to stay. It was the reason he had decided to invest in a practice for Cade as a wedding present for Cade and his daughter.

Lauren was aware that her father had such intentions, but she never said a word to Cade. She was happily waiting for the day that Cade asked her to marry him. On that day, she would feel absolutely secure in his love; then she would tell him. "How could he refuse such a magnanimous offer?" she reasoned, especially considering what he had to compare it with. Life in a wilderness doctoring a group of savages! It simply no longer occurred to her that Cade would refuse, or be angry. She felt the civilized veneer Cade wore was penetrating his heart.

Cade was to take what was an absolutely new thing to the medical world, an examination. Cade's father had helped organize a medical association that worked to enlarge the abilities of the doctor. Until this time, a man served an apprenticeship with a doctor until that doctor felt he was ready; then he opened a practice of his own. It had created a world of quacks and charlatans who killed more than they cured.

The hospital in which Michael worked as chief surgeon was the first to open their doors as a school of medicine. Under these rules, Cade must be examined and receive a degree or he would not be allowed to practice in that area.

Although he had no intention of practicing in Washington, he wanted to satisfy both himself and his father and so he prepared himself to be tested. He studied at night until his eyes blurred and were red-rimmed with fatigue and he worked long hours in the hospital until he almost dropped from exhaustion.

The night before he was to take the first part of the three-day examination, he and Lauren were home in the Brent living room. Alexander had gone out for the evening and Lauren had dismissed the servants for the night. She had been without him a long time and now she wanted them to share this evening alone.

She sat on the floor, late that night, on a soft rug while Cade lay with his head on her lap. They had not spoken for some time. The room was quiet and pervaded with a sense of contentment and peace. She stroked his cheek gently with long slender fingers and his eyes were closed as if he were feeling her with his senses instead of seeing her with his eyes.

"Cade?"

"Ummm?"

"Are you worried about the examination?"

"No, not really. I think I'm only doing it for my father's sake. When I go home, the piece of paper I receive won't mean a thing to the people I'll be caring for."

"You mean the people of your village?"

"No."

"No?"

"When I go home, I will go to our Chief Tekata. He will call a council of all the surrounding tribes. They will come and decide if I can practice my medicine in their villages or not."

"Cade!" she said in surprise and half-anger.

"What?"

"You mean to tell me you have taken almost seven years out of your life, studied, worked, and whether or not you can practice your medicine will depend on a few old men?"

"You don't understand, Lauren. It's . . . well, it's the custom. I could live there for the rest of my life and if the chiefs did not speak the words, I would never be asked to touch one person."

"That is ridiculous!"

"No . . . I want them to want me. I want the old ones to respect my medicine enough to permit me to practice." He sat up and looked at her; for the first time, she saw a hesitant look. "Don't you see, Lauren, I have so many things they need. One day, the white men will begin to move west; it's inevitable. I have seen it and despite all he has done to stop it so has my father. I want to be there when it happens. My blood brother, White Eagle, will one day be chief. He has an open mind and an open heart. We can begin to teach the young. I know it will be hard and slow to start, but think of it. One day, Lauren"—his eyes glowed with an excitement she had never seen before, an excitement he had never felt before—"a school . . . a hospital maybe . . . some kind of link between red and white so they can live in peace."

Suddenly she was frightened. She saw his mind slip away from her and go to a place she could not reach. All her life had been spent involved only with herself. She could not understand or feel what he felt. She knew only her world and it was bright and glowing and she was afraid to step into his world, take his hand, walk with him, for it seemed dark and forbidding.

She realized he had stopped talking and his eyes told her he was reading her thoughts too well. She could not yet face the ultimate test of his love. She reached out and caressed the side of his face.

"Cade," she whispered as she moved into his arms and felt them enclose her. "For tonight let there just be us. Let's shut everything out. Tomorrow, we can face it." Her mouth lifted to his. "Oh, love, let there just be us for tonight."

The wild flame leaped between them as his lips found hers

and his arms pulled her tight against his hard body. She clung to him with a passion she had never felt before and she wanted to cry out her fear that somehow she was losing him.

He pressed her back on the soft rug and bent over her. The fire glowed from his golden-bronze skin and reflected in his eyes as he lowered his head to capture her mouth again. This time, the kiss was a searching demanding one. She surrendered to the strength of his love and felt it begin to lift her beyond reality and into a warm world filled only with Cade. . . . Warm hands, strong searching hands found her cool flesh. Her body called out its need for him at his every move . . . his tormentingly slow removal of her clothes as his hands and lips stopped to caress, to taste, to rouse her to a screaming fury of need.

"Oh, Cade," she moaned as his lips moved across her heated flesh, stopping to nibble gently, then returning to their course traveling across rounded curves to temptingly shadowed valleys until she could hardly bear the sweet agony. He drove her to the brink of wildness, filled her with such a sense of abandon that she lost touch with everything but his urgent and flaming blending with her.

She felt his hard body against her, the iron arms that held her so close she could barely breathe and yet she wanted no freedom from his possession now . . . or ever.

They moved rhythmically together—one passion, one need, one violent and all-consuming climax that left them, in silent wonder, clinging weakly to each other, eyes closed while they regained control of their breathing and their tumbled minds.

It was some time before she regained enough control to speak. She looked up into his warm blue gaze. He was lying beside her now, one hand supporting his head while the other traced lazy patterns with the tips of his fingers down her long slender body.

"Cade?"

"What?" he said softly as he bent down and lightly touched his lips to hers.

"You know how very much I love you."

"Well"—he chuckled—"I'm beginning to get the idea."

She laughed with him. "Be serious."

"I am." He grinned. "I've never been more serious in my life. Lauren . . . after the examination, after everything is over, will you marry me?"

"Oh, Cade . . . yes, yes, yes." She laughed through the tears that glazed her eyes. "Do you know how I've been waiting to hear the words when you asked me?"

She threw her arms about his neck and he held her tight against him. They laughed and talked together speaking of how happy they would be, each of them assuring themselves that the other one would bend. The fire died to glowing embers and they made love together again, this time slowly and luxuriously allowing themselves to glory in the sweetness of it.

It was long after midnight when Cade left. He went home and directly to bed to get enough sleep so that he could face the coming examination.

The examination was long and exhausting. So much so that Cade remained at home after each day, falling asleep almost immediately after dinner. Lauren spent the three days planning a party and an announcement of their engagement.

The party was a success . . . until, after the engagement was announced, Alexander rose from his seat and lifted his glass to toast the young couple. The smile on Cade's face froze as Alexander's words rang clear in the room.

"I have another announcement to make my friends." He laughed. "For a wedding present, I am presenting Cade Holliday with offices in the Manchester Building. Soon, Dr. Cade Holliday will be the second-best surgeon in the city of Washington, second only to Dr. Michael Holliday."

Michael and Cade exchanged surprised looks; then Cade turned to a smiling Lauren whose eyes were alight with pleasure. He took hold of her wrist in a grasp that drew a gasp of shock from her. She looked up into Cade's eyes and saw them wild with fury for the first time in their days together.

"I want to talk to you, Lauren," he said in a clipped cold voice as he drew her behind him and, to the surprise of all the guests, led her out the open doors and into the garden. There he dropped her hand and turned to face her. His face filled with anger and his hands clenched at his sides.

"Tell me," he said in a voice deceptively soft, "what in the hell you think you are doing. Who gave your father the right to do such a thing?"

"But, Cade, it's only a wedding present. It's so much easier than buying your own practice. Cade, really, why in heaven's name are you so angry over a gift? If you think it's too much we'll buy it ourselves and give father his money back."

"Buy! . . . God Lauren, have you heard anything I've been saying to you all these months? Don't you understand me at all?"

"I understand that you are one of the most brilliant surgeons the hospital has ever had, or this city for that matter, and I won't let you throw it away. Cade, darling, we can have the world at our feet. We can enjoy everything money has to offer. Cade, there's nothing in the world that isn't at your fingertips, all you have to do is take father's gift."

Cade stood in silence and that strange unreadable look that Lauren dreaded filled his eyes. Yet his voice was deceptively soft.

"How long?"

"What?"

"How long have you and your father been planning to buy yourselves a doctor?"

"Cade," she cried desperately, this time fear deep in her voice. "Don't say that, you know it isn't that way."

"Isn't it?" he snapped.

"No," she sobbed. "Cade, I love you."

"Do you, Lauren?" he asked. "Or am I proof of your old theory that any man's integrity has a price?"

"No! No, Cade! No! But don't you see the opportunity, Cade? You can pay father back if you're angry about the money. Cade, don't turn your back on this; it's the best chance we'll ever have. You'll be rich . . . famous . . . Cade, don't throw it away!"

"The money," he said in a sorrow-filled voice. "You just don't understand, do you, Lauren? All this time I thought you knew, I thought you wanted to be with me in this fight, I thought . . . now it doesn't really matter what I thought."

She sobbed and took the few steps that separated them and

threw herself into his arms.

"Cade, please listen to me."

"No, you answer a question for me, Lauren." He tipped up her chin and held her face between his hands. His eyes held hers searching for the truth. "Did you ever really intend to leave all your father's money and comforts and come with me, to be my wife, to really share my life, or did you plan all this time for me to stay here and forget everything and everyone? I've got to know the truth, Lauren . . . tell me."

Tears fell from her wide green eyes and she did not answer, but the truth was there for him to see. Suddenly his body seemed to sag and he stepped back from her. She held out one hand to him, an imploring gesture. Her voice thick with tears, she spoke softly.

"Cade, don't go . . . please don't go."

"I have to, Lauren. I've been telling you for years, I have to. If I turned my back on my father and my people now, I would never be able to look at myself again and feel I was a man or a doctor." His eyes held hers in a steady gaze that asked, but would not beg. "Come with me Lauren."

"To what? Look at me, Cade. Do you think I would survive in your world? What does it have to offer me? What are you asking me to give up?"

"Does all this really mean that much to you? Are you so selfish you cannot see what we could have together? Oh, Lauren," he said, anguish tearing at his voice. "I think, if you were not frightened of leaving your safe little world, you would find you are stronger than you think. I don't want to marry a spoiled little child, Lauren. I want a woman to share my life with me, no matter where it is. Grow up, Lauren. You have to choose one way or the other; you can't have both."

"You're not fair, Cade."

"I never lied to you."

"I didn't lie."

"No, you just let me go on believing what I wanted to believe."

"Don't you love me, Cade?"

"I love the woman you are, Lauren; I just cannot live with what you want me to accept. I cannot turn my back on people who loved me, sacrificed for me, trusted me to fulfill my obligations. I want you with me, but the choice is up to you. Next week, I leave for home—with or without my wife. The choice is yours." He went to her and again reached out and brushed the tears from her cheeks with his fingertips. Then he bent and brushed his lips across hers. She closed her eyes and heard his footsteps die away as he left. Her pride, her selfishness, her fear held her immobile.

She stood in the silent garden, her arms folded about herself as if she needed them to contain all the grief she felt.

Alexander had seen Cade recross the ballroom, his face grim, and leave the house. He walked to the doorway and looked across the garden. Lauren stood with her back to him, but he could tell in every line of her body that she was weeping. He walked toward her. She was so enclosed within herself that she did not hear him approach until she felt him turn her toward him and enclose her in his comforting embrace.

"Lauren, child," he said gently, "what is it?"

"Father," she sobbed, "I've lost him."

He held her away from him.

"Do you want to tell me what happened, Lauren?"

She moved from his arms and walked a few steps away. He could see she was trying to regain control of herself. Anger and self-pity began to stir within her. She turned to face her father. "The engagement is over. You can forget the wedding gift you were going to buy; there will be no wedding. Cade has chosen to go back to the savage he was instead of being the man you gave him the opportunity to be."

"But, Lauren . . . why?"

"Because, I would not choose to go grovel in the dirt for him," she said. "Because I choose to live here with all the good things I have. Why should I go there to help people I do not know or care about . . . ? I hate him! I . . . hate . . . him," she cried; then she ran from the garden to her room where she threw herself across the bed and cried until she had no strength left. Exhausted, she fell into a dark and dreamless sleep.

She blinked her eyes open the next morning, aware that they burned and that her body felt exhausted. She lay on her back looking up at the ceiling while last night's memories began to flood into her mind.

"Cade," she whispered softly to herself, yet she knew he was lost to her. She could not, would not, leave the beautiful world in which she lived.

Slowly she rose and sent for a bath. Later, she went down to breakfast, a breakfast she could not eat.

Then she began to lie to herself, console herself. He would come back. He would see how unreasonable he is. They would marry and live happily here. For a week she told herself these lies to hope they would magically soothe the ache within her and the deep sense of loss.

The lies did not work, and by the end of the week she missed him so desperately that she decided to try to see him once more before he left. To somehow try to change his mind from the foolish sacrifice of his talents he was about to make to the safe secure world they could live in.

She dressed with more care than she had ever taken in her life. Then she sent for the carriage and went to the Holliday home. The maid who opened the door blinked in surprise, then stood aside to let Lauren enter.

"Come in the study, Miss Brent. I will go tell Dr. Holliday you're here."

"Thank you."

She went into the study, but she could not sit down. Her nervous impatience could hardly be contained as she searched, as she had for the past two hours, for the words that would help convince Cade to stay.

When the door opened, she spun about, a smile on her face, only to have the smile fade as she saw Michael Holliday in the doorway, a Michael whose face registered as much surprise as hers.

"Lauren?"

She laughed nervously. "The maid made a mistake, I'm afraid. She has sent for the wrong Dr. Holliday."

Michael's eyes became saddened as he said gently, "I'm sorry, Lauren. I'm the only Dr. Holliday who lives here, now."

It struck her like a blow and she stood looking at him. Her face went white and she almost cried out with the pain of knowing it was all in vain . . . Cade was gone.

Michael moved quickly to her side as she swayed on her feet. He helped her sit down; then he sat opposite her and took one of her hands in his. "Maybe you can tell me now what has happened. Cade refused to say anything except that you had changed your mind, the wedding was off, and that he was going home, alone. I couldn't stop him. What happened, Lauren?"

"Oh, Dr. Holliday, it's all such a mess. How can I expect anyone to understand when I don't understand myself? You know what happened at the party last week. Cade and I had a dreadful argument." She looked up at him, her green eyes filled with tears. "Am I wrong to have wanted him to make use of his talents here where he'll be appreciated, even rewarded?"

Michael sighed and patted her hand; then he said the words softly and without reproach.

"It depends, Lauren, on what you consider a reward. Maybe it is for the best. You would never be happy in Cade's world as you are, and despite all the appearances he might have temporarily adopted, Cade was not, nor would he ever be able to live the balance of his life, happy here. You saw him as you wanted him to be, Lauren, not as he really was. You deluded yourself into believing he could tame his wildness and conform to the white society; he can't. It is ingrained as deeply in him as yours is in you."

She buried her face in her hands and cried, broken, heart-rending tears and Michael could offer her no relief except to hold her and try to soothe her.

After a few minutes, she regained control of herself and drew away from him. "I'm sorry," she murmured softly.

"It's all right, Lauren. I know the pain of losing someone you love. I know it's of no help now, but time does ease some of the grief. At least it gives you the strength to bear it."

"You're very understanding. I know you will miss him, too."

"I had him for such a short time. A little over seven years out of a lifetime."

"Would . . . would you mind if I came to talk to you occasionally? Maybe it would be good for both of us."

"Why, child, that is a warming thought. I have just lost a

son, maybe I can gain a daughter." He smiled, with Cade's smile and his laughing blue eyes. It was almost more than she could bear. She rose.

"I must be going home," she said and she laid her hand on his arm. "But I shall come back soon. If . . . if Cade writes to you will you tell me?"

"Of course."

"Thank you."

He watched her climb into the buggy and drive away.

The days were suddenly so long for her and she found she took less and less pleasure in all the things she had enjoyed before. Martin called on her and took her out at least two evenings a week, but she could read the obvious lust in his face when she would catch him looking at her without her knowledge.

She could not adjust to his overbearing sense of possessiveness, as if it were only a matter of time until she fell willingly into his arms; but he was far wrong, for Cade had awakened in her a desire for his gentle love and each time she was with Martin, she longed for Cade more.

She did call on Michael. Often they had a pleasant dinner at his home where, as always, the topic of conversation soon came around to Cade.

As Michael talked to her, she began to see the gulf of differences that existed between her and Cade. She also began to chafe under what she was beginning to think of as a useless and wasted existence. She had told her father of her feelings, and he had helplessly suggested she join some women's groups or clubs to keep her busy.

"I'm going out of my mind," she told Michael one evening. "I cannot function in Cade's world, and I am miserable in mine. What am I to do?"

"Lauren . . . would you like to come to the hospital and donate some of your time? You would be needed and I'm sure you would find it fulfilling."

She looked at him hopefully. "You are not just offering me this to pamper a spoiled child?"

"No." He laughed. "You might find it's not a reward, but a tremendous amount of work. But I think it is work that will offer you some peace of mind. You will be tired enough to sleep, and sometimes that makes the long nights easier to bear."

"You do understand, don't you?"

He nodded. "Loneliness and long sleepless nights. Yes, I do. Work is a tremendous help for it."

"I appreciate how kind you are to me. I would love to work; is tomorrow too soon?"

"No." He laughed and he was pleased to see the sparkle return to her eyes and the delighted smile on her lips. "But it will have to be early."

"How early? Ten . . . eleven?"

"Lauren"—he laughed again—"by ten or eleven we will have five hours work in already."

"Five in the morning!" she said in shock.

"Five in the morning. Do you think you can do it?"

Her chin came up stubbornly. "Of course, I can do it."

"Good. I'll come for you at five tomorrow morning. Don't wear anything good. I'm afraid it would be quite dirty before you get home."

She left, and Michael smiled to himself, wondering if she would be able to handle all the hard work he intended to throw at her. She might find, he thought, that she was made of much stronger material than she thought she was.

When she got home that evening she was happily explaining what she was going to do to a surprised father who could only sit and listen to the bubbling euphoria that surrounded her. If he doubted her ability, he did not say a word about it. It was the first time she had been happy since Cade had gone and he welcomed whatever made her so.

At five the next morning, Michael was just a little shocked to find her waiting outside the front door of the Brent mansion, dressed in a plain green cotton dress and the happiest smile he had seen on her face in a long time.

When they arrived at the hospital, Lauren was immediately recognized and the red carpet was about to be rolled out until Michael took the matronly head nurse aside and explained what the situation was. Elenore Hews had three hard-working daughters of her own. Besides, this, she kept buried just below the surface, the strong feeling that women were more effective in a hospital than men. She smiled at Michael.

"We'll see what the lady is made of by day's end, Dr. Holliday, I assure you."

"I leave her in your capable hands, Mrs. Hews." He grinned. "I suspect by the end of the day, we will have a permanent worker or she will give up and go home."

"What do you think?"

Michael turned and looked at Lauren in laughing conversation with several other nurses. "I," he said quietly, "think she will stick like glue and finish what she started."

"Care to make a wager, Doctor." Elenore's eyes glowed with laughter.

"Five dollars," he responded quickly.

"Done. I'll see you at the end of the day, Doctor."

He bowed slightly and she could hear his chuckle drift behind him as he walked away. Then she turned and walked toward an unsuspecting, smiling Lauren.

If Elenore expected Lauren to quit under the load of work she put upon her that day, she was to be sadly disappointed. Tired, dirty, and aware of hard physical labor for the first time in her life, Lauren clung with grim determination to every ounce of fortitude she possessed. She had seen the sparkle of laughter die in the eyes of Elenore Hews, and a grudging respect replace it. She grasped this with tenacity and hung on. She fetched and carried, lifted, pushed and pulled, mopped, scrubbed beds and bodies until her body screamed for her to stop, and she was never so grateful to see anyone in her life as she was Michael who appeared at her side when it was near six o'clock.

"Lauren," he said, "it's time to go home."

She sighed and rose from a chair beside the bed of an old man to whom she had been reading. Obediently, she followed Michael to his buggy, too tired for any conversation. As the horse clopped a methodical rhythm along the road, she rested her head for a moment and fell into an exhausted sleep. Michael looked down on her pretty face and smiled.

"Good job, my girl," he said softly. "I'm proud of you. If you were my own daughter, I couldn't be happier. There's more to you than anyone has guessed, but the real test is still to come. Will you be on your feet tomorrow?"

Lauren made her way up the steps to her room. A fastidious Lauren Brent who had usually bathed twice a day fell across her bed in a disheveled heap.

Her young personal maid began preparations for her bath, but Lauren called to her.

"Bessie, forget the water, just wake me at five in the morning."

"Five, Miss Brent?"

"Five," Lauren said firmly. They were the last words she spoke for she was completely and soundly asleep.

When she wakened the next morning, every muscle and nerve in her slender body protested violently to every move she made.

Despite this, when Michael arrived for her, she was pleased to see the friendly sparkle in his eyes as she climbed into the buggy beside him. She giggled at his pleasure and her own.

"To work, Dr. Holliday."

"Yes, Miss Brent." He laughed. "To work!"

Inside of six weeks, Michael himself was amazed at the amount of hospital knowledge she had acquired and the ability to handle a great deal of responsibility with complete efficiency.

It was only Martin who frowned on her activities. Then, one day, he made two mistakes, the first to call her down for what he considered unladylike activities and second to do so in front of patients, doctors, and nurses.

When Martin retreated from the verbal attack by Lauren, he was still amazed at what had brought it on, for in his chauvinistic mind, he could not see what he had done to deserve it. He had only informed the woman he intended to marry where her proper place was.

She was leaving a room with a bundle of soiled laundry in one arm and a pail of dirty water in the other when they came face to face.

"Really, Lauren, haven't you had enough of this little charade. It's time you finished with these little games and went home where a lady like you belongs."

Her face reddened, more with anger than embarrassment. Ears listened to every word said.

"Games!" she snapped. "You swell-headed, conceited oaf. How dare you talk to me like that? I probably do more work around here than you do. Get out of my way."

She went to move past him and he reached out to stop her. His luck and his aim were both bad. All he succeeded in doing was to grasp the arm that held the bucket of water causing her to spill it. She knew she would be the one to have to clean it up and her rage exploded.

"Now look what you've done," she choked. "Will you get away from me? In fact, it would please me not to see your arrogant face again. I'm doing what I want and in a place where I'm needed and if you don't like it, you pompous jackass, you can stay away from me here," she snarled, "and outside the hospital. If you are laboring under the misbegotten idea that I need you or anyone else to care for me you are wrong. Find someone else to waste your Machiavellian ideas on and let me live my own life."

She left him staring after her as she turned and walked away amid silent cheers from the onlookers who had no special love for Martin under the best circumstances.

When Martin did call on her for the next few days, he was politely informed that she was indisposed. Finally, he gave up, consoling himself with the thought that a woman of her violent temperament was wrong for a man of his caliber anyway. He preferred his women docile even though the secret desire to have Lauren in his bed was a fantasy he lived with for a long time.

Michael grew accustomed to Lauren going to the hospital with him daily with the exception of Sundays. The relationship between them was the genuine affection of father and daughter. He was pleased with her efforts and her progress and did not hesitate to tell her so, which did tremendous things for the new woman who was beginning to blossom inside her.

The days rolled into weeks, then into months. It was over eight months before the first message from Cade came. It had been sent many months before, and spoke only of the fact that he was well and had arrived safely. There was word that his mother was well and sent her love and a long request for medical supplies, and any useful equipment his father might be able to send. The light in Lauren's eyes died as she met Michael's over the letter and could read in his face that there was no word within for her—or about her.

The change in Lauren was a complete metamorphosis. She could see now what Cade had seen when he had so painfully asked her to come with him. She wanted, more than anything else in the world, to see Cade again, to let him see the person she had become. A whole continent was between them, a barrier she had no way of crossing. It was a complete impossibility for a woman alone to cross half the country and find her way to a small Indian village that was hundreds of miles from any civilization.

She felt more defeat at that moment than she had at any time in her past.

Michael and her father were sitting across the Brent dinner table on a warm Sunday evening. Lauren sat, half-listening to their conversation, half-dreaming.

"I have crossed enough palms with silver," Michael was saying, "to keep that area inviolate. Even if the push west begins again, it will be a long time yet until that particular area is touched."

"Michael, I wouldn't be too sure. Fort Stanton is getting a new commanding officer, I hear, and I hear the man is certainly not sympathetic to the Indians."

"How accurate is this?"

"Senator Mackerin," Alexander said softly. Michael's eyes narrowed.

"Accurate," he murmured softly. "Alex, is there something else going on I don't know about?"

"It seems," Alex said quietly, "Daniel Preston, the wealthy father of one Dr. Martin Preston has been spreading a little money of his own. It seems there is a specific area west of the Mississippi that he thinks should be open to settlement."

Lauren's attention was on Michael now as he spoke.

"The man has a great deal of money."

"And," Alex offered, "owns quite a few influential people in Washington. He's a dangerous enemy, Michael."

"I know. How close is it?"

"I think he can swing enough votes next election to pass the . . . small bill . . . he wants to pass."

"Good God." Michael sighed. "Twenty-three years, and—"

"And I've ruined everything for you," Lauren added softly. She rose and went to Michael's side.

"Dr. Holliday, I'm to blame for this. After all you have done for me. Tomorrow I shall go to Martin Preston and tell him I will marry him. In return he will kill that bill before it gets voted upon."

Michael stood up and smiled down into her eyes. He placed both his hands on her shoulders.

"Child, haven't I taught you yet about the terrible pride of man. I, my son, and all my people would be shamed forever should I let you make such a sacrifice. But even if that weren't so, my love for you would not let me live with it. You, Lauren, are the daughter Waterflower and I never had, and I will not let you do such a thing."

Tears filled her eyes and she put her arms about him resting her head against his broad chest.

"What will we do?" she whispered.

"I," Michael said quietly, "think it is time for me to go home. If I can no longer defend my people from here, I can at least be with them when they need me." He turned to Alexander. "I will have my resignation on your desk tomorrow, Alex. By the beginning of the month, I shall be ready to go home."

Lauren froze into a breathless stillness; then she lifted her head and looked up into Michael's face. She smiled, for she knew what she was going to do.

"I'm going with you."

"Lauren!" Her father stood up. "No, I won't let you."

"You can't stop me, Father. I can go to Cade now; I can be what he wanted me to be. Father"—her voice died to a whisper—"please don't stop me. I need to do this. Even if Cade no longer wants me, I need to do this."

Alexander's shoulders sagged in defeat, for he knew he would not even try to stop her. "Do you know what you are doing, Lauren?"

"Yes, maybe for the first time in my life, I know what to do and how to do it."

"Then . . . I wish you well, child."

She ran to her father and he held her tightly in his arms knowing it would not be for long.

Michael made preparations and gathered all the medical supplies he could get shipped.

Lauren, too, prepared for the future, but if she could have seen it, she would have been surprised at its course, for it wound a path she could not imagine, a path of fear, love and passion, and a path as different from her planned one as day from night.

Chapter Five

The pale sky was streaked with the rays of the first morning sun over the village of Tekata. The women were already moving about in the half-light.

White Eagle lay on his fur-covered bed wide awake and listening as he always did with great pleasure to the stirring and coming alive of his village.

He slept alone by preference, although he could have had any woman of his choice in his bed, and had taken many. He was worrying in his mind about the strange dreams he had been having. He stood alone at the edge of a dark forest looking across a field of white and gold flowers. At the far edge of the field she stood. He could not make out her features for she was bathed in a bright glow of light. He only knew that her skin was white and the sun sparkled from the mists of her golden hair.

He began to move toward her, then stopped short when he realized the field itself was suddenly filled with wild beasts and sounds of danger he sensed rather than saw. He fought his way to her ferociously while he kept his face turned toward her beckoning hands. Panting and weary, he reached her side, but when he reached for her, wakefulness came and he groaned awake knowing again that he wanted this woman with every fiber of his being and yet had never seen her face.

White Eagle had sensed the disturbed eyes of his father on him many times and he knew he had to choose a wife soon. One day he would be chief, and he needed sons to follow him. Yet his dream held him, angrily and reluctantly, but held him powerless to escape.

He was angry with himself also. He was White Eagle! Warrior of his tribe, honored and respected among all. He was strong, a mighty hunter and a brave man! Why then did this misty dream of a white-skinned golden-haired woman hold him in its power and awaken in him a need he could not control.

Disgusted with himself, he rose from his bed and dressed. Taking his quiver of arrows and his bow, he left his tepee. Today, he would hunt. Maybe it would help him to forget the awakened desire within him for something unknown and most likely impossible.

As he stepped out of his tepee, he was met by his youngest sister, Snow Blossom. His hard face softened when he looked at her, for she was the most beloved thing in his life next to his father.

Her eyes were bright with excitement she could barely contain. As always when something interesting, exciting, or troublesome happened in the life of Snow Blossom, it was to White Eagle she came.

"Good morning, Brother. Did you sleep well?"

"Yes," he lied. "And you, little sister? Your eyes are glowing with some secret. Is there something you want to tell me?"

She laughed. He knew her better than any other human in the world—even her father. As brother and sister, they were very close.

"Do your eyes ever miss anything, Brother?"

"Not with you. Come, let us go to the river and swim. There you can tell me this great secret that is so difficult to hold."

He mounted on his horse with one smooth movement, then reached down and drew her up behind him.

They rode to the river a few miles from the village. It was their habit to bathe every morning, although they did not always share the time together.

Between them existed a bond that was unique, and neither felt a touch of shame or a sense of any other thing but freedom—and the comfort of sharing time and pleasure with each other. They stripped off their clothes and dove into the water. He admired her beauty as abstractly as he admired the beauty in the natural scene about him.

When they had exhausted themselves, they lay together on the river bank and allowed the heat of the morning sun to warm and dry their golden bodies.

"Now," he said softly without opening his eyes, "what is this great secret you wish to tell me, little one?"

"Will you always think of me as a child?" she said, a touch of irritation in her voice.

He chuckled. "Only as long as you act like one."

He heard the quick angry sound and laughed again; then she laughed with him.

"Sun Knife is coming home," she said softly.

Now he blinked his eyes open in surprise and heard her laugh of satisfaction. He sat up. "Now I have your attention, Brother?"

"Yes. How do you know? How soon?"

"I heard our father say it and I think it will be in less than one moon."

He lay back down, his hands folded behind his head, a quick smile quirked on his full sensuous mouth.

"So now my sister can smile again. Her warrior returns. I can hear your heart beat from here."

Surprised that she did not respond, he again turned to look at her, only to find a dejected look of sadness on her face.

"I'm sorry," he said gently. "I did not mean to hurt you."

"It is no matter, Brother," she said quietly. "He will probably notice me no more this time than he did before."

White Eagle looked at her critically. Her slender body seemed to glow with an inner warmth; it was as though it had been expertly carved from a piece of golden bronze. He knew that many warriors had tried to take her as wife and failed. He also knew that she had loved Sun Knife with a single-minded passion for as long as he could remember. If Sun Knife brought no wife with him, surely, he thought, he would find it difficult not to return the love of a creature such as the one that lies beside me.

"Why do you not tell him how you feel?" he asked with the typical innocence of the male.

"No."

"Why?"

"I am a woman," she said proudly. "I am Snow Blossom, daughter of the great Chief Tekata and sister of the warrior, White Eagle," she said, her jaw set determinedly. "I would ask no man to come to me. Am I ugly? Have I not rejected brave warriors from many tribes. No, Brother, I go on my knees to no man even if I love him more than life. If he sees me and wants me, I would go to him in joy, if not, he will never know of my love for him."

White Eagle lay back again. "Foolish," he grumbled.

"Not foolish, Brother. You would be the same if you were a woman."

"I'm glad I'm not." He laughed, then his face became serious. "It must be difficult not to be able to say what you feel. I don't know what I would do should I find myself in that position. But I won't," he said positively. "I will always say exactly what I want and think." He laughed again. "I have always found it the best way to get what you want."

These were words that were to come back to him one day and make him realize it was not so easy to reach out and get what one wanted.

"I am going back to speak to our father and find out when he is coming. Maybe I shall go and meet him. I am curious to find if the white world has changed him. Do you want to come?"

"No," she said softly, her eyes far away. "I shall stay here a little longer."

He rose and dressed and left her lying there knowing she was dreaming of the man she had not seen for almost eight years, and wondering, as he did, if the white world had made him different.

He rode back to the village slowly, remembering the time he and Sun Knife had spent together as children. At the village he went to his father's tepee and requested permission to enter and speak. That granted, he went inside and stood before his father.

"I have heard that my brother, Sun Knife, is coming home soon."

"A little bird has told you the truth, my Son." Tekata smiled. "I should always remember her ears are always open for word of her favored warrior."

"It is true, then, my Father?"

"Yes, it is true."

"When does he come?"

"Less than twenty days."

"Good. I shall ride out to meet him."

"Yes," Tekata agreed. "It is good two brothers should meet first, away from the village."

"Just in case," White Eagle said softly.

"Yes, just in case. If he has changed, it would be best for you to know first."

"Sun Knife has not changed," White Eagle said positively.

"You have much faith in him."

"Yes, I know him well, maybe better than any other. He was strong and proud when he left us. He may have gained in the white man's medicine, but he has not changed toward us. You are still his chief, Long Arrow is still his foster father, and I am still his brother."

Tekata's eyes never left his son's face and he knew half the words he said were belief and the other half fervent prayer.

"Then when the time comes, go and meet your brother. It will make him feel more welcome." They talked awhile longer, then White Eagle left to go on the hunting trip he had started that morning.

He rode for some time, less interested in hunting than in being alone. His mind occupied with confused thought, he did not realize the distance he was going until he crested a hill and looked down into a valley which he had never seen before. He was surprised, not only at its existence, but at the white curl of smoke that rose from a campfire. Nudging his horse into motion, he rode slowly and cautiously down into the valley. He was alert for any signs of a trap. The horse made very little noise as he moved forward so that the soft sound of a woman's voice singing came to him from a distance. He stopped the horse and slid from his back. Stealthily, he crept forward, moving closer and closer to the sound of the voice.

He made no noise at all as he gently pushed the underbrush aside and peered out at a sight that left him amazed.

A huge wagon with a white canvas top sat in a small clearing. Beside it a small fire burned and nearby, horses were hobbled and grazing contentedly. There were no people in sight, and it being the first time he had seen such equipment, he remained hidden until he could get a look at the people to whom it belonged. In a few minutes, the singing voice stopped. He became more alert and watchful; then his eyes widened and he almost cried out in shock as a young girl walked around from the far side of the wagon and into his line of vision. His body trembled with the shock of her appearance. She stood with the sun behind her and he could not see her face; he could only see that her skin was white and her hair glistened in the sun like purest gold.

He could feel the heavy thudding of his heart and he knew the hand that gripped his bow was wet with sweat. Still he remained silent, not sure if he should call out to her, or even if he could. Her voice broke the silence.

"Father," she called to someone on the other side of the wagon, "I'm going to the river for water."

"Be careful, child," a masculine voice answered. "Keep on the alert. We don't know where we are or what kind of people live here, be they friendly or unfriendly."

"Father." She laughed, and White Eagle found himself listening with a great deal of pleasure to the rippling sound of it. It reminded him of a stream he knew where rapid waters rippled over smooth stones. "I thought you taught me that all men are made in the image of God and are good unless someone strikes them first?"

His answering laugh came to White Eagle. "That does not mean that I want some friendly savage carrying you away."

Again the pleasant sound of her laughter filled the air and White Eagle was spellbound until he saw that she was walking directly toward where he lay hidden.

An expert such as he had no trouble in silently blending himself into the forest, and she passed him without even knowing he was there, but not far enough away that he could not see the spun gold of her waist-length hair, the smooth creamy skin, and wide violet eyes. He drifted through the forest behind her without a sound, watching the free-and-easy sway of her slender body as she walked. She swung the bucket she carried back and forth to match her steps and hummed lightly to herself. He watched as she knelt by the stream and filled the bucket; then she set it aside and rose to her feet.

She stood erect and lifted her face toward the sun, closing her eyes, and smiling as though she had a deep inner secret she was enjoying. Then she lifted her arms as though she were embracing the warmth of the afternoon sun.

To the girl, it was just that, sheer pleasure in the beautiful place in which she stood and the soft penetrating warmth of the sun. To the superstitious and very religious Indian who watched, she was an omen sent by the sun god and he was watching her, as he thought, communing with the god who had sent her—to him. She was something beyond anything he knew; therefore, she was someone whose path he should not disturb lest the anger of the sun god fall on his shoulders in punishment. No, he decided he would do nothing to let her know he was there. He wanted to move away, but his eyes were held to the rare golden beauty of the girl who stood before him.

It must have struck the caprice of the gods who wondered why this ignorant savage stood paralyzed in awe before the woman he had seen so often in his dreams. Annoyed at his decided lack of inspiration, they took upon themselves a task.

The girl dropped her arms and turned to get the bucket of water. In an instant, she froze and her eyes widened in fear. It was only then White Eagle heard the deadly rattling sound, and his eyes followed hers to the coiled death that lay only a few feet from her.

She stared at the snake, her body rigid with fear. Its flat head with the cold eyes and rapidly flicking tongue drew back tautly in preparation to strike.

He had no choice, nor did he give it a thought. In one swift movement, he reached back for an arrow, fitted it to his bow, drew back, and sent it flying with a deadly aim. It struck the snake through the head and the force of it pinned the snake to the ground.

She spun about, and White Eagle knew it was now impossible to keep himself hidden. An arrow does not come from the sky, though later when he gave it some thought, he began to wonder why the gods did not protect the one they sent. He finally allowed himself the one thought that rationalized all others. The gods had sent him to protect her.

With this thought in mind he rose from where he was hiding and took a few steps toward her. Then he stopped. The last thing he wanted to do was frighten her. At that moment, he was grateful for the teacher who had been sent to Sun Knife, for, from him he had learned the white man's tongue.

"I am a friend, Golden One," he said gently with his hand stretched toward her. "I mean you no harm."

She remained motionless, but the tense quivering of her body told him she was frightened. He stopped, remaining very still.

"The snake would have killed you. I am happy the Great Spirit put me here to kill him in time. Are you all right?"

"Yes," she managed weakly. But he was aware that she was still unsure whether to stand her ground or run. "Who . . . who are you? Where did you come from? I never heard you approach."

"You were too busy speaking to the sun god," he replied.

She looked at him questioningly for she had no idea what he was talking about.

"I am White Eagle. My village is not many miles from here."

"My father and I are just passing through your land. May we go in peace?"

"I would not harm you, nor would any of my people. But beyond our land is a tribe that will not be so kind. You must not cross their land. They have eyes like hawks and hearts like the wolves. They would kill your father and . . ." He stopped for he didn't want to say the things that would be in store for her.

"But we must go on. We are on our way to the coast."

His quick eye had taken in everything. He knew they had been camped here many days. All signs pointed toward it.

"Why then," he asked, "have you stayed here so many days?"

"My father . . . is not well. He has not been able to travel for many days, but he is recovering. If we can stay on your land a few more days, he will be well and we shall leave. We can do no harm to you if we stay for such a short time."

He chuckled, his dark eyes glowing with amusement. He did not see the possibility of them doing any harm should they stay forever.

"Come," he said. "I shall go back to your camp with you and speak to your father."

Still she was slightly afraid to come too close to him. Instead of waiting for her to come to him as he had bidden, he went to her, a gesture completely alien in his society. A brave was the one who ruled. Should he have done what he did in his village in front of any of his people he would have lost face and the respect of his tribe. He knew this, but the urge to stand near her, to look into those wide violet eyes was too much.

When he stood by her side, nothing or no one, no rule of behavior, could have convinced him it was not worth it.

Compared to his huge muscular frame, she was small. The top of her head came to his shoulder and her body was slender, yet softly rounded.

He stood looking into her eyes and did not realize the fear that quivered within her at his overpowering presence.

The gold hair that had caught his fascination held him again in awe. With one hesitant hand, he reached out and lifted one curl between his fingers. It was soft and smooth and he stood enjoying the feel of it.

It was only then he sensed her fear and he smiled. "I mean you no harm," he repeated. "Your hair is like the sun. I have never seen anything so."

"There are many among my people who have hair the same color." She laughed.

He looked at her, wondering if she was speaking truth to him. Then he was immediately angry with himself; a symbol sent by the sun god should not be doubted.

Now she seemed to be regaining control of her fear and she smiled up at him, sensing his peaceful attitude. The smile created a strange twisting feeling somewhere deep within him and a thick constriction in his throat that kept him from answering.

He nodded and she retrieved her bucket and walked ahead of him down the path. He stifled the desire to carry the bucket for her. It was bad enough she was walking ahead of him instead of behind him as she should.

They walked into the camp from the same direction he had originally come. He followed her around the wagon and looked at the man who lay in a makeshift bed beside a low-burning fire. The man was as shocked as White Eagle. White Eagle found the girl had spoken the truth, for the man's hair was as sunny gold as his daughter's with the exception of the gray on each temple.

"Rebecca!" Her father looked at her in alarm. "Are you all right, child? He didn't hurt you, did he?"

White Eagle stiffened and his eyes grew cold. "White Eagle does not make war on women, old Father," he said. "Nor do I make war on helpless men. I am a warrior, son of Chief Tekata."

"Chief Tekata . . . I have heard of him," the man said, relief flooding his voice.

"Of course, you have," White Eagle said proudly. "My father is a man of great strength and honor. His name is sung about many fires."

"I am sorry," the man replied uncertainly. "It is hard not to be able to defend your daughter. Please, come and eat with us. Let me explain to you why we trespass on your land. Maybe then, you will let us go in peace."

White Eagle cast a quick look at Rebecca, then went forward and sat by the man. He was uncertain of what he should do, but he knew one thing: he was going to find every way possible to hold the sun-haired girl called Rebecca here in his valley as long as he could. But along with that, he was going to temporarily keep their presence a secret from all—including his people—until he found what was best to do with them—best . . . and safest.

He ate the food Rebecca silently prepared for him, listening to her father talk, but keeping one eye on her.

"I am a minister of God," her father began.

"What god?" White Eagle asked, his attention finally focused in what he thought was the proper area, for he was still convinced Rebecca was a gift from the sun god his people worshiped.

"There is only one God," the man answered.

White Eagle was doing his best to follow such reasoning, and he forgave a man, who he thought knew only one god, for not recognizing all the other gods of whose existence White Eagle was completely sure.

Ingrained respect for an older man forbade White Eagle from arguing with him, so he silently allowed him obedience to his "one God." White Eagle continued in his own beliefs.

"We are on our way to California where I am to build a church."

"A church?" White Eagle questioned. "What is a church?"

"A place to worship God."

White Eagle blinked. "But you can worship any god anywhere. In the early-morning sun, we praise the sun god at the door of our tepee."

The man's gentle blue gaze fell on the huge Indian who was struggling to understand.

"Don't worry about it, young heathen." He chuckled. "Our religions, I imagine, are not so very far apart."

"What is your illness, old Father?"

"I resent your reference to old." The man chuckled. "But it is a strange fever that leaves me weak as a child and unable to move."

White Eagle nodded. "I have seen it before. It will pass."

"How long?"

"I cannot say. Many days. You are safe here."

"My name is Benjamin Wade." He sighed. "I hope it will pass, but with each attack I seem to get weaker and weaker."

White Eagle watched him closely. The white man was not afraid, he could sense, but he was worried about the welfare of his daughter. "You can stay here for as long as it pleases you. I shall come again and bring you food. When you are well, I shall guide you across the rest of our land in safety."

"Why would you do this for us?"

White Eagle grinned. "No matter what you may think, my people are not wild animals; we do not prey on helpless men and women. We are a brave people. If we ever have to fight you, it will not be because we have wanted to, but because you have pushed us as far as we will stand to be pushed."

Benjamin's eyes softened. "The good Samaritan."

"Who?"

"Never mind. Tell me about your people."

White Eagle and Benjamin talked for a long time; then White Eagle's attention was drawn to the fact that the sun was setting. He rose to go.

"Good night, White Eagle," Benjamin said.

"Good night, I shall come back soon. It has been good to sit and talk with you."

As he turned to walk away, Rebecca came to his side. She reached out and touched his arm lightly and White Eagle could feel the warmth of her fingers send tiny prickles of warmth up his arm. He remained still, his face impassive.

"I want to thank you again for saving my life. I was so terrified I could not move."

"It is best you did not. The snake might have struck before I could do anything if you moved."

"Well," she said softly, her voice hesitant, "I owe you my life and I am grateful. I shall never forget either what you did for me or your kindness toward my father."

White Eagle stood immobile. She had no idea how he was fighting the urge to reach out and touch her smooth ivory skin. At last, his will could no longer resist one gesture. Again, he reached out and lifted one glowing gold curl from her shoulder. He held it a moment seeing it twine around his finger as if it had a life of its own.

"You are truly a daughter of the sky. I watched you today as you spoke with your father, the sun. I am honored you walk in my world, Golden One. White Eagle is the warrior who will guard you with his life. You are safe."

She watched him, then she smiled. "Yes . . . yes, I believe I am. When will you come back, White Eagle?"

"You wish me to return soon?"

Again she could read no emotion in the deep black eyes that regarded her, yet she knew she wanted him to return.

"Yes." It was almost a whisper. "Yes, I do."

For the first time, White Eagle smiled.

It was on the long ride home that White Eagle searched his mind. "Why should he hide the white ones?" he thought. They were the race that were the cause of all the troubles. But the answer came before the question left his mind. "Because, you do not want her to go. You want her to depend on you and stay in that hidden valley as long as you can keep her there."

He arrived home long after dark and went to his tepee where he threw himself on his mat and tried to sleep.

Again the dreams came, only this time, he had no trouble

putting a face to the girl who stood across the field from him. He could still feel the silken touch of her hair as he finally fought his way across the field and stood before her. Only this time, she smiled and reached out, taking his hand in hers. Together they walked to a quiet grass-covered glade where he pulled her down beside him and took her soft willing lips with his.

He was holding his impatience in rigid control as he forced himself to wait two full days before he returned to the valley.

His heart leaped when he saw her bright welcome smile as she saw him coming. She went to the side of his horse and smiled up at him.

"White Eagle, I am so glad you have returned."

He slid down from his horse, seeking words to cover the real reason he had returned. "Your father is well?"

"He had a very bad night last night. The fever was high and he was extremely ill. Oh, White Eagle, are you sure this fever will pass?"

"In time, it will go. And you, Golden One, you are well?"

"Yes, I am well," she said softly, but her eyes escaped his.

"You are afraid?" he questioned gently.

She inhaled deeply as though about to refuse the truth of his words; then her shoulders slumped. "I know I should have more faith as father says, but at night . . . when I'm alone . . . yes, I'm afraid."

"But there is no cause for your fear. Surely the great sun god would not let any harm come to his daughter."

"White Eagle, I don't know what you think I am, but my father is the man who lies there ill. I am no daughter of any god. You do not understand."

"The will of the gods is not for me to understand. I only know you have been put into my care—my vision has told me so—and I will let no harm come to you."

"Vision?"

He knew he could not explain it to her without revealing his real desire to possess her not as a daughter of the gods, but as a real woman. "I will see your father," he said firmly. With her following, he walked over and knelt beside her father. One look told him the man was extremely ill. White Eagle helped her cool her father's fever-ridden body with water from the river, and force down some food, after which, he seemed to rest a little easier.

Together, White Eagle and Rebecca ate the hastily prepared meal she made. Then they sat and talked for a long time.

Her father moved in and out of delirium all day and late into the night; then in the early hours of the morning, he seemed to fall into a deep sleep.

Rebecca was exhausted and White Eagle ordered her firmly to lie down and rest. "I will watch," he said as he pushed her toward the blankets near the fire. "Sleep; tomorrow he may need you. For now, he sleeps and you must, too."

She obediently lay on the blankets and in her exhausted condition, she soon fell asleep.

He watched, as he had said he would. Watched the steady rise and fall of her rounded breasts under the cotton dress she wore and watched as the brilliant gold of her hair spread on the dark blanket. Watched as her soft lips smiled slightly in pleasant dreams. Watched, and knew, she was the one woman he would want until the end of time.

With all the difficulties that were brewing, with all the differences between Indian and white, White Eagle wondered if it would ever be permitted to take a white woman as wife. When the thought came to him, it was followed by the answer—no. . . .

He knew all the arguments that would be presented against it. She was white, was the first. But that, combined with the thought that if the men at the white fort knew, they would come for her and try to take her away from him. That thought raged through him like a flame. No one, he thought angrily, would take her from him if she were willing to stay.

Despite what she said, he still retained the idea that she was some golden goddess from the sun and he kept all his desires to himself, for he was not too sure the sun god would allow him to reach for his daughter. No, he would protect her and wait. If she were meant for him, the gods would give him a vision, show him the path he must take. In the meantime, he would care for her.

In the early hours, just before dawn, when the half-gray

light of day touched the earth, she woke. She stirred sleepily, then opened her eyes. Across the dying fire, violet eyes met black ones. She lay still, fighting a strange new emotion that made her want to go to the safety of those strong muscular arms, lay her head on his chest, and feel secure. It was a new emotion for her, but not so new to the man who sat across the fire from her. He had seen the first dawn of awakening passion before.

If she was gripped by the newness of it, he was held by what he knew existed beyond that look. It took more restraint and control not to go to her, then he had ever had to summon in his life. The moment passed as she shook herself free of the feeling and rose from the bed. She went to her father's side.

"He is sleeping," White Eagle said. "He has been sleeping comfortably for many hours. For now, the fever will go, but it will leave him weak. He must eat well and drink much."

"I'll go to the river for water and make some breakfast. Will you watch him?"

He nodded, then watched her walk away. At that moment, he remembered the snake and the fact that they were often found in pairs. His mind filled with the terror of her loveliness dying. He rose, looked down at the sleeping man for a minute, then on silent feet, he followed her path.

At the river, he did not at first see her for she was a few feet beyond the spot where she usually drew water, and when he did see her, his breath caught and held as he stood unable to move gazing at the vision that presented itself to his hungry eyes.

She had cast aside the dress she wore and the rest of her clothes. She was wading out into the water which swirled about her knees. Ivory and gold, soft curves, high rounded breasts with the sweet pink aureoles. Her soft hips molded into the long slender legs. Desire struck him with a blow that almost made him groan. He stood; the aching need for her filled him like a flaming river, yet he knew he could not, would not, touch her yet. He was unsure, not only of her position in his life, but the fact that the sun god might strike him should he put his hands on his daughter.

It was only his beliefs in his gods that stood between him and Rebecca that day, and she never knew that he stood devouring her beauty until she dressed; then he preceded her silently to the camp. His immobile face showed no signs when she came, but his mind held her beauty in it, and his senses screamed his need for her until he could no longer stand it. He told her he would return and left to spend some time alone.

In the twenty days before Sun Knife came home, White Eagle spent as much time as he could at the Wade camp. Rebecca's father was fighting a losing battle with the strange illness and White Eagle could see he was losing.

As he grew weaker, the burning love in the heart of White Eagle grew stronger. Rebecca turned to him more and more and he knew he had her complete trust.

She would meet him when he came, with a bright welcoming smile, and they often would sit, either at the camp or on the soft grass near the river and talk.

She asked him questions about himself, listening as he told her about his life, past, present, and future. The only thing he excluded from all parts was his deep love and need for her.

He did not question her for he was afraid of answers that might take her forever out of his life. Her past he did not care about, her present he was sharing with joy, but her future and the possibility that he might lose her was something he could not stand to look at.

No matter how well he could hide his emotions from Rebecca, when he began to recover from his last bout with the fever, her father sensed the huge Indian's feelings. He watched silently and realized, for some reason he could not account for, White Eagle had no intention of saying or doing anything about them. Subtly, he began to ask questions, and with White Eagle's full attention usually on Rebecca, he sometimes answered a little too honestly. In a matter of a week, Benjamin knew that White Eagle not only loved Rebecca, but that love was being held on a plane of near worship. He realized White Eagle's superstitious and deeply religious nature. That he thought of Rebecca as something akin to a goddess at first amused Benjamin, then began to worry him, for he, too, knew he was losing the fight and he wondered what would become of his daughter if he were gone. His inherent knowledge of people made him realize she would be safer and maybe happier with White Eagle, a man who truly loved her. For despite all their differences, they were two who were meant to be together.

He began to search for ways to open White Eagle's eyes to the fact that she was a woman and she would need a man not only to protect her, but to love her and fill her life. To his amused distress, most of what he said along those lines did not even dent White Eagle's cool reserve and assurance that he knew exactly what she was—and what she was, was beyond him.

The days were a pleasure for Rebecca, for during the times her father was lucid, White Eagle would spend time with her showing her the ways of the forest and teaching her the way his people thought about the gifts nature had given them. He spoke of the gods with an attitude that she would understand all he said, for she was closer to them than he. No matter what she said, she could not shake the way he seemed to hold her in his mind above and beyond all else. At times, it exasperated her and had she been a little more knowledgeable she might have found the way herself to prove to him she was a woman of flesh and blood and not a woman who wanted to be worshiped from afar.

Though his sister noticed his reticence and frequent absence from the village, no one questioned him and he offered no information, for he kept the secret of his golden one in his own mind and heart.

He had decided to go to meet Sun Knife. If he found him to still be the brother he once was, and being half-white, he would speak with him. Maybe Sun Knife could tell him a way to keep the girl and her father here in the valley.

The time neared for Sun Knife's return. White Eagle had gone to see Rebecca to tell her that he would be gone for a few days. He had brought with him equipment to set up a tepee where they could be more comfortable.

Then, as she walked with him to the edge of the clearing, she felt his reluctance to leave her. She was always more frightened when White Eagle was gone.

"You will return soon, White Eagle?" Her violet eyes revealed her feelings like windows to her mind and he read them as truly as if she had spoken the words.

"Do not be afraid, Rebecca. I shall return soon." He deliberately read the look as fear instead of what it really was. There was a gulf between them that she did not know how to cross and he refused to cross.

Still he could hardly bear to leave her without reaching out to her somehow. Again, his huge hand reached out, but this time, it slid into the depth of her thick hair and held the mass in his hand. Their eyes held for a minute and then he was gone. She watched after him with shadowed eyes, knowing he had touched her more deeply than just with his hand, but not knowing how to reach back to him.

White Eagle went to his village. He gathered all his things and prepared for the few days of traveling it would take to cross Sun Knife's path. He spoke to his father, then left the village.

It was good to have the time alone to try to gather his thoughts. Good . . . but not constructive, for all his thoughts, no matter what path he set them on, came back to Rebecca Wade.

Chapter Six

The stage from Bridger City to Fort Stanton rumbled along the dry rutted road. Cade sat with his feet up on the opposite empty seat and his arms folded across his chest. His head was back against the seat with his hat tipped over it to shield his face from the hot afternoon sun that penetrated through the windows. To all outward appearances, he was asleep; but, as always, his outward appearance deceived everyone. Instead, with acute hearing, he listened to the conversation of the driver and his partner. His body seemed completely relaxed and rolled back and forth with the movements of the swaying coach. He was clothed in fitted buckskin pants and a buckskin shirt that laced at the front. At this moment, the laces were loosened to give as much air as possible. He wore a pair of buckskin and leather boots also; they extended almost to his knees and were laced with ties that circled the strong muscled calves of his legs. On the side of one leg, sheathed in the side of his boot, was a wicked bladed knife. He wore no other weapons.

"That boy don't belong to the military. Wonder why he's goin' out to Stanton? They ain't nuthin' there," the driver's assistant questioned.

"Ain't none of my business. Ain't none of yours either. We just drive 'em where they want to go; we don't ask for no pedigree," the driver answered.

"You sure are touchy, today," grumbled his assistant. "I just asked—"

The driver broke in, "You better quit askin' out here. That could get you real dead, you ask the wrong thing of the wrong man. Just between you and me, I think he's the wrong one to be askin' about."

The passenger could not see the nod of the man's head, but he knew he had.

"Iffen I hadn't seen those eyes, I would have sworn that boy was an Injun. You get a good look at his skin? Same color as an Injun's. Bet he's a half-breed."

"You better shut your mouth. He hears you and you might not be makin' the trip back with me."

"He can't hear us from up here unless he's half-animal. Reckon though he's probably just that. Half-white-man, half-somethun-else."

This remark brought a slow smile to Cade's lips.

"Did you get his name?"

"Nope! And I ain't askin' when he gets off either."

"Ain't you even a little bit curious?"

"Sure, curious as hell, and if he offers any information, I'll lap it up like a cat laps up milk, but if he don't offer, I ain't askin'. That boy's like a curled-up rattler. Don't step on him and he won't bother you. Mess around and you might get a permanent case of snakebite." The driver chuckled.

"Speakin' on Injuns, I hear old Tekata is sick." This remark made the passenger's face lose its smile. He listened even more intently for the answer.

"Yeah, I hear the old man's sick. Hope it ain't nothin' serious. He's a damn' good man. Been a good leader of his people, too," the driver answered.

"What happens if he dies?"

"White Eagle will be chief."

"Know anything about him?"

"Only seen him once. He's young, ain't no more than twenty-seven or so. It's damn' young to be responsible for the situation that's brewin' out here. He ain't goin' to be able to stop Washington if they want the land and they do want it. I kind of feel sorry for the boy."

"They goin' to open up all that land out there?"

"I wouldn't be surprised, one of these days. In fact, I don't know what's been holdin' 'em up all this time, somebody in Washington's been pulling some strings."

"What the hell do they expect all those people out there to do? They aren't even united, just a bunch of isolated villages and tribes."

"Yeah . . . now. If they get pushed hard enough, and they find one strong man to lead them—and that man might just be

White Eagle—they just might not be pushed any further. They might just stand and fight."

"Do you think that might happen?"

"Might . . . they're bein' pushed already. That new commander they sent to the fort after old Riles died, well he ain't got a soft spot for any Indian—man, woman, or child."

"He still can't do anything without the O.K. from Washington."

"Sure he can. Just let a few trappers through, let some kind of incident happen, then when the Indians put up a fuss or try to stop them, he just steps in and takes over. And if he takes over, those poor people won't stand a chance."

"You think anybody'd be fool enough to go out there without the O.K. from Washington?"

"Christ, man, ain't you ever heard of the age-old disease called greed. You give 'em enough reason, enough profit, and they'll go. It won't matter to them if it costs the life of every Indian from here to the sea."

There was a few minutes of silence, then the first man said in a voice that was harsh with anger, "Me, I think I'll go back east. I got a feeling there's going to be something bad happen one of these days and I'd rather not be part of it."

"Yeah, me, too," his assistant said fervently.

The conversation drifted to things now that did not interest the passenger and he ceased to listen, his thoughts held by the words already spoken.

Cade leaned forward and brushed his hand across the black leather case that sat on the seat opposite him. It was a slim case about twenty-four inches in length and about twelve in width and four in depth. On the outside in slim gold lettering were the initials "C.H."

"Brother," he said gently, "maybe I have the balance here—at least I hope so."

The stage rolled through the high gates of Fort Stanton and came to a rocking halt in front of a general store that served as stage depot and post office. The driver and his assistant stepped down, the assistant reaching up for the baggage attached to the back of the coach as the driver pulled the door open. He watched his passenger step down from the coach with pantherlike grace that again reminded him of a wild untamed animal. He noticed the case he carried with obvious care. A million questions hovered on the tip of his tongue, but he knew his men well and this passenger was not a man to be questioned.

"This is the last stop of our route, sir," he said. "We'll be leaving here tomorrow and we won't be back until next month." He added the last in the hope he would be offered some information on his passenger's plans.

"Don't worry about me," came the smiling reply. "I doubt if I'll be leaving for a long, long time." He left the man's questions unanswered and moved around the back of the coach. He bent and picked up a bundle wrapped in soft cowhide and lifted it effortlessly. He began to walk toward the building when a voice stopped him in his tracks.

"Well, Dr. Cade Holliday. It's about time you came back."

Cade spun around, a bright smile lighting his blue eyes. Dropping the bundle with a solid thud, he held out his hand to the man who was walking toward him.

"Grant." He laughed. "The first friendly face."

Grant Garrison was a tall, dark-haired man. His skin, burned brown by the sun, was still a different shade than Cade's. His eyes were a gold brown and had bright gold flecks. He had a thick mustache to match his black-brown hair. Broad of shoulder, he gave the impression of wiry strength magnified by the blue military uniform he wore.

"Well, I sure as hell am glad to see you. God, it's been . . . what . . . years?"

"Eight . . . a long, hard eight."

"But you made it."

"Yes, I made it," Cade answered softly. Grant's eyes narrowed as he watched Cade closely.

"Now you're comin' back to change some things."

"I don't know if I can change anything, Grant. I only know I have to try."

"How long you stayin' here, Cade? Long enough to have a drink with an old friend?"

Cade clapped Grant on the shoulder. "Every friend I've got I can count on one hand, Grant. You're the most valuable thing

I've got."

"Except that case," Grant said, pointing to the case cradled gently under one arm.

"This? . . . this isn't just a friend, Grant, it's a whole new way of life, for me and for my people."

Cade picked up his bundle again and they walked together to the saloon. Inside, Cade went to a table and dropped his bundle beside it. He laid the case gently on the table and sat down in a chair while Grant went to the bar and brought back a bottle and two glasses. He set the glasses on the table and uncorked the bottle as he slid down in his seat. Pouring two glasses half-full, he slid one over to Cade and raised his.

"Here's to your new degree, Dr. Cade Holliday. I hope it does for you all that you expect and more."

"Thanks, Grant."

They drank, then Grant leaned back in his chair.

"Grant, what's been going on here since I left?"

Grant chuckled and Cade grinned in response. "Now you and I both know that by now you know as much as I do. Unless you've slipped some, and I don't think you have, your Indian side has been absorbing information for the past few weeks. In fact, you probably know *more* than I do."

Cade laughed. "Maybe."

"Tell me first," Grant began. "When you left here you were an eighteen-year-old boy with your eyes full of stars and all the education your father had acquired for you. In the eight years have you found out all about your father and his plans?"

"Yes, I have. I only hope I can live up to his expectations and my people's. It's a large bite to take and I have to admit I'm a little afraid."

"Can you tell me all that's happened?"

"I'd like to, but I'm anxious to get home. I'll be back this way when some of my supplies come. We can talk then."

"Sure." Grant laughed. "Sometime is as good as anytime. Are you going home now?"

"As soon as I can get my gear packed on a horse I'll be gone. You did get my message about a couple of horses, didn't you?"

"I did, and they're ready anytime that you are. I'd ride with you, but we have a bunch of new recruits that came yesterday and I've got to get them organized. Say hello to Waterflower for me, will you? Tell her I'll be out soon for a good meal of roast venison."

Cade drank the last of his drink and rose. "I'll tell her. Where're the horses?"

"Livery . . . across the grounds. C'mon, I'll take you over."

They walked from the saloon, across the parade grounds and into the stable. There, Grant gave orders for the two horses to be brought out. He helped Cade put the pack on the horse.

"Cade, a lot of things are changing around here. I hope we can work together to find a way out of this. You and White Eagle, you're like brothers. You two will work well together, but remember, I'm here if you need some help."

"I'll remember that, Grant."

He mounted, and pulling the packhorse along, he waved at Grant and rode toward the gates of the fort he had just entered an hour ago. Grant watched his retreating form until it disappeared; then with a deep sigh, he turned back to the barracks.

That Cade was as at home on a horse as he was on his feet was obvious in the relaxed easy way he rode. Even after eight years of absence he had not forgotten the joy of riding in the freedom of the open country. He traveled for almost two days, pressing as rapidly as possible before he slowed his pace and decided to stop early in the afternoon to give both himself and the horse a rest. Finding a good spot, he unpacked and unsaddled the horses, then hobbled them to graze while he relaxed in the shade of the trees. He chewed on the tough stringy jerky he had brought along to carry him over the trip from the fort to his home. He looked about at the serene and peaceful foothills surrounded by the rugged mountains, the grassy slopes and tall whispering pines ahead. Home . . . he was home. With a small half-smile on his face, he allowed the memories he had kept at bay for seven years to roll over him like a warm ocean wave. Home . . . Cade Holliday had been six years old before he had fully realized he was different from all the other Indian boys with whom he played. It was their sudden interest in why he had such strange-colored eyes that sent him to his mother for answers. Trying manfully not to cry, he had stood in front of his mother as she mended one of his shirts. He had begged her with trembling lips and clenched fists to tell him why. Cade could remember his mother, so very beautiful with her long dark braids and large warm eyes that smiled at him always. "Yes, my Son, you are different. You will always be different. One day it will lead you on a very special path—a path that will make of you the great warrior your father was."

"Was?" he questioned. "But my father is—"

"Sit by my side, Son," she said softly. "Now I must tell you as I think you are old enough to understand."

Cade sat cross-legged at her feet looking up at her with his blue eyes that reminded her so much of his father's. He waited in breathless expectation for the story she was about to unfold before him.

"It was four years before your birth. We lived in a place far from here, across the Mississippi, in a land where the sun rises. We were happy there. My parents and I tended the land and enjoyed the miracles the sun brought. There was some form of peace between us and the white man; we were trying to live together, but the greedy among them decided our land was good and they wanted it. Slowly, they began to push us off it. Then the great white father made a decree, and we were all told we must pick up our belongings and move—not just move to another piece of land, but move across the great river and out to the land where the sun sets.

"I had seen sixteen summers, a woman who had been looked upon by many of the young men of our tribe as a wife. Our life would have been very good, but tragedy replaced it. Women were told to take all their belongings and leave the homes they knew and the land they loved. They walked toward the setting sun, a sun that was setting not only on a land, but on a tribe of people. We began the walk, hundreds, thousands of us. Our escort was a small detachment of soldiers. Among them was a young doctor who was to try to see, to the best of his ability, that as few of us as possible died along the way. The miles, aching, hungry, thirsty miles. I cannot tell you, child, of the terrible things that happened. One day, when you are older, I will say the words to you. For now I must tell you of your father. I would never have seen the man who was your father, for it was forbidden for a young unmarried girl to go to the tepee of an unmarried man. My mother became very ill and my father, Gray Bear, and I could no longer do anything to help her. It was in desperation that we took her to the white doctor—his name was Michael Holliday. I shall never forget the first time I saw him. He was very tall and strong, his hair like the red gold of the setting sun and his eyes as blue as the summer sky."

"Like mine, my Mother?" he asked.

She smiled down on him, her eyes warm with the remembrance. "Yes, my Son, you have his eyes, his smile, and his great loving heart."

"Mother . . . did he—"

"Did he love us, my Son? Yes, but you see a terrible thing separated us and he was forced to leave us. It broke both his heart and mine but it was a thing that had to be."

"Tell me of him, Mother."

"He was a strong man, my Son. He tried with everything he knew to stop the terrible deaths and the sickness. The night my father and I took my mother to him, she was dying. I was looking into his eyes while he raged at my father for not bringing her to him sooner and I saw there, the compassion he felt for our people. I think I gave him my heart at that moment.

"It was an unthinkable thing that I should look upon him, and I tried not to raise my eyes to see him ride among his men. I tried, but I could not help it. I would know without seeing him when he was near and my eyes would flee to him as a child to its mother. I thought it was my secret . . . but again I was wrong.

"I don't know if he had been watching me as much as I had him, but suddenly, he always seemed to be near. Then one day, I was walking back from the river where I had gone for water and suddenly, he was there on the trail in front of me. I shall never forget his words. 'Waterflower, I know this is not proper and your tribe would be upset if you spoke to me. All I want to know is what is the proper way that I must go? For I want to ask permission to court you.' I had no idea what the word 'court' meant, all I knew was that my legs were weak and my heart beat furiously. I told him that if he wanted to speak of me, he must bring gifts to my father and speak to him. He nodded and left me there on the trail without speaking again, for he knew I would be dishonored if we were discovered.

"That night, he came to our tepee and he brought with him

many gifts for my father. They smoked together and talked long into the night. The next morning, my father told me that he wanted me for a wife and that he had agreed. I was so happy I could not speak, and I looked forward to the ceremony that would make me his wife. Michael was surprised, I think, both at the simplicity of the ceremony and that I agreed to marry him so easily. It was only much later that I had the courage to tell him that I had looked upon him long ago and found him pleasing.

"We were married and he was a good husband to me and slowly became a beloved friend of our people. Always his medicine was ready and the magic knife he used to heal with.

"But the days were becoming a nightmare for my people. The land was hard and the white man continued to trespass on it, often violating our sacred burial places. We knew, your father and I, that he would not be able to help us any longer where he was. The only way he could reach out and work for the people he loved was from the white man's world. The day was coming when he knew he would have to leave us if he wanted to help us to survive.

"You were two years old before he could make a decision, and he made it one day when he realized that along with the future of our tribe was the future of his son and the other children who would be his son's companions and friends all his life. He knew he could offer you a greater future there than he could here.

"You will never know of the pain he felt when he left. He held you close to him and promised you that when you were old enough he would see to your education, and he prayed you would be a doctor as he was.

"You have seen six summers, my Son. Next year, when the last winter snow melts, a man is coming. He will stay and teach you until he thinks you are ready. Then . . . then you shall go to your father."

He could still remember the thrill that ran through him as he gazed up at his mother. "I'm . . . I'm to go with him?"

"Yes. I know you do not understand now, Cade, but your father and I have given you two worlds in which you must exist. You are a link between one that is living and one that is dying. Through you, maybe we can find some path to walk better than the one we are on that leads only to death."

No, he did not understand then. All he knew was that from that moment on, he felt even more keenly the difference between himself and all the others. He responded to it as his mother had hoped he would, by opening himself to learning all the ways of both people to whom he belonged.

He grew under the watchful eyes of both his mother and the man he had thought was his father. Long Arrow was a proud and handsome warrior who had been a friend of Michael Holliday. He had been the one chosen to care for the two that Michael loved. He had taken his charge more seriously than anyone thought, and secretly, he held a great love for Waterflower and had accepted this way to be close to the woman he had always wanted.

Cade looked upon him, at six, as the tallest, bravest and kindest man he had ever known. In his small way, after his mother had told him everything, he made it clear to Long Arrow that his feelings for him were still the same. He showed his admiration plainly by endeavoring to walk in Long Arrow's shadow whenever possible and learn from him all that was necessary to make him a strong warrior.

The white teacher came, a small withered man who had lived with the Indians more often than the whites. Cade laughed at the beginning, but as time went on, he began to respect the keen mind that lived in the small wrinkled body.

Cade learned to ride from Long Arrow. He learned to make his weapons and to hunt with the stealth of an animal. He also learned a deep and reverent appreciation of nature and her control of the earth about him. He was taught respect for all life and the dependence upon the gods which the white teacher, Mr. Ebbin McDonnell, never could erase from him with all his talk of Christianity.

He was happy—free to ride, hunt, and sport with the young friends he had, among which was White Eagle, the son of the chief. He and White Eagle had a depth of friendship to which no words could be applied. They realized immediately that each understood the other completely and could depend upon the other implicitly under any circumstances. Often, they were in competition with each other for the shy smiles of the pretty doe-eyed girls that looked their way. In feats that required great strength, White Eagle could be surpassed by no one in the tribe, and that included Cade. In feats that required skill only, there were times that Cade bested him, but they were few and far between. Cade would grin in defeat and White Eagle would clap him on the shoulder with a blow that would almost knock him off his feet; then he would claim that Cade would never be able to claim a wife, first because he was not as handsome as White Eagle, which was an obvious lie, but that he was also second to him in skill. They laughed together, faced sorrow together when White Eagle's mother died giving birth to his sister and were bound together as blood brothers.

Learning to read and write came easy to him, but he struggled with mathematics. By the time he was sixteen and ready to be initiated into manhood in the tribe, he was also said to be a very satisfactory student by his white teacher.

He was seventeen and a warrior in his own right, held in esteem not only by his friend White Eagle but by the elders of the tribe, when the first message came from his father questioning his progress and anxiously awaiting to find out if he was ready to continue his studies at his father's side, to be the doctor he wanted him to be. Cade could admit to no one but himself that he was frightened of the prospect. Afraid that if he were transplanted, he would be so out of place he would not be able to function in the new world. He was a wild and free spirit and the idea of the change they wanted to make in him was hard to handle. His mother, silent but wise to his moods, realized what was going on in his mind. She did not argue or press him, yet she knew he would do as she and Long Arrow wished.

The messages from his father became more insistent, but it wasn't until Cade was eighteen and Ebbin and his mother convinced him he would be able to face the new world and master it, that he agreed to go.

He would never forget that painful parting and his promise to return. It and all the other memories, good and bad, that the last seven years had brought, washed over him.

At first he was homesick and insecure in the confining homes of the white men. But his father, a surprise to Cade because of his awareness, made everything as easy for him as possible. Understanding the Indians, as Michael Holliday did, made it easy for him to close the gap of years between him and the son for whom he had sacrificed so much.

Many experiences were to face Cade. More schooling and working as an apprentice with his father filled his waking hours. Many nights were filled with revelry with some of the many friends he made. He soon found that his untamed look drew women like a magnet and it did not take him long to begin sampling the treats he was offered.

The years began to blend together and the magic day came when his father stood beside him as he picked up the scalpel for the first time. It was an experience so profound that it shook Cade to the core of his being. His eyes met his father's and they silently shared the exuberant joy of returning life to the dying. It was at that moment that Cade truly understood the tremendous sacrifice his parents had made for him and he vowed silently that it would not be in vain. From that moment he was dedicated to the learning and the skill of which he knew his father had just made him a gift.

Then came the day that his father quietly informed him that he thought his education was complete, and that now destiny called on him to be fulfilled.

"You must go home now. What you have learned, what little I have been able to give you must be used to keep your people from dying."

His father had just turned fifty-one, but he was still a vigorous and handsome man and Cade knew without being told that his love for Waterflower and her people was still strong.

"Can you not return with me, Father? Have you not sacrificed enough, you and my mother? You deserve some happiness, too."

"We have our happiness, Cade, in you. When I can no longer serve them here, I will return, for I will live out my last days with the woman I have always loved."

Two months later, Cade waved good-by to his father and began the long journey home. He was twenty-six years old and carried with him the most precious gift his father had given him—the flat, leather case with his initials embossed in gold and inside a set of surgical tools, fine instruments that would mean much to the people to whom he returned.

Chapter Seven

He sighed deeply then stood up. He wanted to take advantage of all the hours he could get before he had to camp for the night. Every day brought him closer to home. He resaddled his mount and repacked the other horse in quick precise movements that told of how accustomed he was to doing it. Within minutes, he was on his way again. Familiar scenery passed him now and often he would smile to himself over some remembrance that a particular spot brought.

It was still four more days of pressing travel before he reached the boundaries of their own territory. He was only two days away from home. He stopped just as the sun began to set and went in search of food. He built a fire and prepared the rabbit he had trapped an hour or so before. When it was done, he reached out with the one and only utensil he carried, the sharp-bladed knife, to strip off a piece. Just before the knife touched the meat, he froze. He listened intently for a minute or so; then he smiled. Again he bent forward and cut off a piece of meat; then he sat back against his blanket-covered saddle. Raising his voice so it could be heard out of the bright range of the fire's glow, he said, "My brother walks through the forest like a wounded buffalo. Has he grown stiff with age like the old ones and cannot stalk his prey any longer?"

A deep throaty chuckle came from the dark area and then a voice filled with good humor replied, "My brother leaves a trail that a papoose fresh from the cradle board could follow. Has he grown soft with his stay with the white man?"

Cade laughed aloud and stood up as the voice outside the light became the shadow, then the substance of a man, and he stepped within the circle of light to stand watching Cade move toward him.

White Eagle was unbelievably huge, yet he gave the aura of having complete control over every muscle of his body. He moved with a lithe grace that belied his size. Cade, as always was impressed with the complete symmetry of him and he, as usual, received the feeling that when the gods created man, it was White Eagle they had in mind. Cade himself was a shade over six feet tall, but White Eagle towered over him by at least four inches. He had a face that could have been chiseled from granite, its jaw, firm and square, its features all sharp-cut planes and angles. Only the dark-brown eyes softened him. They glowed with intelligence and good humor. His body glowed a golden brown in the firelight. He was naked to the waist and wore only his loincloth, leather leggings, and soft moccasins. His huge bow was held unstrung in his hand out of deference to meeting a friend at his own fire. A quiver of arrows in a soft leather case decorated with bright beads hung from his back with the leather band that held it slung across his barrel chest. His hair, long, thick and black was tied back with a strip of leather and another beautifully decorated strip encircled his head. To a stranger, it would have been nothing, but to Cade it meant that White Eagle was the son of a great chief. Where Cade's body was slender, lithe, and sinewy-muscled, White Eagle was heavily muscled and gave the appearance of carefully controlled strength. Cade walked to White Eagle's side and smiled as a huge hand reached out and rested on his shoulder.

"Welcome home, my Brother," rumbled the gentle voice. Cade placed his hand on the huge muscled shoulder.

"It pleases me to see my brother again. It has been long and I have missed his wisdom and his strength. It is good to be among my people again."

He felt the tremble in White Eagle's body, saw the look of relieved pleasure in his eyes, and he instantly became aware that White Eagle had been afraid he would find Cade changed and no longer his brother but a white man.

"Come, sit by my fire, share my supper, and tell me all that has passed since I have seen you."

White Eagle nodded, and laying aside his weapon he dropped cross-legged on the ground beside the fire. Cade sat back on his blanket and looked across the fire at the man who had been closer to him than any other. He was much more mature and

Cade saw a distant look of almost sorrow in his deep-brown eyes. If Cade was surprised at the change in him, he said nothing, keeping his silence until White Eagle decided what he wanted to tell him.

"You are well, Sun Knife? You have succeeded in all you wanted to do on your journey?"

"I have tried to gain some wisdom, White Eagle, but I will not know if I have succeeded until I lay what I know at the feet of our chief and see if it will be of any benefit to our people. If it is, then I have succeeded in fulfilling my parents' dream, if not, I must do the best I can with what I have."

White Eagle grunted his agreement with the words his brother spoke.

"Speaking of our chief, I hear he is not well."

"My father has been ill for the past few months. The medicine men don't seem to know which of the gods are angry with him, or how to appease them."

"Will they allow me to help?"

"Cade, you know our people; you know that the medicine men are quite jealous of their work. It will take some time for you to break that barrier."

"And you, Brother?" Sun Knife asked softly.

"Has there ever been a time I would not have trusted my life to your hands? Do you not remember the many times we stood back to back to protect each other. I will stand so again, Brother."

There was no need for Sun Knife to answer this for the memories were always in his mind.

White Eagle's mouth twisted in a half-smile as he said in a humor-filled voice, "My father was too ill to come with me and I would not bring along the one who really desired to come for it would be unseemly to do so."

"Who?"

"Snow Blossom."

"Snow Blossom." He laughed. "Of course you would not want to bring a child along."

White Eagle grinned at his words. "A child," he murmured softly. "My little sister has been growing for as many years as you have been gone, Sun Knife. She is no longer the little girl you remember. She is a woman ready to be a wife, but she refuses to look at any of our braves."

"Why?"

"Because she carries a memory of the brave she has always wanted. She only waits for his return and prays the gods will smile on her."

"Me?" Sun Knife said softly.

White Eagle nodded, watching Sun Knife in complete amusement. Sun Knife could only remember a small doe-eyed girl, ten years younger than he, who had, most of the time, embarrassed him by her quiet admiration. She had stood beside his horse with her large brown eyes filled with tears the day he had left, but being a proud brave of eighteen, he had no eyes for the grief of a young girl, half his age.

"Tell me of my mother; is she well?"

"Waterflower is well and very excited at the return of her beloved son."

Sun Knife smiled as he sat back and listened to White Eagle describe all that had happened since he had left. They talked late into the night before they both finally rolled in their blankets next to the dying fire and slept.

Both of them rose before the first break of dawn, and in the quiet shadows they gathered Sun Knife's things and packed them on the horse; before the first rays heralded the sun they were well on their way. They traveled the full day without stopping, only chewing on the dried buffalo meat White Eagle carried with him. On the beginning of the last day before they reached home, Sun Knife pulled his horse to a stop.

"Let us stop at the river and swim and eat," Sun Knife suggested. "I would like to look a little better than a sweaty mule when my mother sees me for the first time in eight years."

They let the horses graze without unburdening them, and stripping off their clothes, they dove into the cool clear water of the river. They laughed at the exhilarating chill of the water and began to cavort playfully as they had as children in bygone days.

They rested naked on the bank soaking up the hot sun for

over half an hour until Sun Knife rose to his feet, tied the clothes he wore in a bundle, and added it to the rest. Then he opened another bundle and withdrew from it a new pair of pants and shirt. White Eagle's eyes widened at the beauty of the new outfit. It was white and an intricate colorfully beaded design had been worked into the back. The deerskin from which it was made was soft and pliable and caused it to cling to his body. The arms were heavily fringed as were the sides of the legs. He slipped his feet into a pair of white beaded moccasins that had the same intricate design worked into them in bright colors. About his head, he bound a piece of white leather striped with the design of his family. Then he turned to a smiling White Eagle who said softly, "Welcome home."

Sun Knife smiled and nodded, then wordlessly they remounted and headed toward the village. It was late afternoon and the sun was just beginning to touch the horizon when they crested a ridge and Sun Knife's eyes stung with happy tears as he looked once again on the village of his youth.

Ahead of them in a lush green valley stood over three hundred tepees, imposing painted tepees, most of which had a base of at least eighteen feet; all were elaborately painted. The live and brilliant designs were considered sacred and it was believed that each individual design secured for its owner protection against sickness and misfortune; they were acquired in dreams after long fasting and communion with nature and each was the exclusive property of the owner. A worn-out painted tepee would be duplicated by the owner, but he then must destroy the original, sacrificing it to the sun by spreading it upon a lake and sinking it beneath the water. Each family had its designated place in the camp circle plus its own stylized painting on it. He searched the center area for the chief's tepee because he knew that near it would stand his mother's and next to it Long Arrow's. His heart leaped for joy when he finally spotted it. To him, it suddenly seemed more beautiful than any elaborate home he had accompanied his father to in the last eight years.

He nudged his horse into motion, suddenly wanting to be there, see his family, and feel again the close bond of love with which he had grown up.

They let their horses move at a brisk trot through the wide lanes between the tepees. Sun Knife smiled at a familiar face here and there and occasionally answered a friendly hail. White Eagle rode as the young chief he was, head high and eyes held directly ahead. His manner was almost royal and, Sun Knife thought amused, slightly arrogant. Sun Knife did not miss the swift shy looks of the pretty maidens as they watched White Eagle ride by.

He pulled his horse to a stop in front of his mother's tepee, but almost before he could dismount, she stood in the entranceway. She seemed to him not to have aged a moment since she had bade him a tearful farewell. He walked toward her and stood a few inches away. He could see her large brown eyes swimming with tears as she reached out placing both her palms on his chest. Without a word, he drew her into his arms and felt her clutch him as though she were afraid he would disappear.

"Welcome home, my Son. You are well?"

"I am well, my Mother, and I am pleased to see you are also. You are as beautiful as I have always remembered. May I enter?"

She stepped aside, smiling at his efforts toward the proper formality, and let him enter first as was common among their tribe. She followed him in and he turned to her and reached out his arms. She embraced him and he could hear her smothered sob of joyous tears as he closed his strong arms about her and crushed her to him.

"I have missed you so, Sun Knife. The years seemed never to end. I am grateful that you sent messages so often or the waiting would have been worse. Your . . . your father . . . how is he?"

"He is strong and healthy and very active. Now that I have come home I can see some of the results of his work. I cannot put into words, my Mother, the admiration and love I have for the two people who have sacrificed so much for me. I hope I will never be a disappointment to either of you."

"Always I have been proud of you," she replied.

"Father will come back one day. When his work is finished, he will return here to spend his last days with us."

"He told you this?" she said, her eyes brightening.

"Yes."

"It is so good to hear," she replied softly. Then she stepped back from him and looked at him. "You look magnificent, like a young chief. Where did you get such beautiful clothes?"

"I had them specially made." He smiled. "Could I come home looking anything less than what I'm sure you made the council expect?"

She laughed and he laughed with her.

"You are right, my Son. My tongue has bubbled like an old woman. Come, have you eaten?"

"Yes, White Eagle and I stopped at the river."

"Then sit and rest. We will talk."

"I think it might be best if I went to see Tekata. I was told he was ill, maybe I can do something to help."

"Yes, he is ill, he has been for quite some time."

"Then let me go to him."

"Sun Knife—"

"Yes?"

"Is there not someone you should see for a few minutes first?"

Sun Knife looked at her questioningly for a few moments; then he became angry at his own stupid forgetfulness in forgetting a man who had contributed as much to his life and happy memories—Long Arrow, his honorary father.

"I'm sorry, Mother. It was a stupid thing to forget the man who has given me so much. Where is he?"

"He did not want to force himself upon you. He is in his own tepee. He felt the medicine man his foster son had become would summon him if he wanted to see him. If he did not, then he did not want to embarrass him by forcing himself into his presence."

Steeped in the customs and good manners of the Indian, Sun Knife accepted these words in the way they were meant. He understood that Long Arrow loved him still, but considering the stature Sun Knife could have as a medicine man, he would never press himself forward. Sun Knife smiled at his mother, then turned and left the tepee. It was only a matter of twenty steps to the entrance of Long Arrow's tepee. He stood at the doorway and said in a voice just loud enough to carry within. "My Father, your son has returned home from a long journey and humbly requests permission to again enter your lodge."

The door flap that covered the entrance door was pushed aside and in the doorway stood Long Arrow. He was a man of Sun Knife's height, lean and muscular. His eyes glowed with deep happiness and pride as he looked at the young man who had been as close as if he were a son of his own body. He put his hand on Sun Knife's shoulder in the traditional welcome and his white smile flashed as Sun Knife rested both hands on his shoulders.

"Welcome home, my Son. You have been gone too long. Have you forgotten how to ride and hunt?"

"If I have, Father, I have an excellent teacher to refresh my memory, for who rides or hunts buffalo more successfully than Long Arrow?"

Gratified at Sun Knife's praise, he stepped aside. "Come, Sun Knife, sit with me. We will talk."

"With your permission, Long Arrow, I feel that I should go to Tekata to see if any of my medicine will help cure his illness. May I sit with you when I return?"

"Yes, it is good that you do so. You must establish yourself and your medicine as soon as possible. Come when you are finished, Sun Knife, we have much of which to speak. There are things you should know before you are forced to face them."

"There is great trouble coming."

"The white man moves closer and closer. He builds his cities and destroys as he does so. We have to find a path to walk to keep blood from flowing, for Tekata and the council are sure that the blood will be ours."

"Tekata is right, Father, the white man outnumbers us; he will come like a flood one day. We must learn to fight him with more than weapons; we must fight with wisdom."

"If you are asked by Tekata will you stand in front of the council and speak these words?"

"Yes, I will."

"Sun Knife, what of your true father? He is a white man."

"He is a white man by blood, but his heart rests here with his woman and his adopted people. What more could he do for them than he has done? He fights their battles in the white man's court. He spends his wealth to send food and equipment. Now he has trained me in the ways of the white man's medicine so that I, too, can help. Can they ask any more than he has already given?"

"There are those who speak to the council with warnings of the white man's treachery. They tell of the breaking of treaties, of the stealing of land and the killing of our life—the buffalo. These words urge them to rise up and fight with guns and arrows, to kill the white man, to drive him from our lands."

"Can they not see the future? Can they not see that we must learn to live with the white man, for if we fight, we are doomed? There are good things in the white man's world as well as the bad, just as there is bad and good in the Indian. Is it not clear, Father, that we must learn to live together or surely as the sun god rises, we will die?"

"It is clear to some, my Son, but not to all, and the voice of fear rises up to tell us to defend ourselves and our land."

"Father, as surely as I live, I will tell you what I believe. We must change. We must be able to meet the white man on his own ground. We must establish a way to teach our children the white man's ways. I have done it; they can see that."

"But," Long Arrow said gently, "you carry within you the white man's blood."

"A man is a man, whether his skin is red or white."

"What about our customs, our beliefs, our gods? Are we to just push them aside? If we turn our backs on them, we are asking for their anger and they will show it."

"No, what man turns his back on his heritage? I am only saying we must learn to survive."

Long Arrow smiled and again rested his hand on Sun Knife's shoulder.

"I tire of these words when all I wish is to welcome home the son I have missed. Go to Tekata, then return and let us share a meal and speak of times gone by."

Sun Knife agreed with a broad smile and he left the tepee of Long Arrow only to find White Eagle outside awaiting him.

"I have spoken with my father and told him of your return. He wishes to speak with you."

Sun Knife nodded and followed White Eagle as he strode toward the largest and most brilliantly painted tepee in the camp. There were no formalities when they arrived and White Eagle pushed aside the door hanging and led Sun Knife into the presence of Tekata.

If Sun Knife was alarmed at his first look at Tekata in eight years, he gave no sign of it. He kept his face impassive as he looked at the gaunt old man that sat upon his couch. The inside of the chief's tepee was large, covering at least eighteen feet. It had been painted with a pictorial record of Tekata's achievements. On the sides hung trophies of many wars and feats of bravery, among them many scalps of his enemies.

The couch upon which he sat was covered with a white buffalo robe. A rare thing, but more rare was the fact that Tekata had killed it and had it cured for a robe when he was only sixteen.

He motioned Sun Knife before him and Sun Knife took the few steps, standing before Tekata and waiting for the chief to speak first.

Tekata's dark intelligent eyes missed nothing about Sun Knife. He even gave a faint twist of his lips in recognition of Sun Knife's elaborate dress. He took in the way Sun Knife stood in deference to the chief's honor and again smiled in the knowledge that Sun Knife had not forgotten the people from whom he came. He glanced at his son, who smiled and withdrew, allowing Sun Knife and Tekata to speak in private.

"It is good to see again the son of our friend, Michael Holliday. Your father is well?"

"My father is well and sends his best wishes to his friend, Tekata. He also sends his friend many gifts, hoping they will gladden the heart of his friend and bring him fond memories. I have brought them and they are in my mother's tepee. If you permit I will bring them to you."

Tekata grunted his pleasure. "Sit beside me, Sun Knife, and tell me of your father. We miss our friend."

Sun Knife sat cross-legged on the floor in front of Tekata's couch and again waited for Tekata to speak. While Tekata was contemplating his words, Sun Knife was giving him an examination of his own. His doctor's eye told him that Tekata was very ill. The extreme thinness, the bluish pallor about his lips and the same blue cast to the fingernails of the hand he had rested on his shoulder. He felt a deep pain well up in him when the final realization came to him. Pain at the thought of losing a man who had been like a grandfather to him, and a man he respected beyond any other for his leadership and concern for every member of his tribe. Sun Knife had been so busy searching for signs that he did not notice Tekata had remained silent and was watching him just as closely as he was being watched. When Sun Knife raised his eyes to meet Tekata's he was jolted by the knowledge that the great chief knew he was dying. He wanted to say the words that could chase away the threat of death, but he knew Tekata could not tolerate such a lie. As if to answer his thoughts, Tekata said softly, "It is nothing, this thing of dying, Sun Knife. It is the living that is difficult. Every day I see the end coming for my people and I know that I will not be here to lead them when they truly need me."

"I feel also the wind that comes from the east. It brings with it much unhappiness for my people. If I can be of any help, Tekata needs only to stretch out his hand and I am here."

"You are needed. My son, White Eagle, of whom I am deeply proud, needs the guidance of a man who knows the white man's heart. He will need you like a strong arm if he is going to help our people survive. He will make a great chief, for he is patient and he is strong. But he will need someone to help him protect our people from the mistakes other chiefs have made. He must not be tricked into giving away our land. He must be told how to fight with words as the white man does. The battles to come will not be honorable battles where a strong man may protect his rights and his honor as a warrior. They will be battles of words and slyness like the snake. White Eagle is a man of strong pride and honor; without your help, he will be defeated and the defeat will destroy him."

"White Eagle is my blood brother. Tekata has no need to ask for my aid. Anything in my power to do will be done."

"You will remain here?"

"For the balance of my life. It is where I belong."

"You had not a great love for the white man's world?"

"It is so very different from ours. Had I been born there, I might have liked it more. Had I not been born with mixed blood as I was, it might have been better. But I have known both worlds and I much prefer to be here among the people I knew in my childhood."

"You were not treated well?"

"I was accepted because I was my father's son. His great wealth and power opened doors for me that would have remained closed otherwise. But I saw many examples of how I might have been treated had I been other than Michael Holliday's son and the examples were ugly. No, my heart and my life is here—as my father's is."

Tekata nodded. "It is good, Sun Knife, to know that my second son desires to live among us."

"I want to make use of my medicine. What I have learned could help my people; it could also be of some use to White Eagle. There are many things the white man's medicine has taught me, things that would lengthen life and give more strength. Will I be allowed to use them?"

"The council meets again in two days. I and White Eagle will add our words to yours. I believe they will have enough wisdom to make use of your knowledge."

Sun Knife realized the old man was rapidly tiring, but would never have given any sign if he could help it.

"I must ask the chief's permission to leave. I am weary from the long ride and I have need to bathe and eat. It has been long years since I have been gone and my mother is filled with questions."

Tekata's amused glance took in Sun Knife's beautiful clothes and he knew that Sun Knife, like the other Indians, would never have donned them without bathing first. He knew this excuse was only out of respect to his chief and the knowledge that he was ill. Still he could not resist a jab.

"Of course," he replied with a twinkle in his eyes. "I can see by your appearance that you are definitely in need of a bath and"—he smiled—"obviously a change of clothes."

Sun Knife smiled and Tekata clapped him on the shoulder to

make him understand that his consideration was understood and appreciated. Sun Knife rose and left the tepee.

Outside in the hot afternoon sun, he stood a few minutes enjoying the bustle about him. He made mental comparisons between the places he had been during the last years, and the village in which he stood. He realized that what he had said to Tekata had been true; a sense of belonging prevaded his soul and he knew the pleasing sensation of coming home after a long and tiresome journey.

About two hundred yards away he saw White Eagle standing, his back to him, in deep conversation. Whoever he was talking to was completely hidden by White Eagle's broad back and height.

Sun Knife walked slowly in his direction. He was only a few feet away when White Eagle sensed his approach. He turned quickly and as he did, the person to whom he was talking was revealed and Sun Knife sucked in his breath deeply at the astounding beauty of the girl who stood before him. She was small; he estimated her head would come no more than to his shoulder. She was also very slender, yet her body was rounded and soft. Her hair, black and shiny, hung in two thick braids to her hips. Her eyes dominated her oval face, eyes the color of honey with thick dark lashes. Her cheeks glowed with youth and good health. He had the strange feeling that he should know her, but he could not put a name to the lovely face before him.

She had glanced quickly at him once, then her eyes had been downcast as was proper for a maiden of their village. She waited for him to speak to her first, and he waited for White Eagle to present her while White Eagle waited for it to dawn on Sun Knife who she was. The moment of heavy silence fell as none of them could seem to find the right words to speak first. Finally, White Eagle's humor could take no more. He laughed and the girl's face flushed. At the first sign of her anger, it suddenly came to Sun Knife who she must be.

"Snow Blossom?" he questioned hesitantly.

"This warrior," she said angrily to her brother, "forgets easily the people he left behind, or is it only Snow Blossom who was nothing that he can remember?"

Sun Knife's face reddened and he could feel not only her anger but White Eagle's laughter. He had to try somehow to rectify his mistake.

"When one remembers a big-eyed girl, it is very hard to believe when he sees a woman as beautiful as Snow Blossom has become. Can I be blamed for not being able to recognize the child in a woman? You must forgive me, Snow Blossom, I have not forgotten you, I have even brought you a gift."

"A gift?" she said, somewhat mollified.

"Now that I have seen you, the gift is very inappropriate." He smiled. "I hardly think a doll would be the right gift for you. If you will forgive my immense stupidity, I shall find just the right gift for the beautiful woman, Snow Blossom, and save the doll for the coming of her first child." If he had thought she was beautiful when he first saw her it was nothing until she smiled. It was as if someone had lit a brilliant light behind her face. Her eyes glowed and her white teeth gleamed in her copper-gold face. He stood spellbound watching the startling effect.

"You are forgiven, Sun Knife. I am sorry for my anger; it is a very poor way to greet a warrior who has just returned after so many years. My brother and I were just speaking of a celebration in your honor."

"Snow Blossom was speaking," White Eagle said wryly. "White Eagle was listening as usual."

This time it was Snow Blossom's cheeks that pinkened under Sun Knife's eye. He decided that everything new about her was beautiful. He smiled, hoping she would smile again.

"It pleases me greatly that Snow Blossom would go to such trouble for Sun Knife. It makes my heart light with happiness to find I am so welcome among my people—especially those dearest to me."

Their eyes caught and held, and for Sun Knife it was as though the village, the noise, and even White Eagle vanished and they stood alone somehow touching each other with the fingers of their minds.

How long they stood so, Sun Knife had no idea. A rumble of laughter from White Eagle brought him swiftly back to reality and he realized that again Snow Blossom was blushing under his warm gaze.

He knew that the customs of the Indian forbade such a display. He also knew that as her brother, White Eagle could become angry at what could have been construed as an insult.

White Eagle was not angry, in fact he was exuberant. To have his sister be pleasing to his blood brother, perhaps even to marry, would make him happy.

"Will you join us at our fire tonight, Sun Knife?" White Eagle said. "I'm sure," he added wickedly, "there are many stories you could tell that would interest all who heard."

"I'm sorry, White Eagle, can I join you tomorrow? It has been long since my mother has heard of my father and I'm sure there are many questions she desires to ask me."

"Of course," Snow Blossom said quickly, "you must attend your mother; she has missed your father for so long. I admire her courage and her sacrifice. I do not think I could do what she has done. It must be very difficult to give up the one you love, the father of your son, and the thought of ever having another. She is an admirable woman and an example of what is expected of us."

"She will be pleased to know of your words," Sun Knife said softly, "as I am."

"Will you ride with me at the dawn, Brother? We must have fresh meat for the council meeting. We should have a good day to hunt."

"Yes, it would be a pleasure. I have not hunted since the day I left."

"Good, we will go at first light."

Sun Knife nodded. White Eagle left, and Snow Blossom followed, for it would be very scandalous should she stand and talk openly with a brave if they had not yet spoken for each other. He watched them walk away, enjoying the enticing sway of her slender hips. She turned and cast him a quick glance and another bright smile which he returned.

As he walked back toward his mother's tepee, he agreed with himself that at that moment, he felt happier than he had since he was a child. He also promised himself that he would find a way very soon to speak to Snow Blossom again—alone.

All through the days on his way home, he had done

everything he could to try to exorcise Lauren from his mind and his heart. It was part of the past and he had to cut it away if he was going to be able to face the future.

Now he told himself it would be best if he found a wife among his people, and yet he could still close his eyes and feel Lauren as if she were beside him. His body responded to the thoughts of the soft lips and softer arms of Lauren Brent.

With grim determination, he concentrated on eliminating her vision and the pain she had given him when she had chosen her world instead of his. He remembered the look in her eyes and the knowledge that their two worlds would never be able to survive together. One of them would have to surrender. She would not, and he could not, for he had to return to his people and his parents all that they had given him if he ever expected to walk in pride again.

Chapter Eight

He was right in assuming his mother had many questions for him. They sat together over the supper she had prepared with loving care. All the things he had favored as a boy were there and he ate heartily, telling her with almost every bite how much he enjoyed it and how well-cooked it was. It made him feel good to see the sparkle in her eyes and the quick smile on her lips.

Once she began her questions, she could not stop and he realized how deeply she missed Michael and how very much she still loved him. He promised himself that the first chance he had to contact his father, he would urge his return as soon as possible. Together, they might be able to accomplish more than they could separately.

She had prepared his couch with the softest furs and he knew Long Arrow had hunted the bear and she had cured it so it could be ready for him. He lay in the dark tepee with only the pale light of the now-dying cooking fire in the center. The upper flap of the tepee had been folded back and he could look up at the night sky and the million diamond-brilliant stars that seemed to hover close enough to reach out and touch. It was at times like this when Lauren could creep into his mind. He refused now to let her. He deliberately concentrated on Snow Blossom—Snow Blossom, the exact opposite of Lauren Brent. She might be able to help him erase the gnawing pain that held him every time he thought of Lauren.

He wanted to build the life he had always envisioned and he realized now that Lauren could never be part of that.

He remembered his feelings when he had seen Snow Blossom again for the first time and realized that here was a woman who could give him everything he would ever need, the strength to support White Eagle and his people when he was needed, the strength to fulfill the dream he had carried in his heart the past eight years, to help his people through the storm he knew was brewing.

He wondered if White Eagle was right about how Snow Blossom felt about him. Of course he had known she felt so as a child, but now she was a woman, and a very beautiful woman. Her beauty and her position could give her any brave she wanted either in their tribe or in any of the others.

Then he began to wonder if it would be fair to take Snow Blossom as a wife knowing that he still could not erase the beautiful Lauren Brent from his mind. Would she know somehow or could he keep that part of him forever sealed until it finally died?

Snow Blossom, the daughter of a great chief and the sister of another would be a difficult person to win. It was necessary for her to marry well and he, as yet, was not sure of the position he held in the tribe or exactly what his future would be. He also knew that the bride price for her would be high. He would have to give her father many horses and other valuable things before he could be considered. As he drifted off to sleep, he was already planning on the source of some of this.

He came awake just before dawn with a jolt. White Eagle, who had dumped his clothes upon him, stood over him laughing. "You have acquired bad habits among the whites, lazy one. Lying in bed all day you will never kill anything; the hunt will be over before you can get to your feet."

"All day," grumbled Sun Knife, as he pulled his clothes on in the half-light. "It is still night and you have disturbed some wonderful dreams. And besides, your loud voice has probably frightened all the game away."

"Come." White Eagle grinned. "There are many of us waiting to see if Sun Knife has lost his eye as a hunter. We have your horse all ready. Hurry, white warrior," he laughed, "before the game dies of old age."

He dressed in the same rough buckskins he had worn when he arrived. After he laced up the soft boots about his muscular thighs, he stood and walked to the wall of the tepee where his mother had hung his quiver of arrows and his bow after he had left. It had been long since he had held the weapons. He quickly gulped down some food his mother had prepared and stepped outside. In the gray predawn light, he recognized the small group of braves around White Eagle. All were men he had hunted with and shared many happy days with.

He looked up at a grinning White Eagle. Again the thought crossed his mind that White Eagle was the symbol of all Indians. His strong body glowed bronze gold in the first rays of the morning sun. He sat his horse as though he were part of it and not mounted on its back. He controlled the still half-wild animal with ease. There was laughter in his dark eyes and he seemed completely at one with all the rugged beauty that surrounded them. It was a picture of his blood brother he would remember for a long long time.

He mounted swiftly and they rode from the village to the forest trading small insulting jibes with each other about the other's prowess as a hunter. The great plains country abounded with wild life. All except the coyote and the wolf were grass eaters. All the plains animals were extremely shy, difficult to approach and difficult to kill. Of course the most important was the buffalo, the animal that provided their tribe with almost everything it needed for existence. It provided food, shelter, and clothing. Today, they would hunt either antelope or buffalo, depending on which they found first. The meat would provide the food for the celebration and the meeting of the grand council and the skins would be cured to make robes for the chief.

Killing a buffalo with a bow and arrow from a horse running at full speed took a tremendous amount of skill and no little courage. Sun Knife found that indeed his ability to do so had slipped considerably, and he watched in admiration as they circled a small herd of buffalo, cut two from the herd neatly, and with less than four arrows dropped both of them.

White Eagle, his horse running at breakneck speed, bent sideways on its back and holding onto his horse with nothing but his legs, brought the first one to its knees. Sun Knife was in for some good-natured razzing when he laughingly admitted none of his arrows had found their intended mark and that several times he had to grasp for the reins of his horse in order not to tumble from it.

As they enjoyed a late-afternoon meal, after they had

prepared the buffalo for carrying back, White Eagle said with a straight face that it was time his big brother taught Sun Knife how to ride and hunt lest he starve to death.

They arrived home just before the supper hour and turned their kill over to the women who would butcher the meat and begin preparations on the hide. Then they went to the steam house where they stripped and sat in the hot cleansing steam to clear their pores of all the sweat, blood, and dirt they had accumulated during the day.

After they had dressed in clean buckskins, Sun Knife sat at the cook fire and ate a huge supper. While he did so, he asked his mother questions about Snow Blossom, questions he felt he presented very slyly. But his mother smiled to herself when she realized the depth of his interest.

"She is a good woman. She would be prized as a wife by any brave in the village."

"Has anyone spoken for her?"

"Oh yes, many."

"Oh? And how has she answered?"

"Sun Knife, my Son"—his mother laughed—"do not be sly with me. She has waited for your return for eight years. At the risk of swelling your head like a melon, I will tell you that you are the only brave she has spoken of."

Sun Knife chuckled and rose to his feet. "I have need to walk in the cool night air to clear my head."

Waterflower smiled at his broad back as he left for she knew the walk would soon take him in the direction of the chief's tepee, where he would of course by accident, meet Snow Blossom.

Sun Knife walked through the early evening listening to the bustle of a contented village about him. Soon the council would meet and he would know where he stood and what plans he could make for the future. He tried not to think of what he would do if they refused to let him practice his medicine here.

He was disappointed when he found the area about the chief's tepee vacant. Usually the women would be working there. The chief had four wives, none of which was in view. He stood hesitantly, knowing he could not stand in front of the chief's tepee making it obvious he searched for someone.

He turned and walked across the breadth of the village, past the outskirts, and toward the river which was almost a half-mile away. It was a warm evening and he enjoyed both the walk and the time to think.

As he neared the river, the trees became thicker and he walked slowly. His moccasined feet made no sound on the soft earth so that the figure kneeling by the water did not hear him approach. In deep thought, Sun Knife did not see her until, startled, she stood up swiftly and turned to face him. It was debatable who was the more surprised, Sun Knife or Snow Blossom.

"Snow Blossom!"

She smiled shyly and dropped her eyes from him. "What were you doing?"

"I was casting my fortune to the water gods," she replied softly.

"Oh, there is something special you are seeking from the gods?"

Being in so much close association with nature, and so dependent on it, they always had an awareness of the great forces of it and worshiped it as gods. The water god, as Sun Knife well knew, was a god who was held in great reverence as one who governed not only the people's travels, but the strength of the thing that flowed through them like their blood, their home. All their lives were built around the closeness of the family, and if Snow Blossom was casting her fortune it was to find out with which brave she would spend the years of her life.

Her cheeks pinkened and she seemed in an agony for something to say. He took the opportunity to step close to her. Inches away he could smell the sweet clean scent of her.

"I am glad to find you here. I have not had a chance to talk to you since my return."

Her smile sparkled in the early twilight. "Sun Knife has been very busy," she teased. "He is a warrior too busy to speak to a woman even though she was a childhood friend."

Sun Knife chuckled. "You know that isn't so, Snow Blossom. I was seeking you when I found you here."

Again she smiled, but the teasing look was gone. "We have

missed you, Sun Knife, very much."

"And I have missed you."

"You did not find your life in the white world all you had expected?"

Lauren leaped unbidden into his mind and his eyes became clouded with thoughts of her and the life she had wanted for him. It was a look that did not escape the astute eyes of Snow Blossom, for despite her quiet attitude at the moment, she was not one to let anything pass her by.

"No . . . all I got from the white world was exactly what I went for—the medicine."

In an instant, Snow Blossom knew there was more that he was not saying and with a sinking heart she pictured in her mind the white women he had so obviously thought of.

"Tell me about your time there."

"It was time spent thinking of the day when I could return here," he began. Then he told her of his learning, of the city in which he lived, and of his father. She gazed at him in silence and the knowledge of what he was omitting grew in her mind.

He squatted down and took a handful of stones from the ground and began skimming them across the water. He did this to avoid looking into those searching eyes as he spoke.

"The white world has given you much. You would not have been content to stay with your father?"

"No. I would never have been happy there. One day soon, my father will return. For me, I know my place is here. I am content here with my mother, my friends, and," he added softly, "all the people I love."

Tears of happiness leaped into her eyes, but she would not let him see them. If he felt so then one day he would forget her and turn to Snow Blossom, she thought.

"The council meets soon."

"Yes. I shall go with White Eagle and ask for permission to use my medicine. If they agree, then I can make my plans for the future," he replied as he stood up and turned to her. "This will always be my home," he said gently. "I shall marry and raise my children here, and when the day comes, I will be content to be taken to the burial grounds and buried among our people."

"I am glad, Sun Knife. It makes my heart glad to know you will always be among the people who need you."

He walked to her side and took her hand in his. It was time, he felt, to find out if his brother's words were true.

"And you, Snow Blossom, do you welcome your warrior home as a friend . . . or as a woman?"

Her eyes raised unafraid to meet his. "I have longed for your return, Sun Knife, more as a woman than as one of your people. I am proud of what you have become, but even if you were the lowest, poorest brave of our tribe, I would still feel the same. I think"—she smiled—"you have always known my feelings for you; it was just when you were younger you were too proud to see."

"I am sorry for that." He laughed. "But you have to remember there are many years between us. I was a man and you were still a child."

"Yes, that is so. In fact the day you left you had no words for Snow Blossom at all. You will not know how many tears my child's heart cried over that."

He reached out and touched her cheek with his fingertips and watched with pleasure as her eyes softened to a look he needed to see.

"You are no longer a child, Snow Blossom, but a very beautiful woman. It would please me greatly if you would let me spend some time with you so that we could know and understand each other better."

"We have known each other since our birth, Sun Knife."

"No," he said gently. "I would know you not as friend to friend, but as man to woman. I would, with your permission, ask your father to consider me one day as a son . . . as husband to his daughter, Snow Blossom."

"It would be after you had proven your medicine. You know my father would not want to show you privilege. He is proud that what you have done you have done yourself. He would not want it said that it was done because you are his son."

"I know. It will take some time, but for now, I must know how Snow Blossom feels."

"I will tell you," she said softly. "Always my heart has been filled with Sun Knife. It would please me very much to be part of his world and his life."

He was satisfied for now, mostly because he knew it was as far as he could go. No brave would even think of doing more, for to bring shame to the lodge of Tekata would be a sure way to court death.

"Come," he said. "I shall walk with you."

They walked back to the village talking of anything except the vibrant new thing that was blossoming into being between them.

The next morning he was quiet and preoccupied. Tonight, by the time the fires had been lit, chiefs from many miles and many tribes would gather. They would discuss the politics and well-being of their people and make rules and regulations. When that was over, petitions could be made before them. He would find it difficult to wait.

He was still sitting at the fire in his tepee when he heard the voice of White Eagle requesting permission to enter. He told him to enter, then watched as White Eagle sat cross-legged across the fire from him.

"It is a good morning," White Eagle said. "The sky is bright, and already the chiefs and council members have begun to arrive. There will be much feasting and drinking this day."

"Good," Sun Knife replied noncommittally.

"What is wrong, Sun Knife?"

"Nothing . . . have you spoken to your sister this morning?"

"Which one?" White Eagle laughed, his eyes alite with mischief. "You remember I have several sisters."

Sun Knife chuckled. "You know of which one I speak. Snow Blossom."

"Ah," he said, his grin broadening. "The child I didn't bring along to meet you."

Now Sun Knife laughed outright. "Do you think she'll ever really forgive me for not knowing her when we met? And you, you did nothing to ease the situation."

White Eagle sat opposite Sun Knife and smiled across the fire. "If you hadn't recognized her when you did, I believe your scalp would have been hanging in our lodge."

"White Eagle," Cade said, his smile becoming serious, "is

there any opposition to my practicing my medicine; will anyone speak against me at the council?"

"No one from our tribe, but I expect questions from some of the other chiefs. After all, they all have their own medicine men, and they are sensitive. I imagine they need proof of your feelings before they open their minds to you."

"I have spoken to Snow Blossom. She has consented, if all goes well, to one day be my wife. Does my brother have any objection?"

"Objection to the joining of the two people dearest to me? No. In fact, it is a thing I have hoped for for many years."

Cade remained silent for a moment, then he said softly, "And your father, has he no objection to the daughter of a great chief marrying a man whose blood is half-white?"

"Sun Knife," White Eagle said slowly, "truly my father is a man of great honor, but he also is father to Snow Blossom and not just chief of the village. Do you think he would give her in marriage to a man she didn't want? Many have spoken for her in the past few years, but like I have always known, my father knows where her heart lies, and he also knows you will make a good medicine man and teacher for our people. He sees what is coming and he wants to do something to prepare for the flood."

"And he thinks I can do that?"

"He thinks you can help our people to learn how to live with what is coming. You, like your father, were sent by the gods to help our people."

"Do you believe that?"

"Yes, I do."

"It's not true, White Eagle. I'm a man, like my father is a man. We were not sent by the gods and we can fail like any man can fail. All I can offer my people is all the medicine I know, and maybe I can teach them some of the white man's learning. But I have no special power."

"But you had said in two words what I have known all my life."

"What?"

"My people. We need you, Sun Knife—I need you. Let us not lie to each other. My father is dying. You know it, I know it, and he knows it. He has struggled to stay alive for your return.

He wants you to be at his son's side, and he wants you as his daughter's husband. That way, the three of us united will be able to stand together as some kind of shield for our people."

Cade digested this in silence; then after a few minutes, he looked across the fire at White Eagle and smiled. "Then let us go and welcome the chiefs. Who knows? With the help of Tekata and White Eagle, Sun Knife may have all his heart has desired in the last few years."

"Good." White Eagle smiled again. They rose and went outside and Cade was overcome at all the pandemonium that was going on.

A splendid array of color and activity surrounded him as chiefs of all the close nations and their retinues arrived amid much ceremony.

The day was filled with all types of activities and feasting. Games were played and a considerable amount of drinking was done. Cade abstained from drinking only because he knew he had to stand in front of the council this night to ask their permission to practice medicine here and he didn't want to be falling-down drunk when he did it.

Although he participated in some of the riding games, he was more content to drift about and strike up conversations with members of other tribes. There were also times when he could catch glimpses of Snow Blossom moving among the women. At such times, he would pause and admire her slender graceful beauty and the quick smile that would flash when someone spoke. For him to have gone to her and to have spoken to her would have been an unheard-of thing and would have brought shame on her.

He held his impatience in check, and the hour finally came when the council began to gather in the huge tepee erected for just this occasion.

He knew he was not the only supplicant to face the council and he waited his turn. It was only an hour after the council convened that White Eagle presented himself to Cade.

"Come, Brother, it is time."

Cade rose and walked silently beside an also silent White Eagle. He followed behind White Eagle as he drew aside the door hanging and entered the council room.

The tepee was over twenty-four feet wide and twice as tall as Cade. There had been a large fire built in the center which had burned down to red embers. Nine men sat in a semicircle about the fire, but each about five feet from it, leaving the supplicants room to walk. All the men were aged yet majestically proud. The small couches each chief sat upon were about a foot from the ground and covered with luxurious and heavy furs that were saved only for this occasion.

Cade looked about him trying to find the men whose faces seemed the most sympathetic, but all of them were bronzed masks glowing amber in the light of the fire. Intelligent black eyes watched him silently, waiting for his words.

Tekata's face was impassive, but he would let his son speak for him, and White Eagle stood before them at Cade's side. He stood, his full height proud and straight, his granite face cast in bronze flickering firelight.

"I am White Eagle, son of Chief Tekata who sits among you. I ask you today to recall my friend, Sun Knife, and his father whose long arm has reached out often to help us. Sun Knife has grown among us, and his heart rests here with the people to which he feels he belongs. For long years, he has been gone, to live among the whites and learn their medicine. He has been taught by his father the art of releasing the evil spirits from the body with his knife. Today, he requests permission to speak to the council."

All nine of the old men nodded and White Eagle turned to Cade. He placed his hand on Cade for a moment and then he was gone and Cade stood alone to face the men who held his future in their hands.

"I am Sun Knife, son of Michael Holliday and a daughter of your tribe, Whiteflower. My father walked among you for years and you saw his medicine. It was a great help to you while he was here. The time came when you asked him to return to his own people so that he could use the strength he had to help you with the white man's laws. He has tried his best, always holding you first in his heart. When I was grown, he took me from here and tried to give me the great gift of his medicine. Now, he sends me to you, carrying the knowledge of his medicine. Now I am requesting that the council give me permission to bring what medicines I have from Fort Bridger and use them here among you."

He stood, silent again, waiting for them to question him. He did not have long to wait. One of the lesser chiefs, whose eyes had not left Cade from the moment he had walked in, rose from his seat.

"You have used this medicine among your people?"

Cade felt the stinging reference to his white blood. "You are my people. I was born here, raised here, and I want to live the rest of my days as a son among you. My medicine is all I have to offer outside the strength of my arms. I only ask that you make use of the little I have to offer."

"I have heard," the chief said, "that the white man moves even closer. Where will you stand if one day he comes?"

"I will stand here, beside my brothers. I know that the white man comes. I feel someday we will have to live side by side. I want to be able to help my people so that we may do so in peace."

"Peace!" came the reply. "When the white man wants our land again, are we to move to the sea this time? We cannot live in peace, and I think, Cade Holliday, that one day you will find your white blood convenient."

He felt the anger flood through him, but he also realized he was being deliberately taunted and that all eyes were on him. Slowly, he gathered his thoughts together.

"I am half-Indian, half-white; that is known. But I remind you that my father was all white and he has given to you his heart and his loyalty, not to mention his friendship—a friendship that has given you much. A son does not bring dishonor on his house, and I would not do so to my white father or my Indian mother. If my white blood is convenient, it is because it can provide me with the medicine and anything else that might help the people with whom I will spend my days. I want to live among you for the rest of my life. If the days be bad or good, I want to stand beside the people I call mine. I ask that you give me permission to do so and I tell you that my own honor is something I value above all and I would not relinquish it outside of death."

The chief who had been taunting him nodded slightly and

glanced quickly toward Tekata who had the faintest hint of a smile in his eyes. Cade felt the biggest mountain had been conquered. Another rose.

"How do we know your medicine is good?"

"Test me. I shall do what pleases you at any time. Test me, and let me stand or fall by my own hand."

Again the chief nodded an almost imperceptible nod. Now a man rose who made Cade inhale deeply and hold his quivering breath. This man was not like the others; he could tell immediately by the respectful silence that fell when he rose to speak.

He was not a large man, yet he exuded a feeling of intense power. His eyes gleamed with intelligence and he looked directly into Cade's eyes giving him the feeling his very soul was being read.

"I think you are true, son of Michael Holliday, but I ask you only one thing. If the day ever comes that you must stand at war . . . who will you stand with? Who will you fight beside?"

For a moment, Cade could not speak, and he knew that Tekata and White Eagle waited with the others to hear his answer.

"I am brother to White Eagle. His enemies are mine. If I ever have to fight, it will be at his side. I would pray to the Great Spirit that it never comes to that, but if it does, I stand here with my people."

He could not seem to move until the dark eyes released him. Again the quiet and accepting nod, but the man held up his hand.

"I have dreamed of many white soldiers at war with us. I have seen many battles, much death and destruction. I hear your words, Cade Holliday, and I shall remember them. One day you may face the choice."

He sat down. Cade stood quietly until the aged and very ill Tekata rose to his feet.

"I have questioned the chiefs, the medicine man, and you, Cade Holliday. So that there will be no questions, I tell you this. Go to Fort Bridger, bring your medicine here. When the time comes you will be tested. If the gods smile upon you, then you will be free to work your medicine here. If you fail, you must live among us as a warrior, nothing else. If you do not choose to do that, you will be free to go."

Cade knew that Tekata said what he did to prove it was not his favoritism that worked for Cade. He was relieved when he was given permission to withdraw and he left the tepee to be met by White Eagle who waited outside.

"I have heard," he said. "Do you want me to go to the fort with you to bring your medicine?"

"No, I'll go alone. It should take me only a few days."

"I knew all would be well." White Eagle grinned. "You will have no trouble proving your medicine is strong."

"You've a lot of confidence in me." Cade laughed.

"Well"—White Eagle chuckled—"one can have all confidence in a medicine man when he is not sick. Maybe if you have to work on me, it might change my mind."

Cade laughed. "Tell me something," he said.

"What?"

"Who was the chief, the last one?"

"You've been gone a long time; I had forgotten just how long. You would not know of him, but he is strong and a great leader. His name is Sitting Bull."

"He looked straight through me as though I were made of air."

"Yes," White Eagle said softly. "Some say he sees beyond today. Some say he can look into a man's soul and see what dwells there."

"I can believe that. I've seen no other like him."

"And," White Eagle added gently, "he would be the first to order you killed if he thought you betrayed him."

Cade stopped walking and turned to White Eagle.

"Do you believe I could do that?" he asked angrily.

"Ayeee, you are short-tempered tonight, Brother. Come let us join the others now that the formalities are over. We can tell stories of our great hunting power—at least I can." He laughed. "You can admire my great power and wish you could do as well."

Cade laughed, and they did join the others. He was so happy he celebrated a little more than he had planned to do.

He stumbled to his bed in the wee hours of the morning, only to toss in uncomfortable sleep from the overindulgence.

In the morning, he rose unsteadily and was not quite amused at Waterflower's efforts to keep from laughing at him as he made his unsteady way to the river. There, he threw off his clothes and dove into the chilly water to clear his head.

When he had left the East, he had bought and packed all the medicine and equipment he thought he might need for the first few months and had them sent ahead. He figured by now they should have arrived at Fort Bridger. He knew Grant would have them taken care of.

He made preparations to go, asking his mother if she could see to the setting up of a new tepee near hers, where he could work. She was surprised at the specifications he requested, but she agreed to do her best to fulfill them.

Cade took the horse White Eagle provided for him and a string of others to pack his things on and left early the next morning. It was slower traveling with the string of horses, but he reached Fort Bridger in five days. Grant's sentry had seen him coming and Grant was at the gate to meet him when he arrived.

"I thought you wouldn't be far behind all those packages that came for you. What the hell have you got in all those crates?"

"A hospital and a school . . . I hope."

"If you're going to get it all packed on those horses, you'll have to uncrate it and repack it."

"I know." Cade grinned. "I thought maybe you'd help me do that."

"I thought you might be thinking along those lines so I've already begun the uncrating when I saw you coming."

It was several days before Cade had all the things repacked and was ready to leave. He intended to leave with the dawn, and the night before he and Grant sat in Grant's small quarters and talked. He told Grant all that had happened since he had left.

"Oh, by the way, I almost forgot," Grant said as he rose. "There's a letter here from your father." He handed the letter to Cade who slid it inside his shirt, planning on reading it when he was alone.

Dawn was barely streaking the sky when he again left the fort.

When he camped that night, he sat by the fire and unfolded his father's letter.

My Dear Son,

By the time you read this letter, I shall already be on my way home. There are things happening of which I can no longer be part. I prefer to be with my wife and my son in the times that I see coming.

Congress has allowed homesteading in the unsettled territory just west of here, and I sense that they do not plan to adhere to the treaty. There will be no recognized boundaries to their settling. It will bring a great hardship to our people and I would be there to help.

I am no longer effective here and I find that I miss my family too much to stay any longer.

After having you here for so many years, I see what I have missed.

Cade realized that what his father and the chiefs feared must be bad; his father would never have reacted so if it were not. He continued to read.

Tell Waterflower to expect me soon, but do not make it too well-known among the others. I bring with me many supplies and things that you and I might need.

His reference to things they might need meant medical things so it was obvious his father expected bloodshed. Knowing how unprepared the Indians would be for the quantity of the whites that could overrun them and the superior arms they would bear, he suddenly became afraid, afraid he would lose his world before he had a chance to rediscover and enjoy it.

His thoughts went to Snow Blossom and he decided to ask for her as soon as possible. If things became bad, he wanted her by his side.

He folded the letter and put it in his shirt; then he ate his supper while he contemplated the possibilities of what might happen.

The Indians were not organized; often they fought between tribes. This was the best weapon the white man had. Also the Indian lived under a code of honor that was hardly recognizable to the white man whose greedy gaze turned toward the West.

If his father came soon, they could begin to form some kind of central force and try their best to gather the tribes together to face their common enemy.

He knew trying to get Crow to join forces with Cheyenne, Apache with Paiute, or many other tribes, would be a mountainous job, but somehow they had to convince them it was their only way to survive.

He thought of Snow Blossom and the life they could have—and maybe children. Then he rolled in his blanket and tried to sleep holding onto the thoughts of Snow Blossom, and holding at bay the green-eyed vision that continually threatened to enter his dreams. It was a long time before he got any real sleep, then he was up and on his way before dawn.

Chapter Nine

As he unloaded his animals, the children watched fascinated, along with the women who tried to control their curiosity about the strange things that were taken into the overly large tepee.

He told his mother about his father's letter and she was overjoyed. Then he sought out White Eagle to help him with another thing.

"I want to go on a horse hunt."

"Why?" White Eagle questioned. "If you have need of a horse, I can give one to you."

"It's not for me. Today, I intend to go to your father and ask for Snow Blossom. I suspect I shall have to promise him many horses before he will consider giving her to me."

"Yes, that is so, but—" White Eagle grinned.

"But?" Cade prompted. "What evil do you have in your mind, friend?"

"Evil? Not so, friend." White Eagle chuckled. "But only listen. If we capture wild horses, we must break them before we can gift my father."

"You have another solution?"

"Suppose we count coup." His eyes glittered with laughter. "Not too many miles from here is a tribe of marauding thieves. They have stolen horses from us many times. I thought we might return the favor."

White Eagle seemed to be thinking of the escapade with such delight that Cade could not help joining in. Within an hour, they agreed on the details.

The next morning, the two of them slipped away, accompanied by four friends. They left silently and rode the miles to the outskirts of the village. There they dismounted and waited until dark.

The favored horses of the Indian were tied in front of the

tepee to keep them from being stolen. It was a challenging thing to see if one had the skill to creep close enough to get the ones that were tied so. It was much easier to attack swiftly and run off the other horses that were grouped together and usually guarded by one warrior. Easier, but not challenging enough either for White Eagle or Sun Knife. Like two schoolboys into mischief, they crept slowly and silently through the village. While their foes slept, White Eagle and Cade led away their choicest horses. When they were at the edge of the village, White Eagle gave a wild yelp which was a signal to the others in the group to run off the herd. There was pandemonium as the villagers chased them on foot, wildly cursing them and all their ancestors.

It was a hilariously laughing group when they finally stopped running. When they finally counted, they had thirty-five horses from the main group and six that Cade and White Eagle had taken.

The group insisted that they each wanted only one for their efforts and that the balance would be Cade's. Knowing that a horse was the most valuable thing a man could have, he appreciated their generosity. It gave Cade thirty-one horses in one swoop. He hoped it would be enough to impress Tekata favorably.

They rode back to camp exuberantly; there Cade made arrangements to care for the horses and went to make himself presentable. Again, he sat in the steam cleansing his body. He dressed with elaborate care, went to Tekata's tepee, and requested permission to come to speak to him.

The old man sat upon the couch of thick fur as he had the first time; only now, all four of his wives were present. Not only were they there, but Snow Blossom was present also.

She had been kneeling in front of the fire placing some fresh chips upon it when Cade's voice was heard. She looked up when he entered and again her heart throbbed strangely as it always did when he was present.

As far back as she could remember, Cade had walked in her dreams. When she was twelve, and he was seventeen and a young warrior, he had a way of looking past her that broke her heart more often than she could tell. Of course, he looked upon her then as a little sister to be protected and shielded. She did not look upon him so and when he left she carried him in her heart and mind so strongly that despite the offers of many of the eligible braves of the tribes, she had waited for Cade to return.

She knew she had changed completely since Cade had seen her last, yet it was very rewarding to see his surprised appreciation when he had first seen her.

Now she seemed to quiver all through as he filled the doorway and his eyes found hers for one swift moment. It was unseemly for a girl to look so openly at a brave, so her dark lashes shadowed her eyes and a faint touch of pink tinged her cheeks as she remembered his words at the river.

It had been several days since he had returned from his journey to the fort, but it was not enough days for him to have acquired what her bride price would be.

Even though Tekata wanted nothing more than to see Cade and Snow Blossom married, he could not let her go without the payment of a high bride price to prove her value as the chief's daughter. He hoped Cade had come to seek her and had found some way to get the possessions he needed.

Tekata knew if Cade asked he would give his daughter to him on the promise, because he had spoken to his daughter the day before and was satisfied that her heart lay in Cade's hands.

Cade stood looking across the fire at her, aware of everything about her. The delicate planes of her face caught in a golden glow from the fire; the wide dark liquid eyes that fell before his, the slender curve of her body under the soft deerskin dress that she wore, and the shine of her long dark braids that fell over her shoulders.

"You wished to speak to me, my Son?" Tekata's voice interrupted his study of Snow Blossom.

"Yes, Father," he said respectfully. "Your son comes to sit before you and ask a very great thing."

"Come, sit, and speak to me of what you seek."

Cade sat on the floor and was uncomfortably aware, both of Tekata's whispering wives and Snow Blossom's silent presence.

Tekata allowed his uncomfortable squirming for a time for his own amusement. Then he ordered them in a commanding voice to leave the tepee. They left, laughing and whispering among themselves.

"Now, let us speak. What do you have to ask?"

"Tekata knows that I hold him and his house in great honor."

Tekata nodded.

"I know that I have not yet found my way within the tribe," Cade continued.

Again, Tekata patiently nodded.

"I have come to ask Tekata to look upon me with favor, to give me his daughter Snow Blossom as my wife."

"The bride price for Snow Blossom is high."

"No price would be too high to pay for one such as she. Will you name it, Chief Tekata, so that I may search for ways to acquire it?"

"When the last brave came and spoke for her, he offered a fifty horses, many knives and axes, ropes made by his own hand and other weapons he had gotten from counting coups many times and also blankets and furs to enrich the chief's tepee."

"It was a fair offer," Cade said, dismally aware he could not match it for a long time. "Did it please Tekata?"

Tekata chuckled. "The offer may have pleased me, but he did not please my daughter, and so I refused." Tekata bent closer to Cade. "You have come to make an offer my son, make it."

"I offer Tekata thirty-one horses now, and before we are married, I will gift Tekata with three new bows, arrows, and sharp knives. I will bring him the furs of two buffalo and five blankets. Then to this I will add a fifty horses within the time of ten days. Does Tekata find this small offer acceptable?"

He looked up to find Tekata's amused gaze upon him.

"You know only my daughter's sweet and dutiful side; you do not know her temper. I'm afraid if I refused your offer, I might find my days and nights of living in this tepee becoming very uncomfortable."

He chuckled. "I accept your offer, Cade, and I wish you many years of happiness and strong sons to stand in your shoes when you are gone. I can only pray that the great spirit allows me the time to see them and the grandsons my son will give me."

"White Eagle plans to marry soon?" Cade asked surprised that White Eagle had not told him anything about it.

"I only wish it were so," Tekata said. "He seems not to have eyes for the women of our village. It is time he took a wife and had sons, but he is wordless when I ask him."

"Maybe"—Cade smiled—"if Tekata grants his permission, our marriage will give White Eagle the desire to do the same."

"I hope it will be so. It is necessary for a leader to have sons to follow him."

"Then Tekata grants his permission?"

"Yes, I am pleased to join you to my family. I will make the words before council. When you have acquired the bride price, Snow Blossom will come to you."

Cade was elated; yet he was wondering just how fast he could get what he needed. Now that he knew she could be his, he could hardly contain his impatience.

He told White Eagle all that he would need, but refused to let White Eagle gift him with any of it. If Snow Blossom were to be his, he would pay the price necessary to have her.

He set about making the weapons he had promised and the ropes. The blankets, he intended to purchase. When these were finished, he would go on a hunt for the buffalo robes he had promised. On this, White Eagle insisted he should be able to accompany him. He was joking about Cade's inability to hunt well enough to acquire two buffalo robes when Cade grinned and said, "Maybe White Eagle wants to go on the hunt with me to find a bride price of his own."

A quick fleeting look of sorrow touched White Eagle's brown eyes and his smile faded momentarily. Cade knew then that there was something he was keeping from all of them, and it was something that hurt him deeply.

"We will find the bride price for you first; for me, there is much time," he said gently. Then he turned and walked away leaving Cade watching his departure with furrowed brows. It was not like White Eagle to be this way and he wondered what was bothering him so deeply.

Cade, in the next three weeks, felt a sense of peace he had not felt in a long time. He thought the world could not be a better place for him to live than it was now. "What more could a man want?" he mused. He would soon be able to practice his medicine, he would have a tepee of his own and his parents would be reunited. Along with all these blessings, was the friendship of Tekata and White Eagle. The only thing that bothered him was the remembrance of that shadowed look that he had caught in White Eagle's eyes. It was something he worried over for days before he finally decided, against all protocol, to break tradition and push himself into another's private business. He had to find a way to reach him and find out what the problem was.

He rose very early one morning, went to White Eagle's tepee, and without preamble, he went inside. From the time of birth until he was about eighteen, White Eagle had occupied the tepee of his father. Then, when he had gone through the ceremony of becoming a man, when he had danced the sun dance and communed with the spirits to find out what his guiding symbol would be, he built his own tepee and painted it with the forms and symbols that would be his sign from that day forward.

It was a large tepee, nearly as large as his father's. Emblazoned over the entrance was a huge soaring eagle, the sign that would belong to White Eagle all his life and which he placed with his body when he went to greet the Great Spirit.

Although the top flap of the tepee had been turned back, the first light of dawn did not penetrate it completely and the inside was shadowed. He could see White Eagle's form on his fur-covered couch. He took one quiet step forward, then smiled to himself when he realized that White Eagle was awake and watching him. The soft murmuring chuckle that came from the couch told him he was right.

"I would speak with you, White Eagle."

"Come, I shall have some food brought. We can eat and talk. Is there something I can do for Sun Knife?"

Cade didn't answer immediately, but sat beside the pale embers of the night fire that White Eagle promptly kicked and onto which he threw more chips to bring it to life.

White Eagle stuck his head out the front of his tepee and spoke to the woman who prepared his food. She had risen before dawn and begun the preparations so that his meal could be ready. Blooming Cactus was a woman of unreadable age who had been widowed many years before. She had been without children and had no way to provide for herself. As a single warrior, and son of the chief into whose care all the people would one day be, he had taken the responsibility of providing for her. In return, she prepared his food, mended, and made much of his clothing, and cared for him like a mother.

In respect for her age, White Eagle did not command as he could have; instead, he requested politely if it were possible that she could bring food for both he and Cade. It was the Indian way, this deference toward the old. As the son of the chief and an example to the men of his age, it would never have occurred to him to speak to her with any less respect.

She smiled in quick agreement, and White Eagle returned to the fireside and dropped to the ground. He looked at Cade expectantly.

"White Eagle," Cade began hesitantly, "you and I are men who, over all our years, have spoken to each other openly and unafraid, of all our problems. If there has been any great difficulty in our lives, it has always been our way to share the burdens and in that way make them easier to bear."

White Eagle grunted in agreement. "You have a problem, Sun Knife. Do you need help?"

"No," Cade said gently, "but I fear my brother does, and the thought pains me that he feels he must hold his pain to himself and not share it. What is the thing that darkens your thoughts, Brother, and is there some way that I can help you?"

"You are right, Brother," he said quietly, "but it is not because I wanted to keep it from you. It is because there is nothing you or anyone else can do about it. It is a thing I must learn to live with. I am trying, my Brother."

"Can I try also, can I not reach out and give you support?"

Cade could see that White Eagle teetered on the edge of confidence, yet some fear held him back. He could not believe the courageous White Eagle felt so, but he waited patiently to see if he chose to speak of it or not.

"Sun Knife . . . do you have plans for today?"

"Nothing of importance."

"Then, will you come with me? It is only a few hours away. It is the only way I can tell you what is in my heart. First I must show you. Maybe then you will understand."

"I will come."

"Without questions?"

"Without questions," Cade answered firmly. White Eagle smiled grimly and rose. Cade waited while he washed and dressed; then they walked together in silence toward their horses.

They rode in the same silence. Cade would not question and White Eagle could not speak the words to make him understand.

They had gone several miles, but it was in a direction that Cade thought was devoid of any people. They stopped once to eat a quick cold meal and rest their horses. Finishing rapidly, they were again on their way. It was late in the afternoon when they crested a grade that led down into a small green valley. Cade had been there before as a boy when they had gone hunting. It was exactly the same as he could remember with the exception of one thing—the tepee that sat in the center of the valley, alone.

"Who—?" he began.

"Wait, Sun Knife, will you open your heart and listen to the story I have to tell first?"

"Yes."

"After you have met . . . them," he answered softly, then kicked his horse into motion and descended into the valley and rode toward the tepee.

Cade's mind was filled with questions, but he remained silent until they came to a halt in front of the tepee and he and White Eagle slid to the ground.

White Eagle walked to the entrance of the tepee, and waited while Cade came to join him. Cade examined the tepee closely for some sign as to whom it belonged, but it was completely undecorated.

Once he stood beside White Eagle and White Eagle pulled aside the flap over the doorway, Cade met what he was least prepared for. A white man, Cade guessed, somewhere near fifty lay on a couch. Once he looked, Cade could tell he was extremely ill.

"White Eagle," the old man said, his eyes glowed with welcome, but his voice was hoarse and broken. "I am glad to see you again, my Son. It has been many days since you have visited us."

"Us?" Cade said softly, almost to himself. White Eagle went across the room and knelt beside the man.

"Are you well, old Father?"

The old man chuckled, but he reached out and rested his hand affectionately on White Eagle's shoulder. "Considering the fact that I'm dying, you young heathen, I'm doing quite well, thanks to you."

White Eagle chuckled; then he turned to Cade. "This is my brother, old Father."

The old man's eyes examined Cade. "If he is your brother, then someone from your tribe has kicked over the fence and strayed into a forbidden pasture."

"His father is white; his mother was one of our people."

"Come closer, Son. My eyes are not as good as they used to be."

Cade came forth and knelt beside White Eagle who began to tell him of Cade and his parents, the old man nodded as he spoke. That Cade was overcome with curiosity was clearly visible to the old man who decided with a laugh to explain as soon as possible.

"I am a minister of God, and I was on my way to California when I became very ill. This," he motioned toward White Eagle, "young heathen found us and has been like the good Samaritan and tried, in vain I might add, to nurse me back to health. Without him, we would have died somewhere on this trail and no one would have known—except God."

"Us . . . we . . . you have said that several times; is there another man with you?" Cade questioned. White Eagle and the old man exchanged glances. White Eagle was about to speak when again the flap of the door lifted. Cade turned and his mouth fell open in absolute shock.

The girl who stood in the doorway was so beautiful that she left Cade breathless. If Snow Blossom was the beauty of a star-kissed night, then this girl was the brilliance of a sunny day. Her hair was long and golden, her blue eyes were wide and fringed with thick lashes. She was small and slender, yet her body had the round curves of a woman. She looked like a fragile golden flower. Cade absorbed this, and at the same time he absorbed the reaction of White Eagle who stood at his side. He cast him a quick glance and knew the reason for White Eagle's actions. White Eagle gazed at the girl as if the sun goddess had come to earth. Cade could feel the tremor in his huge body.

"White Eagle," she said softly. Her voice was musical and warm and Cade could sense the sincere warmth in it. "It has been long since you have visited us. We have missed you. Will you and your friend stay and eat with us?"

"This is my daughter, Rebecca," the old man said to Cade. "Rebecca, this is White Eagle's blood brother, Sun Knife."

"Welcome, Sun Knife."

"Thank you."

"Will you join us at our evening meal?"

"Yes," Cade said, amused at White Eagle's wordless admiration.

Rebecca moved quietly about the tepee preparing the food they would eat and White Eagle could barely keep his eyes from following her. All of Cade's answers were there before him; even a blind man could see. Rebecca's father's eyes and Cade's met for a second and he knew the old man knew as well as he did. White Eagle was desperately and completely in love with Rebecca. The laughing man White Eagle always was, was not present. He sat with them while Cade and Benjamin Wade talked, answering softly and seldom as his dark eyes followed the girl. "I know that I will never be able to travel again," Benjamin said.

"Sir—" Cade began.

"No, son, you cannot lie to me. I know that my days are numbered. I am not frightened, in fact I look forward to the day I can meet my Lord. I worry only for my child. She must get to my friends in California. I have asked White Eagle to see if he could help."

"I have told you, old Father," White Eagle said glumly, "I will do everything I can to keep her safe."

The old man's eyes smiled again and Cade could see he held a true affection for White Eagle. "I only wish I could have converted this young heathen to God's way," he said with a laugh. "But I guess I should be grateful he is a good man who has gone to a great deal of trouble to help us."

"What was I to do, leave you to die on the plains?" White Eagle said gruffly as though he was also surprised at what he had done.

"When I first met you"—the old man chuckled—"you did not strike me as a shy boy filled with false modesty. You are a strong man with a kind and sensitive heart. Do not be ashamed of that, my Son; it is the stuff of which great chiefs are made."

The meal over, Rebecca took the two pails and left the tepee to go to a nearby stream for water. It was only a moment before White Eagle left with the excuse that it was dark and she needed protection from night animals.

There was a silence that hung in the air for several minutes after he left; then Benjamin sighed heavily.

"I am sorry for him. He fights a terrible battle within, and I am afraid it is a battle he fears he cannot win."

"I see only a battle, if she doesn't want him," Cade answered.

"He has never, in four months, spoken one word to her of how he feels. I am afraid he never will. He has spoken only to me, and then only of the obligation he has to his father and his people. He is also afraid Rebecca would refuse to come to him, live with him, and turn her back on her own way of life."

"What do you think she feels for him?"

"She respects, admires him, and if it is not love, it is bordering on it. She is young and he knows this. What he doesn't seem to know is that he must reach out his hand to her and lead the way. She is too gentle a creature to reach for him. I have taught her this way and now I am not sure that it wasn't a big mistake."

"She doesn't think of him as a savage?"

Benjamin looked closely at Cade when he said this and his eyes softened.

"So," he said sadly, "you have been in such a position; you know how it feels to be called so."

"Yes, I know. I can understand why White Eagle would

hesitate. Besides the fact that she is white and he is Indian—an almost insurmountable problem, but it has happened before. White captives have married into the tribes. It is that White Eagle will soon be chief and he does have many obligations. He must have a woman who will ease his life, give him sons, and be happy with him—not one who longs for her past."

"Do not delude yourself that Rebecca is weak because she looks fragile. She is like her mother, God rest her soul, a hard core of unbendable iron covered by a fragile exterior. No, Cade, she is everything he might need, and she will never come to him unless he reaches out for her."

"You are not against your white daughter marrying an Indian?"

"A man's heart is not a color, Cade. I can see into the heart of White Eagle and I find there all the things I have ever wanted for her."

"Have you told him so?"

Benjamin chuckled. "It seems amusing, but when he visits us, he does not seem to hear anything I say; his mind seems to be on other things."

Cade laughed. "Do you suggest that we have to hit him on the head to get his attention?" Benjamin joined his laughter.

"I wonder, if Rebecca is in the room, would that do any good? With her the huge man melts like a puddle of butter."

"I will speak to him on our way home."

"Good."

"I'm not guaranteeing it will do any good. When White Eagle gets hold of an idea, he's very tenacious. If he believes his cause is useless, if he thinks it would be wrong for Rebecca, he would say nothing."

"Cade, there are no one's hands I would rather see her in when I am gone."

"She is your only child?"

"She is now. My two sons are dead and my beloved wife followed soon after. Rebecca has been all to me. She has devoted herself completely to my care, like the biblical Rebecca for whom she is named. But soon she will be alone and have to make her way herself. My soul would rest easier if I knew she stood beside a man who had the strength to protect her."

"Rest easy, Benjamin. I will do whatever I can to convince him it would be best for her."

Again Benjamin nodded. Cade could see that he was exhausted.

"Will you let me examine you, Benjamin? I am a doctor. I have brought some medicines with me and maybe some of them will help you. It would be easy for me to come every few days. Besides"—he grinned—"it is a good excuse to get White Eagle here more often."

"A doctor?" Benjamin queried in surprise. "Yes, you may examine me, and while you do, maybe you will tell me the story of how this came to be."

Cade laughed. "It's a strange, long story."

"I'm an excellent listener." Benjamin laughed. "If you want to examine your patient, Doctor, you must supply the aphrodisiac of a good, long story."

Cade made as thorough an examination of Benjamin as he could without his instruments. While he did he told the story of his life in both worlds. When he was finished, he sat back and looked levelly at the man.

"You remind me of another man I know who faces almost the same problem as you. You both have the same kind of courage. You should meet him. You would have a lot to talk about. Despite being from opposing worlds you have a lot in common."

"Who are you speaking about?"

"Tekata, White Eagle's father." Cade went on to speak of Tekata while Benjamin listened in silence.

"You love the man?"

"I love the man, the chief, the leader, everything he represents. I admire his courage and he has been like a father to me."

"Yes," Benjamin said softly, "I would like to meet him. Do you think he would accept our presence in his village?"

"Mr. Wade, Tekata is one of the most intelligent, compassionate people I know. He is also a far-seeing man. No one wants to keep the peace between Indian and white more than he, for he knows what the inevitable outcome would be. While he holds his tribe at peace, he is struggling to give them what they will need to survive in what will one day be a white world."

"Such as?"

"Insight into the white man's world, a way to bridge the gap between them by educating them not only with the white man's learning, but with his tools of survival. Reading, writing, day-by-day endeavors, medicine . . . many ways."

"And the medicine part is where you come in."

"I hope so. I haven't proven myself yet."

"Proven yourself, how?"

"I know not of that yet, either, but the day will come when I will have to show what I can give my tribe as a medicine man."

"You keep talking about giving . . . proving, what are you getting for yourself?"

"If you come to our village, you will see all the rewards I ever hope to have. Peace of mind, pride in what I can give, the friendship of the people I respect and love. Then the best of all, Snow Blossom."

"Snow Blossom?"

"She is the sister of White Eagle and the youngest daughter of Tekata. We are to be married as soon as I can gather the rest of the bride price."

"Bride price?"

Cade laughed. "I'll explain that, too, some other time, it has a long history. Now, I think it's about time we got going. You are tired and it is a long trip home."

"Rebecca and White Eagle should be back in a few minutes."

"Maybe we will be lucky and White Eagle will have gotten up enough courage to speak to her."

"I hope." Benjamin smiled. "I hope, but knowing his iron will, I sincerely doubt it."

Secretly, Cade agreed. When White Eagle put his mind to a thing, he usually carried it through.

"I," thought Cade, "am going to do my best to open that stubborn man's mind."

It was surprising that Cade's thoughts and Benjamin's were identical at that moment.

Chapter Ten

Rebecca walked toward the river humming to herself. She was happy that White Eagle had returned. The feeling of peace and contentment he always gave her were welcome feelings compared to the subtle fear she lived in when he was gone. She found herself wishing she and her father could stay in this peaceful place.

It was impossible for Rebecca to explain to herself the feelings she had when White Eagle was near. She had given them a lot of thought since he had been gone. There was no sign from him, when he had reappeared with his brother, that he had even given her a thought all the time he was gone. The dark eyes had remained unreadable and he had not reached out to her in any way to show he was happy to see her. She was surprised at the hurt she felt when he had remained withdrawn from her.

At the river, she knelt and filled the bucket, then set it aside. She stood listening to the sounds about her, enjoying a cool breeze that blew across the water, and the soft murmuring sound of the river as it moved slowly on. "I could be happy here," she thought. She enjoyed the immensity of the land about her, and the comfort the quietness held.

Rebecca had been raised in a large town, but had been severely protected by her father. Contact with people, who moved in and out of her father's church with their multitudinous problems, had left her longing for a quiet place to give freedom to her own spirit without the clamoring of others. Here, she had found exactly what she wanted, yet she did not allow herself to reach too deeply for satisfaction, for she knew her father, when he was well, would be moving on to California. The thought of not seeing White Eagle again made her deeply depressed. She wanted him to somehow reach out to her so she could tell him how much his friendship had meant to her.

She sat down on the riverbank bending her knees up and wrapping her arms about them. Resting her chin on her knees, she allowed White Eagle to walk through her mind.

She was engrossed so much that she did not hear his quiet approach and he stood watching her, wondering where her mind drifted. His eyes drank in her fragile beauty like a drowning man and he stood immobile allowing himself the luxury of enjoying for this one stolen moment the pleasure that would be his for such a short time. Unaware that he was there, Rebecca's thoughts became verbal, and the softly whispered words came drifting to the man who stood a few feet from her.

"Oh, White Eagle, why don't you talk to me? Why don't you reach out for me?"

The words were spoken in a dreamlike whisper, but they exploded in the mind of the one who heard them. He could not believe the words he heard were meant in the way he had heard them. He clung to his religious beliefs and still found it difficult to attach mortality to the goddess of his dreams. He took a few steps toward her and she turned at the first sound of his approach. She smiled and rose to her feet as he approached her. "White Eagle," she said softly.

They stood close together, her wide violet eyes looking up into his, searching for something within his deep-black eyes to encourage her. The last rays of the setting sun made her hair glow like a golden halo and he not only found it difficult to concentrate, but he felt something drastic was happening to his breathing.

"It is good to see you again, Golden One."

She laughed, a shaky relieved laugh. "I am so pleased to hear you say that, White Eagle. If you had not, I would have no other way of knowing that you knew I existed. I cannot see past those eyes."

"But of course, you know it pleases me to see you are safe and well. I have thought of you and your father much in the past few days. Has your father been well while I was gone?"

"Yes. He had one slight attack, but it did not seem to be as bad as the others; yet he is weak."

"Yes, I can see his weakness. It will be long until he can travel." He wanted to add that he had serious doubts if her father would ever be able to travel again. "You will have to stay here where you are safe."

"White Eagle?"

"Yes?"

"Does it bother you?"

"What?"

"Our staying on your land. Would you feel better if we were somewhere else? Maybe . . . maybe you could help us travel to the fort."

"No," he said firmly.

"But it would be better for you if—"

"Speak no more of it," he said in a gruff firm voice. "You will stay here until your father is well." Or, he thought, until I can find a way to keep you. "Your father is a good man even though he is not wise enough to know all the gods. It pleases me to help him until he is well."

"Is that all, White Eagle?" she questioned softly.

"All?"

"Do you feel nothing for me, or is it only kindness that brings you here? Can you not say one word to me to let me know your thoughts are also of me?"

He held himself with an iron control that required every ounce of will he had. He wanted to reach for her, but he knew all that he could offer her was an empty life as a white slave in his village, for a chief would never be allowed to marry a white girl and stir awake the fury that lingered near. He knew the white soldiers would come for her, and he knew he would fight for her to his last dying breath. No, he would keep her hidden awhile longer . . . at least until he could find out what Cade's thoughts were. All these thoughts burned in his mind; yet he had to say something for he could not stand the pain his silence brought to her eyes.

"My thoughts are of you, Golden One," he said softly. "You walk with me wherever I go. I have found it very hard not to think of you when I am gone from here."

She smiled and he could see the sparkle of unshed tears in her eyes; then she stepped close to him so their bodies almost touched. She reached up and placed both hands on his chest.

"I know my father would call me shameless for what I am about to do, but I have to be honest with myself, my father, and with you. I don't know what you feel for me, White Eagle. I only know the days are long and lonely until you come, that I sleep with dreams of you. That I want to feel again and again the joy I feel when you come. That I want to reach out for you and have you take my hand and keep me with you always."

What control he had over his emotions was rapidly melting in the warmth of her affection. If the gods were angry enough at that moment to strike him dead, still he could not resist the need for her that twisted within him. He reached out and drew her against him, savoring the feel of her slender body that trembled within the circle of his arms.

"White Eagle?"

"Shhh, Golden One, do not speak, listen, I will tell you what I feel. I have dreamed of you so often that I feel you are a part of me. In my dreams I have held you so, and kept you within my arms safe. You are the woman I have searched for and yet the woman I know I cannot have."

She looked up at him, but remained silent while he tried to explain the differences in their worlds that would forever keep them apart.

Her arms slid about his body and she rested her head against his broad chest. He could feel her warm tears against his skin and he tightened his arms about her holding her close to him.

"But I do not want to go back. I want to stay with you."

"They would come for you, believing I had stolen you."

"Who would tell them I was here? Can I not just stay with you without anyone at the fort knowing?"

"For a time, maybe; but, would you really be happy here? Our life is so very different from all that you know. Could you accept our ways? Be one of us, and turn your back on all you have known? It is a great sacrifice, and it is a choice that would take much thought. Our ways are very different, especially for a woman."

While he talked to her he held her against him with one arm and caressed her hair gently with the other hand enjoying the silken feel of it under his fingers. Then he took hold of her shoulders and held her a little away from him. "Think of what I have told you," he said gently. "Speak of it with your father, for maybe he has the words to make you understand what I cannot make you understand: that I cannot make you pay the price for what I feel. He will understand, if you do not, that our worlds are so far apart that no matter how I feel, I must let you go."

If she had accepted his words and moved away from him, if her eyes had not filled with helplessness, he would have been able to continue controlling the situation. But she did not move away from him, and the tears fell heedlessly down her cheeks as she reached up one hand to press it gently against his cheek.

"White Eagle," she whispered softly, "is love not enough between two people? Can it not guard us against all the world? Why is it your people and mine? Why can it not just be White Eagle and Rebecca? Why must we pay the price for the intolerance of others, others we do not even know? I will tell you this, White Eagle. I would come to you, stay with you forever, if you but say the word. Can you be the one who puts away all the fear and hatred? Can you be the one who looks past all the barriers and sees the love within? If I must think of what you have said, then you think of the words I have spoken."

She turned and walked away, leaving him looking after her, amazed not only with the fact that his golden goddess had a very human nature, but that she had echoed the exact words that burned within him as if she were reading his heart.

After a few minutes, he followed her and entered the tepee a few moments after she did. The three of them sat near Benjamin's bed and talked for a while longer, but Cade could see the withdrawal of White Eagle and felt his brother's mind was twisted in deep thought. He suggested they leave and White Eagle grunted his agreement and rose to leave.

"Good night, White Eagle," Benjamin said. "You and your brother return soon. I did not realize how much I had missed you until now."

White Eagle stood looking at him as if he could not decide what to say to him; then without another word to Rebecca or her father, he pushed aside the door flap and left.

Cade was surprised for it was unlike White Eagle to neglect the proprieties or to be impolite. He said good night and left the tepee. In a few minutes he had caught up with White Eagle who was riding along slowly, a deep scowl on his face. They rode in silence for some time, while White Eagle thrashed out his thoughts, and Cade respected his privacy. After a while, White Eagle broke the silence himself with a softly asked question. "Am I a fool, my Brother?"

Cade sighed and thought deeply, for he wanted to say the right words. "White Eagle has never been a fool; it is only sometimes he is blind to the truth that stands before him."

"I see only the truth that it is much to ask for her to give up all she could have to stay with me."

"Could have? What do you know of what she could have? Is it enough for her? Have you spoken to her of the past? Do you know how it has been or if she would give it up with pleasure? In fact, Brother, have you asked her of her feelings or just told her yours?" He remembered too well what had happened between himself and Lauren. "Talk to her, tell her how you feel . . . at least let her choose."

White Eagle explained to Cade all that had transpired between himself and Rebecca, and it was only then that Cade realized, not only the depth of his feelings, but the fact that he held her in awe because of his deep superstitions of her origins. He wasn't quite sure how to breach this gap in understanding and explain to him that Rebecca was as mortal as he.

"White Eagle, when I spent time with my father, I saw many men, women, and children with gold hair. It is not an uncommon thing among them." Knowing how difficult it would be for White Eagle to accept this, he left that thought and opened the door to another he had been trying to bury—Lauren.

He told White Eagle of her only because he wanted to show him that he should not be afraid to love Rebecca because her skin was white and her past different. "If she would have come with me, White Eagle, I would have brought her here and shared my life with her as best I could."

"She refused to come?"

"Yes, because she could not leave the house of her father

and his wealth."

"Ummm," White Eagle said softly. "She was a weak woman."

"No . . . just afraid. I think she was stronger than she thought. Anyway, it is over. My life is here where I belong and my woman is Snow Blossom as the Great Spirit must have wanted from the beginning."

"You have said nothing to Snow Blossom about the white one?"

"No, but there will be no lies between us." Cade smiled. "After I know she is mine, I will tell her. I have a deep suspicion Snow Blossom's disposition is not always as shy and sweet as she pretends."

White Eagle laughed. "You are right, Brother, there is more fire there than you know."

"What are you going to do, White Eagle?"

"I shall speak to my father. If he agrees, I will bring the white ones to our village. Then we will see what happens."

Cade was going to say more to encourage White Eagle, but he held the words. Maybe it would be best if they took one step at a time. He was sure Tekata would approve of Benjamin and Rebecca's being their guests; after that, they would see how Rebecca took to their way of life.

They rode back to the village under the light of a full moon. The village was asleep when they arrived, so they made as little noise as possible as they each found their respective beds—White Eagle to dream of his Golden One, and Cade to worry again over the problems of how the test of his doctoring would come about and where he was going to acquire the rest of the bride's price for Snow Blossom.

The next morning, White Eagle was up with the dawn. He went immediately to his father's tepee where he requested permission to enter. He found his father had just awakened and was still lying upon his bed. He went to his side, and as he knelt down beside him, he realized the great Chief Tekata was growing weaker each day. The heavy load of responsibility would soon rest on his shoulders.

"You are well this morning, Father?"

"Yes, I am well."

White Eagle sat for a moment contemplating the words he would say, unaware that the astute eyes of the older man were reading his beloved son well, as he always could.

"What makes your heart heavy with thought this day, my Son? Of what do you wish to speak to me?"

White Eagle smiled. He should have known better, he thought, than to think he could hide anything from the wise old eyes of his father. "I have come to make a request. Will you listen before you decide?"

"It is of great importance to you?"

"Yes, it is."

"Speak then . . . I will listen."

White Eagle began to explain how he had first come across Rebecca and her father. He went on to tell him of all the visits he had made there. Then he told him of his and his brother's visit there the night before and that Sun Knife had suggested he go to his father and explain his plan to bring the two to their village as guests and keep them there until the white man's health was restored to him.

Tekata not only heard the words his son spoke, but he heard the unspoken words White Eagle was holding within him. Of his six children left living, White Eagle was his favorite. He knew White Eagle would follow him in leadership and he felt secure in the knowledge that White Eagle would make an honest, courageous chief.

"She is beautiful, this white one?" he asked softly.

White Eagle's startled eyes rose to his, but he could hide nothing of his feelings to a man who knew him so well.

"Yes, my Father, she is like a child of the sun. Her eyes are violet and her hair is gold like the first glow of morning. I feel she is an omen sent to me by the great sun god."

"Sent to you . . . you look on this woman as one who would be wife?"

White Eagle rose and moved closer to the fire. There he squatted and contemplated the red embers; then he said quietly, "I know well that the council would frown on my taking a woman who is not of our tribe. I know all the things that stand against us. Yet I feel a great love for her. Yes, my Father, I desire to take her as wife."

"It will be a very difficult thing, both for you and for her. She would have to accept the fact that you must also take a woman of our tribe as wife, and that her children would follow as chiefs, not the white one's children."

White Eagle turned his steady gaze on his father, a bright glow of hope in his eyes. "Then, you are not against my taking her?"

Tekata smiled. "If you feel what you are doing is right, my Son, know that I would stand with you in all things except those that would make you weak. Your difficulties lie not with me, but with the woman herself. For she may not be able to accept our ways."

"When I bring them here . . . after a while, I will tell her. . . . If the Great Spirit is willing, maybe she will understand and accept."

"And if not?"

White Eagle remained silent for a moment; then he said, "I don't know, I only hope. Until that hope is dead, I will continue to hold it. I know whatever the Great Spirit wills will come to pass. We are small in his hands, and all I can hope is that he is merciful and gives me the woman I want, who completes my life. If he chooses not to do so, then I also must learn to accept." He turned to his father. "I love my people, as I respect you, my Father. I will do what I must do. I would let her go if it came to a choice. I only pray that it will not."

Tekata nodded, his heart saddened by his son's obvious pain. He, too, would pray that all would be well for his son.

White Eagle left his father's tepee, mounted his horse, and rode toward the camp of Benjamin and Rebecca.

Cade, standing outside his tepee after the traditional prayers to the early-morning sun in gratitude for a new day, watched him leave and knew the reason for his going. He was so intent on his thoughts of White Eagle, he did not hear anyone approaching. Snow Blossom stood a few feet away from Cade and watched him. She could never remember a time when she had not loved him and now her heart filled with the fact that her almost impossible dream might come true, that one day, she would be his wife. Sensing someone watching, he turned and in the early-morning light, their eyes met and held.

She walked toward him, her smile warm and open and every emotion she felt for him clear in her eyes.

"White Eagle leaves early again. This is a mystery where he goes so often."

"Don't you know?" he replied.

"No, my brother has had something on his mind for some time. As close as we are, I felt it would be only a matter of time until he told me. Now, I wonder. Do you know?"

"Yes, I do."

"Can you tell me?"

"Let us ride together, Snow Blossom. I have an urge to see some of our old places. I will tell you."

Quickly, she went for her horse and within an hour they were riding away from the village and across the grass-covered plains.

Now that they were technically engaged, it was an acceptable thing that they would be allowed to spend some time alone together. A ride during the day and occasional "accidental" meetings would be permissible and it would be purposely ignored if a touch or a stolen kiss or two occurred.

It never occurred to Cade that his environment, free as it was, was more restrictive than Lauren's had been.

They rode along in silence for a while, Cade enjoying every minute of the renewal of his freedom, and Snow Blossom enjoying every minute she shared with him.

As they neared the meandering river, Cade stopped. They dismounted and walked their horses to the shade of a tree that bordered the river. Then they walked slowly along the water's edge.

Cade stopped and grabbed up a handful of small stones and began skipping them across the water.

"White Eagle plans on marrying a white woman," he said abruptly, and waited for the denunciation to come from her. He was disappointed. She did not reply for several moments and he turned to find her watching him.

"Does he love her?"

"I've seen them together. I know he loves her just as I am sure she loves him. I am only afraid, if she cannot accept him and the laws that hold him, what will happen?"

"Sun Knife, if a woman truly loves then she will go with her man no matter what. Nothing would keep them apart. She would change, accept, be what made him happy for that is also what would make her happy."

He walked to her and looked down into her wide dark eyes. For the first time, Cade truly came home, really felt a sense of belonging as he had never felt before. His okipu vision returned and he knew who had touched him, he knew who had whispered the words "You are home." It was Snow Blossom. The Great Spirit had given him a woman of wisdom, strength, and understanding. She was the one who would stand with him in the long dark hours and share with him the joy of the sun. He felt a sudden depth of love for her that left him weak. Gently, he reached out and drew her to him.

"You feel so, Snow Blossom? If I were to tell you I am returning to the white man's world and I wanted you to come with me, would you still feel the same?"

Her eyes smiled up at him. "If you want me as your wife, know this, warrior of my heart. I would follow you to all the ends of the earth. I would stay by your side with you as we walked the path to the Great Spirit together."

He felt the agony of pure joy, and could not speak any words to tell her how he felt. He drew her into his arms and held her, then gently, like the whisper of the water, he took her mouth with his. Her mouth was soft and pliant and her arms circled his neck holding him more and more closely. Snow Blossom was not afraid of the passion she could feel in his hard lean body. She had waited too long, dreamed too often, to be afraid now. Her lips opened to his in joyous giving and she heard his soft murmured groan as he bound her against him with arms that felt like iron.

When he released her, they stood looking at each other, more aware of each other than they had ever been before. It seemed to Cade as if every sense he owned touched her. In his mind, he could feel the smooth texture of her skin, smell the sweet scent of her, and taste her soft honeyed mouth.

That he wanted her more than he had ever wanted a woman before he realized without a shred of doubt. The last clinging shadow of Lauren left his heart and it welcomed Snow Blossom who filled it to overflowing.

He reached out and laid his hand against her smooth cheek. "You are my woman, Snow Blossom. Soon I will have the bride price for your father, but no matter what may happen, I want you to know that my love for you is deep and full. I will try to be a good husband and make you as happy as you have made me."

She trembled with the surge of joy that claimed her and tears of happiness appeared in her eyes.

"All my life, since I can remember, you have walked in my dreams, been the one warrior who has held my heart." She lifted her head proudly. "I am Snow Blossom, daughter of a great chief, and I do not give my love carelessly or lightly, but I give it with my whole being—forever."

Placing his hands on each side of her face, he lifted her lips to his, telling her with the depth of his kiss that his need for her was a fire that raged through him. Their lips clung as he slid his arms about her and in a blaze of happiness he felt her cling to him, moving her body against his as she held him to her in a clinging embrace.

"I want you," he whispered against her silky hair. "God, how I want you."

Her eyes held his as she took his hand. Slowly, she backed toward the grass beneath the trees drawing him with her.

He watched her as she began, with trembling fingers, to loosen the ties of her blouse. It dropped to the ground, followed by the skirt. She stood before him, proud of her rare and blazing beauty, seeing it reflected in his eyes and the love that was written on his face. Then she moved close to him and began, with slow movements, to undress him.

They stood, inches apart, while his eyes devoured her. His hand brushed gently over one rounded rose-tipped breast, then continued down her slender waist to a soft rounded hip. There it rested just for a moment, then with a little pressure he drew her again into his arms as his hungry mouth possessed hers. He felt the unleashed passion within her explode as her mouth opened under his and her hands gripped him. A soft murmured sound escaped her as he crushed her slender body against his and his hands caressed her silken skin.

He drew her down to the soft grass beside him, then slowly, leisurely, as if the whole world had breathlessly stopped for them, he began a gentle and tender capture of Snow Blossom. His hands traced seeking patterns across her skin; his warm seeking lips followed and brought moaning gasps of delight from her. Her slender fingers, too, sought the feel of his lean muscled body. Eagerly and delightedly, they touched, tasted, enjoyed the feelings and the sensuous pleasure they were experiencing, while building their need for each other higher and higher.

Although he was more experienced than she, he was thrilled by the eagerness and obvious pleasure she found. There was no fear, no timid withdrawal. She met him need for need, touch for touch until his mind whirled in a whirlpool of passion. Down, down, down, they tumbled into the oblivion of love, to a place where only they existed.

Within her, he found the sanctuary he had searched for, the one who would share his existence as she shared his passion. Their bodies blended together, and their minds and hearts fused as one, as he lifted her with strong hands and held her writhing body crushed to his and they reached a blinding completion that left them both weak with the wonder of the ecstasy they had shared.

They lay in silence for a moment, neither of them wanting to release this moment of pleasure. He lay beside her, cradling her sweat-slicked body gently in his arms. Their eyes held as he tenderly brushed the soft beads of moisture from her brow; then he held her face while his lips touched hers in gentle gratitude for the joy she had given him.

"I love you, Snow Blossom, more than the very air I breathe. I thought I had known love before, but now I see how wrong I was. You are so beautiful and I shall be so proud to claim you as wife. I only hope I can get the rest of the bride price soon, for you are but a drink to a man dying of thirst. Having you only makes me want you more. I shall never have enough of your sweetness."

She buried her face against his throat and her hands clung to him. He could feel the warm tears against his skin.

"So long I have dreamed, have wanted you. Sometimes, I

could not bear the wanting. Sometimes, I thought, I shall give myself to another and that way, in the arms of another man, I would be able to forget the blue-eyed warrior who held my heart. But I could not, for this thing deep inside me told me that if I could not have Sun Knife, I could have no other. Oh, Sun Knife, my heart sings with joy, to know we will be together forever."

He rocked her in his arms, knowing that no power outside of death could take her from him, and he knew a sense of peace and a oneness with all about him that held him so strongly it brought tears to his eyes. She looked up and a soft half-smile formed on her lips.

"Does a warrior weep?"

"Only if he has come home after a long and weary journey and found all his life needs. Truly, the Great Spirit has given me the greatest gift of all . . . the love of Snow Blossom."

Her soft lips trembled, moistened with her salty tears, and he tasted them again and again until she sighed with contentment and lay against him in complete and all-consuming pleasure.

They talked and laughed together in muted voices as lovers do, as if somehow afraid the world would hear them and intrude. She listened as he told her of his dreams and they talked of their future unknowing that the hand of fate was already reaching for them.

"Let us swim in the river," she said as she rose from his side. He watched her as she walked away from him. She was so unaffected, so unaware of her graceful beauty. She was as much a part of their environment as the sun and the sky. She dove into the water like a sleek young otter and he answered her laughing call when she surfaced by running to the bank and diving in.

Underwater, he swam to her and surfaced close enough to grasp her in his arms. Their lips met as he pulled her beneath the surface and felt her slim body press against his and her arms encircle his neck.

They surfaced again, laughing and holding tightly to each other. He had never felt such joy in his life. All the other memorable events faded into oblivion when compared to the beautiful woman he held in his arms.

They swam to shallow water where she stood squeezing her hair free of water, and he watched the graceful way she seemed to blend with the environment. The sun glistened on her wet body causing her to sparkle in its light. Here, he thought, was a woman beyond compare. She could be the mother of his children and give them the pride and the strength she possessed.

He walked to her side and looked down into the bright depths of her eyes. He bent forward and gently touched her moist lips with his; then slowly, he drew her to him, enjoying the feel of her round breasts as they pressed against his chest and the slenderness of her as he put his arms about her. For several moments, he just held her as if it were something he was trying to imprint on his memory so he could never forget.

Their bodies were cool from the water, but they warmed as his lips found hers and again she surrendered to the magic of the love of the man she had dreamed of so often.

He lifted her in his arms and they returned to the soft bed of their beginning love and renewed their promise to each other of love that would stand the test of time.

It was late afternoon when they mounted their horses and rode back to the village. As they rode he told her as much as he knew about the situation between Rebecca and White Eagle.

"It will be hard for her, Sun Knife."

"Yes, but I don't think Rebecca is weak even though she looks so. I am only worried about what the strength of her religion may forbid her to do."

"Is it wrong in her beliefs for her to marry an Indian?" she asked angrily.

"No. But her religion may forbid her to marry a man who intends to have other wives."

"But my father has many. That is how it should be."

"Snow Blossom," he said quietly as he stopped his horse to look at her, "you are the only wife I shall ever take. You are the only one I want. For this one time, I believe the white man is right."

Her eyes softened as she gazed at him and he reached out and touched her cheek. "There is a special love between a man and wife. It is what I feel for you and I cannot share it with another.

I know it is how Rebecca will feel too. I am afraid it is the one thing that will keep them forever apart."

"Does White Eagle understand this?"

"He worries it in his mind. His heart and his head are at war. I do not see how it can end. If one of them does not surrender, then they can never be together. That would hurt them both for I know they love each other very much."

"I love my brother very much. It will be hard to see him suffer."

"We can do nothing to help him. If Rebecca were Indian—were even half-Indian like me—it would be different. Then he could take her as wife and know his sons would be honored in his tribe."

"If she were—" Snow Blossom stopped her words and sat motionless looking at Sun Knife. Then she smiled. "Come, let us go and see if he has returned. I would like to see a woman who has hair like the sun. I still find it hard to believe."

Cade sensed she had some secret thought in mind, but she kicked her horse into motion before he could question her. They entered the village, and could tell that White Eagle had returned for his horse was tied in front of his tepee. They walked to the doorway and requested permission to enter. When White Eagle called out to them, they went in. Snow Blossom stood still, her eyes wide in surprise at the golden-haired woman who stood at her brother's side.

Chapter Eleven

White Eagle said nothing as the two women's eyes met over the fire. He would never admit he wanted his sister's approval, but deep inside he knew it was so. Snow Blossom stepped closer to Rebecca, her attention still caught by the sun-bright hair. She reached out a tentative hand and touched it; then she smiled and Rebecca's smile came in response.

"Sun Knife has spoken of your beauty and said your hair was made of gold. I did not believe. Now I know it is true. You are truly as he said."

White Eagle could happily have strangled her for making him sound like a young brave excited over his first woman. He knew Snow Blossom tormented him deliberately so he kept his anger under control, promising himself to give her a good slap or two later to teach her to control her tongue. Cade suppressed his laughter at White Eagle's glare and Snow Blossom ignored it.

"Your name is Rebecca," she said as if she had named her herself. "I am Snow Blossom, you will come with me and share my tepee. It is forbidden for you to share my brother's unless you are married."

Again a low warning growl from White Eagle as he took a threatening step toward her, but Rebecca laughed.

"Yes, I know I cannot. It is forbidden among us also. I would like to share with you. I would like to know White Eagle's sister better."

Again, Snow Blossom chuckled throatily at her brother's warning look. "Come," she said to Rebecca, and the two of them left, leaving a Cade who was almost choking on his laughter and a White Eagle who glared suspiciously at him.

Snow Blossom had a plan in mind that might help her brother solve his problem, but first she wanted to decide for herself what kind of woman her brother had chosen.

White Eagle sat before his fire, his face brooding. Cade sat opposite and waited for his mood to change. He had reconsidered the wisdom of laughing at White Eagle when he was already in a mood bordering on violence.

"I shall strangle that woman and her loose tongue one day," he grumbled.

Cade grinned. "You'd best not. I suspect Snow Blossom has some plan to help you."

White Eagle looked up quickly, the frown fading from his face. "Plan . . . What plan?"

"I don't know, it's just a suspicion. But if I read the gleam in her eye right, she has something up her sleeve."

"Up her sleeve?"

"A figure of speech. She has some secret plan."

"How do you know? . . . Besides, what plan could she have? I wonder if there is any way out of this situation other than hoping Rebecca can understand . . . can accept . . . can change."

"Do you think that will happen?"

"No," White Eagle said after much thought. "She and her father worship one god. They must be such single-minded people, for their god allows them only one wife. I don't understand; the work is so much easier with two women to share it. My father's wives all live together well. I don't understand this god. I am sure that my sister understands that you will one day take another wife."

"No, White Eagle . . . I won't. Snow Blossom is the only wife I shall have."

White Eagle was surprised. "Do you believe there is only one god as they do?"

"No, I have our own beliefs. It is just that I love Snow Blossom and I desire to spend the rest of my days with her only. She is the only wife I shall take, for she is the one I know is part of my destiny, part of my okipu vision." Cade went on to tell him about the vision.

"But it did not tell you you could only have one wife."

"It is how I choose, Brother. I want no other but Snow Blossom."

"But what if you did not have children?"

Children were the most prized possession in White Eagle's village. They were cared for carefully and loved more than any other thing a man could have.

"If we have no children, it is the will of the Great Spirit and I will accept it. If we do, I shall love them and be proud of them. But my love for Snow Blossom does not have anything to do with her ability to bear children and work. I love her because she is what she is. I respect both her mind and her feelings. I love Snow Blossom for herself, not for what she can provide for me. Children or no, I will always love her the same."

White Eagle sat in silent contemplation. These ideas were new to him and he had obviously never thought of them before. He had just assumed the choices would all be Rebecca's. He had never realized he would have to make choices of his own.

"Consider it this way, Brother," Cade continued gently. "Suppose it were custom for a woman to take more than one husband. What would you do should you have to share Rebecca with another?"

White Eagle's face became still and his eyes glowed with emotion. "I would kill any man who tried to touch her. She is mine."

"You feel so, how would you think a woman felt when she has to silently share her husband with another. If it would be hard for you, think how hard it is for her."

Again, they were in alien territory for White Eagle. His people had lived the same for as long as he could remember. His own father had taken several wives. He had felt it would always be the same for him. Thinking of a woman's feelings in this matter had never occurred to him. The death rate, due to war among the tribes and the danger of hunting wild animals had always unbalanced the population so that women outnumbered men. To balance this situation men had always taken more than one wife. It was a way of life in which White Eagle had been raised, and the only way he knew. Now confusion took the place of assurance, because he knew he would die before he shared Rebecca with any other brave, and he began to wonder just what her feelings were in the matter. He grunted angrily as he rose to his feet. At the door, he turned and looked at Cade.

"I will think on this. It is a strange way to live. It has not been our way." He paused and frowned at Cade. "Will you truly only take one wife?"

"Truly." Cade smiled. "I feel one happy wife would be much easier to live with than two unhappy ones."

"Ummm." White Eagle grunted and with a thoughtful frown he left the tepee. With a silent laugh, Cade rose and went to his own tepee where he found a warm meal and a very curious mother waiting for him.

Snow Blossom made Rebecca and her father comfortable in a tepee close to Long Arrow's. It was part of a plan that had been forming in her mind to try to make her brother's path a little easier. She took special care in the ordering of the food and necessary material for the tepee, and when she was sure Rebecca's father was being well-cared-for she took Rebecca under her wing to show her the ways of a woman of her tribe.

The women sustained and perpetuated village life, and their labors brought them a measure of tribal esteem. They gathered fruits and nuts and vegetables for their families. Women cultivated the crops and made pottery. They also peformed such heavy tasks as raising and lowering the tepee, bringing in firewood, and digging usable roots.

Far from regarding these tasks as drudgery, Indian women carried them out with a sense of satisfaction and even a joyous camaraderie.

They took special pride in their art. The weaving of baskets and making of a tepee lining was done in a spirit that sanctified the object and dedicated it to the welfare of the family or the tribe.

One of their essential tasks was preparing hides. It was a tedious and time-consuming job and it surprised Snow Blossom that Rebecca took it in stride as she did all the other jobs she had insisted on sharing. She found Rebecca receptive to everything she told her and changed her ideas that Rebecca might be too fragile to be White Eagle's wife.

Snow Blossom found Rebecca easy to talk to and as the days began to pass, their relationship began to warm.

It was several days after their arrival that White Eagle got the opportunity to speak to Rebecca again. Making it appear accidental, he met Snow Blossom and Rebecca at the river when they went in the early-morning light for water. Snow Blossom's lips twitched in a half-smile and she stifled the urge to tease her brother just a little when her astute eyes discerned his tense attitude. Although she could read him well, Rebecca still could not. To her, he looked formidable, somewhat stern, and completely oblivious to her presence. It would take Rebecca a long time to learn to read the face of the man she loved.

White Eagle could see the amusement glitter in his sister's eyes and he controlled the urge to toss her bodily into the river. Instead, in studied majesty, he arrogantly ignored her and this almost made Snow Blossom laugh outright. She took the buckets from Rebecca's hand.

"I shall fill them," she said. Then she walked to the water's edge and drifted far enough away so they could speak without her hearing. There, she sat on the bank and dangled her feet in the water and filled her mind with thoughts of Cade.

"I must speak to you," White Eagle said to Rebecca as soon as Snow Blossom was out of hearing range.

"Yes?"

"You are well?"

"Yes, very well."

"You are pleased with our village?"

"Yes, very much. Snow Blossom has made the days pleasant, and I have enjoyed being here."

"That is good," he said, but the hesitation in his voice made her realize there was much more he wanted to say.

"White Eagle," she said gently. "What is it you really want to say to me? You have been away hunting for the past few days, I thought you had forgotten I was here."

"I have not been hunting, and I have not forgotten you. I have been thinking of the words I must say to you."

"Thinking? Why should it take so much thought to speak to me. I miss your sitting at our fire and talking to us."

"It takes much thought, for I want you to understand all that I say."

"I shall try."

"Rebecca . . . I want to take you as my wife." He said the words slowly and precisely as if he were afraid she would not understand.

"Was that so very difficult for you?" she asked softly.

"For me . . . no, for my love for you is deep. I am only afraid of your answer."

For White Eagle to admit fear of anything was a surprise to Rebecca for she knew now, since she had been among them for a while, that a warrior would admit fear of nothing.

"Why?"

"Because of the teachings of your one god. Because our ways are so far apart." He spoke softly as he began to tell her why he would be forced to take another wife of his own tribe and that he and Rebecca would never be able to see their children follow him as leaders. He watched with pain as the light in her eyes darkened and the smile faded.

"Only because I have no Indian blood," she said in a shocked voice. "Is our love not enough to cross that terrible barrier?"

His heart leaped at her words, "our love," for he desperately needed her to acknowledge it verbally.

"I would change it if I could find a way, Rebecca. Will you read my heart and know that I love you, that I want no other but you? Will you try to understand the obligations I have to my father and my people? I need you, Rebecca, and there is only one way I know. Can you bend in your beliefs this much for me? Will your god not understand what we feel for each other?"

"I am afraid," she whispered.

"Afraid?"

"Afraid that it is not my God that causes me to fear. It is that I cannot bear the thought of another woman sharing your life, giving you children. I love you, and jealousy burns in my heart that one day you will love another."

"Love another? How could I love another? What I feel for you has filled my heart. There is no room for another. I will try to find a way, Rebecca, but if nothing will change . . . I must know. Will you be my wife?"

"I know that my heart shouts yes, but I am confused. I must speak with my father. Will you give me time to think about what you have said?"

"It is good for you to think, but when you do, remember that I love you and I will try to make your life good, try to keep you happy."

Tears glistened in her eyes and she stepped close and put both her hands on his bare chest. She could feel the solid heavy beat of his heart and his eyes held hers in a seeking look.

"I do love you, White Eagle; that is why I doubt my ability to accept the fact that you will not always be mine."

He reached for her, pulling her into his arms. He held her in a tight embrace rubbing his chin against the soft golden hair. At that moment he would gladly have forsaken everything he knew and loved and have taken Rebecca away to a place where they could live together in peace. The moment slipped away when his sister's voice broke the silence. She had seen what was happening. Returning, she had heard some of what was said and she knew an honorable man like her brother would never forgive himself had he taken such a step.

"Rebecca, we must return with the water."

They stepped away from each other reluctantly and Snow Blossom was pained to see the look in her brother's eyes. She decided to try, that day, the plan she had. If it worked it would bring Rebecca and White Eagle together, if not, they would have to face the only other alternative, Rebecca's acceptance of White Eagle's ways. When they returned to the village, Snow Blossom went to the tepee of Long Arrow. She called to him and asked if he would come out and speak with her for it was completely against custom for her, as an unmarried girl, to enter the tepee of an unmarried man. It meant nothing that he was old enough to be her father and was, in fact, the stepfather of the man she would marry. He stepped outside, his brows knit with surprise to see her there.

"You wish to speak to me, Snow Blossom?"

"Yes, Long Arrow. It is important that I ask your advice on a matter of great importance."

"My advice?" he questioned.

"Yes."

"Speak."

She explained her plan to him rapidly and was overjoyed to see his features change from polite curiosity to smiling agreement. "It is a worthy idea, Snow Blossom," he said.

"What do you think of it being permissible?"

"I know it was done once before, but I'm sure no one has thought of it being done with a woman."

"But it is not impossible?"

"No . . . I don't think so. If you desire I shall present it to Tekata and the council. We will abide by their judgment." He smiled at her. "If they agree, it will make your brother very pleased with you."

"My brother is always pleased with me. He has always tried to do as much as he can for me. I should like a chance to return some of his kindness."

"The girl seems pleasant."

"She is a woman of small stature with a great heart, and her heart contains much love for White Eagle. I would like to see them happy."

"You are the one with the great heart, Snow Blossom. My son does well to desire you for a wife."

"Thank you."

"Do you plan to marry soon?"

"Sun Knife has still to acquire all of my bride price. I know he works hard for it—it and the chance to prove his medicine. It would please me if my brother were to marry soon—then Rebecca and I will be truly sisters."

"If our plans work." He grinned.

She smiled at the use of the word "our" in connection with her plan for she knew he would do all in his power to help White Eagle.

"Yes . . . if our plan works."

"You go and talk to Rebecca, comfort her, but do not tell her of our plan for if it fails she will not be hurt, and she may still decide to accept White Eagle on his terms."

Snow Blossom nodded her head and left him. He stood and watched her walk away. "She is a strong and proud woman with much wisdom. My son does well in his choice of wife. Their sons should be warriors of great bravery."

He walked to Tekata's tepee and requested permission to enter. When he heard an answer he went inside and dropped the tepee door cover closed behind him to insure privacy.

Cade had been tenaciously working on the balance of the bride price for Snow Blossom. He had acquired a large amount of weapons and had traded and worked to purchase blankets and furs. With White Eagle and several friends, he had hunted and returned with two buffalo hides which his mother had tanned and prepared for him. All he needed now were the remaining horses he had promised, as he prepared to go on a hunt for wild horses. Fifty horses was a large bite to take, but his desire for Snow Blossom now put all other thoughts from his mind. He would find a way to get the horses, he thought grimly, and Snow Blossom would be his—soon.

He knew White Eagle had weighty problems on his mind so he did not ask him to go along on the horse hunt. It was the reason Cade was not present when the council met again.

White Eagle, as a young warrior, was allowed to sit among the elders at the council, but it was forbidden for him to speak on any subject unless he was presenting a petition or unless one of the elders requested him to do so. It would have shown a complete lack of etiquette should he speak under any other circumstances.

They sat in a semicircle, the elders, smoking the pipe that was passed from hand to hand, for smoke was a sacred thing. It was lifted once in each direction—north, south, east, and west—before it was smoked and prayers were incanted for the benevolence of the gods. The young men sat behind the elders and watched as the ceremony continued. Then those making a request were brought forward. It surprised White Eagle when Long Arrow entered and stood before the council. It was more of a surprise when he spoke the words of his request.

"I am Long Arrow, friend of Michael Holliday and foster father to his son, Sun Knife, a son who lives among us. Long I have walked among you alone and without family so that I could stand as protector of Michael Holliday's son and his wife Waterflower. When Michael Holliday wanted to marry one of our tribe we at first refused because he was not one of us. Then the answer was found. We made him one of us by blood ceremony.

"Now I come to you again to ask if the blood ceremony can be performed again to make two others one of us."

"Of whom do you speak, Long Arrow?" He was asked this question by Tekata in a tone of deep respect for Long Arrow was noted for his honor and his bravery.

"I speak of Benjamin Wade . . . and his daughter, Rebecca."

"This has not been done with a woman before," Tekata said.

"But it is not forbidden, is it my Chief?"

"I am unsure, but leave us. The council and I will speak together. We will call you when we decide."

Long Arrow bowed to his chief, then respectfully to each of th council, then he backed from the tepee. Outside, he turned to find Snow Blossom and Rebecca waiting for him. It was forbidden for a woman to enter the council tepee.

"Long Arrow?"

"They are talking, Snow Blossom. We can do nothing but wait."

They were surprised when White Eagle and all the younger men came out of the tepee.

"Why have you left, White Eagle?" Long Arrow asked.

"My father and the council wish to speak alone. Long Arrow?" White Eagle began. There was a glow of a beginning idea in his head, and it was confirmed when Long Arrow smiled at him.

"Yes, White Eagle, your thoughts run well. When Michael Holliday first came among us, they would not let a chief's daughter marry him because of his white blood. The matter was solved when he was made blood brother both to himself and to me. As a blood brother it was acceptable for him to marry a chief's daughter. As a daughter to me and a sister to Sun Knife, it should be acceptable for Rebecca to marry a chief's son."

"If the council will agree, I owe you a great debt. Know, Long Arrow, that my heart and my strength are at your command."

"It is not me to whom you owe a debt. It was not I who thought of the plan."

"Who then? Sun Knife?"

"No, someone closer to you."

"Who?"

"Your sister, Snow Blossom."

White Eagle turned to his sister who smiled at his surprise.

"It will be well, Brother. I feel it here," she said as she pressed her closed fist against her heart. "Soon you will be able to marry the woman of your choice."

The tears on Rebecca's cheeks told White Eagle just how happy she was and he spoke to his sister in an emotion-choked voice.

"I owe you my life, little Sister. Know it is yours from this day forward. One day, I shall be able to repay you for what you have given me."

The sparkle reappeared in Snow Blossom's eyes. "I shall not hesitate"—she laughed—"to call on you when any need arises. I have longed many moons to have you in my debt."

"Why is it," he responded to her laughter, "that I want to love you in one minute and want to kill you in the next?"

Long Arrow chuckled, then the smile faded. "We are not sure yet what the council will say. Maybe they will not allow Rebecca to become my daughter or Sun Knife's sister. We must pray to the gods that they are willing." There was silence after these words as all of them realized they were laughing too soon. In one word the council could wipe away all their happiness. Three of them wondered then what path Rebecca would choose to take.

"Come, we will go to my tepee and wait." Long Arrow said. "It must appear that we are confident."

They followed, but confidence was still sadly lacking. The time ticked away and minutes turned into hours. Rebecca and Snow Blossom went to Chief Tekata's tepee where they lost themselves in the work of preparing a large meal for the chief and his visitors. It was not so easy for White Eagle who tried to control his impatience.

Then, after three long hours, a young warrior presented himself at Long Arrow's door. "Chief Tekata and the council wish for you to return."

It was a silent White Eagle who walked beside Long Arrow to

the council tepee. Outside he hesitated only for a moment; then he brushed aside the cover and stepped inside standing tall and proud like the chief's son he was.

"Long Arrow," Chief Tekata said. All their faces were still and nothing could be read in any of the dark eyes that watched Long Arrow as he stepped forward.

"I am here, my Chief."

"You are well-known among us, Long Arrow, for your bravery and your honor. It is because of this that the council agrees to grant your request to adopt the white family as your own. The ceremony will be within three days. You must prepare the white ones for the ordeal."

Long Arrow bowed deeply and left the tepee. White Eagle, hardly able to contain his joy, followed him. Away from the tepee, he turned to Long Arrow. "Let me tell them, Long Arrow. I will have to explain the ceremony to them. Especially to Rebecca. It will be difficult for her."

Long Arrow nodded and White Eagle walked with a light step to the door of the tepee in which Benjamin and Rebecca lived. Inside he explained to Benjamin as quickly as he could and was rewarded by Benjamin's blessings on his desire to marry Rebecca and his quick agreement to the ceremony. Then he went in search of Rebecca and his sister, Snow Blossom.

Snow Blossom spotted him first walking purposefully toward them. She watched his face closely as he walked, but even she could not pierce the mask he deliberately adopted.

"Brother," Snow Blossom said in impatience, "you have news?"

"Yes." He smiled at Rebecca who, for the first time began to sense the moods of the man she loved.

"White Eagle?" she said softly.

"Yes, Rebecca . . . they have agreed. In three days, you will take part in the ceremony with your father. In three days, you will be a blood relative of Long Arrow. As such it is permissible to ask him for you in marriage."

Rebecca covered her face and to Snow Blossom and White Eagle's surprise began to cry.

"You are not happy, Rebecca," White Eagle said, dismay cutting through his words.

"I have never been happier in my life," she sobbed. "In three days, I shall have a whole new life and the freedom to marry the man I love."

"Then why do you weep?" he asked.

"She weeps for happiness," Snow Blossom said quickly. White Eagle shook his head. It was beyond him to reason why a woman should cry if she were happy.

"I will explain the ceremony to her," Snow Blossom said.

"No," he replied firmly, "I will. Come, Rebecca, walk with me."

"You will give the village much to talk about," Snow Blossom offered with a laugh. White Eagle shrugged, but his eyes never left Rebecca who moved to his side. He smiled at his sister, then took Rebecca's hand and they walked away from the village.

They walked along in silence for a few minutes, then he spoke quietly.

"The ceremony will not be easy for you, Rebecca. It is much to ask of you. It will take a great deal of courage."

"I am not weak, White Eagle. It is the answer to our problem and I will face it." She was quiet for a moment; then she added, "Nothing could be as difficult to face as having you turn from me to another woman. I think I could face anything but that."

She could see his eyes glow with satisfaction.

"Let me explain the ceremony to you." She listened while he told her all that she would have to do. He noticed that even though her face paled her step was steady and the hand he held in his was firm.

Before they parted, he faced her, reaching out and touching again the golden hair that as always held his attention.

"Once the ceremony is over we will be free to marry. Then you will belong to me; you will be in my care. I find it hard to wait for the days to pass. I would take the pain of it myself if I could spare you. Remember I am near. If you need courage . . . remember I am near."

"I will not forget," she said softly. His eyes searched hers for something and after a few minutes he smiled in satisfaction for he seemed to find what he searched for.

"I love you, Golden One," he said softly, then he was gone and she returned to the tepee to wait for the day of the ceremony.

It was the day before the ceremony, at the crack of dawn, that Cade returned. He returned with a thunderous roar that wakened the entire village and brought them running from their tepees to find the cause of all the noise.

Before he had gone, he had built a corral to hold the horses he would find. Now he came thundering down from the hills shouting at the top of his lungs and driving before him a herd of almost fifty horses. With the help of three friends, he had rounded them up on the plains and driven them home. His friends would share all but the hundred he would need to seal the bride price for Snow Blossom.

She stood outside her tepee and smiled at an exuberantly shouting Cade as he drove the horses into the corral, and, leaping from his horse, closed the gate.

He went immediately to his tepee where he gathered all the things he had promised Tekata. Taking them all he went to Tekata's tepee where he put the required bride price outside Tekata's door as was the custom. Then with a broad and very satisfied smile on his face, he returned to his own tepee to await the formal notice that his beautiful Snow Blossom would soon be his.

White Eagle was the first to come to his tepee to tell him the news of the ceremony soon to come and why.

"That is wonderful, White Eagle. How did this come about?"

"My quick-minded sister," he replied. "She very seldom is lost for a plan or idea and she usually gets what she sets out to get one way or another."

"Snow Blossom?"

"Ummm," he grunted. "I warn you, Brother, she will not be an easy one to tame."

"Tame? I don't want to tame her, I like her the way she is."

"That is because you have not seen her any other way. I hope you are never faced with the other side of Snow Blossom." He laughed. Cade laughed with him, not knowing that the day would come when he would see another side of Snow Blossom—a Snow Blossom of strength and fury.

The day of the ceremony arrived, and it was amusing to Cade

that White Eagle seemed much more tense and nervous than Rebecca or Benjamin.

Rebecca was silent as Long Arrow led her and her father into the council tepee. A small couch had been prepared for them near the fire and both were seated.

Long Arrow made a speech in which he asked the council, his chief, and all the gods to listen to his petition. Then he told of his desire to take Benjamin as his blood brother and Rebecca as his adopted daughter.

"I would share my blood with them so that they may be free to live in our village and share our lives," he said.

"Do they wish to share your life here among us?" questioned the chief.

All eyes turned toward Benjamin and Rebecca. Benjamin rose and said in a firm steady voice, "Yes, my daughter and I wish to be one of you, to spend the rest of our lives among you. We would pray to contribute to the welfare of this village in any way we can. We are proud that Long Arrow, a man of great esteem, has offered us his brotherhood. If it pleases the council, we too would share our blood with a man of such honor and pride."

Chief Tekata and the council nodded a silent agreement and Long Arrow walked to Benjamin and Rebecca. He held both arms out before him with his palms up.

The medicine man walked to his side. Cade, who stood beside White Eagle could feel the tension in his body as the medicine man reached out to lift both Rebecca's and Benjamin's arms. He took a wicked-bladed knife and held it aloft. It glistened in the light of the fire and both Cade and White Eagle could see the paleness of Rebecca's face and the beads of perspiration on her brow. Neither of them made a sound as the knife lowered. Quickly, it slashed a three-inch-long slash in each of Long Arrow's arms about four inches above the wrist. Then, the medicine man made the same cut in Benjamin's arm. He lifted Rebecca's arm and made the cut deep and quick. She made no sound and White Eagle's eyes glittered in pride.

The arms of Rebecca and Benjamin were pressed against Long Arrow's arms so the blood mingled. They were bound together and the medicine man chanted the prayers that made the three of them one family.

It was a long and tedious time for the prayers and White Eagle watched Rebecca closely. Blood stained all their arms and the bindings that held them and he was afraid the loss of blood and the extended time would make her weak or ill. Again he was wrong. She stood immobile, her eyes holding Long Arrow's and her body straight and still.

White Eagle breathed a ragged sigh of relief when the ties that held them together were unbound and each of them had their wounds bandaged. Long Arrow placed his hand first on Benjamin's shoulder. "Welcome to my family, Brother," he said. Benjamin smiled and placed his hand on Long Arrow's shoulder. "Welcome to my family, Daughter," Long Arrow repeated. Then Rebecca instead of putting her hand on his shoulder took his large hand in hers and held it to her heart.

"I am proud to be called daughter to Long Arrow. I hope you are pleased with me. I will never dishonor your name and I shall do my best to be a good daughter. I am grateful Long Arrow, and shall do my best to wear your name with pride."

Long Arrow was speechless and definitely pleased as was Tekata and all of the members of the council. None of them were nearly as pleased and happy as White Eagle.

As they left the tepee, White Eagle stood aside with Cade and waited for Long Arrow and his new family. When they came he made all the proper good wishes, then he spoke softly and firmly to Long Arrow.

"Long Arrow, I wish to ask you for your daughter in marriage."

Long Arrow could hardly resist a little tormenting of White Eagle. He smiled, took Rebecca's hand in his and said pleasantly, "Come to my tepee tomorrow. We will speak of the bride price for my only child. I warn you, she is of much value and it will be high."

He walked away from a stunned White Eagle and a Cade who had all he could do to control his laughter at the look on White Eagle's face.

"Bride price?" White Eagle muttered and he walked away, forgetting that Cade was even standing there.

Chapter Twelve

White Eagle appeared at Long Arrow's tepee the moment he thought he had had enough time to awaken. He sat opposite Long Arrow, after he had been invited in, and tried to control his impatience as Long Arrow continued to discuss everything from weather to hunting. Finally he could stand no more.

"Long Arrow, I wish to discuss the bride price for Rebecca."

"Yes," Long Arrow said gently, "Rebecca is a good woman. She will prove to be a good daughter and I hesitate to part with her."

White Eagle, his patience finally stretched to the breaking point, could not control his words. "What is your price, Long Arrow?"

Long Arrow knew he had pressed White Eagle a little too far. He smiled. "Do not be angry, White Eagle. I have been joking with you. She is my adopted daughter, but I really have no say in her bride price. It is all up to her father. He has told me that he does not understand such things and shall leave it up to me to decide what is fair."

"And you have decided?" White Eagle answered, somewhat mollified.

"Yes."

"I am a wealthy man, Long Arrow, and I consider any price asked for her will be fair. She is the only wife I shall take."

"The only . . . you do not intend to have others?"

"No."

Long Arrow questioned the firm answer no further. "Fifty horses, weapons, blankets, six buffalo robes."

"She is worth more, but I pay it gladly."

"Her father will be pleased."

"I would like the marriage to be soon."

"How soon?"

White Eagle grinned. "Tomorrow."

Long Arrow laughed in response. "You are impatient. Deliver the bride price today, and we will arrange the marriage for tomorrow."

White Eagle grunted in satisfaction as he rose, said farewell, and went in search of Rebecca.

He found her with his sister, on their knees before a buffalo hide that had been staked out so that they could scrape it clean and begin the process of preparing it for use. They were laughing and talking together, Rebecca's golden head bent close to his sister's dark one. Rebecca had changed her cotton dress in favor of the dark fringed buckskin. It was a very flattering outfit for her slender body. He stood for a moment admiring her golden beauty before they discovered his presence. He watched with deep pleasure as Rebecca's eyes brightened when she saw him. He walked to her side as she rose, and looked down into her wide violet eyes. At that moment he felt as if he loved her more than he ever had before. Her golden braids hung down her back and fine wisps of wayward hair blew across her face. She seemed to glow with an inner light that sparkled from her violet eyes and bright smile.

"White Eagle," she said softly, "I am pleased to see you." She raised one arm to brush the hair from her face and he saw the bandage Cade had wrapped about it. Again he realized she had done this thing, taken the pain in silence, so she could be with him. His heart swelled within him, and with great effort he resisted the thought of reaching for her, to hold her for a moment.

"Rebecca, I would speak with you for a minute."

"Of course."

White Eagle cast a quick look at his sister, then grinning broadly, he took Rebecca's hand and began to draw her away.

"We will ride . . . out of the range of big ears."

"But I must help Snow Blossom," Rebecca protested.

"Go with him, Rebecca." Snow Blossom smiled. "We can finish the work later." She was satisfied at the pleasure in her brother's eyes as she watched them walk away.

Rebecca and White Eagle rode from the village. After about ten minutes, he drew his horse to a halt and dismounted. Together they walked, pulling their horses along behind them.

"You have something to say to me, White Eagle?"

"Yes. I have spoken to Long Arrow and he will get the permission from your father. We can be married tomorrow."

"Tomorrow!"

"Yes. I would like it to have been today, but that cannot be, and—" He stopped and looked down into her surprised face. His fingers lightly touched the smooth texture of her cheek. "I cannot wait any longer for I am afraid something might happen. I need you, Rebecca . . . now."

She was silent at the urgent sound in his voice; then she said quietly, "All right, White Eagle. If you desire it so, I will be ready. We will marry tomorrow, only—" She hesitated to say the words in her heart.

"Only," he finished, "you are still afraid I will take another wife. Rest your mind, Rebecca, I shall take no other but you. I will forsake that custom and I feel we shall both be happier because of it. We will share the rest of our lives together . . . only the two of us."

"You do much for my sake," she said. "I will always be grateful, White Eagle, because I know now that my love for you runs as deep as the river, and I can't change the course or the strength of it. I only know that some part of me would die if you turned to another. I want to be with you, stay with you, and I'll be a good wife, I swear. Especially when you have tried so hard to make the way easier for me."

"I love you, Golden One, and I have given much thought to the difference in our ways. I see no barriers between us that we cannot handle if we both try. I want you to know that surrendering the idea of another woman is not so difficult, for I find my thoughts are always filled with you."

"And mine are of you—always," she whispered as he drew her against him. He held her bound tightly against him and pressed his cheek against the softness of her hair, content, only for the moment, to hold her safe and secure in his arms.

When they came back to the camp, Rebecca went in search of Snow Blossom. She needed to learn the details of the wedding ceremony. She was in a state of absolute dismay when she found it usual for a bride to make the clothes in which her husband was married, and her own.

"Oh, Snow Blossom, what shall I do?" she cried in dismay.

"Come with me," Snow Blossom said, and she took Rebecca to her tepee. There she brought out a bundle. When she unwrapped it she brought out a piece of soft white buckskin.

"Oh, Snow Blossom, it is beautiful."

"It has already been cut for a shirt. If we work together the rest of the afternoon, and until time for the ceremony, we could make a shirt."

"I would be so grateful. I want White Eagle to know that I am trying to do things the way your . . . *our* people do."

"I'm sure he already knows." Snow Blossom smiled, then another thought struck Rebecca. "Snow Blossom, you were saving this for Cade, for your own wedding."

"I have time. I can make another. You are my sister and I would make the day of your wedding happy."

"I shall never forget you, dear Sister," Rebecca said softly, tears filling her eyes.

"Come, let us hurry."

Laboriously, they worked all afternoon and until late at night. The ceremony itself would not be until sunset that night, so they continued to work the next morning from the first break of dawn. Just after midday Snow Blossom pronounced the work not only finished, but a beautiful work of art.

It was heavily fringed on the underside of the arms and around the bottom. Across the back, they had created an eagle with its wings spread out of bright beads. There were beaded diamonds down both sides of the chest and about the neck. Rebecca had to agree it was very beautiful.

"Before we begin to prepare you, you must carry the shirt to White Eagle in his tepee. You must not enter, just present it to him and tell him . . . tell him exactly how you feel and why you give him this first gift."

"First gift?"

Snow Blossom laughed in delight. "I'm sure he plans on you giving him another gift later."

Rebecca blushed furiously, but could not contain her laughter at Snow Blossom's obvious amusement. Rebecca took the shirt and carried it openly over her arm as Snow Blossom had told her. It was obvious in the faces of the other women as she passed that they were extremely pleased with her acceptance of their ways and the obvious beauty of the shirt she carried.

At White Eagle's tepee, she stopped and in a soft hesitant voice, she called to him. It was probably the last thing in the world White Eagle had expected. He lifted the flap and walked outside, his eyes full of questions. A pleased smile crossed his face when he saw the shirt she carried.

"I bring you a gift, White Eagle. I hope it pleases you. I bring with it my respect and my love. I hope you'll wear it with pride, and that it brings you happiness."

He took the shirt from her and examined it, holding it so that the beauty of it could be seen by all. Slowly and elaborately, he examined it; then he smiled. "It is a beautiful shirt. I will wear it with pride. You will be a wife of which any warrior would be proud. It pleases me, Rebecca."

She smiled, turned, and left him watching her as she walked back to the tepee to prepare for the rapidly approaching ceremony.

Now Snow Blossom was in for a surprise. She had assumed Rebecca would be married dressed in the buckskin of her people. But Rebecca had saved a gown she had made a long time ago for the day she would be married. She created a beautiful compromise between her people and White Eagle's before Snow Blossom's stunned eyes.

After she had bathed she loosened her golden hair and brushed it until it glistened. She left it hanging in soft waves to her hips. She donned the white cotton dress. It had a high lace neckline and long full sleeves with lace cuffs. The waist was fitted and surrounded with a ribbon embroidered with flowers. The skirt hung full and had a narrow ruffle at the hem. Over her dress, she donned a white buckskin vest, fringed about the edges and beaded in small chains of beads up the front. From her bundle of surprises she took a soft leather headband and a large handful of white feathers. The headband she put about her head and on each side of it, extending down about her face, she put the feathers. The effect was as if her mass of golden hair was being held in place by a soft white cloud. Altogether, the effect was extremely beautiful. Her violet eyes bright, her cheeks pink from excitement, she made a beautiful picture and Snow Blossom told her so. They were finished with the preparations when the sound of softly throbbing drums came to them.

"I'm frightened," Rebecca whispered.

"Why?"

"I don't know. I guess I'm afraid I will disappoint him somehow."

"Don't be afraid, Rebecca. My brother is a good man. He will be a good husband. He is kind and I know he wants you to be happy. Just be as you are and I know you will not disappoint him."

"Thank you. I'm so grateful that you took after your brother. You're kind, and I thank you for all you have done for me."

Before Snow Blossom could answer, her name was called from outside.

"Your father and Long Arrow have come for you."

Rebecca nodded and together they stepped outside the tepee.

Outside Long Arrow held the reins of a beautiful black horse. It was elaborately decorated. Both Benjamin's and Long Arrow's eyes told her just how beautiful she was. Long Arrow lifted her to the horse's back and then taking the reins of the horse, they walked toward the same ceremonial tepee that the adoption ceremony had taken place in.

Outside, they lifted her from the horse and with Benjamin on one side and Long Arrow on the other, they went inside the tepee.

The tepee was lit by a brightly glowing fire. Across it Rebecca could see Tekata seated on a couch. Beside him stood White Eagle. He was dressed in the shirt which clung to his huge muscular frame. His hair was braided on each side of his face, and in each braid were several feathers that told of the bravery of the wearer. His stunned eyes devoured Rebecca's beauty as she was slowly led to his side. Once there, Long Arrow and Benjamin stepped back into the crowd and Rebecca and White Eagle stood alone by the glowing fire facing each other.

To White Eagle, it seemed as if Rebecca's golden beauty reached out and enfolded him in a cloud of flame. She was beyond any dream he could ever have dreamed and he was held breathless in gratitude to whatever power it was that brought her to him. Be it his gods or hers, he thought, he was grateful and he vowed silently to himself that he would try always to keep the look in her eyes he shared now—a look of deep and abiding love.

Tekata rose slowly and laboriously and Cade could see from where he stood that despite the tremendous pride he carried now, it was almost too much for him.

Slowly, he reached out and took his son's hand and Rebecca's hand. Then slowly he placed Rebecca's hand in White Eagle's. In a deep singsong voice, he told of the honor and bravery of White Eagle and the pride of his family. Then he spoke of the beauty and strength of the white girl, Rebecca, of her initiation into the tribe and her belonging to the family of Long Arrow, a man of great courage. Then he spoke of the joining of two such to honor their tribe with their children and to extend the life of Tekata into the future.

He spoke to the tribe in their tongue and Rebecca could not understand the words. The only thing she understood was that White Eagle's hand held hers tightly and his dark eyes held hers as if the words were coming from his heart to hers.

A warrior came to White Eagle as Tekata stopped talking and he placed about White Eagle's shoulders a cape made of beautiful feathers. It was a beautiful thing and it seemed to fit the man who wore it like a shield. He moved closer to Rebecca. Extending his arm with the edge of the cape held in his hand, he placed one arm about Rebecca's shoulder enclosing her within the cloak. They stood side by side as Tekata raised his hands over them. There were a few more spoken words and then a deep silence for several minutes.

White Eagle withdrew his arm. The cape was removed. White Eagle took Rebecca's hand and they turned to face the group. Drawing her with him, White Eagle walked from the tepee into the center of the village. A huge bonfire had been built and a large feast laid out.

A wild shout rang out and the celebration began. It was a celebration that would last the balance of the night—for all except White Eagle and his bride.

A few days before, White Eagle had gone several miles from the village. Near a gently murmuring stream he had erected a tepee. It was here he planned to take Rebecca as soon as the festivities reached their height and few would miss them. They ate, drank, and laughed with the others and when he was satisfied that no one would sense their leaving he drew Rebecca with him and walked to the horse he had waiting.

"Wait, White Eagle," she whispered and he was surprised when she ran back to her tepee and brought with her a small bundle. He mounted, reached down, and lifted her up in front of him. She relaxed against him as he kicked the horse into motion. She did not know where they were going, nor did she care. She felt safe in the circle of the strong arm that held her close. They rode in silence; she, with her head resting against his broad chest and he content to hold her so.

When they arrived at the tepee he slid from the horse and lifted her down beside him. She looked about her at the beauty and serenity of the place her husband had chosen for them to spend their first days together.

"Oh, White Eagle, how very beautiful it is here."

"I thought you might like it here." He smiled. "It is like you, quiet and gentle yet perfect in beauty." He said the words softly as he gently caressed the long silken strands of her hair.

In the pale light of the rising moon, they stood together. She felt his strength and knew the power of his huge muscular frame. Yet she sensed a gentleness that reached within her and touched a need that she could not name. She spoke his name softly as he bent his head and touched his lips to hers. Their kiss began as a feather-light touch and his arms closed about her, drawing her close. Slowly, the pressure of his lips on hers began to warm her trembling mouth. With a soft murmured sound of pleasure she slid her arms about his waist and relaxed against him as his mouth began to search hers for the answer to the hungry need that burned within him. And the answer came, sweet and clear, as her mouth parted and returned his kiss with an urgent need of her own.

He lifted his lips from hers and smiled down into her half-closed passion-filled eyes. His arms tightened about her.

"Come, you must see the tepee."

He led her to the doorway of the tepee, but stopped as she hesitated. He looked at her, searching her eyes for fear, but there was none. Instead, a soft smile was on her lips as she looked up at him.

"White Eagle . . . would you . . . would you give me a few moments alone?"

"Alone?"

"I . . . I would like—"

"Of course." He smiled, and stepped aside. She went inside closing the flap behind her.

He walked a few steps away and leaned against the tree. He looked up at the full moon and his mind echoed a silent prayer of thanks to the gods for such a gift. He stood so for quite some time absorbing the beauty of such a place and promising himself they would return here often to spend some time together.

Thinking of returning here brought his mind back to Rebecca. He had tentatively recovered from the idea that Rebecca was a gift from the sun god, but not completely. There was always an expectancy within him that he was reaching for something meant to be beyond him. He pushed the thought aside and walked to the door of the tepee. Pushing aside the flap he stepped inside.

Rebecca stood in the center of the semidark tepee. She had taken the feathers from her hair and removed the gown she was married in. In its place she had put on a pale-blue gown that hung loose and free about her. Her body could be seen like a pale shadow beneath the gown. White Eagle would have controlled the situation well had not the moon at that time chosen to touch the opened top of the tepee. A bright path of moonlight touched Rebecca and bathed her in its pale-gold light. He sucked in his breath and held it at the sight. If he had pushed aside the idea of a gift from the gods, he renewed it and it was frozen for all time within his heart. It was a gift and he was determined to accept it with thanks and gratitude.

He went to her and stood so close their bodies almost touched. He could see her eyes darken with the depth of her love.

"I love you, Golden One," he whispered as his arms closed about her and his mouth again sought hers. His mouth was hard and hungry. He had waited and wanted her too long to contain the need any longer. With a swift movement he bent and swung her up into his arms and buried his face in the soft curves of her breasts. He heard her soft gasp and felt her silken hair flow about him.

In three steps, he found the soft fur-covered couch and he sat down on it still holding her against him. His lips traced gentle kisses along the curve of her throat. He felt her cool fingers touch his face, holding her against him. He lay back on the couch drawing her with him. Rolling on his side, he pressed her down on the couch. In the light of the moon, he watched the way her hair spread against the dark fur. Her arms about his neck, she drew his mouth to hers again. The sound of their murmured sighs mingled as his hands pushed away the gown that was the only barrier between them. Her body, cool and soft to the touch of his hands became warm and alive. She moved to meet his touch as his hands found the soft curves and valleys that made her moan softly in pleasure. The path his hands discovered, his lips followed, until he felt her tremble with a need that was rising to match the one that almost consumed him. Quickly, he moved away from her for the few minutes it took to discard his clothes. When he pulled her into his arms again, their bodies surged against each other, demanding and possessive.

His heart filled with joy when he could feel the desire in her cause her to lose touch with reality and rise with him to the blinding summit of ecstasy. There was no retreat, no holding away. It filled her with a blinding flame and she searched with her lips, her hands, her body for release from this blinding all-consuming need.

At the height of their passion, when nothing in the world existed but the beauty of the deep-violet flame of their love, when her body writhed beneath him and her soft uncontrolled words of love urged him to possess her, when the need for fulfillment could be denied no longer, he lifted her hips to meet his thrusting body and he pressed himself deep within her, catching her soft murmured cry with his mouth. Gently, he moved her body to match the slow rhythm of his and he murmured her name as he felt her catch the rhythm, cling to him with silken legs, and begin to move with him.

Joyously, they surged together blending, clinging, feeling only the need each to consume the other, to draw the other within, to hold forever the bright glowing love that rocketed them heavenward to burst among the stars, and like a flaming meteor, to skim the heavens in a blazing beauty that left them tumbling together, holding to each other and knowing with a deep and everlasting finality that two were made one, and nothing outside of death would ever separate them again.

He held her against him, cradling her body with gentle arms as he regained control and listened to her ragged breathing and felt the trembling begin to ease. He had no words to say to tell her of how he felt, of the joy that bubbled within him, of the deep pleasure in knowing that she felt the same.

She lay within the circle of his arms and rested her head against his broad chest, hearing the soothing solid beat of his heart.

Safely enclosed in each other's embrace, they remained silent for some time. Slowly, Rebecca lifted her head and looked up into the dark, warm piercing eyes of the man she loved. She saw the reflection of her love and smiled. He caressed the side of her face, then let his hand slide into the depths of her hair. Drawing her lips to his he kissed her gently. "Loving you is a great joy, Golden One. I am grateful to the gods that I have you and I shall love and care for you forever."

With a deep contented sigh, she relaxed in his arms. She had never felt more at peace with the world than she did now. With no doubts and no fears, she knew she was where she belonged and where she would always want to be.

He held her as she drifted into a light sleep, and the late hours slowly faded into dawn. White Eagle was a habitual early riser. The first light of dawn always found him enthusiastic to meet it. It was no different now; in fact he was so filled with happiness he could not contain it. Worse, he had no intention of allowing Rebecca to contain it either. She slept soundly, curled against him for warmth. He smiled down into her sleeping face and gently tightened his arms about her. She stirred, mumbled his name, clung to him a little bit harder, and again drifted into sleep. He chuckled; very gently, he began to brush light kisses across her cheeks, her nose, her chin, and finally her soft unprepared lips. Her eyes blinked open in surprise, then half-closed as his mouth touching hers became insistent.

"Ummm," she murmured as she put her arms about his neck and moved her body against his.

Pleased with this reception, he tightened his arms enough to make her murmur in protest. He could feel her soft rounded breasts against his chest and the length of her long slender body against his.

"Are you awake?"

"I am now." She laughed.

"It will be a beautiful day."

"Yes," she said softly, "but all days with you will be beautiful."

"And all nights with you," he answered gently.

"Oh, White Eagle, I'm so very glad I married you. You're so strong, and I feel so very safe in your arms."

"You are safe, Golden One. You are mine and no one touches what belongs to White Eagle. I would protect you with my life."

"Yes . . . I am yours. It seems almost like a small miracle. We traveled so many miles. It seems almost impossible for us to have found each other."

"It was a thing that was meant to be. I knew of you before I saw you for the first time."

"Knew of me?"

"I saw you . . . in my vision."

"Vision?"

"Dreams. All but your face, but I knew you. I knew you were meant for me. Then, the day came that I saw you for the first time. I could not believe, that first day I saw you, but I wanted you then."

"No one would ever have guessed it," she said wryly. "You

always seemed to act as if you did not know I existed."

His eyes became deep and dark and he said in a quiet intent voice, "I was afraid. It is a thing I would admit to no one but you. I was afraid I could not have you and that I would make myself less than a man, a coward, a man of shame, by allowing my need of a woman to make me do something I could not live with. Rebecca, I shall tell you with honesty, if Snow Blossom had not found this way for us, if I had had to choose between you and the people who need me . . . I would have let you go."

She looked up into his eyes, her eyes soft with love for him.

"I know," she whispered. "Now that I know you, I realize what you face. I must tell you that I wouldn't have wanted to leave, I would have stayed with you, white slave, second wife . . . or anything you had chosen me to be. I love you, White Eagle, and I respect your strength. I only want to add to it, not take away from it. If," she hesitated and gulped back the threat of tears, "you decide you must take another wife—"

"No," he said firmly, "you are my woman. You will be the mother of my sons and they will follow me as chiefs of our tribe. After what we have shared," he said, his voice becoming gentle, "do you think I could ever want another woman? No, Rebecca, White Eagle has found the woman of his vision and he will never let her go as long as there is strength in his arm and the breath of life in his body."

Her eyes glistened with unshed tears as she drew his head down to hers and their lips met in a sealing kiss that bound them.

The fiery need for her leaped through his body as he knew it always would at her touch. He caressed the softness beneath him, enjoying the smooth velvet of her skin. Feeling her hands reach for him made him exultant for he knew that his need was reflected in her. Her hands caressed the broad muscular shoulders and the smooth skin on his back, urging him closer and closer as her hungry mouth parted under his. Slowly, leisurely, he sought to lift her with him. His strong hands and seeking lips changed her from a soft creature to a woman of blazing passion and need. He heard her soft murmur of encouragement, knowing she was unaware of them.

Pure exultant joy coursed through him as she sought, not to take, but to give, and he blended their bodies together molding them again into one flaming pulse of passion. They moved in the rhythmic beat of love that drew its source from the beginning of time and her body lifted to meet his, beat for beat, until they existed in reality no longer, but only in the throbbing pulse of their mutual love.

White Eagle had stocked the tepee well with everything they would need for the days they would be there—everything except meat for which he intended to hunt. They ate a quick breakfast and while Rebecca gathered and put away the balance of the food, her attention was drawn to White Eagle who stood in the entranceway of the tepee facing the morning sun. He stood with his gaze heavenward, his arms spread from his side in an attitude of supplication. She realized, not only that he was praying, but that he did it as habit and she realized it must be a daily occurrence. She smiled to herself, realizing the truth of her father's words, "We are not so very far apart." For in White Eagle's way he worshiped the same God as she, the one who created all things.

He turned as he finished and smiled across the small space at her, extending his hand. She went to him and he drew her into the shelter of his arm. He gestured with the other toward the beginning day.

"I have given thanks to the great sun god for this day. Let us go and see what he has given us."

She nodded and he grinned, knowing she was still too shy to tell him she needed a few minutes alone.

"I shall go and find a safe place for us to swim," he said and she blushed to know he had read her so well. With a quick smile he was gone.

When he came back for her about a half-hour later, he led her to a tree-shaded bank of the river. There they swam, cavorting in the water like children, laughing and playing. Then they lay on the bank, allowing the heat of the sun to dry and warm their bodies. She was warm and content as she lay near him half-drowsing in the sunlight. He turned and placed his hand on her hip.

"I do not want this sun to burn your skin; you are warm and your skin is bright. Come, let us dress and walk through the forest."

She stretched like a luxuriously overfed cat.

"I would be content to lie here all day. It's so warm and comfortable."

He chuckled and bent toward her, brushing her lips with his. "It is comfortable, but I am a greedy man. I do not want you to burn. I'm looking forward to my own comfort later in the night."

"Beast." She laughed. He stood up and extended a hand to her, drawing her up to stand beside him. Putting both arms about her, he hugged her tightly. His hands caressed her slim hips, pressing her tight to him. Then they dressed and walked slowly along the forest bed. White Eagle began the process of opening his world to her. He began to teach her the ways of the forest and the ways of survival. She learned of edible roots, and how to travel in the depths of the woods in a straight direction. As the days and nights passed, Rebecca began to look at her new husband with an ever-deepening sense of wonder and of love.

Sun-kissed days, lazing beside the river, wandering in the forest learning and enjoying their closeness, blended with wildly passionate nights made their time together a joy.

He taught her to shoot with a small bow he had made to fit her size and they hunted together, both laughing in happy pleasure when she finally shot a rabbit. They skinned the rabbit, cleaned, and ate it, then he took the rabbit skin and made her a pair of moccasins with the fur inside.

"They will keep you warm when the snow comes," he explained. "I will also make you a robe out of the coat of the beaver or the fox. When you walk in the snow it will protect you."

"And in a cold tepee," she said.

He smiled and put his arm about her and drew her close to his side.

"The coat will keep you warm outside"—he chuckled—"I will take care of keeping you warm inside."

Her skin became golden tan and her hair brightened under the sun and he enjoyed feasting his eyes on her rare beauty when she was unaware of his gaze. She would sit cross-legged on the ground beside the river while he fished, twisting the wild flowers into a chain. He watched her intent on what she was doing, her head bent forward with her golden hair, which he insisted she let free during their time alone, falling about her face. Love for her would course through him often, drawing him to her side just to reach out and touch, to realize again by her bright rewarding smile she was really his.

He dreaded the knowledge that their time alone was drawing to a close. If he could have had his way, he would have made a permanent home where he was and simply lived there alone with her, but responsibility called to him and he remembered how ill his father was and that at any time he might be needed.

But Rebecca had already begun to learn to read the face and the moods of her husband and that night she came to him.

"I have never been happier in my whole life than I have been for these three weeks," she said gently. She was lying beside him caressing gently the broad muscular chest. "But I know we must soon return home. There are others who need you. I would like to stay here with you forever, but I want you to know that I understand."

"It is only that I worry about my father. If anything should happen, I should be there," he said, the words almost an apology.

"Of course you should. I shall begin to pack our things in the morning. As for tonight," she added in a gentle whisper, "tonight you still belong only to me."

Without saying a word, he drew her across his body and buried his face in her throat. There was nothing in existence for them now but each other and he immersed himself in the depths of her love, feeling it close about him. "Always to you," he murmured.

The next morning, he assisted her in taking the tepee down and packing what belongings they had. As they rode away from the camp, Rebecca stopped her horse and looked back. She wanted the picture to hold in her mind forever; then she turned and her eyes caught White Eagle's. He smiled in response to what he read. Then they urged their horses forward again and headed them toward home.

It was long past midday when they came in sight of the village. They rode in and were overjoyed at the welcome they received. White Eagle was a well-loved leader and they were happy to share his happiness.

Cade and Snow Blossom, accompanied by Long Arrow and

Rebecca's father, were the first visitors to present themselves. Their greetings were warm and very welcome.

"How is my father?" White Eagle asked Cade when they were finally settled and Rebecca and Snow Blossom had gone to White Eagle's tepee to gossip and discuss future things.

"He has been extremely ill, White Eagle. His strength is rapidly going. He is a man of such courage he would never admit the truth, but I know he has been suffering a great deal of pain."

"I do not understand, Sun Knife. What is it that drains my father's strength?"

"A thing that neither the Indian nor the white man has a cure for. His heart is losing the battle for life. I am afraid one day soon, it shall simply give up the battle."

White Eagle's face was grim. But his eyes carried a deep sadness and a sense of loss for he had a great love and respect for the man who had always been the guide and the strength for him. White Eagle went directly to his father's tepee. As he raised the flap he was surprised to find Rebecca already there kneeling beside the old man's couch and holding one of his rough weathered hands in hers while she laughed gaily and chattered to him about all the plans for her and White Eagle's future.

"We will have sons one day soon, I hope, Father, and you must regain your strength so that you may teach them all they should know. I would not want them to miss the guidance of a man who was responsible for a man such as White Eagle. If you will help us guide them, Father, I know their future as men of honor and courage will be secure."

White Eagle was delighted by the bright light of pleasure in his father's eyes and the way the old man seemed to be drawing strength from the woman kneeling beside him. Again, as he had so often in the past weeks, he gave thanks to the gods who had seen fit to give him such a woman.

He went to her side and knelt beside her. He put out his huge hand and laid it over their hands.

His father's eyes held his, and he was eased with the knowledge that the blood of such a man would be extended into another generation.

Chapter Thirteen

Cade rode toward the fort to talk to Grant. He wanted to invite him to his wedding and to find out if there had been any word of when his father could be expected. The bride price paid and the day for the wedding set, Cade felt completely satisfied with thoughts of his future.

He chuckled to himself remembering how he had tried to explain the bride price to Rebecca's father who was unsure that it did not smack of selling one's children.

"It seems a very primitive idea."

"A brave does not 'buy' a bride, Benjamin," he explained carefully. "It is a thing that is done more to prove his worthiness as a son-in-law. He is trying to prove, the only way he can, that he is a good provider and will take good care of his wife and that he considers the woman he is getting very valuable. How else can he prove such things?"

"It is difficult for me to understand easily, young man. You all must bear with me. Your customs are so very different from ours."

"If you think the marriage customs are different, you should see the customs of divorce." Cade laughed.

"Oh?" Benjamin said wryly. "Tell me. I didn't know you have divorces."

"It is rare, but we do. If a man wants to divorce his wife, he simply takes a stick, goes to the center of the village where all can hear him and shouts 'I divorce this woman. I no longer want her.' Then he tosses the stick. If another man wants her, he simply catches the stick. It is a thing of great shame for a woman so you can see why divorces are few. Besides that"—Cade smiled—"the wife gets to keep all the horses and personal possessions."

Benjamin laughed. "And a woman, what does she do if she wants to divorce her husband?"

"Well," Cade replied, "she takes all of his personal belongings, dumps them outside their tepee and closes the flap."

"That's all?"

"That's all."

"Sounds extremely simple. Have you had many divorces?"

"I cannot remember any in my lifetime."

"Why do you think there have been none?"

"I would say it has much to do with a sense of honor. No man or woman could easily bear the shame that goes with being discarded. Especially a man who would not be able to face others after it had been announced he was a poor provider or a man who beat his wife. Yes, I guess marriage, like all other commitments, brings honor and pride."

He thought of those words as he rode along and thought he might have added that fact that marriage, to the Indians, meant not only a wife, but children. And of all his possessions, he valued his children the most.

When he arrived at the fort, he was met by Grant who seemed overly subdued and quiet. He rode through the doors of the fort aware that the eyes of everyone inside followed him. He was used to this, so he paid it no attention. When he dismounted in front of Grant's quarters, the door was opened before he could reach it. Grant held out his hand and Cade took it with a smile.

"I was told an Indian was riding this way. In fact, a cocky savage who expected the doors to open for him."

Cade chuckled.

"They got quite a shock," Grant added blithely, "when I told them it was the doctor I knew who was going to help me with some sick soldiers."

Now Cade laughed outright. "I can imagine how well that went over."

Grant stepped aside and ushered Cade in before Cade actually realized what he had said. "Sick soldiers? What's the matter with them? Where is your own doctor?"

"Doc's one of 'em. I don't think it's serious, but we have a few boys down with somethin'. Can you spare a day or two?"

"Yes, I can."

"Got a letter from your father for you." He took the letter from a case on his dresser and handed it to Cade who started to put it in his shirt.

"Go ahead and read it; what I have to say can wait."

Cade tore open the letter and scanned it swiftly. It contained nothing except to tell Cade when he could expect his arrival and the fact that he had sent a lot of equipment. It had not occurred to Michael to tell Cade in the letter that Lauren was accompanying him. Cade thrust the letter into his pocket, pulled out a chair, and sat down.

"What's been going on here since I've been here? You seem kind of quiet."

"Major Riles was transferred," Grant answered.

"Bad news?"

"Not that so much as the one we got to replace him."

"Who is he?"

"Maj. John Chivington."

"What's so bad about him?" Cade laughed. "Is he a disciplinarian?"

Grant's face was grim as he answered softly. "He's an Indian hater. He'd like to see every Indian from here to the sea dead."

Cade was speechless for a moment. "You're not exaggerating?"

"No. Why do you think you got such a quiet reception. I think most of my men have run across a few of your people from time to time as I have. The meetings were all very friendly. . . . I don't think there will be any more. The only reason I didn't ride out to meet you, to stop you, was because he found out you were a doctor and he feels he can . . . 'tolerate a savage' for a short time. Just time enough to use your services; then he'll find a way to kick you out."

"Grant . . . what's happening?"

"Territory is about to be opened I think. They're letting trappers through. Cade, for God's sake, warn your people not to let any incidents happen with any of the trappers moving about. I don't think there will be many and you can keep peace. Don't let this man have any excuse or he'll come down on your village like a tornado. I don't want to be ordered out. . . . I don't think I could obey a command like that. But he would.

He's a martinel and a man who's looking forward to a big political future and he doesn't care who pays the price—especially if they are Indian."

"Of all the times—" Cade began.

"Why?"

"Tekata is very ill. In fact he is close to death. White Eagle will have a very difficult time containing some of the hotheads if those trappers do anything foolish. If White Eagle could have just a little more time to fit the burden of leadership on his shoulders. A little more of his father's wisdom, and time to build his own family to keep him anchored. He has just been married to a—"

"To a what?"

"To a very beautiful woman."

Grant's eyes were intent on Cade.

"Is there something about this woman I should know? Something you're trying not to tell me?"

Cade found lying a difficult thing to do, especially to Grant who had been such a good friend to him.

"She's white."

Grant sat down as though his legs refused to hold him. "Good God, Cade, it's just the kind of thing this man needs to stir up a war."

Cade told him how Rebecca and her father had come to their village, how White Eagle and Rebecca had fallen in love and how her father had approved, and even blessed the union.

"She loves him, Grant, and he loves her. He will be a good, strong leader and she will be the quiet strength behind him, if they only have a chance."

"He'll never find out from me. I'll keep an eye out here, and you and White Eagle keep control out there. As long as there's no incident, no legitimate excuse, he can't do a thing and you can bet your bottom dollar, I'll make sure he has a damned good reason before he does anything."

"I'd best get back and talk to Tekata and White Eagle."

"Just take a look at my men and see the doctor, and you've got to meet our commander. He'd have my head on a plate if I let you go before he . . . looked you over."

"All right, let's look at the men first."

Grant nodded and took Cade to the makeshift hospital that had been set up to accommodate the number of men who had been stricken. Cade went from man to man and made a thorough examination. When it was finished, he prescribed some medicine, assured Grant that it was nothing serious, and suggested they go to meet the man whom he felt he should know and understand in case they should ever come to a conflict. They walked across the compound and were told to go right in since Major Chivington was expecting them. When Grant opened the door, Cade stepped inside and looked across the room at a man who would one day have a profound effect on Cade's life and the lives of his people.

"Major Chivington," Grant said, standing at stiff attention, "this is Dr. Holliday. He has already seen to the men, sir and assured us it is nothing serious."

Maj. John Chivington stood ramrod straight. He had the slim muscular build of a man who had seen many hours of physical endeavors. He was about fifty years old; his face was leather-tan and his hair a remarkable white with a full white mustache to match. He would have been handsome if it were not for his eyes, Cade thought. They were a strange color that seemed to waver between brown and gold, but they were the coldest eyes Cade had ever seen. They made the hair at the back of his neck prickle as though he had been touched by some evil lifeless thing. A strange premonitional feeling touched him. This man would let nothing in the world stop him from succeeding at anything he wanted and Cade felt he knew what he wanted—the death of the Indians.

"Dr. Holliday," he said, and his cold voice matched his cold eyes. He made no effort to extend the hand of friendship and Cade was not sure he would have taken it if he had. He did not like or trust him, and he was well aware the feeling was mutual.

"Major Chivington."

"You say my doctor will be well?"

"In a few days, he will be fine. I take it he has just recently been stationed here?"

"Within the month, why?"

"It's just a thing that seems to strike newcomers to this area. He will be fine."

"This area," the major said in disgust, "is fit only for wild animals and savages. I intend to help change that."

"Why not," Cade said softly, "leave it to the . . . savages and take your men back to . . . civilization where they belong?" He could sense Grant stiffen and he regretted the words as soon as they left his lips.

"I would expect a man who has such blood not to understand, but I thought you might have gained some insight in how decent people lived in your short stay with the white man. I see I was wrong. No matter how much you polish the outside you cannot remove the ignorant savage from the tainted blood."

Cade felt such rage he could barely contain himself from striking the man. Instead of doing that he smiled.

"I've tried both worlds and for civilized people I will take the Indian every time. At least he has to have provocation to kill."

"He is a beast, and as a beast, he will be eliminated so that decent civilized men can live in this country. I thank you for seeing to my men. If your visit here is complete, I suggest you leave. And I suggest you warn your people that I will tolerate no infraction of the law . . . none."

"And you'll be looking closely," Cade replied softly.

Major Chivington smiled and his eyes became even colder. "Very, very closely."

Cade would not make things deliberately more difficult for Grant. Without another word, he turned and left the room. Outside he stood in the sun realizing he was trembling with fury and his hands were clammy with sweat. He waited, and a few minutes later Grant joined him.

"If it wouldn't cause the complete annihilation of every Indian village around here, I would like to see some warrior hang his scalp from his war lance," Grant said angrily.

"For the first time in my life, I felt the urge to deliberately kill a man," Cade said, his voice vibrating with the anger he felt.

"Come to my quarters and have a drink with me," Grant offered.

"All right, one quick one. I want to start for home. I have to tell Tekata what is happening. White Eagle will have to talk to his people. I don't want them giving that man any reason to come after them. There's no more mercy in that man than in a rattlesnake."

They walked across to Grant's quarters and after Grant poured the drinks, he handed one to Cade and he smiled. "You came here for a reason, Cade, what was it?"

"I came, old friend"—Cade laughed—"to invite you to my wedding."

"Wedding?" Grant said, his eyes lighting with pleasure. "Who's the lucky girl?"

"White Eagle's sister, Snow Blossom."

"Snow Blossom, you've good taste."

"The best, my friend, the best."

"When's the wedding?"

"The end of the month . . . about two and a half weeks."

"I have some time due me. I think I'll come out in about a week or so and stay for the wedding."

"My mother would be pleased to have you as a guest and I'm sure Tekata and White Eagle will have a million questions to ask."

"I wouldn't miss your wedding for anything. You can look forward to sending a scout out to guide me; only don't let him come into the fort. I'll have a watch kept for him. Have him stay at the edge of the forest. It will be safer for him."

"All right."

"Cade . . . I have to say something, something that scares the hell out of me."

"What?"

"When Major Riles was transferred I had a feeling somebody in Washington was beginning to breathe heavy. I think someone sent Chivington here for a very special reason, and I think I know what it is."

"What do you know, Grant?"

"Chivington used to be stationed at Fort Bradley. It was somewhere south, anyway; he took his wife and two kids with him. He was heavy-handed then, and he was facing Comanches."

"Comanches don't know the words surrender or fear, but they wouldn't have attacked a fort first. What did he do?"

"I'm not sure of all the details." Grant sighed. "All I know is he was responsible for the hanging of the local chief's two young sons. Said they were caught stealing."

"Hanging?" Cade said in shock. "Why hanging?"

"He knew it would be the final blow that would incite the chief to attack . . . it was a success. The chief attacked, Chivington called in all kinds of forces—in short, he killed the chief and wiped out three-fourths of his village . . . most of which were women and children. It seems the man has a firm belief that all Indians should be killed for, as he says, the young boys grow into the men and the young girls bear the children and you must stop the flow of the river at the source."

"That's not all, is it?" Cade asked softly.

"No, it seems the chief had a brother. The brother gathered all the warriors from the camps all around the territory. When he attacked the fort, they had no chance. He took Chivington and his family as prisoners. His wife and children were tortured to death and Chivington would have died too, except he was rescued at the last minute. He hates all Indians with an undivided passion. He doesn't care what tribe they come from. Do you see, Cade, why I tell you that you must walk carefully. It doesn't matter to him who your father was. He hates you and every man, woman, and child with Indian blood, and he'll wipe them out if you give him one small spark of a reason."

"Grant, I'll do my best to see that we have no contact. My father should be arriving soon. He'll know more about what's happened. Maybe then, we can help keep control of this situation."

"I'll be watching for him."

"Good," Cade said. He rose from his chair and set his empty glass on the table. "I'd best be on my way; about ten days, I'll send a guide."

"I'll be waiting." Grant smiled. "I'm looking forward to seeing you get married."

"See you the end of the month, Grant." Cade laughed as he extended his hand and Grant took it in a firm friendly grip.

As he rode home, Cade turned Grant's words over and over in his mind and he came to one final conclusion. He would do anything in his power to keep his people from following the path the Comanche had taken to Chivington's mercy.

He was about a mile from the village, just cresting a hill, when he heard the clatter of a horse coming toward him. He pulled his horse to a halt and waited; then his face lightened with a broad smile as Snow Blossom rode toward him, her face bright and flushed with the pleasure she always found when she saw him.

"This is the nicest welcome committee I've ever had." He laughed. "And I must say it's the prettiest one, too."

"I've been waiting for you. I thought it would be nice if we rode back together."

"It certainly would be."

"Did you see your friend at the fort?"

"Yes, I did."

"Will your father be coming soon?"

"He'll be here in time for our wedding, and I think then I'll have everything in the world a man needs to make him happy." He said the words softly as he turned to look at Snow Blossom.

He was rewarded by the bright light of happiness in her eyes and the quick reach of her hand toward his. He took it and they rode along slowly, letting their horses drift side by side.

"Tell me how things have been at home."

"Oh, Cade, White Eagle and Rebecca are so very happy with each other they hardly know there's anyone else in the village." She laughed. He laughed in response more to her happiness than anyone else's.

"It's a warm day," he said gently.

"Yes."

"It would be nice to go down to the river and sit in the shade of a tree. We could even swim."

He watched her face soften when their eyes held and she nodded her assent.

They rode to the river and hobbled their horses so they would not wander far. He took her hand in his and they walked along the sandy shoreline for a while. He put his arm about her slender waist and she rested her head against his shoulder.

"I love you very much, Snow Blossom; you know that, don't you?"

"I know, Sun Knife." She smiled. "But it is good to hear you say it again . . . and again and again." She giggled as he tightened his arm about her in a laughing ferocious hug. She turned to him and put her arms about his neck as he lifted her from her feet to hold her tight against him; then he kissed her in a most thorough fashion—thorough enough that she murmured soft approval. He let her slide slowly down his body until her feet touched the ground, but he continued to hold her close to him.

"The time goes so slowly, it seems so long until we stand in the council tepee and hear the words that will make you my wife. I wait, but not with much patience. I've tasted, and the taste has filled me with a fearsome hunger—a hunger to possess you, hold you, love you for the rest of our lives."

"And I, my love," she whispered, "suffer from the same hunger. Only I have suffered more years than you. I am even more impatient to belong to you."

"My dear love," he whispered as he took her lips with his in a shattering kiss that left her weak and trembling in his arms and him aflame with the burning need for her.

With a quick bend of his knees, he lifted her in his arms holding her tight. He carried her to the deep cool shade of a tree and they sat together on the ground.

With gentle hands, he held her face and softly kissed her brow; then her cheeks. She closed her eyes as he touched them lightly and then his mouth drifted down to hers. Slowly, gently, a soft sigh spoke of her surrender. She felt the cool grass beneath her as he laid her back on the ground and his hands slid to the hem of her skirt and touched the soft velvety skin of her thighs.

Seeking hands removed the barriers of their clothes as she joined him in the passion that had begun to build. The feel of her body, cool against him, was a pleasure he intended to savor for a while. He held her, letting one hand slowly caress her soft skin.

"If I could just hold this magic moment forever, Snow Blossom, maybe in that much time I could find a way to tell you just how much I adore you." His lips discovered her slender throat, smooth rounded shoulder, and round firm breasts that trembled under his seeking lips. Unhurried, they sought to learn the touch of the white flame that began to lift them. Her hands caressed the lean rippling muscles of his arms and back as he in turn discovered the sweet taste of the loveliness he held. Eliciting soft sounds of pleasure from her, his lips continued their journey of discovery.

She writhed in his arms, her body seeking his, knowing the answer to this burning need lay with him. But he wanted to carry her with him, to share with her the passion that sent searing tongues of flame that threatened to consume him. Controlling the deep need for her that grew within him, he sought to give, not to take. He absorbed with deep pleasure the way she clung to him, the words of wild encouragement that she was unaware of. He heard her soft moaning sobs as his lips touched the center of her pulsing flame. Her body trembled beneath his and he could contain his need no longer. He lifted her hips gently and sheathed himself deeply within her. Silken legs enfolded him and soft hands pulled him closer. She moved with him as the flame licked to a white heat and burst about them, leaving them only each other in the great void of desire that enclosed them. There was no tomorrow, no yesterday, only now. Now and the beauty they shared.

They lay side by side, holding on to each other's hands, silenced for the moment at the wonder they had just shared. He turned on his side and as their eyes met, she smiled a soft dreamy smile of pleasure that crept to the heart of him where it would live forever.

"You have added to the fire that will always burn within me, Snow Blossom. Now, having you a million times will never be enough."

He looked at the sweet beauty of her and suddenly he became afraid, afraid a man with cold eyes in a fort many miles away could separate them, harm them and those they loved, in fact kill them. It struck him so fiercely that he drew her into his arms and rocked her tightly against him.

She sensed his urgency immediately. "What is it, Sun Knife? What makes you fear? Is it for me . . . for us?"

Quietly he explained to her how he felt and what had transpired at the fort. She shuddered at the story of the killings, but said nothing until he finished.

"He is an evil man," she whispered.

"Not only evil, he is powerful. Unless you have been to the white world as I have, you've no idea what a reserve of men and arms he has. We are disorganized and unprepared to meet such a force; I doubt if we will ever be. You see how important it is for us not to come to conflict here. We would be playing directly into his hands."

"My brother is a very brave man."

"In this case, Snow Blossom, it is not a matter of bravery. It is a matter of trying to keep the peace against incredible odds, and to help his people survive against a man who is dedicated to eliminating them. One mistake on his part can cost the lives of many. No, it is not bravery, it is a kind of inner strength and a great amount of cleverness. He's going to need every ounce of help and encouragement he can get, from all of us."

"Don't you think my brother can do this thing?"

"Of course I believe in him . . . but Snow Blossom, he fights with honor. Chivington does not. The most difficult thing facing us is to make an honorable man like White Eagle think like the man he faces. For White Eagle that will be the difference between protecting his people and bringing peace or having them herded like animals to a reservation where their freedom-loving souls will die."

"I have heard of the reservation." She shuddered. "I do not think I could exist there either."

He looked down into her wide dark trusting eyes. "Don't you know," he said softly, "I would have to be dead before I would let a man like Chivington touch you. Together, we are strong. My father comes soon, and with him comes a kind of force Chivington will understand. We will make a force that he will have to recognize."

She smiled and put her arms about his neck. "Yes, my warrior, always it will be us against the world. With you and your father our people will find the strength to stand. But know this, warrior, you are my strength always. As long as you love me, as long as I can feel your strength in my arms, I will be happy."

"And I will love you," he replied as his lips touched hers, "until there is no breath in my body."

They shared a new knowledge of each other, and a strength

that lifted their love beyond anything they had ever known before.

The day grew older and they did not want to leave the place where they had found such love. It was already close to sunset when they mounted their horses and rode to the village.

After Cade had eaten supper he went to Tekata's tepee. After he requested permission to enter, he found Benjamin there. The two older men, so very different in culture and beliefs, had found themselves understanding each other. Each tried to gain knowledge of the other and finding that rewarding, had continued on to develop a friendship.

The occasions of conversations between them were enlightening to say the least, and sometimes amusing, as when they came to verbal conflict over how many gods there were. Benjamin would chuckle when Tekata, acting as a gracious host, smiled condescendingly at what he thought was Benjamin's naïveté in believing in only one god.

"The son is very much like the father," Benjamin said to Cade as he entered. "He is a stone wall against which no force can prevail."

"Do I not bend, white one?" Tekata said, the soft glow of humor in his eyes. "Do I argue with you when you speak of your one god? Do I not let you believe as you want to believe?"

"Meaning"—Benjamin laughed—"that it is I who will not bend. Maybe you are right, but I would like to discuss it and other matters with you again."

"You are most welcome in the tepee of Tekata," the old man replied with grave dignity, but his eyes twinkled with humor.

It is good for him, Cade thought. He waited until Tekata and Benjamin finished speaking and Benjamin had left before he spoke of what was happening.

"Sit, my Son."

Obediently Cade sat close to Tekata, for he did not want his words to carry to ears that might spread the word and create fear before Tekata had had some time to think of what he would do. Tekata listened in silence, his eyes seeming to hold something at a distance.

"Maybe," Cade said hopefully, "we could move the village farther west. Find a place the white man does not know. It would take Chivington a long time to find us and we would be far enough away from him that he could not send men out without them dying."

"Listen to me well, Sun Knife. It is no use for a man to try to outrun his destiny. It is better for him to stand and face the wolves like a man. Even if he is brought down, they will know they were fighting a man of courage, not one who runs. We should try to gather the tribes of our people together. Maybe in that way, we will hold off the flood of whites a little longer. I have seen, as have others, the white force that comes. In what time I have, I shall try to tell my son. The time has come for us to face what the Great Spirit has ordained for us. For me, it will not matter; but for my son, his children, and all the children that follow, it will be a heart-breaking thing. There is no place to run, so we will stand here, and we will survive. One day, you, your children, White Eagle, and his children will have to hold our people together with the force of your wills. This is the thing I seek from you. Combine your will with my son's. Together you will help what is left of our nation to survive." His eyes held a depth of sadness that Cade could not stand.

"I will do all that I can, Father."

"Yes, I know. Soon, you will marry my daughter. I welcome you not only as a son-in-law, but as a medicine man and a warrior. I have seen, Sun Knife, a long future for you and my son. You will be the ones that finally help overcome the white man's presence in a land to which he does not belong." He reached out his hand and gripped Cade's arm. Cade was surprised at the strength in it. "When a tragedy strikes, the strong survive and their will to live leads them to rebuild . . . to change. The tragedy is come, but the strong will is here. We may change, but we will survive."

When he returned to his tepee, he was exhausted and he went immediately to his couch and fell into a restless dream-filled sleep.

In the next few days, he talked with Tekata often, and he realized White Eagle was at his side also.

A few days after his return from the fort, he took a young warrior, Leaping Bear, aside and asked him to go to the fort and to guide Grant to the village.

"Camp on the edge of the forest; Grant will be looking for you. Above all, do not go to the fort. I want no incidents to set fire to this situation."

Leaping Bear nodded agreement. Then he mounted his horse and left. Cade watched him leave and knew he would live in an agony of suspense until he returned.

Cade had given much thought to what they would do after the wedding. It was a usual occurrence that a brave found a nice secluded spot, built a tepee and made it a nice comfortable place for him and his bride to spend the first few days of their married life.

Cade decided to do the same, so he spent three days finding the place he thought would be perfect. It took him another day to erect the tepee, and supply it with all the things he thought they would need. Satisfied, he returned to the village. Now came the hard part for Cade, the few interminably long days until the wedding.

He spent the days checking over the health of the tribal members although they were decidedly abundant with good health. He hunted, spent long hours with Benjamin and Tekata, and as much time with White Eagle as he would spare from Rebecca.

The time finally narrowed down to two days and Cade began to wonder where Leaping Bear was—and Grant. He had risen early in the morning and had eaten; then he decided it was time to take inventory of his supplies and his surgical equipment. It would keep his mind busy and off Snow Blossom until the wedding day.

He was sitting with a small case of tools open before him. Carefully he cleaned each one and replaced it in its proper place in the case. It had been so long since he had used them. He held his hand out before him. It was steady, the palm wide and the fingers long and slender. Would he ever have the chance to use them again? He was so engrossed in his thoughts that Snow Blossom, who stood outside, called to him several times before the sound of her voice registered in his mind. He rose swiftly and went outside. She stood waiting and he knew why she was there. Over her arm, she carried the clothes she had made for him. It was a custom, and he knew she would have spent many long hours working on them. They would be observed by every woman in the tribe.

"I have brought you a gift, Sun Knife," she said softly. "I

hope it will please you." She held it out to him.

As often as Cade had seen this done before, as many wedding clothes as he had seen laboriously made, he had never seen one before that was as beautifully made as this one was. The deerskin from which it was made had been tanned and worked until it was feather-soft to the touch. The pants had fringe down each leg. The top had the sign of Cade's vision in fine beadwork on the back. The design was done in bright beads which contrasted beautifully against the ivory color of the shirt. There was heavy fringe down each arm and on each side of the row of fringe was an intricate design worked in the same minute beads. A border across the chest consisted of a fine row of beads and below it another row of soft colorful feathers. Altogether it was a beautiful work of art that he knew had required a tremendous amount of labor on her part—labor and love. She may have been proud of it, but no sign showed on her face. Solemnly he took it from her and held it so that he could be sure every watching eye could get a good view of it.

"Snow Blossom, I will be very proud to wear this thing of great beauty. It would make the shabbiest man look like a brave and noble warrior. You are a woman of great ability and you will bring pride and honor to my lodge."

His eyes were warm with love as he spoke to her, and she felt her eyes sting with tears of pride and happiness.

Without another word, she turned and walked back to her father's tepee. Her head held high with pride, she walked with her beautiful free and easy stride. "I am Snow Blossom, daughter of a great chief," her walk said proudly.

Cade was about to turn back to his door when he looked out toward the horizon and was surprised to see Leaping Bear riding toward him.

He waited until Leaping Bear entered the village and rode up to Cade. He dismounted, a wide smile on his face.

"Leaping Bear, where is my friend, Grant?"

"He comes, Sun Knife."

"You had no trouble at the fort?"

"No, no trouble. We had to wait for the big tepee on wheels to be packed."

"Big tepee . . . a wagon?"

"Yes . . . a wagon."

"Why did Grant need a wagon?"

"To pack all the things," Leaping Bear said with extreme patience as if he were explaining something difficult to a child.

Cade laughed. "All right, Leaping Bear, just what did Grant have to pack that he couldn't put in a saddlebag? He's only staying a few days."

"It was not what he was packing of his own, it was the things he was packing for your father."

"My father is here!" Cade said in an excited voice.

"Yes. It is why the blue shirt did not come sooner."

"I shall ride out to meet him. My thanks, Leaping Bear."

Leaping Bear nodded and went to his own tepee. Cade walked swiftly to the tepee of Tekata. There he requested permission to enter. Inside, he quickly asked Snow Blossom if she would like to ride with him to meet his father.

"Your father is returning now?" Tekata asked him.

"Yes, he is not far from the village. With your permission, my Chief, Snow Blossom and I will meet him and bring him to you."

"Yes, yes, my Son. Go quickly. It will be good to see our friend again."

Cade took Snow Blossom's hand and went to find his mother who was gathering firewood.

"Mother," he said as he gently took the bundle of firewood from her hand, "my father has returned. He is not far from the village. Will you ride with me to meet him?"

Waterflower gasped in surprise and her eyes filled with tears. "Michael," she murmured.

"Come, Mother," Cade said. She moved quickly to the horses and the three of them left the village.

As they crested the first hill, they saw the huge wagon headed their way. It stopped and Cade could see his father jump from the wagon and start toward them. With a cry, Waterflower slid from her horse and ran toward the man she had loved for so long. Cade and Snow Blossom smiled at each other when they saw Michael grab Waterflower up in his arms, laughing and kissing her.

Chapter Fourteen

Grant had been watching for his guide and spotted him immediately. The last thing he wanted was for him to come to the fort so as soon as he knew from the spiral of smoke from the campfire that he had prepared to wait, he went out.

Leaping Bear was a man of about eighteen years. He was an easy-dispositioned person who found pleasure in most things in his life.

He had reached that point in his life among his tribe when he would step from boyhood to manhood. He had already made his journey into the wilderness, and slung on the side of his horse was a shield bearing the symbol of a huge bear, claws outstretched and teeth bared. He was destined to take part in the next okipu ceremony, and his eyes had already fallen upon a pretty young maiden among them. Her name was Little Bird, and they had tentatively reached for each other, speaking when the rare opportunities came to do so. The only thing that troubled Leaping Bear was to gather together the bride price. Her parents, Great Horse and Laughing Water, had valued her high, which was very proper in his mind for he did also, but the gathering of it had been a long and tedious thing and his great fear was that someone else would be able to pay the price before he could and he would lose her forever.

He was sitting before his fire nibbling on the rabbit he had roasted and thinking about Little Bird when Grant approached. Leaping Bear's astute hearing had told him Grant was coming long before he saw him. He rose to meet him and invite him to sit at his fire and talk, and Grant smiled at the very proper manners, for he obviously held Cade in great esteem and would therefore extend to a friend of Cade's all the hospitality and good manner he knew.

"I am Grant Jameson. I believe you came to guide me to your village?"

"Yes. I am Leaping Bear; Sun Knife has sent me to bring you for his wedding to our chief's daughter."

Again Grant heard the depth of respect in the way Leaping Bear said Cade's name and for a minute, he envied all that Cade seemed to possess.

"It will be another day or two before my chief gives me permission to leave. You will wait?"

Leaping Bear shrugged his shoulders and smiled. "It is no difficulty to wait. I am by nature a very lazy man and lounging by my fire and eating while I wait for you will not be a problem."

Grant laughed, for he knew there was probably not a lazy bone in the boy's body. And that he would probably rove the area around the fort until he knew every inch of the ground.

"Good; I shall meet you here as soon as I can." When Grant returned to the fort, he began to pack not only what he would take for himself, but the few gifts he had bought for Snow Blossom and Cade's wedding.

For Snow Blossom, he had brought things he knew she would need, a set of sharp-bladed knives and two iron cooking kettles for there were few of them among the Indians. Usually they had built a tripod over a fire and hung meat to roast, or if cooking a stew, had used an imaginative device by tying the four ends of a buffalo's stomach to the poles; then to make it boil they dropped in hot stones, about fist size, that were heated on the fire. He knew she would appreciate the gifts. For Cade he had brought other things and he knew also the need Cade would have for them. Three repeating rifles and two hand guns were wrapped securely and secretly for he knew Chivington would never have let him out of the fort with them. He hated the idea of such gifts, but more, he hated the reason for the need of them.

He went to sleep the following night in readiness for leaving the next morning. It was just after dawn when his orderly shook him awake.

"Lieutenant Jameson, sir."

"What is it?"

"Major wants you in his quarters, sir, as soon as you can. We have some guests, sir . . . a . . . Dr. Michael Holliday."

Grant was on his feet in a minute and reaching for his clothes. Within half an hour he was walking rapidly across the compound to the major's quarters. As he approached, he could tell by Michael's stiff shoulders and cold eyes that he and the major had already locked horns.

"I'll be leaving as soon as possible," Michael said. "I should prefer to be anywhere but in this fort with people so prejudiced they think other people should die for their benefit."

"I repeat my advice, Dr. Holliday. Don't encourage those savages to do anything foolish. My job is to keep this area peaceful and I intend to do it to the best of my ability. There will be no margin for mistakes."

"Don't worry, Major Chivington, your reputation is well-known to me. I have no intention of making a mistake myself or letting my people do so."

"Your people? . . . hardly, Dr. Holliday."

"Yes, Major, *my* people. I intend to live among them the balance of my life. Major . . ." he began softly, "I am not a man of threats. I have a great many friends in Washington. Now, I want no trouble with you, but if it comes to trouble I would not hesitate to use every friend I have in any way I feel necessary. We want to live in peace. Leave us be and you will have no problem with any of my people, that I promise you."

Major Chivington was angry but he contained it well. Only his eyes spoke of the violent hatred he felt.

"Then I've your word of honor, Doctor, that your people will cause me no problems?"

"As long as you cause them none."

"Agreed, Doctor, but if they step out of line once . . . just once, I shall make an example of them that will thoroughly impress every other tribe in the territory. Now, I see another of your kind has come to join you. I hope you both have a safe trip."

Grant paid no attention to the last thrust at him; instead he extended his hand to Michael.

"Welcome back, Doctor. I know there are a great many people anxiously awaiting you. If it pleases you, we can be on our way immediately. I have a guide waiting for us."

"Thank you, Grant. I must say it is good to see you again."

"Thank you, sir. I've horses ready; would you like to leave now?"

Michael nodded, said a quick good-by to Major Chivington and he and Grant left the major's quarters.

"What a cold-eyed bastard he is," Michael said.

"I agree. Dr. Holliday, I would suggest that you be very careful with him. He is a man filled with hatred."

"Don't worry, son. When I leave this fort, I doubt if Major Chivington and I will ever cross paths again."

Michael laughed, but Grant was not so very sure.

"We'll need a wagon," Michael said.

"Why?"

"I'm not traveling alone."

"Oh, you've brought friends with you?"

"Well not exactly a friend of mine, more a friend of Cade's."

"Someone from medical school?"

"No, Lauren is the daughter of an old friend of mine."

Grant had a sudden suspicion that this "old friend" was going to be rather upsetting to Cade. He would have questioned Michael further, but they had reached the room that had been provided for Lauren. Michael knocked and the door was opened by what Grant thought was the most beautiful woman he had ever seen in his life.

"Grant, this is Lauren Brent; Lauren, this is one of Cade's best friends, Grant Jameson."

"Hello, Lieutenant Jameson."

"Hello, Miss Brent. You are a good friend of Cade's?"

She smiled. "We were just a little more than that. Cade and I were once engaged to be married. We've had a . . . ah . . . misunderstanding. I would like to change that if possible."

Grant was stunned. He didn't know what to say, but he knew sometime between now and the day they reached Tekata's village he would have to tell her. He just couldn't let her walk into Tekata's village just in time to see Cade marry another woman.

Grant invited them to join him for a meal before they left. While they ate and changed their clothes he had the wagon packed and prepared for travel.

They left the fort just after noon. Grant was amused at

Lauren's first reaction to Leaping Bear, and even more amused at his reaction to her. He acted the part of a young gallant more effectively than any dandy Grant had ever seen before. Leaping Bear went out of his way to make Lauren's trip comfortable.

They had been on the trail for three days before Grant got the opportunity he was looking for. The four of them sat about the campfire after a late meal chatting. Michael was the first to claim he was tired and he went to his bedroll which was only a few steps away beneath the shade of a tree. Lauren slept in the wagon and Leaping Bear and Grant slept under it. Leaping Bear followed Michael to bed in a few minutes leaving Grant and Lauren alone. Neither of them spoke for a few minutes, then Lauren said in a quiet voice, "Grant, is there something you think is wrong about my being here? Somehow my presence seems to upset you."

"No, Lauren, what makes you think that? It's not often one gets to travel out here with a woman as beautiful as you." He grinned. "It's enough to unnerve any red-blooded man, and I assure you, madam, I'm as red-blooded as any man."

"I thank you for the compliment," she answered softly. "Now tell me the real reason."

Grant's smile faded. "Lauren, it would have been best if you had stayed at the fort until Cade could have come to talk to you."

"Why?"

He hesitated. "I was leaving to go to Tekata's village before you and Cade's father came."

"To visit with Cade?"

"Not exactly."

"Then why? From the way your commander talks of Indians, I wouldn't think he would want you visiting among them."

"He couldn't have stopped me on this occasion."

"What occasion?"

He sighed, staring at the fire so he would not have to meet her eyes, then said quietly, "Cade's wedding."

She was silent and he looked up to find her eyes wide with shock and her face drained of all color.

"Cade's wedding?"

"He's marrying Chief Tekata's daughter, Snow Blossom. She's a beautiful woman."

"When?"

"In a few days. Lauren, I should have told you to stay at the fort."

"No, I would not have stayed anyway. Tell me about Snow Blossom."

"What can I say, Lauren? She's beautiful, she's a fine woman—and she belongs here."

"And I don't?"

"Lauren, you're a lady who's been raised among the best that money could buy. Life out here is different. There are no luxuries, in fact all there really is is a lot of hard work. The Indians are slowly going to be driven from this land to reservations. I know it, Michael knows it, and so does Cade. Cade wants to make this transition as easy for his people as he can. At the risk of hurting you, I will tell you that Snow Blossom is the woman he needs to stand with him. She is strong and her people respect her father, her brother White Eagle, who will be the next chief, and her. She can be of great help to him. Lauren, I think it would be easier for you to let Leaping Bear take you back to the fort and get an escort back home."

"Easier for whom, me or Cade?"

"For both of you. I don't know what happened between you, I only know that Cade and his medicine are needed here, desperately needed. Tell me, Lauren, deep in your heart, would you be happy living out here, in a tepee? Away from everything you know . . . music, books, good food, parties?"

"But we wouldn't have to stay out here always. We could visit New York from time to time."

"That will never happen. Cade will never leave his people again. He'll spend the rest of his life trying to build a hospital and educate their children so they can survive the white flood. You're trying to hang on to your old life and have this one, too. The day will come when you'll really have to choose. Think about it, Lauren, don't you think you'd best choose now before you cause a very serious problem?"

He rose with those words and left her beside the fire to think about all that he had said.

And Lauren did think . . . she thought about how much she still loved Cade and how much she had tried to change. But she knew she could not forsake her past life permanently. She still felt it would be possible to have both if she played her cards right. After they arrived at the village, there would still be a few days left in which she could get Cade to change his mind.

"Snow Blossom," she murmured, "princess of an Indian tribe. Let us see if you can hold him now that you have him. I can offer him more than you can. We will see, princess, just how strong your hold really is."

She thought for a long time, and the fire was dying into red embers when she went to the wagon and slept.

She was up early the next morning and took the first opportunity to talk to Grant alone.

"Grant, I gave a lot of thought to what you said last night. I imagine most of what you said was right, but I want to go on to the village. I would like to see the wedding and since I am an accomplished nurse, I feel I can be of some help to Dr. Holliday—both Drs. Holliday."

She smiled, and her eyes were bright, yet Grant could not shake the nagging thought that there was more brewing in her mind than nursing sick Indians. He wondered just how much of a problem she would be for Cade and Snow Blossom.

As they came closer and closer to the village, Michael became more tense. After all these years to see his beloved Waterflower again. In his mind's eye, he could still see her as she as the day he had left. It was a picture he had always held. Now, he wondered if she remembered him as well. If anything would be different, he knew that his love for her was as deep and lasting now as it had been before. When they were less than a day's ride from the village, he sent Leaping Bear ahead. The wagon rolled on slowly. To Michael, it seemed it had never moved slower. He was in deep thought when Grant's voice broke in.

"Look, sir . . . there's Cade."

Michael looked up at the crest of the hill ahead of them. He saw his son, but his eyes were on the slender woman who slid from her horse and started toward him. He leaped from a wagon that to him moved entirely too slowly and ran to her.

His outstretched arms lifted her against him. Half-laughing, half-crying, he heard her say his name over and over as he crushed her to him. His lips found hers in a kiss that bridged the years. He kissed her again and again, capturing her face between his hands. He laughed exultantly . . . he was home.

He paid no attention to anything until the wagon stopped beside him and Cade and Snow Blossom were dismounting nearby. With one arm about Waterflower's waist, he turned to the wagon. It was at that moment that Lauren appeared from inside. Cade was so shocked that he stood still, his eyes filled with surprise, and it was at that moment that Snow Blossom's and Lauren's eyes met, held for a moment, and each of them knew in the age-old wisdom of women from the beginning of time that the other threatened her world.

"Lauren," Michael said, "this is my wife, Waterflower. My love," he said to Waterflower smiling down into her eyes, "this is Lauren Brent."

Grant helped Lauren from the wagon and the four of them stood together. Cade had not moved, nor had he said a word. Snow Blossom stood beside him and waited. She would not go to the white woman first, of that she was certain.

It was Lauren who took the few steps toward them. She looked at Snow Blossom for a minute without saying a word, then her eyes lifted to Cade.

"Hello, Cade," she said softly. "I understand congratulations are in order. From what Grant tells me, we have come just in time for your wedding."

"Lauren," he replied, "I had no idea you were coming with my father. Just why did you come out to this 'savage' country? I'm sure there's nothing out here your father's money couldn't buy for you at home."

"Cade, that was a little unjust," his father replied. "Lauren—"

"It's all right, Dr. Holliday, I guess Cade has a right to be bitter. I'm sorry this has been such a surprise to you, Cade, but it might surprise you even more to find I'm quite accomplished in nursing. Your father intends to build a hospital one day and I intend to be the first nurse who works in it. Now, since your manners have deteriorated since we knew each other in New

York"—she smiled at Snow Blossom—"I'll introduce myself. I'm Lauren Brent and I imagine you are Snow Blossom."

Snow Blossom's smile was just as cool as Lauren's as she said in a deceivingly sweet voice, "Yes, I'm Snow Blossom and since Sun Knife has not, I would be pleased to invite you as a guest to our wedding."

"It seems I've come at just the right time. Is the wedding soon?"

"In two days; you are welcome to stay with us."

"Thank you."

"I think it's best we return to the village," Cade said. He took Snow Blossom's hand and started back toward the horses.

Michael led Waterflower to the wagon. "Ride back with me. Now that I'm home, I find it hard to let you out of my sight again."

She smiled up into his eyes as she said softly, "My horse can carry double, and I know of a place near here that is filled with old sweet memories. Shall we go find them, my Husband?"

Without a word, Michael looked up at Grant and Lauren, now seated on the wagon seat. "Take the wagon on straight ahead, Grant. I'll ride back with my wife."

Grant slapped the reins against the horses' rumps and the wagon moved toward the village. Michael turned and looked down into the eyes of the woman he had loved faithfully for so many years and he saw his own love mirrored in her eyes. She reached up and laid her hand against his cheek.

"It has been so long. You have not changed, my Husband. You still are the handsomest warrior I have ever known."

"And you are the most beautiful woman I have ever seen."

Slowly, he drew her against him and his head bent so that he could touch her soft lips with his.

"I have loved you always, Waterflower. I told you I would return. I am home where my heart has always been. Shall we go and find those memories?"

She nodded and they walked to her horse. Quickly, he swung up into the saddle, then he reached down and drew her up before him.

He did not need a guide now to take him down an old remembered path to a green-tree-shaded valley. They had ridden here together the day they had been married. He had followed the old custom of a honeymoon tepee secluded from everything. It was to this spot that he returned.

Waterflower relaxed against him, enjoying the feel of his arm about her and the warmth of his body as he pressed her tight against him.

When he stopped her horse it was almost at the exact same spot they had spent their first days together. She smiled up at him pleased that he had remembered it so well.

"Did you think I would forget? Do you think I could forget the best thing that ever happened in my life?"

He slid down from the horse's back and lifted her gently down beside him; then he hobbled the horse so it would be free to graze yet would not drift too far away. When he went back to her, he extended his hand. She took it and they began to walk back into time. Suddenly, she felt shy and afraid, almost the same way she had felt the first time they had walked here. Her hand trembled in his and he sensed her fear. As if they had spent all of their days together, he began to talk to her. He spoke of the past years and the work he had done, he told her of the people he had met and amusing anecdotes that made her laugh. Slowly, he could feel her tensions relax; he saw her smile brighten and her eyes grow warm. He felt the way her hand now gripped his in a firm almost possessive hold. It was only then that he stopped, turned her toward him, gently pulled her into his arms, and kissed her the way he had wanted to all those lost years.

"I have missed you so desperately, Waterflower. Sometimes, I longed for you so much that I would consider leaving it all behind and come home. The lonely nights that I needed you, missed your gentleness, your sweetness. I love you Waterflower. I have loved you in my mind a million times over the years. Now . . . I need you, Waterflower. I need to hold you, to know for now and for always you are mine."

"I am here, my Husband. My love is as strong today as it was at the beginning." She said the words quietly as she slid her arms about his neck. His strong arms enclosed her and his mouth searched hers and found the answer to his needs.

He lifted her in his arms holding her tight, burying his face in the soft curve of her throat and hearing with joy, her soft murmurs of pleasure.

He carried her to the soft bank of the river and with gentle hands, he slowly removed her clothes, caressing the soft skin beneath each piece. It was as if he were worshiping something sacred to him. She closed her eyes and savored the joy of being loved by him.

His arms closed about her and gently lifted her against him and with a half-groan, half-cry of pleasure, he blended their two bodies together. Neither of them moved for a heart-stopping moment; they seemed frozen in time, each wrapped in the close embrace of the other. With their bodies joined, he touched her lips again and again with his, each kiss becoming deeper, clinging longer until he heard her throaty sob of desire and felt her hands urgently drawing him nearer and nearer, caressing his back and sliding down to his hips to urge him deeper and deeper, to reach the fire that burned within. Slowly, leisurely, he began to move, holding her slender hips in his huge hands. It was as if he wanted to sink to the deepest depths of her, as if he could not seem to hold her close enough, possess her deeply enough.

"Waterflower, my love, my wife. I love you more than life itself," he whispered.

"Oh, Michael, Michael," she sighed as they filled the empty void within each other the years of separation had created. They moved now with a throbbing rhythm lost in the magic of each other that had always filled their lives in past days.

It was a thunderous, blinding completion that left them clinging to one another as if they were the only two people left in existence. It was some time before either had the strength or the inclination to speak. It seemed to be enough for the moment just to hold each other and enjoy the renewal of their love.

"You are all I ever remembered completely about home, all I ever remembered with perfection. Now, I know why. You are home. It is not a place; we could be anywhere—and anywhere with you would be home."

She sighed and turned to lie against him, her head on his chest. "I have missed you so much, Michael. It was only the possession of your son that has held me together."

"*Our* son. I am very proud of him. You and Long Arrow have done well in raising him."

"Yes." She laughed softly as she ran her hand lightly across his chest. "I am quite proud of him myself."

He laughed and she could feel the rumble of it beneath her touch. It pleased her. "Michael?"

"Yes."

"Tell me why you brought the white girl with you. You need not tell me what was between her and our son; that I felt when they first met. But why did you bring her here if he had chosen to leave her behind?"

"I don't know if I'll regret bringing her or not. She is, as she said, a good nurse. And I will need her help for all I have planned to do. She is also well-educated and we can certainly use her teaching abilities."

"Michael, you have not been away from me so long that I do not remember how you feel and think. It wasn't a nurse or teacher you brought. It was Sun Knife's woman, was it not?"

"To tell you the truth, my love, I'm damned if I know."

He told her all that had happened between Cade and Lauren, why he had left, and all that Lauren had done since. He explained that Lauren had begged to come along and he had felt she would really be an asset to him and that her coming would prove to Cade that she loved him.

"My God, Waterflower, I did not even think that Cade would find a woman and plan to marry so soon."

"Michael, you do not think that our son has only turned to Snow Blossom because he lost the one he loved? It would hurt her beyond anything, for she has loved him with a great love since they were children."

"I will tell you one thing of which I am certain."

"What?"

"Cade will marry Snow Blossom, and no one besides him will know if he loved Lauren or not. She can stay here the rest of their lives and find he will not change. If she had come with him it would have been different, but she chose not to. Deep within, he does not trust her love now, nor will he ever. No, in my heart I feel he has chosen right. He belongs here and his woman should be a strong woman. Is Snow Blossom that?"

"She is. She will make him a good wife."

"Then Lauren will find that she has lost her chance and that she must build her life in another direction. She has come, she has seen, maybe she will choose to go home, but as it was before, the choice is hers."

She sighed and nestled closer to him, feeling his arm tighten about her. "Much as I hate to leave this place, we had best return to the village," he said.

"Yes, you must speak with Tekata and Long Arrow, but," she whispered, "remember I am waiting for you."

He pulled her against him and kissed her again and again. "I have never forgotten, nor will I ever. I love you." Again, he kissed her, then reluctantly got to his feet. He reached down and pulled her to her feet beside him. He held her possessively against him. "Let us hurry to the village. I would get the reunion over with quickly; then I can relax and begin to renew our days together."

They dressed and returned to the village, riding leisurely while Michael absorbed and renewed his memories of the land about him and Waterflower relaxed against him, now knowing with finality that her beloved husband was home to stay. However, she began to worry about the situation that might be developing with her son, for she knew Snow Blossom was not a woman to be second to anyone. She also knew Snow Blossom would be a fury that Lauren Brent would find very difficult to handle, if in fact, she could be handled at all.

Grant and Lauren rode along in the wagon slowly and in silence. Lauren's eyes were still on the two figures who rode together far ahead of them and rapidly disappeared from sight. That her eyes were filled with tears, he refused to see, for he knew she was trying with valiant effort to hold them back.

"She's very beautiful," she said softly.

"Yes."

"Cade is so . . . different here."

"No, Lauren, you're seeing things backward. Cade is not Cade; he is Sun Knife. He is not different here; he was different there."

"Yes. I guess it is what you and my father have been trying

to tell me. You have the answers, but how am I to cope with the fact that I still love Cade . . . and I love Sun Knife?"

"I don't think that is true," he answered.

"Why?"

"Because you did not know Cade as well as you thought, and you do not know Sun Knife at all." His words were blunt. "I think that you still have a lot of growing to do. I think you are placing yourself in some magical dream that does not have a ghost of a chance of coming true." He looked at her. "Lauren, don't do anything foolish. Snow Blossom is no fool and Cade would never forgive you."

Lauren was silent, but her thoughts would have made Grant more taut than he already was.

Lauren's nature was to fight back at any obstacle that stood in her way. It was the natural reflex from her environment. She had always gotten what she wanted. She had worked hard to be the kind of woman Cade wanted and she was making the mistake of thinking of Snow Blossom as an ignorant savage. She still, deep within, felt that Cade's future was in the white man's world. She still could not think of Cade as a savage, but only as a surgeon who was blind to his potential. She was silent, but she did not plan to back away from this confrontation so easily.

They rode along without speaking until they could see the village in the distance. Lauren was surprised at the quantity of the tepees and the bustle and activity within them. Grant began to explain the background behind the tepees and their brilliant coloring.

Cade and Snow Blossom rode along in a silence neither of them was sure how to break. Cade wanted to explain to Snow Blossom about Lauren before her imagination carried her away. He had no idea that Snow Blossom was also searching for a way to tell him that she had sensed his knowledge of the white woman long ago and in no way intended to condemn him for what she knew was past.

"Snow Blossom," Cade began, "we must talk."

Without a word, Snow Blossom guided her horse away from the well-worn trail. They rode a few minutes until they came to a meadow; there she dismounted. He followed, searching his mind for what he wanted to say. He hobbled both of the horses so they would not drift away; then he took Snow Blossom's hand in his and they walked slowly across the meadow.

"I should have told you about Lauren, and I'm sorry I didn't. I can excuse this situation only by saying that I thought she was part of a past I never intended to see again. I left the white world finally and with no regrets. I have not looked back since then—at anything. Snow Blossom, I had no idea she was coming with my father, believe me. I may have left out things I should have told you, but I have never lied to you and I will not lie to you now."

"She is beautiful, this white one. Did you love her, Sun Knife?"

"There was a time when I thought I did," he replied honestly, "but that was before I knew what love was. What I felt for her could only be a pale shadow beside what I feel for you. Will you listen, and I will tell you now what I should have told you before?"

She nodded. Slowly he began to explain all that had happened between him and Lauren. Her face was unreadable and she remained silent while he spoke. When, at last, he came to their parting, she listened for pain or bitterness and found none. When he finished, he waited to see just what her reaction would be, prepared to fight for her should she be angry or jealous. "I feel very sorry for her."

"Sorry?"

"She is a foolish woman with very little wisdom." Snow Blossom came close to Cade and put her arms about his waist. She looked up into his searching blue eyes and smiled. "When I first saw her and the way she looked at you, I was angry and filled with jealousy. I am glad you have told me all you have, but I must tell you this, she will never have you while there is a breath in my body. Snow Blossom's loves and hates run deep, and I would see her dead before I would surrender. She must beware, Sun Knife, for I will tolerate no one trying to take what is mine. All my life I have loved you. Now that I know your heart feels the same for me, I will defend what belongs to me. I am the daughter of a great chief whose pride runs deep. I would warn her not to tread on it lest it spring up and devour her."

He laughed as he put his arms about her, drawing her tighter against him. "And I thought you had such a sweet and gentle nature, my love. Maybe I'd best be careful."

Her eyes were still and dark. "Sun Knife, the heart of Snow Blossom is not so easily forgiving. What this white one feels and wants I understand and I can fight . . . but I do not think I could easily forget or forgive betrayal by one I love as I love you. You possess every ounce of love within me; only you have the power to turn that love to hate. I will do all that is in my power to make you happy. But I think I would die a little if you turned from me to another."

"No, Snow Blossom, don't think such a thing. Now that I've known you, I know I have never known love before you. I will never betray you. I love you with a depth I did not even know or understand myself until the sudden fear a short time ago that I could lose you. Don't think that I would turn to another for there is no other such as you. In a few days, you will become my wife. I would like to think of myself as a man of honor and that I would keep my vows sacred, but it is not just that; it is that I love you and I shall continue to love you until I die."

"Then I repeat," she said softly as she put her arms about his neck and lifted her lips for his kiss. "I feel sorry for the white one for she has not yet found her path in life and I am lucky to have found you."

He would have liked to stay where they were, but they both knew they would be expected at the village. After a few kisses, they reluctantly mounted their horses and headed back.

Michael's arrival was welcomed by pandemonium. Drums echoed through the village and the older ones who remembered Michael's generosity and kindness during his short stay with them rushed to meet him. Young people who had been hearing stories of Michael, or who were friends of his wife and son called out welcome as they rode in.

Lauren and Grant had arrived before Michael and Waterflower. Grant was made comfortable in the large tepee that had been erected for that purpose and Lauren found herself sharing a tepee with an older widowed woman. She was amazed at the size and comfort the tepee offered and the remarkable way in which it was provided with all the things a family might need.

Among the many things of which Lauren was aware were the amazed, respectful, and interested looks of the young braves as they watched her disembark from the wagon. She could literally feel their dark eyes warm upon her. She also felt the eyes of the young women who were not quite as warm and friendly.

Leaping Bear stood in the company of several other young braves, watching in appreciative silence as Lauren arrived.

"Who is the sun-haired white one?" one questioned.

"She belongs to Michael Holliday," Leaping Bear answered.

"Is she his wife?"

"No, you should remember the white man only takes one wife," Leaping Bear answered, then he smiled. "I think she is his adopted daughter."

"Is she married?" one questioned hopefully.

"No, I think she has come to be Sun Knife's second wife. You would be wise to ask before you speak."

The excitement of the day turned into a celebration that night. Tekata, with Benjamin on one side and Michael on the other, watched with quiet eyes what he thought might be one of the last celebrations, besides his daughter's wedding, that his tribe would be able to enjoy. After his long talk with Michael that afternoon about the information about the new commander of the fort and his feelings toward the Indian, he realized the inevitable course they were on. He watched his son whose eyes were bright with laughter and he wondered, sadly, just how long the laughter would last.

Chapter Fifteen

White Eagle was immensely amused when Cade managed to be absent from the village almost up to the time of the wedding. With a few friends and White Eagle, Cade had gone hunting. It turned out to be less of a hunting trip and more of a chance to stay out of Lauren's vicinity, which called for much in the way of humorous banter from White Eagle.

"I understand you've learned well the other side of my sister's disposition."

"We've had no arguments." Cade grinned. "And I intend to see there's no cause to have one. There's too much time for Snow Blossom to change her mind, and I won't give her a minute's cause to do so."

"Sun Knife," White Eagle said seriously, "your white woman—"

"She's not my white woman," Cade said in exasperation. "White Eagle, I've told you how it was between us and how it is. There's nothing between us now, nor could there ever be again. I love Snow Blossom and I don't want any problem with her."

"That is what I was about to say. It seems she came here thinking you would welcome her. It must be difficult for her. And—" He did not smile but his eyes twinkled suspicously. "You ran from the village at the first opportunity. Don't you think you at least owe her something—at least to talk to her, make it easier for her?"

"Ran! I did not run!" Cade sputtered.

"You didn't?" White Eagle said innocently.

"I just thought it would be less trouble for her until she decided to leave."

"What if she decides to stay?"

"Why should she stay? She'll go back with Grant. In a few weeks, she'll be back in her comfortable mansion and she'll forget all about life out here. It is a life she can't handle."

"Maybe you're right, but I'm not so sure. I think she wants to do more with her life than that."

"What can she do here?"

"Your father seems to think she can be of some help to him, and to us, Sun Knife," he said softly. "Wouldn't it make it easier if you were friends? If she decides to stay and help your father—help us—then one day you will have to face each other. Wouldn't it be better as friends than as enemies?"

"Snow Blossom," Cade said softly.

"Do you think my sister is a foolish child? She is a woman. Do you think she is not a woman wise enough to know in her heart that your life and hers are meant by the Great Spirit to be shared?"

Cade sighed. "Yes, I guess you are right, just as I knew I was trying to force out any idea of facing it. I guess I was hoping my attitude would drive her away. It was a stupid thing to do. We'll go back and I'll try to put things right. If she can be of some help to my father and my people, then it is unfair that I would try to stand in her way."

White Eagle chuckled. "I always knew my brother was a man of great courage."

They laughed together, then breaking camp they headed back to the village. The next day was to be Cade's wedding day and he decided to smooth all the paths in his life in preparation for the future.

They arrived at the village just before dark, White Eagle to return to his tepee and explain to Rebecca why he had stayed so long on this hunting trip and what was happening between Cade and the other white woman. Cade went first to the tepee of his parents. He had moved into his own as soon as his father had arrived. Now he wanted first to talk to his father. When he sat with his father at the fire his first question came directly to the point, and he was answered in the same way. Michael told him how well Lauren had learned nursing and how hard and dedicated a worker she had become. He also said he felt that with her education, Lauren could be one person who could help more than any other.

Resigned now, and feeling slightly guilty, Cade vowed

silently that he would, after he and Snow Blossom had returned, go to Lauren, try to apologize for his rudeness and try to mend the breech between them. He left his father's tepee, after eating the meal his mother had literally forced on him, and went to his own. He went to bed hoping the night would pass quickly and looking forward to the new day that would give him Snow Blossom forever.

The day dawned bright and warm. Cade knew he would not see Snow Blossom until time for the wedding which would take place just as the sun set. Both of them would be going through a preparation time. Cade sat in the steam lodge as water was poured over the heated stones to produce cleansing steam. He was to make himself both physically and mentally prepared to face the responsibility of the coming ceremony. He controlled his thoughts rising them to the gods he was raised to believe in—gods that would guide his and Snow Blossom's life together in the village, gods that would, he hoped, one day bless them with children.

He wiped everything else from his mind except his fervent prayers for his marriage and for his future.

Snow Blossom herself was undergoing almost the same thing. She had been wakened by her step-mother who had sat with her and spoken ritual words of instruction; then she had gone to the cleansing steam and then to scented bath water. Her hair had been washed and brushed to a high glistening sheen. She was dressed in a soft white elaborately beaded buckskin dress; then her hair was braided and decorated with beads and feathers.

As the sun slowly began to set, Cade walked to the council tepee. He waited outside while his eyes watched the pathway between the tepees. In a few minutes, he was rewarded. Mounted on a beautiful black stallion, she made a magnificent picture as she was led to his side.

When the horse stopped beside him, he reached up and lifted Snow Blossom down. Hand in hand, they entered the tepee and walked together to face their chief.

The marriage of the chief's daughter had been an occasion that had brought many chiefs and subchiefs and their women from other villages.

The men of importance crowded the huge tepee. A few women, wives of important chiefs, surrounded the inner circle of men. Benjamin, Rebecca, and Lauren stood close to each other, fascinated both by the elaborate colorful ceremony, and the huge gathering of men and women from many other tribes.

Lauren had been watching Cade and Snow Blossom, as had all the others, unaware that her face clearly showed the combination of pain and jealousy she felt. It was sometime along in the ceremony when she felt the gaze of someone near. She could actually feel eyes watching her and slowly she turned her head to find out where the feeling was coming from.

He stood on the opposite side of the huge room from her; yet she had the breathless feeling he was standing close enough to touch her. That he had been watching her for some time she knew; his dark eyes were intent on her and his face was an unreadable mask. She tried to concentrate on the ceremony, but her eyes were drawn again and again to the bronze immovable man whose eyes never left her.

He was tall and solidly built. That he would be very strong she could see by the heavy ridged muscles across his chest and the rippling muscles of his arms, all that was visible to her at the moment. His face was granite-hard and sharp of features yet ruggedly handsome. There was an aura about him that would command attention no matter where he was, she could feel the tingle of it across the crowded room.

With deliberate and intense concentration, she focused her attention on the ceremony. Again a flicker of misery crossed her face as the ceremony drew to a close, and again it was read by the hawk-faced man whose eyes had never left hers.

She watched as Cade enclosed Snow Blossom in the feathered cape he wore, his strong arm drawing her close to him. She watched his blue eyes soften with love and his smile grow warm as Snow Blossom looked up at him. At that moment she felt as if she could easily kill the girl who stood within the arms of the man she still loved. Hatred, too, could be felt across the room. The ceremony was over and the celebration began. There was no way, as Michael's and Waterflower's guest, that she could refuse to remain. She wanted to make a useful life here helping Michael and she was not going to antagonize

Michael and Waterflower, or the tribe by refusing to remain at the celebration.

She struggled through it, constantly aware of her deep inner pain, and the eyes of the man who continued to watch her.

After Cade and Snow Blossom had left, she finally found a chance to escape. She went to the tepee and found herself finally alone. She threw herself down on the furs and let the hot tears fall.

The night was velvet black with a huge yellow moon that hung near the horizon. The sky sparkled with a million diamond-bright stars. A soft breeze ruffled the trees and the soft sounds of night animals were the only things that disturbed the silence surrounding the tepee that sat nestled on the edge of the woods.

Inside, the lovers knew nothing but the joy of each other. The sound of gentle laughter, of softly spoken words, lingered inside the tepee away from all intruders. He held her close to him as they lay together on the soft fur couch. "Do you know this is the beginning of all I've ever dreamed of? You have made everything complete," he said.

She smiled, her head resting against his chest; she let her fingers gently caress his skin.

"And you for me, my Husband, have made my life begin."

He rolled on his side and looked down into her wide dark eyes. The fire had died to bright glowing embers and her golden skin glistened in the half-light. She raised her hand to caress the side of his face, absorbing the soft glow of love in his eyes.

"I hope," she said, "this night I carry within me your seed, my Husband. I would give you a son as good and loving as his father. It would give me joy beyond all else."

He held her hand against his lips. "Only the gods could know how much I love you, Snow Blossom," he said gently, as he bent his head and touched her lips with his.

Her arms reached to hold him close and her lips, warmed by his passion, became seeking and soft. Her body moved against his as he joined with her in a blinding, burning need that consumed them.

* * *

Lauren wakened the next morning before the first light of day. Her eyes were heavy from crying and her body felt weary and tired from tension. She rose quietly, not wanting to disturb the others. Outside, the first pale streak of light rimmed the horizon, yet the stars could still be seen in the half-night sky. Without realizing where she was going, she walked the well-known path to the river. When she got there, the first morning sun dappled the wind-ruffled water. She bent and touched her fingers to the stream; it felt cool and inviting. She knew it would be an hour or so until the women came to the river for the morning's water. Making her decision quickly, she slipped out of her clothes and waded into the water until it was deep enough, then she pushed forward and swam. The water cooled her heated flesh and soothed her jangled nerves. She floated on her back a few minutes then dived below the surface.

Tired, she swam back to the shore. She squeezed the water from the long braid of her hair, then patted herself dry with her petticoat and slipped her dress over her head. Sitting on a flat rock, she watched the sun come up. She had been allowing her thoughts to drift aimlessly when she again became aware of the tingling sensation of being watched. She turned quickly toward the stand of trees that stood between her and the village and gave a startled gasp.

He sat motionless on his horse at the edge of the trees and some inner instinct told her he had been there for some time. When he knew she had seen him, he nudged his horse into motion and walked slowly toward her. She stood up and watched him come, determined to find out not only who he was, but why he watched her so closely. It was the same man who had been watching her the night before. He stopped his horse close to her and looked down on her with a face that showed no sign of the thoughts behind his dark eyes.

"You are the woman of Michael Holliday?"

"No, I am only a friend," she replied.

"Then you are Sun Knife's woman?"

"No," she replied. Now she was slightly angry at his persistent questions since he had not offered any word about who he was or what he wanted. "I am no one's woman," she snapped.

"Then to whose lodge do you belong?"

Now she was really becoming angry. With quick, clipped precise words, and eyes flashing with anger, she told him she was here to help Michael with his hospital and his school. In conclusion, she added, "I was unaware that it was considered good manners to make a guest feel like she was a prisoner under question."

He chuckled deep in his chest, and with one lithe movement, he slid from his horse and stood beside her. He was taller and more powerfully built than she had thought, but she refused to let his overpowering masculinity overwhelm her. She looked up at him defiantly and he smiled down into her anger-clouded green eyes. His smile was broad and friendly and it made an amazing difference. He suddenly seemed much younger and not in the least as stern as she had at first thought. His teeth, white, strong, and square flashed back, but she held herself under control, continuing to glare at him with anger that was rapidly fading.

"I'm sorry if I frightened you."

"Frightened!" She smiled now. "Why should I be afraid of you? I'm sure if you were invited to the wedding of the chief's daughter you are an honored guest who would bring no dishonor to the village of Tekata."

That she had struck home she could tell by his speechless look of surprise.

"Of course I would do nothing to anger Tekata," he replied in a voice stiff with pride, and tinged with a bit of anger that she had struck back at him so easily. "I wished only to speak to you. I searched for you during the celebration but you were gone."

"I . . . I was tired. I went to bed early."

"You were also very unhappy. It is why I wanted to speak to you."

She turned away, prepared to leave him where he stood, but his next words held her. "I wondered why a marriage could bring such sadness to the eyes of a beautiful woman. It is the reason I thought you might be Sun Knife's woman, for your eyes were only for him."

She spun about. "Who are you, and why do you think you

have the right to question me?"

"I am Running Wolf. My village is at the foot of the mountains," he replied as he pointed to the ridge of mountains that stood in the distant horizon. "And I do not mean to upset you. I only meant . . . I only wanted to say something that might help your pain. You are too beautiful to mourn the loss of any man for long. You would need only to smile and any wise man would be at your side."

"Thank you." She smiled again. "I'm sorry I snapped at you. That was good for my badly bruised ego."

"Ego?"

Now she laughed. "Never mind. It was good for my pride, too. I must go back."

"Wait—"

"Thank you for your kindness, Running Wolf," she said softly, "but I must handle this myself."

"May I talk with you again? We will be in your village a few more days."

She looked at him steadily for a few minutes; then she smiled, shrugged, and walked away. He mounted his horse, his eyes still on her, enjoying the enticing sway of her slender hips as she walked away.

"What is your name?" he called.

She turned. "Lauren Brent."

"I will speak with you again," he said more to himself than to her; then he smiled and his eyes twinkled mischievously. "Lauren Brent!" he called.

Again, just at the edge of the trees, she turned to look at him.

"You swim well," he called and was pleased at the expression of shock on her face as he kicked his horse into motion and rode away.

Lauren walked back to the village. It was time she sent her life in some definite direction, yet she felt lost, wandering in a strange world. She no longer belonged in the world of her past and she could not find her way in this new world.

She wanted Cade now more than at any other time to comfort her, to hold her, to tell her that everything would be all right.

At the village, she joined Waterflower and Rebecca in their

daily work, fighting the pictures that burned in her mind of where Cade and Snow Blossom were now.

For the next two days, she managed to stay out of Running Wolf's path, although she knew without looking toward him that his eyes were often on her. She was kneeling on the ground with Waterflower, a digging tool in her hand, digging strenuously for edible roots. Concentrating on her inner thoughts, she did not realize how vigorously she was digging or that Waterflower had stopped and her eyes were upon her.

"Lauren, why are you so troubled?"

Lauren sat back on her heels, wiped the perspiration from her forehead, and looked at Waterflower. "I'm fine."

"Is it my son?"

"I thought it was, but now I know it is me. Waterflower, what am I to do? I cannot seem to find myself."

"Maybe you are searching too hard, and in the wrong place."

"You mean I should go home; I don't belong here."

"No, I didn't say that. My husband is proud of your qualities and he thinks you have a great deal to contribute here."

"Then why do I feel so . . . so miserable . . . so very unhappy?"

"Do you want me to speak the truth?"

"Yes, yes I do."

"You have the body of a woman, yet your heart is that of a spoiled child who feels all things must bend for her. It is not love of Sun Knife; it is love of Lauren that makes you so. Put away small jealousies for they burn only your own heart. Open yourself to the love and need of all others around you. Then and only then will you find what you are searching for."

"Help me," Lauren said softly. Waterflower smiled and reached out her hand to cover Lauren's.

"All of us will help you. Michael, me, Long Arrow, and . . . all others who care for you. As my husband has told you, you have a gift to give. Think of what you have to give, not what you need, and in that you will find all you have ever wanted."

Lauren smiled and both women went back to the work they were sharing.

* * *

Cade bent low over his horse's neck; his laughter filled the air as he watched Snow Blossom ride beside him. They raced toward their tepee, after a day of enjoying the sunshine, for supper. They skittered to a stop in front of the tepee and Cade slid from his horse's back and went to lift her down. He kept his arms about her and laughed at the wicked glitter in her eyes.

"I won," she said.

"You ride like a warrior," he protested. "I thought I would have to let you have an advantage so I let you start first."

"I did not! I did not! We started at the same time. Aren't you ashamed of such a lie?"

"I have to save face somehow," he said. "I can't have it spread all about the village that a great warrior such as I was beaten by a woman, can I?"

She laughed. "Maybe," she said softly, "if I am rewarded well I can be bribed not to speak of such a terrible thing."

"Rewarded." He chuckled. "That's blackmail, madam."

"Blackmail?"

"You're forcing me to do something against my will."

"Against your will?" she said softly.

"Maybe," he said gently as his arms tightened about her and he brushed her lips with his, "it is wise that I surrender to superior forces and just give in to your demand. Just what kind of reward did my lovely wife have in mind?"

She put her arms about his neck and pressed herself close to him.

"I am afraid I do not discuss small terms. I insist on complete surrender."

"Your word is my command, love," he whispered. "Your word is my command."

Her throaty laugh echoed on the still evening air as he swung her up into his arms and entered the tepee with her. He stood for a minute contemplating the meat that hung suspended over a low-burning fire.

"What is it?" she asked.

"I was just making a momentous decision," he said in a serious voice.

"Decision?"

"Yes, I was wondering which appetite has the upper hand—my stomach"—he grinned down at her—"or my lust for you."

She gave a muffled laugh, tightened her arms about his neck, and he yelped in surprise as she bit the lobe of his ear.

"Well," he said, "if you are going to get violent, I guess I can surrender a meal for a short time. Especially since the dessert is much more appetizing than the meal." They laughed together and he let her feet slide to the floor.

They had shared the tepee for six days and five long and beautiful nights that felt, to Cade, like the swift passing of minutes. He would have liked to stay lost in this time and place, to try to forget what he knew would one day face them. There was even one night, as he held a sleeping Snow Blossom close to him, that he wondered if White Eagle and the rest of the village would move, take all their possessions and make the long journey to the border of Canada. There he thought they might be safe. When the thought came, it died, for he knew that neither White Eagle nor any of his people would run from the threat of the white man. He knew their pride would allow them to run no farther. He searched his mind for any way he could think of to protect them.

They were small individual tribes and villages. If only there were some way to unite the tribes . . . it would not be enough to stop the flood, but it would be enough to slow it—to give them time.

In time, he and his father would be able to start their people to learn. Time . . .

"What are you thinking, Sun Knife?"

"What?"

"You were so far away. What were you thinking?"

He looked into her deep, trusting eyes and the urgency to hold her, to be part of her, filled him until it was a deep poignant pain within him. He reached out and took her into his arms, pressing her close, needing the feel of her. He bound her so tightly against him that she could feel the depth of his need. She looked up at him, and he cupped her face in his hands and looked down into her questioning eyes.

"I want to do all I can, Snow Blossom. Will you understand if it isn't enough? Will you be where I can reach out for you, hold you, and know that you love me? I love you," his voice rasped in a whisper. "I love you and I need you."

"What is it, Sun Knife?" Her voice was frightened.

"I guess it's that I'm afraid, suddenly I'm afraid. I've found the place where I belong and the one woman who makes my life whole. I am afraid. I could bear anything but losing you."

"But how can you lose something that is a part of you? We are not two any longer; we are one. We will always be part of each other. No matter what happens, we will always have a part of each other. My love for you is great, Sun Knife. Great enough that I shall remain with you even if we find a time when we are separated." She took his face in her hands and drew his mouth to hers. "I love you . . . I love you."

He drew her with him to the fur-covered bed they had shared in happy joyous love. But this time was different. Snow Blossom sensed that this time would live in her memory as the perfect time when the forces of their love combined and forged into a solid single force that would hold them together for always.

They lay together, relaxed and unhurried, touching, tasting, exhilarating in the joy of giving so totally that they were lost to any other thought but each other. His lips searched hers, finding them soft, warm, and willing under his. His hands caressed the slender body beneath his, finding the sensual pleasure in the touch of her cool soft skin that he always found.

His lean hard body pressed her almost savagely against the fur-covered couch. He drove within her as if he were literally trying to become one with her. She closed her mind against his savagery knowing the love for her that drove him, and knowing that she wanted him with a fierceness of passion that matched his.

She drew him within her, holding him as if to comfort him without fully realizing the source of his need. The gentleness of her body reached the source of the need that burned within him and eased it, and he whispered her name softly against the smooth skin of her throat as, with joy, he became aware that she knew and understood and was willing to be his fountain of strength no matter what they had to face.

It was much later, when he had drifted off into sleep, that she quietly rose from their bed. She removed the half-burned meat from the now almost dead fire, then she threw on a few more twigs and sat by the fire thinking. She looked across the small space at her sleeping husband. For a moment she closed her eyes and said a silent prayer of gratitude to all the gods she had prayed to for so very long.

She sat in deep thought for a long time. When she finally rose to return to her bed, it was with the silent vow that she would hold always to the peace she had found in her husband's heart. Even if it meant extending the first hand of friendship to a white girl, who at one time had shared love and, she suspected, the bed of the man who was her husband.

She nestled into his arms and smiled as they closed possessively around her even in sleep. He mumbled her name, drew her close against him, and they both drifted off into sleep.

Running Wolf was frustrated for one of the few times in his life. Being a young subchief in his tribe he was used to having his own way about most things. In his tribe, he would have been sought as a husband by any of the young maidens. He was strong and handsome and had always been aware of the welcoming gazes of women. He also was well aware of propriety and knew that the male head of a household must be approached first if a man intended marriage. He was completely frustrated now by three things. Lauren continued to ignore him, his time was coming to return home, and he could not get it straight in his mind just who was the head of the household to which she belonged; in fact, even where she belonged eluded him.

That she was deliberately evading him, he sensed, but he wasn't sure what to do about it for fear of offending any one of the men to whom she seemed to be attached.

It was obvious that the white doctor held her in great esteem, for they worked together in the large tepee they called a . . . hospital, and it was also obvious that Tekata's tribe was accepting the white girl with more and more respect each day as she helped doctor their children and began trying to teach the women more and more methods of sanitation that would help fight disease and lengthen their lifetimes.

All this he saw, and yet he was firmly told that Michael was not the head of the family to which she belonged. Leaping Bear had also told him that there was a possibility she was to be Sun Knife's second wife, so he was in a state of deep confusion.

Finally he decided to let the warriors who had come with him return home. He would wait for the return of Sun Knife. If the white girl with the beautiful green eyes was not meant to be Sun Knife's woman, he would then ask her bride price and to whom he should pay it. It would be a simple thing, for he was the son of what would have been considered in any tribe a wealthy family. He felt certain she would be happy when she found out what honor he was planning to bestow on her. It simply never occurred to him what a drastic mistake he was about to make, or that Lauren was in control of her own life.

It was the day before Cade was to return that Running Wolf was somewhat rudely awakened to a surprising fact. He had been looking daily for an opportunity to talk to Lauren alone again. It was a difficult thing to do for during the day she was always busy in the company of Michael or Waterflower and Rebecca. At night it was impossible to get too near to her tepee for fear he would alarm the rather formidable woman who lived there with Lauren. She was a widow of, in his estimation, innumerable years, who seemed not only to have eyes in the back of her head, but to be aware of every thought in his.

Running Wolf had just ridden back from hunting. He dropped the deer he had shot in front of the chief's tepee where it could be cleaned, skinned, and the meat divided among any who needed it. He dismounted and was about to enter the tepee allotted him when his gaze lifted to a small hill not far from the village. He could pick out Rebecca's golden hair and with her was Waterflower. Not far from them was another woman, and from all the times he'd held her vision in his mind, there was no doubt it was Lauren. They must either have been picking berries or gathering nuts, but gradually they had become separated from each other. Lauren was alone. He lost no time leaping on his horse's back and setting off in her direction.

Lauren was doing more drifting and daydreaming than she was picking berries. That was probably why she did not hear the horse until he was almost beside her. She looked up at the approaching horse and rider. She recognized him immediately, and also knew this meeting was no accident. He slid down from his horse and walked to her side.

"I am surprised to see you, Running Wolf. I thought all your people had gone back to their village."

"They have all gone. I . . . I am waiting for Sun Knife to return."

"Why?"

"I have a thing I must ask him."

"I see." She smiled and started to turn away.

"What I have to ask him concerns you."

"Me? Why should you be asking Cade anything about me?"

"I must know if you belong to him."

"Be-belong?" she repeated.

"If you are to be his second wife," he replied.

Storm clouds began to gather in her green eyes that Running Wolf did not see. He continued to make matters worse.

"I am not sure who to ask, or to find the bride price from, or I would have made arrangements to have taken you back with me and we would have been married by now."

"Married . . . bride price?" she sputtered. "What do you think I am, you arrogant savage, a horse or a blanket you can buy?" She was so angry now that he took a step back in surprise and she followed after him, her cheeks pink and her eyes aflame. "I told you once that no man owns me; now I will tell you again in the hopes you will understand. There will be no bride price paid for me, there will be no man's permission to ask. I will marry when and with whom I choose."

"I meant no offense," he said quickly. "I know of no other way to get you."

"Did it ever occur to you to ask me?"

She could tell by the look on his face that it hadn't and that he was beginning to get amused at her anger. There was a suspicious twinkle in his dark eyes and his lips quirked as if they were struggling not to smile.

"Our ways are different. Our women are much more gentle. I am sorry if I have offended you, but you must understand that I intended only to honor you."

Now it was her turn to be struck by the humor of the situation. Her eyes laughed before her lips and he saw them change.

"You are a very beautiful woman, Lauren Brent. Maybe if you had given me the chance to speak to you before, this would not have happened."

"It would not have changed things, Running Wolf. I do not wish to marry anyone now. I have other things I plan to do and many things to think over before I do."

"And," he added softly, "the man you want to marry is married to another."

At any other time, Lauren would have lost her temper, but now she realized that she had found her barrier. She could do nothing with her life until she faced the fact once and for all that there was nothing in the future for her and Cade.

"Maybe you are right, Running Wolf. Maybe, despite what I thought, I was still clinging to Cade. Everyone has been trying to tell me to grow up; well maybe I am. I know that I like being here, I like working with Dr. Holliday and I enjoy my friends, Waterflower and Rebecca. I will stay, I will work, and I will make peace with Cade and Snow Blossom."

"Then . . . one day you may look for a husband among us." He smiled now and the infectiousness of it caught her and she smiled back. "I will visit here often. If you are a little girl, I want to be near when you are grown up. Will you welcome me back as a friend?"

"I can promise you nothing but friendship now, Running Wolf."

"Friendship is more than some marriages are based on. Of course"—he grinned—"I shall remember your temper, and I shall not offer a bride price. I will ask you again one day when you have discovered what a good friend I am."

She laughed and placed her hand on his arm. "I shall remember and be on the alert for you."

His eyes grew dark and intent and he reached out and brushed his fingers across her cheek and touched her hair lightly.

"Grow up quickly, Lauren Brent. I find it very difficult to wait."

He was gone before she could reply and she watched him ride away without looking back while far away another situation was fermenting that would throw them together in a storm of violence neither of them could imagine.

Chapter Sixteen

Three riders crested the hill that led to Fort Stanton. All three were dressed alike, in worn buckskin and even more worn boots. Their hair was long and all three were bearded. Mo Mackin, unspoken leader of the three was a man of about forty-two. He had been born and raised in the hills of Kentucky, one of sixteen children. His life had been bleak and hard and had left him the same. He had cold blue eyes that squinted continuously. His face was narrow, sharp, and hard. One jaw bulged with a continuous chew of tobacco and his teeth were stained with it. Mo Mackin loved no one and no one loved him. Many feared him for his disposition could have been, and often was, compared to that of a rattlesnake. His hatred of people was more pronounced with Indians. He hated them with a passion that went beyond any normal emotion. The only time in his life he had opened himself in any way had been with an Indian girl he had bought and with whom he fell in love. It was the first and last time he had cared for any other human. Incapable of knowing how to treat a person, he had beaten her into submission. He had bullied her and made her life such a hell that she had finally run away, and in his mind the blame was hers. Now he turned his violent hatred toward all Indians. He was a trapper by trade and a troublemaker by choice.

Leach Bosley was a small wiry man who was weak and had to be attached to someone who would be his courage for him. Mo had found him drunk and unconscious in an alley and dragged him out, sobered him up, and given him what was to Leach the closest thing to kindness he had ever known. They had spent the past three years trapping together. Leach gave Mo the one thing he needed, which was to be superior to another human. Mo spoke the command and Leach followed like an obedient puppy.

Josiah Tucker was the enigma of the group. Dressed the

same, bearded and ragged the same, there was still a subtle difference between him and the other two. First, he was several years younger than the others who were in their early forties. As aged as his clothes were, he himself was clean which was quite a difference from the other two. His eyes were a clear deep gray and did not slide away from another's gaze as the others' did. He was tall and broad-shouldered. His disposition was reserved and quiet and the other two knew no more about him now than they had six months ago when he had first met and joined them.

"Mo, why the hell we comin' clear out here? The trappin' was good where we was," Leach asked plaintively. "Besides, they's a passel of redskins out here I wouldn't look forward to tanglin' with."

"We got a job to do, Leach. The pay is goin' to be good and we don't have to do much work to collect it."

"You don't never tell me nuttin, Mo. What kind of a job do we have to do?"

"I ain't told you because I don't know all the details yet. Soon as we get to the fort, and talk to the man we been sent to talk to, we'll know for sure what we're supposed to do."

Josiah absently touched his pocket where several letters rested that were to be delivered. He had definite instructions on whom they were to be delivered to and why. He was pretty sure of the effect that was planned also. He reserved his thoughts, not wanting to know or care about what would be happening or the lives it might cost. In fact, there was not too much in the world that Josiah cared about at all. He had left all the love he had known buried beside a cabin that had been destroyed by fire at the hands of a band of marauding Indians. He had sealed his pain in a small corner of his cold heart. There had been no violent swearing of revenge, no fire, no anger, in fact no emotion at all. Josiah was a very dangerous man, flint to the gunpowder that was about to explode in this area of the frontier.

They entered the fort, tied their horses, and asked directions to Major Chivington's quarters. Inside, they were ushered into the major's office. Once the door was closed, Major Chivington held his hand out to Josiah.

"Josiah," he said quietly.

"John," he answered gruffly, but there was no light of friendliness in his eyes. He took the packet of letters from his pocket and handed them to the major. John motioned them all to sit; then he opened the packet of letters and read them. A faint half-smile twisted his lips and he seemed pleased with what he read. Finally he folded the letters, put them in the drawer and looked at the three men who sat in front of him.

"I will provide you with horses and pack mules and enough furs to make your story look legitimate. I want you to find and map every Indian village between here and the White River. It would be best if you would find the outlying tribes first and end up spending the winter in Chief Tekata's village. You can be accidentally caught there when the winter's snows come. Of course, they will allow you to spend the winter with them; they are too ignorant to do otherwise."

"Ignorant?" Josiah said with amusement. "Or hospitable?"

John flushed. "I should think you, too, would not find any redeeming qualities among them."

Josiah shrugged, but the amused smile lingered in his eyes.

"You will report back to me in the spring." He stood up and said the next words slowly and precisely so there would be no misunderstanding of what he wanted. "I cannot move against these heathens unless I have just cause. I want an incident—any incident that will give me an excuse to wipe these red savages from my area. I expect you to come back in the spring and give me that incident. Do you understand?"

They nodded. "We'll manage to get what you want one way or the other," Mo replied. "And I'd like to be along when you come down on them."

Neither of the other men said a word. John nodded and the three men left his quarters. Slowly, he sat down in his chair, his eyes frigidly cold; his clenched fist lay on his desk.

Two days later the three trappers left the fort again, this time headed toward the plains and the mountains beyond.

They were welcomed in the first small tribe they found. They were offered food and drink and given accommodations in which to sleep. Slowly, leisurely, they moved from one small tribe to the other, accepting their good will and marking their location on a map made of a piece of soft buckskin that Josiah carried folded inside his shirt.

The first snow covered the ground with several inches when they finally headed their horses in the general direction of Tekata's village. It was a bright day with huge flakes of snow filling the air when they finally spotted it. They camped just a few miles from it that night, prepared to let the Indians find them rather than to ride into the village. It would look more of an accident that way.

It was Leaping Bear who ran across them first. He had been returning empty-handed from a hunting trip. Cold and aggravated because he had found no game, he was making his way as rapidly as he could toward the village for a warm fire and a hot meal.

He saw a spiral of white smoke from the campfire and made his way toward it, wondering who else was as foolish as he to be out in such weather. Long before he arrived at the campfire, he knew the men who camped there were not Indians. The trail they had left made that obvious. Alert now, he walked his horse slowly toward the camp. The three men around the fire watched him approach with mixed emotions that if he had understood at the time, might have given him the wisdom to have turned from there and gone to warn his people. Instead, he stopped a few feet away and raised his hand in a peaceful gesture. Josiah, who spoke several different tongues, rose and raised his hand in reply.

"We are glad to see you, friend," Josiah said. "We are lost and would find a safe place to wait out the storm."

"It is dangerous to be out here in the winter season," Leaping Bear replied. "Many have been lost forever here and not found until spring."

"We were just talkin' about that when you found us. We heard talk there's a small village around here. Maybe we could find a place to hole up for a while until the snows pass."

"The village of my chief is not small. Tekata is a great warrior and he leads many people. I am sure he would find a place among us for you. If you will come with me, I will take you to him."

Leaping Bear waited patiently while the three repacked their equipment, put out their fire, and mounted their horses. He did not see the smile on Mo's lips as he turned his horse toward the village.

The wind began to stir and swirl the snow about, and by the time they were over halfway home, it was almost a blizzard. Josiah thought if Leaping Bear had not been guiding them, they could quite well have gotten lost and never found their way out. He watched as Leaping Bear moved with unerring aim toward the village.

When they entered the village the blizzard was in full force. Leaping Bear guided them to Tekata's tepee where they were made welcome and offered food. Later they were escorted to a tepee that had been erected while they ate. A fire had been built within and it was warm and welcome.

The next morning the weather abated a little, but the snow was still falling heavily. The trees about the village had heavy-laden branches and the air was still as if the world were awaiting something.

Everyone they saw was bundled so thoroughly in furs that none of them recognized the fact that a white woman was among them as the men moved about the village.

Their paths crossed Rebecca's and Lauren's only two times; both were occasions when their faces could not be clearly seen.

It was over a week since they had arrived, and they had been invited to White Eagle's tepee for a meal. White Eagle had wanted to speak to the white men for some time, but this was the first opportunity he had found.

Mo, Leach, and Josiah walked toward the tepee designated as White Eagle's.

"White Eagle is the chief's son, ain't he?" Leach asked.

"Yes. Maybe he might be a link to finding this 'incident' the major wants. Did you bring along that bottle of whiskey? We might just find out if our red-skinned friend has any capacity for drinking," Mo replied with a chuckle.

"Yeah, I brought it."

"Well, here we are. Now, keep your ears and eyes opened and Leach, try to keep your mouth shut, and for Christ's sake, stay away from that bottle."

"O.K., Mo, O.K."

It was custom for a woman to prepare a meal when her husband had guests, then retire from the main fire while they ate and talked. White Eagle would have put aside this custom, except there was something about these three white men that made him uncomfortable and just a little hesitant at letting them see Rebecca. Deep inside, he still harbored the fear that if and when the white world found Rebecca was there, they would try to find some way of taking her from him and he knew without doubt he would kill all three of these men before he let that happen.

He asked Rebecca if she would be very upset if, for this one time, she left their tepee before his guests arrived.

"Why?"

"Because . . . Rebecca, I don't want them to see you."

"I don't understand. White Eagle, they have already seen me."

"Not really." He grinned and drew her into his arms. "Your beautiful golden hair wrapped in furs and your equally beautiful body wrapped in layers of fur is not really seeing you. In that condition, I don't believe they even looked at you, but"—his smile faded—"if they see you as you really are, they might get the idea you need rescuing. I would hate to have to prove to them just how I would object to such a move." His voice was joking, but his eyes were serious, and Rebecca had long since begun to learn to read the face of her husband. She wrapped her arms about his waist and looked up at him.

"White Eagle, tell me the truth, I am not a child you have to protect, I am your wife."

"If they should happen to return to the fort and mention you are here it might draw the blue coats down on us. Rebecca"—his voice softened as he gently caressed her hair—"I will never let you go if I have to fight all the white man's army."

She smiled, put her arms about his neck, and lifted her mouth for his kiss.

"I shall do as you say, White Eagle. I want no trouble for my adopted people because of me. I will go to Lauren's tepee and visit with her. Will you come for me when they are gone?"

"As soon as they leave," he said softly. "I do not like this tepee as much without you."

He kissed her again, holding her close to him. "White Eagle, surely they will see me sometime while they are here."

"I must speak to them first. I want to know how they think. If they seem to be honest it will be all right. If not, it might be best if Leaping Bear took you and Lauren to another village for a short time."

"Separate us!"

"Only for a short time. I would follow you soon."

"I hate this pretense, this sneaking about. It is my choice to be here; why should it be in their power to stop me from being where I choose to be?"

He sighed and moved away from her. "Why should it be in the power of the white man to steal our land and push us farther and farther from the world we know. I don't know or understand the white man's greed, Rebecca. I only know that I will do all in my power to keep you and if that means fighting the entire white world, it is what I will do."

He stood with his back to her and she went to him. Putting her arms about his waist, she laid her head against his back. "I shall do willingly whatever you think is best, White Eagle, for I love you. I will do nothing to cause such a terrible thing."

He turned and took her in his arms, rubbing his chin against the softness of her hair. His thoughts, once started on such a path, conjured up pictures of Rebecca being taken from him. His arms tightened in involuntary reaction and he heard her startled gasp as he crushed her to him.

"I'm sorry; I didn't mean to hurt you." He touched the side of her face with gentle fingers. "I love you Rebecca."

"I know, White Eagle, I know," she whispered as he bent his head and took her mouth with his.

"And now for a few hours I must let you go. I will come for you when the white men return to their tepee."

She nodded, kissed him once again lightly, and was gone. He stood watching the empty doorway through which she had gone and knew the emptiness he would feel if she were ever out of his life.

White Eagle had been wise enough to warn all the others not to reveal the existence of white women in the village, but he was unaware of Josiah's knowledge of Indians. Josiah had asked many questions, among them whether or not White Eagle was married. His inner instincts told him, by the evasive answers he had received that there was some reason White Eagle's wife was a subject they could not, or would not discuss. He made up his mind to find the answers on his own, in his own way.

Cade joined White Eagle in his tepee before the others arrived.

"You have spoken to Lauren?"

"Yes," Cade replied as he looked back on the conversation he and Lauren had had. "It is as you say, White Eagle, both of us will try in the future to at least be friends. It is a step. Lauren has changed a great deal from the girl I once knew. When I apologized I did so sincerely. I think she knew it."

"Did you ask her to stay out of sight?"

"Yes."

"And?"

"She agreed."

"Sun Knife, I have a bad feeling about these men."

"Why?"

"I don't know. For some reason I feel they bring bad medicine."

"Let us at least give them the benefit of the doubt. We will talk to them. If it is as you think, we will do what you suggest, and move Lauren and Rebecca to Gray Cloud's village."

White Eagle nodded, but before he could speak again, the white trappers were brought to him. With a smile, he waited to face them. When the three entered, they stood and faced White Eagle.

"I am White Eagle, welcome." He motioned toward Cade. "This is my blood brother, Sun Knife."

Cade acknowledged their greetings, smiling to himself at their obvious surprise at his blue eyes.

"You have not met my father yet. He is the doctor here and"—he smiled pleasantly—"he is a white man."

"I would have known from those eyes." Josiah smiled. "He couldn't have been anything else unless there is a white woman here."

White Eagle was silent, but Cade laughed. "My mother is

Waterflower and my wife is Snow Blossom, daughter of Chief Tekata."

He went on to tell them of his past, answering their questions while White Eagle, adding some things to the conversation, spent most of his time studying the men and listening intently not only to what they said, but to what they did not say.

After the meal was finished, Leach brought out the bottle of whiskey.

"We ought to have a drink to celebrate being found. We was real lucky."

"Yes," White Eagle said softly, "you were very fortunate."

"Neither of us will be drinking," Cade said. "It is enough that you were all safely found."

"Yes," Josiah replied. "I have not met your wife, Sun Knife."

"I shall introduce her to you at the first opportunity."

"And your wife," he said quietly to White Eagle. "I have not met her either."

"My wife is visiting friends in another village."

"Oh, where?"

"The village of Great Bear, near the mountains."

"I see, well, maybe if we visit again sometime, we will meet her." He got to his feet. "I thank you for the meal and your hospitality. Good night, White Eagle." He smiled. "And you, Sun Knife."

They left the tepee walking slowly, each to his own.

"What is the matter, Josiah?"

"White Eagle was deliberately lying."

"About what?"

"If you gentlemen will remember, one of the villages we have mapped was the village of Great Bear. There was no sign that the wife of a chief of the caliber of White Eagle was anywhere near there. No, my friends, our young chief was lying and I'm going to find out why."

"What are you going to do?" Leach asked.

"I'll tell you later. For now, you two go back to our tepee and stay quiet. I have some looking around to do."

They stood and watched him walk away, his feet scrunching

the frozen snow.

Cade and White Eagle remained silent for a few minutes after the men had gone.

"What do you think, Brother?" White Eagle asked.

"I don't like Leach and Mo, but I think the other one is the one we'll have to watch. I think they're here for some reason we don't know."

"What reason could they have? What makes you suspicious?"

"I'd like to know if they stopped at Fort Stanton on their way in. If they did and they met the major, it would give us a lot of answers."

"Maybe it would be best if we sent Lauren and Rebecca to Running Wolf's village for the remainder of their stay."

"I agree it might be wise at least until we find out if our major is behind this."

"I will tell her tonight." He smiled. "She will not be too pleased."

Cade and White Eagle left together, Cade to return to his tepee and White Eagle to Lauren's. Rebecca drew on her furs and walked back to their tepee with White Eagle who kept a watchful eye for any of the white men to appear. It did not occur to him to look about his own tepee.

After he and Cade had left a dark form moved from one tepee to another until it found the one it wanted. With a knife that glittered in the pale light of the moon, he cut a small slit in the skin of the tepee, then he silently waited. When he heard voices inside, he put his eye to the slit. In a few minutes, a half-smile crossed his face.

Inside, a smiling Rebecca threw off the furs she wore. Her bright gold hair glistened as she bent over to renew the fire. White Eagle took her in his arms and kissed her as if she had been gone from him for an eternity.

"Rebecca, I must talk to you of these white men. They are a danger both to our tribe and to us."

"I have a feeling I know what you have in mind. White Eagle, must I leave?"

"Do you think I want you to go?" he said half in anger half in misery. "But I cannot let them see you. Both Sun Knife and

I have a suspicion they were sent here."

"What for? Not to find me. There would be no reason for them to be looking for me. No one knows my father and I stopped here."

"I don't know their reasons yet, but I intend to find out. If they are what they say they are, they can go in peace, but if they are here to bring harm to my people . . . I shall kill them."

The figure outside the tepee had seen and heard all he wanted to know. Quietly, he moved away from the tepee and made his way back to his own.

"Rebecca, you and Lauren must leave in the morning. Leaping Bear will guide you. I want you safely there before the snow falls again."

She sighed, went to him, put her arms about him, and rested her head against his chest.

"It will be hard to be away from you for so long," she whispered.

He tipped her chin up to look into her eyes and smiled.

"I shall come often. It will probably amaze my tribe how often White Eagle goes hunting. Especially a White Eagle who has never cared much for the cold and the snow."

She laughed, but pressed herself closer to him as if she were afraid.

"You tremble, Rebecca. Why are you frightened? It is for your safety I send you away."

"I know. I just have this feeling that if I do not hold you now, it will be a long time before I hold you again. White Eagle, something is happening and I am frightened of it."

White Eagle, always superstitious, and still almost sure Rebecca had some close connection to the gods, felt the chill of her fear and another greater one . . . that she was, in some way, telling him what was to happen. His arms bound her to him as if he could fight away the specters of avenging gods, by holding her. She was brought by the gods, she could be taken by them, and it shook him with real fear, a thing White Eagle had never known before.

He told her in the only way he knew. He kissed her gently at first, then the kiss grew deeper and deeper due to the combined fear and love he could not control.

Without a word, he lifted her in his arms and carried her to the fur-covered couch. There he dropped her feet to the floor keeping one arm about her. She whispered his name as she pressed her hands against his chest. He dropped his arm and stood watching while she loosened the ties of the buckskin dress she wore and let it drop to the floor.

"You are mine, Golden One," he said gently as he reached for her, "and no one will take you from me." His mouth found hers and he drew her down with him. His hands explored gently and possessively the soft warm creature that lay beneath him. She wanted to weep at his gentleness and his deep need to tell her how strong and all-consuming his love for her was. He held her slender body with infinite tenderness as he joined them together moving deep within her to blend them in fiery possession.

Josiah went back to his tepee to find the other two had consumed over half the bottle of whiskey.

"I want you two to stay calm and peaceful. Stay out of everybody's way, and don't cause any trouble. When spring comes, we'll leave as easily and peacefully as we came."

"That ain't our job," Mo said. "We have to find some excuse so the major can move in."

Josiah smiled. "I've already found it. Tell me, Mo, just what would the major do if he found a white woman living here?"

"I don't know, I suppose he'd come and get her."

"Well, suppose a little further. Suppose he thought she had been kidnapped and held against her will."

Mo's eyes began to glisten. "He'd hit this village so hard they would never know what happened."

"It would set fire to every village in this area and make our major a very happy man," Josiah replied.

"I'd like to see every Indian put on the reservation where they belong," Mo said.

"I know about you, Mo," Leach said, too drunk to realize he was treading on dangerous ground, "but what's got *you* so fired up against these Indians?" he said to Josiah. "What did they ever do to you? I heared once you was married to an Indian girl."

Josiah's eyes glittered dangerously. "Leach," he said softly, "if I ever hear you mention that to another living soul, you're a dead man. I'm none of your business; don't be foolish enough to pry into my private affairs. I don't take well to intruders."

Leach began to sweat when he heard the softly spoken words and saw death in the eyes of the man across the fire from him. Leach gulped heavily. "I didn't mean nothing by that, Josiah."

"Forget it, Leach."

There was quietness in the tepee now as all three found their beds. Mo slept solidly as a man without conscience is apt to do. Leach lay trembling for a long time over the mistake he had made with his loose tongue and Josiah lay awake a long time living with an unwelcome memory Leach's words had resurrected.

The next day, White Eagle wakened Rebecca before dawn. Quickly and quietly, she prepared herself and they slipped quietly to join Lauren and Leaping Bear who waited for them. White Eagle watched them ride away until they disappeared from sight. Then he turned back to what to him would rapidly become a lonely empty place where he would do little but sleep and eat. He was satisfied that he had gotten Rebecca safely. He did not see the shadow that stood in the entranceway and watched him reenter his tepee.

"Too late, my friend," the shadow said softly. "Much too late."

Leach and Mo lazed around the tepee enjoying the hospitality of the warm-hearted people, but offering nothing in return. It was Josiah who roamed the village talking to everyone, making himself as pleasant as possible. He met Benjamin who told him he was living with the Indians by choice and mentioned nothing about having a daughter. Seeing Benjamin it did not take Josiah long to connect him to the golden-haired wife of White Eagle.

He hunted with some of the young warriors who were fascinated with his guns, and he even tried to teach them to shoot, knowing that any instruction he gave them was like throwing a pebble into the sea.

They had been in the village for almost a month before

Josiah had the opportunity to actually meet Snow Blossom. Cade had done his best to keep their paths from crossing. He, too, knew the dangers of Mo and Leach, but he did not know, nor did Snow Blossom, that an even greater danger lay in the meeting between Snow Blossom and Josiah Tucker.

Snow Blossom had walked into the woods to gather firewood. She enjoyed the time alone and the silence of the woods muffled by the blanket of undisturbed white snow. It was at such a time that she had been born, during a deep quiet winter. On his way home from hunting her father had spotted a bright red blossom on a rocky ledge. Surprised that a flower grew at such a time, he had plucked it and carried it home. He arrived home to find that his wife had presented him with a daughter whom he immediately and happily named Snow Blossom. She had enjoyed hearing the story often from her father, and she enjoyed the winter snow. She walked along now, gathering small pieces of wood and not realizing how far she had drifted from the village until the ground became rocky and cliffs began to climb on each side of her. She paused for a moment to admire the beauty before her and that is when she spotted the bright red clusters of small flowers that were defying the winter snow and sending forth their color against the rocky cliff.

Determined to get one, she laid aside the bundle of wood she carried. She found small niches in the rocky surface and began to climb. She was about fifteen feet up, close to the red blossoms. She reached out her hand to grasp the flowers and suddenly her foot slipped. Helplessly, she grasped for another hold, but one could not be found. She tumbled. If she had not been unlucky, she would have been all right, but on the way down, her head struck sharply against the rock and she landed in a crumpled heap . . . unconscious.

Josiah had been separated from the men with whom he was hunting. This was the reason he was alone when he spotted the crumpled form in the snow.

Quickly, he dismounted and ran to her side. Gently, he turned her over and a gasp of shock was drawn involuntarily from him.

"Two Moons," he whispered. A look of joy crossed his face,

followed by one of intense pain. It was at this moment Snow Blossom opened her eyes. Her wits returned quickly. She knew instantly who was bending over her, and struggled to rise.

"Wait, lie still for a moment until I see if you are hurt," he said quickly. He reached out to brush back the hood of her fur coat to look closer at the cut on her head. It was a small cut, but it was bleeding freely. He took a handful of snow and washed away the blood and examined it carefully. All this time, Snow Blossom was watching him closely.

"It's not deep. I think you will be all right. What in heaven's name were you doing?"

Snow Blossom smiled. Feeling a little foolish, she explained about the flower she had been after. He smiled.

"Let me help you back to the village."

"I'm all right," she insisted, but when she went to get to her feet a cry of pain came. Her ankle was already swollen and she could put no weight on it.

"I will take you back," he said firmly. "You could never get back on that ankle."

There were no words of protest that could have effectively stopped him. Quickly, he mounted his horse; then effortlessly, he reached down and drew her up in front of him. They rode back to the village without a word exchanged between them. Cade, who had been working with his father in the treatment of a few small illnesses and injuries, was told by a breathless child that the white man was bringing Snow Blossom home.

Cade ran to his own tepee and found Josiah lifting Snow Blossom down from his horse.

"What happened?"

"She's had a nasty fall. Her head is all right, but I'm afraid she's sprained her ankle." He carried her inside and laid her gently on the couch while Cade bent down beside the bed to examine her ankle. Almost immediately Michael and White Eagle appeared. Josiah explained what had happened and the three of them stood watching as Cade finished examining her.

"It is not broken, but you won't be able to walk on it for a few days." He smiled down into Snow Blossom's eyes and reached out and took her hand. He held it while he turned to Josiah. "My thanks for finding her and bringing her back safely."

"You're welcome. I'm just glad I was there."

When everyone was gone, Cade again knelt by his wife's bed. He brushed a quick kiss across her cool lips.

"I must demand that you be more careful of yourself, my love." He grinned. "You had me scared there for a minute."

"I am fine." She answered his kiss by reaching up and drawing his mouth to hers in a kiss that was meant to do exactly what it did. It took Cade's mind from the cause of the accident and centered it on the soft responding woman in his arms who proceeded to prove that, in fact, she was quite well.

When Cade finally returned to his father's side, Snow Blossom relaxed against the furs and slept for a short time. She was wakened when a voice outside her door asked her permission to enter. It was Josiah and in all honor, she could not refuse him. When he came in, he was smiling and holding one arm behind his back.

"I must thank you for rescuing me," she began. "I would have had great difficulty getting back to the village by myself."

"You needn't thank me. It was my privilege to be there when you needed me. It is an honor to be able to come to the aid of such a beautiful woman."

"Nevertheless, I am grateful."

"I thought I might make the fall worth the while."

"What do you mean?"

"You were climbing for something?"

She smiled. "It was foolish of me."

"No, not foolish. If you wanted the flower, I felt you should have it," he said softly. He brought out his hand from behind his back and in it, he held the blood-red snow blossom.

His eyes were intent on her and he smiled when he saw her eyes light with pleasure.

"You went back for it," she breathed softly as she accepted the flower. "Again I must thank you. It was a kind thing for you to do considering how childish I was to climb for it anyhow."

"Childish?" he said softly. "No, you are a very beautiful woman. A woman who seeks beauty should have it."

Her wide eyes watched the expression in his change and deep

within her a deep tingle of fear began. There was something mysterious and deep that lurked in his eyes and she could not quite understand. All she knew was that she was suddenly extremely afraid, an emotion she very seldom had felt, and that she wanted Cade more deeply and desperately than she ever had before.

He must have read the fear also, for he smiled and turned toward the door. "You must rest."

"Thank you again for the flower."

At the door he turned to face her. There was no smile again and the words he said echoed through her mind and she would one day remember them vividly. "Your husband is a very lucky man. He should be careful to guard and protect a rare thing such as you. Carelessness could cost him a great deal."

Before she could answer him, he was gone, leaving her alone with that unnamable feeling of impending disaster that she could not control or prevent.

Josiah walked slowly back to the tepee he shared with Leach and Mo. His mind was caught now in a memory he had tried for a long time to exorcise from his mind and his heart.

When he entered the tepee, Mo questioned him on where he had been.

"Hunting."

"Get anything?"

"Yes . . . I did."

"What?"

"Something I've been looking for for a very long time, and this time I don't intend to lose it again."

"Huh? I don't understand."

"Never mind, Mo. It's not meant for you to understand. I do, and for now, that's enough. When spring breaks and the major wipes out this village, I intend to take what I want. Then it will all be returned to me and everything will be even. . . . I'll have what always should have been mine."

Mo didn't understand a word Josiah said, but he knew Josiah was a man who could not be pushed. He shrugged and returned to his own thoughts.

Josiah threw himself down on his couch with his hands behind his head . . . and began to plan.

Chapter Seventeen

It was a six-day journey from Tekata's village to the village of Gray Bear. Leaping Bear traveled much slower than he would have, had he been alone, in deference to the white women. A pleasant, happy man by nature, he made the trip easy for Lauren and Rebecca by explaining how he found the path from village to village, and much about the birds and animals they saw along the way.

Rebecca, made aware of nature and the Indians' affinity with it by White Eagle, enjoyed the trip, but for Lauren, it was an experience. She began to realize how well the Indians lived with the world given them. Instead of trying to make it conform to them as the white man did, they conformed to it, blended with it until nature and the Indian were one.

She also began to realize how difficult it must have been for Cade to move from one world to the other, and deep inside she began to understand Cade's preference for this one.

There were always outlying watchers and guards for every village. Mostly men who were hunting the area around their village. This was the reason Running Wolf knew of the approach of the strangers two days before they arrived. When the white women were described to him, he realized that the golden-haired one had to be the wife of White Eagle and also that the other had to be Lauren.

Leaping Bear and the two women were riding along when suddenly Leaping Bear stopped.

"What is it, Leaping Bear?" Rebecca asked.

"Someone comes to meet us."

"How did they know we were coming?"

Leaping Bear grinned. "I am surprised they did not come sooner. I am sure," he said with amusement deep in his voice, "there are those in Gray Bear's village that are happy to see the visitors from Tekata's village."

Lauren and Rebecca could see the rider approaching and in another few minutes, Lauren could tell that the rider was Running Wolf. He reined in his horse close to them. His words were for Leaping Bear, but his eyes were on Lauren.

"Welcome. Chief Gray Bear sends his greetings to the visitors from Tekata's village."

Rebecca smiled.

"I bring the white ones to stay with you until White Eagle comes for them. There is danger to them in our village."

"Danger?"

Leaping Bear explained hastily the three white visitors and White Eagle's feelings. "He would keep his woman safe from the prying eyes of the white ones he does not trust."

"Our brother does not need to fear, his woman will be cared for carefully," Running Wolf said quietly. "Come, I will travel with you."

Mischief in his glittering eyes, Leaping Bear said, "I am sure we are safe now. We do not want to take you from your hunting."

Running Wolf grunted and replied gruffly and firmly, "I will travel with you." He was aware that Leaping Bear was laughing, but was silently hoping Rebecca and Lauren didn't notice. It would have been beneath a warrior's dignity to care for women in place of hunting meat for his people.

They traveled together the balance of the day and no one but Leaping Bear noticed that Running Wolf kept his horse as close to Lauren's as possible. He pointed out things of interest and chatted with her amiably hoping she would not realize that his eyes devoured her and his fear was that she would hear the pounding of his heart from where she was.

They camped that night and just before Lauren fell asleep, she smiled at what the people of her world would say if they could see her now, camped in the wilderness with two "savages" and, she thought, never had she felt safer or more protected in her life.

Running Wolf sat by the dying fire for a long time watching the sleeping girl who lay curled in her blankets and furs across the fire from him. They had built a hasty lean-to to protect them from the wind, and with the fire in front of it, Lauren slept, comfortable and warm. The glow of the fire picked up the rich gleam of her auburn hair, and his mind could envision her slender body beneath the bundle of furs, the rich golden body he had watched avidly the day he had found her swimming.

He thought of his hunger for this woman and deep inside lingered the knowledge that her heart still turned toward Sun Knife. The one thing that irritated him was that he could not hate Sun Knife. He had been in his village less than two weeks and had developed a deep respect, both for Michael and his son.

Running Wolf had shared physical love with enough women to know that he would never take a woman against her will. He realized that he wanted desperately for Lauren to return what he felt for her. He wanted to cleanse her heart of what thoughts she had of Sun Knife so that she could find a place in it for himself. He also knew if it was not this way, it would be no way. He, too, was proud, too proud to keep a woman who thought of another. If he ever held her in his arms, he wanted her thoughts to be of him and only of him.

He had infinite patience and would do everything in his power to keep her now that she was joining them. His thoughts sank themselves in pleasant dreams as he drifted off to sleep.

Running Wolf had a way of coming completely awake instantly. He opened his eyes before dawn broke. The others were still asleep, so, moving silently, he rebuilt the fire and saw to the care of the horses.

When the women woke, they ate, and by the time the sun was fully up they were mounted and on their way.

By the time they arrived, they were relaxed and laughing together in friendly camaraderie. Rebecca's golden hair caused quite a stir in almost everyone, including wide-eyed shy children. Rebecca was delighted with them and soon she and Lauren were absorbed in the daily routines of the village.

Running Wolf found every opportunity he could to be in the same vicinity as Lauren and soon, she found herself depending on seeing him every day; yet between them, there were the words left unspoken.

They spoke of trivial things, and Lauren kept the conversation on that plane.

Lauren made immediate and fast friends with the children and young girls of the camp, sharing confidences and enjoying the games they played.

She laughed in sheer delight at the competitive yet friendly spirit in which they competed.

Two weeks after their arrival, White Eagle came. He remained in the village for three days, then returned home.

To Lauren, it was a time of relaxed play. There was little work to do, and what there was, was done in a united way to leave time for gossip, which the women seemed to thrive on, and time to play. She would watch the children sliding about on the ice-covered river and marvel at their seeming resistance to the cold and their delightful joy in their play.

Each day she seemed to find something new and interesting and each day she reached out for the friendship of these warm loving people, and it was given. Without restraint they accepted her as one of them.

No one accepted her more than Running Wolf who wanted her to stay among them forever. He came to her one bright afternoon. Fresh snow had fallen the night before and there was an atmosphere of majestic beauty in the snow-covered mountains and still trees that towered about them. She had been watching the antics of some of the children as they tumbled in the snow. Her cheeks were pink from the cold and her eyes shone with a rare contentment she didn't even know she felt.

"Will you ride with me, Lauren? I have a place I would like you to see."

She agreed immediately and they left the village.

He led the way on a path she would never have found if he hadn't been leading. She realized she would be totally lost in this enormous wilderness, yet she felt the spirit of oneness with all nature as she watched the splendor of it unfold before her.

They reached a tree-covered ledge and Running Wolf dismounted. She slid from her horse as Running Wolf came toward her. He tied both horses.

"We will have to walk a short way."

"What are you going to show me?"

"I would rather have you see."

She sighed and began to follow him. The path led upward and with a suddenness that took her breath away they were standing at the edge of a rocky cliff and the scene before them left her speechless. They faced another rocky wall about five hundred feet down where a waterfall must have fallen in the warm days of summer. Now, it was frozen in a state of suspended animation as if waiting for the sun to start it to life again.

"Oh, how very beautiful," she breathed as she turned toward him. "Running Wolf, thank you for bringing me to see this; it is breathtaking. I should like to see it in the summer."

"Stay," he said softly. "I will bring you back to see it."

She turned back to face the waterfall. He came up behind her, close enough for her to feel his presence, yet he did not touch her.

"Look at the falling water, Lauren. In the summer, it falls with a great roaring sound, but now it stands still. . . . It waits for the touch of the loving sun. It is like me, Lauren. Since I have seen you, my life seems to have become frozen like the water. It awaits only the warmth of your smile or the touch of your hand to send it thundering into life again."

She was suddenly frightened . . . frightened by the immensity of the land, of the emotion that threatened to overwhelm her. It was too much; she felt hot tears in her eyes and knew the taste of fear in her mouth.

She was not sure anymore even of the love she had felt for Cade. She knew that during the weeks she had been here, Cade was seldom in her mind. They had been filled with absorbing, learning, and sharing the joy of these open, giving people. She had been finding a place to stand on her feet. Running Wolf's love was an immense thing that she could feel.

"Lauren?"

"I don't know." The whisper was almost a sob. "Maybe . . . maybe I should go back to my safe little world. Maybe I'm fooling myself into believing I can do something."

"No!" he said sharply. He took hold of her shoulders and turned her to face him. "I swore by all the gods I would not say anything to force you, but Lauren, I have seen you here, among the children, among the women. You have a great strength and love to give. Michael and Sun Knife do not need you, but we do . . . I do."

"I cannot offer you yet what you need or deserve, Running Wolf. I am not sure of myself."

"I am a patient man, Lauren. Stay with us for one summer. Let me share it with you. Then you can decide and I will understand your decision whatever it is."

"Even if I decide to go?"

"Even if you decide to go," he replied softly.

The tears escaped and rolled down her cheeks as he drew her into his arms. His lips tasted her salty tears, then moved slowly and gently to her mouth. A new and strange sensation took her completely by surprise. A feeling of peace of warmth that flowed through her like a slow-moving flame. His arms bound her to him while his mouth explored hers with an expertise that swept her senses away. A newness, a brightness exploded within her, and she clung to him as her lips parted and she returned his kiss.

Slowly they parted and his intent dark eyes held hers.

"Stay, Lauren, stay. One summer. Stay and let me prove to you, you have been seeking what you want in the wrong place." His voice was gentle.

She closed her eyes and laid her head against his chest. He held her in silence as he waited for her answer. She would never know that he could hardly breathe in suspense, that he held himself quiet only by sheer determination, that he would never beg her to stay. When she lifted her head to look into his eyes, her green eyes glistened with tears, but the answer was there and he smiled, controlling his urge to shout with joy.

"You will stay," he said.

"Yes, I will stay . . . one summer."

"I will change that in time." He laughed with new-found assurance. "I will make you love me as I love you."

"Running Wolf—"

"No, Lauren, there will be no lies between us. I know what you feel for me is new; you are unsure. I also know Sun Knife lingers in some shadowed place in your mind. But I intend to force him from your mind and from your heart."

"It is unfair to you for me to say anything. I cannot make a promise."

"We will not speak of what is fair or unfair. You have agreed to stay; that is enough for now. We will take one day at a time. I love you, and I am willing to fight for what I want."

"I will stay. . . . I will try," she said softly.

With a soft exultant laugh, he kissed her again, enclosing her in an embrace that made her gasp.

They walked back to their horses and rode back to the village.

In Tekata's village, the three white visitors had become model guests. They were polite, quiet, and helped the men of the village provide sustenance for the winter days.

Mo and Leach were assured by Josiah that their quest for the "incident" the major had required was complete. He told them of Rebecca's presence and how she had been temporarily sent away.

"When spring breaks and we leave, White Eagle will bring her home. When he does, the major will have all the incentive he needs to do what he plans."

"Good," Mo replied, "we'll leave at the first sign of spring. The major will be glad to hear this. Breaking up a village the size of Tekata's will shake up every small village around here. When they get all the territory opened, it will be easy to shove them on a reservation."

"I'm sure that is less than what the major has in mind," Josiah said dryly.

"What do you mean?"

"He don't care if they get on a reservation or not. Can't you two see what's in his mind?"

"What?"

"He wants them dead—as many of them as he can get that way."

"Well, I'll tell you," Mo replied casually, "I don't care what he does. When we get our money I'm heading east. He can do what he wants out here."

"Yeah," Leach echoed. "We did our job. We'll take our money and get out. He can kill 'em all for all I care."

Josiah looked at the two for a minute; then he turned and

left the tepee.

"What's eatin' him?" Leach asked.

"Don't worry about him. Spring's only a few weeks away and we'll be gone from here with some good money in our pockets."

The two laughed together.

Outside, Josiah started from the village. He often walked alone, thinking out the plan he had in mind for one member of Chief Tekata's tribe . . . his daughter, Snow Blossom.

Returning to the village in the company of two other women, Snow Blossom saw Josiah making his way toward her. Again, that tingle of expectant fear touched her and she could not understand it. He had always been courteous and kind to her, from the day he had rescued her and brought her the flower. She had only just begun to realize how often she found herself in his company and that it was more and more often when he knew Cade was busy. She frequently felt his eyes on her, and then she found herself seeking the safety of others. She never went anywhere alone. She was angry at herself for fearing a man who had not only come to her aid, but who had never said anything to her that was in any way wrong.

"Hello." He smiled. She nodded her head in response. "I think we're going to get the first break in the weather."

"There will be more snow; there always is. It is not time for father sun to rule again."

They spoke of the weather, yet again, she felt the strange feeling of an impending force, as if some dark thing reached out and touched her. His eyes seemed to absorb her, hungry eyes that took in everything about her and stored it in a safe place to be withdrawn and examined more leisurely. What he wanted at that moment was to drag her to a quiet place and kiss those soft pink lips until she surrendered to him. "Soon," he thought, "your half-breed husband will be dead and you will belong to me."

Quickly making an excuse, she left him. His eyes followed her. Again, he cautioned himself to patience. One day soon, there would be no one left in her world but him.

Returning to her tepee, Snow Blossom found Cade there. It was a surprise to her for he was usually busy either with his father, hunting, or making new equipment. She must have looked at him in surprise for he laughed. His blue eyes sparkled with the love he felt for her and she felt it spark between them. Suddenly, the fear she felt near Josiah surfaced and she went to him, she put her arms about him and pressed herself close to him.

"I'm not complaining, my love." He chuckled as he kissed her several times. "But whatever I have done to deserve this tell me so I can do it more often."

"Oh, Sun Knife, I love you so much, sometimes I'm afraid."

"Afraid of what?"

"I don't know. Afraid that something will come along and take you away from me."

"Snow Blossom, nothing is going to happen." He held her close to him wondering if his uncomfortable feelings about their white visitors were being transferred to her. "We have nothing to be afraid of. It is the long winter that depresses you. Soon it will be spring, and we can be free of this confinement. You will find this will all pass."

She was sure it was more than just the winter that seemed to smother her, but she also knew she did not have the words to make him understand. She wanted to tell him how afraid she was of Josiah, but there was no real complaint she could make. Josiah had always been polite and friendly. No, there were no words, but now they were unnecessary. Warmed by her clinging, Cade's mouth was seeking hers in a more demanding way. She stirred against him, feeling the deep pleasure she always felt when he reached for her.

"God, I love you, Snow Blossom," he whispered against her hair. "Do you have any idea how often I thank the gods for giving me you? You have made my life a full and beautiful thing."

His lips stopped any words she might have said in reply. Letting everything but him slip from her mind, she clung to him and her lips parted in fervent response.

She felt his hands fumble for the ties on the clothes she wore and soon, she felt their always gentle touch against her skin.

He lifted her gently in his arms, rocking her against him. She put her arms about his neck and closed her eyes savoring the strength and the warmth of the deep need she always felt for him.

There was no hurry, as he joined her on the couch and drew her cool slender body close to his. She could feel the length of his lean muscular frame as they lay against each other.

His lips now were gentle, touching her lightly and tracing the soft line from her jaw to her throat down to her rounded breasts. He heard her contented murmur of his name as he continued his path, tasting and touching until she moved against him in a burning, searching need that matched his own.

Her hands clung to him, feeling the taut muscles of his back, caressing and pulling him closer and closer.

The desire to possess her was a need that would always remain with him. He knew with every fiber of his being that if he possessed her a million times, the need would remain. It had burned to a depth in his soul that would forever reach for the other half of himself, the being that made him whole.

He lifted her body to meet his as he joined them. With slow easy movement, allowing his desire to mount to a pitch almost beyond control, he moved within her, building the flame higher and higher until neither of them knew of the existence of anything but the fire that molded them into one.

In the stillness they lay together, contented and relaxed. He held her in the curve of one arm with her head resting on his shoulder while he absently caressed her.

"Snow Blossom?"

"Yes."

"When you came in, something was bothering you. Is there something wrong, something you want to talk to me about?"

She thought of the loving gentle man who held her and she did not want to turn that gentleness into anger. Josiah had done nothing to her, she rationalized, and he would be gone soon, so she would say nothing to create trouble.

"It was nothing; maybe I was just a little impatient for the winter to be gone. I miss Rebecca and Lauren and I miss the warm sun."

She stretched luxuriously. "I should like to be lying in the warm sun near the river with you now. We could swim and then—"

"And then what?" He laughed.

"And then we could make love again. I would stay in your

arms always."

He turned on his side and looked down into her eyes, his blue eyes alight with the pleasure of knowing she wanted him as much as he always wanted her. He bent his head and brushed a kiss across her lips. "You are good for me, love." He chuckled. "You have a way of making me feel as if I could conquer the world or any other problem we might face. I thank you, but make no mistake, you are my strength, my hope, and every other thing I have of real value in this world."

"Sun Knife," she said, a deep urgency in her voice, "don't let us ever be separated—not by anything. I don't think I could bear it."

"What is it, Snow Blossom?" he said, his eyes holding hers. "Why are you afraid?"

"I don't know. I have seen it in dreams and felt it when I am alone. Something dark that takes you away from me."

He held her close to him. "You and I both know that we live our lives by what the Great Spirit wills. I cannot believe he would have given me the gift of you if he had not meant it to be. We cannot live in fear, Snow Blossom. We will live our lives together and be happy with each other as long as he wills. You may feel sure of this. Outside of the hand of the Great Spirit, nothing will separate us, for outside of death, I will never let you go."

"I know." She smiled. "Forgive me for sounding like a child." She kissed him quickly. "And now tell me why you were home doing nothing when I came." She made a mock face. "What kind of a lazy husband do I have?"

"If you must know, impudent woman, I just came to look into your pretty eyes for a few minutes."

"Serpent tongue, why do you lie to me?" She laughed.

He pulled her roughly into his arms again, then reached out and smacked her solidly on her bare buttocks. "Is that any way to talk to your hard-working husband? I should beat your bottom until you learn to respect my . . . ouch!" he yelped as her teeth found a vulnerable ear.

"Beat me, would you?" She laughed again as she leaped to straddle him and pressed her small fists against his chest. He was suddenly still as he looked up at the beauty that bent laughing over him. Her eyes sparkled and her heavy braids fell over her shoulders. That she was completely unaware of her extraordinary beauty, he knew, but he was held breathless by it. There was laughter in her eyes and a glow of love about her that gave her a look of vibrant life. He reached up and gently touched her cheek. She remained motionless as he slowly let his fingers trail down her slender throat, linger for a second on the curve of her shoulder then move down to slide over one pink-tipped breast. They paused for a moment then moved again to travel the curve of her waist . . . down to one rounded hip. There he let his hand rest. Then slowly, he reached up with his other hand and took hold of one long braid. Gently, he pulled her toward him and she bent forward until their lips met. Then, with a soft murmured sound, she was in his arms again seeking the renewal of their promise of love.

The sun grew warmer and the snow began slowly to melt. Ice on the small rivers began to splinter then melt and the streams grew rapid again. Small buds began to appear on the trees and in small spots in the meadows and valleys, valiant blades of grass and flowers began to push their way up from the still half-frozen ground.

The cool breeze from the north turned and began to blow with a warm touch across the village.

Children began to play outside and their shrill laughter filled the air, a pleasure to the elders who could now sit outside the confining tepees that had held them all winter.

Young warriors made their weapons, anxious to make their way into the forests to prove their bravery.

It was spring, a spring that would be marked in the memory of the tribe of Tekata for all time.

Mo and Leach were anxious to go back to the fort, but Josiah was not ready to leave yet. He lingered for a little longer to antagonize Sun Knife and White Eagle with questions and to talk as often as possible with Snow Blossom.

She managed to stay away from him, but the day came when she could not. She was walking back into the village and for the first time, she became careless—she was alone.

She walked slowly, literally tasting the still, cool breeze. She was not aware of his presence until he stepped from behind a tree directly in her path. There was no way she could not speak to him for her debt, in her mind, was still there.

"Good morning, Mr. Tucker."

"Must you still call me Mr. Tucker? I thought we were friends?" He smiled. "Can you not call me Josiah?"

"Yes," she replied softly, "Josiah."

"Yes." His voice was gentle. "I like that."

Her heart thudded heavily as his eyes seemed to devour her. All she wanted was to be away from this spot.

"May I walk with you?"

There was nothing she could do but nod, grateful that they could be moving closer to the village. They walked along slowly together.

"We will be leaving the village soon," he said softly. "It has been a long winter. I am glad the spring has come."

"So you can go home?"

"No, so I can see you again."

She remained quiet. He stopped and reached out to touch her arm so that she would stop, too. Snow Blossom had been pushed as far as she intended to be. She was not a woman to stand in fear for very long. Now, she looked up at him her gold eyes aglow with fire.

"What do you want here, Josiah? There is nothing here for you now that spring has come and it is safe for you to travel. It is best that you go."

"You are very beautiful, Snow Blossom."

"I am married, Josiah, very happily married to the only man I have ever loved or ever will. It is not the custom of our village for an unmarried man to pursue a married woman. You are our guest. I suggest, so that you do not anger Chief Tekata or my husband and my brother, that you go. I will say nothing to them unless you continue to follow me. Think well, Josiah, there are many of us and few of you."

"I am sorry if I have offended you, Snow Blossom; it was not my intention. I wanted to tell a very beautiful woman that I appreciate her beauty. I . . . I once knew another woman as beautiful as you. In fact . . . you look so amazingly like her. She had that same . . . glow of life about her as you do. She loved everything and everybody—she even loved me." He said the last words softly and there was a faraway glow of pain in his eyes that reached out to her.

"Where is she now?"

"She is dead, or"—his gaze returned to her—"I thought she was dead."

"I'm sorry."

For a moment he remained silent; then he smiled. "I did not stop you on a beautiful day like this to tell you my troubles."

"I am also sorry for my rudeness," she said.

"It is all right. We will be leaving tomorrow. I wished to tell you good-by . . . for now."

"For now?"

"Maybe . . . we will meet again one day."

"I doubt it. Good-by Josiah. I wish you well."

"Thank you, Snow Blossom," he said, his voice quiet; then he turned and walked back toward the village. She stood and watched him go, and again she was possessed with an inner vision of darkness and blood. She shook the feeling free, telling herself she was imagining all kinds of dark things about this man because she had feared him. Placing her mind on other things, she went back to the village.

The three white men packed their equipment and made preparations to leave the village the next morning. Tekata had a small feast prepared for them that night. Cade, White Eagle, Tekata, and Benjamin ate and talked with them and wished them a safe journey.

The next morning just after the sun rose, the three slowly made their way from the village. Snow Blossom stood in the doorway of her tepee and as Josiah reached the edge of the village he turned and saw her.

"Soon," he whispered.

They traveled slowly, camping late at night and rising early in the mornings. It was still several days before the fort came into view on the horizon. At sundown that night, they rode through the doors of the fort and into the fate of the village of Tekata.

Josiah, Mo, and Leach were given supper and quarters. The next morning Josiah took the map and went to Major Chivington's office. Inside, he spread the map on the major's desk.

"There are many isolated villages," he said as he pointed to the map. "Here, here, here, and here are the four closest to the large village of Tekata."

"How many fighting men?"

"Singly the only village that could get enough men to do you any harm is Tekata's. He could probably muster five hundred warriors."

"The others?"

"None of them could get up more than about two hundred apiece."

"Singly . . . singly," he repeated.

"John, if ever Tekata were able to get all those small villages together he could give this fort some real serious trouble."

John Chivington smiled. "You have a plan in mind, Josiah?"

"Yes."

"What?"

"Before I tell you, I want a promise from you."

"What?"

"I'll give you your incident, John, all the reason you need to go in and do what you want."

John looked across the desk and smiled.

Again, "Anything you want is yours; give me what I want."

Josiah paused for a moment, then he said the words very quietly.

"A white girl. The young chief has a wife who's a white girl."

John slammed his hand down on the desk, and a harsh laugh echoed in the room.

"A promise, John?"

"Yes . . . yes, what is it?"

"The chief has a daughter. Her name is Snow Blossom. I want her."

"An Indian girl!"

"I want her, John."

"All right. It is a bargain. Both of them are to be brought here. The white girl . . . what is her name?"

"Rebecca Wade . . . now she's White Eagle's wife."

"She's no Indian's wife. Both of them will be brought here—the rest will be wiped from the earth."

"Let me tell you one thing, John. Make sure you kill the chief, his son, and the husband of Snow Blossom. Any one of them left alive will have all the force to gather the tribes together. If they did, I warn you, this fort would be in real danger."

"You needn't worry about that, Josiah. I shall make a point of killing those three personally, if I can. But they will be dead. Do you want to come with us?"

"Mo and Leach will go; they'll point out the women. I . . . I will stay here."

"Have it your way. I am going to perfect my plans and start getting my men prepared. In about three weeks, we will leave here in force. In a month it will be all over. The white girl will be here and so will that pretty little Indian squaw and you can do what you want with her." He grinned lasciviously.

"She is not a squaw, John, she is a lady."

"A . . . a lady, this little Indian whore?"

Josiah stood up, his face frozen and his eyes burning with an emotion that made a distinct pause in the major's thoughts.

"She is not a squaw," he said firmly. "She is not a whore. She is the woman I intend to marry."

"Marry?"

"She is the daughter of Chief Tekata. When you see her, you will understand. She is not the kind of woman a man forces; she is the kind of woman that you enjoy like fine wine."

"Well, no matter. In a month she'll be here. From then on, she's your problem. Now, show me how this village is laid out and where the tepees are located that we'll find those women in."

They bent over the map for a long time before the major was satisifed that he had everything straight in his mind. He went to a cabinet and took out a bottle and two glasses. He filled one and handed it to Josiah and then he held up his own.

"Here's to the elimination of a plague," he said softly; then he sipped from his glass not noticing that Josiah did not drink.

Josiah rose from his chair, set his glass on the table, and walked to the door.

"Good night, John," he said quietly; then he went out and closed the door behind him.

Outside, he walked in the warmth of the sun and thought of Snow Blossom. He washed all thought of any others except two from his mind—Cade Holliday, whom he wanted to see dead, and Snow Blossom whom he wanted alive, very much alive.

Chapter Eighteen

With a speed that brought laughter to all his friends, White Eagle made preparations to go and bring Rebecca home. He smiled pleasantly at their laughter and admitted freely it had been the longest winter of his life.

He made what would have been a trip of several days, in much less time. He traveled until the depth of night forced him to stop and he rose long before the sun. As he traveled, he chewed dry corn and strips of dried buffalo meat to keep from stopping. It was only in consideration of his horse that he rested at all.

Rebecca, since the first thaw, had watched the trail entering the village. Every day, she had kept one eye on it and one on her daily work. To Lauren, this was also a source of amusement.

In the early dawn, they had brought water from the river and prepared breakfast; then they had gone about their daily chores, sharing the work and the close feeling that had developed between them, for it was to Rebecca that Lauren turned with her troubled mind, and in a few words, it was Rebecca who opened her eyes to a new way of thinking.

"It is stubborn determination that blinds your eyes," she had told Lauren. "You cling to thoughts of changing others and their feelings while you refuse to change yours. And . . ." she said softly, "you refuse to look at love because it demands of you what you are afraid to give."

"I am not afraid."

"Are you not? I will admit that I also was afraid, for life here is more demanding than I have ever known. But I have allowed myself to see that love for White Eagle will be a strong thing on which I can lean. You know, in your heart, that will never exist with Cade. You have seen with your own eyes how much he loves Snow Blossom, but still you hold to thoughts that cannot be. You refuse to let a strong love that stands near you, support you. Lauren, what do you feel for Running Wolf?"

"I am confused."

"What has happened between you?"

"I have promised to stay when White Eagle comes for you. I have said I will stay for one summer."

"Will it do any good to stay if you do not open your heart and allow yourself to feel. Forget all else that came before and try to let yourself see what Running Wolf promises. Maybe for the first time you will understand."

Lauren sighed. "I know you are right, Rebecca. I just don't know about me. Maybe . . . maybe I should just go home. I cannot seem to find my footing here."

"If you run away from facing one problem," Rebecca said quietly, "it will become easier and easier to run away from the next one, and one day you will find that you have run away from everything."

Lauren was about to reply when Rebecca's gaze was caught on the horizon. Although still far away, she knew the rider as only a woman would know the one man in her heart. Slowly she rose to her feet.

"Rebecca?"

"White Eagle is coming," Rebecca said softly; then suddenly her feet were flying as she ran toward him. At that moment he, too, saw her coming and kicked his horse into a run. When he got to her side, he pulled his horse to an abrupt halt, slid down from its back, and gathered her into his arms. He could hear her happy laughter as he swung her up against him and crushed her to him with iron arms. She gasped at the breathless way his mouth sought hers and it was several minutes before he deposited her again on her feet and stood looking into her eyes.

"Come home, Rebecca." He smiled. "It has been a long lonely winter."

"I am ready. I have prepared my things from the minute of the first thaw. I have waited impatiently for you to come for me."

"I came the moment they left. I will go and thank the chief for caring for you while you and Lauren get your things together."

"White Eagle, Lauren is not returning with us. She has promised Running Wolf to stay for the summer."

"It is good, Rebecca. I had hoped Lauren could find some kind of happiness. Running Wolf is a good warrior and a strong man. He is the kind of man she needs."

"I don't know if anything will happen; I only hope she will open her eyes to see."

"That is something only they can solve," White Eagle said firmly as he tightened his arms about her. "Let us leave today."

She nodded. In one quick movement, he leaped upon his horse, then reached down and lifted her in front of him. They rode slowly back to where Lauren stood, smiling and awaiting them.

"White Eagle," she said as they dismounted beside her. "It is good to see you again."

"And you, Lauren." He smiled. "You are brown and beautiful. Your green eyes smile, that is good. You are content?"

Lauren looked at him, aware for the first time that she was growing content here. "Yes," she replied. "It has been good. Did Rebecca tell you that I am not returning with you?"

"Yes, Lauren. I think it is good if you stay. It will give you a better chance to find yourself and what you need to make you happy. It is good to spend quiet time away from all you know, to think of your future and what you will do with it."

She smiled at his understanding. "Will you come and eat before you begin your journey back?"

"Yes, we will eat, but I would begin our journey back soon. I would like to be well on the way before we camp for the night."

The sparkle in Lauren's eyes and the swift blush to Rebecca's cheeks brought a deep rumbling chuckle from White Eagle as they walked toward the tepee Rebecca and Lauren had shared and in which they would eat.

They ate what Lauren would laughingly refer to as the hastiest meal ever, and then White Eagle went to thank the chief of the village for caring for his most prized possession—Rebecca.

Within two hours, they were on their way and Lauren stood

and waved farewell until they disappeared from sight. She stood and watched the empty horizon, wondering if she was doing the right thing or not.

Lauren turned back to the tepee, spending the rest of the warm afternoon within, thinking. It was just at the supper hour when she rose from her couch and went for a walk.

That first touch of spring still held a mild touch of winter in the air. She wrapped a small warm blanket about her shoulders and walked slowly along the path through the woods. There she sat by the rapidly moving water. It was like her life, she thought, a rapidly moving thing with depths she did not know yet or understand. She felt herself caught in those depths now and her mind floundered in search of a strong rock on which she could cling until she could find a solid shore on which to stand.

It was dusk and the last rays of the sun touched the horizon when she rose to return to the village.

She had just entered her tepee again when she heard Running Wolf call to her. She pushed aside the flap and stepped outside to speak with him.

As always, his intent dark eyes regarded her with an expression she could not read.

"Rebecca has gone with White Eagle?"

"Yes, they left a few hours ago."

"I know. I was told he was seen coming. I . . . I was afraid you might have changed your mind and gone."

"I would not lie to you, Running Wolf," she said softly.

"I know in my head"—he said the words quietly as his eyes held hers—"but my heart was afraid."

"I will stay . . . stay until I find my answers."

"I am glad. The snow melts; soon the waterfall will fall with a mighty roar. I want to take you to see it. I want you to see many things with me. It will be a good summer."

She could not answer the searching look in his eyes, the look that sought a matching response to his love.

"Yes . . ." she said softly, "it will be a good summer."

He stood without speaking and the long shadows of early darkness cast his face in deep shadows and she could no longer read his eyes; yet she could feel the emotion that exuded from him and reached to touch her. They had stood so for several minutes, then he reached out and brushed his hand against the softness of her hair. In a moment, he was gone and she stood staring into the darkness still feeling his presence. After a while, she turned and reentered the tepee to lie long into the night unable to sleep.

Rebecca and White Eagle had traveled slowly, yet they had covered many miles before the sun began to set.

They made camp and cooked a meal, and talked together as they ate. He told her about the white man's stay and all that had transpired since she was gone. She spoke of a pleasant time spent in Running Wolf's village and a long uneventful winter. They spoke words that slowly drifted away unheard and uncared for. Their eyes met and held and with a half-smile on his lips, he reached out and drew her beside him on his blanket.

She sighed contentedly as she nestled in the safety of his arms and rested her head against his chest.

"It is good to feel you in my arms again, Golden One. I cannot tell you the loneliness of the long nights without you."

"You need not try, White Eagle. I know well, for I felt as if I were lost." She caressed his broad chest with slender fingers. "White Eagle . . . I will never be separated from you again."

He drew her body across his and she smiled down into his eyes. Then she repeated in a slow firm voice, "I will never be separated from you again. It is my only wish to live and die here, in your arms, where I belong."

He bound her against him, his lips searching for hers as he murmured softly, "Never, Golden One . . . never."

He tasted gently her soft giving mouth with several light kisses that sent her heart skipping madly.

"Oh, White Eagle," she murmured softly, "I have missed you so terribly."

His hands caressed her with a memory of their own and his lips grew more and more demanding.

She closed her eyes and allowed herself to be immersed in the warm depth of his love.

It was a thing of beauty such as she had never known in all the times they had been together. She felt him reach within her to touch a place that she had never known existed. She heard him say her name softly against her hair as she clung to him and reached to possess him as he was her.

It was a joyous and fulfilling blending that left them silenced and spellbound by what they shared. He held her until she slept in his arms. For several hours, he did not sleep, but lay holding her and caressing her soft hair.

"You are mine, Rebecca . . . mine. There is no power on this earth strong enough to take you from me," he whispered. It was a long time before he closed his eyes in sleep.

The soft call of a bird wakened Lauren and she smiled. Rising from the couch she gathered a few extra clothes. In the half-gray light of dawn she went back to the river. Quickly stripping off her clothes, she waded into the water. Its coolness felt good against her skin. She swam, luxuriating, then walked ashore, dried herself, and put on the extra clothes she had brought.

It was breaking day when she reentered the outskirts of the village. There would be work for her the moment she arrived; yet today, she felt the urge to play the truant, to go somewhere and enjoy the warm spring day, to watch the budding of the trees and smell the clean fresh newness of the world about her. She was deep in thought, so deep that she almost bumped into Running Wolf before she saw him. Startled, she gasped his name.

"Running Wolf!"

"Good morning." He smiled. "Your hair is wet; you've been swimming?"

"Yes."

"It is a beautiful day. Would you like to go with me?"

"Where?"

"Fishing."

"Fishing?"

"I am hungry for fish and I know a quiet little place where the fish are big—like this." He laughed as he held his hands about three feet apart.

Catching his humor, her green eyes sparkled with laughter. "Are they really that big?" she inquired, doubt glowing in her eyes.

He looked at her with wide innocent eyes. "Would I not tell

you the truth? If they are not that big, I'll cook them myself."

"I have half a notion to call your bluff just to see the strong warrior, Running Wolf, cook a meal for a woman." She laughed.

"You'll come?" he asked and she could hear the hopefulness in his voice.

"Yes . . . I'll come."

His quick smile flashed. "I had hoped you would so I had two horses made ready."

Their laughter blended as she walked with him to the horses. He helped her mount by easily lifting her from the ground and placing her on the horse's back. Leaving the outskirts of the village, they rode for quite a while before he began to edge his horse from the path and toward the sound of the river. At the river, they dismounted, and Lauren watched while Running Wolf tethered the horses. From the side of his horse, Running Wolf took a long spearlike object that had, instead of a weapon's sharp point, a trident-type head.

They walked to the edge of the water and Lauren sat on a large flat stone while Running Wolf waded out into the water until it came to mid-thigh.

She watched as his lean brown body became motionless. He stood, poised like a young Adonis with the spear raised and his dark gaze on the water. She sat very still, her eyes on him, and admired his muscular graceful body as he stood like an immobile statue. Time moved slowly by and she was amazed as minute after minute passed without a single movement from him. Dressed only in a breechcloth, the sun glistened across his bronzed skin. It was the first time she had really studied his features without those dark eyes reading her thoughts.

He had strong features, the nose hawklike and the jaw square and solid. High cheekbones made his broad, easily smiling mouth seem more vulnerable. His hair, thick and dark, hung in two braids at his shoulders bound with rawhide ties. He was, she realized suddenly, an extremely handsome and masculine man. The hand that held the spear aloft was large, but the fingers were long and tapered. He stood, unmoving while she studied him, seemingly unaware of anything else but the slow-moving water. It fascinated her that he had such absolute control of his body that he did not stir a muscle.

It was the first time she had ever seen anyone fish in this manner and she was absolutely sure it was near to impossible to spear a swift-moving fish. She had seen the others in the tribe fling nets into the water and drag in fish, but nothing like this.

As he walked into the water, he had cautioned her to absolute silence, and she had complied. Minute followed minute and she found herself stiff with expectancy. Suddenly, in a movement she could barely follow, the spear flashed downward and she heard his sudden laugh as he turned toward her holding the spear aloft with a huge fish pierced and wriggling at the end of it. Her laughter answered his as with a mischievous look in her eyes she opened her hands to the size he had mentioned before. She tipped her head to the side and said, "It is a lovely fish, Running Wolf, but I do believe it is a *little* smaller than you had promised."

He chuckled, and his dark eyes sparkled in return. "Then you must have your wish and I shall have to cook it, but of course," he said humorously, "you must also help me eat it if I cook it."

He waded ashore and neatly flipped the fish to the grassy bank.

"Are you hungry?"

"If you are going to cook, I'm hungry."

They laughed together. She helped him gather the wood for the fire. After it was built, he set about swiftly cleaning the fish and preparing it. At the edge of the fire, he had placed a flat rock. As the intensity of the fire grew, the rock became hotter. As the fire slowly burned down, he placed the pieces of fish on the hot rock. They began to sizzle and within a few minutes, were cooked, juicy, and crisp at the edges. She enjoyed them thoroughly, giving most of the credit to her hunger and not to the fact that she was enjoying Running Wolf's relaxed happy company. They talked and ate and completely enjoyed the bright spring day. Not once did he speak of their relationship. Instead, he told her amusing stories and enjoyed her relaxed laughter. The day, he thought, was more than rewarding, for he had seen the beginning of the loss of fear in her. It was enough for now, he thought, as they rode slowly home.

It was an occasion that opened the door for more, and she soon found that she was in Running Wolf's company often in the days that followed.

When he hunted, he would bring a choice piece of the meat to the tepee she shared with an older woman who was amused also. Running Wolf would studiously ignore the glittering eyes of the older woman.

Lauren found herself a source of sincere interest to the children of the village to whom she told fascinating stories of the white world, sang songs, and extended the hand of gentleness to any that were hurt. They would gather about her and listen with rapt faces. Among the children was a small wide-eyed child about ten whose face seemed strangely familiar. When she finally managed to pull a few words from her, she found out why. She had just finished the telling of a story and the children had begun to drift away—all except the little girl who sat at her feet and looked up at her.

"Don't you want to go and play with the children?"

The small head shook negatively.

"Why? Do you want to hear another story?"

Again, the negative shake.

"What is your name?"

"Little Dove," came the soft reply from the shy little girl.

"What a pretty name. Who is your mother?"

"She was Clearwater. She is gone now."

"Gone?"

"The Great Spirit took her."

"Oh," Lauren said helplessly. "Who cares for you?"

"My father, Great Wolf, and my brother, Running Wolf."

"You are Running Wolf's sister?"

Again the quick affirmative nod and a timid smile.

"I see. Do you have other sisters and brothers?"

"No, only Running Wolf."

"Well, would you like to come and stay with me while I am here? I would like your company."

This time she was surprised at the quick negative shake of the head again.

"I will stay with my brother."

"You love your brother?"

"Yes . . . when will you go home?" she asked bluntly.

Lauren was so surprised by the question that she could not answer for a moment. Then she realized the emotion that created the question. Running Wolf was looking at Lauren and Little Dove was jealous and too young yet to handle the emotion. She wanted to reach out and comfort the child, but did not know what words to say to her.

"Little Dove," she said softly, "why do you want me to go home?"

Her small head bent forward so that her eyes escaped Lauren's.

"Little Dove?"

Lauren reached out and tipped Little Dove's head up so she could see the glistening tears in her eyes. "Why did you come?" the child said softly. "My brother is different since he has looked at you. He . . . he does not see Little Dove anymore. His thoughts are all of you. He . . . he wants you to stay here."

"How do you know this?"

"He told my father. He wants you to marry him and stay with us." The tears were falling now. "If you do he will never remember Little Dove again."

"Little Dove, I am sure your brother's love for you grows every day and that he could not love you less no matter if I chose to stay or not."

Doubt filled the child's eyes and Lauren could see her refusal of this.

"Little Dove, why do you not speak with your brother? Why do you not tell him how you feel? He will tell you the truth . . . will you listen?"

"He will be angry with me that I spoke to you with disrespect."

"I think not, Little Dove. I think he will want to ease your troubled mind. Do you want me to be with you?"

"No." The child rose, looked at Lauren with puzzlement in her eyes, then turned and ran quickly from the tepee. Lauren followed to see her small figure crossing the fields and running toward the river.

Without hesitation, Lauren ran to Running Wolf's tepee. When she called out to him, he came out of the tepee, surprise in his eyes.

"Lauren, what is wrong?"

"Running Wolf, I must speak to you."

"Of course, are you all right?"

"Yes, but I think someone else close to you has a serious problem."

"Who?"

"Little Dove."

"Little Dove—my sister," he said. Alarm was clear in his voice as the frown on his face deepened. "What is the matter, is she hurt? Where is she?"

Quickly, Lauren tried to explain what had occurred between them. Running Wolf remained silent and listened until she was finished. "The child has only known me and my father since our mother died. I was thinking of myself so much I had forgotten how she must feel. I will speak with her. Is she in your tepee?"

"No, I think she is down among the trees near the river."

Running Wolf walked rapidly in that direction with Lauren following close behind. It took them several minutes before they spotted the small form near the base of a tree. Running Wolf went to her and knelt beside her. Lauren kept herself a little distance away, yet she could hear his words. Little Dove's eyes were filled with remorseful tears as Running Wolf asked gently. "Little Dove, I must speak with you. Will you listen?"

She looked up at the brother she worshiped and felt she was losing.

"I am shamed, Brother. I will understand if you choose to punish me. I spoke with hate to our guest."

"I do not punish you, Little Dove, you punish yourself. Look at me, Little Dove."

Her large, tear-filled eyes looked up at him.

"You do not hate, my little flower, you just do not understand."

He sat back on his heels and held out his hands toward her.

"Look, Little Dove." He spread the fingers of one hand, then he held out the other and wiggled the fingers. "Both of my hands are the same. If I take a knife and cut one, it hurts. If I cut the other, it hurts also. They are both different, yet their loss would hurt the same. Love is like that. You can love more than one person and the love is the same. The hurt or the loss of that person will be the same. Yes, I love Lauren, but I love you, too, and like part of my body, I would feel pain at the loss of either of you."

Lauren looked at Running Wolf, feeling the truth and the warmth of his love even more than the trembling, wide-eyed child who slowly rose and threw herself into her brother's arms. She watched the way he held the child close to him and caressed her long dark braids. With gentle words, he comforted her. "We are one, Little Dove," he said softly, "like the sun and the trees, the river and the earth on which we stand. You and I came from the same father, were carried in the arms of the same mother. My love for you could never change." He held her away from him and smiled down into her eyes. "Was I not the one who made you your first doll, guided your first steps, taught you to ride and to swim? I hold those memories in my heart and they will remain so until the Great Spirit calls for me."

Again he held the small child away from him. "And now, little one, I think there is something you must say to Lauren."

Little Dove nodded and walked to Lauren. "I am sorry I spoke to you with disrespect. I did not mean what I said; I wanted to hurt you."

Lauren smiled down into the troubled eyes. "I know, Little Dove. It is all right."

"I can come again to your tepee and hear the stories?"

"Yes, I would be happy if you would be my friend."

With a quick smile and a swift look at her brother, she turned and ran back to the village. Lauren watched her small figure disappear; then she turned to face Running Wolf. He still stood where he was, and she knew he had absorbed every word, every move she had made. A feeling of sureness and peace seemed to descend on her as for the very first time in her life she realized the giving not the taking in honest love. She could see with a clearness she had never had before.

Slowly, she walked to him. He did not move, but watched her with a face that told her nothing of the tumultuous emotions that raged within him. She stood only inches away; then gently she reached out and placed her hand against his broad muscular chest. She could feel the heavy beating of his heart, yet he did not move. "I have never really looked. . . . I have never really seen the heart of Running Wolf before. I have only felt for myself, never reaching for another before. It is the first time that I know what love is, this feeling of peace—of knowing that you are so much to another. Oh, Running Wolf . . . hold me," she said softly.

He reached for her, drawing her against him, enfolding her in his strong arms. She laid her head against his chest and put her arms about his waist. She felt the strength of his love enfold her like a shield and she heard the gentleness in his voice as he spoke.

"To me, you have always been the one I have sought. There is no way for me to tell you how you fill my heart with love."

She looked up into the face that was now open for her to see. "Running Wolf, if you still want me . . . I will stay."

"You are sure, Lauren?"

"Yes, I am."

He gave a quick laugh and again drew her close to him.

"I have wanted you for so long I am no longer sure I can believe what I hear. You will be my wife? You will live here with me . . . for always."

"Yes, this will be my home, you will be my husband and, oh, Running Wolf I shall try to be a good wife to you. It will be a difficult thing for you"—she laughed shakily—"to have a spoiled little white girl for a wife. I have much to learn. Look how long it took me to recognize love when I saw it."

He caressed the side of her face with trembling fingers. "I would spoil you more. . . . I would give you the sun from the sky if you were to ask. Lauren . . . come with me now."

"Where?"

"To a place near here, where the warm water falls and the shade of the trees is cool and sweet smelling. Lauren . . . to the place that belongs to us."

She looked up into his dark warm eyes and again the feeling of sureness, of rightness and peace touched her. "Yes," she whispered. He took her hand and they slowly began to walk . . . to the place they had first reached for each other . . . to the place where they would again reach for the elusive touch of love.

At the village, he drew her up behind him on his horse. Her arms wrapped about his waist, he rode in silence. Every sense he had was filled with the need for Lauren, and the deep pleasure he still felt when he had heard her whisper yes.

The sound of the waterfall filled the air as they walked to the grassy ledge that faced it. It was as if they were alone in the center of the world. He turned to her, watching as the mist dampened her hair and made it curl waywardly about her face. He reached out and gently touched her soft, moist lips a moment before he bent to kiss her. Her lips were trembling. It was a gentle kiss that ended as quickly as it began. His eyes held hers, searching for fear or doubt and saw none. He drew her into his arms and this time, the mouth that claimed hers was seeking, the arms that held her were strong and forceful. She was his, and his need of her was the only thing he knew at the moment.

With a quick effortless movement, he bent and lifted her in his arms, resting her head on his shoulder. She closed her eyes and savored the strength and the possessiveness of him.

Beneath the shade of a huge towering pine, the ground was soft and dry. They lay together, touching, tasting, sharing the joy of finding each other. There was no hurry. He intended to seal her within him; every inch of her was precious and he wanted to commit her to his mind and his soul. Her skin was soft and cool to the touch of his hands and his lips. And he savored the touch of her cool hands against his skin as she sought to discover him as he did her.

He heard the soft murmured words as he crushed her to him, felt her cling to him as he blended them together, listened with all his being to her answering need for him. For a long time, he held her without speaking; there were no words in his mind that he felt would tell her how he felt. Blindly, he searched for a way to tell her.

Lauren sensed his quietness and she raised herself on one elbow and looked down on him. Her bright auburn hair caught a ray of sunlight and the look of intense love in his eyes brought a smile to her lips. Then he knew. There would never again be a need for words between them. They knew each other as the earth knew the gentle kiss of the sun.

"I love you, Running Wolf," she said gently.

"And I love you. You are no longer Lauren."

"No? . . . Who am I, Running Wolf?"

"You are Summer Rain. The magic that gives new life to the earth like you have given to me. You are mine, Summer Rain, and soon I will stand before our chief and tell our village."

Again he heard her softly murmur, "Yes."

As he drew her again into his arms, his hungry need again searched for her.

Chapter Nineteen

Tekata was dying. There was no one about him who did not know the truth. White Eagle sat beside his father's bed late into the night. He had sent an exhausted Rebecca back to their tepee to sleep. She had spent many days and nights by the old man's bed because it seemed to bring him pleasure to see her there. Now, Cade had told him that the final hours were near and nothing in his or his father's medicine could do anything to stop the progress toward death.

They were alone. White Eagle thought his father slept so he sat quietly looking at the man's lined and weathered face. "What a good father he has been to me," he thought. "What a great leader he has been to his people. Great Spirit," he prayed silently, "can I walk in his shoes?"

"My Son?" The gentle voice startled him in the silence of the tepee.

"Father?"

Tekata's hand reached for his. White Eagle grasped his father's hand in both of his and held it, surprised at the thin dryness of his fingers.

"I am here, my Chief," he said quietly. The dark old eyes sparkled with love for his son. Slowly, he raised his other hand and placed it on White Eagle's shoulder.

"I have always been proud of you. From the day of your birth you have walked with honor and pride."

"It is because of your strength, my Father," White Eagle replied in a hoarse grief-filled voice. "I can only stand in your shadow."

"No. We both know that soon the Great Spirit will seek my spirit. I am not afraid, my Son, for I leave my people in safe hands."

"Father—"

"Listen to me, my Son. The days that are coming will be hard for you and for our people. You are strong, but you are not alone. Sun Knife will be your right arm. He knows the white world and how the white man thinks. Seek his advice and the advice of the elders; seek their advice but follow your heart."

"Rest, Father, rest. Do not excite yourself."

Tekata's hand shook and beads of perspiration touched his brow. He lay back on his couch, his breath coming in short hard gasps. "White Eagle"—the old man chuckled—"I would have liked to have seen your children."

"Rest. One day soon, you will teach your grandsons to hunt and to fish. Rest, Father."

The old man nodded and his heavy eyes closed. The time ticked by and only White Eagle knew when his father's spirit left his body.

When the first light of dawn touched the sky, Rebecca returned to Tekata's tepee. When she stepped inside, she found White Eagle slowly and steadily preparing his father's body for burial. She went to his side and knelt beside the old chief she had grown to love. Her eyes glistened with tears of pain for herself and for White Eagle. She knew the depth of White Eagle's pain was a thing that could not be touched with words. She remained silent until he finished. He had put his father's body in the white buffalo robe and bound it with rawhide strips. When he was finished, he lifted his head and looked at Rebecca. It was the first time she had ever seen such contained grief. Tears glistened in his eyes as he rose and extended his arms to her. She went to him, feeling his arms close about her as he drew from her strength, too.

Determinedly, White Eagle held Rebecca away from him. "I must tell my people. We must send my father on his last journey with the honor and respect he deserves."

She nodded, knowing he was grasping for a way to control the grief that racked him and the new subtle fear that lingered within him that the leadership he had just received was more than he could handle. White Eagle was still young to be chief and he knew that he did not yet possess the wisdom of his father's many years.

The preparations were made. Tekata's body, wrapped securely in the white buffalo robe, was taken to a high hill overlooking the village whose people he had loved so well. There, a high scaffold was built out of four slender but sturdy trees that had been cut especially for this occasion. On this was built a platform. Tekata's body was placed on the platform that was built high enough to keep it safe from animals.

All of his personal belongings, such as his shield, bow and arrow, and war lance were also placed beside him. The pipes he had smoked both for peace and for battle were added. His favorite horse was led under the scaffold and killed so that he could accompany a great warrior such as Tekata on his last journey. It was considered important that Tekata should be mounted on his war horse and supplied with all his equipment when he entered the happy hunting ground and met his father and all the others who had been friends and had gone before him.

The mourning was intense, for Tekata had been a beloved chief. Eerie mournful cries came from the women and the warriors chanted a death song to accompany them. Snow Blossom and White Eagle stood beside the platform; unashamed tears glistened on their cheeks.

It was only at the close of the day when they were alone, that Cade could comfort a sobbing Snow Blossom. He held her close, sharing her grief for a man who had brightened his life by his kindness and his teaching.

The days went by, and they all knew that the day was coming when White Eagle would officially be made chief.

Two days before the ceremony, White Eagle took his bow and a quiver of arrows and left the camp. It was custom that he would take these days to meditate and pray to the Great Spirit for guidance. Rebecca waited for his return, praying that he would find his way and return more at peace with himself.

White Eagle traveled the entire day without a morsel of food or a drink of water. He traveled on foot at a smooth loping run that covered a great deal of territory. When he stopped, the stars were already bright and the moon had risen. He built a fire and knelt beside it. Slowly, he relaxed his mind and his body and allowed his exhausted thoughts to reach out.

The village awaited his return; a quiet expectant emotion lingered in them all. White Eagle would either come home strengthened by his journey and prepared to accept his obligations, or he would come home prepared to hand over his authority to another. Cade, Rebecca, and Snow Blossom felt in their hearts that White Eagle would stand like a rock and accept the tremendous task which lay ahead of him.

On the morning of the third day, Rebecca, who had not been able to sleep the nights through since White Eagle had been gone, stood at the doorway of their tepee and watched the mist of early dawn swirl about the village. She had been looking toward the path that led to the village and slowly, out of that mist, the form of a man moved toward her.

A smile formed on her lips as she observed the pride in his carriage and the positive way he walked. When he reached her side, she smiled into his tired but peaceful eyes. "Welcome home, Chief White Eagle. I have been waiting so that I could be the first to call you so."

He smiled and reached out a hand to gently caress her golden hair.

"Was there a doubt in your mind, Golden One?"

"No, not for a minute. It is more than my eyes and my body that know White Eagle's heart. My heart knows him also. He is too strong and brave a warrior to turn his back on the people who need him."

"I am tired."

"Come, I've kept some food warm." She took his hand and drew him inside. He sat on the couch while she knelt by the embers of the fire to which she added some twigs to make it burn again. She took a bowl and ladled some warm stew into it; but when she turned to give it to him, she found that he had lain back on the bed and was now sound asleep. She returned the stew to the larger container and left it near the fire to stay warm so that he could eat when he awoke.

It was past noon when he wakened. He wakened to find Rebecca seated beside the bed, her head resting against it and holding one of his hands in hers.

She looked up quickly when she felt him stir and was relieved and pleased when she saw his relaxed smile and the reappearance of the warmth in his eyes. "You were afraid for me?"

She flushed a little at the laughter in his voice. "I . . . I didn't want you to go away from me."

"Away . . . why would I go away?"

"Not in body, but in your mind, in your heart. I want you to know I am always here."

He drew her up beside him on the couch and held her close to him.

"I know, Golden One . . . I know."

They lay together for some time, wrapped in the closeness of the moment, each of them wanting to hold this time for as long as possible.

"I must rise. There are many things to be done."

"What will happen now, White Eagle?"

"There will be much feasting and dancing, and in a few days, the council will meet and announce that White Eagle, son of Chief Tekata, is now chief of this village. It is only then that the real problems begin. I am sure my father had more faith in me than I do."

"You are blind, White Eagle." She laughed.

"I? . . . How?"

"Do you, for one minute, believe your father is the only one who has complete faith in you? You forget I am a woman. I can gossip with the others and they tell me how their men think. There is not a warrior in this camp that would not follow you to his last breath if need be. They love you, White Eagle, as they loved your father, and they respect you—as a warrior, as a man, and as a leader."

She was pleased to see his eyes brighten at these words.

"You are a good right arm to have in this camp. Your encouragement was something I needed. But you are wrong about one thing."

"And what is that?"

His arms tightened about her and there was a sparkle in the depths of his eyes that sent a tingle through her body. "Not for a minute could I ever forget you are a woman." He chuckled. "You are more woman than I have ever seen before and I love you, Golden One . . . very much."

He kissed her soundly, then rolled off the bed to his feet.

"If I stay here with you another minute, I'll get nothing

done the rest of the day. You make it inviting to stay."

She laughed, pleased that his sense of balance was regained. She knew in his heart he would mourn a long time for a father he had deeply loved, but she also knew he was ready now to continue what was expected of him.

It was exactly as he told Rebecca it would be. There was a two-day celebration in which many ceremonial dances were held. White Eagle took part in these and Rebecca sat with the rest of the women at a distance. Women very seldom took part in any ceremonial dances except on rare occasions. One of these could be if a woman chose to make a blood sacrifice during the okipu ceremony.

Now she watched White Eagle's bronzed body as he danced about the blazing fire. His body gleamed in the light and she was fascinated by his often ferocious leaping and stomping. The dance was primeval and yet had a deep sensuality that kept her eyes on him in fascination and quickened the blood in her body. The rumbling thunder of the assorted drums, the call of the flute and the other musical instruments filled the air.

Cade and Snow Blossom were well used to these extraordinarily colorful ceremonies, but they were unusual and exceptionally exciting to Benjamin and Rebecca who asked continual questions about them.

The third day of the ceremonies, the council sat. Everyone knew it was a formality for White Eagle was popular and strong. There was unqualified acceptance of him both by the people and the council.

Six days after his father's death, White Eagle was made chief of the tribe.

Both Michael and Cade were deeply involved in caring for the injured and ill in the village. They had set up, with what little they had to work with, a semblance of a hospital that fascinated the people. They would come with imaginary ills just to see the equipment. There were times when it was deeply amusing to both doctors who struggled to keep a straight face as they listened to the accounts of how and why injuries and illnesses came about.

Spring began to drift toward summer, and a relaxed easy atmosphere of contentment pervaded the camp and its inhabitants—a contentment that was soon to be replaced by a more evil and unbelievable fear. On a warm day that found everyone a little lethargic and reluctant to find work to do, White Eagle and Rebecca and Cade and Snow Blossom were absent from the village when Running Wolf and Lauren arrived. White Eagle and Cade, ostensibly going to hunt, had left the village early. Rebecca and Snow Blossom had gone to the river and were swimming in the cool water.

Lauren went immediately to Michael and Waterflower. She explained their visit. She wanted to be married by Benjamin, in the white man's way, but she also accepted the fact that when they returned to Running Wolf's village, she would be married again in the Indian ceremony.

Both Michael and Waterflower were pleased to see Lauren happy and when White Eagle and the others returned they made a celebration of the wedding. For the first time since her arrival, Lauren and Cade found it easier to talk. She told him that as Running Wolf's wife, she would be allowed to work among their people with what limited knowledge of medicine she had. Cade replied that if any emergency came up that she could not handle, she need only send for him or his father and they would be glad to help. He was still amazed at the change in her. She seemed gentler . . . calmer, as if she had tapped a source within her and found a well of strength and contentment.

Benjamin supervised the simple ceremony that married Running Wolf to Lauren. Snow Blossom stood beside Cade and watched with deep interest as Benjamin read from the Bible, then spoke the words that joined them. It was later that she asked Cade a million questions. "I don't understand," she mused after he had tried his best to explain to her; "there is nothing happy about the ceremony. There was no—"

"Color," Cade supplied with a laugh. He remembered well the colorful and rather noisy ceremony that accompanied his wedding.

"Sun Knife, how can the gods be happy with this ceremony? Surely, they did not know about it. The white one did not call the gods' attention to it."

"Snow Blossom, the white man believes in only one god. So

it was only His attention he wanted to call to the ceremony."

She stared at him doubtfully. "But, Sun Knife, surely the other gods will be angry."

He knew he would never get Snow Blossom to understand. "Snow Blossom, when they return to Running Wolf's village, they will be married . . . colorfully . . . noisily . . . and with the attention of all the gods they can call on."

"Do not laugh at the gods, Sun Knife; they might not like it."

He put his arms about her and held her close. "I would not laugh at gods who were good enough to give me you. I am very grateful to them."

She smiled, pleased at his words. "You should be. It is not every warrior that the daughter of a great chief would marry."

He tightened his arms about her and chuckled. "I do love you, Snow Blossom."

"I know," she said softly as his lips touched hers.

Running Wolf and Lauren had planned on staying several days in the village, but three days after the wedding these plans were suddenly changed.

Running Wolf was wakened very early in the morning and told to come to White Eagle's tepee. Surprised and aware that something very unconventional must have happened, he went to White Eagle immediately. There he found a young warrior from his own village. The young man was nearing exhaustion and White Eagle had found that he had made the journey traveling day and night until both man and horse were near a state of collapse. Running Wolf was alarmed, for no warrior would have pressed himself or his very valuable horse had it not been a very serious emergency.

"Gray Cloud, what is wrong?"

"The council has sent me for you and your medicine woman, Running Wolf. There is a strange sickness in the village. Many are dead already."

"What kind of sickness?"

"The day after you left a white trapper came to the village. He was sick so we took care of him. Three days later, he died. Since then, one after another, they fall to the strange sickness."

"Tell me about it."

"It strikes suddenly with fever, then the body is covered with spots and it makes you very ill. Soon the fever rages and the victim dies. Some of them tried to cool their bodies in the river, but it only made them worse . . . soon they died."

"How many?"

"When I left, twenty were already dead and many more were ill. We need help."

"White Eagle," Running Wolf said quickly, "I must return to my people. Maybe it would be best if my wife stayed here among you. I would not endanger her life."

"Yes. Before you go, speak to Sun Knife. Maybe he or his father will have some medicine to help you."

"I will go and tell Summer Rain."

Running Wolf went back to his tepee where he found Lauren by the fire she had rekindled waiting for him. Swiftly, he told her the situation. When he finished she rose and began packing their things.

"What are you doing?" he demanded.

"I am going home with my husband and help him care for our people."

"No!"

She turned to him, surprise and a spark of anger in her eyes. "Running Wolf?"

"No, I cannot let you return."

"But I must."

"Why?"

"First because I am your wife and I belong with you when our people need us, but second and just as important, I can help with the disease."

He went to her and took her shoulders in his hands. She could see the fear he tried to hide.

"I cannot let you go. . . . What if . . . I cannot."

"Running Wolf," she said gently, "you must listen to me. I will return either with you or after you."

"You would disobey me?"

"Only in such a thing as this."

He drew her against him and held her. "I could not bear it if you became ill. If anything happened to you part of me would die."

"And I could not bear to be away from you if you should happen to become ill. We are faced with the same problem, my love. Why do we not face it together?"

He sighed. "You are a stubborn woman."

"Yes. I could have warned you before you married me, but I was afraid you might change your mind."

He laughed, but it was a strained laugh and his arms bound her against him as if he were afraid it might be the last time he would hold her. She knew how he felt and remained silent; yet she clung to him, too.

"Would you truly follow me, Wife?"

"Yes, I would."

"Then I must surrender. But if you show one sign of becoming ill, I shall return you immediately."

Lauren refused to answer, just as she knew she would refuse to leave him as long as he needed her.

Silently she left his arms and resumed her packing, but a few minutes later, Running Wolf's name was called and Cade and White Eagle entered.

"I am going with you," Cade said. "I have packed some of my medical supplies. My father will stay here to protect our people in case it should become an epidemic."

"Epidemic?" Running Wolf questioned.

"We think the disease may be smallpox. In case it is, it is very serious and could spread like wildfire."

"What of Snow Blossom?"

"She will remain here."

They made the trip as rapidly as possible, and when they reached Running Wolf's village, they found an unbelievable disaster. A disease, common to the white but completely unknown to the Indian, raged through the village claiming life after life. There was no immunity to it and it struck in the most severe form. As quickly as possible, Cade and Lauren set up a large tepee in which they would confine the people who were extremely ill or showed any signs of the sickness. Cade ordered the belongings of each person who was confined to be completely destroyed by burning them.

"Everything?" Running Wolf asked.

"Everything they have touched, even the clothes they wear. We must stop this from spreading any further."

"But if they get well they will have nothing."

Cade looked at him, a deep frown between his eyes; then he realized Running Wolf was trying to cope with something he had never seen before and did not understand.

"They will have their lives, Running Wolf. For now, that is all we must worry about. After we have beaten the disease, then we will help them rebuild. If there are any left, they can join our village."

"If . . . if there are any left, Sun Knife?"

"I will not lie to you, Running Wolf. This could kill every human life in your village."

Running Wolf thought of his small sister, Little Dove, and all the other children of the village. Determinedly, he clenched his jaw and he straightened his shoulders. "I will do whatever you say needs to be done. We must save as many as we can."

Four strong warriors were chosen to help. And a huge fire was built at the edge of the village. Amid the cries of fear, belongings of the sick ones were taken and burned.

Rapidly the tepee filled with the stricken ones. Lauren worked from sunup to the wee hours of the morning. She and Cade treated them in the few ways possible. Cade knew if they had been whites in a white city, the majority of them would have been well in a few days. Instead, they grew rapidly worse and worse.

The fire raged higher claiming all the worldly possessions of family after family. Cade did not allow a single healthy person near the confinement tepee or the fire on which their things were burned.

The days moved slowly by and the death rate climbed. Out of a village of over a hundred and fifty tepees containing over five hundred people, over a hundred were already dead and more than fifty crowded the huge tepee where Lauren and Cade worked day after day, night after night, until they were near exhaustion.

Cade made up a detachment of men whose only job it was to care for the dead. He would not allow their families near them. Running Wolf was the only contact between them, and Cade made him take elaborate precautions. He made a boundary over which Running Wolf could not cross. Lauren would meet him there and they would stand a distance apart while they spoke either of the dead or the arrival of another victim.

Running Wolf's eyes would hold hers, seeing her exhaustion, wanting to help, yet unable to reach out for her. Then came the day that Lauren walked to the boundary, her feet slow and dragging. A low moan escaped her when she saw Running Wolf standing there holding in his arms, Little Dove. She ran as close to him as she could get and said angrily, "Running Wolf, you should not have touched her. Now you can catch it."

He smiled. "I want to be with her if she needs me, and I no longer want to be alone. I would cross over and be with you."

"You took the chance of catching this terrible disease just to be with Little Dove and me?"

"I cannot stand the thought of being here alone, not being able to help. She needs me . . . and I need you. It is better this way," he said gently.

She watched as he stepped over the barrier, knowing the possibilities of death, yet loving enough to willingly make that sacrifice. One of the warriors who had survived the disease and worked as a carrier took Little Dove from Running Wolf's arms. In a moment, he was beside her and Lauren cried out with joy as she felt his strong arms close about her. She closed her eyes and allowed his strength to flow through her.

"The days and nights have been too long without you, Summer Rain," he whispered. "I would rather be with you even if the time is little than to be alone."

She looked up at him with tear-flooded eyes and tried to smile. "Oh, Running Wolf, I am so glad you are near. I need you."

"I will always be here."

She touched his face. "Promise me. I could not bear to lose you now. I have only just found what love is and I want to be able to tell you for the rest of my life."

"I promise," he said softly as he again drew her close to him and held her.

"Come, Running Wolf, we must see to Little Dove."

They went back to the tepee where Running Wolf stood silently and let Cade rage out at him for crossing the barrier. Finally Cade could see he was getting absolutely nowhere so he smiled ruefully and pointed at Running Wolf.

"If you get sick, you stubborn ox, I have half a notion not to take care of you."

Running Wolf smiled. "But you would, Sun Knife. You are a healer and even if I am stubborn, you will not turn your back to me."

"Stubborn ox," Cade grumbled as he walked away. Lauren and Running Wolf exchanged amused glances, then went to join him.

It seemed with the coming of Little Dove, the illness reached its peak. For the following three days, there were no new cases and there were only four deaths which was small in comparison to the preceding days. Little Dove remained critically ill, moaning and calling for Running Wolf who stayed by her side. The very rare moments he was away from her, he spent with Lauren, both of them too tired even to talk. They would merely sit in the shade of the trees and absorb the comfort of each other's presence.

Finally the day came when Little Dove's slim young body was the only one left. Cade worked to save her hoping she was the last one and the disease's hold on the village was broken.

He had forced Running Wolf and Lauren to lie down for a few minutes. They agreed, but made a bed close to where Little Dove lay. He watched them now as they slept exhausted, yet their bodies seemed tense and prepared. Running Wolf's arm protectively held Lauren close to him.

The hours dragged slowly by. It was in the wee hours of the morning that Lauren awoke and saw Cade bending over Little Dove's bed. Sure that a tragedy was occurring, she slipped silently to his side. If Little Dove was dying, she wanted to know before Running Wolf. Maybe, she thought, she could help make the pain of it a little easier to bear.

She moved close to Cade's side, and when he realized she was there he cautioned her to silence.

"Cade?"

"She sleeps."

"Sleeps?"

"The fever has broken. She sleeps a natural sleep. In a few days, she will be well."

"Oh," Lauren whispered as hot tears flooded her eyes. "Thank God . . . thank God."

"Lauren, it is safe to leave her now. I think both of us need some sleep."

"Especially you. I'm grateful, Cade. Both for your allowing me to help and for caring for Little Dove."

"I have meant to tell you for a long time, Lauren. I don't think I would have been able to do much without your help. You have changed a lot since the first time I knew you. You have turned into a very loving, compassionate woman and I am proud to be your friend."

"Thank you." She smiled the old mischievous smile. "And I must thank you again for being responsible for bringing me here. If not, I would have missed the best part of my life."

"He's a good man, Lauren . . . be happy."

"I will."

"Good night."

"Good night, Cade."

She watched his tired body move slowly to the door and exit, closing the flap behind him. Tears, both of happiness and relief, fell and she turned back to see Running Wolf awake and watching her.

The tears meant to him something completely different. His heart thudded painfully and he could not bear to look at the small form that lay under the blanket across the room. His eyes held hers as he said painfully, "Summer Rain, is she—?"

"She's going to be well, Running Wolf. She's sleeping now, but it's a good healthy sleep. The worst is over."

He rose and went to Little Dove's side and lifted one of her tiny hands in his. Unashamed tears of relief fell unchecked and his throat was so restricted he could barely breathe.

Lauren stood watching him. She knew she was as close to exhaustion as he was, yet she could not seem to understand why his figure seemed to wave in front of her. She began to feel uncomfortably warm and she could feel the perspiration on her face.

"I . . . I'm so tired, Running Wolf," she said softly.

"I know. You must lie down, Summer Rain." He held out his hand to her. Her arms were heavy and she could not seem to lift them. She wanted to move, yet her body would not obey the commands of her mind.

He saw her waver on her feet and realized suddenly it was more than being tired; she was going to collapse. In two quick steps, he was beside her, just as her knees buckled and she fell unconscious into his arms.

He lifted her slight body as a whole new fear began to build. He had almost lost Little Dove; now the black fear held him that he could lose Summer Rain, the one other person in the world that he loved.

Chapter Twenty

The village slept, the tepees surrounded by the rising mist of early dawn. White Eagle had gone the day before with most of the men from within the village to hunt a herd of buffalo that was reported seen not too many miles away. Rebecca was sleeping, too, curled warmly in the fur robes as was her father in a tepee not far from hers.

Snow Blossom, who still missed Cade very much, was in a state of half-wakefulness, filled with fitful, disconnected dreams.

In another tepee, Long Arrow lay. He also could not sleep well. Some untouchable feeling made complete rest elusive.

In yet another tepee, two people slept silently and contentedly, clinging to each other. Michael and Waterflower, warm, comfortable and happy.

The rumbling noise began as a small sound in the distance that at first did not disturb the sleeping dogs, or the quiet groups of horses. It began to build slowly; dogs wakened, and began to bark. The horses, restless, whinnied softly, confused by the noise.

It grew and grew. Long Arrow was the first to hear it, yet it did not register in his mind exactly what it was for several minutes. By the time the realization came to him and he leaped from his couch grasping for his bow and war lance, the blue-uniformed soldiers had already reached the edge of the village and begun to sweep through it in a wave of destruction.

By this time, most of the occupants of the sleeping village had been startled into confused wakefulness.

Long Arrow ran from his tepee to witness a sight that would live in his memory for the rest of his life.

The soldiers attacked; women who ran out of their tepees with children, were cut down indiscriminately. Children were slaughtered without mercy. For a moment, he was stunned, then white rage overtook him. Holding his war lance high, he screamed a war cry and lunged at the first blue coat near him.

By now, every member of the village was awake. Shouting, screaming, and the thunder of horses filled the early-morning air.

Michael had run to the door of his tepee, seen what was happening, and run back for his guns.

"Michael!"

"Stay in here, Waterflower; do not come out."

He ran outside, but Waterflower screamed and ran after him. She was out the door and running toward him when she saw his body stiffen as a bullet found its mark, followed by another. She ran to him, but just before she reached his side, something struck her side and she fell unconscious.

Rebecca had gotten up from her bed, but the scream on her lips froze as the door flap was torn open and soldiers seemed to suddenly fill the tepee. She felt herself grasped by hard iron hands. She was dragged from the tepee and shoved up on a horse in front of a large soldier who held her firmly despite her struggles.

Snow Blossom, too, did not have any opportunity to leave her tepee, but her capture was not as easy as the attackers had thought it would be. Their orders were to take her alive, but she had grasped Cade's war lance in one hand a wicked-looking knife in the other and stood with her back to the wall of the tepee, prepared to defend herself to the death. They charged her only to be rewarded by a slashing cut on the arm of one and a severe jab on the shoulder of another.

Again and again, they attacked, but it was only after several more joined them that they captured her and tied her firmly. They carried her, kicking and screaming insults and curses at them, to another horse and threw her up on it. Immediately, she tried to control the horse and get it to run away, but a man mounted quickly behind her. She was shocked and felt the first tug of fear when she heard Leach's voice in her ear.

"Ain't no use to fight no more, sweet thing," he chuckled. "We's takin' you and they's nothing you or that half-breed husband of yours can do about it. He's probably dead by now—most of 'em are."

She realized they must not know that White Eagle or Cade were not in the village. She tried to calm herself and look about. It was then she saw Rebecca held captive on another horse. She was disheveled and fighting, but she was alive.

Snow Blossom looked about her. Men, women, and children littered the ground. Some of the tepees were burning. Among the mass of corpses, she saw Michael and Waterflower a few feet from each other, their bodies still and stained with blood. She cried out thinking of Cade's pain when he returned and found them.

They rode from the village. Snow Blossom remained quiet, her agile mind seeking any means of escape. She would never allow the man who held her so tightly, to think for a moment that she was afraid. If they stopped, and any opportunity arose, she would kill him. She would wait, she would watch, and if it were possible, if they dropped their guard for a moment, she would escape. Somehow, she would find White Eagle and Cade and they would seek revenge for the deaths of their people and the kidnapping of their chief's wife and his sister.

They rode all day and far into the night before they stopped. They were allowed to rest only three hours; then they were roughly fed and both women were guarded even when they had to retreat to the brush to relieve themselves. Rebecca cried with shame, but Snow Blossom's anger grew. It began to boil into a sincere and deep hatred.

Again they were mounted and traveling. The pace increased until even Snow Blossom was in a state of exhaustion. It was another day and night before they sighted the fort.

Once inside, Rebecca and Snow Blossom were thrown into a small dark room and the door was locked.

"Rebecca, are you all right?"

"I'm not hurt. Snow Blossom, why . . . what could any of our people have done to provoke this terrible thing?"

"I don't know. Our village and those around us have been peaceful. We have not approached the whites even to trade."

"Snow Blossom . . . my father . . . ?"

"Did you see him?"

"Yes . . . they . . . they killed him."

"Michael and Waterflower . . . I think they are both dead. I don't know for sure."

"It was a massacre. . . . No one stood a chance; I cannot believe this."

"We must be strong, Rebecca," Snow Blossom said firmly. "You are the wife of a chief and I am the wife of Sun Knife. We must not let them know that they can make us fear. Listen, they believe White Eagle and Sun Knife were there and are dead. We know they will come for us as soon as they find what has happened. Until then, we must remember who we are. We will wait with patience and if we find a way we will escape."

It seemed hours, and another new day was dawning before the key turned in the lock and the door was opened. Two men came inside, one holding a gun that pointed at Snow Blossom. The other went to Rebecca and grasped her arm pulling her from the room.

"Remember who you are . . . say nothing, Rebecca," Snow Blossom shouted. She turned her eyes on the young soldier who held the gun on her and the violent hate in them caused him to back up quickly. He left and she heard the lock again.

She sat down on the edge of a small bunk wondering just why she and Rebecca had not been killed with the others, and who had led the white soldiers to their camp.

Grant cursed and rose to pace the small room in which his anger and disagreement with his commanding officer had put him.

He had found out what the intentions of the major were only a half-hour before his detachment was to leave on what he thought was maneuvers. His anger had burst when he found out the plans for the unprovoked attack on the helpless sleeping village.

"There is a white woman there whom this red-skinned savage has taken as a wife. I will not allow this animal to keep a woman of white blood."

"Go to them . . . let me go to them. At least find out the facts before you do this," Grant had shouted.

The major had smiled with a malicious smile, and clasping his hands behind his back, he had said softly, "I already know all I want to know."

Grant had frozen, reading the major's eyes as accurately as

he wanted them read. "You will kill as many as you can."

"Yes."

"And when White Eagle comes for his wife?" Grant asked softly.

"If the Indians attack this fort," the major said as he slowly bent forward and put his hands on the desk, "I shall wipe this area clean of every Indian within two hundred miles."

"You want him to come; you want a war?"

"There will be no war."

Grant stood up and glared at the major. "I will have no part of this. I will put myself on record now. You are a fool, and you are judging White Eagle and Cade to be fools, too; they are not. If you do this, White Eagle will see you dead. He loves Rebecca and she loves him. He will come for her, and when he does, you will regret that day and many many more."

"Go to your quarters, Lieutenant. You will be confined there until further orders."

"Major, don't do this, please? Let me—"

"Lieutenant, must I call the guard?"

For the first time, real fear struck Grant. The major was insane and he knew there was no way to reach him. Another plan formed.

"Yes, sir," he said; then he saluted and left. He went straight to the stables. If he could get out, he would go and warn White Eagle. He would worry about the major later.

He pulled his horse out and threw the saddle on his back. He was busy tightening the cinch when an amused voice came from behind him.

"Are you deserting like a coward, or do you intend to go warn the enemy?"

He spun around to find the major and two men with rifles pointing at him.

"The enemy," Grant said softly, "women and children?"

"Nits grow into lice."

"Major—"

"Take the lieutenant to the jail. Lock him up and keep him there until I return. I want no lily-livered coward at my back."

There was nothing more Grant could say. With two guns prodding his back, he walked to the jail. He heard the detachment ride away. The days passed in agony. He pictured in his mind what was happening. He sat and buried his face in his hands when he heard the soldiers return for he knew of the death they had left behind.

Major Chivington paced the floor slowly, a pleased half-smile on his face. Josiah sat and watched him, knowing the evil gloating that lingered in his mind.

"She is here, Major?" he said softly.

The major stopped pacing and turned to look at Josiah as if he were surprised he was there.

"She . . . yes, of course, she is."

"I hope you plan to keep your side of the bargain, Major."

"She is yours, Josiah. Take her and get out of here. I don't want the dirty little savage here any longer than necessary. She has served her purpose."

"The other one, the chief's wife, what do you plan to do with her?"

"I don't know," he mused. "I didn't realize the woman was so beautiful. She might prove . . . interesting. We shall see."

"I have my things packed and ready to leave. I will take her now."

"Yes." The major reached in his desk drawer and took a key out. "Here is the key to her room. Take her."

Josiah took the key, then looked at the major who seemed to have forgotten him again. He left and went to where he knew Snow Blossom waited behind a locked door. Quickly, he unlocked the door, stepped inside, and closed the door behind him.

Snow Blossom looked up when he entered. Their eyes met, and all the pieces of the puzzle fell into place. She knew now who was responsible for the massacre and who had her brought here. Grim and quiet-eyed, she rose and faced the man who walked slowly toward her.

White Eagle rose with the dawn, pleased that the hunting trip he was on had been rewarding. They had killed a medium-sized buffalo, a number of rabbits, and a large deer. The hides had been removed and the meat cut into large pieces which could be carried back. The deerskin was a rare beauty and he intended it to be softened so that Rebecca could make it into a dress.

His mind on Rebecca, he urged his friends to more speed and when the camp was broken, they headed back toward the village. They were less than half-day's ride from the village when the circling predatory birds warned him that something was wrong. As he kicked his horse to greater speed and grew closer, he could see the fine haze of smoke rising slowly. A feeling of intense fear twisted within him. No longer waiting on the others, he urged his horse ahead. When he crested the hill that led to the village a cry of mingled fear and rage came from him. He rode into the village at a full gallop, his eyes hardly believing the death and destruction about him.

He was about to dismount and begin a frantic search for Rebecca when a voice called to him. His attention was drawn to a stand of trees at whose edge Leaping Bear stood.

Quickly, he rode to Leaping Bear's side. "Leaping Bear, what happened?"

"The white soldiers from the fort," he began. The whole story followed and White Eagle listened without interruption. "I have gathered the ones left alive, and we were going to prepare the others for burial."

"Rebecca?" White Eagle asked softly, afraid of what he would hear.

"She was taken."

"Taken? She is alive."

"Yes, they took her with them. They also took your sister, Snow Blossom."

White Eagle jumped down from his horse.

"Tell me . . . who is alive . . . who is dead?"

"White Eagle, they have killed Dr. Michael, Benjamin Wade, and seventy more of our people. Over a hundred are seriously wounded."

"Long Arrow?"

"Wounded."

"How badly?"

"Very badly."

"Waterflower?"

"Wounded also, but I do not know how serious."

White Eagle was momentarily stunned with the immensity of the unprovoked destruction. Then he turned a cold angry face toward the white fort. He stood for a moment allowing seething hatred to boil within him.

"Come," he said softly, "we must bury the dead. Send a rider to Running Wolf's village. Tell Sun Knife what has happened and that we need help. Then"—again his eyes turned toward the fort—"we will go to the fort and take back what is ours. It is best to give them time to pray to their one god for they will need his help. If Rebecca or my sister have been harmed . . . even their God will not protect them from my vengeance."

There followed two days of agony and abject misery as the survivors prepared their dead for the ceremony of burial. They were stunned with the violence of the attack, and a soft murmur of mourning hung like a heavy dark cloud over everyone.

White Eagle personally prepared Michael's body, for Waterflower had been seriously wounded as had Long Arrow. He worked methodically with frozen face and a heavy control over the emotions within him.

Slowly, they wandered through the destruction trying to put together some personal possessions. Many had been left completely destitute.

White Eagle seemed to be tireless as he supervised the sharing and rebuilding. He knew that the summer was short and if they were not prepared to face the winter, many of them would die. He was not tireless; he was working with desperate energy. He knew if he stopped, his mind and heart would dwell only on Rebecca.

He waited only until Cade returned, for he knew Cade's anger would match his and that he would want to be with them when they went to the fort.

Cade had fallen asleep as soon as his head touched a pillow, his mind too numb even to dream.

It seemed that he had just fallen asleep when Running Wolf bent over him to again shake him awake. It was only habitual reaction that brought him instantly awake.

"Running Wolf, what is it? Are there more?"

"It's Summer Rain."

"Lauren . . . where is she?"

"I put her in the bed next to Little Dove."

Cade and Running Wolf went back to the room that had held so much silent agony for them. Running Wolf's silence told Cade as no words could, how afraid he was. He bent over Lauren's still form. He examined her quickly but thoroughly, then he stood and looked at Running Wolf.

"I don't think it's the same, Running Wolf. I think it is just complete exhaustion."

A harsh breath escaped Running Wolf, a deep sigh of relief.

"She has a very high fever, but I think with a little care and some good food, she will be all right."

"Then I will take her back to my tepee. I will care for her. You are sure it is not the spotted sickness, Sun Knife?"

"About as sure as I can be."

Running Wolf looked down on Lauren's slender form, still and quiet in sleep. Her cheeks were flushed from the fever and damp tendrils of hair lay on her sweat-coated forehead. Gently, he reached down and brushed away the drops of perspiration. He bent and slid his arms beneath her and lifted her up, cradling her gently against him. Without a word, he took her to the small tepee they shared. He laid her on the bed. With gentle hands, he removed her clothes and bathed her heated body with cool water. Then he covered her and sat on a rug by a half-dead fire waiting and watching for a word or movement from her.

It seemed hours that he sat and listened to her moan softly in the depths of her sleep and stir restlessly. When she finally came to semiwakefulness, the fever raged. Her eyes were glassy and he knew she did not recognize where she was, why she was there, or who bent over her.

Again, he bathed her, but it was impossible to get her to swallow anything. As the hours passed, the fever grew worse. She thrashed around on the bed and fought him as he tried to cool her.

A day passed, then another and another, and Running Wolf began to fear for her life. Her body became dry, her lips cracked with the severity of the fever.

He stayed beside her, trying in vain to get her to swallow water or some of the broth he had made from a piece of venison. She gagged and vomited violently and her body, slim before, grew gaunt and weak.

Cade tried forcing enough medicine down to calm her and get her to sleep, but that, too, was useless for she would vomit it up as soon as it struck her stomach.

Two more days passed and she remained the same. She would call out to Running Wolf and he would hold her and tell her he was there, knowing she did not hear him.

It was a still night, with only the soft night sounds to break the quietness. He sat on the floor with his back braced against her bed. Occasionally, he dozed, but it was sporadic and light sleep that gave him no real rest.

The fire had died to glowing red embers and he listened to her rasping breath and heard her soft sounds of complaint.

As the night began to fade into a pale misty dawn, he dozed again, his body stiff and uncomfortable. He startled awake when he heard her say his name—once, and very softly. He looked closely at her to see that her eyes were clear and she recognized him. She tried to smile, but her lips were too dry and cracked. Weakly, she tried to lift her hand, but was even too weak to do that.

He took her hand in his and painful relief flooded him so suddenly he could barely speak past the constriction in his throat.

"Running Wolf," she said in a cracked whisper.

"I am here, Summer Rain, I am here."

"I dreamed."

"You have been very sick; it was not a dream. For a while there I was afraid you were going to leave me."

"How long—?"

"Six days. It feels like a lifetime, you were gone from me; and I realize how much I would have missed you, how much I love you."

Again she tried to smile.

"Will you try to eat or drink a little? You must do so to get your strength back."

"I will try."

He put one arm about her shoulder and lifted her. She drank a little, but her stomach was still too weak to handle it. Resting her head against his shoulder she closed her eyes. "Oh, Running Wolf, I feel so weak . . . so tired."

He eased his body down beside her and held her against him.

"Sleep, Summer Rain," he said gently as he caressed her. "Rest, soon you will be well . . . sleep."

She drifted into a deep restful sleep, at peace with the steady strong beat of his heart and the gentle hands that held her.

When she woke again, bright sunlight filled the tepee and Running Wolf was no longer at her side. She tried to rise and found she had no strength. Lifting her hands to her hair, she was distressed at the dry sticky feel of it. Her skin felt parchment-dry and she knew she looked worse than she felt. At that moment, Running Wolf came in, his face brightly smiling. A low groan from her and she turned away from him. Quickly, he was beside her, the old worry drawing lines on his face.

"Summer Rain!" he said in alarm. "You are sick again. What is wrong?"

"I'm not sick," she mumbled, hiding herself in the fur robe that covered her.

"What is wrong?"

"Oh, Running Wolf," she cried an anguished cry.

"Look at me, woman!" he said sharply, fear causing his voice to roughen.

"I can't. . . . I can't," she moaned.

Running Wolf was tired and worried and his taut nerves could accept no more. He took hold of her shoulders and turned her to face him. Her wide green eyes filled with tears and he studied her face for any sign of the recurring fever.

"What is it—are you in pain?"

"I'm so ugly," she sobbed.

"What?"

"I look so terrible, my hair is so dirty, and I . . . I smell."

He sighed in exasperation. "You cry for that? You have frightened me into thinking you were sick again."

"How can you even look at me? I look so terrible."

"Summer Rain," he said gently, "to me you look beautiful because you are alive. There was a time a few days ago when I thought I was going to lose you. I can only see that you are alive and well and my heart is filled with the joy of it."

"I dreamed . . . I dreamed you held me and I could feel your strength call to me."

"I did. I prayed to every god I knew . . . even"—he grinned—"your own. I would have fought the Great Spirit of death with my two hands if he had come for you."

Suddenly alarm filled her eyes. "Little Dove?"

"She is well, thanks to you. Soon she will come to visit you."

"The others?"

"There is no more sickness. It is over. We have lost many, but now Sun Knife says the battle is over. We can begin now to concentrate on getting you well."

"If I could get up and wash both myself and my hair. Clean clothes would make me feel better."

"Well, you cannot get up so I will wash you, and put clean clothes on. Maybe if I can move you, I could wash your hair."

"But you cannot!"

"Why can I not?" He laughed. "You are too weak to stop me. For once in your life, you will be obedient. It is a rare occasion and I think I will enjoy it."

She was helpless to do anything to stop him, and he was surprised when she blushed as he removed her clothes and gently bathed her body.

"I am so skinny and so ugly. How can you touch me?" she said half in anger and half in helpless embarrassment.

"Soon, with all the food I intend to stuff down you and all the care I intend you to have, you will be soft and pretty again. I wait without a great deal of patience, little one."

Holding her with her head suspended from the bed, he washed her hair the best he could, rubbing it briskly to dry it; then he put clean clothes on her and again laid her against the pillows.

She drew her long hair over her shoulder and braided it. She watched as he knelt by the fire and ladled out a small bowl of the broth and brought it to her. She took a small taste and grimaced.

"Ugh, that tastes terrible."

"It is the best I can do," he grumbled good-naturedly. "I never was taught to do a woman's work. I am a warrior."

"And," she said softly, her eyes softening, "a warrior bathes and dresses a woman like she is a child, and nurses her for hours and hours?"

He knelt beside her, his eyes filled with laughter. "A warrior as wise as I am, does. He is too clever to let such a beautiful thing slip out of his life."

"Even when I am not beautiful?" she teased.

"You are always beautiful," he said seriously. "Get well, Summer Rain, my life is lonely when I cannot share everything with you. The days are beautiful and I would have you walk in the sun with me."

He refused to let her rise until Cade came and told him she was well enough to do so, which forced her to stay in the bed another two days. Then Running Wolf helped her to her feet and she stood on wobbly legs, pleased with herself. He helped her as she began taking tentative steps. In another two days, she stepped out of the tepee and lifted her face for the warm kiss of the summer sun.

Soon, they were riding together and walking the shaded paths. The village was regaining its equilibrium. New tepees began to slowly replace the ones that had been burned. Men, including Cade, hunted so that the skins and meat could be prepared for the winter to come.

Cade and Running Wolf were on their way back to the village after a successful hunt. "Now that I am sure Lauren and all the others are completely well, Running Wolf, I plan to start back to my village."

"When will you leave?"

"I imagine in a day or two. There are a few of the children I'm keeping my eye on."

"Is there a chance that—?"

"No." Cade laughed. "Don't be worried, Brother. I'm sure they are all right . . . just double checking."

"It was a terrible thing, and I do not want to ever see anything like it again."

"I agree with that. I don't know of much else that could be as bad." They had reached the fringe of the village and dropped the carcasses of the deer they had shot at the first tepee.

Running Wolf looked toward the tepee he and Lauren shared and saw a strange horse tethered there.

"Sun Knife?"

"What?"

"One of the warriors of your tribe is here. There must be a message for you."

"They rode up to the tepee and dismounted. When they went inside, they saw an ashen-faced Lauren with tears in her eyes and a somber-faced young warrior who sat by the fire. The first thing that came to Cade's mind was the terrible disease he had just fought at such a great loss of life. His heart pounded in an agony of suspense. The young warrior rose as soon as they entered. He was much younger, almost a boy, and his face showed the hard way he had traveled. He waited for Cade to speak to him first.

"You are Little Buffalo?"

"Yes. I have been sent by Chief White Eagle."

"He has a message for me?"

"You must come back. The village has been attacked by soldiers of the fort. They have killed many, and many more are wounded. We need you."

"My father!" Cade said, but he knew the answer before he heard it and the pain struck him a blow that left him breathless.

"He is dead, Sun Knife," the boy said gently.

"My . . . my mother?"

"She is badly wounded and needs you."

"Snow Blossom?"

"They have taken her to the fort."

"Taken her . . . why?"

"I don't know, Sun Knife."

"Long Arrow?"

"Wounded also. White Eagle fears he may die."

"I will get my things and start back now. You rest here for a day or two and follow me."

"No, Sun Knife," the boy said firmly. He squared his shoulders and his jaw clenched firmly. "I shall go back now. White Eagle goes to the fort. They have also taken his woman."

"I don't understand this," Cade said, the anger darkening his blue eyes. "Why? What could anyone have done to provoke it? Why would they take Snow Blossom and Rebecca?"

"White Eagle does not know the answers, but his anger is great. He waits only for you. He will go to the fort and take his woman back and repay the white soldiers for their treachery."

"Yes," Cade said softly, "we leave now. If they have touched Snow Blossom . . . if they have harmed her or Rebecca in any way . . . then we must see to it that they answer for it."

It was in silence that Cade gathered his things and he and Little Buffalo prepared to leave.

"All our warriors will follow as soon as they are gathered together," Running Wolf said.

"Cade," Lauren said softly, pity in her face. "Your father . . . I'm sorry."

"I know, Lauren . . . we had such a short time together. He wanted so much for his people. I shall have to try to finish what he started."

"I shall come to be with Waterflower. . . . Find Snow Blossom, Cade. I know now how much you love her. Bring her back safe. . . . I . . . I feel we could be friends now."

"I shall bring her back," he said with much more confidence than he felt. He, of all people, knew the white man's mind. He also knew as an Indian, she might not receive the gentlest treatment at the hands of white men. The thought of them mistreating her caused the rage in him to flame.

He mounted and he and Little Buffalo began a long and rugged journey. When he came in sight of the half-destroyed village, he could hardly believe his eyes.

On the hill overlooking the village, he saw row upon row of the high scaffolds of burial platforms that stood near Tekata's. He knew his father was there and fresh anguish filled him.

He rode down into the village filled with pain, anger, and the need for violent revenge.

Chapter Twenty-One

"Brother," White Eagle said quietly when Cade came to him. "I am glad you are here. We share a great sorrow. Your father is a great loss to all of us and we mourn with you."

"Tell me what happened, White Eagle."

"They attacked at dawn. Many of the warriors and I were gone on a hunt. No one can say why they did such a terrible thing. Sun Knife, you know they have taken both Rebecca and Snow Blossom?"

"I know. I can't understand this. There is no reason for such an attack."

"It seems they do not need a reason. We are here and that seems to be enough for the white chief."

"White Eagle . . . my mother . . . Long Arrow?"

"We have tried our best to keep them alive until you came. I know what you have done at Running Wolf's village, and I know you are weary, but they need you desperately."

"I want to see them now."

White Eagle nodded. Cade was surprised at the calm way White Eagle seemed to handle everything, and then he realized that White Eagle was walking a tightrope between control and violence. The control he had now, but the violence was breeding beneath the surface and soon it would erupt.

His mother lay frighteningly still. When he gently spoke to her, her eyes fluttered open. "My Son," she whispered softly; warm tears rolled down her cheeks.

"I am here, Mother. Are you in pain?"

"It is a pain that cannot be healed, my Son. He is gone . . . gone."

"I feel what you feel, Mother, but we must not let his memory and all he worked for fade. I will help you, Mother; you will fight, you must fight. I cannot bear the grief of losing you both." He lifted her hand in his and felt her try to grip it.

He knew she would fight the death that hovered near.

He examined her. The deep cut on her head was severe, but it was not the vital problem. She had been struck low on her right side by a bullet that had exited a few inches away. It must have been shot at an angle for which Cade was grateful, for he realized if it had been aimed directly at her, she would be dead now.

There was no sound from her as he cleaned the wound and bandaged it. He realized she had lost a great deal of blood, and thought how he would have liked to share some of his blood and his strength with her.

When he was finished, he mixed a powder in water and made her drink. In a few minutes, her eyes closed in a deep and healing sleep.

"Now I will look at Long Arrow and then the others."

White Eagle nodded.

Long Arrow suffered the gravest wounds for he had fought valiantly. It had taken several bullets to drop him. One wound was high in the left shoulder. It was clean and already beginning to heal. Another was just above his hip and was deep. The third, and the one that worried Cade, was low where the thigh joined the abdomen. There was a profusion of smaller cuts and wounds over parts of his body. Cade felt if he could help the wound in his abdomen, he could save him, but he was afraid. When he finished his ministrations, he looked up to see Long Arrow awake and watching him. He knew Long Arrow must be in excruciating pain, but no sound passed his lips. The dark eyes questioned Cade, who knew what news he sought.

"She is alive and I think she will be all right, Long Arrow," he said softly. "My father is dead."

Pain, deep and powerful, touched Long Arrow's face. A man he had called brother, whom he had loved like a brother, was dead and the woman he had loved for as long as he could remember lay wounded. His pain turned to a cold, deep hatred.

"Sun Knife," he gasped. "They attacked without warning. I could do nothing."

"I know, Long Arrow, rest easy. When you are better, we will do what must be done."

"Snow Blossom . . . Rebecca, are they well . . . ? They're not—"

"No, they are alive. . . . They have been taken to the fort."

"Why?"

"I have met the major at the fort. He has a deep hatred for all Indians. I suppose he took Rebecca only because he could not stand the thought of a white woman married to an Indian. I fear for the reasons he may have taken Snow Blossom, unless he knows that she is my wife and wants to pay my father and I back for our defense of the Indians. Whatever reasons he may have, he has made a very bad mistake. White Eagle will not tolerate this and neither will I. If we have to fight we will."

"I would fight by your side."

"You will not move. I am going to save your life if I can; then we will fight together."

Long Arrow was about to speak when Cade spoke again. "I have lost my father, Long Arrow. I would not lose you, too; it is too much to bear."

Long Arrow's eyes spoke eloquently of his feelings and Cade smiled in response.

When Cade stepped outside, he was struck by the silence of a village that had always been filled with laughter, the strong voices of men, and the joyful sound of children. Now a thick sense of grief hung over it. He walked slowly through the half-desecrated village. The burned debris of some tepees remained and the scent of death hung in the air. A feeling of lonely desolation suddenly seemed to smother him like a thick blanket. He felt again the pain of losing a father he had known for such a short time and the misery of his mother and the man who had been dear to him. But it was the need to reach for the gentle understanding of Snow Blossom that intensified the ache within him. With the thought of Snow Blossom came a white-hot anger against a man who had so coldly done such a thing. He knew he had to go and speak of future plans with White Eagle, but his pain-numbed mind rebelled. His mind involved, he allowed himself to move slowly toward the towering burial scaffolds until he stood beside his father's.

He looked up at the fur-shrouded form and the heat of tears

burned his eyes. He was overwhelmed by the exhaustion that had hovered over him since the days in Running Wolf's village, and the final knowledge that in a matter of weeks, his whole life had been shattered. His father dead, Tekata dead, his mother nearing death, and Long Arrow's silent bearing of pain were a load to bear, but the thought of Snow Blossom in the hands of a man whose viciousness and hatred of Indians he well knew, was the crowning agony.

"Snow Blossom," he whispered, "have courage, my love. I will come for you and if he has harmed you, I promise his life will be the price he will pay."

He remembered Sitting Bull's words. "One day you will have to choose between white and Indian; you cannot be both."

Now he silently but firmly made that choice. He was Indian; his life, his people needed him, and he would not turn his back on them. Silently and firmly, he made a sacred vow at the feet of his father.

Through anything the white world brought against them, he would stay and work for the benefit of a strong and courageous people who were being pushed beyond what any people could stand. He would do whatever was in his power to do, but even if he failed, his life would be lived and ended here, in the place he loved, and with the people he loved. His heart cried out only for one gift from the gods. "Let me find her, Great Spirit. I need her strength and courage, and I need her gentleness and fulfilling love. . . . Please let me find her."

He had sat on the ground beside his father a long time before he realized that again, White Eagle was beside him. He had no idea how long White Eagle had been there. He stood up stiffly, his body protesting every move.

"Come to my fire, Sun Knife," White Eagle said. "We must talk."

Cade nodded and they walked back in silence. Inside, White Eagle had built a fire. Cade sat in front of it and waited for White Eagle to speak.

"I have sent warriors to all the villages. I have called all the warriors to come here. There will be many." He bent forward, and for the first time, Cade saw the fury and violent revenge in his dark eyes. Death was there and Cade knew it. "We will burn the white man's fort and kill them all. Then we will take back what they have stolen from us."

Cade searched for words to tell White Eagle that he was heading down a trail that could only bring retaliation and death. Against the white army with its cannons and guns, poorly armed Indians had no chance. He knew they would have to find a way to get Rebecca and Snow Blossom out of the fort, but no idea would penetrate his weary mind. He only knew he had to stop White Eagle from heading for certain and more permanent destruction.

"White Eagle . . . will my brother listen to me?"

"I have always heard your words."

"We cannot attack the fort until we get Rebecca and Snow Blossom out of there. I know the white leader. He is a heartless man. If we attack he will kill them both—and what of Grant and the few of his friends who are also our friends?"

"Why do you speak these words to me, Brother? Look around you. Look at what the white soldiers have done. They have struck me a blow that no leader of his people can take. I must do something or lose face. If that happens, who will lead them? And you? They have struck you, too, Brother. . . . I am sure Snow Blossom has faith that you will come for her."

"Do you doubt for a minute that I will get her back, Brother?" Cade asked softly.

For the first time, a small flicker of a smile touched White Eagle's lips.

"And you are telling me to wait to go for Rebecca?"

"No, I'm not telling you to wait. I am telling you to use caution."

"What kind of caution?"

"While the braves are gathering, you and I will ride to the fort and speak to them. We will demand our women back."

"And then?"

"If they will return them, we will rebuild."

"No, Sun Knife."

"White Eagle."

"No . . . I shall get Rebecca back and you will get Snow Blossom . . . but I will not spare the man who took the lives of women and children. As a chief I can do nothing else."

"It will bring another attack. . . . There are white men like the leaves on the trees."

For a moment, White Eagle was silent; then he said softly, "My father spoke of this. I know what we face, but, Brother . . . I cannot give up the pride of our people. I cannot lay down my arms and simply surrender without trying to defend my people. What else would be left, Sun Knife, if we did not pick up our war lances and fight like men? Are we women? Are we children? No, we will be warriors until we have no strength left, and the Great Spirit will know we walked the last trail with courage."

Cade knew there were no words he could say that would stop White Eagle. He could see the determination in his eyes. An overpowering weariness swept over him.

"Will you at least try to get Rebecca and Snow Blossom back by peaceful means first?"

"You think," White Eagle said quietly, "that the white major would kill them if we attacked?"

Cade was silent for a long time, remembering the look in Major Chivington's eyes. Then he said the words softly that he knew were true.

"Yes . . . yes he would."

"Sun Knife." The words were said quietly. Their eyes met and held. "I will go with you to the fort. I will ask for my women back. If I do this, will my brother ride at my side should they refuse?"

Cade knew that White Eagle was retreating as far as he could only out of love and respect for his brother. Again, he was faced with a choice, a choice that would be final. He looked at White Eagle, remembering their childhood days. He remembered the sweet gentleness of Snow Blossom, the dedication of his father, the guidance of Long Arrow, and the devotion of his mother. He knew what would happen, and yet he felt a stir of pride when he again held White Eagle's eyes and said, "I will be by your side, Brother; my shield will protect your back as yours protects mine. My war cry will echo yours and my life will be offered to the Great Spirit for the benefit of my people."

"Yes." White Eagle smiled for the first time. "I knew

you would."

White Eagle rose and Cade followed. They stood outside and looked across the destruction of their village to the shadows of the burial scaffolds.

"We will go to the fort tomorrow, Sun Knife. I cannot stand the thought of Rebecca being in their hands."

"As soon as the sun rises," Cade answered. He walked away leaving a silently brooding White Eagle whose eyes were still held by the burned tepees and the silent village.

Cade went to his tepee. Things inside were in a shambles proving what a struggle Snow Blossom had put up before they took her. He lay on the bed, but as tired as he was, sleep would not come. Instead, painful memories came, and it was a long time before he won the battle and slept a dream-filled sleep. He was awake before dawn. The first thing he did was to go to his mother's side. She was extremely weak, but she smiled at him and clung desperately to the hand he offered. There was still the glassy, half-fevered look in her eyes and he knew she still hovered dangerously near death.

"You are looking well, my Mother. You must get well soon. I have not eaten a good roast venison in a long time."

She tried to laugh, but it brought a grimace of pain. "Yes, you were always hungry. My son's medicine will make me well. . . . Sun Knife?"

"Yes."

"Your father—"

"Mother, please don't . . . not yet. When you are stronger we will talk."

"I must know if he has been prepared as he should be; does he have all of his things? I would not have him enter the happy hunting ground unprepared."

"Mother, rest easy. Everything has been cared for. White Eagle has seen to it."

Again he gave her something to make her sleep; then he held her hand and talked with her until she closed her eyes.

From his mother, he went to Long Arrow. He found him grimly clinging to life and a determination to join White Eagle and Cade in finding revenge for all they had suffered. He took the time to swiftly check all the others. When he started back to his tepee, he found White Eagle mounted and waiting for him. White Eagle had dressed in all the accouterments that spoke of his leadership and his bravery.

He was mounted on his best war horse. He wore a heavily beaded and fringed shirt, and a full-feathered headdress that reached his hips. The lance he carried was also fringed with feathers, feathers from the eagle that spoke of the bravery and courage of the warrior who carried them. Again Cade was struck by the thought that White Eagle was the perfect symbol of the Indian. He sat majestically straight, and in every inch of his bearing was the warrior, the strength of the Indian tribes.

Cade went inside his tepee and made the same elaborate preparations he had made when he had first left to meet his father. He wore the same elaborate beaded headband and the white and black feathers of the eagle. He donned the white buckskin shirt and pants. Saying a small private prayer, he took from the wall of his tepee his bow and arrows and his shield and war lance. Inside the tepee he left Cade Holliday, the doctor; outside, Sun Knife, warrior and medicine man, joined his brother, White Eagle, in a quest for the return of his woman. He left every semblance and thought of the white man. He was now only Sun Knife—Indian.

They traveled rapidly, stopping only when the horses absolutely required rest. They ate dried meat and corn and drank from their water pouches while still in the saddle.

Several days later, they sat their horses in the shade of the trees a half-mile from the fort. Without speaking, they nudged their horses forward and rode slowly toward its huge closed gates.

Snow Blossom had stood in silence and watched Josiah walk toward her. When they were a few inches apart, he stopped.

"I am pleased to see you are safe, Snow Blossom."

"I do not think I am safe here, Josiah. Return me to my husband. Let Rebecca and me go home."

"Go home to what? Your husband is dead, your brother is dead. All the warriors in the village are dead. You have nothing to return to. There is nothing for you anywhere except with me. You are going with me."

The words froze in her mind. He did not know that Sun Knife and White Eagle with most of the warriors had been away at the time of the raid. Snow Blossom knew it would only be a matter of time until White Eagle and Sun Knife came for her and Rebecca.

She did not want to give him the knowledge that Sun Knife and White Eagle were still alive. She must do something to give them time.

"Are you proud of what you have done? Is it a sign of courage in the white man when he slaughters innocent women and children?"

"I did not go on that raid. I am responsible for killing no one."

"And you think you carry less guilt because of that? Speak the truth to me, white man. Why were you and your friends in my village all winter?"

"We told you the reason we came. We were afraid winter would find us in the open."

"I don't believe you. You led the white major to our village."

"Snow Blossom, that is not true. I had nothing to do with what happened in your village."

"Then why are you here?"

"I would protect you."

"From what?"

"From a man who hates the red man, hates them enough to take his hatred out not only on the innocent men and women of your village, but . . . any prisoners he may have."

"I do not want your protection. I do not want you or anyone else to do anything for me except to release me. I will find my way back to my people. If you want to do anything for me, speak to the major, tell him to let me go."

"He will not listen to me. He will never release the white woman."

"She is my brother's wife."

"He does not recognize a marriage between a white girl and an Indian. He plans on sending her east . . . soon . . . and besides, what would he release her to? You would not survive the coming winter out there."

"Let me go," she said, holding herself as proudly and firmly as possible. "I will survive."

"Yes," he said gently as he moved even closer to her. "You will survive. You are as strong as you are beautiful, but you will survive with me. No matter what you say, I am taking you with me."

"Do not do this, Josiah; I warn you. It is a thing you will regret. Do you not think other warriors of our tribe will search for me? Do you think the daughter of Tekata could be stolen without them coming for me? This could cost you your life, Josiah."

"They will not search for us. The major intends to make it impossible. There will be no one left to do the searching; they will need all their strength to survive."

"You are underestimating us, Josiah. . . . I warn you again. Do not do this. I will never belong to any man other than Sun Knife."

"He is dead."

"No matter. His memory lives within me and I would rather be dead than belong to any other."

He reached out and gripped both her wrists, drawing her resisting body close to him. "It no longer matters what you want. With or without your consent, you are going with me. In time, you will learn that I am your way of existence. There is no other man to protect you. In time you will learn. We leave here tomorrow morning. I am taking you far enough away from here that no one will find you even if he were foolish enough to try. From this moment on, you belong to me."

He turned and left the room, locking the door behind him. Snow Blossom stood still, her cold eyes watching the closed door.

"You are a fool, Josiah," she said softly. "Never will I belong to you or any man other than Sun Knife. I will die first . . . but you may also die when Sun Knife and my brother hunt you down for the ungrateful traitor that you are."

She sat down on the edge of the bed, in complete control of herself. In her mind there was no doubt that Sun Knife would be returning to the village soon and find her gone, there was also no doubt in her mind that he would come for her. The only thought that did surface was that if they left tomorrow, just how would she leave a trail for him to follow?

Major Chivington had stood in silent thought a long time after Josiah had left him. His mind dwelt on the golden-haired beauty that they had brought back to the fort with them. Her amazing loveliness had stirred something within him that had lain dormant for a long, long time—the desire for a woman.

His deep hatred for the Indian people filled him with the firm belief that any white woman who allowed herself to be touched by an Indian was defiled and a woman of no morals.

To his rigid code, any woman should choose death before allowing an Indian to touch her. If he had taken her by force, she should have found a way to kill herself over such dishonor.

His mind held Rebecca in only one light, the shaded scarlet light of a wanton woman to whom any man would be welcome. He thought of her unusual and fragile beauty and his blood quickened at the thought of her. It would be amusing, he thought, to possess her for a time before he sent her east. She would make a warm and exciting mistress of pleasure on the long nights.

Once the fantasy of her entered his thoughts, he could not let it go.

Josiah would leave with the Indian girl and the other two trappers would be paid and sent on their way. Yes, he thought, he would keep her as long as she pleased him, then pass her on to any of his officers who wished to share her. What did she matter? he reasoned. A woman who would consort with an Indian was less than a woman and would not care who shared her favors. Like a bitch dog in heat, she would welcome what small amount of security he and the fort offered. It would be better than to be thrown to the mercy of the wilderness where she would surely die in a short time. Thoughts of her soft beauty in his arms built until they seemed real.

Slowly, he turned from the window where the last light of the fading sun grew dim. He went to his door and opened it. He walked with a purposeful stride from his quarters, across the compound, to the rooms in which Snow Blossom and Rebecca were held. A guard stood outside each door. They saluted him when he approached.

"These women can do no harm and will not try to escape. I see no reason for them to remain under guard. You are both relieved of duty. Good night, gentlemen, get some sleep."

"Yes, sir," they both echoed, their eyes avoiding each other's, but each man's thoughts were the same. They both wondered just which one of the beauties behind the closed doors the major would be lucky enough to have.

Major Chivington threw away the butt of the cigar he had been smoking. A pleased half-smile touched his face, a smile of expectant pleasure. He took the last step to Rebecca's door and reached for the key to unlock it. The key clicked in the lock and released it and he pushed the door open and stepped inside.

When Rebecca had been dragged from Snow Blossom's side, she had been taken to a small room and thrust inside. The door was securely locked, for the first thing she did was to test it. All the things that had happened in the past few days had left her shaken. She might have been frightened had not Snow Blossom's last words echoed in her mind.

"I am White Eagle's wife. No matter what these people think, I am proud of it. I will not let them frighten me." She also knew that White Eagle, Sun Knife, and many of the warriors were still alive. It would be a matter of time before White Eagle came for her. She, above all others, knew his pride and dignity. She also knew that White Eagle loved her too much to allow her to be taken from him. She had only to hold on to her nerve and her pride until he came.

What crushed her most was the knowledge that her father was dead and she could not even be there when he was buried. Silently, she prayed for his soul.

She was very tired. The pressured trip from the village to the fort had been a strain; now she trembled with fatigue—that plus the unknown factor; she had no idea what they intended to do with her. She reasoned that there was logically not much more that they could do other than send her back to the remains of her family. She knew she had an aunt and an uncle somewhere back east, but she had been a child the last time she had seen them. No matter what they tried to do, she had no intention of leaving this area.

She wondered why she and Snow Blossom had been separated. Snow Blossom's presence had lent her some semblance of courage and she would have liked nothing more than to be with her now.

Determinedly, she held herself under stern control. She refused to give way to the tears that hovered near. Eventually, she would be allowed to speak to the commanding officer. Whether he approved or not she would tell him that she would rather return to her adopted village; that she was happy there and chose to stay. Surely, she thought, once she had made her feelings known he would allow her to return.

When her mind returned to the village, she thought of the brutality of the attack and the pain White Eagle and Sun Knife would feel when they returned and found such death and destruction. She wished she could be at her husband's side to help him in this dark time.

Rebecca stood by the small window watching the shadows lengthen across the parade ground. Men moved about and conversed in small groups and occasionally, a look would be cast in the direction of her cell.

Slowly, the groups broke up. Men drifted away to their lonely beds, dreaming of the warmth and softness of the women who were held in captivity.

Now the grounds were empty and the only soldiers she could see were the guards who paced the platforms that overlooked the walls and the area beyond. A complete and utter silence pervaded the room. Rebecca shivered as if a cold hand had suddenly reached out to touch her.

She turned from the window and went to sit on the narrow bed. She was exhausted, yet she knew she would not be able to sleep. Slipping off her moccasins, she sat back on the bed with her back against the wall. Absently, she loosened the braids and ran her hand through her hair. She smiled in remembrance of White Eagle's fascination with her golden strands of hair. For him it had been a never-ending source of pleasure to slide his hands into the thick heavy mass of her hair and bury his face in it.

Drawing up her knees, she put her arms about them and allowed herself the pleasure of drawing on her memories. The strength of White Eagle seeped through her and she knew that as long as they both were alive, they would find a way back to each other.

"White Eagle," she murmured softly, "I will be the strong wife your love has taught me to be. You have shared with me your pride, and the pride of your people. I shall not shame you. Whatever happens, I know Snow Blossom and I will walk with that pride in our hearts."

Rebecca was worried about Snow Blossom and the treatment she might be receiving at the hands of the white men. Snow Blossom, full-blooded Indian, might be treated more severely than she. It never occurred to Rebecca that she, a white woman in a white world, might be in more danger than Snow Blossom.

Her mind, caught up in reverie, did not at first hear the fall of footsteps across the wooden porch outside the door. Nor did she hear the soft murmur of voices outside her door. She became aware only when the door swung slowly open.

She watched as the major stepped inside and slowly and firmly closed the door behind him.

Slowly, she stood up from the bed. They stood across the small room from each other, and their eyes met and held. She knew, without doubt or hesitation, what he was thinking. She saw his disdainful, lust-filled look and her heart began to beat furiously. His eyes took in her slender trembling form, her wide violet eyes and the long golden hair that fell in profusion about her.

With all the strength and courage she could gather, she held herself erect and her eyes met his steadily.

"I am Rebecca Wade. I am the wife of White Eagle. I demand you release me at once and let me return to my village with my sister, Snow Blossom. We have done nothing to be held, so let us go, and White Eagle will spare your life. Keep us and he will kill you and burn your fort to the ground."

Major Chivington stood watching her for several minutes; then he threw back his head and laughed.

Rebecca watched as he slid the bolt home, turned, and walked slowly toward her.

Chapter Twenty-Two

"This is insanity, Major," she said coldly. He was taken aback by her lack of fear, not knowing she was trembling within. He stopped and looked at her. "All of this is insanity. Your attack on our peaceful village was brutal premeditated murder. Was it your order to slaughter innocent women and children?"

"Our?" he questioned.

"Yes, our. I am the wife of White Eagle, chief of the Cheyenne. White Eagle is a peace-loving man, but do not mistake that for weakness. Let me go, let me return to my husband, and maybe he will spare the lives of you and your men."

The major's face became dark with anger. "No decent white woman would become the wife of a dirty filthy Indian," he raged. "My life! The lives of my men! I shall kill every savage from here to the mountains; I shall wipe this area clean of this vermin. Wife to an Indian! You slut, to allow yourself to be touched by him."

He took several more steps toward her. "Yes, let him come. I welcome him coming. Let him see that I have sent his sister away to become the slave of the white trapper, let him see that I can take his wife as casually as I would any other whore. Let him know before he dies, that I am going to strip him of everything and make him grovel on the ground before I give him the mercy of killing him."

"White Eagle will grovel to no man."

"What can the sad remnants of his warriors do? If he is still alive, and I doubt that, for we tried to kill every warrior in sight. It has been several days since your capture. If he were alive, if he had followed, he would be here by now."

"White Eagle is not the animal you are. He has probably stopped to bury the dead . . . and to prepare himself to destroy you."

He laughed and reached out to grasp her by the shoulders. "His bones are being picked clean by the vultures at this minute, and I shall enjoy that thought as much as I shall enjoy the whore he calls wife." His gloating angry face was close to hers and Rebecca was more afraid than she had ever been in her life. Her strength was no match for his and she knew it. Her mind searched desperately for a way to stop him.

"Major," she said, her voice frigid and firm. He stopped, surprised both at the tone and the look in her eyes. "It might be overlooked by everyone should such a thing happen to Snow Blossom, an Indian, but how will you explain to the world that you raped a white woman, a white woman whose family is well-known and not exactly powerless."

He seemed stunned, and not as sure of himself as he had been. She relentlessly pressed her advantage. "Has no one told you I am also the granddaughter of Senator Wade?" She said the words, grateful for the fact that there was a Senator Wade in office and in her desperation she had remembered it. She had met the senator at a tea, when he and his wife had attended her father's church.

"What?"

"Senator Nathanael Wade is my grandfather. He would be shocked should the world find out his granddaughter had been raped by an officer in the U.S. Army."

"I don't believe you; besides, there will be no way of his knowing."

"Everyone in this fort knows by now you have come here. Unless you kill me, I shall shout it to the world. Even if you do kill me, do you really believe not one of the men in this fort will one day whisper it to another? It is a secret you cannot hope to keep. Let me go, major, do not let your lust lead you to a deed you will surely deeply regret."

He did not quite believe her, yet he could not take the chance that what she was saying was not true. There was no way to assure absolute silence of over five-hundred men. He thrust her away from him.

"Damn you! I would not touch you. You are filthy from that Indian's touch. But I will tell you that if your Indian is not dead, and he and his tattered ragtag stragglers come here, I shall make sure this time that he is. If he is alive he has no men left to follow him. His are few against over five hundred men." He bent close to her, his hate so violent she could feel it pulse from him. "I shall personally drag him into this fort and hang him in front of you; then I shall send you back, labeled a whore, and return you to a white world where they do not accept the leavings of an Indian."

He spun about, unlocked the door, and slammed it behind him. Again she heard the click of the key in the lock and his rapidly retreating footsteps.

Reaction set in. She began to tremble. Her weak knees refused to hold her and she collapsed on the bed. Hot tears started and she could not control them. She lay on the bed, pulled the blanket tight about her, and cried until she was exhausted and a dream-tormented sleep overcame her.

She was startled awake by the sound of Snow Blossom's protesting voice. It was barely dawn and she ran to the window to look out. Snow Blossom, tied securely, was struggling as she was put up on a horse. Rebecca recognized Josiah immediately. He put Snow Blossom on the horse despite her struggles and tied her feet together under the horse. Then he mounted and reached down and took hold of Snow Blossom's horse's reins.

Major Chivington and several men were standing near, laughing at Snow Blossom's struggles. "You'd best tame that wild one fast," one shouted.

"A horsewhip across those pretty hips might straighten her out," another jeered.

"I'd suggest you do other things with those hips than whip them," one taunted. "It might make the tamin' a little more fun."

"Sure you don't want me to come along and show you how to housebreak that little filly, Josiah?"

"Housebreak hell, how about bed-break?"

Snow Blossom remained silent. Her eyes turned from the men who shouted, her shoulders square, her back straight and her determined chin high, she ignored them with the royal disdain of a queen.

Josiah smiled at their jeers and kicked his horse into motion, drawing Snow Blossom's after him. Fresh tears burned in Rebecca's eyes as she watched the doors of the fort open and Josiah and Snow Blossom ride through and disappear.

She returned to the bed, pain for Snow Blossom within her, and the fear that what she had said to the major would not hold him off for too long. She feared he would think of some way to surmount all the obstacles. She closed her eyes and prayed silently for White Eagle.

Grant had paced the floor of his cell hour after hour. He knew what must have happened at White Eagle's village, but he knew nothing else. The men who came to give him food and water were under orders to tell him nothing. He did not know yet that Rebecca and Snow Blossom were prisoners also.

He heard the laughter and talk, but could not see the grounds from the window of his cell. In angry frustration, he threw himself across his bed. His vivid imagination pictured White Eagle's village destroyed, White Eagle and Cade dead, Rebecca and Snow Blossom . . . Waterflower . . . Long Arrow . . . dead. He vowed silently to himself that if his life was not taken by the monster who commanded this fort, he would do all he could to see that he paid somehow for what he had done.

The approach of footsteps drew his attention, and in a few minutes his cell door was opened and a young boy, about sixteen, came in carrying a tray of food.

"I got your breakfast, sir."

"Thanks, Will." He smiled as he stood up. He watched the boy set the tray down. Will Trumpp had been at the fort less than a year. He was, as Grant knew, a strong and loyal boy, but lacking somewhat in mental faculties. Grant wondered if he could get him to say something careless.

"Will, there's a lot of fuss going on out there so early in the morning. Someone get in a little trouble?" Grant asked the question so carelessly and smiled in such a friendly way that Will smiled back.

"No, sir. It's just that trapper takin' that Indian girl away."

Grant froze; the smile on his face remained intact, but his mind raced forward. "What Indian girl?"

"The one the major brought here after they hit that village. I heard they killed most all the men and women. This one is young and real pretty. One of the men said she was the old chief's daughter, but I don't believe him. Jake talks all the time like he knows more than he does."

"Snow Blossom," Grant murmured.

"Yes, sir, that's her name. I don't know the name of the other girl."

"What other girl?"

"The white one."

"White . . . Rebecca . . . For God's sake, was that man fool enough to bring both of them here? Will, was the girl blond . . . really pretty?"

"Yes, sir."

"What did the major do with her?"

Will's face turned crimson. "I don't know, sir. I only heard some of the other men talkin'."

"Talkin' about what?"

"How the major went to where he had her locked up and sent the guards away so he could be alone with her for a while. They . . . they said all kinds of things."

Grant sat slowly down as if there were no strength left in his legs. Will saw the stricken look on his face and quickly left the cell so the lieutenant could ask him no more questions.

"God," Grant murmured. "If White Eagle is alive, the major just signed his death warrant and everyone else's in this fort."

Snow Blossom and Josiah rode along in silence. She had tried to get free of the bonds that held her hands tied to the pommel of her saddle, but it was useless. Her mind searched for a way to leave some kind of trail to follow.

It was in the late afternoon before they stopped, and many miles separated them from the fort.

He came to her and untied the bonds that held her feet, but he left her hands tied together, simply releasing them from the saddle horn. He lifted her down and set her on her feet.

"Don't try to escape, Snow Blossom. It's useless with your hands tied. You'd die out there." He went about hobbling the horses so they wouldn't drift away. She stood watching him; then her eyes fell to the hoofprints she saw in the dirt and she knew Sun Knife would find her. Satisfaction welled up inside her. Indians never had their horses shod, and there, firmly printed in the dirt was the clear print of an iron-shod hoof.

Josiah made some food quickly and was satisfied when Snow Blossom obediently ate. He thought she had finally surrendered to her circumstances, but that was not so. She was doing her best to keep up her strength for when the chance to escape might come, or for when Sun Knife came after her.

In less than an hour, they were again on their way. They traveled at a slow but steady pace and Snow Blossom was dismayed at the miles they had put between them and the fort and the fact that the sun was touching the rim of the horizon and she was not sure of what to expect when it finally set and night would be upon them.

He had spoken very little to her, and she found herself wondering what was going on in his mind.

He lifted her down from her horse and again left her hands tied; then he unsaddled the horses and hobbled them for the night. He built a fire and told her to sit and eat. She obeyed, watching him closely.

The moon had risen and the fire had burned to glowing embers. She watched his face as he contemplated the embers in silence. She could see that his mind was somewhere far away, and she did not want to draw his attention to her, so she remained quiet. Then he spoke softly and she realized he had always been aware of her.

"Your husband is dead, Snow Blossom," he said softly as if it were only a thought for himself. She did not answer, and he looked at her across the fire. He smiled, a sad smile. "Do you think I intend to rape you?"

"What do you intend?" she questioned softly.

His eyes held hers as if he were searching for something; then he sighed deeply and again the sad smile appeared.

"I intend to keep you safe and well. I intend to take you far from here; then . . . one day, we will marry. I will build a cabin and we will have children. I like children." He said the words slowly and gently as if they had often been repeated in his mind. "You must forget him, Snow Blossom. . . . I will make you happy."

"And you, Josiah?" she questioned gently. "Who are you trying to forget?"

A fleeting look of pain crossed his face and was gone. He looked at her. "What makes you think I'm trying to forget something?"

"Not something, some*one*. Tell me, Josiah, who is it that I remind you of?"

He smiled. "You are as wise as you are proud and beautiful. Yes, you remind me of someone I loved very much . . . a long, long time ago. She was like you, strong, proud, and so very beautiful."

"What was her name?"

"Two Moons."

"What happened to her, Josiah?"

He remained silent, but his face had closed against her.

"Go to sleep, Snow Blossom. You need not worry; I will not touch you. It is not the time and place of my choice. When we get there, then . . . you will belong to me."

For some strange reason, she believed him. She curled herself on the blanket near the fire and drew it close around her and tried to sleep. She knew in the near future, she would need all her wits and strength. He was still sitting in silent contemplation of the glowing embers when she drifted off to sleep. He watched her eyes close and saw her drift into sleep. The look in his eyes, had she seen it, would have frightened her, for it was a look of intense and all-consuming hunger. After a while, he, too, lay on his blanket and closed his eyes in sleep.

She could barely make out his form in the half-shadows of dawn when he wakened her. They ate swiftly, and before the sun rose, they were on their way again.

For five days, they traveled at the same pace. They were now in territory she did not recognize, although she was trying to watch the way they traveled in case she would have to try to find her way back alone.

She wondered where Sun Knife was at the moment and if he had been able to find and follow the trail. She was constantly watching behind her, but there was no sign of anyone.

On the sixth day, they slowed their pace and in the early

afternoon, they stopped. She looked about her, aware of the beauty of the place. It was an area of rolling wooded hills. They sat atop one and looked down into a green valley. There was a small meandering stream cutting through it and when she looked closely she could see what seemed to be the burned-out remains of a small house. It was in this direction that they rode. When he stopped beside it, she realized this was the final stop. He came to her, carrying a large wicked-looking knife. With it, he slashed the bindings about her wrists and legs and helped her down from the horse.

"Here," he said softly, "here we will build a house and live. It is a beautiful valley, is it not, Two Moons?"

Her eyes lifted to his; he wasn't even looking at her. His eyes were on the remains of the house and the narrow river just beyond. It was as if he were living, clinging to some faded dream world.

"I am not Two Moons," she said firmly. This brought his attention back to her.

"No, of course you're not," he said. "Don't try to escape, Snow Blossom. I know this place like the palm of my hand. You are here with me, and here you will stay. Now, help me with the horses; tomorrow we will start to work. For today, we will eat and rest."

He walked ahead of her to the overgrown remains of the house. It suddenly seemed as if he had left her and walked in a place she could not see. She watched as he stood among the ruins in a silent aura of sorrow.

Slowly and as quietly as she could, she mounted the horse; holding the reins of his, she began to back away. If she could get a running start, he would not be able to follow her. A few feet farther and she kicked the horse into motion, pulling his horse along.

Now they were in a full run and her heart thudded as she realized the possibility of escape. Then she heard a sharp crack and the horse beneath her stumbled and went down, throwing her free. She fell with a solid thump that momentarily stunned her and knocked the breath from her body. She lay still, and in a few minutes, he stood over her, the still-smoking rifle in his hand. "That was a foolish thing to do. Did you think I would let you go even if it cost a horse?"

She tried to get up and he knelt and pushed her back against the ground roughly. His eyes were hard and he spoke coldly. "Don't try that again, Snow Blossom. I would hate to hurt you. If you try leaving me, I shall make it impossible for you to ever be able to again. I could do that, you know." The words were cold and soft and yet she knew he meant every word of them.

He pulled her to her feet, and surprisingly his hands again were gentle. They walked to the horse and he mounted. With a gesture, he motioned her to mount before him, but she turned away from him determinedly and walked back to the ruins. She could feel his eyes on her all the way.

To the Indians, a horse was one of the most valuable things they had. She knew if Josiah had shot a horse so easily, he would not hesitate to stop her from running in any way he could.

Rebecca saw no one for the next few days, except the young soldier who was sent with food and water. She paced the floor, tense with worry over Snow Blossom, and White Eagle. There were too few men in their village to overcome the soldiers at the fort, and she was sure, once he found where she was, White Eagle would do just that. He would not stand a chance with all the soldiers and their guns. One agonizing thought led to another. She pictured White Eagle dying outside the gates of the fort and being unable to go to him.

Grant, too, was in a state of anxiety over all the things his imagination had envisioned.

It was in the early morning of the days after she had been captured that Rebecca heard men moving rapidly and exicted conversation. She went to the window, but no one was close enough or showed any inclination to stop and tell her what was happening.

Grant heard the confusion, and though he did not know exactly what was happening, he knew it had to be something very unusual. . . . *It was.*

Major Chivington had been at breakfast when a young trooper, excited and rather breathless, came to his quarters.

"What is it, Mason?"

"There're two Indians outside the fort, sir. One of 'em speaks English. They're askin' to talk with you. I don't know if I'm right or not, sir, but I'd swear one of 'em is that half-breed doctor who came through here awhile back, and some of the men think the other one is that young White Eagle. He's dressed like a chief; do you think old Tekata might be dead?"

The major rose and accompanied the soldier across the compound and up the steps that led to the guard platform. He looked down and a smile crossed his face. Despite his Indian dress, he recognized Cade Holliday immediately, and he knew the Indian with him could be no one but White Eagle.

"Corporal Mason."

"Yes, sir?"

"Tell the . . . gentlemen that I shall send someone out to speak to them."

"Yes, sir, shall I open the gates, sir?"

"No! I want none of those savages within this fort. Simply tell them I will send someone out. If they want to talk, they will wait."

He chuckled a grim mirthless sound. "I guarantee you, Corporal, they will wait."

"Yes, sir."

The major returned to his office. Deliberately, he alloted himself two hours before he sent for a messenger. The young man came rapidly. No one in the fort moved slowly when Major Chivington sent for him. He stood at rigid attention.

"I want you to go and bring Lieutenant Jameson to me."

"Yes, sir."

He spun about and left, crossing the compound almost at a run.

Grant was surprised when his cell was unlocked. He could tell by the combination of excitement and fear in the boy's eyes, that something unusual had happened.

"The major wants you in his office, sir. He said immediately."

Grant was just as anxious to see the major as the major was to see him. Within minutes he was at the office door, his hand raised to knock.

"Come in."

Once inside, Grant stood at attention while the major's eyes appraised him with cold amusement. "There are two of your friends outside, Lieutenant. It seems they have come to talk to me. I choose not to talk to such vermin, so I am sending you."

"I don't think it's talk, sir," Grant said bitterly. "I think White Eagle wants his wife back."

"Wife! How dare you suggest I let a white woman mate with an Indian? Have you no respect for your own kind? She will be returned east, under guard if necessary."

"Major, may I say something?"

"What?"

"You are misjudging White Eagle. That is a very dangerous thing to do. He is a strong and well-loved leader as is his father Tekata. Their tribe outnumbers this fort. The wisest thing to do would be to return his wife to him. It would save a lot of bloodshed and keep the peace with the Cheyenne."

Again the major laughed. "You are wrong on several things."

"Sir?"

"My scouts have reported Tekata is dead and White Eagle is now chief in the Cheyenne village."

Grant was jolted and felt a deep sympathy for White Eagle and Snow Blossom.

"Of course," the major continued softly, "there is very little of his village left. Most of that blight has been cleared from the face of the earth."

"Then . . . then you did attack?"

"Yes, I did. Quite successfully I assure you. I should not be surprised if there were less than two hundred men at White Eagle's disposal. With that kind of force, he can do this fort no harm."

"They were unprepared—the women and children . . . you—"

"Destroyed as many as possible."

"Oh, my God," Grant said painfully. "He will never forgive you."

"Forgive me! Who asks for his forgiveness? I want you to go out and tell that scum to round up what is left of his village. It will be moved out of this area to a reservation."

"White Eagle on a reservation? White Eagle not seeking revenge . . . ? Never."

"He will go," the major said softly, "or I will round them up personally and drive them . . . drive them like a herd of cattle."

"You cannot treat him like that. He is a chief, a great warrior. He will fight. . . . You have killed his people and stolen his wife, what is it you expect him to do?"

"Leave, before I have to teach him another lesson . . . maybe a more fatal lesson."

"At least give him back his wife. Maybe we can prevent bloodshed that way."

"No."

"Major—"

"No! Lieutenant, you are under direct orders. . . . You will go and talk to your aborigine friends or I shall have you shot for desertion from duty."

"Yes, sir," Grant said as he grimly held himself from throwing himself across the desk at the man who stood behind it. He saluted, turned, and left the room.

After they had been told to wait, White Eagle and Cade sat on their horses in silence. Cade watched White Eagle as the time moved slowly by. He gave no sign of knowing how long they sat outside the fort or the deliberate insult in making him wait so. His face remained unreadable and frozen. But Cade had known him for too long. He saw the boiling fury, the contained violence beneath the surface. Cade knew that White Eagle's anger was growing into a dark and violent thing and the longer they waited the deeper and deeper it grew.

It was almost three hours and White Eagle had not moved a muscle. He controlled his horse and remained still. Cade was finally about to break the silence and speak when the gates of the fort opened and a rider came out. In a few minutes, Cade recognized Grant.

He rode up to them and Cade could easily read the look in his eyes. He could, and he knew White Eagle could also.

"Cade," Grant said quietly, "White Eagle."

"I would speak to your leader," White Eagle said coldly.

"He will not come, White Eagle. He has sent a message

with me."

"He will not speak with me? Go to him and tell him, White Eagle demands the return of his woman."

"White Eagle—"

"Grant," Cade interrupted, "are Rebecca and Snow Blossom all right?"

"I think so."

"You don't know?"

"No, I have been locked up for refusing to go on the raid of your village."

Grant could see the flicker in White Eagle's eyes and the relief in Cade's.

"I'm glad you weren't along, Grant. I could not believe you would be party to such a thing."

"Go and tell the white major to release my wife and my sister or I shall kill every soldier within and burn this fort to the ground. If he harms her in any way, I will make sure he takes a long, long time to die."

"White Eagle, if I can get Rebecca and Snow Blossom out, will you take them and go in peace? You are few and unarmed. It would be another massacre."

"Go where? This is our home. You are the trespassers. Give me my woman and my sister and I will consider your words."

Cade knew in his heart that White Eagle never intended to let the deaths of his people go unpunished. He said nothing, for he, too, felt the savage need of revenge.

"You will go north—to the reservation."

White Eagle looked at him, disbelief clouding his eyes. Cade felt the major had just struck the fatal blow that sealed his fate. White Eagle would never willingly go to a reservation. To be caged like an eagle with a broken wing would be like death to him.

"Go to your major, tell him White Eagle camps here one night. When the sun rises over our heads tomorrow, he will return my woman and my sister or . . . he should begin to sing his death song."

"Cade?" Grant said imploringly.

"No," Cade replied softly, but firmly. "Sun Knife, and it is also my woman he holds. I want her back, Grant. I stand with

White Eagle and my people."
"Does your father condone this?" Grant said.
"My father is dead," Cade replied gently.
"Michael," Grant whispered softly; then his eyes searched Cade's. "Waterflower, Long Arrow?"
"Alive . . . barely. Your major is a very thorough man."
"God, Cade, I'm sorry."
"I repeat, Grant. Cade Holliday died with his father. Sun Knife is here to seek revenge for a man whose heart was good, a man who was a warrior, not the kind of a man who took his life. We will wait here one night and until noon tomorrow. Advise him, Grant; it would be best if he returned Snow Blossom and Rebecca to us."
"Cade . . . Sun Knife, you know him and his kind. He intends to kill you all. He is using Rebecca as an excuse. He can send one of his endless lying reports to Washington. The Indians rose up and he was forced to eliminate their entire village. For God's sake, listen to me!"
"We have listened to all we want to hear," White Eagle replied. "Talk to him; tell him we will wait. We will be here tomorrow. Send out Rebecca and Snow Blossom."
White Eagle spun about and galloped away toward the edge of the woods, where he dismounted and began to make preparations to camp.
Cade watched Grant. He would have liked to speak the words Grant wanted to hear, and save the bloodshed he knew was to follow. Grant had been a friend to him; yet he knew he had to stand beside White Eagle now, just as he knew he had to have Snow Blossom back.
"Grant," he said gently, "do everything in your power to get Rebecca and Snow Blossom out of there by noon tomorrow. Major Chivington might get a surprise at White Eagle's ability to make war. He has pressed a strong and honorable man against a wall and given him no choice but to fight, and fight he will. It is a warning for a friend."
He rode away to join White Eagle and Grant watched him go. Then he sighed deeply and rode back through the gates of the fort. He went directly to Major Chivington's office and was told to go in immediately. Major Chivington was awaiting his

return. He went in and closed the door behind him. John Chivington stood with his back to Grant looking out the window. His hands were clasped behind him and he rocked gently on the balls of his feet.

"Well, Lieutenant?"

"After what you've done, you knew they would refuse. For God's sake, Major, give them their women back."

"Women?"

"I know Snow Blossom is here, too. Give them back; we might still avoid a conflict." Grant told him word for word what White Eagle and Cade had said.

"I repeat these words slowly, Lieutenant, so you will understand. One, I will not release any white woman to these savages. Two, she is the only one here, the other one I gave to the white trapper, Josiah Tucker, as a reward for leading us to Tekata's village. Three"—he turned to look at Grant; he smiled but his eyes were cold as ice—"I intend to make an example of this savage and all his friends. I intend to wipe them from the face of the earth. After this example, the other tribes will move to the reservation without problems."

"You . . . you gave Snow Blossom, a chief's daughter, the wife of Cade Holliday, to a trapper! Are you insane? If there ever had been a slight chance to prevent a war, you have killed it."

John Chivington stood immobile, his hate-filled eyes turned on Grant.

"You, Lieutenant Jameson, will go tomorrow and give White Eagle my final ultimatum. Gather his people and take them to the reservation. If he does not, I shall finish what I started and wipe it clean. Do I make myself clear, Lieutenant?"

"Yes," Grant said hoarsely. "I will tell him, but I will also tell you that I intend to go to Washington. Cade's father has many friends there. I intend to make a full report of what you have done. I intend to shout it to the world, print it in every newspaper. If it is in my power, I intend to see you get court-marshaled and hung for the atrocities you have done and those you plan to do."

"Get out of here, Lieutenant!"

"I'll leave. I don't think I can stand to be in the same room with a man such as you. I have met these Indians, I have been treated with honor and respect, and I will tell you that I sincerely hope White Eagle has the ability to destroy this fort and all that is in it, for it is an evil that deserves to be destroyed."

Grant turned and left the room, not bothering to close the door behind him. John Chivington stood watching him, a faint twisted smile on his face.

"You will be nothing more than a casualty of war when this is finished, Lieutenant, a very tragic casualty of war."

Again he turned to face the window and clasped his hands behind his back; again he began the slow rhythmic rocking on his heels as his mind returned to the strategy he planned to use for the destruction of White Eagle, Sun Knife, all their people, and . . . one white officer.

White Eagle and Cade camped at the edge of the woods so that everyone in the fort could see them. They sat together, neither of them hungry enough to eat the meat they had roasted, and each of them thinking of the women they loved in the hands of Major Chivington.

"White Eagle," Cade said quietly. "Is there a way we can save Grant, too? He has been a good and loyal friend. He is helpless when his chief speaks." White Eagle remained silent for a long time; then he spoke. "My warriors remember coming home from a hunting trip to find their tepees burned, their wives and children dead. Do you think they would listen to my words if I asked them to spare any of the soldiers? The white chief has made it impossible. They have done to White Eagle and his people more than he can tolerate."

It was in the wee hours of the morning that they rolled in their blankets and tried to sleep. It was an elusive thing, for each of their minds were on the two women held prisoner in the fort, a fort White Eagle intended to destroy. Dawn found them both up and preparing themselves for the long wait until noon. There were no words to say, so they waited in silence as slowly and steadily the sun began to rise.

Inside the fort, Grant was already prepared to go to them, but the major had obstinately refused to let him go out until the very last moment.

Slowly the doors of the fort swung open and a heavy-hearted Grant headed toward the two warriors who sat on their horses in expectant silence.

Cade was determined that he would still try to find some way to ease the situation and get his wife returned without bloodshed.

"You have spoken to the white chief?" White Eagle said.

"Yes, I have spoken to him."

"He has agreed to send my woman and my sister back to me? I have thought on this matter. I will let his men go free if he agrees. The fort must burn and another must not be built."

"White Eagle . . . he will not set them free. He says you are to go to the reservation with all your people. He is sending Rebecca back east."

White Eagle's face smiled grimly. "Tell your white chief to sing his death song. His time is over. White Eagle talks no more. I will come for my woman." He turned his horse and rode away.

Grant would have still held a small touch of Cade's loyalty had he not been forced to say the next words.

"Sun Knife," he began, his voice slow and agonized, "Snow Blossom is no longer here. The trapper . . . Josiah Tucker . . . he took her . . . five days ago."

Cade's face filled with disbelief and rage. All support he had for his father's people melted away and in its place sprang hatred and a deep need for revenge.

Without a word to Grant he turned and followed White Eagle.

Chapter Twenty-Three

They waited together, Sun Knife and White Eagle, in a deep black silence. The sun climbed higher and higher in the sky. When it stood directly overhead, White Eagle, without a word, turned his horse away from the fort and rode toward home. Sun Knife had told him what had become of Snow Blossom.

"I will follow his trail, brother," Sun Knife said. "He will not escape if he travels to the end of the earth. I will repay him for every moment she spends with him."

"The white chief of the fort knows which path they took."

"Of course, but would he tell me?"

"He will tell you, Sun Knife," White Eagle said firmly. His eyes were cold and hard as death. "Soon we will drag him from his fort where he feels so safe. Then he will tell us where to find my wife and my sister; then he will wish he had returned them this day."

Silent, burning with a deep anger held in check only by strong wills and plans of revenge, Sun Knife and White Eagle returned home.

They found the village swollen with warriors, with more arriving every day. All of the small villages had been contacted; all knew the names of Tekata and White Eagle, and all picked up their weapons to answer the call. The invading white man had begun to push the Cheyenne as far as they would tolerate being pushed. They were not, in all, a warlike people. Their one enemy was the Crow and these they fought sporadically and usually by stealing their horses and leaving negligible fatalities.

Now, warriors donned their paint and decorated themselves with bright feathers in preparations for battle.

War was a very serious thing to the Cheyenne and he brought to it all the supernatural aids that he could muster. A warrior decorated his face and torso with designs intended to protect him as he went into battle.

Besides painting his face and body for battle, the Indian dressed for the occasion, but except for his shield, most of the things he wore or carried were of no practical use as armor. Rather, they were part of his personal medicine, or spiritual armor. His shield was thought to embody more magical qualities than physical protections; yet its physical qualities were impressive.

For all the Indian's trust in his spiritual protection, in the heat of a battle, every Indian warrior bet his life on the effectiveness of his weapons.

Every warrior owned a knife, which he usually wore under his belt. He also carried a bow and a quiver of arrows, a war club which he used for hand-to-hand combat, and a tomahawk. The bow and arrow, in the hands of one of these warriors, was accurate at over one hundred yards, and could be fired more rapidly than muskets or rifles.

Mounted, they formed what many white officers referred to as the greatest cavalrymen they had ever seen. They rode as though they were part of the half-wild animals beneath them, with a phenomenal control over both the horses and themselves.

Sun Knife knelt on a buffalo skin and opened his small containers of paint. They had been wrapped in his medicine bundle for years. He had hoped he would never have to use them. He looked at his hands . . . a doctor's hands, meant to heal and bring life; yet now he could only think of death, death to the man who had stolen Snow Blossom from him, death to the man whose treachery had brought such grief to his people.

Slowly, he put a finger in the white paint and drew a zigzag streak of lightning from the inner corner of his lips to his jawbone on each cheek. Then he touched the red paint and drew a corresponding red streak below the white. From his lower lip to the curve of his chin, he drew two lines, one red, one white. Across his brow from temple to temple, two lines of red and one white. He removed the band he wore about his head and donned a war bonnet that extended to his hips and was decorated with the feathers of the hawk and red and white beading.

He picked up his war lance and his bow and arrows, after he had tucked his knife in his belt.

Silently he repeated the prayers to the gods to protect him in battle and to protect his wife until he could find her.

When they were ready to leave the warriors were fifteen hundred strong—fifteen hundred of the strongest, ablest men the tribes had to offer. With White Eagle at their head, they rode toward the fort.

Rebecca found her door unlocked the morning after the major's visit. She was told she had complete freedom to move about, and immediately took advantage of it. It was a thing she wished afterward she had never done. She walked from her room to the general store, aware of all the eyes that watched her. There were a group of soldiers inside that looked at her with such suggestive leers on their faces that their thoughts could hardly be mistaken.

She turned to leave and found her way blocked by a tall, rather handsome young lieutenant. Obviously, he considered himself a lady-killer and Rebecca open prey, for he grinned suggestively at her.

"Hello, pretty lady."

"Let me pass, Lieutenant," she said quietly.

"Now, that would hardly be good manners on my part to let a pretty thing like you spend a nice day like this all alone."

She could hear the snickers and soft laughter behind her.

"If you don't want to go for a walk in the woods, pretty lady, I'd be glad to take you back to your room."

"Thank you, no, Lieutenant. I would rather go alone."

"Oh, now, pretty thing, you aren't used to being alone. I heard you had plenty of company out there in that Indian camp. You aren't implying that some dirty savage is better than one of your own kind, are you?"

"If you are speaking of my husband White Eagle, Lieutenant, yes, I prefer his company to anyone's, and I agree on another thing, he is certainly not your kind. He would never accost a woman and make such ugly innuendos. He is too much of a man to push himself on a woman who did not want him."

"Why, you little tramp!" the lieutenant replied angrily,

after hearing the laughter that followed his remark. He gripped her roughly by the arm. "You need a lesson in good manners after keeping company with those animals. I'll show you how to treat a real man."

"Let me go, Lieutenant," she said. She was trembling now; yet her eyes held his and her chin was stubbornly set. He drew her close to him, his hand gripping her arm until she cried out with pain.

"You," he snarled softly, "need to be mounted by a man who knows how to pleasure a whore like you. After sleeping with that savage, it ought to be a treat."

Pure red rage flashed in her mind and she drew her other hand back and slapped him across the face with all the strength she had. It surprised him and caused him to step back. Now his eyes narrowed with hate.

"You little bitch, I'll show you some manners."

He reached out and slapped her smartly across the face. Before she could stumble back he again grabbed her by both arms and drew her roughly into an embrace she could not wriggle free from. His lips began to lower to hers, but before they could touch, a soft voice spoke from the doorway.

"Let her go, Carroway."

The man holding her dropped his hands so abruptly that she staggered back from him. Tears of pain, frustration, and anger clouded her eyes as she looked toward the doorway; then with a soft cry she moved toward him. Grant stood still, the anger within him so strong that he was afraid if he moved he would leap on the man.

"Defending private property, Indian-lover?" the lieutenant snarled.

"No, just defending a woman against an animal. It is a thing I would do even for your sister. Don't you think your family would be proud to know you treated a defenseless woman so?"

Lieutenant Carroway's eyes fell from Grant's and all present remained silent as Grant took hold of Rebecca's arm and led her from the store.

They stood on the porch several minutes without speaking while Rebecca tried to regain control over her trembling body and tear-filled eyes.

"Oh, Grant," she whispered softly, "I have never felt such hatred before. Why, why should they hate the Indians so? Especially a man like White Eagle?"

"Ignorance, Rebecca, ignorance. They don't know them as we do. All they know is the fear and greed that governs them."

"Why," she gulped, "why do they hate me so?"

"It is a hard thing to try to explain, Rebecca. You are beautiful and their opinion of all Indians is so low they think you have degraded yourself. In their ignorant minds, it makes you fair game. Rebecca, try to forget it. I'll walk you back to your room. It . . . it might be best if you sent for me before you went out again."

"Grant, it is so unfair. They should at least give us a chance. White Eagle is a peaceful man. Why do they judge us so?"

"It is something I cannot explain even to myself. Come, Rebecca, I'll take you back." Holding her elbow, they walked back to her room. Once inside, Rebecca threw herself across the bed.

"Oh, White Eagle," she said softly, "come for me. I do not think I can stand to live among such people again."

The days drifted slowly by. Rebecca never left her room unless accompanied by Grant.

Major Chivington gloated over his "victory" over the Indians, continually referring to it as a major campaign, assuring everyone that this particular area was under his complete control. He took every opportunity to make it clear to both Rebecca and Grant that he, in one move, had broken the spirit and will of her Indian friends.

He forced Rebecca to eat at his table at mealtimes and, though he tried to separate them, Grant would be there, too. These times were tedious for Rebecca, and often her nerves were so frayed she had to keep herself under rigid control. She was determined he would not bend her and make her submit to him.

Over two weeks after she had been taken, Rebecca woke one morning to an insistent rapping on her door. She put on her robe and went to asnwer it. When she opened the door she stood facing a young corporal. He had bright-red hair, a profusion of freckles and a grin that nearly split his face. It was a sincere smile, so sincere she could not help but smile in return.

"Major Chivington would like to speak to you, miss. He says it is important and would you please come as soon as you can."

"Yes, I will. Thank you, Corporal—?"

"Glazer, ma'am, Timothy Glazer."

"Well, Corporal Glazer"—she smiled—"would you be kind enough to wait and escort me across the compound. I . . . I prefer not to walk it alone."

"Yes, ma'am," he said. "You needn't be afraid, miss."

"Thank you; I'll only be a minute."

She closed the door and began rapidly to change into her clothes. When she opened the door again, she found him patiently waiting and his admiring gaze told her how well she looked. She took his arm and together they crossed the compound to the major's office.

The sergeant who worked in the outer office rose to his feet when she walked in. Rebecca was surprised at his good manners in regard to her, then remembered having seen him in Grant's company several times. His smile, too, was friendly and it was the first day she had felt welcome since she had come.

"Good morning, Miss Wade."

"Good morning, Sergeant—?"

"Sergeant Price, miss."

"I'm a married woman, Sergeant." She smiled.

He chuckled in friendly response. "What do I call you, ma'am? Mrs. White Eagle?"

Now she laughed, too. "Call me Rebecca."

"Thank you, Rebecca; I'm honored. The major will see you now." He took her elbow and guided her to the door. When his knock was answered he opened the door and she walked in and he pulled the door shut behind her.

She stood facing the major's desk while his eyes moved slowly over her. "Come in, sit down. I have some news for you."

"I'd prefer to stand, Major. What is your news?"

"You will be leaving soon."

"You are sending me back to my husband?" she said hopefully, her smile brightening.

"Hardly. I could not allow a white woman to . . . join those savages. No, you will be going east—to some friends of mine. They will care for you until my duties are over here. Then"—he smiled—"I shall join you."

"And your duties here are to butcher," she snapped.

"What is there left to butcher? Your Indian lover could hardly scrape up enough men to annoy me. No, I intend to herd them to a reseration and then . . . we will make millions from this land."

"You are a wretched beast. How can you give the name 'savage' to the men who defended their own in honor when you fought with such despicable treachery?"

He chuckled. "Such vehemence is useless, my dear. You shall be leaving soon and I will join you when this dirty little business is finished."

"I would rather die first."

"No, no, my dear. I don't want you dead," he said softly. "I want you very much alive."

"White Eagle will never let you get away with this. He will kill you."

He began to laugh and moved toward her, but before he could reach her a knock sounded. He glared at the door. "What is it?" he called.

Sergeant Price opened the door. The smile was gone and his face was pale.

"Sir, you had best come at once."

"What's the matter?"

"I . . . I don't believe it, sir. There must be over a thousand of them, sir." His voice grated with amazement and a little fear.

"A thousand what?"

"Indians, sir. Led by those two that came here a few days ago."

"White Eagle came here?" Rebecca asked quickly.

The major's face was unreadable as he roughly took Rebecca by the arm and pushed her toward Sergeant Price.

"See that she is returned to her room. Lock the door and bring me the key."

"Yes, sir," Price replied, but the look in his eyes told Rebecca many things. One, that this job was distasteful to him, and two, his respect for his commanding officer was negligible. He was quiet as he walked across the compound with her.

"Sergeant Price, White Eagle has been here before?"

"Yes, Rebecca; he came for you. He and one other man."

"Sun Knife!"

"The major refused to return you to him so he left. I'm sure the major thought that would be the end of it. He was certain White Eagle was defeated and couldn't rouse enough men from the scattered villages to do any harm."

"What a fool he is," Rebecca said softly. "He does not know what kind of a man White Eagle is. He is honorable and proud, Sergeant Price. He is also stronger than the major realizes. His father's name and his would draw warriors to him just for the honor of fighting by his side. The major should return me to my husband. I cannot bear the thought of being responsible for anyone's death."

"I don't think it's just you, Rebecca. The major is a hate-filled fool as you said. He has done to White Eagle what no man would be able to stand."

They arrived at Rebecca's door. She turned to him and smiled. "I want to thank you for your kindness and consideration. Whatever happens here, Sergeant, I want you to know I'm grateful."

He smiled. "It's quite all right, Rebecca. I'm glad I could be of some help."

"Sergeant?"

"Yes?"

"Would you . . . could you tell me what happens? It is so difficult to be in the dark, to wait without knowing."

"I'll do my best."

"Thank you." She touched his arm lightly, then turned and went inside. In a few minutes, she heard the lock click. She slowly sat down on the edge of her bed to wait.

Major Chivington stood and stared with disbelieving eyes. On the horizon, fifteen hundred painted, feathered Indians sat their horses, motionless and silent, waiting only a sign from

White Eagle to attack the fort that contained less than a third their number.

The air crackled with soundless expectancy. Slowly, Sun Knife and White Eagle rode forward until they had covered half the distance to the fort. There they sat their horses and waited. There was not a man watching who did not know what they waited for.

"Bastards!" he muttered. "Dirty red-skinned bastards!"

He turned to Timothy Glazer, who still stood in dumbfounded wonder, his eyes wide and his face very pale.

"Tell Lieutenant Jameson I want him now."

"Yes, sir," Timothy replied. He left and ran to find Grant who accompanied him at a fast run back to the major. He looked out over the silent line of Indians, saw Sun Knife and White Eagle waiting motionless, and he knew the finality of everything. The few they were stood no chance with the number facing them, even with superior weapons.

"Well, Lieutenant?"

"Do you want my honest opinion, sir?"

"Of course!" the major snapped. "Why did you think I sent for you?"

"We don't stand a snowball's chance in hell of coming out of this alive."

"I detest the thought of surrendering one inch to a bloody savage, but until I get reinforcements, I will do so. Send the woman out to him. . . . I will be more thorough next time."

Grant turned to him. "Do you honestly think sending Rebecca back to him now will be enough? He has passed the time when he will listen or speak to you. He is a proud leader and you have pushed him to a place where he cannot retreat."

"He wants his wife, Lieutenant, and you have been able to speak to him before."

"Now you will admit she is his wife?"

"Temporarily. Find out just how and why he was able to acquire so many warriors. I want to make sure that never happens again. Go, and take the woman with you."

"Yes, sir." Grant turned away; he could stand no longer to look at the man who understood the Indians so little that he had deliberately signed the death warrants of so many men out of ignorance. There was no use talking to him. He had to let the major find out for himself that White Eagle intended to attack whether Rebecca was returned or not.

Taking Sergeant Price with him, he went to get Rebecca.

When the three of them rode from the fort, even Rebecca was aghast at the number of Indians and their silence.

White Eagle and Sun Knife, seeing them coming, exchanged glances. Then White Eagle raised a hand and two of his men rode to his side.

"Take the two soldiers," he said quietly. Neither of the two warriors had to say anything to acknowledge his words, he knew his orders would be carried out.

When Grant and Rebecca reached White Eagle, they stopped, facing him. "White Eagle," Rebecca said softly and was rewarded by the glow of love in his dark eyes.

"Come here, Rebecca," he said and she rode to his side. He reached out and touched her just for a moment. "You are well, Golden One?" he said softly. She nodded; then he turned back to Grant.

"Let the men in the fort go free, White Eagle," Grant said. "They are not responsible for this."

"Grant," Sun Knife said, "do you know where Josiah has taken Snow Blossom?"

"No, I don't . . . the major does."

Sun Knife did not say another word, he just nodded his head.

Grant was about to speak to White Eagle again when he realized that he had slowly been surrounded by silent warriors. It was only a second before he realized what was happening.

"No! White Eagle, no!" he shouted, but it was already too late. He felt himself gripped by several hands and lifted from his saddle. His arms were bound behind him. He could see Sergeant Price was getting the same treatment. "Let me return to my duty, White Eagle," Grant pleaded, but he might have been talking to a statue.

"Sun Knife!" he shouted. "Don't do this!"

But Sun Knife was already turning his back to him to rejoin the line of Indians. Rebecca, accompanied by two warriors, Grant, and Sergeant Price, was taken behind the line where they could see, but not be in danger.

Grant and Sergeant Price watched in frustrated misery as fifteen hundred Indians, with shrill war whoops attacked the fort of less than five hundred men.

There was no way they could withstand the force of the attack. Slowly but surely, small parties breached the defenses in one place after another.

It was over three hours of severe battle, before the strength of the fort broke. The huge gates of the fort were thrown open by the Indians who had reached the inside. In a roar of thundering hoofs, White Eagle led his warriors inside. A few minutes later, the battle was over. Several prisoners were taken at White Eagle's orders; among them was a stunned Major Chivington and a very frightened Corporal Glazer.

There were no more than twenty men herded from the fort, shocked, bloodied, and frightened. They were forced to walk the distance from the fort to White Eagle's village. What had been a six-day trip by horseback was a shattering and almost unbearable ten-day trip for the prisoners driven almost to the limit of their endurance.

They lay in complete exhaustion in a large tepee, well-guarded by silent stone-faced guards.

Rebecca had been taken to White Eagle's tepee where she waited for him to come to her. She had closed her eyes to the violence of the battle, knowing that White Eagle's pride left him no alternative. She hated the deaths of her own people; yet she knew that the tribe had been pushed to this violence against their will.

She, of all people, knew the generous and gentle nature of her husband. But she knew that the white world would only see what he had done as the act of a bloodthirsty savage.

It was very late at night, and Rebecca had tried to wait for White Eagle, but exhaustion overtook her and she drifted into a light sleep. She came slowly awake to the realization that White Eagle was standing just inside the doorway. He stood silently watching her sleep. His war paint and bonnet had been removed and he wore only buckskin pants and shirt. His immobile face seemed carved from bronze granite and he seemed to be waiting for something. It was then she realized he did not know how she would accept him. Would she understand what he had done, or would she condemn him for the deaths of her people? Understanding him more now than she ever had before, she slowly rose from the couch and went to him. His dark unreadable eyes watched her come and she could sense the tension deep within him. She stood close to him and gently raised her hand to touch his face.

"It is good to be home, White Eagle. I have longed for the safety of your arms."

He seemed to relax and he drew her into his arms and held her.

"I thought I had lost you, Golden One. My life would have been a shadow if you had left it. All I could see in my mind was the long lonely days, if you had been gone."

He lifted her chin to look into her eyes, and what he saw there returned the warmth and the love to his.

"Death is the only thing that will separate us, White Eagle," she replied gently.

"After what I have done, the wrath of the great white father will fall on us. It will be very difficult."

"Are you suggesting that I have a choice?"

"You do."

"No, I don't. White Eagle, the man who will always live within my heart, will always possess me. I cannot, I will not live without you. There is a part of the teachings of my church I will tell you. It is 'whither thou goest, I go; thy people shall be my people; thy home, my home.' It is my belief, it is the way I must go."

"Your god must be a very wise man. One day, you must tell me more of the god who makes you believe so. For now, I am grateful that he has returned you to me."

With his arm about her, he walked toward the couch. He sat down, and she could see the tired lines on his face.

"What will you do now, White Eagle?"

"I must make the white chief tell us where the trapper has taken Snow Blossom," he replied.

"What if he refuses to tell you?"

"He will tell me," White Eagle said grimly. "He would be wise to do so for Sun Knife will kill him slowly if I give him the chance. His anger is so great that only my will is keeping him from doing so now."

"When will you question him?"

"At first light. Let him sit with the survivors for a while and think. Maybe he will develop more wisdom than he had when he refused to return you to me, and chose to give Snow Blossom to a man as if she were a slave."

"White Eagle?"

"Yes?"

"The survivors," she said softly. "What do you plan to do with them?"

He sat quietly for a moment in deep thought; then he turned to look at her. "Many of my people died at their hands. Do you think I should not punish them for what they have done? My people seek revenge."

"White Eagle, you know of the major and what kind of man he was. He is to blame. Some of the men you hold had no choice but to follow orders. Some of them were kind to me. Sergeant Price and . . . a young corporal went out of their way to defend me and protect me." She slid to her knees at his feet and placed her hands in his. "Can I ask for their lives? Can I ask mercy from a man whose heart is compassionate?"

"I cannot free the major; he has brought too much death."

"But Grant . . . and the others, White Eagle, can you set them free?"

He sighed tiredly. "I shall see what can be done, Rebecca."

"It is all I can ask of you. Rest, White Eagle."

He lay back on the couch, drawing her with him, holding her against him.

"All the nights you were gone from me, Golden One, all those hours I spent remembering your softness in my arms. I long for comfort, but not for sleep."

She rose on one elbow and looked down into his warm dark eyes; then slowly she bent her head and touched her lips to his. With one hand buried in her thick hair, he drew her body across his and his hungry mouth searched her willing one.

She closed her eyes and savored the warmth of him, the joy of feeling his deep hungry need for her.

His hands caressed her gently, pushing aside the clothes she wore and brushing her skin with gentle searching fingers.

After the deathlike struggle of the battle, he sought the sweet release her love gave him. He murmured her name softly as he buried his face against her breasts.

She could feel their bodies join and blend together, and she accepted with the deepest pleasure the knowledge that he found his peace within her, that she could give to him the love, strength, and courage he sought.

They lay together in silence for a long time and he must have thought she slept for he slipped quietly from the bed and went to the dying fire. There he threw on some twigs and chips and when it burned brightly, he sat before it to think of what he would do to the survivors of the battle. Sun Knife, his brother, waited for White Eagle to give him access to the major, and he knew Sun Knife would find where Snow Blossom was. His main thought was what he would do to the remaining white soldiers—and Grant, his friend.

"White Eagle," she said softly, and he looked up in surprise; then he rose and went to her. He sat beside her on the couch.

"I thought you slept," he said.

"I was watching you. You have made a decision?"

He played absently with strands of her hair, then he said firmly, "I will give the major to Sun Knife to do with him as he pleases. My people will not like it, but I will release the others. If they can find their way back alone, they will live; if they cannot . . . then the Great Spirit will have seen fit for them to die." She took one of his hands in hers and held it close to her breast.

"Can I ease some of your pain if I tell you that I shall return to the tribe a life for the great gift of mercy?"

"Golden One?"

"Yes, I carry a child, White Eagle. I would give you a son, out of love and gratitude for all you have given me. I only hope and pray it will be a sign of peace and love."

He lifted her against him, holding her close. He buried his face in her soft hair and rocked her gently.

"You could have given me nothing greater in this world to bring me joy. A child, Rebecca, is a blessing to any tribe; but this one will be more special. He will be the peace after a war;

he will be the life after death. I am grateful. I promise I will do my best to create a peaceful world in which we can raise our son."

"I had never thought you would do anything less." She smiled. "And I hate to annoy you, my dear husband, but what if the child is a girl?"

He grinned and kissed her lightly. "Then she will be beautiful like her mother. She will be her father's pride and the bride price for her will be so high that only a wealthy chief could afford it."

"White Eagle, I don't care if she marries a chief or not. I would only pray she finds a man such as her father. Then I would be assured of her happiness."

"You fill my head with conceit, little one. I will try to be a good father to our child, whether it is boy or girl. Rebecca, I am afraid after Sun Knife gets the information from the major and we release the prisoners, we will have to leave this village."

"Where would we go?"

"I don't know yet, but we must find a place that the white man has not touched yet. We must join forces with other tribes, even some that have been our enemies. It is the only way we will be strong enough should the whites come again. I will send scouts out to speak with the Comanche and Crow and the other tribes that we know. Maybe we can bring them together and talk. Then we will search for a safe place to live. You . . . me . . . and our child."

Her arms crept about his neck as his lips touched hers and his arms bound her against him.

"Wherever thou goest," she murmured softly as she surrendered to his all-consuming love.

Chapter Twenty-Four

Sun Knife paced back and forth in his tepee. Sleep was something he could not achieve. When the warriors had returned to the camp, he had gone directly to the tepee where the prisoners were held only to be told that White Eagle allowed no one in. In a black rage, he had gone to White Eagle and demanded to know why.

"As he is now," White Eagle replied, "having faced such a defeat, his pride and anger would forbid him to tell you anything. Let him be the rest of the night, let him hear the drums of the victory song. Let him see the misery of his remaining warriors. By morning, he will see the wisdom of telling you what you want to know."

"It is hard, Brother, to wait."

"I know. Why do you not go to your mother and Long Arrow, and see to the welfare of the wounded? It will help the time to pass." It was the only thing that he could do for he knew if Sun Knife remained idle for long, he would force entry to the prisoners' tepee and in his anger he could kill the major.

He washed the war paint from his face and went to his mother's tepee where he found her awake and listening intently to all going on about her. There was no need for him to tell her much of what had happened; she already knew.

Her hands reached for him as he knelt beside her; she gripped his arms, reached a hand to touch his face.

"You are well, my Son, you are not hurt?"

"No, Mother, I am well. I have come to see if you are well also."

"I walked a few steps before your return. I am weak, but my strength returns rapidly thanks to the magic of my son's hand."

"That is good. I expect to see you on your feet soon."

"Yes," she said softly, her eyes intent on him. "Tell me, my

Son, what is it that still grieves you? Snow Blossom, was she well when you found her at the fort? They did not hurt her, did they?"

His blue eyes darkened and she knew, with a sinking heart, she had struck a spark of pain. "Sun Knife, she is not—?"

"No . . . she . . . she was not at the fort."

"But where—" she began, fear and tension in her face.

"Rest easy, Mother. I'll tell you all I know." He went on to explain all that had happened. Anger replaced fear.

"That he would do such a thing to a woman like Snow Blossom is unforgivable. Has he told you where she is?"

"No." He again explained how White Eagle felt and that they planned to question the major early in the morning.

"Do not worry, Mother; he will tell us where Snow Blossom is or I shall rip it from him."

Tears filled her eyes. "Such violence and hatred was not what your father and I had planned for you. It hurts to see your eyes angry and the hands that were meant to heal hold a war lance."

He knew their conversation was exciting her and upsetting her beyond what her healing body could stand.

"You must rest, Mother, and forgive me for leaving you so soon, but I must see to the others. Long Arrow—"

"Long Arrow has been to visit me already."

"What! He's been out of bed? Impossible!"

"What I saw and talked to was not a vision, my Son. I will admit he was very weak and tired, but he was here at my side as he always was when he was needed. He is a good and dear friend."

Sun Knife's eyes held his mother's, wondering if she knew, as he did, that Long Arrow's love for her had grown stronger every year. "I will go and see him, Mother." He pressed her hand between his. "I shall be back tomorrow. In the meantime, you must sleep."

"Sun Knife?"

"Yes?"

"You will tell me when you hear any news of Snow Blossom? You will not do anything without letting me know, letting me see you?"

He smiled. "Don't worry, Mother. I will not do anything before I tell you all the news."

"She will be safe, Sun Knife. I will pray to the gods; they will protect her for you."

He smiled reassuringly, more reassuringly than he felt. Everything hinged on Major Chivington telling him in which direction Josiah and Snow Blossom had gone. Grimly, he rose to his feet, knowing the doctor, the healer, the pride of his parents, his friends, and his tribe would resort to any method to find out where Snow Blossom was.

He made his way to Long Arrow's tepee, walking slowly. He went inside without asking permission and found what he expected to find: Long Arrow seated by his fire working slowly and laboriously on the making of arrows. He had several finished beside him and was just putting the finishing touches on another. He looked up in surprise when Sun Knife entered without asking; then he grinned sheepishly, aware that his doctor was less than happy with him.

"Long Arrow!"

"Do not be angry, my Son. I could lie on that couch no longer."

"You have not healed; you are not well enough to be up, much less moving about. My mother told me you walked over to see her today."

"Do not shout, my Son." He waved his hand toward the fire. "Come, sit with me. There are many things of which we have to speak." His voice had faded to a quiet whisper on the last words, his dark eyes warning Sun Knife he would do what he felt was right to do.

Sun Knife sighed in exasperation, but sat down by the fire facing Long Arrow.

"Tell me . . . why did you not bring your wife from the fort? What have they done to her?"

Again he repeated the story of what had occurred at the fort. Long Arrow listened in silence, but his eyes did not miss any unspoken signs or words. "Tomorrow he will speak the words I want to hear. By the time the sun rises overhead, I will be on the way to bring my wife home."

"And kill the man who stole her?"

"Yes . . . and kill the man who stole her. Would you have me do anything less? Would you have me walk in shame by allowing him to live?"

"No . . . I would go with you."

"Impossible."

"I would have you know that I have ridden already."

"But it has only been . . . what? A month since you were wounded? You are not well enough to ride."

"Let me tell you, Sun Knife, I will go whether you think it right or not. This man is responsible for stealing your wife, but he is also responsible for the death of a man I called friend, and the pain of near death to a woman who is much to me. I will go with you." He smiled now. "Besides, I know you would feel better if I was with you so you could watch me, instead of following, where I might die all alone . . . at the mercy of the wild beasts."

The glitter of laughter in his dark eyes brought a responding laugh from Sun Knife. "You are as stubborn as my horse," Sun Knife grumbled. "Is there nothing I can say to stop you?"

"No."

"Let me look at your wounds, Long Arrow."

"There is no need. They are nearly healed. I have walked daily and rode many times. Put no more barriers before me, my Son. I will go. The soul of my friend, Michael, calls to me. I could not face his spirit when I reach the happy hunting ground if I did not right this wrong."

Sun Knife nodded. Against these words, there was nothing he could say.

"I will sleep here with you tonight, Long Arrow, if you don't mind. Going back to my tepee makes sleep too difficult."

"Of course; roll your blanket near the fire."

Unrolling a blanket, Sun Knife sat on it and watched as Long Arrow gathered his arrows and rose slowly and with difficulty to put them away. Long Arrow lay on his couch with a deep sigh. There was silence as both tried to sleep, and both knew the impossiblity of doing so.

Sun Knife lay watching the fire die to embers while his memory reached for every moment spent with Snow Blossom. With grim determination he put from his mind the thoughts of what had happened to her. For his own sanity and the control of his anger, he had to think of the good things. Close to morning, he must have drifted off to sleep.

The rumble of methodical drumming brought him awake. The time had come to try to discover the truth. For one moment, deep poignant fear struck him. What if he refused to speak? What if he could not make him tell where Snow Blossom had been taken. Could he live the balance of his life in peace if he could not find her? He turned his eyes toward Long Arrow. He was awake and watching him with eyes filled with compassion and understanding. They both rose and prepared to meet whatever might come together.

Grant, too, had been unable to sleep. He sat in the tepee with the other prisoners from the fort. His thoughts were on the man who sat a few feet away from him—a man who was responsible, Grant thought, for the deaths of over four hundred of his own men and those of the uncountable Indians who had died in the mass slaughter of their village.

As if sensing his thoughts, John Chivington raised his head and their eyes met. In one, there was lingering surprise at what had happened and in the other hatred for the man responsible for so much destruction.

"What will these savages do now, Lieutenant? Torture us to death? These brave and noble people you defended, will they butcher us?"

"They will do," Grant said in exasperated anger, "exactly what you have pushed them into doing."

"You are a stupid man, Lieutenant," Chivington replied softly. "Don't you see how futile their fight is? They must make room for another civilization. Since they will not surrender, then they must be pushed into the sea if necessary. They are a lost race of people. It is inevitable they will die."

"I don't believe as you do. The red man and the white could live together in peace if Washington would stop blundering by sending people like you here."

"You damn fool," Chivington replied. "Don't you know there are men in Washington who want this land? Do you think a few thousand savages are going to stop them? Are you that naïve? God, you fool!"

"I'll stay a fool. I would rather believe there was a way we could share this land. They are good, intelligent people. If we helped them build schools, send teachers, doctors—"

"Like your friend, Cade Holliday?"

"I don't think you will hear about Cade Holliday again. You have pushed him from the path he was on. He is Sun Knife, and as Sun Knife he will find revenge for the man who was fool enough to give a princess of the Cheyenne tribe to a trapper, as if she were nothing—the daughter of a chief, the sister of a chief, and the wife of a man who could have been the bridge between us."

"Well, I will admit a small mistake in judgment giving her to Josiah."

"A *small* mistake! You can actually call that a small mistake?"

"A mistake we might just turn into our passport for freedom. This . . . friend of yours wants to know where his wife is."

"Where is she?"

"I'm not fool enough to tell you, Lieutenant. You would tell him immediately and our fate would be sealed. No, I'm going to buy our way out of here."

"How?"

The major chuckled. "By depending on this fine sense of honor you claim they possess. If they want to know where their princess has gone, they will give me all I ask for."

"I wouldn't push them any further if I were you. They might try tracking her themselves. They are expert trackers, and you might find we're all expendable."

"No, I think not. I think your half-breed warrior would give anything to know where his wife has gone—anything."

Grant was silent, listening. The sound of the throbbing drums must have been penetrating his mind for some time before he really heard them. At his attitude of silent listening, the major listened, too, as did all the other half-awake men.

"I believe," Grant said quietly, "you are about to find out what you want to know."

The door flap was pushed aside and several solemn-faced,

bronzed warriors came in. Without a word, they grasped Grant, the major, Sergeant Price, and two others. Binding their hands behind them, they pushed them ahead of them, out the door and across the compound to the council tepee. Roughly, they were pushed inside to face their trial.

The council fire lit the faces of the men who sat about it—all dark unreadable faces who watched the white men that stood before them.

White Eagle sat at the head of the council, dressed in the brilliant regalia of a chief. It did not take any of the white men a moment to realize, by the cold dark obsidian gaze of the handsome chief, just what danger they were in. His eyes showed no compassion or mercy.

Beside White Eagle, sat Sun Knife whose cold blue gaze was just as merciless and had not left Major Chivington since he had been pushed into the room. He felt cold rage at this arrogant, unfeeling man and would have loved to have attacked him with nothing but his bare hands and squeezed the breath from his lungs.

Beside Sun Knife sat Long Arrow, whose emotions were so completely under control that no one in the room but him knew how dangerously close to murder he was. He thought of Waterflower and Michael and his dark gaze remained on the man who had killed one and wounded the other. His heart thudded painfully from his hot desire to attack him and the strain of exercising his determined will to control that desire.

There was a deep silence for several minutes while they studied each other.

"Your fort is burned, white Chief," White Eagle said quietly. "Your warriors are dead. All that is left are you and your few warriors. I warned you what would happen. I told you to sing your death song. Do you think now I will let you live?"

"I did not sing my death song, White Eagle, because it is not my time to die."

Grant looked at the major in surprise when he heard him. He had not realized the major even knew what the death song was.

"It is not my time to die," repeated the major. "Nor is it the time for my warriors. We will live to fight you again."

"Major," Grant said quickly, "you are only making this

more difficult."

Chivington ignored him and his eyes moved to Sun Knife, who had not moved or said a word since they had been brought in.

"I have something very valuable to give in return for my life and the lives of my men."

Both White Eagle and Sun Knife stiffened as the major continued to speak. "Do not misunderstand me, either of you. I am the only one who knows where your sister is, White Eagle. Listen to me and believe me. I will die before I speak the words to tell you where she is. I will die and my information will die with me."

"I will make you speak," White Eagle said angrily.

"No . . . listen again, White Eagle. I have faced the Comanche. You and I both know they are fierce warriors. I have seen the worst they can do and I will tell you there are ways to die and I know them. I will take my secret to the grave with me."

White Eagle did not have to look at him to know of the tension in Sun Knife's silent face.

"What do you want?" he demanded.

"Freedom for me and my men, horses, food, water, and arms to help us back to our own people."

"Then you will tell me what I want to know?"

"Yes."

"What is to stop me from killing you after you have spoken?"

Chivington smiled. "As I know the Comanche, I also know the Cheyenne. You will give me your word and I will not be stopped. I know the word of a chief like White Eagle will be honored by his warriors, just as I know you would die before you would break it."

White Eagle's eyes remained unreadable, but Sun Knife's did not. At that moment, he would have loved nothing more than to leap on the major and beat him to death with his fist. The emotion was so strong there was not a man in the tepee who did not feel it, especially the major, who suddenly felt the first tingle of real fear he had ever felt in his life. The last thing White Eagle wanted to do was to release the man who had caused so much grief in his tribe, and who, if set free, would undoubtedly cause much more. Yet Snow Blossom hovered between them. Could a chief set aside his sister, and the wife of his medicine man as if her life amounted to nothing? His blood bond to Sun Knife would forbid him from doing so. He did not have to look at Sun Knife to know his reaction. Sun Knife would wait, out of respect to his blood brother and chief, for White Eagle to speak. He knew that, just as he knew Sun Knife would be the first to reach the major to try to get the information from him.

At his extended silence, the tepee was held in excruciating tension. No man would speak before White Eagle.

Grant found his mouth dry and his body weak from the strain of wondering if his next breath would be his last.

White Eagle rose to his feet.

"You are filled with evil spirits, white man. As a warrior of the Cheyenne, I would kill you for what you have done. As a chief and blood brother to Sun Knife I must listen to you, for my sister is part of my own heart and blood. Listen to me well, white man. I must let you go, I must give my word that you and your warriors are free. You will tell me where my sister is. If you have lied, Sun Knife and I will hunt you down and kill you in a way that would weaken even the Comanche." He continued, his voice frozen and hard. "Do not walk on my land again, white one, for if you do, it will be the last of your days. White Eagle does not give his word easily, but he does not threaten carelessly either. Tell me where my sister is, then go and do not let your shadow fall on my land again or you will surely answer to me for the murders you have committed."

"I have your word we will not be touched?"

"You have my word."

"Where is my wife?" Sun Knife demanded in a cold piercing voice.

"Beyond the high peaks, many miles across the plain is a small river called Dry Creek. Do you know of it?"

"I know of it," White Eagle said.

"When you reach the edge of the creek you follow it up about three days' ride. There is a place there, a small cabin which the Comanche burned. It is where Josiah and his

Comanche wife, Two Moons, used to live. It is there you will find him. He, somehow, has connected Snow Blossom with his wife, Two Moons. I'm afraid he is a little . . . ah . . . unbalanced . . . and, very dangerous."

"Dangerous?" Sun Knife said. "To himself, to others . . . or to Snow Blossom?"

"If she fights him . . . if he becomes angry enough or convinced she is not connected to his wife . . . I'm afraid he's dangerous to her."

"And yet," Sun Knife replied softly, "you gave her to him. Knowing what he was, you gave her to him."

"It was part of our bargain."

Sun Knife's face hardened and again his blue gaze turned to ice.

"A bargain," he replied, his voice soft, yet Chivington paled at what he saw and heard. At that moment, he was nearer death than he had ever been in his life and he knew it.

Without moving, White Eagle said softly, "I have given my word, Sun Knife."

For a moment it was as if his words had not been heard; then Sun Knife's body relaxed and everyone present began to breathe again.

"I will honor your word for now, Brother," Sun Knife said softly. Then he looked at Chivington. "But if I find my wife harmed in any way, I will follow your trail. There will be no place you can hide. I will find you and I will see you die. You had best pray she is well and unharmed."

Sun Knife's eyes never left the major's as he said the words softly and Chivington did not doubt the truth behind his words. His immediate thought was as soon as they were set free he would put as much distance between himself and this savage as possible.

True to his word, White Eagle gave horses and food to the white soldiers and he and Sun Knife stood with Long Arrow and watched them ride away from the village.

Grant and Sun Knife had spoken together a few minutes before they departed.

"Cade, I'm sorry for all of this. It is a thing that makes me ashamed of my people."

"It is a thing of great sadness, Grant; we were friends once. We can no longer be friends again. We part now, and one day you and your blue coats will be sent again and we will fight each other. It is a bad day when brother fights brother, no matter the color of their skin."

"No, Cade, you are wrong. I will never come here with a gun in my hand to kill your people. I will fight, but it will be in Washington where I might do some good. Lauren's father will want to know of her and with his considerable influence and your father's name, we may still swing open some doors."

"Grant, my father left a considerable amount of money. I'll give you authorization. I want you to take that money, and as quietly as you can, see if it is possible to buy as much land out here as you can."

"You think the white man will really push you all out?"

"It's inevitable. They outnumber us. I want enough land to build a school, a hospital, and to make room for as many as I can."

"It's a big step."

"It's the only way."

"Cade, come back with me. It would be more effective if you did it."

"No, my place is here. The day is coming when my people will really need me. I will stand by my brother, White Eagle, when the time comes. For now, I must find Snow Blossom, and . . . I must find the man who took her."

"You intend to kill him, Cade?"

Sun Knife looked at Grant, and it was the first time in all the years he had known him that he saw cold, naked savagery in his gaze. The words he spoke were softened, but the eyes were not.

"What would you do in my place, Grant? My mother almost died from her wounds. Long Arrow also hovered near death"—his voice dropped to a whisper—"my father died. I cannot touch the man responsible for that. I cannot touch the man who gave my wife away like she was nothing. But I will tell you this; I will find the man who took her and he will pay for every moment he had her."

He turned from Grant and walked back to his tepee and Grant felt the separation of Cade and Sun Knife and he knew

Sun Knife would never be able to cross the barrier between white and red. He wondered if he and Cade Holliday would ever meet again.

As he mounted his horse a young brave ran up to him and handed him a folded piece of paper. "Sun Knife sent this to you. He said he wishes you safe journey, and that you would know what to do with the message."

Grant took the paper that gave him access to all the Holliday money, and the responsibility weighed heavily on him. Sun Knife stood in the doorway and watched the line of soldiers leave the village. His eyes remained on the stiff-backed man who led them until they were beyond his sight. He was unaware that Long Arrow already stood beside him until he spoke.

"Sometimes the gods have strange ways of balancing things, Sun Knife. I have a feeling we have not seen the last of the white chief."

"It would be best for me if he did return. It would save me searching for him."

"Sun Knife?"

"I will find him one day . . . someday . . . I will find him and he will remember well the vengeance of Sun Knife."

"Sun Knife, our chief has given his word. We are honor-bound to it."

"He gave his word that we would not do anything to stop him. I won't, but the day will come when our paths cross again and my brother's word will not bind me. Are you ready to leave now, Long Arrow?"

"Yes, I am ready."

"Good. I expect to cover many miles before we camp for the night."

They mounted their ponies and left the village moving in a direction completely opposite from that of the white soldiers.

White Eagle was wakened early the next morning with news that several warriors were headed toward their village. They wore no war paint, their bows were unstrung, and their shields hung on their saddles. It was obvious they were on a peaceful mission and they were from villages that were not known to White Eagle's people.

When they rode closer and could be seen clearly, it shocked

everyone for they were Comanche, Arapaho, and Kiowa, usually deadly enemies of the Cheyenne. Why they came to them now in a peaceful gesture was a wondrously amazing thing for the small Cheyenne village.

They rode slowly and sedately into the village and stopped in front of White Eagle's tepee where he, dressed in full regalia, stood in silent pride and awaited them.

Dismounting, they walked to White Eagle, showing the proper respect for a chief. They were young men and they awaited acknowledgment from White Eagle first.

"Welcome to our village. I am White Eagle, chief of the Cheyenne."

The first young man, obviously a fierce, proud young Comanche, spoke. "I am Little Hawk. I bring you greetings from the chief of the Comanche, Gray Calf. We would bring to you a message from our chief of much importance."

"Come into my tepee. We will bring you a cool drink; then you must tell me of this message of great importance."

Inside they were seated about White Eagle's fire while food and drink were brought by Rebecca who watched the visitors with curious eyes and a million questions forming that she would ask White Eagle later.

After the meal, the ceremonial pipe was passed from hand to hand, each puffing and blowing the sacred smoke skyward.

It was only after all this that words were spoken.

"You have come a great distance to speak to me," White Eagle said. "What message does the chief of the Comanche send to the chief of the Cheyenne?"

Little Hawk bent forward slightly so he could study White Eagle's face closely. "The white man moves closer and closer to our land."

White Eagle nodded without speaking.

"We have sent scouts out to watch. They tell us that the white man kills the buffalo, not for food, but for the hides alone. They leave the meat on the prairie to rot. He slaughters the buffalo in great numbers, so great that our chief fears the spirit of the buffalo will draw all the buffalo away. Our people would go hungry, we would have no hides for our tepees. The white man destroys."

"I know all this, Little Hawk, but all white men are not the same." He continued to tell him about Michael and his son, Cade.

"Where is your brother?"

Reluctantly, White Eagle told him the story of Snow Blossom's capture and Cade's search for her.

"I would not offend you, Brother," Little Hawk said, "but your wife is a white woman and your brother carries the white man's blood. Does your heart listen to the white man's words too closely and forget that they are reaching for our land?"

"I am White Eagle, chief of the Cheyenne," White Eagle said proudly. "My wife is one of us, she is blood daughter to Long Arrow, one of our bravest warriors, by her own choice. My brother, Sun Knife, is true to his Cheyenne blood. He will never turn his back to us should we make him choose. I know always the feelings of my people and I will never harden my heart to their needs. You have not come here to question the loyalty of White Eagle."

"No, our chief asks a peace council. He would make an alliance between our people. He would have us put down our shields and war lances and speak as brothers. We have made war among ourselves too long, and we have blinded our eyes to the coming of the real enemy—the white man."

All the men about the fire were silent at these words. The Cheyenne, Arapaho, Comanche, and Kiowa had been enemies for as long as most of the men present could remember. The Comanche were fiercely proud. They would never call for a joint effort with their enemies if they had not seen a dark threat on the horizon. Little Hawk continued to speak. "We know now of the treachery of the white chief who took your wife and your sister. We also know that you have destroyed his fort. We ask why you let the white chief go. The honor of the Comanche would have seen him tortured to death very slowly for what he had done."

"As would the honor of White Eagle; but in return for the place my sister was taken, I promised him his life. I know him. . . . One day he will return. White Eagle's memory is long. One day he will pay in full for what he has done."

"We must go and tell our chief your words. Do you come to

the council or not?"

"When will it be?"

"We have brought the counting sticks." At these words, he took a bundle of small sticks bound together and laid them in front of him. "It is many days. We must go to more villages and take the words of our chief."

"I will wait for my brother, Sun Knife, to return; then we will come. I will send word to our friend, Chief Gray Bear, but I feel sure he will also come."

"Good."

"Rest and eat before you continue your journey. You are welcome in the village of White Eagle."

"Our thanks, Chief White Eagle, but our chief has told us to make our journey as fast as possible. We will eat and take fresh food and water with us."

"We will give you fresh horses to make your trip easier. When you have eaten, go to the herd of White Eagle and choose the horses that please you."

"We are grateful, White Eagle," Little Hawk said, his eyes bright with respect for a chief who had the intelligence to meet those who had always been his tribe's sworn enemies with an open heart and offer them the hospitality of his camp and even more valuable, his beloved horses.

While food was brought, the warriors talked about the fire. They spoke of past glories of their own individual tribes, and though their words were full of laughter and wild, sometimes unbelievable stories, there lingered in them the fear of an unknown danger they still were not sure of how they could fight.

When the meal was finished, White Eagle accompanied them to his own private herd of horses, where, with expert eyes, each picked out a horse that pleased him. They were surprised to find that White Eagle did not want their horses in trade, but intended his horses as an outright gift. White Eagle watched them ride away. He stood looking after them, his brow furrowed in a deep frown. He was unaware that Rebecca had come to stand beside him until she spoke.

"It worries you, this coming council?"

He smiled down on her. "And how did you already know

about the council? You were not even in the tepee when we spoke."

"You forget that word travels like fire among women. A snatch of conversation here, a word there. We are very clever."

"It is not only the council that worries me; nor is it the threat of open warfare against the whites."

"Then what is it, White Eagle?"

"I worry if Sun Knife will find Snow Blossom and be able to bring her home safely."

"You want Sun Knife at your side if you are forced to fight."

"Yes. My life and Sun Knife's are bound together. I would feel his loss deeply. I pray he finds her soon, for Sun Knife's anger against the whites will be even deeper than mine. I will fight for my land . . . for my family . . . for my people as I hope my brother would do. I would not like to see his only reasons be hate and revenge. Sometimes those feelings hurt the possessor more than his enemies."

She remained silent as he laid his arm possessively over her shoulder and they walked back to their tepee together.

Chapter Twenty-Five

Lauren and Little Dove worked together over the softening of a deerskin they planned to make into a new outfit of clothes for Running Wolf. Lauren listened to the bright chatter of Little Dove with half her mind; the other half was filled with thoughts of Running Wolf and his expected return from hunting after three days of absence. She worried over the fact that they had received no news from Cade or White Eagle since word had come of the attack on their village. Her heart was saddened over the death of Michael and she was going to ask Running Wolf if it would be possible to visit soon, so that she could speak with Waterflower. She knew about the abduction of Rebecca and Snow Blossom, but felt sure, since no other word had come, that the women had been found and returned to their village. The bloodshed and hatred that had really occurred had never entered her mind. Days filled with sun and laughter and the love of Running Wolf had made all such thoughts an impossibility for her. She thought with amusement of the changes in her life in the past year, of the spoiled little girl who would never have thought of laboring so hard over something to give someone else pleasure. With these thoughts her mind turned to Running Wolf. As always, she felt the sense of wonder within her that thoughts of this man could make her feel. She held the secret of his love within her, and she waited with expectant pleasure to see the look in his eyes when she told him.

She bent forward on her knees. Bracing one hand on the ground, she scraped methodically toward her. She smiled as Little Dove's words came to her.

"Running Wolf has promised me the new pony that is to be born soon."

"That is good. I have seen you tend his horse; you do it well. I am sure he thinks you deserve it and that you will take good care of it."

Lauren continued to work, unaware that Little Dove had sat back on her heels and was watching her. At her prolonged silence, Lauren looked up from her work.

"What is it, Little Dove?"

"Nothing. I was just thinking how happy I am that you decided to stay. You are good to me, Summer Rain, and my brother is happy. He sings sometimes and he smiles more. I am glad that you did not become angry with me and leave us. I am sure it would not be the same here without you."

"Why, thank you, Little Dove. I'm pleased that I'm so welcome now."

"You . . . you will never leave us, Summer Rain?"

"No, Little Dove, I have no intention of leaving."

"Even if the white man comes and makes us leave this land? You would go with us, wouldn't you? You would not let them take you away with them?"

Lauren smiled at the worry in her eyes. "I am Running Wolf's wife and Little Dove's sister. I will not leave my family no matter what. Even if the white man comes, I'm still going to stay here with the people I love."

Little Dove sighed with relief and her shy smile reappeared. "I am glad. I know Running Wolf will be glad, too."

Lauren looked intently at her. "Little Dove, has Running Wolf believed that I would not stay?"

"He has never said so, but I know he always fears that the white world will call to you someday and you will listen. He has said, sometimes to himself, that you had everything in the world before and he cannot give you all you had. He is afraid one day we will not be enough to make you happy and you will again turn your face toward your past."

Lauren was surprised at the astute reading of her brother by this child, just as she was surprised that Little Dove and Running Wolf still did not really believe she was happy here. Determinedly, she decided that once and for all, she would put aside these fears. "Little Dove, look at me."

Brown eyes met green ones as Lauren said firmly, "I love you as a sister, and I will never leave here. You're my family and I'm content to spend my days with you. Do you understand, Little Dove?"

"Yes." Again, the shy dimpled smile appeared. ". . . Sister."

Lauren smiled. "And say nothing of our conversation to your brother. When he comes home, I will make him understand. It is time he realizes finally that our lives are permanently combined." She rose to her feet. "Let the skin dry for now and we will work to soften it together tomorrow. Why do you not run and play with your friends for a while? You have helped me with enough work for today."

She watched a pleased Little Dove run to join her friends; then slowly she walked back toward her tepee.

Her dark-auburn hair hung in two thick braids and her skin, tanned a deep golden brown, magnified the bright green of her eyes. Dressed in the soft buckskin dress and leather boots, she was extremely beautiful. Gently, she allowed her fingers to lightly touch her belly where a small unnamed life was growing. A deep warm pleasure filled her as she remembered the gentle nights of love that had created it. Ever leaving Running Wolf was something that had never entered her mind. In fact, in the past few months she had forgotten about her other world. Now, she thought purposely, she must make her husband do so, too.

Inside her tepee, she knelt by the fire and began to prepare a small supper, for she was not sure Running Wolf would be there to eat.

She had just finished its preparations when she heard approaching horses. In a few minutes, the tepee flap was pushed aside and Running Wolf was there.

Suddenly, she was in his arms and she could hear his quick laugh as he embraced her. She looked up into his eyes and smiled at the bright laughter there.

"Welcome home. Was your hunt a success?"

"It was. There will be meat for everyone."

"Good. I have prepared food. Are you hungry?"

"Yes," he said as he sat down on the couch and lay back, his hands folded behind his head. "Crying Wind hunted with us. He has a gift for you."

"For me . . . why?"

"Because he is grateful for the way you took care of his little girl when she was so sick. He will come and speak to you."

She did not reply, but knelt by the fire and put the food into his bowl. She was unaware that his dark eyes studied her closely. There was a look of restrained fear in his eyes as he watched her deftly ladle his food. It faded quickly as she turned to hand it to him. Silently, he took it and began to eat.

Still kneeling by the fire, Lauren watched him. His strong hands held the bowl, hands whose gentle tenderness she knew so well, hands that caressed her, giving as much pleasure as he received.

"Running Wolf, when you have finished, I would speak with you."

He hesitated momentarily in his eating; then he laid the bowl and spoon aside. "Come, speak to me now. Is something wrong?"

She went to him and knelt on the floor beside him. "Running Wolf, sometimes I have the feeling that you are not sure of my love."

"That is not so, Summer Rain," he protested.

"You ask if something is wrong as though you expect there to be."

"Summer Rain—"

"When we married we went to Rev. Wade and had him marry us in my ceremony. Would you do something for me?"

"Of course . . . what is it?"

"I would marry you in your tribe's ceremony. I would have you know once and for all that Lauren Brent is gone and only Summer Rain remains. I would have you understand that I am now and always will be part of your world. I want you to know how very happy being the wife of Running Wolf has made me."

The pleasure in his eyes was enough reward for her words, but he took her in his arms and held her against him.

"Summer Rain," he said softly, "I know these things in my heart. Sometimes, when I look at you laughing with the women, or walking with the sun in your hair, I think, what if she were to go away, to go back to her own people? What if she is lonely for the things she knew and had and cannot find the words to tell me? What would you do, Running Wolf, if she were to come to you one day and tell you she hungers for another world? A world where there is no room for Running Wolf."

She reached up and placed both hands on his cheeks. "Running Wolf, I love you. Please believe me when I say that you are all the world I need. I have found happiness here, and I feel I am useful here."

"You are. The children love you for your stories, your songs, and the way you cure their little sicknesses and injuries. You are medicine woman to most of the tribe and considered very important to us all. You have found a place in the hearts of many. It is only my disbelief in my good fortune that brings the dark thoughts."

"I could tell you over and over again that I love you and maybe you might still have the dark thoughts." She took his hand and pressed it against her belly. "I will tell you in a way you cannot doubt. I carry your child, Running Wolf. I carry the chain between us that will always keep us bound to each other. Now will you put the dark fears to rest? Now will you believe?"

She could see the flame of joy leap in his eyes as his hand remained pressed against her. "My child . . . Summer Rain, you will give me a child . . . when?"

"After the snow falls. I imagine at the beginning of the new year."

He enclosed her in his arms and his happy laughter rang out.

"Now do you believe?" She laughed. "And the ceremony?"

"We do not need any other ceremony. I believe, Summer Rain. I am sorry for the doubts. I would have you forgive me if they caused you pain. A child . . . Summer Rain." He laughed again. "We will have a celebration when he is born. I will teach him to ride and hunt. He will be the bravest warrior of them all . . . we—"

"Running Wolf, we might have a girl child."

"Of course." He paused, then laughed again. "What does it matter what the child is? It is ours; that is all that matters, ours! Yours and mine! I do not think I have seen a happier day since I found you. You, my beloved wife, have made me the happiest warrior in the village of Gray Bear . . . no, in all the villages . . . no, in the whole nation . . . no—"

"Running Wolf." She laughed with him and then delirious laughter filled the tepee with the joy of their shared pleasure.

Running Wolf's exuberant happiness spilled over her like a warm blanket of love. That night was filled with their shared pleasure in each other.

At first he seemed hesitant to touch her, but assured that the child was completely safe, he drew her into his arms. They lay together for a long while, talking, touching, kissing, and sharing the quite moments of closeness. When his hands and lips became more insistent and searching, she pressed herself close to him and held him, whispering words of encouragement and love that added fuel to the fire that consumed them both.

To both Running Wolf and Summer Rain, it was the first, the last, and the most loving time they had been together. They sought to learn, to reach, and to touch the place they had never been able to reach until now. With all finality, Running Wolf knew that Summer Rain was his completely.

As dawn crept in, Running Wolf was the first to waken. Summer Rain slept, her body curled against his, seeking his warmth. He looked at her, and the constriction in his throat made breathing difficult. Gently, he brushed strands of hair from her face; then he lowered his head and touched her cheek, eyes, and forehead with soft gentle kisses.

Drawing her more closely he let his hand brush her soft skin until it lay gently against her belly.

"My child," he thought and the keen pleasure of it moved through him again. Gently, they lay together, she sleeping and finding him in quiet dreams. He, awake, and finding her in the same dreams.

Too soon for him, the bright rays of the sun touched them. She stirred and wakened.

"Good morning," he whispered.

"I have slept late; the whole village will think I am a lazy wife."

"No." He laughed. "I know many who will think that lucky Running Wolf is able to stay abed late with his beautiful wife in his arms. How I envy that warrior."

She sighed and nestled closer to him, closing her eyes to

savor the warmth and strength of his arms.

"How I love you, Running Wolf," she said softly. He tightened his arms in agreement.

"What will we call our child, Running Wolf?"

"If it is a boy child, I would be pleased if we could name him for his grandfather. He is a most honorable and brave man, and I know it will give him pleasure and make him proud."

Summer Rain nodded. She, too, liked the man who was grandfather to her husband, and his name sounded brave and strong. "White Fox," she said. "It is a good name for the son of Running Wolf; and a girl child?"

"If it would please you, we could name her Falling Water. Each time we looked at her we could remember our special place. It would be a sweet and warm way of remembering."

"How very wonderful. It almost makes me wish for a girl instead of a boy. I would like to have a daughter."

He chuckled and bent to brush her lips with his. "I will make you a bargain. Give me a boy first and we can have a girl the next time."

"And just how many times do you think there will be?" She laughed.

"As many as the Great Spirit pleases," he answered. "And I hope it pleases him for us to have many. Children are a special blessing, a gift from the gods."

Content with his words, she repeated the names softly. "White Fox, Falling Water." Then she smiled, crossed her fingers, and despite Running Wolf's thoughts prayed silently for a girl child.

For the next few days, Summer Rain was pleased in the more relaxed presence of Running Wolf. She could see in his sister's face the fact that she knew her brother had put aside the problems that had troubled his mind and accepted the fact that he was secure in the knowledge Summer Rain would never leave him.

Five days later, they had just begun to prepare the evening meal when two riders were seen approaching. It did not take long for them to identify the riders as warriors from White Eagle's village. After all that had happened they were prepared for bad news.

Running Wolf went to the council tepee and Summer Rain impatiently awaited his return. It was late at night when he finally did.

"Running Wolf, what has happened? Have Rebecca and Snow Blossom been returned? Do you know why they attacked the village?"

Running Wolf explained as rapidly as he could all that had happened. She was shocked that Snow Blossom was still gone and afraid when she heard that White Eagle had attacked and destroyed the fort.

"Running Wolf, this will bring a disaster. What in the name of God could the major have been thinking of when he took Rebecca and Snow Blossom? He should have known what would happen."

He told her all that had occurred after the attack, how the major had been set free and Sun Knife had gone after Snow Blossom.

"I will prepare my things and go with you. With Cade gone they might need me. I would like to speak to Waterflower now. It must be so hard for her to have lost a man like Michael. Then to have to face the disaster in her village."

"It would be too much for you."

"No, I am strong and healthy. Besides, I want to tell Rebecca about the child and spend some time with her. I would feel better if I was there to help in case . . . in case Cade could not get Snow Blossom back. Running Wolf, do you think this council is called because White Eagle intends to go to war against the whites?"

"I don't know. What else can we do? A man cannot stand and see his women taken, his village destroyed, and do nothing."

"Running Wolf, I come from the white world. I can tell you that they are more than you. There is no chance of success if you fight." Fear held her at the sudden thought that Running Wolf could be taken from her. He saw the fear and he went to her. Taking hold of her shoulders, he looked into her eyes.

"Summer Rain, would you have me run and hide like a child afraid of a dark night?" She put her arms about him and rested her head against his chest.

"I would not lose you," she whispered. "I would not have my child without his father. I have only just found my world. I am afraid it will be taken away from me."

"Don't be afraid, Summer Rain. I will go to the council and find out what is happening. Maybe the chiefs only intend to move the villages." He said this to comfort her, but neither of them believed it.

They put their things on their horses and began the journey to White Eagle's village. Running Wolf would not allow Summer Rain to travel long hours each day. Despite her protests that she felt fine, he started late in the morning and stopped early at night with a prolonged stop in the middle of the day. Consequently, it took them many more days to travel than usual.

When they arrived at the village, Summer Rain was surprised at what she found. The place she had known as happy and filled with laughter was quiet as if an invisible blanket smothered all the joy within.

Children did not run and play, but gathered together in small clusters and remained unusually quiet.

They rode through the village slowly, seeing the half-repaired destruction, observing women who had cut their hair and slashed themselves on their faces and arms out of grief for their lost husbands, sisters, brothers, and children.

Tears stained Summer Rain's face and Running Wolf's eyes were dark with disbelieving pain by the time they stopped in front of White Eagle's tepee. Friends he had known were no longer here, and he could feel the ghosts of those slain without warning call to his pride as a warrior. As he helped Summer Rain down from her horse, the flap of White Eagle's tepee was opened and White Eagle and Rebecca came out to greet them.

"Running Wolf," White Eagle said, "welcome to our village."

"I was told we were called to a grand council, White Eagle. I knew there had been a battle here, but I did not know there had been such destruction. My heart is filled with pain for White Eagle's people. It is also filled with anger. I would help White Eagle seek revenge for all that happened here."

"I thank you, Running Wolf, and I shall remember your

words. Has Gray Bear come?"

"My chief is coming here. Summer Rain and I have arrived ahead, but he will come soon."

"Good. When the counting sticks are gone we will go to the grand council if—"

"If?"

"If Sun Knife has come back with his woman."

"There has been no word from Sun Knife, no sign?"

"Nothing. He has been gone many days, he and Long Arrow."

"White Eagle," Summer Rain said softly, "do you believe he will find her?"

White Eagle looked at her. "I hope so. . . . If he comes back without her . . . the white major will regret all his days the attack of White Eagle's village."

"Lauren, come and let me get you some food. You have had a long journey; you must be very tired."

The two women went inside the tepee followed by White Eagle and Running Wolf.

White Eagle and Running Wolf sat by the fire and smoked their pipe while they talked of all that was happening—and more, the fear of what they thought was going to happen.

Rebecca and Summer Rain sat a few feet away, their voices low. They, too, discussed all that had happened. As women, white women, who knew their own world, they were even more afraid of what was going to happen.

"So," Rebecca said with a pleased smile, "Running Wolf has changed your name."

The smile was turned to a pleased chuckle as the reply came. "Running Wolf has changed everything in my life."

"Summer Rain—it is very beautiful."

"Yes . . . they have such a way of seeing something beautiful in everything. I had never known until now how very close to everything God-given they were."

"I hear many stories of you . . . Summer Rain."

"Stories?"

"Word travels fast. . . . The drums . . . the smoke, those who travel through tell us of a medicine woman with white skin who heals the sick, who sings to and teaches the children."

"I know so little, Rebecca. I try to help, to return to them some of the love they give me."

"I am afraid, Summer Rain," Rebecca said very softly, her eyes on White Eagle making sure he had not heard her. She knew that Lauren and Cade were the only two people in the world who would understand what she meant.

"I know . . . I know."

"He . . . he sees the white men like any other enemy. A force to face with honor. He does not really see that . . . that they want to destroy him. If Sun Knife were back, he might be able to speak at the council . . . to tell them what is coming."

"He will come."

"Do you believe he will find Snow Blossom?"

"Yes. Don't you?"

"I don't know. I don't see how he can find her or how he can get her back. If he doesn't, he will be changed. There will be no way of getting him to try to stop what is happening." Summer Rain reached out and laid her hand on Rebecca's arm.

"Believe, Rebecca. I know Sun Knife, maybe better than anyone else other than Snow Blossom. He will find her and he will return and speak to the council. He will speak of peace and try to find a way to help White Eagle lead his people away from this tragedy."

Rebecca smiled through tear-filled eyes.

"Do you still love him?"

"No . . . no, not that way. I love Sun Knife as a friend, as a doctor, as a strong man. As a leader I respect him. No, my love is for Running Wolf who has given me all. . . . It is not the same. I have found something with Running Wolf I never thought to find. I have a place with our people, with Running Wolf that fills me with a sense of peace. I do not have to search anymore. I am home and now I must cling to the belief that we will find a way to peace and freedom. I . . . I pray . . . both to Running Wolf's gods and to ours, Rebecca. I carry Running Wolf's child, and I want a world like Running Wolf's to raise him in."

Their voices were kept low so that the men who were in deep conversation would not hear them.

"Then we are really like sisters. We come from the same

world, you and I, and we have both found everything we have always needed to make us happy. I, too, carry a child. I hope one day they are brothers as Sun Knife and White Eagle are brothers."

"Let us hope Sun Knife comes soon."

"Yes . . . let us hope."

"Summer Rain," Running Wolf called to her. "I will take you to the tepee White Eagle has given us. You must rest; the trip has been long."

Summer Rain smiled at Rebecca; then she rose and went to stand beside Running Wolf.

"I have told my husband again and again that I am strong and healthy. Still he treats me like a child."

"No." Running Wolf grinned. "I treat you like the woman who carries my child."

"A child?" White Eagle laughed. "Rebecca, too, carries a child. It is a good sign."

"Yes," Running Wolf agreed. "A good sign. Soon Sun Knife will come and bring Snow Blossom. We will go to the grand council and we will speak for peace."

White Eagle smiled and rested his hand on Running Wolf's shoulder. Both Rebecca and Summer Rain watched, both aware that the two men who faced each other were the breed of men that would be the strength of their homes, their people, and their nation.

Given a tepee, Summer Rain and Running Wolf made themselves comfortable as they awaited the arrival of both Gray Bear and Sun Knife.

Summer Rain, against Running Wolf's will, threw herself into helping the women repair the burned out tepees, dry meat for storage, grind grain, and seek out any who were ill or hurt to try to help.

Running Wolf hunted with the men. The time was short to replace the winter supplies that had been destroyed by the white soldiers. When he was not hunting, to Summer Rain's distress, he and the other warriors made new weapons, weapons he hoped to use for peaceful hunting, but weapons he knew he would use if he were forced to defend the people and the land he loved.

Several days after Running Wolf's and Summer Rain's

arrival, Gray Bear and five of his warriors arrived and were given a welcome befitting Gray Bear's stature as a chief.

A small celebration was held. Food was prepared to honor a chief. The drums and flutes sounded and the young people danced a slow rhythmic dance. The couples danced shoulder to shoulder, their hands crossed and held in front of them. It was a laughing, happy dance and the enthusiasm caught Running Wolf, who pulled Summer Rain up beside him and coaxed her to learn the dance. She caught the rhythmic beat of the music and picked up the steps with ease. Memories of a Strauss waltz, of rustling silk, and a tiled dance floor crossed her mind and she clasped Running Wolf's hands tightly knowing she held the better world of the two and she pushed her memories aside as Running Wolf's eyes met hers and his hands clasped hers tightly.

After the dance, he drew her with him and they walked from the outskirts of the village down to the bank of the softly flowing river.

They walked in silence, enjoying the black velvet, star-studded sky, the soft rustle of the breeze through the trees and the rippling water.

"You are happy, Summer Rain?"

"Yes, I am happy." She smiled. "I hadn't thought I'd be able to say that. A few years ago I thought it would take so much to make me happy. Now I know that one has to look carefully so as not to overlook the most valuable things in life."

He reached out and drew her into his arms. Holding her close, he brushed his cheek against the softness of her hair. "I must tell you," he whispered, "I listened to your words with Rebecca. I know that I should not have, but it pleased me to hear them. There were many times that I have been jealous of Sun Knife. It is good that all the old ghosts are gone. You will never know what pleasure your words gave me. I felt I had to tell you."

She lifted her arms and put them about his neck. "Now, I shall ask you; you are happy, Running Wolf?"

"Yes, I am happy."

"Good." She laughed as she drew his head down to hers. Her parted lips and warmth in his arms pushed everything in his mind away except Summer Rain, which was exactly what she intended. He drew her down on the soft grass of the riverbank. Gentle, seeking hands found soft flesh as he caressed her.

"Just the touch of your love is all it takes to push any other thoughts from my mind but possessing you."

"Good," she murmured. "That was what I had in mind."

She heard the rumble of his laughter as he tightened his arms about her and her answering giggle came. He silenced her with a hard, seeking mouth that left her gasping and clinging to him. His broad, strong body blotted the moon from her sight. She closed her eyes, feeling only the joy of their blending.

Strong arms lifted and held her as he joined them and she caressed the heavy, rigid muscles of his back and whispered soft murmured words of encouragement.

"Oh, Running Wolf, I love you so, I love you so."

The flame engulfed them both, lifting them together, carrying them to a world where only they existed, and only their love was reality. She felt the iron strength of his hard, lean body. Willingly, her body picked up his urgent rhythmic movement and she drew him within her. She heard him call her name softly; then suddenly, she was beyond knowing anything but the flame that licked through her body, mind and soul, a flame that drove her beyond anything she had ever known before. All the world was gone; it was not only Summer Rain and Running Wolf, it was man and woman locked together in the eternal need for the warmth and the peace of love.

He held her trembling body close to him as they tumbled slowly from the heights to the reality of the world around them. It was as if he wanted to protect her from this reality and keep her locked in some safe place within him. His hands caressed her as his mouth gently touched hers again and again. They lay together, content for a while before either of them spoke. Neither wanted to speak the words that would break the spell of this rare and magical moment. Then her mind touched on Snow Blossom and she shivered as a touch of fear found her.

"You are cold?"

"No."

"Why do you tremble?"

She drew herself even closer to his warmth. "I have thought

of Snow Blossom and Sun Knife. I'm afraid, Running Wolf. It is a fear I can't put into words."

"I can name it—the white man. He intrudes not only on our land, but within our villages. I would hope that White Eagle would let us move rather than fight, but whatever he chooses to do, we must all stand together. Maybe if Sun Knife comes soon—"

"Yes, if Sun Knife comes soon."

He rose to his feet and drew her up to stand beside him.

"Whatever happens, Summer Rain, we are together. We will face whatever comes when it comes. For today, I have you, and soon our child. We have much to be thankful for. Maybe this threat will pass and we can move to a happier hunting ground and live in peace."

"At the council will you be asked to speak?"

"No, I do not think so. I am only a subchief. Gray Bear will speak for our village."

"Will you be able to say nothing?"

"Only if Gray Bear should ask." He grinned. "And I seriously doubt if he will. Gray Bear is a very strong and wise man. The words of a man as young as I will not be heard."

"How do you think he will feel?"

"Gray Bear is a very peaceful man. I think he will try every path to peace if he can. The sickness in our village was enough death for us all. If I had to guess, I would say Gray Bear would speak for moving."

As they finished dressing, they walked back to the village slowly, where the drums and the laughter could still be heard.

Yes, she thought, the old chief, filled with wisdom and a deep hatred for death, would speak for moving and for peace. But would the white man let it go at that, or would he follow until there was nowhere to go, until their backs were to the wall and they were forced to fight?

She thought of Sun Knife and Snow Blossom and knew if he did not come back with her, as far as White Eagle was concerned, they had already reached the wall and—the knowledge made her weak—that Sun Knife with Running Wolf beside him would fight the unstoppable white flood, fight until their last breaths.

Chapter Twenty-Six

Sun Knife knelt and examined the dry earth closely. Long Arrow watched as he expertly read the signs of the passage of the two people for whom he searched. With a satisfied grunt, Sun Knife rose to his feet. "It has been several days since they passed here. The foolish man leaves an iron print a child could follow."

"It may be," Long Arrow replied, "he does not think you or any of the tribe would be able to follow."

"Most likely, we should reach the river soon; then we will follow. We will give him a big surprise."

Sun Knife stood watching the horizon, his eyes blank as if he were looking at another time and place. Long Arrow was saddened by his gaze. Hatred was a thing he did not want his foster son to feel. Sun Knife had taken enough in the past few weeks: the death of his father, his mother's brush with death, the sickness in Running Wolf's village, and now the abduction of his wife. He understood why he would feel so; still it hurt him to know what was in his mind.

"Sun Knife," he said softly, "Snow Blossom is a very brave and courageous woman. You will find her soon."

Sun Knife turned his bleak gaze toward Long Arrow. For a minute he looked at him as if he had not quite understood what he was saying. Then he shook himself as if coming awake from a bad dream.

"Yes . . . soon," he replied quietly.

Long Arrow knew the signs of death for Josiah Tucker, just as he knew there was nothing he could or would say to stop Sun Knife. Within him he carried the tear-stained face of Waterflower and he knew to save her more grief, and to save his foster son from the deed, he would see personally that Josiah paid and paid well for all the misery he had caused. He remained silent, for if Sun Knife had read his thoughts he would have separated from Long Arrow, and he could travel much faster than Long Arrow could.

Long Arrow knew that despite his urgent need to move rapidly, he had slowed his pace so that Long Arrow could keep up. It was a supreme sacrifice, for Long Arrow above all, knew the fiery need that burned within him, to find his enemy before him and know of the safety of his woman.

Sun Knife mounted his horse, and without more words kicked it into motion. There were still several hours before dark and he intended to make full use of them.

It was a still, dry day, as if the world was held in a state of suspended animation. The place they were traveling now, with its heat and dryness, seemed forbidding. A cloud and its shadow on the ground were a relief to the eye, a single hawk wheeling in the air was a thing to watch. The cottonwood trees that grew near the approaching river seemed like giants. Their whitish-gray furrowed trunks were larger than a man could reach around, and some towered four times as high as a tepee. Their leaves rustled continually, gently whispering of shade, bathing, and the pleasure of making camp. But Long Arrow knew pleasure was not in Sun Knife's mind and that he would not even give a thought to making camp until it was too dark to follow any trail.

They had been traveling several days now in the sun, the heat, and the blanket of tension that rode with them. As Long Arrow thought, the moon was high and the stars had already begun to glitter in the night sky when they made camp and ate a hastily prepared meal. This was the time that Sun Knife dreaded most, those hours between the time they stopped and the moment when restless, dream-filled sleep found him.

He wore a mental armor against the words he feared from Long Arrow, words that would deny him the anger and hate that kept him going, words that tried to return him to rational thinking. He wanted only to think of two things: the recovery of Snow Blossom and the death of Josiah Tucker.

Sun Knife lay with his hands folded behind his head, caught in the thoughts that continually haunted him, thoughts of Snow Blossom wondering when he would come, of her fear that he would not be able to find her and that she might be lost to him and her people.

He tore his mind away from these thoughts with an effort for if they remained they would drive him frantic during the inactivity of night. He knew he could not follow the trail well at night, yet stopping filled him with almost uncontrollable tension. He tried to concentrate on other things.

"You are well, Long Arrow?"

"Yes. It is not too painful. I think I am healing well. Most of my stiffness"—he grinned—"I'm sure is old age."

Sun Knife grunted with laughter. "You, old?" He looked at his foster father with critical eyes. Long Arrow's long, lean muscular body looked as if it could belong to a man half his age. His black shining hair, braided and tied with rawhide, had not a single gray hair. His face, unlined and dominated by dark intelligent eyes and a wide humorous smile, also spoke of youth. As Sun Knife looked at him, he again realized what this unselfish man had contributed to his life, and what he had sacrificed to do so. It was brought sharply to him that Long Arrow had respected and loved his parents so much that he had silently sacrificed his life for theirs. When he thought of this, he remembered that many of the joys and happiness of his young life could be laid in this man's hands. He loved his father, but he had known him for such a short time. His love for Long Arrow was filled with good memories.

"My mother is healing well also. By the time we get back, she should be completely well."

"Yes, Waterflower is a strong woman."

"She will be lonely with my father gone," Sun Knife suggested.

"Yes, she will be lonely."

"The pain of my father's death is enough to bear; she should not be lonely also."

Long Arrow's eyes glittered with laughter at the obviousness of Sun Knife's blatant suggestion.

"Are you by any chance suggesting she should marry again?"

"My mother is young. She has many years ahead of her. I would hate to see her spend them in loneliness. I would like to see her smile and be happy. I loved my father, but he is gone, and she must live out the rest of her years. I would see them happy years."

Long Arrow was silent for a moment; then he said gently, "There is no man who could fill the place in your mother's heart as your father did. Always she would be living with him in her mind. It would be a difficult thing for any man to accept."

"A man of strength would understand that. With patience he would find his own place in her heart. Of course she could never forget him, but time has a way of healing wounds and allowing you to put them where they belong, as beloved memories."

Long Arrow contemplated his words for some time, then he replied, "Sun Knife . . . if you cannot find Snow Blossom, if she is lost to you forever, will you be able to accept it and find a new path for your life, perhaps marry again?"

"I have never thought of not finding her. I will follow until there is no trail, maybe even longer. I cannot honestly say that I could accept that, for I know she is not dead. It is different with my mother. My father cannot possibly return. Snow Blossom can."

Long Arrow nodded at this logic. They remained silent for some time each contemplating his private thoughts. After a while, Long Arrow spoke again. "It is best we sleep now, Sun Knife. Dawn will come soon."

Nodding his agreement, he rolled in his blanket and each sought elusive sleep, but each had his dreams—Sun Knife of finding Snow Blossom and Long Arrow of the possibility that the woman he had loved for so many years might someday turn her eyes toward him. He was pleased at the thought that he would have the blessings of her son.

Many miles away, another group of men lay about a low-burning fire. Most of them were asleep with the exception of two. Grant was unable to find sleep, his mind and heart were filled with too many pain-filled thoughts. His anger and dislike had not lessened for the man who lay across the fire from him. Major Chivington slept as a man with a free conscience would, and Grant wondered how he could ever sleep again after the actions for which he was responsible. He thought of Michael, his friend, dead at the hands of this man. He thought of the loneliness of Waterflower and the misery of Cade as he parted from him. It was a thought he could hardly bear, that he and Cade would never again meet as friends, and that White Eagle, a peaceful man, was slowly turning his face toward the white man in hatred and distrust. White Eagle had done what he would have done had he been pushed into the same position. Yet Grant was a knowledgeable man. He knew of the Indians' perilous position, and he knew their chances of survival lay in their changing. The children had to be educated and a man had to lead them who knew what changes were necessary. Despite the fact that he admired and respected White Eagle, in this he felt Cade would be a better leader than he. If they could combine, he thought, then there would be a slim possibility they would have the wisdom and strength to help hold back the flood that threatened to destroy them.

Grant again looked across at Major Chivington. There was the enemy of the Indian, the man who was convinced of the superiority of the whites; the man whose prejudices led to the death and destruction of an entire nation. Determinedly, he decided he would fight men like Major Chivington in the white world, and in every way he could. He could not, he reasoned, fight him from the military for they would find a way to silence him even if they had to transfer him to some godforsaken place where he would never be heard from again. He knew Chivington's power. He decided then that the first thing he would do when he returned was to resign his commission. The second would be to find Lauren's father and enlist his continued help. With the wealth of the Holliday family and the help of Lauren's father, they would have a weapon of power that would give men like Chivington a reason to stop and think.

He sighed deeply and turned over, and his eyes met Sergeant Price's. He lay as wide awake as Grant. He watched as Price slowly rose from his blanket. He gave a silent motion with his head and Grant rose and followed him . . . away from the fire and any ears that might hear them.

"You wanted to talk to me, John?"

"Grant, I got a feeling you've got definite plans when we

get back."

"Yes, I guess I do, why?"

"I rode with him on that last raid."

"I know."

"I haven't been able to sleep a night since without seeing it all over again."

"What are you saying, John?"

"I'm saying that I'm sorry for what I've done and I'd like to try to do something to help make up for it, at least something that will let me live with myself the rest of my life without seeing all those innocent people dying in front of me."

"Like what?"

"I don't know, but somehow I think you do and I'd like to be with you."

"You got a family, Price?"

"Just a brother."

"You making a career out of the army?"

"I was plannin' on it . . . until I did what I did. Now . . . I ain't so sure. Why?"

"Because, when I get back I'm resigning my commission." He went on to tell Price all he intended to do.

"That's a hell of a big bite."

"I know, but Cade's money and Alex's influence should swing a lot of weight."

"Boy, if he knew that—"

"What?"

"He might try to see you never lived long enough to talk about what you know, let alone to do anything about it."

"He won't know until it is too late for him to do anything about it. Once I'm out of the army, there's no way he can stop me from carrying out my plans."

"Lieutenant, I don't think that man would stop short of having you killed, no matter what."

"That's a risk we all take. Death can come any way, any time. We can't stop doing what we think is right because we're afraid. I have to shave in the morning and I can't look at myself and live with what was done without doing something. Even if it's not effective, even if it's not enough. I have to try."

"Yeah . . . yeah, I guess you're right. I sure ain't been the same since it happened." He looked back over his shoulder toward the campfire. "I don't know how he can sleep so easy."

"He hasn't got a conscience. I don't think," Grant said softly, "he's even got a soul. If he did, he would be living in fear of answering to God for what he's done."

"Grant, I want to join you in whatever it is you decide to do. Somehow I've got to try to make up for some of it."

"You're welcome to join me, Price."

"Thanks," Price replied, and he extended his hand to Grant who took it with a firm, hard grip and a deep feeling of gratitude. They went back to their blankets and found what sleep they could, but both of them were up and preparing to travel before dawn and long before everyone else.

Only after many days of hard travel did they reach the outskirts of civilization, and many more days passed before they came into sight of the first fort. It was on that last day that Chivington and Grant could no longer ignore each other. Chivington showed no consideration for or interest in the young men who surrounded him. He had pushed them beyond endurance and Grant's patience had reached the exasperation point where he could no longer tolerate Chivington's inhumane attitude toward all others. What occurred began as a trivial matter but ended with a violent explosion of tempers that caused Grant to say much more than he intended and Price to commit himself earlier than he'd intended.

It was Tim Glazier who began the whole confrontation. The fort was still two days' ride away, and it was late in the afternoon. Any reasonable man, Grant thought, would have known that both men and animals were too exhausted to push any further. They could rest that night and be able to reach the fort in better condition. It was what Grant thought, but not what the major had planned.

Tim's horse, weary and suffering extreme thirst, was the first to stumble. Tim, anxious about the welfare of his horse, dismounted and began to unsaddle his mount. The major, surprised when the group stopped, turned and rode to the boy's side.

"Corporal Glazier, what is wrong with you? Mount your horse; we do not have much time."

"I can't, sir. She won't carry me any farther unless she has some rest and something to drink."

"Mount up, Corporal."

"Sir, she'll die before we get there."

"If she falls, Corporal," the major said coldly, "you will shoot her and ride double with another trooper. I won't have a horse keep me from what I have to do."

Tim gazed up at the major in both shock and beginning resistance to the heartless order. Grant could see what was coming in the cold gaze of the major, and what was coming meant only trouble for Tim. Without another thought, he moved toward the major to intercept what was inevitable.

"Major, the boy is right. One more night won't make any difference. The horses need the rest and so do the men."

"Lieutenant, I did not ask for your advise. One day's difference means one day more that arrogant savage and his bloodthirsty warriors will be alive."

"You . . . you don't mean to come back here? Haven't you done enough to these people?"

"I not only mean to come back here, but I intend to see that not one of those animals is left alive when I do, and I suspect, Lieutenant, you think you can do something to stop me."

Heat, exhaustion, and rage combined to make Grant answer honestly.

"I'll do anything in my power to stop you. I'll go to everyone who has the power to do anything, I'll shout it from every rooftop in Washington, and one day, someone will listen."

They looked at each other, both knowing each spoke the truth.

"I'd be careful, Lieutenant," the major said softly. "You might find things becoming very difficult for you in this army. You seem to have forgotten I have some influence and power."

The threat, unveiled, was like a dash of cold water to Grant who immediately came to his senses and began to regret having spoken so soon, but it was too late to back down.

"Major?"

Both men turned to face the questioner. Price looked at them.

"I'm requesting the major to give the horses at least an

hour's rest and some water. If you do, I feel sure most of them have a good chance of making it. If you don't, White Eagle has succeeded in doing what he wanted to do. We'll kill ourselves and he'll have the last laugh."

He looked at the major, his face impassive.

Chivington had thought only on his anger and striking out at Grant. He had given no thought to how much White Eagle would enjoy the fact that they had not survived.

"Yes, that would satisfy him, wouldn't it? All right, Price, one hour."

Price gave the order to dismount and the men quickly obeyed before it could be changed. Grant was unsaddling his horse, when Price approached him. Grant was angry with himself for having allowed the major to reach a place within him that he should have kept hidden until a more opportune time.

"Lieutenant?"

"Price . . . that was probably the stupidest thing I have ever done. I'm grateful that you did something. I'd already said too much."

"You sure left yourself wide open. Now, he knows for sure where you stand. Does he know just how much damage you might be able to do to him?"

"No." Grant laughed. "You had enough sense to stop me before I gave myself completely away. Thanks, Price."

"You're welcome, but I'm still worried."

"Yes, so am I. I can't resign until we get to Washington. A lot of things can happen between here and there."

"Make you a deal, Lieutenant?"

"What?"

"Let's stay close. I'll watch your back and you watch mine."

"It sounds good to me. Nice to know I've got a friend at my back."

"Lieutenant?" Price laughed. "Out of these twenty men, you've got twenty friends. The major will not do anything here. It is later that I am concerned about."

"We'll cross that bridge when we get to it. For now, let's see if we can get these boys home before he kills the rest of them."

"He's insane, you know," Price stated softly.

"Yes . . . yes, I know. I pray I can find some way to help those people before he's let loose on them again."

"You will . . . remember, you've got friends watching out for you. . . . Sleep easy."

Price shook his hand and turned to walk away, but froze in his tracks. Several feet from him stood Major Chivington, a full knowing smile on his face. There was no doubt in Price's mind that he, too, was on the major's list of enemies.

It was late evening the following day that Major Chivington led his tired, hungry, thirsty men through the gates of the fort.

After spending a week there, they were rejuvenated, and began to journey back to Washington where the enlisted men would wait for further orders and Grant, Price, and Major Chivington would begin to seriously fight their battle.

Grant's and Price's first step was to tender their resignation. The next step was much easier as they made preparations to visit Alex Brent, Lauren's father.

Alex, impatient and anxious to hear news of his beloved daughter, met them at his door with a warm and enthusiastic greeting. He ushered them in, poured them large cool drinks, and when he had made them comfortable, he pounced on them with a multitude of questions about the welfare of his child.

"Tell me, Grant; I've heard no word. Is she well, is she happy? I know she loved Cade so much. Did they ever meet; did they ever marry?"

"I will tell you the whole story, a story I think will surprise you. When I have told you, you will see why we . . . *they* so desperately need your help."

Alex sat back in his chair.

"Tell me."

"First I must tell you that Lauren is still beautiful, and very, very happy. She is married to a young man named Running Wolf."

"She and Cade never married?"

"No. They both are very much in love with someone else."

"But, is she happy?"

"Yes, but not only is she happy, she has found a place in life where she is desperately needed. She is medicine woman to her tribe, much like Cade is in his. They love her, respect her, and value her as a bringer of laughter, knowledge, love, and medicine."

"This is such a relief to me. I have worried so long for her welfare."

"I did not say you should not worry," Grant replied gently.

"Then there is something to worry about?"

"Yes, there is."

"Something that endangers my daughter?"

"Your daughter and all the people she loves. It is not something, but someone."

"Is it someone I know?"

"I believe you might."

"His name?"

"Maj. John Chivington."

"Chivington . . . I don't think I know him."

"Then"—Grant leaned forward in his seat and spoke quietly—"let me introduce you to Maj. John Chivington and some of the men I know are behind him, and their bloody mercenary ideas."

"You are an angry man, Grant."

"Yes . . . yes, I'm angry. I'm angry at men who will ruthlessly kill innocent women and children to acquire wealth and land. I'm angry at politicians here who will send out against these unsuspecting, defenseless gentle people a bloodthirsty man like John Chivington."

"You know all these men?"

"Not all, but most of them."

"What has happened?"

Quietly, Grant told him of the massacre of the women and children in White Eagle's village. Then, he told him the balance of the story and of their trip home.

"You mean this man actually stole the wives of these men?"

"Not only stole them, but he gave Cade's wife, Snow Blossom, to a fur trader who had betrayed the exact location of White Eagle's village to him."

"*Gave?*" Alex said in a deeply shocked voice.

"Gave, as if she were a nothing."

"My God, what kind of a man is he?"

"A man who will stop at nothing to get what he and the men behind him want—the land of the Indians."

"And where are they to go?"

"Alex . . . he wants them all dead. Every man, woman and child."

Alex was shaken, his face pale. He rose and poured another drink which he gulped down. Then his face hardened and he walked back to Grant.

"I'll do anything to help. Can you tell me the names of these men and how we can stop them?"

"Yes, I can. Before I left, Cade gave me the power of attorney to handle all his funds. He wants me to use all the money to protect his people."

"You can have anything else you might need. And all my help. After this is over, I will go there with you. I want to see my daughter, and I want to be around to see any grandchildren this new and wonderful daughter I have might present to me."

Grant and Price both smiled as Alex said firmly, "Tell me what we have to do to stop these scoundrels. Tell me, gentlemen, the names of all the men behind this."

They talked for long hours deep into the night. While they talked and prepared to fight a battle, Sun Knife, too, was preparing himself to do the same.

They had trailed the iron-shod hoofprints to the banks of the river, then had begun to follow the winding stream in search of the place where they were told Josiah might take Snow Blossom.

They had spent the days mostly in silent travel, each of them caught in his own worries and thoughts. In Sun Knife's mind, one thought was always first. Would he find Snow Blossom where he was told she would be, or had it all been a lie? If he did find her . . . would she be well? If Josiah had a suspicion he was being followed would he leave her, take her someplace else, or . . . would he kill her so he could travel faster?

They had traveled up the path of the river for two days. At the dawn of the third day, Sun Knife noticed that Long Arrow had been more than usually silent. He watched him and could immediately see that he was losing strength. The healing wounds had sapped most of his energy and he was silently and determinedly traveling on by sheer will.

He knew that Long Arrow's pride would never allow him to stop. Before Long Arrow could rise to help him break camp, Sun Knife made a pretense that his horse was becoming lame and would need at least half a day's rest and some close tending, too.

Although it was hard on Sun Knife to wait those few hours, he knew he could not sacrifice Long Arrow.

Before he said they could travel again, it was long after noon, so that the hours would be shorter until they camped. By daylight the next day, he could see the rest had done Long Arrow a great deal of good, so he prepared to push on. As they crested each grade, passed each curve, he expected to find those he sought, only to be disappointed. He began to suspect that the major had lied, and that he would never find them. He clung only to the sparsely scattered iron-shod tracks that they had found occasionally. Now he worried a thought over in his mind, wondering if at the end of this trail he would find some trapper or hunter, if all this time he had been following a false trail and that Snow Blossom was being carried farther and farther away from him. Would she believe he would find her . . . would he ever find her?

One more night they sat around a campfire morosely brooding on these possibilities.

"Long Arrow, do you think we are following the right trail? I keep thinking this is false, that we are going in the wrong direction. I keep seeing Snow Blossom's face and wondering if she is being carried farther and farther away from us."

"It is possible, Sun Knife, but I don't believe it is so. It is only because we do not know their destination that we travel slower. I feel we will find them soon."

"I hope so. Snow Blossom is not a woman to submit easily, and we have been told of the nature of Josiah Tucker."

"Snow Blossom is not foolish. She will not cause him to hurt her. No, I believe she will wait and watch and if he lets his guard drop, she will seize the chance and be gone."

"One thing is as bad as the other. If she is alone . . . if she had to cross this country alone, it will be because she is running; she will be unarmed, defenseless." Picturing her so in his mind, roused him almost to panic. He could see her attacked by some wild animal, or dying of exposure or thirst in some dry unhappy place where he would never find her. Silently, he prayed, realizing one situation was as bad as the other.

He didn't sleep; he couldn't. His mind relived and renewed every poignant beautiful memory—childhood days, when he considered himself too grown a warrior to look at a child; the times he was away when the only thoughts of her that crossed his mind were of a wide-eyed little girl; the day he returned to discover her beauty and a love such as he had never known before; the first day she had come to him with her rare and exceptional beauty; their wedding day and the joyous days that followed. He clung to them as he hoped she would be doing.

The half-gray light of dawn found him up and preparing to travel. Wordlessly, Long Arrow joined him, and before the night was completely done, they were already moving along the banks of the river.

They moved with plodding slowness as they searched the ground for more telltale tracks. On a patch of moist ground, tracks were found. They pushed on; then suddenly—they rode over a grass-covered grade to look down at a half-finished cabin, with no sign of life about it.

He pulled his horse to a halt as did Long Arrow. They would not ride in abruptly and possibly cause Josiah to do something foolish. They drew back beyond the crest where they could not be seen and dismounted.

"Long Arrow, did you see anyone?"

"No, did you?"

"There's not even the sign of a fire," Sun Knife said worriedly.

"It would be best if I went to the other side and we approached from two different directions. If he is prepared for us, he cannot defend two positions at once and still keep an eye on Snow Blossom, and she is the one that would need watching."

"Good."

"Give me enough time for the shadows to move from that

tall tree," Long Arrow pointed. "I will signal you from that hill and we will approach slowly and quietly."

Sun Knife nodded agreement and Long Arrow left him. He moved on foot, like a shadow through the trees, and within minutes disappeared. Time seemed to stand still. A breeze touched him, rustling through the trees. Birds sang, undisturbed by the silent passage of Long Arrow. Sun Knife crept to the top of the hill where he could watch both the half-finished cabin and the hill from which Long Arrow's signal would come.

It seemed an agonizingly long time until Long Arrow's signal came, a time of motionless, breathless expectancy. He rose, slid his bow over his shoulder, and began to work his way toward the ominously silent cabin.

From tree to tree, from one shadowed spot to another they silently worked forward until they were a few feet from the cabin. Still no sign that they were seen, or even that anyone remained inside.

In one quick explosive moment, Sun Knife leaped inside the remains, his knife in his hand, prepared to meet force.

There was no force; there was nothing. The remains of the cabin were empty and gave the eerie sensation they had been for some time. Within a few minutes, Long Arrow joined him and they looked about the empty room in surprise and fear.

A few minutes later, Long Arrow grasped Sun Knife's arm and quietly pointed to a spot near the back door. They went to it and knelt beside a pool of blood that had already begun to dry.

They looked at each other; then another spot caught their eyes. Blood stained the lower part of the door and trailed outside.

"Someone was hurt here and dragged himself away," Long Arrow said softly.

"Or was dragged away by someone—or something."

Sun Knife's heart thudded furiously as slowly they traced the path of blood stains. It took them time to go from one to the other until they could see that the general direction was a small grove of shade trees that stood on the ridge of a nearby hill.

They walked toward the trees, both of them reluctant to face what they were sure they would find.

At first, beneath the shade of the trees, they could see no one. Then, simultaneously, their eyes caught the form that lay in the shadow of a great tree half-braced against the trunk of the tree. From the way the figure was lying they were sure death had already struck. The only fear that dwelt within them was . . . who?

It was Sun Knife who finally acquired enough courage to look closer. He had to know if his beloved Snow Blossom was lying there, even in death, waiting for him.

He walked to the figure, knelt, and turned it over. Death stared back at him. Death, final and complete.

Chapter Twenty-Seven

Snow Blossom stirred and tried to turn in her sleep, but her bound hands made comfort impossible. Josiah slept across the room from her, but he slept so quietly, she was not sure he was not pretending while actually watching her closely.

After her attempt at escape, Josiah had watched her carefully. He had bound both her legs and her feet while he prepared food. He ate first, then unbound her and watched while she ate.

She ate what food he offered, for she was determined to keep up her strength for whatever she might have to face. She was surprised when he spoke to her in pleasant conversation. It was as if, in his mind, they were two people enjoying a pleasant time together.

"This cabin was once very warm and secure. We will make it so again, Two Moons."

"I am not Two Moons," she said angrily. His eyes clouded as if a memory was slipping away.

"No . . . no, you're not. But you will stay. . . . You will stay."

She watched him closely, then replied softly, "Why did Two Moons not stay, Josiah?"

His eyes snapped from his reverie and turned to her. "Eat your food. We will work on the cabin today."

She obediently ate, but her eyes never left his. Again, he seemed to be gazing inward, looking at a long-lost scene that had brought him much pain. She knew the name Two Moons reached a sensitive, well-protected spot and decided that she would watch and question him until she found the reasons.

"You once told me I remind you of Two Moons. Was she your woman, Josiah? Did she leave you for someone else?"

Again he turned to look at her, but this time, his eyes were filled with brilliant anger. "She would never have left us," he said. "Be quiet and eat, we have work to do."

"Us?" she thought.

After she had eaten, she was prepared to have him tie her hands again, but instead he came and squatted down in front of her.

"I have a horse and a gun; you have nothing," he began. "If you run, I can track you within minutes. Out there"—he pointed in the direction from which they had come—"you stand no chance of survival. No food, no water, would find you dead within days. I am not going to tie you, but I am warning you"—he grasped her chin in his hands and lifted her head to hold her eyes with his—"I will not kill you," he said softly, "but I will make you wish I had, many times over. Do you understand, Snow Blossom?"

"I understand, Josiah," she replied calmly. "But you must understand. I am Sun Knife's woman. I will take any opportunity that comes that will let me escape safely. I will wait, but if the time comes, I will find my way to my village and my people."

"They are no more. With the winter snows, they will not survive. Why must you insist on being so foolish? You cannot go fast enough or far enough that I cannot track you. I would find you long before you could make your way back to them. And," he added, "he is dead, this warrior of yours. I am all you have."

"I am Sun Knife's woman," she replied obstinately, "and I will remain so until I see his body to prove his death."

"You are a stubborn woman, but no matter what you think or say, the facts are still the same. You are here, you are mine, and I intend to keep you. One day soon, you will finally realize that no one is coming for you. That day you will know that you belong to me."

Her eyes remained steady on him. He smiled and caressed her cheek with his fingers lightly. "I will not hurt you if you do not force me."

"No," she replied coldly, "you would only dishonor me. You would only make me whore before the eyes of my people."

"No . . . you will be my wife. The wife of Josiah Tucker is no whore."

"I cannot—"

"Shut up! Speak to me no more of your dead husband or your escape! You might as well accept the fact . . . you are mine!"

She did not reply again. She saw the dangerous gleam in his eyes, and she did not want to be bound again.

Satisfied that she was submitting to him now, he rose and pulled her to her feet.

"You will do the cooking from now on. I will repair the cabin. When we are finished with it, I will take you to the fort on the other side of the river. It will be many more days of travel, but we can be married there."

Again she pretended submission, and he smiled and turned from her.

They began work that day, and she kept a close eye on him mostly to see if his guard would drop. It didn't. She knew that at any given moment, he knew exactly where she was and what she was doing.

This went on for another three days. She worked until she fell into an exhausted sleep at night, too tired to care what he was doing or thinking.

The third night, she awoke from a deep sleep in the wee hours of the morning to find that Josiah was not within the half-repaired cabin. Slowly, she rose from her blanket and searched about. She looked outside and saw no sign of him. Going to the back door, she looked out. A few feet from the cabin was a small hill. Atop the hill was a grove of trees. Outlined against the starlit sky, Josiah stood motionless.

Quietly, she slipped from the cabin. Using the cover of trees, she moved from one to the other and made her way to within a few feet of where he stood. It was only then she noticed he stood at the foot of two mounds of earth—graves whose grass-covered tops told her they had been there for some time. There were two, and one was suspiciously small. She felt sure one must belong to the phantom of Josiah's mind, Two Moons . . . but to whom did the other belong?

The sound of his voice broke through her thoughts.

"You've come back to me, Two Moons. I knew you would. Soon our child will join us and we'll be happy again—happy, like we were a long time ago."

"His child?" she thought. "His wife and child are buried here. Poor Josiah. It was obvious that grief for his great loss had unbalanced his rational thinking. She felt a deep sympathy for his grief and understanding for his reaching back into his past for lost love. She moved from behind the shadow of the trees and walked to his side. For a few moments, it was as if he did not know she was there; then he turned and looked directly at her, his face clouded with anger.

"What are you doing here? Must I tie you up again at night? Go back to the cabin!"

"Josiah . . . maybe if you tell me what happened, maybe if you say the words, you will realize that Two Moons is gone and you can find no happiness in stealing someone who looks like her. She is buried here with your child, isn't she . . . isn't she, Josiah?"

"Go back to the cabin!"

"It is not enough, Josiah. You will find no happiness with me. You are looking for a ghost, and you will find the hurt and pain still there. Even if you take me, and you have the strength to do that, you will find it empty and unfulfilling. You will still be searching for your lost spirit. Tell me, Josiah, and maybe you and Two Moons will be able to rest."

"Two Moons," he whispered.

"Yes, tell me of Two Moons, Josiah; then maybe you will find some peace."

He stood silently looking at her, yet she was aware he was seeing the past.

"It . . . it was so long ago. I came out here on a fur-trapping expedition and found I had lost my way. I came across the village when I was desperately cold, hungry, and thirsty. They took me in, cared for me, and nursed me back to health. I stayed with them until spring. There was to be a big celebration, for the chief and his son expected members of another tribe who were to bring with them a maiden who had been promised to the chief's son by her father.

"I went out with several warriors to escort the visiting party back, and there I saw Two Moons. She was so beautiful, so young, and the marriage was against her will. We traveled for two days, and I knew it was against her wishes, when I found a way to meet her and speak to her. We met several times, then finally she told me the truth. The marriage was to have been between the chief's son and her older sister. The sister had become ill and died so she was sent to fulfill the promise. She did not love the chief's son. As the time went on, we met more and more often and I knew she loved me as I did her. Then, one day, we were caught together. Both tribes were in a terrible rage. We had shamed them, they claimed. We had brought disgrace on both tribes. They were going to punish us both—her by slitting her nose, cutting her hair, and branding her 'whore,' then throwing her from the village; and me by simply burning me to death. I thought of the only way out. I called the chief's son a coward and challenged him to fight me for the maiden. If I won, I could take her and go. If I lost, they could kill us both. He was so arrogant, so sure, he accepted my challenge. We fought, a terrible, horrible, bloody fight. For him, it was anger, for me it was for the life of the woman I loved. I won. But in doing so, I angered both tribes. I had killed the chief's son. They could not kill me, for they had agreed and must honor their promise. We were brought in front of both chiefs and told to go and not be seen in the area again. The father of the man I had killed swore that one day he would avenge his son's death. . . . Oh, God . . . he did, he did. The revenge was more than any man could bear.

"We left the village, traveled for weeks, and finally came here and built this cabin. The days and weeks passed and we thought we were safe.

"As time went on and we shared so much happiness . . . I was a fool. . . . I dropped my guard. . . . I trusted. A few months later, Two Moons told me of the expected child. I was so happy. I could not believe my good fortune; the woman I loved and a child to hold us closer together. He was born, and I was happier than I had ever been in my life before." His voice softened as he remembered a gentler sweeter time. "He was so strong, so handsome. We called him Swift Deer, for she laughed at his long legs that reminded her of mine. She swore he would be swift as a deer. He grew tall and handsome. It was nearly four years and I had put aside all thought of the revenge-seekers. When I was happy, when I had a perfect world and all I needed in it . . . it was then they struck. I knew they meant only to kill me. Instead, their revenge was more than complete. They left me alive and took from me everything in my life that made it worth living. They took the lives of my wife and my son. They left me with an emptiness and desolation I could never imagine existed. For a while, I thought the world had stopped . . . and then the dreams began. In the dreams, she would call to me. Sometimes . . . sometimes, I could not tell the dreams from reality. They blended into long days and nights of wanting. I left this place; I thought I could run from the pain. I was wrong. It followed me wherever I went. I began to hate, to hate those who had taken from me all that I had to live for. I began to kill."

She gave a surprised start. "I have killed many. Anywhere I can find them," he replied in a deadened voice. "That did not ease the pain either. Then the major sent me a message. He said I would have the chance to eliminate many." He looked at her now with eyes as cold as ice. "I wanted to see every man, woman, and child dead—dead like mine were. It was the only emotion that kept me alive. He sent me to map out the villages, and I did that." His eyes softened on her again and he reached out and touched her with gentle fingers. "And then I saw you. It was as if she had reached from the grave and touched me."

Desperately, her mind fought to help him rationalize what he felt, to make him understand that the peace he sought was not with her.

"Maybe she did, Josiah," she said softly. "Maybe she was trying to speak to you with love. To tell you to stop the death with which you lived."

He was listening and she continued searching for the words he needed to help him, for despite all he had done, she felt a deep sympathy for the agony in which he lived.

"Maybe she wanted to tell you to stop the running and the killing. Maybe she wanted to bring you a touch of peace."

"Two Moons?"

"No, Josiah. Look at me! Look at me! I am not Two Moons; you are searching for what cannot be found. No one can replace the love you have lost. When you separated Sun Knife and I, you did to another what has been done to you. Do you think Two Moons' spirit can rest in peace when she knows what road you travel on? It is why she comes to you, Josiah. She grieves that her warrior walks the wrong path, always away from her, never to her. You will not find your peace with me, you will find only emptiness and a longing for what you are destroying."

His ragged breathing and the tears on his cheeks told her of the agony he was enduring. "The blackness—" he said hoarsely. "The loneliness . . . I cannot stand it."

Tears filled her eyes as she watched the emptiness and pain cross his face.

"Your heart has been so filled with hate and death," she said, "with the guilt of the deaths of many innocent ones, that Two Moons' spirit can no longer find a place within it. You must find peace, Josiah, by pushing all these things from your heart and remembering only the good of what you shared with her. It is only then she can find her way back to your heart and give you the peace you need."

"I have lost her."

"No, Josiah, we never lose those we love. The spirit of them lingers within our hearts to give us the joy of memories. She has only left you because you have left no room within your heart for her. Find peace, Josiah. Take me home to my husband; live with us. Let us help you day by day to find your lost love."

"That cannot be possible. I have killed your husband."

She was aware if she told him Sun Knife was still alive, he might turn on her, but she knew also that she had a tentative hold on his thoughts and if she did not speak, she might lose that hold completely and irretrievably.

"No, Josiah," she said softly. Again he turned to look at her, his eyes questioning.

"The day of the attack, Sun Knife was not in the village. White Eagle and many of the warriors were hunting. When Sun Knife returns, and finds me gone, he will feel the same fear and grief that you did when Two Moons was taken from you. As you would have done, he will follow. Meet him halfway, Josiah; still his anger by returning me. I will speak to him, and he will understand. Sun Knife has a good and open heart as you must have had before this terrible thing happened to you. Let us help you find the way back, Josiah. Please, Josiah," she pleaded softly, "return me to my people, to my husband. Take the first step on your journey back to Two Moons and your son. Let us help you."

She watched the battle on his face as grief and hatred warred with reality, as his mind reached to understand and to grapple with the dark pain he was trying to exorcise. Slowly she watched his clouded eyes clear as hope began its victory over death. He looked at her with eyes that held glistening tears, and sought to find the answers in her face. She smiled and reached out a hand to lay against his broad chest.

"I would help you, Josiah," she said softly.

"Even after what I have done?"

"Yes, even then; for I understand the darkness and the pain that made you do it."

He reached up and placed his hand over hers.

"You are like her in every way," he said. "She, too, had a kind and forgiving heart. I have not felt so since the day I found her. I will return you to your warrior, and I will search for the peace I need." For the first time tears of relief filled her eyes, and she began to cry. He drew her into his arms and held her, but it was only a comforting embrace and she felt the need he, too, had to hold her and to receive comfort.

The first gray light of dawn had just touched the sky and awakening birds began to fill the air with a new morning song. A new touch of life filled the heart of Josiah Tucker as he took Snow Blossom's hand in his and stood before the graves of his beloved wife and son. For the first time in several years, he felt her reach out and touch his spirit as she had in life.

In that quite morning light, he washed himself clean by telling Snow Blossom about her. It seemed to strengthen him, so she stood quietly and listened, listened to a man pick his spirit up from the deep pits of hell to walk again on a peaceful path brightened with hope and sunlight.

He talked for a long time, as if he were washing himself clean. Snow Blossom laughed with him, cried with him, and mourned with him, and felt with joy his renewed life begin to flow. It was as if his feet again walked the path to the safety and love of Two Moons.

The sun warmed them with its rays before he ceased to talk. Then for a few minutes, they stood in silence. He became aware of her again, not as the ghost of Two Moons, but as Snow Blossom.

"Come, we will go back to the cabin. You must eat. Then we will begin our journey home."

Gratefully, she put her hand in his and they turned to walk back down the hill to the cabin. Suddenly, he stopped. Her eyes followed his to the distance where two riders could be seen approaching.

"You are truthful," he said. "I think Sun Knife comes for you. Let us go and wait for him in the cabin."

They walked down the hill and entered the half-repaired cabin through the back door. Inside, Josiah began to gather his things together. In a few minutes, the sound of horses could be heard. Snow Blossom ran to the porch followed by Josiah; but no sooner were they on the porch and the riders had become visible, that Josiah grasped her arm and pushed her forcefully back into the cabin.

"Josiah!"

"It is not your husband," he said quickly. "I must get you out of here to safety. They would like nothing better than to kill you slowly in front of me, thinking you are my woman."

"Josiah," she said, fear gripping her voice. "Who is it?"

"Two Hatchets . . . Kiowa," he answered.

"Who—?"

"He is a warrior known for his fierceness and bravery—also for his heartlessness and his long memory for grievances. He is . . . or was, brother to Watchful Fox, the warrior I killed for Two Moons. He has come for me. He must not find you here."

"Where can I hide? They are almost here."

"Snow Blossom, listen to me. We have not much time. Stand by the back door. I will go out to them. When I have their attention, you slip out and go to the safety of the trees. You will find my horse there. Head into the sun by day as it rises, and let it fall over your left shoulder as it sets. You will find your way home. Do not forget to gather the water sack and food or you will die out there."

"Josiah, what of you?"

"I will be all right. I can handle Two Hatchets. Get to safety. I will come to your village when I can."

"I hate to leave you."

"Snow Blossom, I cannot do anything if you are here. I must know you are safe. Please do not let them get you. There is no way we could convince them you are not my woman. Death by their hands would not be fast or pleasant. Do as I say."

"All right."

He smiled at her; then he drew her into his arms and brushed her lips with a gentle kiss.

"Good-by for now, Snow Blossom. You are a true and beautiful woman. I am sorry for all the grief I have caused you. Say I am forgiven."

"Yes, Josiah, I forgive you."

"Good, tell your husband of me. I will come if I can. Good-by, Snow Blossom."

"Good-by, Josiah."

He smiled at her, went to the door, and stepped outside to face his enemies. It was only then that she realized he had gone out—unarmed.

She stood by the open back door until she heard the two horses stop, and the sound of voices reached her.

"Two Hatchets," Josiah said quietly. There was a new sound to his voice, a stronger sound as if he were no longer haunted by black memories; was, in fact, amused at Two Hatchets' cold, dark look.

Two Hatchets was a tall imposing man, his features dark and sharp. A scowl on his face and death in his eye, he spoke to Josiah.

"I have come to repay you for the death of my brother, white one. Every year, I have come to this place. I knew one day you would return here."

"You will not die easy, white one," Two Hatchets' voice assured him.

"I will not die at all. Two Hatchets is a snake that comes bringing death; only he comes like a coward, with help in case he is too weak to do it alone. At least your brother faced me man to man, not like a coyote—in a pack." After these insulting words, Josiah made it more pointed by laughing.

Rage filled Two Hatchets' face at this open insult to his manhood. "I do not fear you, white one. I will kill you myself. I need no help."

"Then"—Josiah chuckled—"why did you bring your brother? Unless"—now Josiah's voice hovered near laughter—"you want him to bring the news back to your village of how Two Hatchets, mighty warrior," Josiah scoffed, "died like a whimpering dog at the hands of a white man who did not even seek his death."

As Josiah spoke, he moved a small distance away from the doorway. He was deliberately trying to draw their eyes away from the door so she could slip out the back. She would like to have cried out and run to help him, for she knew he was trading his life for hers. Yet she knew his sacrifice would be useless if she were caught.

Slowly, she edged her way toward the door, keeping her eyes on the open doorway. The men were not in her range of sight; yet their voices still came to her.

Josiah faced Two Hatchets with a calm that surprised even him. He was no longer afraid of death, and he felt a deep comforting peace surround him. He looked up at Two Hatchets' enraged face.

"Come down from your horse, Two Hatchets. I will meet you man to man."

"I do not need to fight you on your terms, white man. You cannot escape me. I will decide what will be done."

"Do not tax your overworked brain," Josiah drawled. "Just finding me here was enough thought for you. Sit on your horse, it will keep your brain warm while you try to decide if you possess enough courage to get down and face me."

This was the last insult Two Hatchets and his brother could tolerate. They nearly leaped from their horses and walked to Josiah. As they moved to Josiah, Snow Blossom slipped from the door and turned to run, only to come up against the broad muscular chest and hard arms of another warrior. She cried out Josiah's name as the warrior pinned her hands, lifted her fighting body with ease, and walked through the cabin to join the three surprised ones who stood on the other side.

"Snow Blossom," Josiah cried. He tried to move to her, but Two Hatchets' voice stopped him. "If you move again, white one, Spotted Bear will slit her throat."

Josiah stopped and watched as Spotted Bear dumped Snow Blossom at Two Hatchets' feet. For a few minutes, Two Hatchets was silent as he watched Josiah's face; then he threw back his head and laughed exultantly.

"So the great white warrior has another woman. He forgets easily what happened to his last one. We will enjoy her, white one; we will enjoy her as we watch you die and for a long time after before she dies, she will curse your name for bringing her here."

Josiah searched desperately for some way to get Snow Blossom away from here and out of danger.

"Two Hatchets is still a fool," he said coldly. This stopped Two Hatchets' laughter for a minute.

"You call me fool again, white one? Was I the fool who brought another woman here to pay the price for my stupidity? I am not the fool, white one, you are."

Josiah looked at each face, trying to find the weaker or more honorable one of the three. Of Two Hatchets, there was no hope. Death was in his eyes both for him and Snow Blossom. The one called Spotted Bear seemed slow of thought and followed Two Hatchets' way. But the one who had accompanied Two Hatchets was a much younger man, and for a moment, Josiah thought he saw a flicker of compassion as he looked at Snow Blossom.

"I said you were a fool, Two Hatchets, and I repeat it. You will cause your tribe much more trouble if you harm this woman. She is not my woman. I was returning her to her people. She is Snow Blossom, sister to Chief White Eagle and daughter of Tekata, chief of the Cheyenne. Not only that, she is wife to their medicine man, Sun Knife. Do you see what vengeance you will bring down on your village should you harm her? The anger of Tekata is not to be taken lightly, nor is the anger of White Eagle and Sun Knife."

Two Hatchets did not answer, but Josiah saw the quickly veiled look of concern on the younger man's face as he spoke to

Two Hatchets.

"Brother," he said softly, "our chief will be angry should we harm the family of Chief Tekata. Long have they lived in peace."

"You speak too much, Little Mountain," Two Hatchets said quickly. "How do we know the white one speaks the truth?"

"I am as he says I am," Snow Blossom said proudly. She stood erect, her chin lifted in defiance. "My father and brother will demand much in payment for my life, and my husband, Sun Knife, medicine man of our tribe, will not stop until you are dead if you touch me."

Two Hatchets was angry at the turn of events, but genuine concern was in the face of his brother, Little Mountain. It was clear, both to Josiah and to Snow Blossom, that he had little liking for this vendetta in the first place. "Let us take the white one to our village and let our father decide," Little Mountain said.

"No!" Two Hatchets said quickly. "This white one is mine and I will not have my revenge taken from me."

That Two Hatchets was confused and angry, Josiah knew. He intended to keep him off balance as long as possible.

"Let her be taken to your village. Let Little Mountain take her and they can return her to her people."

"No! Josiah!" she cried. "Two Hatchets, let us both be taken to your village. My tribe will repay you both for my life and the white one's life."

"I will tell you what is to be done," Two Hatchets stormed angrily. "Little Mountain, you take the woman to our last camp and wait for me. I will fight the white one, and when I have killed him, I will join you. Then we will find out if she speaks the truth. If she does not"—he grinned—"I will give her to you as a slave to do with whatever you want."

"Brother—" Little Mountain began.

"Take her and go before I change my mind. I might decide to torture her in front of the white one for my pleasure."

Josiah stiffened in alarm, but Little Mountain moved swiftly. He grabbed Snow Blossom, and despite her battling, he bound her securely. Then he mounted his horse and Spotted Bear threw her up in front of him.

"No! No! Josiah," she called as she writhed and fought the strong arm that held her.

"Snow Blossom," Josiah said angrily, "do what must be done. Do not make my regret for getting you into this any deeper. If I live, I will find you and your husband and ask his forgiveness for what I've done. Please, Snow Blossom, do not make it any harder for me."

She ceased to fight, but tears blinded her eyes as Little Mountain turned his horse away. She looked over Little Mountain's shoulder and saw a smiling Josiah wave as they rode away.

Now Josiah turned his face toward Two Hatchets. "And now, my enemy," he said softly and calmly. "How do you propose we end this? Are you going to give me a chance to fight you one at a time with honor, or are you going to be a coward and fight me two against one?"

"Where are your weapons, white one?"

"In the cabin."

"What weapons do you have?"

"A gun, a knife, and"—Josiah smiled—"my bare hands."

"Go and get his gun, Spotted Bear," Two Hatchets ordered. Spotted Bear obediently went inside the cabin and brought out the gun.

"Destroy it," Two Hatchets said firmly.

Josiah watched as Spotted Bear smashed the gun against the side of the door until it fell in pieces on the ground. Then he and Josiah both turned to look at Two Hatchets to await his final words.

"I fight only with my knife, white one," Two Hatchets snarled as he threw aside all other weapons. "It is all I need to kill you."

"And what of your friend? Does he attack from the back?"

"No, we fight alone. In a place of your choosing."

"I know the best place to end all this. At the grave of my wife and son who died at your hands. I would like to kill you there more than at any other place," Josiah said quietly.

"Good," Two Hatchets grinned. "Where is this place?"

"Up on that hill . . . beneath those trees."

"Spotted Bear, you wait here. I will return soon," Two

Hatchets said. "As soon as I soak this one's blood into the grave of the whore who caused my brother's death."

Josiah would not let his violent anger control him. He knew if he did, there would be no doubt Two Hatchets would win. Instead, he went into the cabin and took his hunting knife from its sheath. He went back to Two Hatchets, and in silence they walked to the shade of the trees where the two graves waited for the blood of one of them.

They reached the top of the hill and each stood for a second in silence as they looked at the two grassy mounds. Then they turned to face each other.

They crouched low, their arms outstretched and the glistening knives held firmly, and then circled each other, looking for a weak moment to attack. Two Hatchets thrust with his knife and leaped back as Josiah slashed at him. Again he leaped forward and struck with the speed of a snake, but the knife whistled harmlessly in the air as Josiah jumped back. They circled slowly, each seeking to find the one right moment to strike. Again and again each slashed out only to find his adversary gone. Time after time, their wicked knives flashed, and then they began to reach their goals as both men began to tire. A long gash in one arm drew a stream of blood from Josiah. He returned by touching a vulnerable shoulder and making Two Hatchets jump back as a bright-red stain flowered on his bronze skin.

Josiah knew in his mind that Two Hatchets, being the larger of the two, stood a better chance than he. The only advantage he had was that he was calm while Two Hatchets was becoming angrier and angrier. He grasped what he thought was his only chance for survival as he felt his strength beginning to ebb. He began to tease and taunt Two Hatchets with laughing remarks about his inability to carry out his threat to kill him.

"You should have sent your mother or your sister to fight for you. Even an old woman would have done better."

A low, muttering growl from Two Hatchets told him his ploy was working.

"I lied to you, Two Hatchets," he said, "she *was* my woman and when I return to her, she will laugh with me at the weak warrior, Two Hatchets." It was the final straw. Tired, covered with blood, Two Hatchets leaped at him. It was the one thing he had wanted. Stepping quickly to one side, he thrust his knife upward. It caught Two Hatchets low in the belly. With a gasping moan and a look of complete surprise, he fell to the ground.

Panting and exhausted, weak from loss of blood, Josiah knew he was no match for the one who waited. He had to take him by surprise; he had to strike first. Slowly, he worked his way toward the cabin. He was surprised when he found no sign of life as he drew near. He knew he was dripping blood all the way from the hill, but he had no way to stop it until he could get into the cabin. He stood outside the door, but still heard no sign within. Peering around the door, he was even more shocked to find it empty. Crossing the room, he looked out. Two Hatchets' horse was there, the other was gone. Then it came to him. He had seen the final blow, knew that Two Hatchets was dead, and had no desire to meet the same fate. He had ridden away, and, Josiah thought, was on his way home to tell some story to justify what had happened. At least he had a horse on which he could follow Spotted Bear's trail.

As he grew weaker, he searched for something to stop the flow of blood. When he found it, he sat down by the back door where a small pool of blood formed before he could bind the wound.

He rested for a while, but he knew he had to follow soon or he would never be able to find them.

White-hot agony ripped through him as he drew himself up. He was grateful for one thing, the wound was well-bound so the bleeding would soon stop.

He went outside, mounted Two Hatchets' horse and headed in the direction Snow Blossom had been taken, praying he was not too late to save her.

Chapter Twenty-Eight

From the bundle of counting sticks, White Eagle removed another. The bundle had shrunk considerably in size and the number left worried White Eagle. There was still no word or sign from Sun Knife. The days had passed one after the other as everyone watched and waited. All eyes turned toward White Eagle. It was his sister and his blood brother who held the entire village and its chief in expectant suspense.

He placed the bundle of remaining sticks away, hoping Sun Knife would return with Snow Blossom before the day for leaving came. He was contemplating what he would say at the grand council, how he would speak to the chiefs of the other tribes to make them understand his still strong desire for peace. He did not understand the white man's mind and at this time desired the presence of his blood brother to help him weigh his thoughts and his words.

A voice requesting permission to enter broke his reverie and he called out. Running Wolf pushed aside the tepee flap and entered. It took him only a moment to read the dark, unhappy gaze of his host. His eyes fell on the bundle of counting sticks and noticed quickly the small number left.

"The time grows short," he said. "There has still been no word from Sun Knife?"

"No . . . no word."

"Do you believe he will find her?"

"If anyone can find her, it will be Sun Knife."

"White Eagle, what if he does not?"

White Eagle sighed deeply. "If he does not, there will be no way I could get him to speak for peace at the grand council. He will be filled with anger and hate. Until now, I always felt some part of Cade Holliday lived within him. If he loses Snow Blossom forever, he will also lose Cade Holliday. There will be no one left but Sun Knife, who will turn his face away from any thought of peace between us and the whites."

Running Wolf remained quietly thoughtful for a few minutes; then he said, "Gray Bear will stand with you and speak for peace, of this I am sure, but of some of the others . . . Black Kettle and Walking Man, some of the Comanche and Kiowa . . . of these I am not certain."

"I have had word from the village of Sitting Bull and Crazy Horse. It is the first I have known that they, too, will be at the grand council. Sitting Bull may bend toward peace, but I am not too sure about Crazy Horse. He is much younger, and filled with a deep anger toward the white eyes."

"The white man," Running Wolf muttered softly, "how I wish he had never found us."

Amid all this worry and strain his statement struck White Eagle as suddenly amusing.

"Would you like the white man to disappear, and take Summer Rain with him? After all she is white."

Running Wolf chuckled. "I should like them to disappear, but leave Summer Rain with me. I believe I can stand the presence of two such peaceful whites as Rebecca and Summer Rain."

They laughed together, grateful for this mild touch of sanity in a world that was rapidly going out of control.

Rebecca stepped into the tepee in the middle of this pointless laughter and smiled. It was good to hear White Eagle laugh; he had not done so for a long time.

"Has Summer Rain returned with you?" Running Wolf asked.

"She is in the tepee of Dark Cloud. His wife has been ill since the birth of their child."

"But she carries a child, too, and she does too much for everyone else but herself," he replied. "I think I must go and force her to go home or she will find someone else to care for on her way to me."

Rebecca laughed again. "I believe your sympathy is all for yourself, Running Wolf."

He grinned happily. "It is. If I thought I would get away with it, I would keep her in our tepee and never allow her to stray."

"I never thought a warrior would admit such a thing. How

could she stop you from doing so?"

"By looking at me with those green eyes and saying nothing. She has a way of turning my anger into nothing but hot air." He laughed.

Again, White Eagle and Rebecca joined him, pleased in his and Summer Rain's complete happiness with one another.

"I will send word if there is any news of Sun Knife or Snow Blossom," White Eagle said as Running Wolf turned to leave.

Running Wolf nodded and left. He walked the wide pathway between the tepees. After he had passed several, he stopped in front of one. A warrior sat outside in front of a small fire. He had a blanket about him and was peacefully smoking and watching the antics of two young boys who played at war a few feet away. It was simply out of the question for a warrior to go about asking for his wife. His pride would never allow it. To make his mission less obvious he sat down beside the warrior and began to converse about the weather, hunting, arms, and anything else that came to Running Wolf's mind.

In his search for words, Running Wolf missed the mischievous twinkle in the eye of the man he sat beside.

When he could think of nothing else, he came to the point he had been artfully dodging since his arrival. Of course, he came to it in the most roundabout way he could find.

"I have been told, Dark Cloud, that your wife has given you another son."

"Yes, she is a good woman. I have three sons now."

"I only hope my wife will give me a son as strong as yours."

"Ummm," Dark Cloud grunted. "She is good, your woman. Her medicine makes my woman smile again. She is with her now. It is good you came." He chuckled. "She is very tired and you can walk with her to see that she gets safely home."

Running Wolf laughed with him when he finally realized that all his diplomacy had been for nothing and his worry about his wife had been obvious to a man who had had the same feelings only a few hours before.

At that moment, Summer Rain stepped out of the tepee.

"Running Wolf," she said, doing her best to cover the surprise in her voice. "I thought you were hunting."

"I have just returned."

"I will go and warm your food; you must be hungry."

She started to walk away. In a few minutes, Running Wolf caught up with her. She was pleased at the grin on his face, but just a little curious as to what brought it about.

"What is so funny?"

"I have just been told that I should take better care of my wife. 'She carries your child,' he told me, 'and you should not let her do so much.'"

Summer Rain laughed. "I'm as strong as a horse, and I have never felt better in my life." She laid her hand against her belly that still did not show much sign of her burden.

"Little Doe's child is so handsome, Running Wolf."

"But not as handsome as our son will be," he said positively. "Of course, he will look like me."

"Conceited oaf." She laughed. "What if he has my hair and skin and green eyes; will you still take credit for his looks?"

"Of course, am I not the cleverest warrior in the Cheyenne nation to have had the wisdom to have chosen a woman as beautiful as you to be the mother of my children?"

They entered the tepee and she turned to him laughing, to find herself bound against him and being thoroughly and effectively silenced.

"Three days is a long time to be away from you," he said. "You are well?"

"Yes, I'm fine," she replied. "Was your hunting a success?"

"Yes, but we have to do much more before the snow falls or there will not be enough to last the winter."

"The rebuilding is going well. Those whose tepees were destroyed are joined by all, and they have made it a community project. Maybe we will have them all rebuilt by the time the leaves fall and the ones who are sharing can have their own again. Sometimes, I feel guilty that we have a place all to ourselves."

"Well"—he grinned—"if you insist on sharing, Red Blanket has a daughter of about sixteen summers. I'm sure she wouldn't mind . . . ugh," he grunted as a well-aimed fist found a sensitive spot on his body.

"You wicked man. She smiles at you constantly. Have you been giving thoughts to returning her smiles. If you are, think well. My skinning knife is sharp and under those circumstances, I wouldn't hesitate to use it."

He laughed, his eyes alight with the pleasure of knowing she was jealous of him. He drew her tighter against him.

"I am not a jealous man, nor am I foolish. Why would I sacrifice the most complete meal at home for a handful of scraps outside? But it is good to know you are jealous."

"I am not jealous," she claimed as she laughed in return. "But I am possessive. You are mine, and I will share you with no one. I know by now of your people's customs to take more than one wife, and if you care at all for her well-being, do not bring her to this tepee."

His dark eyes held hers. "You are the only woman I want. I have given no thought to another since the first day I saw you here when Sun Knife married. I loved you then and I love you now. It has been difficult enough to capture you; I will take no chances on losing you."

She raised her arms to twine about his neck. "I know," she said softly. "I love you, Running Wolf, I love you."

His lips claimed hers and he heard her murmured sound of pleasure as her warm body melted against his.

Every homecoming, to him, seemed to be warmer and more pleasant each time. He wanted to drink deeply of the joy of it. It was as if every sense in his body was always aware of her. He knew she could walk into his presence at any time and even if his back was turned he seemed to know she was there. A vibrant current lingered between them; he was constantly aware of it. The flame of love licked through him like wildfire.

"You are hungry," she protested mildly as he drew her with him toward their couch. He sat down and drew her gently down onto his lap.

"My hunger is not for food," he whispered as his mouth again claimed hers. His hand touched and caressed a soft warm thigh. She sighed contentedly and nestled more closely against him.

It was always his pleasure to undress her slowly, to linger over each touch, each kiss, until he drove her desire to a frantic pitch. He had a way of drawing from her the deepest fiery need, and holding her enmeshed in it until it drove both of them wild.

He had the patience of an expert and he used every ounce of it to drive her senses to the brink of abandon. Warm lips traced patterns over her body and he held her as she reached for him. He would carry her higher and higher, lift her to a need that matched his own. He heard with exuberant pleasure her uncontrollable words of love, felt her body seek his in a blaze of desire. Still he held her away; still his mouth and hands lifted her farther and farther, beyond thought, beyond knowing, beyond anything but the two of them. She cried out his name again and again; her hands caressed the length of his body. He could feel the pressure as they slid down the heavy muscles of his back to his hips to urge him within her.

When his mind and his body could bear no more of the sweet agony, when the need of her seemed to explode deep within him, he allowed himself the final and heart-stopping joy of joining their bodies. Slowly, with easing sensuous movements, he sank into the depths of her. He heard her ragged gasping breath as he began to move within her slowly . . . slowly until neither of them knew any longer of the existence of the rest of the world. In a breathless voice, she begged for more; her body lifted to meet his, demanding and urgent. The rhythm slowly increased as they released their final hold on all reality and tumbled together into the flames of complete and utter surrender.

Stilled, they lay together, bodies entwined until they regained some control over their minds and bodies. Neither could move, neither wanted to. They did not speak, there was no need. Each of them knew that they had found in each other the total of their love and their pleasure for a lifetime.

After a time, he stirred and pulled the fur robe about her, thinking she slept. She lay with her eyes closed so he tried to move from the bed without disturbing her. As he did, her arm encircled him and she nestled closer to him.

"Don't go yet," she whispered.

He smiled as he lay back down beside her and drew her into the circle of his arms. Her head rested on his chest and her long slender legs entwined with his. He lay still, drawing all the pleasure from feeling her need of him. Absently, he caressed her hair with his fingers.

"What are you thinking?" she asked softly.

He chuckled lightly. "I have no strength left for thinking."

Playfully, she squeezed her arm about him. "Good, then Red Blanket's daughter can smile for nothing."

Their laughter blended as he hugged her tightly to him.

"I was thinking of Sun Knife and wondering how the gods can give me everything to make me happy and yet take so much from him. I grieve for him at the loss of Snow Blossom. I know how empty it would be for me if you were gone."

"Yes," she answered gently, and as they lay contented together, her mind, too, went to Snow Blossom and where she was now.

Little Mountain pulled his horse to a stop beneath the shade of a grove of trees. It was obvious from all the signs that they had camped there previously. She was heartened by the fact that when he lifted her from the horse, his eyes refused to meet hers and he seemed troubled by the events that had just occurred.

"Untie me and let me go, Little Mountain. You know what you are doing is wrong. The strength of my brother's and my husband's hands will be stopped if you return me to my people. Our villages have lived in peace for a long time. Would you end that now by doing something foolish?"

"Be quiet, woman," he snapped.

She was quiet for a few minutes, watching him. He was uncomfortable and aware of her scrutiny. It was also clear to her that he had no taste for holding a woman against her will, no matter who gave the order.

He was a young man, not much older than she, she surmised. He was a handsome, well-built young warrior who had obviously just acquired his status as a man and a warrior. His pride was at war with his responsibility and respect to his brother.

"Is it wrong for you to talk to me; does your brother forbid it?"

Stung to anger, he snarled at her. "No one forbids Little Mountain to do as he pleases." He doubled his fist and struck his chest. "I am a warrior! No one tells me which path to take or to whom I can speak."

"We may be here for some time. I don't know the reasons for all that has happened," she lied. "Can you tell me why Two Hatchets wants to kill the white man?"

Despite the fact that she knew the story well, she feigned interest while he told her the story of the promised marriage, of Josiah and Two Moons, of the fight, and of his older brother's death.

"It seems your older brother fought with honor and lost. If the chiefs gave them permission to leave, why did Two Hatchets follow?"

"Two Hatchets would avenge our brother's death!"

"How old were you then?"

His face turned away from her.

"You were a boy. If that is true, you are following the wrong path. Two Hatchets would lead you to a path of death to ease his own jealousy!"

She knew she had struck the right place when his eyes snapped back to her and she could clearly read the doubts and fears in his eyes.

"He was, wasn't he . . . jealous of his own brother? He, too, wanted Two Moons. He would kill the white man, not for his brother, but for Two Moons and his own black heart. Will you allow him to cause a war between our people for such a reason?"

He rose angrily to his feet and walked away from her. He began to slowly build a fire, but she could see his mind was deep in thought. She had planted the seeds of these ideas and now she must wait for them to grow. She only hoped it would happen before anyone else came. She prayed Josiah would win the fight, but against the odds of two to one, she doubted it. If she could get him to take her to his village before Two Hatchets came, at least she stood a better chance.

"If you will untie me, I will prepare you some food. It is safe, there is no place for me to run. I would not survive long out there alone."

Knowing she was right, he came to her and cut the bonds that held her; yet he warily watched her as she went about preparing him a meal from the supplies he carried in his saddle pouches.

She began to talk to him in a relaxed and easy way as if she were unafraid of her situation and was rewarded by watching him unbend and occasionally smile.

She told him of Tekata and White Eagle and watched his eyes register interest and dawning respect. She told him of Sun Knife and his medicine, and slowly he began to unbend. He was a good-natured boy and his brother had drawn him into this situation by shaming him, telling him that he was a warrior afraid to fight for the spirit of his dead brother.

"Tell me of your older brother," she asked gently.

He began to talk and it soon became evident to her that although he had loved and respected his older brother with the admiration of a child, it was not so with Two Hatchets, whom he followed because he was forced to save his pride. At his age, pride was a large and very vulnerable thing.

The time passed and it became clear to them both that too much of it had passed and that neither Two Hatchets nor Josiah had appeared.

Nervous and unprepared to take charge, he was emotionally ready to accept an idea.

"Maybe you should take me back to the cabin. Maybe they are all three dead. We should see if they need our help."

"Two Hatchets said to wait here—we will wait."

She shrugged and remained silent, but she knew once he had the idea he would not easily let go of it.

As the time went on and on, they both knew that none of the three they had left behind were going to join them. He was in a position now where he had to be the one to make the choice. She remained silent, praying he would make the right decision. Finally, he turned to her.

"Come, woman, we will go and see what has happened. My brother may be wounded and need my help."

She could have cried out in delight, but she kept her face still. She rose swiftly, and in a short time they were mounted and on their way back.

They had ridden for only a few minutes when Little Mountain pulled his horse to a halt. She stopped beside him and in a few seconds they heard the sound of an approaching horse. He grasped the reins of her horse and drew her after him to the shade of some trees where they could be hidden from the path.

The sounds of the horse drew closer and closer and a cry almost passed her lips when Josiah rode into sight.

Little Mountain, armed as few Indians were, with the white man's gun, drew it from the buckskin shield that hung on the side of his horse.

"Speak one word, woman," he hissed quietly, "and you are both dead."

Josiah was almost beside him when he kicked his horse sharply. It leaped from the shelter of the trees directly into Josiah's path. It was so sudden that Josiah's horse reared. Wounded and unprepared, Josiah fell from the horse and landed with a solid thud on the hard ground.

It was a difficult thing, but he staggered to his feet to look up into the face of Little Mountain and the barrel of the gun, pointed at his heart. He remained motionless, waiting for the death blow.

"My brother?"

"He is dead."

There was still no sign of Little Mountain's intent. "Where is Spotted Bear?"

"He ran, like a coward."

Little Mountain chewed his lip thoughtfully. His brother should have a proper burial, yet he could not leave these two or they would escape. It would be a sad tale to return and tell his father and mother, he decided and motioned to Snow Blossom.

"Tie him. We will go to my village and I will send someone to get my brother's body to give it proper burial."

Obediently, Snow Blossom dismounted and took the rope Little Mountain handed her. Trying to be as careful of his wounds as she could, she tied him.

"I will care for your wound as soon as we make a camp," she whispered. He smiled at her, but before he could reply, Little Mountain ordered her to mount. Forcing the two of them ahead of him, they began the journey to Little Mountain's village.

It was close to sundown and Snow Blossom knew they would

have to camp soon. She watched Josiah as he weaved in the saddle, weak from the loss of blood.

The sun had completely set when Little Mountain called a halt and prepared to camp for the night. After building a fire and preparing food, Snow Blossom went to Josiah's side and began to care for him. Ripping the shirt from his arm, she washed and bound the wound. She worked, unaware that both men watched her with conflicting emotions.

"You can still tend me after what I have done to you, Snow Blossom? Most women would not be able to forgive me. You could have him leave me here to die."

He watched her, and they were both unaware that Little Mountain, too, waited for her answer.

"No, Josiah, I could leave no man here to die. It would not make me feel any better about what has happened to see you dead. I hate what has happened, but I understand why it did. When we get to Little Mountain's village and explain to his chief what has happened, he will let us go."

"No, my dear. You, maybe, but me never. I am the man who has killed two of his sons. Do you think he can forgive me? No, he will kill me."

"No! Josiah, I will ask for your life. He will listen to my words."

Josiah sighed. "You are a kind and very compassionate woman, but you are no fool. You and I both know it would take a miracle to soften the chief's heart toward me."

"Josiah—"

"Snow Blossom, please. I . . . I don't mind. I am not afraid of death. Sometimes it seems welcome. I only regret what heartbreak I have caused you. I am glad it has worked out this way. If you get back to your village, remember me without too much pain. It is better this way."

Tears stung her eyes and she turned away and went to her blanket; there she muffled her tears and cried until she slept.

Little Mountain had been listening and watching. He was thoroughly and unhappily confused. Two Hatchets had made Josiah seem a bloodthirsty monster and he had thought this woman the same. Now, her gentle words to a man who had, it seemed, done her a great wrong, and his words, sent him into thoughts he was emotionally unprepared to handle. Angry at his own thoughts, he, too, rolled in his blanket and sought sleep, preferably without dreams.

The morning sun rimmed the horizon when Snow Blossom woke. She found that Little Mountain was already awake. She moved to Josiah's side to find that her care the night before was good. He had no fever, the arm seemed to bother him less, and he had a warm smile for her.

Little Mountain watched as Snow Blossom gathered sticks for the fire and began to prepare some food. He decided to see to the hobbled horses. He walked to them and reached down to loosen the length of rope that hobbled them.

He had wondered why the horses had been so jittery and frightened. They moved restlessly as though frightened. When he reached for the rope he found out in one shocked second why. The snake struck like a bolt of lightning, and he felt its fangs sink deep into his arm before he could shake it free and move rapidly away from it.

Snow Blossom heard his startled cry as did Josiah. They saw him shake the huge snake free from him. Snow Blossom leaped up and ran to his side.

"Little Mountain!"

"Shishinowuts," he said in a rasping whisper, "the snake with the rattles." Quickly, Snow Blossom grasped the handle of the sharp hunting knife he carried. She cut away his sleeve. Little Mountain was now on his knees. She took a piece of the sleeve and tied it above the bite; then she took the knife and cut deeply into the bite. She lowered her head and sucked at the wound. She spat and sucked again and again.

Little Mountain lay on the ground, his face bathed in sweat and his breathing labored. She knew the poison was already in his system and that only prayers and his own strong constitution and youth could save him.

She ran back to Josiah and slashed at the bonds that held him. "Quickly! Help me! We can save him!"

Josiah got to his feet, and together they dragged Little Mountain's half-conscious form back to the fire.

"He is strong," she said. "I have seen others live with the bite of the snake."

Josiah watched her as she labored over the boy who lay still and quiet beside her. She wrapped him in a blanket and cooled his fever-wracked body with water. His arm was now almost double its size and Josiah could see that his breathing was shallow and forced. Hour after hour, she worked. Again and again she reopened the wound and let it bleed, then rebound it.

Through the day, they listened to his restless babbling and held his tormented body still.

When night came, he was quiet, but Josiah knew it was because he had reached the crucial point and was as near death as he ever would be.

Snow Blossom sat beside him through the entire night, and Josiah could see that often she prayed. He was fascinated by the fact that this man was the one who held her captive, might have even taken her life, yet when she had a chance to escape him and let him die, she chose to remain at his side and help him.

After the sun had risen the next day, Josiah went to her side. Little Mountain lay very still, his face ashen and his breathing slow and very quiet.

"Will he live?"

"Yes, I think so."

"Thanks to you. Why, Snow Blossom?"

"Why what?"

"Why did you work so hard to save him when he was your enemy. He might have been responsible for your death."

She smiled at him, softening the words she spoke. "He was not my enemy, Josiah. He was only following his brother in vengeance. It was easy to see his heart was good and that he would not choose to kill me."

"You were so sure?" he asked gently. Again the quiet smile flickered in her eyes.

"As sure as I was of you."

"I envy your warrior." He chuckled. "I wonder if he knows how lucky he is."

She laughed with him. "When I return to my husband's side, I shall remind him again and again of my great value."

Slowly, Little Mountain's eyes flickered open. His deep delirium had passed and Snow Blossom could see rational thought in his eyes. He looked from one to the other, then tried to rise. Snow Blossom put both her hands on him and pressed him gently back.

"Rest, Little Mountain; you have not the strength to rise. The worst part has passed. You will be well soon. In a few days, we will be able to return to your village."

He obeyed, his eyes filled with wonder. "You could have left me to die. You could have gone from here."

"No," Snow Blossom said softly. "No, Little Mountain, we could not have left you to die, as you would not have left either of us had we been bitten. Rest, Little Mountain, and when you are well, we will return to your village with you, not as captives but as friends. Maybe your father will remember that Josiah helped save the life of one son and will forgive him for the deaths of the others—deaths he did not want."

Little Mountain looked at Josiah, who returned his gaze. Then he closed his eyes and said softly as he drifted off into a deep exhausted sleep. "Yes . . . I will speak with my father. I will tell him . . . all."

Josiah and Snow Blossom exchanged glances, wondering what he meant.

Little Mountain slept all that day and all the following night. When he woke the next morning, he was weak, but both Snow Blossom and Josiah could see he was mending and that soon his strength would return. Still, it was over four more days before they could begin the trip home. They resumed the journey in easy stages. Both Josiah and Snow Blossom noticed Little Mountain's prolonged silence as if he weighed something deep in his mind.

They traveled for almost three days before Little Mountain told them they were in the territory of his village and would be seeing it soon.

Nearing the end of the day, they crested a hill, and Snow Blossom could see a lone tepee in the distance. It was a surprise to her to see one tepee alone when Little Mountain's village was so close. She pointed toward it and questioned Little Mountain.

"It belongs to a woman who is not of our village. We know her; she came to us many years ago. She chooses to live as she does; yet I and many of the warriors have hunted and given her food. She lives with her child, and they would keep their past life to themselves. We respect their ways and do not question them. If it is a path they choose to walk, then we must not interfere."

"How old is the child?"

"Maybe ten summers."

"Does he not hate to live alone without others to learn from and hunt with?"

"He has many friends in our village, but he is a boy who keeps much to himself. He cares well for his mother and if he chose, they both would be well-accepted in our village."

"Can we stop and speak to them?"

"If you wish."

Snow Blossom did not herself understand her urge to stop and see the woman and her child. She only knew she suddenly felt it was right.

They rode up to the tepee and Little Mountain called out to the ones within.

"Tzia, it is Little Mountain."

The woman who stepped out of the tepee was still very beautiful; yet hard lonely years had taken their toll of her. Snow Blossom smiled at her and Tzia smiled in return.

"Come, Little Mountain, you and your friends are welcome to eat at our fire."

They dismounted and walked toward her; Tzia turned and called within. "Little Eagle, come, we have guests."

The flap of the tepee was pushed aside and a young boy stepped out. Snow Blossom stopped in her tracks and the smile on her face froze as she looked into the blue eyes and smiling face of a young Sun Knife.

Chapter Twenty-Nine

If her eyes widened and her face expressed knowledge it did not pass the quick gaze of Tzia. She sensed immediately a hand from her past that had reached out to touch her.

Snow Blossom gazed silently at the boy. He was tall for his age and his crystal-blue eyes seemed shadowed as if he were well used to keeping his thoughts and emotions bottled within him. His body, though slim, gave promise of the same long, lean, muscular one she remembered so vividly. His features were even, and when he hesitantly smiled in return to Snow Blossom, it was a wide easy smile that brightened his otherwise solemn features.

"This is my son, Little Eagle," Tzia said, her voice alternately possessive and frightened. It was then that the burning sensation of truth crowded all thought from Snow Blossom's mind except the fact that she was looking at Sun Knife's son. Who else but a woman who had been raised in the same village as Sun Knife, known him as a child, and had watched him grow, would recognize the father in the boy. Her mind seemed stunned with the recognition and she hardly realized that the boy had spoken to her.

"Today I hunted," he said proudly. "And my mother has two fat rabbits roasting."

"Wonderful," she replied. "I am very hungry, and I know Josiah and Little Mountain are, too."

She said the words to the boy, but from the corner of her eyes she watched Tzia's face. Without doubt, she recognized the emotion that crossed it—fear.

The two men and the boy went in first as was common custom. The women followed, avoiding each other's eyes.

The meal was good and Snow Blossom listened to the happy laughter between Little Mountain and Little Eagle. Again it was obvious to her that the boy was well-liked and even, at his young age, respected by Little Mountain.

Tzia was silent throughout most of the meal, speaking only to answer Snow Blossom's questions or to follow a request for more food from one of the men.

It was dark before the meal was over and Little Mountain rose.

"If we travel for an hour or so, we can be at my village. Even in the dark, I can smell home." He laughed.

Josiah rose also from his seat, but turned questioning eyes to Snow Blossom when she remained seated. He did not know that her mind was searching frantically for a reason to stay longer and a way to speak to Tzia alone. It was Little Eagle who gave her the answer.

"But, Little Mountain," he protested, "can you not stay one night? I would show you the horse I captured—by myself. If you stay this night, I will ride to your village with you tomorrow."

It was as close to pleading as he would go.

Both Josiah and Little Mountain looked at Snow Blossom, who was relieved to find the way. "It would be better to stay. Our horses are tired and so are we. One more night makes no difference."

Josiah was surprised, but knowing Snow Blossom as well as he did now, he realized there was more reason behind her words than he knew.

Tzia had been standing very still, and suddenly a look of pain crossed her face and her shoulders slumped in resignation. It was recognition of something she had always known would come eventually. She had always put off answering Little Eagle's questions about his father. She had eased her own mind by thinking that if the gods wanted him to know, they would find the way. She was a wise woman who recognized the will of the gods when she saw it.

She prepared room for them all to stay, then she and Snow Blossom rolled in their blankets, away from the area of the fire around which the men were talking. Tzia listened to her son's deep voice that had only this summer broken from that of a boy to that of a man. She wept silent tears when she heard him, for she knew she had had him for as long as she could. She knew the day had come when he would find his father. He had always respected her and loved her; yet she had known he longed for the father he had never seen. All was quiet finally and the men slept. When she was sure all were asleep, Tzia rose quietly from her bed. She did not have to waken Snow Blossom for she had been waiting, too. Quietly, she rose and followed Tzia outside. They stood in the pale moonlight facing each other.

"Did you wish to talk with me, Tzia?"

"Tell me who you are," Tzia requested.

"I am Snow Blossom, daughter of Chief Tekata of the Cheyenne, sister to Chief White Eagle and wife to Sun Knife, medicine man of the Cheyenne."

"Sun Knife," Tzia whispered softly and her eyes saw the handsome blue-eyed brave who had changed her life and given her the great gift of Little Eagle.

Snow Blossom remained silent, waiting for what she knew must come. Then softly, Tzia told her, told her of that hot and beautiful summer when she had found love for the first and last time. She told of their days together and how she had seen Sun Knife's bright and shining future. She told her of the day she had gone away carrying his son and leaving him the future she knew he should have.

"You are braver than I, Tzia," Snow Blossom said softly, "I do not think I would have had the courage to leave him."

"Have you borne him any children?"

"No, not yet, but I hope to give him sons. The Great Spirit has not willed it yet."

"You knew Little Eagle was Sun Knife's son?"

"Could I have mistaken him anywhere? He looks like his father, and his blue eyes could have been the gift of no other."

"He is a good son, obedient and well-mannered."

"Yes, you have raised him well."

Tzia's chin lifted proudly. "He loves and respects me."

"Why should he not? Are you not the one who gave him life?"

Tzia's eyes filled with tears. "And yet," she said softly, "he longs to have and to know his father. He hasn't said so to me, but I can see it in his eyes when he sees the others with their fathers, and I hear it in his voice when he talks to them."

"What will you do, Tzia?"

"Do? I will do what your coming has forced me to do. I will surrender my son."

"No, Tzia. You must not surrender him. Is it wrong to let him know his father, to share him with us? We would not take him from you. Your sacrifice and love have earned you more than that, but does Sun Knife not have the right to see him and to offer him the love of a father? Does Little Eagle not deserve that, too?" Snow Blossom's voice was gentle, and this gentleness was what touched Tzia.

"What can I say to Little Eagle? Can I tell him of my past? Would I not shame him to let him know what I was? He is young and filled with pride."

"We will tell him nothing."

"He will question. He is a very curious boy and would find the answers to his questions. It would crush him."

For some time Snow Blossom thought, then she said to Tzia, "We will tell him this: when you were young, you lived in the village of Tekata. You and Sun Knife met and fell in love. Your mother was from our tribe, but your father was not. One day, he became angry with Tekata and took your mother and you away. You did not know you were carrying him at the time. On the way home, your father and mother became ill and died. You were afraid to go back to Tekata's village and so you made your home here for your father's people were, in your heart, partly responsible. You gave birth to him and have raised him here, until now, afraid to take him back to Tekata's village. Tell him of his father. Ask him then if he would like to see him. Tell him he can come back to see you often. It would be good for him to know he can have both his mother and his father."

"You . . . you would not keep him from me?"

"No, it would be unfair to all of us. I could not take your place as mother, and Sun Knife would never want it so."

In the moonlight, Snow Blossom could see the crystal tears on her face. For her life would never be different, but now she could offer him the love and pride of his father and a tribe to which he would belong. She had always known of his longing and his loneliness. Little Eagle was young enough to feel the need of roots, of a sense of belonging. He needed now a man to teach him the way of the world. And what better man than his father, a father who was strong and well-loved in his village? She looked at Snow Blossom warm and compassionate. "When I left Sun Knife, it was because I knew he was meant for a woman such as you. His heart must be filled with love and pride in you. I hope you give him the sons he needs, and I hope you can make room in your heart for my son."

"Tzia, what do you plan to do?"

"As Little Eagle grows older, he will begin to question. One day, if he keeps coming here, he will find out the truth. It . . . it is best he does not see me again. I have always known that one day he would go. You would make the kind of mother a boy such as he should have. I give him to you and Sun Knife. I would not break his pride and shame him. I would always have him remember me with love."

"But he will return."

"And he will not find me."

"But it will be painful for him."

"Painful for him and for me, but better for him in the future."

"You have much love, Tzia, to give your son so much, and to be hurt so badly."

"I have lived a life of quiet pain, always knowing, always fearing the truth. Now it is here and I must face it. Little Eagle is my life. I would have him happy and grow tall and strong with pride and love. It is a thing I know now I cannot offer. He does not know I have given myself to many men to get the food and things we need to live. The pain would be much more for me if I were to look into his eyes one day and see hatred and disrespect. This hurt," she whispered, "will be much less than that."

Snow Blossom went to her and put her arms about the weeping woman.

"I can only promise you that he will have all the love and care that we can give, and one day, when he is man enough to face it, I will tell him of the sacrifice of a mother who loved him too much to let him be hurt."

They talked for a long time. Tzia told Snow Blossom all she knew of her son, his likes and dislikes. His ways were well-known to Snow Blossom after this. Snow Blossom in return told her all that had happened to Sun Knife since she had gone. They laughed and cried together and formed an alliance that would help mold the boy who quietly slept.

The next morning, Tzia took her son and left the tepee. Both Little Mountain and Josiah were surprised when Snow Blossom said they would wait for their return.

It was over two hours, but when they came back, Snow Blossom could see the light of excitement in Little Eagle's eyes and the quiet sadness in his mother's. He came to Snow Blossom.

"My mother has told me the story of my birth. She says that you know my father and will take me to see him?"

"Yes, that is so. Will you come with us now?"

"Yes, I would be grateful if you would let me travel with you. After I meet my father I will return for my mother."

Tzia and Snow Blossom exchanged glances.

"Did your mother tell you I am your father's wife?"

"Yes, but she could be his second wife," he said hopefully. "My mother works hard and cooks well. She would make the work easier for you. I will be an obedient son to you, too. I promise. Do you think my father will consider this?"

"Yes . . . yes he would consider it," Snow Blossom said softly.

The boy seemed overjoyed and gathered his small possessions together quickly. He laughed at his mother's tears.

"Do not cry, Mother. I shall return soon."

"No." She smiled through her tears. "I will not weep, for I know you will be well, my Son."

She would not embarrass him by embracing him in front of others, but she could not resist one last touch. She reached out and placed her hand on his shoulder. He looked up at her, a small frown between his blue eyes, as if he were strangely aware she was saying a final good-by.

"We must go, Little Eagle," Little Mountain said.

Tzia stood in front of her tepee until they disappeared; then she went inside, threw herself on her bed, and cried.

When the four of them rode into Little Mountain's village, everyone watched and as they stopped in front of Chief Long

Bow's tepee all eyes were upon them.

Snow Blossom, Josiah, and Little Eagle remained outside while Little Mountain requested permission to enter his father's tepee.

Inside, he began to explain to his father all that had happened. Chief Long Bow listened quietly, and when Little Mountain was finished he stepped outside to face the three who waited. He gazed at Josiah.

"So we meet again, white one."

"I do not wish it to be so," Josiah replied. "I did not search out your son to kill him. He found me."

"Yes, I know. Little Mountain has told me. He has also told me how you saved his life when you had the chance to leave him to die. Long Bow does not forget the gift of the life of his only son."

He turned to Snow Blossom. "He has told me of you also. I know of your father, Chief Tekata, and your brother, White Eagle. The name of your husband, Sun Knife, has been sung in all the villages. We know of the light-eyed warrior." His eyes fell on Little Eagle, who gazed at him in wide-eyed admiration. "And this is the son of the light-eyed medicine man?"

For the first time in his young life, Little Eagle's chest swelled with pride as he answered, "Yes, I am the son of Sun Knife." He could almost have cried out with the joy that filled him.

Again Chief Long Bow's eyes came back to Josiah. Their gazes held for interminable minutes as Chief Long Bow read the depths of his thoughts.

"My son, Little Mountain, is now my only son. To you, I owe the deaths of my other two. I weigh this with the thought that I also owe you the life of Little Mountain. The debt is paid, Josiah Tucker. You are free to go with your friends, for the value of the life of Little Mountain is very great, and I would take it and set free the spirits of my other two."

Josiah breathed a sigh of relief. "I am grateful, Chief Long Bow. I would have wished that none of this had happened. Now, I seek only to go in peace."

"Yes, go in peace. You return to the village of White Eagle?"

"Yes. I have to face another and ask his forgiveness for a great wrong I have done him."

"Seven of my braves and I will travel with you. A great council has been asked by the other tribes. We would meet and speak of the paths to peace. Chief White Eagle has asked me to come."

"I will travel with you, my Father?" Little Mountain said swiftly.

"Yes, my Son, you will ride by my side. I would have you go to the council and listen to the chiefs. One day, you will be chief of this village and it is best you know all of your friends and your enemies."

"When do we leave?" Josiah asked.

"In three days. It will give us enough time to get to White Eagle's village before the counting sticks are gone."

Chief Long Bow made them comfortable to wait out the three days. Snow Blossom took the time to become closer to Little Eagle. The closer she drew, the more she could see Sun Knife in his thoughts, beliefs, and loves.

By the time they were prepared to leave, Snow Blossom and Little Eagle were becoming friends. Friends enough, she hoped, to help soften the blow when he returned one day to find his mother gone from his life.

Sun Knife and Long Arrow stood and looked down at the body of the man neither of them knew.

"He is Kiowa," Long Arrow said, a frown on his brow. "He is a long way from home."

"And where is Josiah and Snow Blossom? This is the place we were told they would be."

"Let us look around for more sign. Maybe then we can tell what has happened here."

"Let us prepare him for burial. It is not right a man should be left for the animals."

Long Arrow nodded. They wrapped Two Hatchets' body in a blanket, built a small scaffold in a nearby tree, and put him in his final resting place, facing the place the sun would set. Then they set about studying the area to try to piece together some of what had happened here, and where Snow Blossom and Josiah might have gone.

It took them several hours before they stood together and discussed what they had found.

"Three of them left here," Long Arrow said.

"Yes, Josiah, Snow Blossom, and . . . who?"

"Ummm, we do not know that. It might have been three warriors that came with the Kiowa. They may have taken Snow Blossom and Josiah as prisoners and forced them to ride double."

Sun Knife sighed. "That could be so. Shall we follow the trail?"

"No. Many days ride from here is the village of Chief Long Bow. He is Kiowa. It may be the tribe from which these came. The tracks go in that direction. We could take the chance and go there. It would save much time. If this is the place they were taken, we would lose many days if we slowly followed their trail."

"Will he meet us in peace?"

"We have been at peace with his village for a long time."

"Good, let us go there then. The faster we go the sooner I can taste the blood of Josiah Tucker."

"Sun Knife," Long Arrow said softly, "for all you know by the time we get there, they may have already tasted it."

"And Snow Blossom?"

"The women of the Cheyenne are known everywhere for their beauty and ability. Snow Blossom would be of much value to one of them as a wife."

"She would never go to one."

"With or without her consent, one of them could take her to his tepee. We must be prepared to face such a thing. If we do find her there, you may have to fight one or many warriors for her."

"I would fight the entire nation for her. I only hope they have not killed Josiah Tucker. I have other plans for him. I want him to die slowly as he remembers what he has done to earn this reward."

Long Arrow knew no words would change Sun Knife's white-hot anger at the man who had stolen his wife. Maybe, he hoped, if they found Snow Blossom alive and well, he could help ease some of the anger, at least ease it enough so that he would not kill. Long Arrow knew that Sun Knife was, at heart, a healer not a cold killer. He would do his best to stop him from becoming one, for it would injure him more than anyone.

They left the remains of the cabin and the unknown warrior and headed in the direction of the village. Without need to follow the trail signs, they moved more rapidly. Sun Knife only stopped when he could see the pace was too much for Long Arrow, and he bore his impatience stoically when the need came. They camped at night only when it was too dark to travel any farther. They rose before the sun came up. Going at this pace, it was not many days before they rode over the rise of the hill and saw the lone tepee that occupied the valley before them.

As they drew closer to the tepee they were aware of the air of abandonment and loneliness about it. They stopped outside and called out to whoever was within, but no sound of movement came to them. The fire outside the tepee was cold, and when they finally entered it was to find the tepee deserted and stripped of everything.

"Whoever was here, left in a hurry and meant to travel very fast. It is odd that a family would not take their tepee, especially one as good as this one," Sun Knife said.

"Something bad must have happened, first to make a family live alone this close to a village, and then to leave it in such haste as to leave behind something of such value."

They left the tepee and rode away, but before they left the valley, Sun Knife stopped his horse and looked back at the tepee. A wave of unbelievable sadness seemed to touch him like a breath of wind. He remained motionless, held by an emotion he could not understand. Had Snow Blossom been there? Is that why he felt so, did her presence linger? Was she well? Had she given up hope that he would ever find her? As these thoughts flowed through his mind, other more bitter ones followed. Was Josiah still with her or had others captured them both? Determinedly, he shook himself free of these evil thoughts and turned to look at Long Arrow, whose gaze was gentle and filled with understanding.

Now that they knew the village was near, they rode a little

faster. Yet it was over half a day before the sight of a cluster of tepees came into view. It was not long before, to the surprised look of the tribe, they rode into the outer circle of the tepees and toward the tepee of the chief.

They stopped and dismounted, but before they could speak, the tepee flap was pushed aside and a woman of undetermined age stepped out.

"If you seek Chief Long Bow, he is not here."

"We seek a white man and a Cheyenne woman," Sun Knife said. "They would have come from the direction we did. She is young and very beautiful. He is tall and some years older than I. We have followed their trail here. Have you or any of your tribe seen them?"

She watched him through dark intelligent eyes and heard the hopeful sound in his words.

"You speak of the young woman, Snow Blossom, daughter of the chief of the Cheyenne and the white trapper, Josiah Tucker?"

Sun Knife could have shouted for joy, and had to restrain himself from grabbing her and shaking speedier answers from her. Long Arrow was the first to speak.

"Snow Blossom is the sister to our chief, White Eagle, and she is wife to this one, Sun Knife, our medicine man. She was stolen from him by the white soldiers and given to the trapper. We have followed their trail many days. Sun Knife would find his wife and meet the man who has taken her. Was she captured and brought here by force or did Josiah bring her here himself?"

"It is a strange thing," she answered.

"Strange, why?" Sun Knife questioned.

"If she was taken from you by the white trapper, why would they come here freely, and then consent to go to the village of White Eagle again?"

Sun Knife and Long Arrow exchanged surprised looks. "Will you explain to me what happened when they came?" Sun Knife requested.

She explained Josiah's and Snow Blossom's arrival with Little Mountain, going into explicit detail on every event that had taken place since Little Mountain and Two Hatchets had gone in search of Josiah. "Your chief and the chiefs of many other tribes have sent word of the gathering of a great peace council. They asked Chief Long Bow and many of his braves to come. The white trapper and your woman spoke with our chief for a long time; then they all prepared to travel together. It has been many days since they have gone, but I know they went to the village of White Eagle."

"I do not understand this, Long Arrow."

"I do not either."

"If he comes there, he knows what will await him."

"Yet he comes. The woman would have no reason to lie. To me, her eyes spoke the truth."

"Yes, I believed her, but it is beyond sensible reasoning. He knows that return to our village means death to him. Why would he be such a fool?"

"We will not discover his reasons if we remain here. She has told us the council will be called soon. If we try to go to our village we might be too late. Why do we not go to the place of the council and await them."

Sun Knife turned to the woman. "Where is the council to be held?"

"The ones who knew the location have already gone. The rest of us were never told exactly where, except it is to be held on the banks of the great river."

"But that could be anywhere; the great river is many miles long."

"Yes, warrior," she answered softly, "but neither I nor any of the others left here know exactly where on its banks the council will meet. If you would find your woman soon, maybe it would be best if you traveled as swiftly as you can and pray the gods get you there in time. It is rumored that many seek war. If the white soldiers hear of the council, they may come again, and this time they will destroy more."

"Sun Knife, she is right. We will travel fast. If we reach home before they leave, we might be able to warn Chief Long Bow of Josiah's treachery, for if we do not, he might find a way yet to rid himself of the one person who might warn Chief Long Bow and his braves, Snow Blossom. This might be another trap to extinguish another village as White Eagle's almost was."

"You are nearly exhausted, Long Arrow."

"I am strong enough yet for what must be done."

"The travel will be very difficult. It must be fast, with little rest, little water, and little food."

Long Arrow chuckled. "And who was the man who taught this arrogant warrior to travel so? Do you think I am too old to remember my own teachings? Insolent one, when we reenter our village, it will be I who will be dragging you, for the young still do not know as much and some of them are soft from the white man's ways."

Sun Knife grinned at the sparkle in Long Arrow's eyes. "Then I shall do my best to keep up with you. Shall we go?"

It was a very long and somewhat silent trip. Each of them reserved his strength to concentrate on keeping himself from giving in to the heat, the hunger, and the thirst such a trip entailed.

What they carried in their saddle pouches had to carry them through the day and if both of them were not too tired, they would hunt for a rabbit, or something edible they could shoot in the short time between when they stopped and the night fell.

Over and over, Sun Knife turned the idea in his mind as to why Josiah would travel in a large circle and come back to the place where he had committed such a crime. He wondered what had happened to Snow Blossom since she had been taken. Thoughts he could hardly bear crossed his mind and he deliberately blotted them out. He knew Snow Blossom too well. She was the kind of strong-minded woman who could not easily turn from the one she loved, and he was as sure of her love as he was of his own heartbeat. The thought opened his mind to much more pleasant ones, and he clung to them, savored them, and relived them until sleep found him.

As they began to enter familiar territory he felt the urgency that drew him home, but with it lingered a strange uncomfortable feeling, as if something unusual was about to happen.

In the distance, he saw the tepees of his village. He knew that the same moment he was aware of them, they knew of him.

Would they be here? he wondered. Or was it all another of Josiah's tricks? Would he find her or was she already being taken farther and farther from him on a trail he had never followed?

It seemed an unbelievable amount of time from the first sight of the tepees until they entered the first outer circle of them.

Then he could see his mother's tepee and his heart gave a violent lurch. In front of it stood his mother, and beside her was Snow Blossom. They stood with expectant smiles waiting for him.

It was not at them he was looking at the moment, but at the man who stood a few feet away—Josiah Tucker.

Deep and raging fury struck him. He was tired, hungry, and thirsty, but all these feelings ran second to the anger that crowded every other thought from his mind. He drew his hunting knife from its sheath, and kicked his horse into motion. With a wild victorious war cry on his lips, he thundered toward the man who stood with a paralyzed and shocked look on his face as violent death thundered upon him.

Josiah grasped for his knife-wielding arm as Sun Knife slammed into him. They both fell to the ground, rolling in the dirt, Josiah defending himself as best he could and Sun Knife determined to bury his knife deep in the heart of the man beneath him.

Chapter Thirty

When Snow Blossom and Josiah had ridden into White Eagle's village, they had been greeted by surprised faces. It took only a few minutes for White Eagle to learn of Josiah's presence and even less time to have him bound and brought to him. He was surprised when Snow Blossom came with him, and even more so when she pleaded his cause.

"Why do you speak for him, Sister, after what he has done?"

"Because I want you to understand the reasons before you condemn him to death. He made a map and gave it to the white soldiers, yes, he is guilty of that. But they would have found us anyway, even if he had not. He did not come with them when they attacked."

"He took you," White Eagle interrupted. "Sun Knife has been following your trail since then. His anger will not be so forgiving when he returns."

"Will my brother listen to me just for a moment? Will you hear my words first? You will understand why I ask mercy for him. He has done me no harm, Brother, and I think the gods willed it so for on my journey, I found a great treasure my husband lost a long time ago. It is only because of Josiah that I return to Sun Knife a thing that will give him great joy."

"What is this treasure you return?"

"I bring my husband . . . his son."

White Eagle stared at her, for once taken so by surprise he hardly had the words to speak.

"His son!"

"Do you, Brother"—she smiled and her eyes sparkled mischievously—"remember a woman named Tzia?"

The name brought an instant flood of memories. He remembered her beauty, and he also remembered her sacrifice. She could have stayed, he knew, and Sun Knife in his young years would have married her. He knew, as she had, that it would have cost Sun Knife much. He also remembered that he had promised if he ever heard of Tzia again he would find a way to repay her for all she had given up.

"Yes, I remember Tzia."

"I met her. She told me of the reasons she had left here."

"Is your heart hardened toward your husband because of this?" he asked her gently.

Snow Blossom gave this much thought. "Maybe at first it was so, but I remember when I was still a child and Sun Knife was a grown and handsome warrior. I loved him then, and I can understand how a woman as lonely as Tzia was, could love him too. No, Brother, I am grateful that she chose to leave for I know I would have shed many tears had she stayed. I would tell you of our meeting."

He nodded, and she began to speak, telling him everything that had happened since the day she had been taken from the fort. He was silent as he listened, and his thoughts toward Josiah changed. He heard with sympathy the story of Tzia's sacrifice of her son for the promise of his future.

"She would give him the chance to grow into the strong honorable man I think he will be. Will you see him and speak to him, Brother? Then you, who knew Sun Knife better than any other, will see and understand."

"Yes, I will see him."

Snow Blossom left the tepee and went to bring Little Eagle to her brother. She found him sitting in front of her tepee patiently waiting for her.

"Why did you not join the other children?"

"I would wait for you, second Mother. I did not know if you chose for me to do so, but . . . I . . . I would see my father," he added softly.

"Your father is not here now, but he is expected to be soon. For now, my Brother, Chief White Eagle, would speak with you."

His eyes widened, and his young body trembled. "To me, second Mother?" he gasped. "Chief White Eagle wants to talk to me?"

She smiled down at him. "Chief White Eagle is my brother,

and he is also blood brother to your father. He was once a young boy like you. They played together. He is not a monster as you might think and even as his fierce appearance would make you believe."

He walked with her in silence to White Eagle's tepee. There she could see him gather himself erect and lift his chin determinedly as they entered. White Eagle stood looking at the boy, his dark eyes showing nothing of what he felt.

"He is exactly like Sun Knife at the same age," White Eagle was thinking. There could be no doubt in anyone's mind who had been his father.

He had no idea what effect his immense size and dark scowling face had on the boy's thudding heart until he heard the soft chuckle from Snow Blossom.

"You would have the boy think you a fierce beast, White Eagle?"

White Eagle's face softened with laughter, and he smiled at Little Eagle.

"You are Little Eagle?"

"Yes, Chief White Eagle," came the proud reply.

"There is no doubt in my mind whose son you are. It is like seeing my blood brother himself when we played together as children."

The questioning eyes looked up at him.

"My father is a great warrior, is he not Chief White Eagle? I have been told he fights with honor, that his arm is strong, that he can shoot an arrow farther than any, that his war lance and shield are sung about with fear around the fires of his enemies, that—"

Both White Eagle and Snow Blossom laughed at the obvious desire in Little Eagle to hear of the great powers of the man of whom he had always dreamed but never seen.

"Your father is all things a good warrior should be, and I think he will be very proud when he sees you. It is always the hope of every man to have a good son to follow him. I have looked at you and I see your father. You have much to be proud of, Little Eagle. Your father comes soon."

"Where is he?"

White Eagle and Snow Blossom exchanged glances. She

shook her head negatively. If the story had to be told, it would be better all things were discussed between father and son. Sun Knife would tell him all he wanted him to know, especially about Josiah.

"He has been on a journey, but we expect him soon. For now, you will stay with Snow Blossom." His voice became commanding. "You will soon be a warrior. It is for you to care for your foster mother until your father returns. It is also for you to see to any guests we may have. Do whatever necessary to make them comfortable. Make yourself of use to them and to the elders."

The boy's eyes glittered like sky-blue glass. He was being accepted among his father's people as almost a warrior. His ghost-like father hovered before his eyes and at that moment, he would have died to prove his worthiness before him.

"Yes, my Chief. I shall do as you say. Do . . . do you think my father will allow me to stay and live with him?"

White Eagle smiled again. "I think your father will find great happiness to keep you by his side. He and your foster mother will give you a good place to live and grow."

"And someday soon, with my father's permission, I can bring my mother here?"

Again an imperceptible negative shake of Snow Blossom's head silenced White Eagle.

"That will be for you and your father to discuss. Go now, and remember what I have told you."

"Yes, my Chief." His eyes smiled, though he struggled to keep his happiness from bubbling up in a shout.

He left the tepee. Now White Eagle's attention returned to his sister.

"He knows nothing of his mother?"

"Nothing, and I think it is best he does not. In time the wound of her leaving will heal. It is as she would have it. Soon Sun Knife's presence will help him."

"Your husband will worry over what effect this will have on you."

Snow Blossom's white teeth sparkled in a quick smile. "For a short time, Brother, it will do good for him to worry."

He laughed. "But not for too long?"

"No, not for long, for I have missed him so, and I know all the worry and strain he must have gone through for the past weeks. What will you do with Josiah, White Eagle?"

"I shall let him have the freedom of the camp, but still, I will guard him. When Sun Knife returns, he shall decide what will be done with him."

Snow Blossom nodded. "Sun Knife has a merciful heart. He will understand."

"I am not too sure. With anything else maybe, but not with the man who stole you from him and kept you for so long. He will want to see him pay for this."

"Do you think my husband will not believe my words when I tell him Josiah did me no harm?"

"If he takes the time to think, but all this time his mind must have been carrying thoughts of his treatment of you. His anger might be beyond control."

She sighed. "Then we can only wait for his return. I shall try to talk to him before he sees Josiah."

White Eagle nodded his agreement to this. The order to allow Josiah freedom of the camp was given and Snow Blossom watched the trail that led to the camp daily.

Waterflower, recovered, yet still a little weak, found Snow Blossom constantly at her side to help her and share talk with her of the one thing that interested them both the most—Sun Knife.

Waterflower had been overjoyed to find she had a grandson, and even more when she saw Little Eagle and looked into the bright eyes that were the legacy of Michael Holliday. She insisted that her grandson should share her tepee and he was more than pleased at the one person who could talk to him for hours of his father.

So the days passed and Little Eagle's head swam with visions of the man who had given him life.

He had gone to the forest with several other children, to practice at being warriors. Snow Blossom and Waterflower stood in front of Waterflower's tepee and talked of him. They were standing so when Josiah approached them.

"Snow Blossom, I have not yet had the chance to thank you for my freedom."

"There is nothing to thank me for. White Eagle will say or do nothing until my husband returns. He will decide then what is to be done. I will speak to him first if I can, but I can only obey what he demands."

"That is more than fair; even more than I expected. I still thank you, for many things."

"You are welcome, Josiah."

Josiah turned to walk away. Several feet from them, he stopped to watch several children at play.

At that moment, Waterflower looked across the village and saw Sun Knife and Long Arrow approach.

"Your husband comes, Snow Blossom," she said softly.

Snow Blossom spun about, her heart beating wildly with a joyous smile on her face. She was frozen to stillness as Sun Knife kicked his horse into a run, rode rapidly past her and with knife in hand leaped on an unprepared Josiah.

Josiah defended himself as best he could, the wound in his arm making him weaker. It was only a matter of seconds before he was pinned to the ground and the sharp blade of the knife lay against his throat. He looked up into cold blue eyes filled with death. He knew at that moment, he was as close to death as he ever would be.

Recovering from their shock, Waterflower and Snow Blossom ran to them. Snow Blossom fell on her knees beside them while Waterflower went to Long Arrow.

"Long Arrow, stop him, stop him!"

Long Arrow could not reason, in his tired state, why he should, but the habit of responding to Waterflower's needs was too great. He slid from his horse and went toward the place where Snow Blossom was pleading with Sun Knife not to kill.

Her hands about his arm were ineffective. She felt his iron muscle contract against the pull of her hands.

"Sun Knife, please do not do this. Let me talk to you. He did me no harm, Husband. Let me explain; please, Sun Knife, do not kill him!"

For a moment, Josiah thought he had not heard her for the pressure of the knife continued and he could feel a trickle of warm blood on his skin.

Long Arrow took hold of his shoulder and Waterflower knelt

at his other side.

"Let him go, Sun Knife," she said, her voice quiet. "Let Snow Blossom speak with you first."

"Please, Sun Knife," Snow Blossom pleaded. "He has done me no harm."

Sun Knife shook his head as if surfacing from a bad dream. He turned and looked at Snow Blossom, seeing for the first time the look of fear on her face and the tears in her eyes. "I would not have you kill like this, Husband," she said softly. "Please let me speak to you first. Josiah will not be allowed to leave the village."

He stood up, his eyes cold and his jaw hard. "It is too easy a way for him to die anyway. All these days, I have planned it better. You will die, Josiah, but it will not be swift, with a knife. It will be a way of shame and pain so that your spirit may walk in the dark always and you may never find your way to the happy hunting ground."

That he had reverted to the savage there was no doubt in Josiah's mind, for the mind of the white man would never have thought such a thing.

Angry at himself and still murderously furious at Josiah, Sun Knife turned away and walked to his tepee. Snow Blossom followed.

Sun Knife could not contain the conflicting emotions he felt—his hatred of Josiah, his painful relief of finding her alive, and anger at the three people he loved most for stopping him from killing the man he felt responsible for all their grief. As Snow Blossom entered, he turned to face her. There were no words he could find to express all he felt. He held out his arms to her and she went to him. With her eyes closed and her arms about him, she felt the joy of holding him again.

"Snow Blossom," he whispered. "I had feared you dead. I pictured so many things in my mind that I find it hard to believe you are real and this is not a dream from which I will awaken still wanting you and not knowing where you are or how you are."

"I am well, my Husband. No harm has befallen me except the terrible separation from you. I have many things which you should know."

"Tell me," he whispered as he drew her close to him, "that you love me as I do you. That is all I need to hear now."

"I do love you, Husband, more than I have ever loved you before, but there are serious things of which we need to speak. Our happiness depends on it."

Now he looked at her closely, a frown on his face and angry suspicion beginning again. "He did not harm you?"

"No, he did not."

"Then what is so serious?"

"Sit down, Sun Knife. You are tired and what I have to say is very lengthy."

"Snow Blossom?"

"Sit or I will say nothing."

He looked at her and knew argument was worthless; besides, he was too tired to do so. He sat.

"Now will you speak, woman, before I lose my temper and beat you?"

She laughed at his threat, and came to her knees in front of him. Slowly, she explained all that had happened from the day Josiah had taken her. He listened without interruption until she finished that story; then he said quietly, "And you think I can be medicine man and warrior in this village and not punish a man who has stolen you and kept you for weeks? Would you have them laugh and say Sun Knife is too weak to protect his woman? No matter the reasons for what he did, I cannot do nothing."

"What will you do?"

"I don't know, but I must punish him somehow just to show everyone that no man can touch you and go free."

"Do not kill him, Sun Knife," she replied gently.

"Maybe," he muttered, "he will not die, but the debt must be honored. I will think on this."

"If you give him the gift of life, I will return to you a gift that will bring you great happiness."

"What gift is this?"

"Your son."

"My . . . you are going to have a child?"

"No."

"Impossible, woman! You speak in riddles," he said,

exasperation in his voice. "It is impossible to have a son if my wife is not pregnant."

"Even if the son was born to you eleven years ago?"

"Now I truly do not understand. I had no other wives, either then or now."

"Did I say you had a wife, noisy one? I said you had a son, and I'm not too sure the news does not still anger me for I would have been the first to give you a child."

His eyes narrowed at her and he gripped her shoulders in two iron-hard hands. He gave her a thorough shaking.

"Maybe that will loosen your words," he said. She knew if he were not so exhausted, he would never have done such a thing; yet she wanted to punish him just a little. She rose to her feet and said gently, "Come with me, Sun Knife."

He followed her as she walked out of the tepee and toward his mother's.

"Where are we going?"

"You will see," she said firmly.

At his mother's door, she stood aside and let him enter first, then followed. Waterflower was there preparing a meal. Seated opposite her was Little Eagle, who slowly rose and faced the man who he knew by the silence and tension in the air was his father.

"This is your son," Snow Blossom said in a quiet voice. "His mother is Tzia."

She said this, then turned and left the tepee. In a few minutes Waterflower, too, rose and quietly left them. A frightened and shaken boy stared at a more frightened and shaken father. After one look at the boy, there was no doubt in his mind about his parentage. He let his memories open to Tzia. He could see her in many of the boy's features.

Now he suddenly realized how he must look to the boy who stood trembling before him; yet his chin was lifted bravely.

"You are called Little Eagle?"

"Yes, my Father," the boy's quiet voice came.

"Your mother was Tzia?"

"Yes, my Father."

"I . . . I never knew of you."

"I have always wanted to know you. I always dreamed you

would be what you are."

"What I am?"

"Yes. I have heard many stories of you from my grandmother and others since I came. I am very proud to be the son of Sun Knife."

Sun Knife walked to him. With a trembling hand he lifted the boy's chin. It was all there in his eyes, eyes too young and inexperienced to hide their emotions. With all his heart he wanted and needed his father.

"And I, too," Sun Knife said softly, "am proud to have a son such as you. We must learn of each other. We must become friends. You are welcome here, Little Eagle, and I am grateful to the gods that you were found and brought to me."

The boy manfully gulped back tears that threatened to overcome him until he saw the glint of tears in his tall father's eyes. Suddenly, he was held in strong arms and his young heart nearly burst with the sheer joy of it. Sun Knife held the boy away from him.

"I must go and speak to Snow Blossom. Wait here for me until I come for you."

"Yes, Father."

Sun Knife smiled, patted his shoulder, then turned to leave. Slowly he walked toward his own tepee trying to form words in his mind to reach the heart of Snow Blossom.

Inside, he stood looking across the room at the slender form of Snow Blossom who stood with her back to him.

"Snow Blossom?" he questioned softly.

"Yes," came the gentle reply.

She is angry, he thought, and she has every right to be.

"I did not know of him."

"I know you did not."

She will never forgive me. Have I found such a son only to lose the woman I love?

"I would have told you if I had known."

"Yes, I know."

"I was very young, and Tzia was—"

"Do not speak ill of her, Sun Knife. She has sacrificed much to do this thing."

"I would not speak ill of her. I would only have you

understand. I was a boy and she was very beautiful. I never meant for her to get hurt. I never meant for you to be hurt either."

He came up behind her and gently touched her shoulders with both hands.

"I would have you forgive me for any hurt, Wife," he said softly, "and I would keep the boy close to us. He is my blood. Can you not love us both? Is it too hard for you to forgive me?"

She could hear the pleading in his voice. He had said the words which she had wanted to hear. He had totally accepted the child she was beginning to love. He waited in suspense for her answer. He knew he would throw all pride out the door and beg her if necessary.

"There is one thing I find it very difficult to forgive."

"Tell me what it is. If it is in my power, I will change it."

"It is in your power," she said.

Would she ask him to leave, would she tell him she could not accept the fact that his son had another mother?

"Tell me."

"I would have your child, too, husband, and I will find it very difficult to forgive you if you do not give me one."

He spun her around and looked down into laughing lips and sparkling eyes. It was only then he realized she was tormenting him as just a little punishment for Tzia.

"Snow Blossom." He laughed. "Your punishment is a complete success. I have never been afraid of anything in my life until now. I was afraid I would lose you."

"No, Sun Knife, you will never lose me for my love for you is greater now than it ever was. It has given me great joy to see you accept your son so. You could have hurt him badly by turning your back on him or speaking ill of his mother."

She went on to explain all Tzia had said and done. He was saddened by the tragedy in the life of Tzia. But he would not put aside the joy in his.

"We will remember her always, Snow Blossom. The boy will stay with us. And"—he grinned wickedly—"I shall do my best to gain your forgiveness by giving my son a brother or sister as soon as possible."

They were interrupted by a call from outside. Waterflower

and Long Arrow came in.

"We have been waiting. I have explained all to Long Arrow and now we wait for the word of Sun Knife. Does my grandchild stay?"

"And my foster grandson?" Long Arrow grinned.

"I am outnumbered, and being a very clever fighter, I shall retreat. The boy stays, for he is my son, your grandchild, Mother, and your foster grandson, Long Arrow. Another boy to teach, teach him as you taught me and he will be a reward for us all."

They were all immensely pleased with this news, only to have it interrupted by Sun Knife's next words.

"It is good we have found him, but that still leaves one thing to which I have to attend."

Long Arrow was the only one who knew of what he was speaking.

"What?" questioned Snow Blossom.

"Josiah."

"Sun Knife . . . you will not kill him?"

"I think not."

"What will you do?" Long Arrow asked.

"Where is he?"

"In the center of the village . . . waiting for word. He will not run away, for he desires to face you and ask your forgiveness for what he has done."

Sun Knife turned to Snow Blossom. "Take my mother and go to the tepee with the boy. Wait for me there."

"Sun Knife—?"

"Wait there, Snow Blossom," he said firmly. He told her in more than words that he would not take any interference from her this time. Obediently, Snow Blossom and Waterflower left.

Sun Knife stood awhile in deep thought; then he turned to the wall of the tepee. He lifted down a rawhide whip and walked out with a silent Long Arrow following.

They walked toward the center of the village. Josiah saw them coming, yet he did not move a muscle. Any chance of his staying in this village would be gone forever if he did not face Sun Knife now. If he ran . . . he was lost.

Sun Knife walked to within five feet of Josiah and they stood facing each other. All eyes watched and waited to see what Sun

Knife would do. Even White Eagle and Rebecca stood by the door of their tepee as did Running Wolf and Summer Rain. None of them would interfere with justice.

Josiah watched Sun Knife closely. He still wore the close-fitting buckskin pants and shirt and high, fringed boots in which he had traveled. His lean muscular body seemed relaxed. His hair was braided on each side of his face and tied with white rawhide thongs. About his head was a beaded headband. His dark skin glimmered in the late summer sun. Nothing about him spoke of white man except the cool blue eyes that watched Josiah intently. "You have stolen from me, Josiah Tucker."

"Yes, Sun Knife, I did. I admit my guilt. Yet I ask you to remember that I returned to you all that I stole and brought you more."

"I have given that much thought." He raised his voice so all could hear. "Josiah returned my woman unharmed; with her he brought my son, a son, whose existence I knew nothing about until today, yet a son I welcome in joy and in pride. My wife also welcomes my son into her tepee to accept him as her own." He gazed at Josiah intently again. "But his existence does not free you of the guilt, Josiah. I would kill you if it were not for the boy."

He loosened the whip in his hand, drew it back, and snapped his arm forward. The whip struck like a snake leaving a long gash down Josiah's cheek. Sun Knife threw the whip aside.

"In my heart, the debt is balanced. You are free to draw your knife and fight me, or to leave your knife sheathed and remain in our village. Know that I have washed away all that was between us unless you choose to fight. The choice is yours."

For a few minutes, the pain and the blood from the dripping wound on his face angered Josiah; but then he saw the wisdom of what Sun Knife had done.

He, too, knew Sun Knife could have killed him, or better still, had him tortured to death. Because he wanted the debt balanced without death, he had chosen this way to keep his pride among his people.

He threw back his head and laughed; then he walked to Sun Knife and held out his hand. Sun Knife accepted it with a very relieved smile.

Josiah lifted his hand to touch his bleeding face and

chuckled. "You bloody savage, you've marked me for the rest of my life."

"Yes, the next time you choose to do such a thing you will remember. When you look at the reflection of your face in the water, you will remember. Always you will remember what belongs to Sun Knife."

"Yes, I damned well will. Sun Knife . . . you had every right to kill me. Why did you not?"

"Snow Blossom told me everything. Maybe I felt you, too, had suffered enough. It is time you looked forward into a new life instead of back into the past. Stay with us, Josiah. Maybe you can find some happiness here."

"Thank you, Sun Knife. I will stay."

"Good."

There seemed to be an air of gentle relief in the entire tribe as Sun Knife turned and walked back toward his tepee. Waterflower and Snow Blossom, who had been watching with Little Eagle, were pleased with how everything had turned out. It was Little Eagle's rapturous gaze of absolute worship that brought a warm smile to Sun Knife's lips.

"Mother, take Little Eagle with you for tonight. Snow Blossom and I must spend some time talking of things to be forgiven. I have much to ask forgiveness for." His smiling eyes caught and held Snow Blossom's and her heart leaped at the thought of him.

"But, Father," Little Eagle protested, for the last thing he wanted was to leave the presence of his father now.

"Little Eagle," Sun Knife said firmly, "one of the first things you must learn as a man is when to be obedient. What good is a warrior to his chief or his village, or even his parents if he cannot do this? You and I will ride and talk tomorrow. I have a new pony that needs caring for. I will give him to you. For tonight, you will go with your grandmother."

"Yes, Father."

Waterflower bore a reluctant Little Eagle to her tepee where soon she had him in a deep state of interest over the deeds of his father when he was a boy.

Sun Knife turned to Snow Blossom and held out his arms. When she stepped inside he gathered her close and rocked her.

"It is good to hold you again. For a long time, I had the terrible thought I might never see you again."

"There was a time when I felt the same. It is good to be back in your arms, Husband."

He bent his head and touched her warm willing lips with his.

"Let us speak of things that need forgiving, Wife. I believe you spoke of a child?"

She laughed and pressed herself closer in his arms. "You must do what you can to return my good feelings, Husband. Would you have people say Snow Blossom cannot give Sun Knife a child as another has done? Maybe, they will say, she is not the woman for him and tell you you should choose another."

"Do not joke with me of such things, Snow Blossom. I once told you I don't intend such a thing. I do not weigh our love by the number of children you could bear. I love you. If the Great Spirit sees fit to give us children, I will love and care for them. If he does not, then we will be happy with Little Eagle and I shall still love you more every day."

"I do not mean to joke, Sun Knife. I know of your love. Maybe I envy her a little, but then I think, I have Sun Knife and his son. What more could a woman ask but for the love of such a man?"

She drew his face to hers and their lips met in a kiss of gentle understanding. He lifted her from the ground and carried her to the bed they shared.

There, they explored, touched, and blended in a gentle giving that molded them forever into one.

He came to her with a warm seeking love that was more than they had ever shared before. There was a newness to it, and yet it was the touch of the memories past.

She was his, totally and beyond any doubt, and he was hers.

The night drifted on, but they did not sleep. It was as if they were afraid to waste one moment. They talked, caressed, kissed, and blended again and again until all need was swept from them. Then they lay together and felt the warmth and peace of one another. Then there were no words, for none were needed. It was the beginning of a love that would carry them forever.

Chapter Thirty-One

The last counting stick was gone. It was time for the tribe to gather its belongings and go to the council.

It was late summer, the days hot and bright and the nights cool and peaceful. White Eagle would have chosen for his people to live always like this, at peace with the land and at peace with each other. He thought of all he had, Rebecca with her golden hair and sweet ways, the child she would bear him when the snow fell.

He had watched Sun Knife and Snow Blossom with their son and longed for the new happiness his child would bring. He laughed to himself, knowing Rebecca still thought of a girl even though she spoke to him only about a boy, yet truly, he did not care. His thoughts dwelt most on Rebecca's well-being.

The women were working on taking down their tepees and packing their belongings while the men saw to the health and welfare of the horses and talked of what would be said.

Long Arrow stood at a distance and watched Waterflower labor over the packing of her belongings and the dismantling of her tepee. It was more of a job than she should have been doing; yet she would ask for no help.

He watched her until one of the poles fell and nearly struck her on the head. This was more than he could stand. He went to her and began to help. Startled, she looked at him.

"Long Arrow, this is not a warrior's work. You will have the whole village talking of you."

For the first time in his life that he could remember, he became angry with her. "Do you not think," he snapped, "that you mean more to me than what the loose tongues in this village can chatter about? Be silent, woman. I will help if I choose and no one will speak to me of it or I shall silence them."

She blinked in surprise at the first harsh words Long Arrow

had ever spoken to her. They began to work together and soon everything was organized into bundles and prepared for packing on horses.

As she finished working, her thoughts dwelt on Long Arrow. She began to realize just how much he had done for her, how often he had been there to support her through all the problems in her life. After Michael had left to return to his people, it was Long Arrow who had unselfishly cared for her and Sun Knife. It was he who had hunted for her meat, who had cared for her and Sun Knife when they became ill or needed his help. It was he who had taught Sun Knife to walk in the honorable way he did and had, with gentleness, trained him well in the ways of a warrior. It was Long Arrow who mourned with her the death of her husband, and still Long Arrow who reached out to help her in all things.

Suddenly the knowledge of his love for her reached in and shattered her quieted heart. She had thought there was no love left but Michael, and when he was gone, some part of her heart remained frozen and untouched. It was this controlled peace that Long Arrow broke.

The pain of it was that he had never once reached for her or given any sign of the love he felt. Such unselfishness overwhelmed her, and left her weak. He had given her his life asking nothing in return.

She was overcome with the thought of it, more so because she felt she had unfeelingly taken from him all his life and given nothing in return. She had cheated him! Cheated him! She was overwhelmed with shame and anger at herself for taking so much with no concern for the one she took from. Her mind had always been on Michael and Sun Knife, never on the quite gentle love that had supported her through the years.

As they finished the work, she watched him. He looked up at her suddenly as he was tying the last bundle and their eyes met. It was difficult to know who was more shocked, she because his unshielded gaze told her the truth, or he, because for the first time he saw awareness in her eyes.

He rose slowly to his feet, watching the realization in her eyes followed by tears. "Do not weep, Waterflower," he said gently.

"You have never spoken to me, Long Arrow."

"Would I speak to you when I knew your heart belonged to my blood brother?"

Her head dropped and her eyes avoided his. "I am ashamed."

"Ashamed?"

"To have been so unfeeling, to have spent my life taking from yours."

He walked to her side, his eyes gentle, smiling. He lifted her chin and their eyes met.

"You have taken nothing I was not more than willing to give. I do not regret a moment of the life I have lived. It is impossible not to admit the truth to you. I would never have spoken had you not seen the truth yourself. That I love you and think of Sun Knife as my son is a secret to no one but you."

"I . . . I owe you—"

His smile ceased and he stepped back from her. "Do you think I could accept something like that as a payment for a debt? I would rather have it the way it was when you did not know. I, too, have my pride Waterflower. I am a man, a warrior of the Cheyenne. I do not need to take a woman because she is in my debt. We will not speak of this again. I do not wish any woman to come to me with such a feeling in her heart. If I had chosen to marry there were many women who would have smiled at me. I chose my way out of respect for Michael, love for you, and love for my foster son. Do not make that a little thing by dishonoring my love, by offering a reward. If I choose to take a woman, it will be because she respects and loves me. Hear me, Waterflower, for I will not speak to you so again."

That he was both hurt and angry at her was clearly seen in his stormy dark eyes and the stiffness in the back he turned to her. He walked away and mounted his horse; then he rode from the camp without another look at her. Waterflower was left facing her own deep and innermost thoughts.

Clouds of dust followed scattered groups of tribes as they headed toward the Arrowpoint River. This gathering on the riverbank was a result of careful consideration by tribal leaders. They knew that their way of life was in a state of flux. It was a time of movement, new homelands, advantages gained or lost, new enemies or new friends made, new and better trading situations. Relationships were changing, not only between Indian and white, but between Indian and Indian as well. It was clearly a time for discussion and cooperation, and the first step necessary was intertribal peace.

It was the time of year when the buffalo had shed most of their long hair and the brown calves followed at the cows' flanks; when prairie plums were hard and green and the sun bore down hot on the rolling plains. A great Indian peace council was gathering; altogether some five thousand Indians were gathering here.

The valley widened to a broad plain on either side of the river with ample groves of cottonwoods and willow clumps—an ideal campsite, with space and shade and water and wood. Grass was plentiful and would supply grazing for the horses.

White Eagle and Sun Knife rode at the head of their tribe with Gray Bear beside them. Running Wolf, Little Mountain, and many of the younger warriors rode in groups that would hunt along the way. The women for the most part, walked. They could ride if and when they chose.

Long Arrow rode alone, deep in miserable thought. "Why," he contemplated, "did his pride stand between him and the woman he had wanted all his life?"

He loved her, yet he knew his manhood would die should he take her that way. If she could have met him halfway, told him she cared just a little, it would have been different. He would have taken her and tried the rest of his life to make her love him. Why did she have to say "I owe," as if she would give herself to him in payment of a long-standing debt. The two words crushed him as thoroughly as if she had struck him. Angrily and bitterly, he rolled the words about in his mind; they lingered there, and he knew he would never forget them.

Waterflower, too, was sharing the same angry thoughts. "Why," she demanded of herself, "did you speak to him so?" To a man who had given her everything she had said the words "I owe," as if he had sold her a horse or a trinket of little value.

The days of travel passed and Waterflower saw little sign of Long Arrow except to see him riding in the distance.

Day by day, she thought of what she had said. She thought over her life, and she thought of how she could heal the dreadful wound between her and Long Arrow. They had traveled for three weeks, and were in sight of the Arrowpoint River when she found her answer deep within herself and began to plan what she would do about it.

The Cheyenne and Arapaho arrived first on the north bank of the river. They must have entered the valley with conflicting emotions. It was always good to come to a river, and this river was like an oasis in a desert.

This plain was no ordinary campsite. No sooner did the Cheyenne and Arapaho arrive than they began to look south with anticipation—and perhaps some apprehension. One does not meet with once-deadly enemies without wondering, even at a peace council. Yet these former enemies were bringing a promise of peace.

The Cheyenne made their camp in a circle, with a break in the circle toward the east where the sun rises. Everyone in the tribe had his precise and appointed place. This was why Long Arrow found his tepee next to Waterflower's, where it had always been.

The Cheyenne, observing all their traditional formalities, pitched a large-scale camp. A circle was not necessarily the most convenient arrangement, but it was impressive. Let those people from the south who had asked for peace see how a proper, disciplined tribe camps. And another thought had occurred to White Eagle. If the southern leaders would willingly enter the heart of the Cheyenne circle, it would prove their sincerity and trust.

A special lodge was built in the middle of the Cheyenne camp circle, a framework of poles shaded on one side with lodge coverings and open on the other. It was large enough to entertain all the visiting chiefs.

Now it became quiet and still. Every Cheyenne was settled and everyone waited for the coming of the tribes from the south.

The third night they had camped was clear, with diamond-bright stars and a large golden moon.

Long Arrow stayed away from the camp until after dark for he still did not want to look into the eyes of Waterflower and feel the same pain again.

Now he rode through a silent camp and stopped in front of his own tepee. He unsaddled his horse and secured it for the night. Tired, and annoyed with the fact that he knew he would not be able to sleep, he pushed open the tepee flap and stepped inside. Shock held him motionless when Waterflower stood up from the couch where she had been sitting and waiting.

"I would speak with you, Long Arrow," she said, a note of gentle pleading in her voice.

He walked to her and angrily took hold of her arm. "Are you stupid, woman? Do you not know what people would say if they knew you came to my lodge alone?"

She smiled and repeated his words. "Do you not think that you mean more to me than what the loose tongues in this village can chatter about? Be silent, warrior. I will come here if I choose and no one will speak to me of it or I will silence them."

His words thrown back in his face did not make him feel any better, but he dropped his hand. Her nearness was an upsetting thing also, for to have her here so had been one of his best loved dreams. He moved as far away from her as he could without looking foolish.

"Of what would you speak to me, Waterflower?"

She went to him and stood looking up into his dark gaze. The firelight touched her face with shadows, and the glimmer of her smile reached out to him.

"I would speak of two foolish people, two people who would be happier sharing each other instead of walking their last days alone; two people who have good memories and many happy days ahead of them. I speak of us, Long Arrow, you and I."

"Stop, Waterflower."

"Why?"

"I do not need your pity."

"Stupid man!" she said angrily. "Waterflower would give herself to no man out of pity. Must I humble myself before a stone-hearted warrior before he will understand?"

At her anger a small smile cracked his face.

"Do you laugh at me, stone heart?" She, too, smiled a little.

"No, I do not laugh at you, only at your very good description. I am not stone-hearted, Waterflower."

"You are if you let your pride trip and fall over my very stupid words. Words I did not intend to say. Let me speak the words that are in my heart. Then I will listen to yours."

"Speak then."

"I cannot say to you that my love for you is what I felt for Michael. I would not lie or try to deceive you. Yet I do feel for you a love that is peaceful and sharing. I would ask you, Long Arrow, if it is enough for us to build a new life on? I have looked into my heart and found a place where only you live. I am lonely and you are lonely, yet it is not only loneliness that draws me to you. It is the strength of the love in your heart that I can feel for the first time. It has reached out to touch me many times and I was too blind to see it. I am no longer blind, Long Arrow. I would be your wife. I would come to you honestly and truly and try to make you happy. Can you put aside the foolish words I spoke and listen only to my love? Can your pride overlook my stupidity? Can you find a place in your life for me, for I have missed you much since you have stayed away from me?"

Long Arrow's heart was stricken to its depths. He stood for a long time thinking how often he had dreamed these words. He loved her and wanted her more at that moment than he ever had before. He stood in silence letting the joy of those words wash through him and drain away the arrogant and foolish pride that had almost taken her away from him. But he stood in silence too long. She took his prolonged silence as refusal. With a soft sob, she turned toward the entrance.

He reached out and spun her about and caught her to him. He could see the tears on her face. He held her bound against him and looked down on her.

"Again, I say do not weep, Waterflower. Your tears tear my heart as nothing else can. You spoke words I desire very much to hear again."

"What words?"

"I would be your wife, Long Arrow. I have missed you much. They are sweet words to my heart, woman, for I have dreamed of you saying them to me many times."

She laughed softly and slid her arms about his waist. Then she repeated the words in a half-whisper. "I would be your wife, Long Arrow. . . . I have missed you much . . . very much," she added quietly.

She could feel the tremor of pleasure as it rippled through the muscles of his tense body. His arms tightened about her and slowly his head bent and he tasted gently the lips of the woman he had wanted for so long.

For him, it was the knowledge of the sweetness he had dreamed. The years faded away as did all thought of the camp that surrounded them. He only knew Waterflower and her sweet-dreamed surrender to him.

When he lifted his lips from hers, he searched her eyes for any sign of the past. He saw only gentle giving love and his heart sang.

He would keep her here, he thought, for he wanted her with the desperation of a dying man. Yet, he knew he could not, for all would frown if they saw her leave his tepee in the morning. He would have her, but it would be with honor and pride. What better way to begin a great peace council than with a marriage? Reluctantly, he held her a little away from him.

"You must go for tonight. I would not have any speak of my wife with disrespect. It would please me to go to White Eagle in the morning and ask if he will marry us. Until then, I must let you go, no matter how badly I want you to remain here beside me through the night."

"Of course, I understand," she said. "I will go. I will prepare my things for our wedding. Long Arrow, will we live in your tepee or mine?"

He laughed happily. "Waterflower, we could live under a tree for all I care. Nothing is of any importance to me now, but the knowledge that you will soon be mine. It is all my overburdened heart can think of."

"We must be practical, too," she replied smiling.

"You be practical, my soon-to-be Wife, and let me enjoy the thoughts of our marriage."

"Your tepee is better," she said firmly. "In the morning, I shall begin to move my things in."

"That is settled," he replied. "Now I will walk you to yours."

Outside, they walked in the clear night air.

"You will speak to Sun Knife?" he said quietly.

"You know my son will be overjoyed. No man has held his affections more than you."

"Still, I would like his blessings."

"I will speak with him tomorrow."

She turned to him when they arrived at her tepee. He reached out and laid his hand against her cheek.

"Long I have thought of you, Waterflower. Know that I will try to make you happy. We will try to make it a good marriage for both of us."

"Yes, Long Arrow," she whispered. "We will try."

"Good night."

"Good night."

She turned and went inside. Long Arrow walked slowly back to his own tepee. Again, he was sure sleep would escape him, but at least he would find pleasure in the thoughts that kept him awake.

There was no doubt of everyone's pleasure the following day. Of them all, Sun Knife was the happiest for he and White Eagle had almost always known of the great love for Waterflower in the heart of Long Arrow.

It was a celebration within a celebration and many of the elders predicted good fortune, both for the council and the newly married couple.

Long Arrow stood proudly, dressed in his finest clothes; he watched the beautiful woman who was now his wife with an almost shy look. He took great pride in her beauty and he wanted others to admire her, yet it warred with the deep desire to have her alone.

The throbbing drums and bright fires that night drew all to the celebration. When it reached its heights of merriment, Long Arrow took Waterflower's hand and drew her into the shadows.

"You know if we return to our tepee tonight, we will be harrassed until morning?"

"What will we do?"

"Let us go from here. Ride down along the river to the far grove of trees. I will bring blankets. We can spend our first night there and fool all of them."

Like two young children, they smothered their laughter, gathered their blankets, and stole away while several young braves, with wicked thoughts of annoying them all night silently surrounded their empty tepee.

Once alone it was Long Arrow who seemed unsure. He stood and watched while Waterflower arranged the blankets on the ground. Then she rose and looked at him.

White moonlight bathed her skin and made the beaded white buckskin dress she wore glisten in the night. Used to hard work, she was still supple and slim. She had married Michael at fifteen and so her years were a little over thirty-five. To Long Arrow, she looked as young as she had been at her first marriage.

He walked to her side and drew her into his arms.

"I have dreamed so long; yet I feel like a boy with the first woman he has known." He laughed and looked down into her eyes. "I see you as you were so long ago when I first wanted you."

"You flatter me, Husband. I am almost an old woman. Did we not"—she giggled like a girl—"plan to marry to share our old days together?"

Falling in with her teasing, he drew her with him to the blanket. "Come then, old one, let me protect you from the cold night."

He pulled her down on the blanket beside him and found her soft lips in something quite different from an old man's kiss. She twined her arms about his neck and responded in a way that assured him the woman he held in his arms was far from old.

They lingered, with the patience and assurance of ones who had loved before, over each kiss, each touch, until they found in one another a warmth that built from a flicker to a flame.

There was a response in her that told him with a certainty she was withholding no part of herself. She was giving her all to this marriage and he accepted it with gratitude and deep pleasure.

He found in her all he had expected, hoped for, and more. There was no way to contain the immense joy her complete giving had brought him.

She, too, felt the depth of the love he offered. The door to the past remained closed and bolted, and she saw only the open door of her future filled with sunlight, pleasure, and the love of Long Arrow.

Chapter Thirty-Two

Long Arrow and Waterflower returned to the village the next morning, riding double on his horse, and acting as if this were any other ordinary day. The ones who had done their best to torment them during the night were subject to many jokes and laughter. It was a day that added spirit to all who awaited the coming of the other tribes.

Little Eagle, who had been granted consent by Sun Knife to keep watch, climbed a high cottonwood each morning to scan the horizon for any sign of the expected tribes.

Other half-grown boys who were rapidly becoming Little Eagle's friends, scrambled up with the aid of rawhide ropes or sheer agility to gain a better vantage point.

Then the morning came when clouds of dust could be seen in the distance. Excited voices called to one another.

"I see them coming!"

"Straight out there, a village of people!"

"Packhorses! People riding! Loads of travois poles!"

"How many horses?" someone called.

"It looks like a hundred—more than a hundred!"

And from another tree. "Look to the left, just under the dust! Many horses!"

"Loose horses? Count them!"

"It must be five hundred!"

And from still another tree, "Eeee! A thousand coming over the ridge! They keep coming! More than a thousand!"

Little Eagle climbed agilely down from the tree and ran to his father. Sun Knife stood outside the tepee. He already could tell that many were on their way; yet he greeted his son's enthusiasm and breathless words with patience and interest.

"There are many, Father. More horses than I can count. Will you come and see!"

Sun Knife smiled and took hold of the boy with one hand.

"Have patience, Little Eagle. Would you have our visitors believe we are not warriors well used to entertaining visitors? And have we not seen many horses before? Have patience."

Little Eagle looked up at his father. Sun Knife had dressed for the occasion, in his best finery. His feathers in his braided hair and all his weapons laid aside, he would greet the newcomers with pride in his own people.

Containing his impatience with tremendous effort, he stood quietly beside his father and waited. He did not see the smile that touched his father's lips or the pleased glow in his eyes.

Finally they could hear a trembling thunder of hoofbeats on the earth. The newcomers were bringing eight thousand horses, more than most of the encamped Cheyennes had ever seen or dreamed of. They converged on the peace-council site from the grassland. All six divisions of the Kiowa in dozens of bands—men, women, and children. With them came two large proud bands of Comanche.

The men and boys herded the horses to water at convenient spots along the stream.

The women brought the hard-working pack and travois horses into the sandy flats south of the stream and began to spread up and down the valley. The band chiefs selected general locations for their followers: the women, significantly, chose lodge sights. Nominally unimportant in the hierarchy of the tribe, the women actually held considerable influence simply by virtue of doing most of the work around a camp.

They looked for shade, for firewood, for nearness to water, for grass on which to picket a special horse or two, for closeness to friends or prestigious people of the band.

They thought of picking a place with good drainage in case of a shower.

The best spot was northwest of a giant cottonwood, where the midday sun could be blocked off, but not directly under the branches, for the leaves would drip for hours after a rain.

As the new women raised their lodges, they were aware that the curious and critical eyes across the stream were appraising their skill.

The Kiowa women bound their three main tepee poles with rawhide toward the tips and raised the tripod, added extra poles to the circular framework, tied the poles again at the tips, hoisted the heavy fitted cover of buffalo hide with a final pole and unfolded it around the framework to a beautiful cone. They would show those Cheyenne how to make a proper camp. Why did those superstitious people insist on camping in a circle? Some of them were a long carry from water. The Kiowa women, with great cooperation and good nature, set up a camp that filled the flood plain south of the river.

Some of the tepees on both the south and north banks of the river were decorated with geometrical designs, religious symbols, or simple pictures commemorating a warrior's deeds. A few were painted solid red. The owner of one of them was appropriately called Red Tepee.

When the newcomers had settled, the Cheyenne chiefs rode across the river. They invited the southern chiefs to come over and feast in their special lodge. Their offer was accepted.

They gathered together to cross the river, dressed, like the Cheyennes, in their finest, but with no war paint, weapons, or shields.

After White Eagle had ridden among the Kiowa and Comanche unprotected, and the southern chiefs had come to the Cheyenne meeting lodge, any remaining tension between the tribes relaxed completely. It now became a gala occasion.

Naked children ran squealing among the tepees, riding stick horses, chasing each other, pausing sometimes to gaze wide-eyed at the spectacularly dressed chiefs as they passed by. The peace council was about to begin.

Little Eagle knew he would not be allowed within the space where the chiefs sat. He was allowed to walk beside his father and White Eagle on their way.

He posted himself as close as would be permitted and watched his father and White Eagle enter. As was customary for every serious or important occasion, it began with smoking.

Ceremonial pipes were the personal property either of a chief, a medicine man, or an important warrior. They were smoked according to grave ritual. In it was used a mixture of tobacco and various aromatic herbs. When an Indian filled his pipe his intent was usually deadly serious.

The eight honored guests and White Eagle, with Sun Knife

at his left side and Long Arrow at his right, sat in solemn silence as the pipe was filled. It was lit and passed first to the oldest. He raised the pipe first east, west, north, and south, then he puffed and blew the smoke out slowly. The smoke he exhaled was seen as a breath of prayer, and the pipe itself was regarded as the ultimate channel of communication to the spirit world, and between men. It was passed solemnly from one chief to the other to solidify their hearts and minds so they could make some achievement at this council.

Of course on this day, the one who would rise to speak first would be the most honored and the eldest. In this case it was Chief High-Backed Wolf, old and much honored chief of the Kiowa. He rose and stood majestic and proud. His feathered headdress fell to his feet and he carried the scars and memories of many days.

He spoke of his people and their desire to live in peace. He spoke of the battles he had known when Indian fought Indian. Now, he said, the enemy was different. He had more weapons and more warriors than the stars that lit the night sky. He had heard many stories from those who had come from the east. They told of the number and strength of the white man. "We must make peace with them so that no more will come," he said. "If we show them we stand together in our desire for peace, they will go and leave us alone. If we decide to fight, they will bring the white man's guns—cannons—and destroy us all. It must be peace for the benefit of our children and their children after them."

After he had spoken he returned to his seat and waited to hear the words of the next chief.

The next one to speak was a warrior of the same nation, Spotted Calf, a man known for his courage and his constant battle for the welfare of his people. He spoke long, and of the courage and the strength of his people. He spoke of their ways as people of peace. He spoke of their desire to live in peace with all men. He had found, he said, that many things could be settled better with the peace pipe than with the war lance. He, too, had heard of the numbers of the white men, but he rationalized they did not know our ways. It would be best to wait and see if they would talk in peace or if they came with their guns. He and his tribe would speak for peace.

The third chief rose, Tall Bull, chief of the Comanche, and there was not a man there who could not tell by his hot glowing eyes and his scowling face how he would speak for his people.

"The white man will push us from our land if we allow it. We must kill him before he can take our land away and make us weak. I have not just listened to the stories, but I have gone to the lands of those who have heard the white man's word and made peace with them. It is always the same. They ask for peace and when you hand them the pipe, they meet it with a gun. They take away our land, they take away the buffalo. Soon, they will take away our strength to fight. Then it will be too late. Then we will have only two ways to choose. We will let them put us on the reservation where our pride will die in the dust, or we will sing our death song, for the whites will settle for nothing less than to conquer us forever. I say we fight. I say we drive the white man out while there are still young men to do battle, while they still have the strength in their arms to pull a bow. I say we kill him now . . . or the white man will kill us. It is impossible for us to live together in this land. One of us must go. It is our land. We must hold it or die."

His words were accepted in contemplative silence as the next chief, Gray Bear, rose to speak. He, too, spoke of moderation, of patient waiting, of trying to meet the white man halfway. All the time the chiefs were speaking, White Eagle, Long Arrow, and Sun Knife kept respectful silence. They would carry their thoughts of the speakers home to think over during the night for after Gray Bear had spoken, it was time to conclude for the day.

Already the drums were speaking, calling all warriors and maidens to come to the great feast of celebration. Tomorrow would be time again for others to speak.

Women threw new wood on the fires to make light for games and dancing. Drummers brought out their painted drums and set them up, several men about one instrument. The beat rose. *TUM! tum, tum, tum. TUM! tum, tum, tum.* Men and women danced side by side, forming a circle that contracted and expanded, following each other in a snakelike parade. Men sang in deep voices, women sang in shriller tones. Hand rattles made of gourds or stiffened hides swished to the measure of the drums.

The fires scattered through the valley cast their glow on the trees and the moving people. The tribes did not visit across the river this night, but each side knew that the same celebrations were taking place on both shores of the Arrowpoint.

It was as if none of these people had ever been enemies. Rebecca and Snow Blossom kept all their questions to themselves that night, for both White Eagle and Sun Knife were in deep serious thought over what they would say if their opportunities came the next day.

The next day dawned bright and warm. The same ceremonial pipe was smoked with the same attention to ritual as the day before. It was obvious, after a short time, that neither Sun Knife nor White Eagle would have an opportunity to speak this day. Their youth left them to be the last speakers, for neither of them would have broken protocol in such a thing.

The next speaker was Otter Belt, a well-known and highly respected chief of a tribe of the Comanche. He was about five feet eight inches tall, not as tall as most of his fellow tribesmen, but lithe and sinewy, quiet and dignified, with a reflective and melancholy face.

He spoke in a quiet voice, yet it touched the people who listened to him. He, too, had seen firsthand the works of the white man. He, too, had been subject to their justice when they had made forays into his land to kill the buffalo. "It is not only the buffalo they want to kill, it is us," he said quietly. "This land is mine. Not only the earth as deep as it goes beneath my feet, but the air above it as high as it goes up. The stars over this land are my stars. The trees with which we make the poles for our tepees are mine. The rivers that flow across it are mine. The animals that give me food and warm clothes are mine. We do not ask the white man to give us the things which he needs to live. We would take from him nothing, but let him live in peace—on his own land. My father and his father before him have lived and died here. The breath of my spirit lies over this land and I believe if we are pushed from it that breath will leave and we will die. I am not afraid of any enemy. I have fought many battles and my bow and war club are ready to defend what is ours, for if we do not . . . our days are numbered. I say that we find a way to defend what is ours."

He sat down, and the group remained silent for some time thinking on his words.

The next speaker was a Kiowa chief. Particular Time of Day was a tall emaciated man with dark intelligent eyes.

"I have come to this council to speak for peace," he said in a deep resounding voice. His straightforward honesty drew their minds to him. "A nation is nothing except the people who exist in it. We must find a way to peace so that the white man will not shatter us to pieces. We must learn. Those who have no learning have only their bodies and they can see only the glory of fighting. You who have wisdom in your heads, you have a treasure that should not be spilled like blood. It should be kept for the day when we must have the wisdom to tell our children how they must live. It is during times like these that we must hold ourselves from war. The white man is in the East. We must talk to him before he comes to our land and find a way to live with him. I speak for peace, yet I speak for peace with honor. Talk first—we can always answer the war drums when we have tried every other path."

Wandering Horse, Kiowa chief, was the next to speak.

"It is easy to overlook one man or several men who come to us in peace to trap furs in our streams and dwell among us. But it is the beginning. One day the man comes with his woman; then they bring the children and begin to sink roots in our land. The thought of this troubles me because in their way, women and children are more dangerous than the soldiers, for the soldiers will go away to return to their families. With soldiers, it is easy to keep the hate alive, but how can hate persist when enemy families come and make their homes? Here is a great evil. If we do not stop them now, slowly they will drive away the buffalo, build their lodges of stone and wood. I would speak of meeting the white ones with our war weapons. We must keep them from our land for their greed is known. They will take it from us unless we defend it here . . . and now."

Then he, too, dropped cross-legged on the floor about the ceremonial fire. Now rose a man that Sun Knife remembered well. Sitting Bull. Although he had the respect of many years, Sitting Bull was not much over thirty. He rose and looked at all those about him. Sun Knife, as he had before, had the distinct feeling this man could see within his soul, knew every thought that existed in his mind.

"I and my people can tolerate the presence of the greedy white man no longer. You have not seen all his evil yet. Yet I must listen to the words of the honorable men who sit about the council fire. I will agree to what this council decides if it decides that all must do the same."

Now it was White Eagle's turn to speak, for Sitting Bull had made his sentiments clear. He did not trust the white man, but he would refrain from war if the council promised to remain united. If they had to go to war in the future they would be allies, not enemies.

White Eagle rose slowly. The night before, he and Sun Knife and Long Arrow had agreed on the words he would say. He would speak for the three of them.

"All of you know White Eagle and his people. You have known of my father and his father before him. We are not afraid to war against the white man. I have spoken with my blood brother and medicine man, Sun Knife. I have also spoken with Long Arrow, a man of wisdom. They have agreed my words are their words, too.

"Always we have fought one another as tribe against tribe, as warrior against warrior. The white man is very clever. He knows this, too. Yes, he is clever, he draws all his warriors together. That is why he is strong, and that is why he does not fear us.

"Fear of another's strength can sometimes keep an enemy from attacking him. My brother, Sun Knife, has lived among them for eight summers. He knows their strengths and their weaknesses."

At these words, Sun Knife could feel Sitting Bull's eyes on him.

"It distresses my brother deeply, yet he must say the truth. The white man numbers more than we do and they have guns with which to kill. Even though many of us have found ways to get the white man's gun, still there are not as many. Sun Knife says the way to defeat the white man is to learn, to teach our children, to be able to face the white man on his own terms. We can only do this if we present a united front to the white man. If we educate our children to know the white man's laws, if we teach them to read their language and understand, then maybe we can extend the hand of peace to them and let them know we, too, are united. Then we cannot be tricked or cheated from our land by the white man's paper and we will not be forced from our land because we stand together defending each other and defending our land and the way in which we live."

Sparkling dark eyes looked at Sun Knife as White Eagle sat down. He could not tell what any of the impassive silent men were thinking. Now came the time to decide what they would do.

While the tribes at the ceremonious council on the Arrowpoint River looked toward peaceful coexistence on the high plains, the highest government in Washington had very different plans for them—in fact for all Indians. Some people with great influence in the government regarded them as a lesser race that must be expelled—if not eradicated or driven onto reservations.

A rainy night in Washington, the dark streets were quiet except for the occasional passing of a horse and carriage on some speedy nocturnal business.

John Chivington sat in one of these, his face grim. He was on the way to meet a very wealthy and influential man, a man he had not met before, but a man who had a cause in mind that corresponded with his.

The buggy was pulled to a stop and its door opened by a blank-faced carriage man who had found it wiser not to see or recognize the men he carried to and from nighttime rendezvous.

"You will return for me in two hours?" he demanded.

"Yes, sir."

John nodded, paid the man, and walked up the steps to the door. He knocked twice. He was surprised to find the door opened by the man he had come to see instead of a servant.

"You are John Chivington?"

"Yes, I am."

"Come in, come in. We have been waiting patiently for

your arrival."

"We? I thought this visit was to be confidential."

"It is, it is. It is only my son and I. We both have an interest in this affair. I in money and land, and he in a little revenge against a man who took something from him he wanted very badly."

The two men entered the library where they found another man, a glass of brandy in his hand, seated in front of the window, waiting for them. He rose when they came in.

"Martin," John's host said, "this is Maj. John Chivington. The . . . ah . . . gentleman I have been telling you about."

"Major Chivington." Martin extended his hand.

"Mr. Preston."

"John," the elder Preston said. "Will you have some brandy and a good cigar? We will talk of some . . . ah . . . mutual problems later."

Chivington accepted the brandy and the cigar. He sat opposite Martin on a rich brocaded love seat. Martin's father sat beside him.

"Here is a toast," he said, "to the acquisition of a rich piece of land."

"I didn't know that much land was ready to be sold," John replied.

"It is not, yet." The older man chuckled. "But I have good authority it will be soon. You will certainly get your share, John. I am seeing to your orders. The next time you meet these savages, you are to exterminate them . . . completely. We will see to it you get a good piece of land. In fact, come to the desk with me."

They walked to a large mahogany desk where large rolls of paper lay. Martin unrolled one and placed a weight on each corner. He tapped the map lightly with his finger.

"Here is the location of a tribe of Cheyenne. Here also, between these four peaks, lies a rich piece of land out of which you could stand to make a great deal of money. All you need to do is eliminate the Indians on it, while we negotiate its purchase here. By the time you return, it will be yours. After that, there may be other opportunities to make more. Make no mistake, we do not want these people moved to a reservation where they might cause us future problems. We want them where they can cause us no problem at all—in fact . . . dead."

John's gaze held Martin's. "I do not think it is all land that causes this."

"No, it is not. There is a white girl living among them. I want her brought home where she belongs."

"Is her name Rebecca Wade?"

"No, it is Lauren Brent."

"Ah, Miss Brent, or rather should I say Mrs. Running Wolf? She is married to one of them."

"She married an Indian? She did not marry Cade Holliday?"

John laughed. "Cade Holliday is Sun Knife, doctor to the Cheyenne. Lauren is wife to Running Wolf. She is almost a miracle to them with her medicine that Sun Knife helps her with. I do not think she will come home very easily."

Martin slammed his hand down on the desk. "I did not ask if she wants to come home. You will bring her here to me where she should be."

"And you?"

"I," Martin said firmly, "will teach her to act the fool and marry some animal. When I get her back, she will learn many lessons at my hand. One of them is to be obedient to me. No one else will even spit on her when they find what she has done."

"You intend to marry her?"

"Are you stupid, sir? Marry that little whore? By no means. I will keep her as my mistress just long enough to teach her to be obedient and well-behaved. After that, I shall turn her over to some friends who will gladly teach her . . . other things."

John laughed and soon the two Prestons joined him.

At the same time, Grant Jameson and Ruben Price were also headed for a meeting. "This man has a lot of political pull?" Ruben asked.

"More than anyone else I know."

"I hope he has some answers."

"At least to whether or not the rumors are true that the land is to be sold."

"I'll bet there aren't too many poor farmers who know about this."

"No, I doubt it. Someone plans to make a hell of a lot of money. I want to know just what plans they have for the Indians who live there. The next thing is to find out who can get hold of some of this land and how much it would take to buy it. I sure as hell have access to enough money." Grant laughed. "At this minute you are looking at a man who controls several million dollars."

The carriage came to a stop and both men disembarked. They walked to the door and knocked. The servant who opened it seemed to have expected them even at this late hour. They were shown into the library.

"Mr. McGibbon will be with you in a moment, sirs. Can I get you anything while you wait?"

"A little whiskey would be fine, thank you," Grant said. The man nodded and disappeared. In a few minutes, he returned with a tray on which was a decanter and three glasses. Behind him, James McGibbon came in. "Lieutenant Jameson." He smiled.

"No longer, James. I'm now a private citizen."

"You've resigned?"

"Yes."

"But I thought the army was your life?"

"I have found a better cause in the past few years. I need your help and your power, James."

"You do not need to ask, Grant. You saved my life once. I have long been in your debt. What can I do for you?"

Grant explained everything to him while James sipped his whiskey and listened without interruption.

"I know that you could help me buy that land, James, and I'm willing to pay anything they ask."

"Grant, I shall find out what is going on and if the land is going to be sold—privately, if it is—I shall certainly see to it you get your hands on the piece you want. Can you show me exactly where it is?"

"I've brought a map," Grant said as he rose, took the map from his coat, and unfolded it. He laid it on a table and pointed to a spot.

"Between these four peaks. All I want is to buy it in name only, to be held by the Cheyenne tribe that lives there."

"You must love these people to spend so much money to keep their land safe."

Grant told him of Michael, of Cade, of Lauren, and her father.

"Alex Brent is behind you?"

"Yes, he is."

"Do you know the law concerning the Indian holding land?"

"No."

"They can't."

"They can't?"

"Can't buy it, farm it, hold it, or anything else for that matter."

"But Cade's half-white."

"Then he can't do anything, because he's also half-Indian."

"But damn it, man! It's their land!"

"Not for much longer, Grant. Have you not heard the President's speech?"

"No."

"Here's a copy. Read it."

Grant took the paper and read.

". . . My convictions upon this subject have been confirmed. That those tribes cannot exist surrounded by our settlements and in continual contact with our citizens is certain. They have neither the intelligence, the industry, the moral habits, nor the desire of improvement which is essential to any favorable change in their condition. Established in the midst of another and superior race, and without appreciating the causes of their inferiority or seeking to control them, they must necessarily yield to the force of circumstance and ere long disappear. Such has been their fate heretofore, and if it is to be averted it can only be done by the reorganization of their political system upon principles adapted to the new relations in which they will be placed. . . ."

"James, if Cade can keep his people here he plans on helping them change, to learn to build. He would help educate them. All he needs is time to help them. They are not inferior as he says. They are intelligent people who love their land. Will you help me?"

"Yes, Grant. I will help you. But we've got to find someone

in whose name you can buy this land."

At that moment the door to the library swung open and a woman stood in the doorway.

James rose to his feet, a smile on his face and a mischievous twinkle in his eyes.

"My dear Martha, you are finally home."

"James." She laughed, as she moved across the room. She held out both hands and James took them. He kissed her on the cheek then turned to Grant.

"This is my sister, Martha. Martha, this is an old friend. I've told you of him often and of how he saved my life that winter in the wilds of Missouri."

"But of course." She smiled as she extended her hand to Grant. "Lt. Grant Jameson."

"No longer lieutenant, madam." He smiled, for her smile and the friendly glow in her eyes drew his smile automatically.

She was not a beautiful woman, for her features were strong for the style of the day, her eyes wide and brown, her nose straight over a mouth a little too wide. Dark glossy-black hair had been twisted intricately on her head. She was a year or so younger than Grant's thirty-five years, but no one would have thought her over twenty-five.

"Where have you been gallivanting to now, my dear?" James smiled.

"A ball, James, a very boring ball. This town is ever so dull, at least"—her eyes contemplated Grant—"until now."

James's eyes grew serious as he watched her; then they brightened as she again turned to him.

"Well, I must go. It is very late. You will call on me with any news tomorrow, won't you, James?"

"Yes, Grant, I will. Good night."

"Good night, Miss McGibbon."

"Mrs. Sanders," she repeated and her eyes smiled again when she recognized disappointment in his gaze. "I'm a widow, Mr. Jameson."

"Oh," he replied softly. His eyes held hers for another moment. Then he and a very silent Ruben turned and left.

The next day, Grant and Ruben stayed near their dwelling because they expected word from James at any moment.

Neither of them were surprised when a visitor was announced, but both of them controlled their shock when the visitor turned out to be Martha Sanders. It was a quick-witted Ruben who found an excuse to leave her and Grant alone.

"I was expecting word from your brother."

"I know. He was on his way, but I begged him to let me come."

"Why?"

"Because I wanted to see you again. Are you shocked? Do you consider me a very forward woman?" Her eyes shone with teasing laughter.

"Certainly the most interesting one I've ever met."

"Thank you. I do have word from James. He has found someone else who is trying very hard to buy the same land you are. Do you know a Mr. Preston and his son Martin? I believe he is a doctor here."

"Martin Preston. Yes, I know them. They have no love for my friends. Above all, they must not get hold of this land."

"My brother has the signed papers in his hand," she said softly. "The Prestons will not know this until you find a legal name under which to buy it. The buyer must be white."

Grant was smiling.

"You know someone?"

"I know just the name to ruin any plans Martin Preston may have."

"Who?"

"A woman with the same strength and courage as you have. Who else," he exclaimed happily, "than Lauren and Alex Brent."

He went on to tell her Lauren's story and she, too, smiled with pleasure at the strange way fate could turn the tables on the Prestons by using the one person they least expected—Lauren.

They went to supper together, then visited Alex Brent who enjoyed the idea most thoroughly. The next day, the papers were signed and Lauren and her father became legal owners of all the land between the four peaks that held the territory of a tribe of Cheyenne, the tribe of White Eagle who had no idea of this turn of events.

When word came to the Prestons they were astounded, then angry. After these emotions had cooled somewhat they suddenly thought of another thing. John Chivington, with the help of the Prestons, had received his orders to go back and force the Cheyenne from their land. They knew he would force a fight and eventually kill them all. He did not know what he was about to do was illegal, and that even if he succeeded in accomplishing it, none of the land would ever belong to him.

It was three weeks later that Grant, who had been keeping an eye on Chivington, found this out.

Immediately, he packed. He said a fond and prolonged farewell to Martha and promised to return soon. Then he began a mad dash to the valley of the Cheyenne to see if he could avert a useless tragedy.

Chapter Thirty-Three

Fate was the only thing that held John Chivington from doing what he came to do. Fate and the weather. Before he could prepare his men to leave the fort for a confrontation with the Cheyenne, winter fell.

Snows on the open plain made it an impossibility to make war on the Indians. Maneuvering huge guns was completely out of the question.

He waited, as a spider awaits his prey, for he knew no matter how long it was here, winter had to pass—spring had to come.

Grant followed as far as the weather would permit. Sixty miles from the fort, in the last town in civilized territory, Grant stood at the window of his room and watched the thick white flakes fall. He knew, just as he was held here, John Chivington would be held at the fort. His friends were safe for the winter.

But he also knew, as his thoughts drifted back to a dark-haired woman whose mystery-filled eyes tempted him, that spring would come. When it did, he would move as fast as he could to intercept the major and claim the land in the names of Lauren and Alex Brent. "Yes," he thought, "spring will come."

The council had ended in peace. Some of the tribes remained at the site several days to wade the river back and forth, to make new friends, to gamble and continue with the other rounds of games and sports. The old griefs and hatreds were wiped out, for the tribes had finally agreed with White Eagle. They would try to form a united front to the white men. Maybe with this show of unity, they could convince the white men they were not welcome on this land. They had then placed individual marks on a piece of buckskin with a pictorial drawing of the council. They had signed a nonaggression pact with each other and now turned their faces toward the east.

The cold winds began. Soon, the snow would follow. White Eagle took his tribe home. Running Wolf and Summer Rain decided to stay with the tribe until the winter was over. Lauren knew, of course, that Running Wolf wanted her here when the baby came so Sun Knife with his magic medicine could see to her care.

The first snowfall came like a thick white blanket. It began during the night and the village rose to find a soft white world. Mother Nature gave them a beauty beyond belief. Children ran half-naked in the snow, pelting each other with balls of it and rolling about as if they could not feel the cold. It amazed both Rebecca and Lauren that the children seemed impervious not only to it but to the sickness that could have followed it.

They both wore the fur coats of animals that their husbands had killed for them, and heavy moccasins lined inside with rabbit fur warmed their feet.

At Sun Knife's insistence, they both walked often, sometimes in the day with one another or at night with Running Wolf and White Eagle.

Summer Rain seemed to burst with good health; yet Running Wolf kept one eye always upon her. He had lost his mother to childbirth and the thought of losing Summer Rain gave him many uncomfortable days and sleepless nights.

White Eagle, too, kept a close eye upon Rebecca. Although she claimed good health, she seemed to him to have lost the glow in her cheeks. Often he knew she was very ill in the mornings and the burden she carried seemed to him to be overly large. He had looked closely at Lauren whose time was about the same and could see that Rebecca was considerably larger.

There was no price that a Cheyenne warrior would put on his children. They were the pride and joy of their life. In a Cheyenne village, children were accepted as a blessing and very seldom punished. They were taught with patience both by parents and grandparents who had much to do with their raising. Often children lived for days with grandparents to give a young couple time to spend alone. They seldom shouted at them and very rarely beat them. They gave the small ones a great amount of freedom, including the freedom to get hurt—

and thereby to learn. The children lived within an extended family; uncles, aunts, all assumed part of the parental role.

Among the tribe every child was supplied with what was called a second mother and father at birth, usually close friends of the family. In this case, Rebecca and White Eagle would serve as second parents to Summer Rain and Running Wolf's child and they to theirs.

The second mother would see to enough of the child's care so that the child would be safe from an overprotective mother.

Snow Blossom did her best to keep her innermost thoughts a secret, but her desire to have a child was never a secret from Sun Knife. He could see her quickly averted look when he noticed her watching Rebecca or Summer Rain and he knew of her continual reaching for Little Eagle. To try to help her peace of mind, he decided to take the chance and speak to his son.

Little Eagle seemed to find his place in the village of White Eagle. He was proud of his father and his unique place in the tribe. He did his best to please his father in every way he could conceive, and his little heart would be near to stopping if Sun Knife should frown in his direction.

Yet he seemed to accept Snow Blossom only as the woman of his father, only as the one who cared for him until he could go for his mother. Often, Sun Knife would catch him staring thoughtfully toward the north, and he knew his mother was in his mind. Nearing his twelfth year, Sun Knife thought it time he learned the truth and learned to accept things not as a boy but as the warrior he hoped he would be.

It was early in the morning when Sun Knife rose. He went to Little Eagle and shook him gently.

"Quiet, Little Eagle," he cautioned. "Do not wake Snow Blossom. Would you like to go with me to hunt this morning?"

With as much alacrity as he could command without making any noise, Little Eagle fairly leaped from his bed.

"I will wait for you by the horses. Dress warmly and do not take too long."

Sun Knife left and Little Eagle dressed rapidly. Snow Blossom was already awake, yet she stifled her laughter at the boy's clumsy attempts to be silent as he literally tripped over almost everything in the tepee.

She was pleased with the relationship that had developed between father and son, yet her arms longed to hold him and call him son.

"Oh," she cried softly, "if I could only give him a child, too, I would not be so miserable. Great Spirit, please bless me this month and let me be carrying his child."

She wrapped herself in her fur robe and contemplated the imagined boy she would have. It did not surprise her much to know that her imaginary son resembled Little Eagle amazingly.

Little Eagle walked rapidly across the village and found his father waiting for him by the line where the horses were tied.

"I am ready, my Father," he said.

Sun Knife looked at him closely.

"I think you are not."

The boy's eyes widened with questions.

"I think," Sun Knife continued as he reached to the back of his horse and drew from its shield a well-made bow, "you are not yet equipped to hunt. How can a warrior hunt without his bow?"

"For me? Father, I have seen you work many hours on this. It is a thing of great beauty. Do you really mean it is for me?"

"It is for you. A small reward for your obedience and good behavior. You have pleased me in all things but one."

The boy's eyes blinked as if he had been struck.

"Father, in what way have I displeased you? If you will tell me I shall do my best not to do it again."

"Come, Little Eagle, we will ride together as warriors and speak of this thing. You are no longer a boy, for you walk the path of a man. It is a thing which men must speak of alone, out of the range of other's ears."

The gift and the words of praise were enough to get Little Eagle's spirits back on an even plane. "If my father speaks to me so, surely this thing is not a serious thing to make him angry," he thought. He mounted and he and Sun Knife rode through the early-morning light across the white snow, through the forest.

They rode for some time before Sun Knife slowed his horse and allowed the boy to come alongside him. He looked down into the wide, trusting blue eyes. His heart swelled with pride and love for the boy who gazed back at him. He had been a joy to Sun Knife since the day of his coming. Now he had to say words that would hurt him, words that would either make him grow or fill his heart with bitter anger.

A fallen log made a good place to stop and talk.

"Little Eagle, we will stop here and talk."

Little Eagle nodded and dismounted and they sat side by side on the log. Little Eagle listened while Sun Knife began to speak.

He told Little Eagle of his childhood and his growing years, told him of the brotherhood between him and White Eagle, told him of the sun dance where he had acquired his name, his symbol, and his first step into manhood. Then, in a quiet voice, he told him of his meeting with Tzia and the summer they had spent together. He told him as much as he knew and suspected about Tzia's past. He dwelt long on her great sacrifice for him and how he honored and respected her courage. Then he told him of her sacrifice for him. He spoke of how his mother's love for him had made her choose a way of life she felt he should walk. Tears were in the boy's eyes when he finished, tears he could no longer control.

"You mean if I return I shall find she is gone?"

"I came to the tepee in search of Snow Blossom. It is empty. Your mother is gone and has left no trace of her trail."

Little Eagle remembered silently his mother; then he turned and looked up at his father. His face was filled with conflicting emotions; yet he had gained a new control over himself.

"Father, what is the thing I have done that displeases you?"

"You have shown no concern or love for the woman who gladly accepted you even though she could have pushed you aside. Snow Blossom does not wish to remove your mother from your heart, only to fill an empty place that might bring you sorrow. She would be mother to you; she would love you as her own son. She offers you a gift of her love and you have turned your face from it. She asks only to share your life, Little Eagle."

A choking feeling filled Little Eagle as he realized he had refused to see Snow Blossom, because he had thought his mother would someday come. Shame overcame him as he understood that he had allowed the idea to exist that Snow Blossom would be pushed aside and his mother would be first wife to Sun Knife. He had taken what care and love she had to offer and tossed it aside as if it had no importance. The warrior struggled within the child. He knew the respectfulness into which he had been trained and the thought of his carelessness almost overcame him. Mixed with all these emotions was grief at the permanent loss of the only mother he had known. Sun Knife read the young face well.

"It is impossible to take your love from one person and give it to another. It is a thing that must be shared. I would not ask you to love your mother less; I would ask you to love Snow Blossom more. Reach out to her and you will find much happiness. The grief you bear for the loss of your mother is like the grief many men bear; yet they hold it within and remember only the good things."

"I shall try, my Father," came the soft, broken voice heavy with tears.

Sun Knife reached out and drew the boy into his arms. "I would grieve with you my son, and yet I would tell you that my pride in you is great. There is no shame in tears, for I wept for my father. But the tears must pass. Someday, you will be a warrior for whom Snow Blossom and I will receive much praise, and I will know that it is the strength in your own heart that has made you so."

The boy clung to him for a moment, then sat erect and wiped the tears from his face. Then he smiled shakily at Sun Knife.

"Let us hunt, Father. I would bring my mother a rabbit fur to make a new pair of winter moccasins."

"Yes," Sun Knife agreed with a laugh and in comradeship clapped the boy on the shoulder. "Let us hunt. It would be good to make a kill the first day you have your new bow."

They laughed together, drawn closer by their words, and mounted again for the hunt.

Running Wolf dropped the bundle of firewood down in front of his tepee and went inside. Although it was a woman's job, there was not a warrior in the camp who would not accept such work if his woman was near her time.

Inside, he saw Summer Rain seated on the floor bent over a shirt she was sewing for him. She looked up when he came in and smiled. Her face glowed with the good health of her mind and body.

"You should not sit so"—he laughed—"my son will be smashed into a little ball."

She tried clumsily to rise and giggled at her immobility. He lifted her from the floor and stood with one arm about her.

"Smashed into a ball, is he?" she said. Taking one of Running Wolf's hands, she placed it on her belly and told him to wait. In a few minutes, a resounding kick from the child within told its father it was well and very active. He chuckled, deep pleasure in his dark gaze.

"You are more beautiful every day, Summer Rain. Why is it some women just become ugly when they are creating life? You—you are like life itself. Your cheeks are pink, your eyes shine, and you are simply more beautiful. I do not understand."

"It is because I am completely happy and because I have a secret."

"A secret?"

"Yes, one I do not need to tell you."

"You mean," he said slyly, "that you have been wishing for a girl child, and the old woman has told you it is so?"

"Running Wolf!"

He laughed. "Is it not so? Did she not tell you that only a few days ago, and"—he glared in pretended anger at her—"do you not secretly wish for a girl child?"

She laid her head against his chest and felt the warm welcome feel of his arms about her.

"Are you angry with me?"

"Angry, no. I would wish only for you to be well. What the child is, matters not. I am afraid sometimes; when Little Dove was born our mother died." His arms tightened. "I would not lose you. If you are well, then the child can be whatever it chooses."

"Good," she said with a soft laugh. "Then Falling Water does not have to face her father's angry face when she first comes into the world."

They laughed together, holding to one another and enjoying the close bond that held them.

In the tepee of White Eagle it was not the same. Since the heavy snows had fallen, White Eagle spent more and more time in his tepee. He told Rebecca it was because there was nothing else to do until spring. He did not tell her that his frantic worry over her kept him close to her. She was determined to be as strong as the other women seemed to be and did as much as she could do, until White Eagle firmly and angrily forbade her to do such things.

He sat now working on a new shield which he would give to Running Wolf for being his child's second father at its birth—if it was born.

Rebecca lay asleep on their couch. In her sleep her face twisted in pain and a soft moan escaped her pale lips. White Eagle rose quietly and went to her side. She was pale and beads of perspiration lay on her forehead. Again he thought that her body seemed much larger than normal.

Gently, he touched her swollen belly. The child within stirred so he knew it lived; yet he worried that it was slowly sucking the strength of its mother. Rebecca's eyes fluttered open and she smiled. "I did not mean to waken you," he said softly. "I was only feeling our child move. Rebecca—you are well?"

"I am fine, White Eagle. Some women just have a little trouble carrying children. I am afraid I am one of them. I am weak and it makes me ashamed."

He lifted her into his arms and held her, caressing her hair as he always did. "You are not weak, woman. Did I not have to shake my fist at you to stop you from doing more than you should? Rebecca"—his voice became caressing—"I would call Sun Knife to come to you."

"No!"

"Why?"

"I am well, White Eagle. It is just that the time is close. Maybe . . . maybe I'm a little afraid."

"If it were I," he said, "I would have been trembling with fear long ago. It is good the Great Spirit knew who to give the work of bearing children to. I do not think I would be as strong as you are. Rebecca, it would be good for my weak heart if Sun Knife came."

"No, I will be better tomorrow. There is only a month to go, White Eagle."

"I am not too sure I can stand another month."

"I can, only if you are near," she whispered. He shifted position and drew her against him so she was resting upon him.

"I am here, Golden One."

They sat together, she drawing strength from him and he with the gnawing worry deep within that something was wrong. The darkness of a life without her made him catch his breath from overpowering fear. He caressed her hair and held her until again she slept. Long after her eyes closed, he sat watching her and resting his hand against her belly as if he could force his strength through her flesh to the life within.

The snowdrifts remained and new snow fell upon them again and again until the tribe lived in a brilliant white world. Hunting still went on. They made snowshoes of buffalo rawhide and tracked buffalo. Unable to carry their weight, the buffalo sank helplessly in the deep snow and were easily speared with the long lances.

Running Wolf came for Summer Rain one morning. "Come, I will walk with you."

"Where?"

"I want to show you something."

Summer Rain threw on her heavy fur and walked with Running Wolf to the river. There, she saw a scene that brought happy laughter to her lips.

The river had frozen solid. Children, a large group of them, ranging from two-year-old toddlers to those twelve and thirteen years of age, had brushed the snow away. With bones of buffalo tied to their feet, they had made ice skates and were convulsed with delighted squeals and laughter as they tried to keep their feet under them.

Some of the older ones finally did so, for a little time, but would land solidly on the ice amid jeers and laughing insults from their friends. The younger ones copied the older ones as best they could and Summer Rain was filled with the pleasure of seeing Little Eagle skate nonchalantly by, drawing with him by means of a short rope several younger children.

"He has changed somehow. I don't know how. All I know is it is a good thing. He seems to be at home here, now, and I have lately heard him calling Snow Blossom mother. She, too, smiles more," Summer Rain observed.

"Yes, he and Sun Knife seem much closer, too. It is as if they had suddenly become a family."

They watched the skaters until Summer Rain shivered with the cold. His astute eyes missing nothing, he took her arm and smiled.

"Come, woman, would you keep my child out in the cold so long? Eeee, what a stubborn woman I have chosen for my child's mother. She will not care for herself, so I must do it for her."

Summer Rain laughed, but walked along with him. They stepped inside the tepee and she loosened the heavy fur and threw it from her. When she did she suddenly gasped as a pain struck the center of her back. Running Wolf was at her side.

"Summer Rain?"

"It is all right. It is gone." She smiled.

"It is time?"

"Yes, I think so."

"I will bring Snow Blossom and Waterflower to you."

"Yes, Running Wolf," she replied. He was gone quickly and as the tepee flap closed another pain gripped her. She went to the bed and started to sit down. When she did a flood of warm water soaked her legs and dress.

She knew the signs, had in fact helped in the delivery of many babies. She was surprised that she was not afraid. She took off the dress and wrapped a blanket about her and began to mentally count the time between pains.

Running Wolf returned with Snow Blossom and Waterflower who immediately ejected him from the tepee. He sat outside and tried to remain calm. He even took his pipe and began to puff nervously, unaware he had placed no tobacco in it.

The hours seemed to drag by. Several times he decided to walk away only to find himself drawn back to sit helplessly and wait.

Within, Summer Rain labored. Her strength was good and

the supervision of Snow Blossom and Waterflower left nothing to be done but comfort her when the pain swept over her, and wait.

It was less than six hours until the child lustily screamed its anger at being taken from its safe warm place and cast into this cold alien one.

After she had cut the umbilical cord, Waterflower cleaned the child and wrapped it. Then she carried it out to a tense and waiting Running Wolf.

"Waterflower?"

"It is a girl child, Running Wolf, a very beautiful girl child."

Running Wolf grinned, took the baby from her arms, and held it close to him.

"Falling Water," he said softly, "my daughter."

His eyes found Waterflower's. "She is well? Summer Rain, she is well?"

"She is very well. She said to tell you as soon as you have gloated over your prize to bring her back to her."

Waterflower smiled to herself for Running Wolf's face as he looked at the small wriggling red child was as near to foolish as it would ever be.

Carrying the child, he went into the tepee. "Your daughter is beautiful, Running Wolf," Snow Blossom said.

"Yes, she is beautiful. My thanks to you, Snow Blossom. I shall not forget."

Snow Blossom knew the ways of her people. He would probably give Waterflower and her an outrageously rich gift he probably couldn't afford and his pride would forbid them not accepting it.

She left the tepee so Summer Rain and Running Wolf could share alone the joy of the child they had created.

Running Wolf was fascinated with her tiny hands and feet. He examined them closely.

"Yes, Running Wolf,"—Summer Rain chuckled—"she has all ten toes and fingers."

He laughed and laid the child beside her. His eyes sparkled with unshed tears of joy. "You have given me much since the first day you came to me, Summer Rain, but this is the greatest gift of all. Falling Water."

"Falling Water," she repeated softly. "Are you pleased she

is a girl?"

"I am pleased she is our child," he replied as he took one of her hands in his and one of the child's. "We are one, you, me, and Falling Water."

Their eyes held as he bent forward and touched her lips with his.

Snow Blossom and Waterflower walked slowly back toward their tepees. They came to Waterflower's tepee first only to find White Eagle there in intense conversation with Long Arrow and Sun Knife.

"What is wrong, White Eagle?" Waterflower said.

White Eagle's eyes were filled with worry. "Rebecca . . . the child comes. She is in much pain and she is very hot."

"Snow Blossom," Sun Knife said, "go to our tepee and bring me my case of medicine and"—he paused—"bring my case of instruments as well."

Snow Blossom ran, and silence greeted his words. Long Arrow and Waterflower clasped hands in fear for the fragile golden woman that lay in the tepee and the fear-stricken man that stood before them.

"Sun Knife?" White Eagle questioned softly.

"Let us go, White Eagle. I must see her before I can say what will be done."

They walked together to White Eagle's tepee in silence. One look at Rebecca told Sun Knife all he needed to know. She was laboring to bring forth more than her body would bear.

Kneeling down beside her, he pushed away the blanket that covered her and placed his hands upon her belly. Firm, sure fingers felt the size and shape and suddenly he looked up at White Eagle.

"White Eagle, wait outside with my mother and see if Snow Blossom comes with my things."

White Eagle nodded and left. In a few minutes Snow Blossom was beside him. She laid the instruments on the floor and opened the case. She saw the wicked-looking tools before her and they made her shiver. After Sun Knife had examined Rebecca completely, he turned to Snow Blossom.

"You will have to stay and help me. I must take this child if they are to live."

"Take?" she whispered raggedly.

"Snow Blossom," he said firmly, "I need your strength; can you help me?"

"Yes, yes, Sun Knife. Tell me what I must do."

He smiled and reached out and touched her. "Good. Now have someone go for water. Put it on the fire and boil it. When you have done this, dip my instruments in it. Then lay them on the cloth after you have also soaked the cloth in the water. Do not touch them after you put them there. Do you understand?"

"Yes, Sun Knife."

She worked and after he had watched her for a minute he was satisfied she would do well. He returned to Rebecca who was moaning on the bed. He bent over her.

"Rebecca," he said softly, "will you trust me if I tell you I must take this child from you if either of you are to survive?"

"Sun Knife," she gasped. "Save my child . . . please."

"I will, Rebecca, I will," he answered, unsure if he could do what he promised.

Taking a bottle from his case, he mixed a liquid in some water and made her drink. Then he placed a small piece of cloth over her nose and dropped on it a drop or two of a liquid he had never tried before. He watched her body relax as she drifted into a deep sleep. Then, under the wide and very frightened eyes of Snow Blossom, he reached for a slender scalpel.

He drew it down over her belly and a thin red line followed. Snow Blossom felt a momentary touch of dizziness; yet she took hold of herself. She could not leave him now.

The miracle of Caesarean birth opened before her eyes and she stared in open-mouthed wonder. Again she looked at the hands of her husband as he labored over the girl before him and a new sense of love and wonder filled her. She had always hated the days he had been gone from them, but now she could see what he had brought with him.

Another sight caused a startled cry of surprise and Snow Blossom and Sun Knife smiled at each other over Rebecca and the great gift she was producing. By the time Sun Knife stepped out of the tepee a new moon had risen in the heavens and one star hovered near it. White Eagle rose from the place he had sat like an immobile statue from the minute Sun Knife had sent him from the tepee. He turned bleak dead eyes toward

Sun Knife.

"She is dead," he said with desperate finality.

"She lives now, and will, I hope, live a long productive life."

White Eagle seemed to quiver with relieved tension; then his eyes searched Sun Knife's again.

"The child, it lives, too?"

"Yes."

Again the huge man sighed. "I was afraid," he whispered almost in awe of the great fear that had held him.

"What was the child?"

"What did you want?"

"A boy?" White Eagle asked hopefully.

"Yes, a boy."

White Eagle smiled.

"What did Rebecca want?"

"She always told me she wanted a boy for me; yet I know she really wanted a girl child."

"Well, she had her way."

"What?"

"She got her girl child." Sun Knife grinned.

"But you said . . . you said a boy child."

"Yes, I did."

"Sun Knife, I am tired and confused. I do not understand how you speak. How could it be a boy child if it is a girl child?"

"It could if it were two."

"Two?"

"Ignorant one." Sun Knife laughed. "Your wife has just given you two children. Twins, a boy and a girl."

Now White Eagle's eyes were lit with shock and unbelievable happiness.

"Can I speak with her now?"

"She sleeps. I have given her a drug to make it so. White Eagle, there is more I must tell you."

"What is it?"

"She will be able to bear you no more children. It was a difficult thing and it took away her power to bear again."

"But will she be well? She will be able to walk in the sun and enjoy her children?"

"Yes."

"Then that is all that matters. I have a son and a daughter. I have a wife who is a woman beyond any. She has filled my life with happiness. I shall try to fill the balance of hers so. Two children are enough. I have her and that is all that matters."

Sun Knife nodded and watched White Eagle go into his tepee to look for the first time on the faces of his son and daughter. He picked up the boy and held him. "Night Sky," he whispered softly as he named the child. Then he went to the girl and lifted her. "Lone Star," he said. "My children!"

Sun Knife and Snow Blossom walked back to their tepee. In the dark he could not see the peace and love on her face; yet he could feel her beside him.

Once inside their tepee, she turned to him. "It is a wondrous thing you have done, Husband. I want you to know that never in our time together have I felt so close to you or loved you as deeply as I did when you gave life to those children. You are a giver of life to others and to me. I am so proud to be the woman of Sun Knife. I am filled with the joy of being your wife."

He drew her into his arms and tasted her sweet, giving lips.

They joined that night in a new and overpowering love that transcended any emotion they had ever felt before. She prayed silently that the giver of life who slept beside her later had again given life, this time within her. She knew that Little Eagle gave them both great pleasure, especially since he had come to her finally in love. Now she would add another child, one conceived on this night when she had watched a miracle.

A huge celebration was held for the birth of the chief's two children. All the tribe stood in awe of the two who were born at one time.

The winter days began to pass and the snow began to melt. Grass began to appear in small clusters and trees began to bud.

White Eagle, when Rebecca was well enough to travel, gathered his people together. He announced they would fold their tepees and head for the valley between the four peaks where they would spend the summer.

The tribe was at peace. Happiness filled it. After all, had they not had the miracle of two born as one! And were not their chief and his people happy. They would go home. It was time. It was spring.

Chapter Thirty-Four

The tribe traveled in a long straggled trail, each member at his or her own rate of speed. Young warriors, such as Little Eagle would dash ahead on their horses, too excited to keep pace with the slower moving women.

White Eagle, Long Arrow, and Sun Knife rode ahead to guide them; they made short journeys each day with early camping at night, and each night was given over to happy relaxation and celebration. The summer home was always returned to like this, with vibrant enthusiasm.

Running Wolf often pulled his horse up beside Summer Rain, who carried their child in a cradle board hung from her saddle. The easy rocking motion of the walking horse and continual activity about it kept the baby's attention.

He had no need to ask about her health. She bloomed, like a flower opening to the spring sun. Her hair glistened like dark fire in the sun, her tanned body, slim again, was like it had been the first time his appreciative gaze had seen her. No matter how often he looked at her, he could never seem to get enough. He rode beside her now.

"You are well, Summer Rain?"

She smiled at him. "Must you ask me that question every hour on the hour? Do not your eyes see that I abound in good health?"

"Falling Water takes the trip well, too, I see. She seems to be enjoying herself."

"She is ever curious, like her father. As soon as she is on her feet, she will be running out to see what the world is about."

He laughed. The sheer joy of existing seemed to fill him to capacity. Was ever a warrior as lucky and as happy as he?

If these thoughts were in his mind it was because they mirrored the thoughts of the woman who rode beside him.

She watched his tall muscular body sway with the easy stride of the horse, his white smile that made his eyes crinkle at the corners. He is so handsome, she thought. It would be good to have a son that looked like him. She reached an absent hand down and lightly touched the round soft head in the cradle board. He watched her gesture with satisfaction.

It had been over a month since the birth of her child. He would not come near her for some time yet, for in their superstitious ways they considered it a bad omen to touch a woman until the allotted time had passed. It did nothing to ease the hunger to hold her that lived constantly within him.

It would be another two weeks before they reached the summer camp. He thought of the sunlit tree-covered valley. He remembered the first day he had seen her there. He had sat on his horse among the trees, and watched her walk from the river, saw the sun kiss her slim golden body. The need for her had claimed him then and never left him. They would have many happy days in the sun here. Now they could swim together in the river. He could almost feel her water-slicked body in his arms. The idea played havoc with his body. He thought it best to get out of her vicinity for a while for his own personal peace of mind.

He kicked his horse into motion and rode to the front of the caravan where White Eagle, Sun Knife, and Long Arrow were in conversation. He joined them, but did not speak. He would not, out of respect to the chief, speak until he was spoken to. To make it easier for him, White Eagle looked in his direction.

"It is a good day, Running Wolf. Your woman and child are well?"

"Yes, White Eagle, they are well, and I"—he laughed—"I feel the need to arrive in the summer valley."

Sun Knife laughed, as did White Eagle.

"It is amazing," White Eagle replied humorously, "but I feel the same need."

Running Wolf chuckled.

The deep love White Eagle had for Rebecca was a well-talked-of fact among the people. They had all come to look at the two children who came as one. They looked in wonder and amazement. White Eagle's pride came near to bursting. He stood over the children as if he himself had produced this miracle.

If he guarded the children it was more so with Rebecca. It took a fit of temper on her part for her to be allowed to rise from her bed two weeks after their birth, and another to keep him from hovering over her as if she were so fragile she would break at any moment.

Now, though he pretended differently, he had one eye always on her and the two cradle boards that swung gently on either side of her saddle.

Her skin had taken on a healthy glow again, and her hair had already begun to brighten under the new summer sun. She smiled easily and often and White Eagle would watch her over the glow of their evening fire as she nursed first one child then the other. His emotions would swell within him and he would sit beside her and gently touch her golden hair as he smiled down at the child suckling lustily at her breast.

It was a time of peace, and all of them would have had the balance of the days the Great Spirit planned for them remain so.

The entrance of the valley was a very welcome sight. In the distance they could see the four majestic peaks that shadowed this rich place. With the slow caravan and herds of horses, it took three more days of travel before they entered the mouth of it. Up to the center of the valley where its banks widened to broad plains, they followed the wide river that split the valley in two. It was here they had made their summer homes for as many years as White Eagle could remember.

The tepees were raised amid much laughter and confusion. Horses were herded to the grass-covered hills to graze.

That night a celebration fire was lit and again they danced and sang in celebration of homecoming.

John Chivington inspected his troopers as they stood in a long blue line before him.

Scouts had already told him the Cheyenne had returned and were camped again in the valley. He was pleased with this information.

It would take him a few days to get from where he was to the ruins of the old fort White Eagle had burned. He intended to use the remains of the old fort to tell his men his own version of what the Indians had done. He was glad these men were all new and did not know anything of the past. It would make belief in his words much more acceptable. It would open their minds to what he planned to do and enrage them toward the "wicked savages" who had attacked and killed without mercy.

Having ordered his men to mount, the blue column moved toward the ruined fort.

Grant, Price, and Alex left the last town that bordered civilization from the open territory. They were mounted on good horses and each drew a packhorse behind him. Grant knew well the direction and location of the old fort. It was the trail from there to White Eagle's village of which he was not sure. He was determined he would find it, for he knew he was only a day or two behind Chivington.

Each night they camped, Grant grew more nervous and tense at the thought that he might not remember as well as he thought he would. Alex questioned him about Tekata, White Eagle, Sun Knife, and Lauren, mostly of Lauren, not because he did not feel now that she was where she wanted to be, but to keep Grant's mind off the worry.

It was over a week of intense travel, rising before dawn and going to bed long after the moon had risen, until they came in sight of the ruins of the old fort. Wordlessly, they rode toward it. Dismounting, Grant and Price began looking for signs of the presence of others there.

"They've been here, Grant," Price said. "From all the signs, he's brought along enough equipment to blow that whole valley to smithereens."

"How long ago, Price?"

"'Bout two, maybe three days."

"God, three days. They could wipe them out before we could get to them."

"No, sir, we can travel faster than they."

"Yes, I know we can, but"—he gestured toward Alex—"what about him?"

"It's his daughter he's worried about," Price said softly. "I'd say he could make it."

"O.K., we'll give it a try."

They walked toward Alex, who waited patiently.

Price began to unload a packhorse, while Grant went to Alex.

"Alex, it is going to be impossible for us to get to them in time unless—"

"Unless what?"

"Unless we strip all equipment and push both us and our horses day and night until we get there. It's hard, Alex . . . very hard."

"And if we don't make it, my child might die. Which do you think is harder, Grant?"

Grant nodded and they set to work. The packhorses were unloaded and left to graze. All their equipment except their guns and two small pouches of dried meat and corn were left. This and two water canteens would have to carry them to White Eagle's village.

They mounted again, and this time Grant set a pressure pace that he would hold until they arrived . . . or until they dropped.

Two young braves moved about the camp in the gray early dawn. Today they would go out into the plain and seek the great herd of buffalo. When they found it a large hunt would be held. The men would kill many and the women would follow to skin, clean, and cut meat that would be carried back to the camp.

Amid quiet laughter and whispers they made ready. Mounting, they rode along the river until the mouth of the valley came into view. They left the valley and started across the plain. Both boys had been victims of the first attack on their village. They remembered it well . . . too well.

They rode for a while, then began to show off their horsemanship to one another. The first swung his legs over his horse and rode backward shouting happy insults at the other who quickly took the challenge. He swung down from the saddle and while gripping the saddle with his hands, struck his feet against the ground and was back in the saddle.

Now the first one, his laughter carrying in the light morning air, looped his leg over his horse's neck and swung down to touch the ground with his fingers.

Trained as they were from childhood, they were prime examples of the expertise with which all the warriors could ride.

They were enjoying each other's capabilities immensely, but a stranger, hearing their wicked and sometimes pointed insults at each other, would have thought them enemies.

They stopped when the sun was high overhead and ate the small amount of food they carried. When night began to fall, they would hunt for their supper.

"Tall Grass, Long Arrow says we should sight the herd within two days' ride."

"Yes, Long Arrow usually knows." Tall Grass smiled. "You are anxious to return to the village?"

"Why should I be more anxious than you?" the second boy, Walks Tall, said humorously. "You mean you will not dance with Cactus Flower this night? If not"—his eyes sparkled happily—"I would be glad to keep her from weeping for you."

Walks Tall laughed and gave his companion a friendly if somewhat forceful shove.

"You will walk carefully, Brother, or I will separate parts of your body and plant them so the Great Spirit will never find them."

They had been companions from childhood and the taunting was done in friendly camaraderie.

They sat about talking for a short time, then remounted and began again their search for buffalo.

It was late in the day when they hunted for a rabbit, cooked it, and ate. They sat by their small fire and spoke of their friends, their people, and their village.

As the stars began to glisten in the distance, Walks Tall rose to stretch.

Suddenly, in the distance he saw the glimmer of many fires.

"Strangers," he said softly.

Tall Grass rose to look. There was no doubt in their minds that a great force of men were camped on the plains. The only question was . . . who?

Immediately scattering their fire, they both ran to their

horses. Within an hour, they knew who.

They would not stop to camp any longer or go near the white man's army. They turned and rode at the most rapid pace their horses could maintain.

White Eagle lay, half-awake and half-asleep. He was content to hold Rebecca close to him and listen to her deep breathing.

As he often had before, he thought with deep contentment of his life and all he had. There was nothing, he mused, that he did not have to make him happy. He and Sun Knife had spoken of beginning to build the places Sun Knife wanted. White Eagle did not understand, but he had faith in his brother. After the miracle of what he had done for Rebecca, Sun Knife could have asked for anything and White Eagle would have given it to him.

This thing called a school would be done as would the thing Michael and Sun Knife had called a hospital.

He was drifting away into sleep when the sound of rapidly running horses came to him.

Memories ran deep; in one swift movement he was out of the bed with his lance and shield in his hand. A few steps took him to the door of his tepee and outside.

He watched as the two young warriors came to a halt and leaped from their horses. In a few words, they explained what they had seen.

His heart felt like a rock within him and his anger coursed the blood through his veins like fire.

"Make smoke; send signals to Gray Bear and all our friends. It is time we proved if our treaty is as powerful as we have said. How soon will they be here?"

"They have many heavy guns; they travel slow. What would take a rider a day will take them three."

"Send scouts out to watch. Gather our warriors together and take the women and children to the hills." He turned his cold angry eyes toward the enemy that approached. "This time the white man will not take us by surprise. This time he will face armed warriors, not women and children."

All warriors were wakened, and within minutes, Sun Knife and Long Arrow were at White Eagle's side. Rebecca, when

White Eagle told her what was happening, remembered the attack on their village before.

"White Eagle," she said, her wide blue eyes on him. "Our children . . . will they be safe?"

"I will keep them safe, Golden One. You must do as I say. Take the children and go with the others to the hills."

She came to him then and put her arms about his waist and rested her head against his chest. She could feel the gentle touch of his hand on her hair. "I love you, White Eagle. If something should happen to you, I . . . I do not think I could live."

He held her from him.

"Listen to me well, Rebecca. No matter what happens to me, I give you the care of my son and my daughter. You will keep them well and safe. You will teach them how to live. It is no longer you and I; it is our children. We are the only ones who stand between our children and that death out there." He drew her close and held her. "We will each do what must be done, won't we?" The last words were whispered softly and he could feel her tears against his skin.

"Yes, White Eagle, I understand."

"Good." He smiled at her, kissed her, then turned her away from him. In a moment he was gone.

Snow Blossom, raised in the customs of the tribe, said nothing. She called Little Eagle to her and made ready to leave. She looked at Sun Knife who had been watching her. She went to him and in silence he gathered her in his arms.

Summer Rain was frightened, frightened in a way she had never been before. Running Wolf took up his shield and bow and turned to her. "Take the child to the hills with the women, Summer Rain," he said gently.

"Running Wolf."

"Summer Rain, do as I say."

"I don't want to leave you."

"Do you think I want to send you? I could not fight knowing you are here, and that our child might be—"

"No!"

He dropped his weapons and went to her. Taking her in his arms, he held her tightly. "When they struck the village before they tried to kill everyone, everyone. I need to know you are safe. I need to know our child is safe. Summer Rain, please, do as I say." He tried to laugh. "At least for once. I shall not ask you to do it again."

Her tears choked her and she clung to him. "What of you, what of you? With their guns, they will kill you."

"Summer Rain, would you have us run in fear from the white man? Would you have us throw our pride in the dirt and kneel at the white man's feet? I think not. I will fight, I hope with courage, and you will wait with more courage than I will ever hope to have."

Quietly, she nodded. Holding back her burning tears, she gathered their child to her. He kissed her gently and in a moment he stood with empty arms and watched the doorway through which she had gone. He stood for a moment, then again picked up his weapons and left.

The signals for help had been sent, the women and children were as safe as they could be in the face of what was coming. The warriors waited and watched the horizon where the new sun was rising, armed, tense, and prepared to defend their lives and their future.

The wide mouth of the valley was filled with soldiers. They, too, waited for their orders.

But Major Chivington made his one last final mistake. He had to gloat; he had to make them know who had trapped them.

He took with him three men, and with flags flying, they rode to the crest of the hill overlooking the village.

White Eagle saw them coming and with Sun Knife and Long Arrow at his side, he rode out to meet them.

When they recognized who it was they faced, shock came first, then intense and violent anger. Only immense restraint prevented them from killing him then. A code of morals the major did not have prevented his death.

"White Eagle," the major said smugly.

"You have walked on my land again, white one. You have not listened to my words. I will say again, sing your death song, for I will not die before I see you dead."

"Oh, yes, White Eagle," the major said softly, his eyes glittering with hate. "You will die. I will see to it. I have guns that will blow your tepees to dust. I have enough men to wipe you and the remains of your people from the earth."

Sun Knife felt the heat of a violent passion such as he had never felt before. This was the man who had killed his father. This was the man who had brought his mother and Long Arrow as close to death as they ever would be, and most of all, this was the man who had treated Snow Blossom like a worthless whore. It was only intense and deep respect for White Eagle that held him silent.

"I am going to allow you enough time to pray to your pagan gods, whatever they may be." With elaborate production, he took a gold watch from his pocket. "You have six hours to surrender this valley. If you do not bring out all your people by then . . . and I do mean all, White Eagle—men, women, and children—I shall open fire and eliminate them completely."

Without another word, he turned his horse about and rode away.

"We will stand and fight will we not, White Eagle?" came the soft question from Long Arrow.

"Yes, Long Arrow," White Eagle said, "we will stand and fight."

With these words, they rode back to the village and prepared to wait.

Grant, Price and Alex could see the lines of blue soldiers prepared to move into the valley. Ahead of them about a mile was a line of Indians. It was White Eagle he could pick out from the group because of his majestic appearance and his full-feathered headdress.

He knew they were prepared to strike and he knew White Eagle and his braves did not stand a chance.

Urging their nearly exhausted horses forward, they rode down into the flats that led to the valley.

Everyone was startled at this surprising intrusion. Grant rode the path between them and stopped in the center.

"Maj. John Chivington," he shouted.

"Get out of our path, Jameson," Chivington called, "or I shall be forced to fire on you."

"If you do fire on us, you fire on the U.S. Government. We

are here to tell you that this land is now under private ownership. Beside me is Mr. Alexander Brent. He has a paper signed by the President. Will you fire on that?"

He motioned both White Eagle and Chivington toward him. They came reluctantly.

"White Eagle," Grant said, "I have a paper here to tell you this land is safe for you and your people." He turned to Chivington. "You will withdraw your men."

Furious, yet helpless, John Chivington rode back to his line of men.

It would have been over then, but Sun Knife could not bear the thought of him going completely unpunished. He knew he could not kill him without starting a war . . . unless the major attacked him.

He rode forward to the surprise of White Eagle and Grant.

"Sun Knife, no!" White Eagle called.

Sun Knife turned to face White Eagle. "I respect your words, White Eagle, but I must do this. I call on a debt."

White Eagle nodded, and Grant looked at him in surprise. "White Eagle?"

"He has given me the gift of my woman's life and my children. It is a debt I can never repay, but I will let him do this thing, even if it brings us to war. He will never rest or be happy until he repays the major in some way for what he has done. He has wisdom enough to know not to kill him."

Within a few hundred feet, he stopped. Raising his voice, he called not to Chivington, but to the men behind him.

"I would speak to you," he called. "I would speak of a coward. I would tell you to take these words back to your land for all to hear and know what he is."

Chivington chose to ignore him as he began to ride up and down the line. He told them of the attack on the village and about the women and children who died there. It made the line of men stir restlessly and look at the major. He spoke of burned homes, crippled and dead babies, and all that had occurred. Now the men were staring at the major, who turned to face Sun Knife.

Then Sun Knife turned to him. Methodically and viciously he insulted him in every way known. He called him everything from a blatant coward to an abuser of women. He told him what kind of man would steal the women of others. He implied in well-chosen words that the kind of man who would do this was not only physically defective, but mentally defective also.

The major's rage was only held in check by the knowledge that he could not attack him and go free.

Sun Knife began to arouse laughter in the men by turning to insults more personal and decidedly funny. This kind of insult Chivington could not take. With a loud shout, he attacked Sun Knife, who smiled when he saw him coming.

The major leaped at him and they both tumbled to the ground.

Sun Knife had succeeded in doing what he wanted. He had forced the major to attack him. He knew he could win for the major was softer and more dissipated, and he was in a completely insane rage.

Methodically and with infinite care to do as much physical damage as possible, Sun Knife proceeded to beat him until he was nearly unrecognizable and had fallen unconscious at his feet. He stood over him a moment, feeling release wash through him; then he left the major lying there, went to his horse, and rode back to White Eagle's side.

"It is over," Grant called to the men. "Take the major and leave."

They watched as the soldiers withdrew from the valley.

Grant and Sun Knife greeted each other with enthusiasm and Grant answered all their questions as to how he came to be there. Running Wolf was sent for, and when he came, he was told that Alex was Lauren's father. At the look in Running Wolf's eyes, Alex laughed.

"I did not come to try to take her away, Running Wolf. I would just like to see my daughter and this beautiful grandchild of whom I have been told."

The women were sent for and Alex waited with Running Wolf in front of his tepee for Lauren to come. They began to come, one by one, and in small groups. Alex must have been looking at her for some time before he realized it. She was tanned, dressed in soft buckskin, her hair, braided and tied with rawhide. She walked with a free and easy stride.

When she looked up and saw her father, her eyes widened in delight. She handed the child to the woman next to her and ran to him, throwing herself into his arms.

"Father," she cried. "Father."

"Oh, my child," he murmured as he crushed her to him.

Rebecca was overjoyed when White Eagle came himself to bring her home. He lifted her onto his horse in front of him and told one of the women to bring the babies.

They rode slowly while he told her all that had happened. She lay back against him and closed her eyes listening to his words, but enjoying more the feel of his hard arms about her and the strength of the body she lay against.

"Rebecca," he said gently, "you would welcome me in your bed tonight? It is lonely without you."

She laid her hand over the arm about her.

"You are most welcome, my Husband. I long to hold you and to know this day is over and you are safe."

She was pleased as his arm tightened possessively about her.

Sun Knife, too, was anxious for Snow Blossom to return to him. When she did not come quickly, he went in search of her. He found her walking the path to the village alone. He saw that she was weeping—or had been. He went to her, slid down from his horse, and stood beside her.

"You weep, Snow Blossom. Why? It is over."

"I know. I also know that you chose to fight for me anyway. You have repaid all debts, Sun Knife. We are free to live our life."

He reached out his arms and she came to him. He murmured the words she wanted to hear before his lips claimed hers.

"We are free. . . . I love you, Snow Blossom, and I shall love you forever."

Epilogue

The village rang with lusty laughter. It was a happy place. The coming of the soldiers had long been forgotten.

Three children, all about nine years of age, were at play on a grassy patch. The two who watched them stood at their tepee. Long Arrow and Waterflower took great joy in these children for the two whose appearance was identical were the children of their chief and the other was the child of Summer Rain and Running Wolf. Summer Rain was held in high esteem by her tribe as a bringer of medicine and much love.

A young proud warrior rode by and the eyes of one of the children followed him intently.

He was a handsome boy with a pleasing disposition and blue eyes that laughed easily. He stepped down in front of his parents' tepee and went inside. In a few minutes, he returned, casting a quick look about him.

The little girl ran to him and he smiled at her which caused her to blush and tremble.

"Have you seen my parents, Lone Star?"

"No, Little Eagle, I have not."

"Have you seen my little sister?"

"No, but I will search for her if it pleases you."

"Yes, it would please me. Father will be angry if I have let her slip away to the river again."

The adoring child ran to do his bidding, and he promptly forgot her.

Long Arrow laughed. "He is like his father. He is too much a warrior and too proud to see a little girl. It was the same with Snow Blossom."

"Yes," Waterflower said wisely, "and you remember well how that ended." They laughed together.

"Where are Snow Blossom and Sun Knife?"

"They have gone for a ride to be away from prying eyes,

Husband," she replied. Again their eyes were drawn to the other two at play. Night Sky and Falling Water were inseparable.

"One day soon," Waterflower said softly, "those two will find each other."

"Oh, woman of great wisdom," chided Long Arrow. "How do you know?"

"The same way I knew Snow Blossom would one day belong to Sun Knife. I know."

He took her hand and smiled at her. She had been his wife for nine years, and he had loved her all his life, yet never more than at this moment of peace when their hearts were filled with each other and the children.

It was not surprising that the children were also the subject of conversation of two others who lay together in the soft grass beneath the shade of a tree.

"Little Eagle has grown into a handsome man, Sun Knife."

"Yes, he has. I am proud of him; I am also proud of his sister. She promises to be the same beauty her mother is, if she does not kill herself trying to keep up with the boys. How many times have you reminded her she is a girl child?" He laughed.

"So many I cannot count. Little Eagle helps in looking after her, Sun Knife?"

"Yes."

"Lone Star looks at our son."

"She is a child."

"So was I when I looked at you. Her heart breaks as mine did when you did not see me."

"Well," he said as he turned and drew her into his arms. "Maybe he will be as lucky as I and find a treasure one day as I found you."

"Your school is almost built, and Rebecca and Summer Rain have agreed to teach. Josiah brings the supplies for your hospital. Grant has at last found himself a wife. I cannot believe the world can be as happy as I am."

"You are happy?"

"Completely." She drew him closer to her. "I have you and nothing else matters as much. All the rest of our days will be happy."

He held her, caressed her, and made love to her, but in the back of his mind lingered the thought that one day the white man would come again; this time they would not be stopped. With her love and help, he would be prepared. They would face all tomorrows united—he and Snow Blossom . . . he and White Eagle . . . he and his people.